THE ROMANCE OF THE THREE KINGDOMS

LUO GUANZHONG was a Chinese writer who probably lived during the fourteenth century, during the Yuan and Ming periods. Very little is known about his origins and life, but the writing of *The Romance of the Three Kingdoms* has been attributed to him, as has the editing of *The Water Margin*. These works are the first two of the 'Four Great Classical Novels' of Chinese literature.

MARTIN PALMER is Director of the International Consultancy on Religion, Education and Culture (ICOREC) and Secretary General of the Alliance of Religions and Conservation (ARC). His previous translations include *The Book of Chuang Tzu* and *The Most Venerable Book* (both Penguin Classics), *The Dao de Jing* and *The I Ching*. He is visiting professor in Religion, History and Nature at the University of Winchester, UK.

HE YUN has studied in China, Australia, the UK, USA and the Netherlands. She specializes in the relationships between traditional Chinese culture and ecology, and is Head of China Projects for ARC.

JAY RAMSAY has collaborated with Martin Palmer on a number of Chinese texts as a poet since 1991. Author of *The White Poem, Alchemy, Kingdom of the Edge, Crucible of Love, The Poet in You* and *Out of Time*, he also works as a psychotherapist in private practice and runs poetry and personal development workshops worldwide. His latest collection is *Monuments*.

VICTORIA FINLAY is the author of *Colour: Travels Through the Paintbox* and *Buried Treasure: Travels Through the Jewel Box*.

THE ROMANCE OF THE THREE KINGDOMS

LUO GUANZHONG was a Chinese writer who probably lived during the fourteenth century, during the Yuan and Ming periods. Very little is known about his origins and life, but the writing of *The Romance of the Three Kingdoms* has been attributed to him, as has the editing of *The Water Margin*. These works are the first two of the 'Four Great Classical Novels' of Chinese literature.

MARTIN PALMER is Director of the International Consultancy on Religion, Education and Culture (ICOREC) and Secretary General of the Alliance of Religions and Conservation (ARC). His previous translations include *The Book of Chuang Tzu* and *The Most Venerable Book* (both Penguin Classics), *The Dao de Jing*, and *The I Ching*. He is visiting professor in Religion, History and Nature at the University of Winchester, UK.

ZHAO XIAOMIN has studied in China, Australia, the UK, USA and the Netherlands, and specializes in the relationships between traditional Chinese culture and ecology, and is Head of China Projects for ARC.

JAY RAMSAY has collaborated with Martin Palmer on a number of Chinese texts as a poet since 1990, author of *The White Poem*, *Alchemy*, *Kingdom of the Edge*, *Crucible of Love*, *The Poet in You* and *Out of Time*. He also works as a psychotherapist in private practice and runs poetry and personal development workshops worldwide. His latest collection is *Monuments*.

VICTORIA FINLAY is the author of *Colour: Travels Through the Paintbox* and *Buried Treasure: Travels Through the Jewel Box*.

LUO GUANZHONG

The Romance of the Three Kingdoms

Translated by
MARTIN PALMER

Assisted by HE YUN, JAY RAMSAY
and VICTORIA FINLAY

PENGUIN BOOKS

For my grandson Alfie – whose safe if somewhat dramatic arrival we all celebrate.

PENGUIN BOOKS

UK | USA | Canada | Ireland | Australia
India | New Zealand | South Africa

Penguin Books is part of the Penguin Random House group of companies whose addresses can be found at global.penguinrandomhouse.com.

This translation first published in Penguin Classics 2018
017

The character illustrations in the Introduction are from a nineteenth-century Chinese edition of *The Complete Three Kingdoms Novel*. The door god illustrations in the main text are from *A Design Books For Posters: Spring and New Year Design for Printed Paper Pictures* (1981), a reissue of a Chinese text from 1890

Set in 10.25/12.25 pt Sabon LT Std
Typeset by Jouve (UK), Milton Keynes
Printed and bound in Great Britain by Clays Ltd, Elcograf S.p.A.

A CIP catalogue record for this book is available from the British Library

ISBN: 978-0-241-33277-1

www.greenpenguin.co.uk

Contents

Chronology

All dates are AD.

168 Death of Emperor Huan (reigned 146–68) and start of the rule of Emperor Ling.
168–89 Reign of Emperor Ling. During this time Yellow Headbands revolt and power of eunuchs rises.
189 Brief reign of Emperor Shao (15 May–28 September). Deposed by Dong Zhuo.
Start of reign of Emperor Xian, brother of Shao.
190 Yuan Shao heads the confederation of nobles against Dong Zhuo. Dong Zhuo destroys the capital at Luoyang and moves the emperor to Chang'an.
191 Yuan Shao defeats Gongsun Zan and captures the area north of the Yellow River.
192 Spurred on by his love for Diao Chan, Dong Zhuo's adopted son Lü Bu murders Dong Zhuo. Start of the rise of Cao Cao.
194 Xuande recruits Kong Ming to be his adviser and seizes Xuzhou.
195 Emperor Xian is forcibly removed from Chang'an but requests help from Cao Cao.
196 Cao Cao takes command of the emperor and brings him to Xuchang.
197 Lü Bu attacks Xuande, who turns for help to Cao Cao, while Yuan Shu in the south declares himself emperor.
199 Cao Cao executes Lü Bu, and Emperor Xian plots to overthrow Cao Cao through the 'secret edict' plot. Yuan Shu dies. Yuan Shao takes over.

200 Cao Cao attacks Xuande, who sides with Yuan Shao. So Cao Cao attacks Yuan Shao and captures Guan Yu, whom he treats with honour.

199–200 Sun Ce dies, and Sun Quan takes over, declaring himself emperor of the Han. Cao Cao defeats Yuan Shao and takes power in the north.

201 Yuan Shao finds refuge in Jizhou, while Xuande goes to Liu Biao in Jingzhou. Guan Yu brings Xuande's wife through terrible times to be reunited with Xuande. The three brothers are together again.

202–4 Death of Yuan Shao and capture of city of Ye by Cao Cao.

205–8 Sons of Yuan Shao take refuge with the Wuhuan tribe but they are conquered by Cao Cao.

207–8 Xuande falls out with Liu Biao's wife Lady Cai. Shan Fu recommends Kong Ming to Xuande. After three attempts Xuande meets and is joined by Kong Ming. Liu Biao dies. Battle of the Red Cliffs.

209–10 Xuande marries Sun Quan's sister Lady Sun. Lu Su tries to get Jingzhou returned by Xuande to Sun Quan. Xuande and Lady Sun flee Wu.

211 Cao Cao threatens Zhang Lu in Hanzhong, so he starts to plan to attack Shu ruler Liu Zhang. Liu Zhang sends Zhang Song to ask for help from Cao Cao but is rejected so goes to Xuande instead and is warmly welcomed.

212 Xuande marches 'to the assistance' of Liu Zhang in the Shu.

212–13 Cao Cao attacks Wu (the south). Xuande invades Shu (Riverlands).

214 Xuande takes over Shu.

215 Cao Cao seizes Hanzhong.

216 Cao Cao makes himself king of Wei (the north).

217 Cao Cao attacks Wu again.

218 Revolt against Cao Cao breaks out and is crushed.

219 Cao Cao settles in Chang'an. Xuande is declared king of Hanzhong. Guan Yu is captured.

220 Sun Quan has Guan Yu and his son executed. Cao Cao dies, and his son Cao Pi forces Emperor Xian to abdicate. Cao Pi makes himself emperor of Wei.

221 In reaction, Xuande declares himself emperor (first ruler) in order to continue the House of Liu/Han of Shu. Sun Quan of Wu agrees to be ruled by Wei. Shu invades Wu.
222 Lu Xun defeats the Shu invasion. Wei then attacks Wu.
223 Xuande dies, and his son Liu Shan succeeds as second ruler of Shu. Sima Yi attacks Shu, resisted by Kong Ming.
224 Cao Pi invades Wu.
225 In seven battles Kong Ming captures and then releases the king of the Man tribes. He eventually wins their submission.
226 Cao Pi dies, and Cao Rui becomes the next Wei emperor.
227 Kong Ming invades Wei and is resisted, but not very well, by Sima Yi.
228 Kong Ming attacks Wei again.
229 Sun Quan declares himself emperor of Wu.
231 Cao Zhen dies, and Kong Ming is caught up in plot to discredit him and has to retreat from Wei. Having foiled the plot, he returns to invade Wei.
234 Kong Ming dies while invading Wei.
239 Cao Fang becomes Wei emperor, with Cao Shuang as his most senior adviser. A decade of growing corruption in Wei.
249 Revolt led by Sima Yi overthrows Cao Shuang, and Sima Yi becomes most powerful man in Wei. Jiang Wei starts invading Wei to fulfil dream of Kong Ming. Over the next many years he invades eight times.
251–2 Death of Sima Yi – succeeded by his son Sima Shi. Sun Quan dies.
254 Sima Shi deposes Emperor Cao Fang and puts puppet ruler Cao Mao on the throne.
255 Sima Shi dies, and Sima Zhao takes over, despite revolts against the Sima clans, seizing power.
257 Sima Zhao defeats the rebels. Shu again gives up its invasion of Wei.
258 Sun Chen overthrows the Wu emperor Sun Liang but is then killed when Sun Xiu takes over. Deng Ai takes over responsibility for the Wei defence against Shu.
260 Cao Mao is assassinated, and Cao Huan becomes the puppet emperor for Sima Zhao, who becomes prime minister.

263 Wei invasion of Shu reaches Chengdu.

264–5 Liu Shan, second ruler of the Shu, surrenders to Deng Ai, and the Liu (Xuande) dynasty comes to an end as Shu is reunited with Wei and the Three Kingdoms period is over.

265–80 Jin dynasty of Sima clan rules a united China.

Introduction

> I was fifteen when I followed the army
> And forty when I returned.
> I met a man from my own village
> And asked him: whom will I find at home?
> 'Your house is that ruin over there,
> overgrown and deserted.'
> I found rabbits running in through a hole,
> And pheasants were roosting in the roof.
>
> (Anon., 'Ancient Poem', *c.* AD 200)

When civil war rages, virtue is forgotten. When mighty men tear apart a country, they carve their own kingdoms from the ruins. This poem, written at the end of the Han dynasty, is a lament for the ordinary folk whose lives are broken by violence and the collapse of government, and whose voices we rarely hear in official histories.

The Romance of the Three Kingdoms tells of this same collapse in the form of an epic novel. It is set historically in the time of the disintegration of the Han dynasty (from around AD 168 to 280), though written a thousand years later. Most of the key events described in the book actually happened. The murder of emperors and empresses; the betrayal of loyal advisers; the breakdown of central government; the burning of a great, historic capital city; the many, many battles – all these took place. They were recorded in the official history of the period primarily written and compiled at the very end of the third century AD. But while the true events form the skeleton of the book, its beating heart is the epic retelling of the story with heroes and heroines, scoundrels and betrayers. This was done initially by the oral storytellers of folk legend and drama, and much later by a novelist, who wove it all together into this book and whose identity is still debated.

To the people and dynasties that came later, the fall of the Han and the rise of the Three Kingdoms from its ashes became a classic symbol of dynastic decay and collapse. Previous dynasties had fallen, of course – either overthrown, like the Shang in the eleventh century BC, or gradually failing, like the Zhou, whose empire founded in the same century eventually fell into feuding kingdoms. By the Warring States period from the fifth century BC, the pretence that the Zhou was still the ruling dynasty was maintained even as the actual states – kingdoms in all but name – fought each other for centuries. In the end it was the triumph of the state of Qin that reunited the empire, only for it to fall due to the cruelty of the first emperor – he of the terracotta warriors – less than twenty years after he was declared emperor. In 206 BC, Qin was overthrown by the Han. The Han rulers controlled China for over 400 years (punctuated by a brief period in the middle, when a rebel named Wang Mang seized power AD 9–25. In roughly the same period, the Roman republic became the Roman empire and rose to its greatest height. In many ways the Han was the first fully recorded Chinese dynasty. Earlier periods of Chinese rule, including the Shang and the Zhou, are half hidden in myths, legends and magic, which swirled around the key historical facts available from inscriptions, tombs and annals. But the Han is as fully recorded as any later dynasty and for many Chinese it stands as the model of what a dynasty should be.

This is why its fall was so traumatic and why it has acted as a warning to successive dynasties and regimes ever since about the failure that so often follows excessive ambition. This is also why poems written about the suffering of the ordinary folk during the Han's collapse, such as the one at the start of this Introduction, have been passed down from generation to generation. The fall of the Han has become the archetype of how justice, morality, stability and wisdom can be threatened by greed, plotting administrators (often here in the guise of eunuchs), ambitious women, audacious men, warlords, abuse and extravagance. It has become the key story about the rise and fall of fortunes; about virtue and lack of virtue; about abuse and kindness. Its enduring prominence in the Chinese imagination explains why a novel would seek to tell the story of a dynasty's decline and fall at such great length and why that novel would be so popular.

In the centuries following it, the fall of the Han became one of the favourite stories to be retold in the evening around fires or to be acted out at local folk and religious festivals. It provides so many of the larger-than-life characters that make great tyrants and heroes in Chinese opera and folk plays. There's the evil Dong Zhuo, who early on in the novel overthrows the legitimate emperor, places his own candidate on the throne and then subverts his power. There's the hero Zhao Zilong, whose arrival at a battle ensures success because of his outstanding

Lü Bu

courage, and the heroine Lady Sun, a warrior and then a wife to the most virtuous of the founders of one of the Three Kingdoms. And there are plenty of wickedly scheming courtiers such as Wang Yun, who plots to overthrow Dong Zhuo by setting him against his adopted son Lü Bu but then hastens the collapse of the empire. Alongside these key characters there are many lesser characters whose betrayals and intrigues bring the people involved to horrible and bloody endings: perfect for dramatic re-enactments.

The period in Chinese history after the Han and after which the novel was named is called the Three Kingdoms. This is because as China fell apart and into a dark world ruled by warlords and thugs, three key leaders emerged. Each ended up founding his own dynasty and each carved his own kingdom out of the dying body of Han China. The three were Liu Bei (or Xuande, which is how I refer to him throughout the book, to distinguish him from all the other Lius), Cao Cao and Sun Quan.

Xuande appears right at the start of the action in Chapter 1, and it is his fortunes that determine the pace and direction of the beginning of the novel. The first description of him is famous in Chinese storytelling:

> While he is not a scholar, he is a good man: generous, reserved and modest. His greatest aspiration is to befriend the worthiest men of the empire. He is a tall man, with arms that reach down below his knees. He has long earlobes, and his eyes are so wide apart he can actually see his own ears. His face is as pure as jade while his lips are bright-red. (p. 3)

In the same chapter we are also introduced to two other major characters – the erratic, violent but deeply loyal Zhang Fei and the gallant, much more noble and equally loyal Guan Yu. They are each, for different reasons, on their way to offer help to the local governor after a revolt has broken out, when they all meet, by chance, in an inn. Soon afterwards they take one of the most famous vows in Chinese history, known as the 'vow of the peach orchard', promising to support each other, to defend the people and to seek to die side by side on the same day. From

Liu Bei (Xuande)

Zhang Fei

that moment on they are a band of brothers with Xuande as their leader.

In real life Xuande was declared the emperor of the kingdom of Shu (sometimes called the Shu Han) and tried almost single-handedly to keep the Han dynasty alive through his own distant links with the imperial family, even though the dynasty had in truth fallen. Xuande's kingdom was based in Sichuan province in the west of China; his tomb in its capital at Chengdu is still an important place of pilgrimage and veneration to this day.

In the novel, almost immediately after having taken their vow, the three brothers-in-arms come up against the second of the main historic characters, the ambitious, ruthless Cao Cao. A famous story tells of how, when he was young, one of his uncles had complained about his behaviour to his father, who punished him. The next time Cao Cao met that uncle he dropped to the ground as if he were having an epileptic fit. Then, when his father was called, Cao Cao told him that nothing had happened at all, but it was just another of the uncle's lies. From then on he got his own way, and the father did not listen to anyone criticizing him.

Cao Cao effectively held the real Han emperor, Xian – the

Cao Cao

last of the true Han emperors – under elaborate house arrest and made him his puppet. Cao Cao later took the title of the king of Wei, a reference to the entire northern area of the empire. When he died in 220, his son Cao Pi forced Xian, the last Han emperor, to abdicate, allowing Cao Pi to become the emperor of Wei. The exact whereabouts of the burial of Cao Cao remain a matter of controversy. Certainly he was never accorded the reverence that Xuande was.

The founder of the third kingdom was Sun Quan. His family had already ruled an area in the south for three generations. As the Han empire fell apart, Sun Quan watched, often from the sidelines, often in uneasy alliances with either Xuande or Cao Cao. Eventually in 229 he declared himself emperor of the kingdom of Wu in its capital, known today as Nanjing. This kingdom covered the east and south of China and included some of today's Vietnam. A much more shadowy figure in the novel, Sun Quan was renowned for two things: his habitual indecision

Sun Quan

and for being the man who eventually ordered the execution of one of the three brothers of the peach orchard, Guan Yu. In southern China, Sun Quan is still revered, and his tomb is located within the stunning setting of the Ming Xiaoling Park in Nanjing, with its sacred path marked by huge statues of animals, mythological beasts and officials. It is less visited as a place of worship and reverence than the tomb of Xuande, but the tomb mound is still very visible, and an exhibition hall praises Sun Quan as a model emperor and enlightened ruler.

The other great figure in this story is the Daoist magician, strategist and official Kong Ming, also known as Zhuge Liang (I have used the former name throughout to distinguish him from the many other Zhuges). He is the most fascinating and enigmatic of all the characters in the novel and, true to form, we first meet him by not meeting him.

In the story, Xuande is advised to seek this Daoist master in order to learn from him. And he tries unsuccessfully time and time again to do so, to the intense annoyance of his peach orchard brother Zhang Fei. When they eventually meet, the die is cast. Kong Ming not only outlines immediately what course of action Xuande should take but also joins him as his military and civil adviser. The first description of Kong Ming is famous:

> When Kong Ming appears, Xuande is truly impressed because he looks like such a gentleman. He is tall, with a complexion like jade, and is dressed in a long cloak of crane feathers; his head is bound with a silk scarf. To be honest, he looks like a god or an immortal. (pp. 189–90)

With Kong Ming on his side, Xuande moves from being a support character to being the main driver of the narrative along with Cao Cao. And at this point the Three Kingdoms becomes an inevitable consequence of the collapse of the empire. A special shrine dedicated to Kong Ming is to this day beside that of Xuande and, like that of the man he guided into a position of such power 1,800 years ago, it is still a major focus of reverence, and even worship. His actual tomb near Hanzhong is likewise a place of pilgrimage.

What is surprising is that the most visible of all the figures of

Zhuge Liang (Kong Ming)

the Three Kingdoms today is Guan Yu, the gallant second member of the peach orchard brotherhood. In the long period since his death in AD 220 he has been elevated to divine status by various emperors. In 1120 he was made 'the most loyal and faithful duke' when the Song dynasty was under dire threat by northern barbarians, and the empire needed a hero who had fought against the northerners before. In 1330 the Mongol emperor, seeking to legitimate the foreign rule of the Mongols over the Chinese, elevated him further with the title 'warrior prince and civilizer'. And then in 1594 the Ming emperor Wanli made him a god and awarded him the title 'faithful and loyal great emperor, supporter of heaven and defender of the kingdom'.

Today Guan Yu's image is everywhere in Chinese culture, for he is both the god of war and the god of literature. He is shown in statues, on posters, in prints with his two supporters and almost always with his faithful horse Red Hare, who died of sadness shortly after his master was executed. Hopeful scholars and schoolchildren pray to him before their exams, in his role as god of literature, and as god of war he has been invoked by

Guan Yu

just about every commander of Chinese forces since the Ming dynasty. His temples are among the most common in China and abroad in Chinese communities. Yet he is almost entirely the creation of fiction – without doubt his towering status is down to the virtuous and loyal starring role he plays in folk stories, dramas and *The Romance of the Three Kingdoms.*

The core historical facts of the fall of the Han are attested in the *Records of the Han Dynasty*, compiled initially in the very late third century but then expanded with much additional material until a final *Imperially Approved Record* was authorized in 429. Over the succeeding centuries, poets, writers and others called on the lessons from this particular period in the past to shine light on the problems of the present. The Three Kingdoms offered them both poignant images and philosophical lessons in abundance, and many of their responses would later find their way into *The Romance of the Three Kingdoms.*

In the Tang dynasty (AD 618–907) poets were acutely aware

of the historic events of the Three Kingdoms and of their great moral and spiritual significance. The major eighth-century poet Du Fu (AD 712–70), for example, wrote of visiting the tomb of Kong Ming in Chengdu and brilliantly described the break-up of an empire. His poem, reflecting on the death of Kong Ming, which is included in Chapter 105, is a key moment in the novel:

Where can I find the prime minister's shrine?
Beyond the town where the cypresses stand vertical.
Here's sunlit, lush grass – a perpetual spring.
Orioles sing in the branches – but who to?
Three times his lord had to beg him to help the
  kingdom.
He served two terms with all his heart,
But died with all his plans unrealized –
And ever since, truly heroic men weep at his death.

Kong Ming's illustrious name is known worldwide,
Highest among the high, famed for his kingly mien.
Three kingdoms split into being: he used all his skill,
One-pointed as a feather, to reunite them again.
His reputation as great as the legendary ones:
Even in his failures, he still ranks among the greatest.
The stars turned . . . the Han were fated to fall,
Working to the end, his body scarred, he never gave up.

The ninth-century poet He Zeng wrote about Kong Ming's most famous military exploit, in which he pardoned the tribal leader of the Man people, Meng Huo, seven times – a central story in the later chapters of the novel. His verse is reproduced in Chapter 88:

For five months on campaign in this desolate land,
Going by moonlight to the river of deadly mists,
His outstanding audacity more than justifies the three
  visits,
And yet despite his attacks on the Man liberty is given
  seven times!

Du Fu was writing in the mid eighth century, when a major revolt had nearly toppled the Tang dynasty, and He Zeng was writing as the dynasty fell, in the years running up to 907. Bad times on both occasions increased interest and reflection on the lessons to be learned from the fall of the Han and the rise of Three Kingdoms.

Once the Tang had fallen, a period of anarchy erupted, followed in 960 by the Song. The new dynasty faced huge challenges, not least from the north and from barbarian tribes. In this era the famous poet Su Dong Po (1037–1121) wrote of one of Xuande's famous exploits – a dramatic escape from his enemies on a horse that leaped a raging river, told in Chapter 34:

> I'm growing old, the leaves drift from the trees;
> I journey, on official business, by the Tan River.
> Halting my carriage, I get out and walk beside it.
> Catkins glisten, stirred by the wind:
> I see the dying virtue of the Great Yang!
> How dragon fought tiger; and tiger, dragon.
> At Xiangyang, the nobles gathered round their king,
> And among them, Xuande, as if doomed to die.
> But he rides for his life out of the western gate,
> Escaping, but as soon, pursued with a vengeance.
> He's stopped by water, the water of the Tan.
> The enemy ploughs on, intent on his death:
> 'Go!' he shouts at his faithful horse –
> Heaven's whip-like golden wind urging him on.
> The sound of a thousand horsemen clattering
> behind him.
> And into the thick of it, these two dash like dragons:
>
> The one, born to rule the west,
> The other, for this dragon horse to bear him.
> The Tan's waters race, streaming eastwards . . .
> Dragon horse and brave warrior, ah, where are
> they now?
> I'm standing by the riverbank, perplexed,
> As the sun's last rays light on the hills.

Was it just a dream, these Three Kingdoms?
What will it be for the future . . . just a dissolving
memory?

The Song dynasty collapsed, losing northern China to invading tribes and resettling in the south, not long after this poem was written. As a result the conflict between the barbarian tribes of the north and those in the south and west under mainstream Chinese rule became a theme which found a focus in the historical story of the struggle between Cao Cao in the north and Xuande in the west and in the south. The antagonism between these two key characters is there in the historical records, but there is no doubt that the development of stories about them through poetry, folk theatre and opera from around AD 1100 onwards considerably heightened the dramatic tensions. Later, the *Romance* would exploit these tensions still further, using the antagonism of characters such as Xuande and Cao Cao as a means of illuminating the whole historical period – much as Shakespeare would do with the kings and villains of his History Plays.

As we have seen with the inclusions in the book of classical verses from great poets such as Du Fu and Su Dong Po, the *Three Kingdoms* makes extensive use of poems, which are scattered through the body of almost every chapter. The use of poems in classical novels is fairly typical; *The Water Margin*, another of the 'Classic Novels' of China, also has poems scattered throughout. But what is more unusual about the *Three Kingdoms*, apart from the use of major poems by great poets, is the way the author introduces additional, essentially anonymous poems, often preceded by the phrase 'a poet has written'. These poems sound like the sort of summing-up speech an actor would recite to remind the audience of what has happened so far in a play: not on the whole gems of poetry but useful encapsulations of what has just happened to whom. It is likely that these are derived from the folk plays and operas that developed in medieval China and travelled from place to place.

Thus, we have historical records as the bedrock, we have

the dramatic use of the material, primarily in temple or village storytelling and theatre, as well as the famous verses composed by poets such as Du Fu and Su Dong Po. The third layer is the work of the author of this novel pulling it all together.

That there was a novelist of considerable skill is without doubt. *The Romance of the Three Kingdoms* is a magnificent work of creative writing and has enthralled readers for over 500 years. But who exactly was the author? Convention says it was the writer Luo Guanzhong. Almost nothing is known about him except that he lived somewhere between 1315 and 1400. He is first listed as the author in a 1522 edition of the novel, which contains a preface written in 1494 that mentions Luo as the author. This would put the composition of the novel somewhere between 1350 and 1380, which is almost exactly the time of the English poet and storyteller Geoffrey Chaucer (*c.*1343–1400), who in a similar way took old stories, shook them around a little and created and recreated wonderful tales to enthrall audiences.

However, these dates are not agreed by everyone. Some specialists prefer to date the novel to the middle of the fifteenth century, which would take Luo Guanzhong completely out of the picture. Whoever wrote it, in its current form, the one thing we know is that the novel dates from some point in the first hundred years or so from the beginning of the Ming dynasty (1368–1644) and reflects a rising national pride in the unification of China. The fourteenth-century uprising against the Mongols, whose Yuan dynasty had ruled China for nearly a hundred years, was a powerful anti-foreigner and anti-northern movement launched by Chinese nationalists. There was a strong revival of interest in Chinese dynastic history when at last the empire was ruled by Chinese emperors from the late fourteenth century onwards.

The pride felt in the rise of the Ming was to be cast down in 1644 when yet another Mongol invasion conquered the whole of China and the Manchu Qing dynasty took power. Once again northern invaders subjugated China and once again the novel attained a sort of iconic role because it was not only about revival of the empire but also powerfully nationalistic and anti-northerner in orientation. It held out hope of a change and of Chinese domination once again. In 1911 the Qing finally fell, and the republic came into being. In the 1920s and 1930s warlords ruled over a chaotic land, and it seemed as if the Three Kingdoms was being repeated, only this time as an epic of Seven or even Eight (Little) Kingdoms. In this context the fact that military officers on all sides, but especially in the republican army of the Kuomintang, were recorded as studying *The Romance of the Three Kingdoms* to help them plan military action is highly significant. But in the end it was to no avail, and in 1949 the Communist People's Republic of China was formally declared, once again uniting China under one dynasty.

Today, the popularity of the *Three Kingdoms* is as great as it has ever been. Movies, manga books, cartoons, TV series, computer games, comic books – the *Three Kingdoms* story is more accessible now than ever. However, it is a vast book – just short of a million Chinese characters – and requires some considerable effort to read. This was why Penguin Classics asked me to produce an abridged version. An abridgement is always a challenge. What do you leave out? How do you connect the segments? But it is also exciting.

The text in this book is about a third of the whole, and I have sought to ensure a flow of narrative with no breaks. In order to do this, I have simplified the background information, trimmed down the many, many long descriptions of battles (which are all remarkably similar) and tightened the narrative. As a result I hope you will be able to travel the length of the novel's span in time, narrative and adventure without the risk of getting bogged down in minor details.

Where a major story takes place – such as the fascinating plot by Wang Yun and his servant girl Diao Chan to destroy the dictator Dong Zhuo through romantic intrigue setting father against son, or the story of the terrible misunderstanding leading Cao Cao to kill an innocent family – I have translated the whole text. Likewise, I have fully translated major discussions, such as when Xuande meets his future mother-in-law, who responds to his virtue with virtue of her own.

I have included just over a third of the original poems,

Diao Chan

including all those by great poets such as Cao Zhi (who was the actual son of Cao Cao and a renowned third-century poet) and of course Su Dong Po and Du Fu, as well as those anonymous poems which shed light on a key moment in the narrative. I am grateful to poet Jay Ramsay for working with me to turn my translations back into poetry.

This is not the first abridgement of one of the so-called Four Classic Novels of China undertaken for Penguin Classics. In 1961 Penguin published the abridged edition of Wu Cheng-En's *Journey to the West* – *Monkey*, as it is also called in English – translated by Arthur Waley and originally published in 1942. Waley's approach was to omit 'many episodes, but translat[e] those that are retained almost in full'. Large as *The Romance of the Three Kingdoms* is in Chinese, it has serious competition from the size of the full edition of *Monkey*. I have adopted Waley's policy of full translation of key episodes while ensuring that the flow of the story is also retained.

You will find a list of the main characters just before the text starts (pp. xli-xlv); this will be useful, as there are lots of Caos,

Lius, Suns, Yus and others. In the Chinese text many of the characters have several names, and I have on each occasion chosen just one, for clarity. The map will also help you follow the major events and remember where Wei is in relation to Wu and Shu.

The chapter titles are essentially traditional ones. However, I have added key events – such as the death of major figures – which help us to follow the plot but which are not in the original text of the chapter titles.

It has been an adventure translating and then abridging this astonishing novel. I find myself using stories from it in discussions with people because this is in the end a vast human drama about leadership, power, decline, abuse, loyalty, heroes, villains, magic and the supernatural, ghosts and virtue. It truly is one of the classics, not just of China, but of the world.

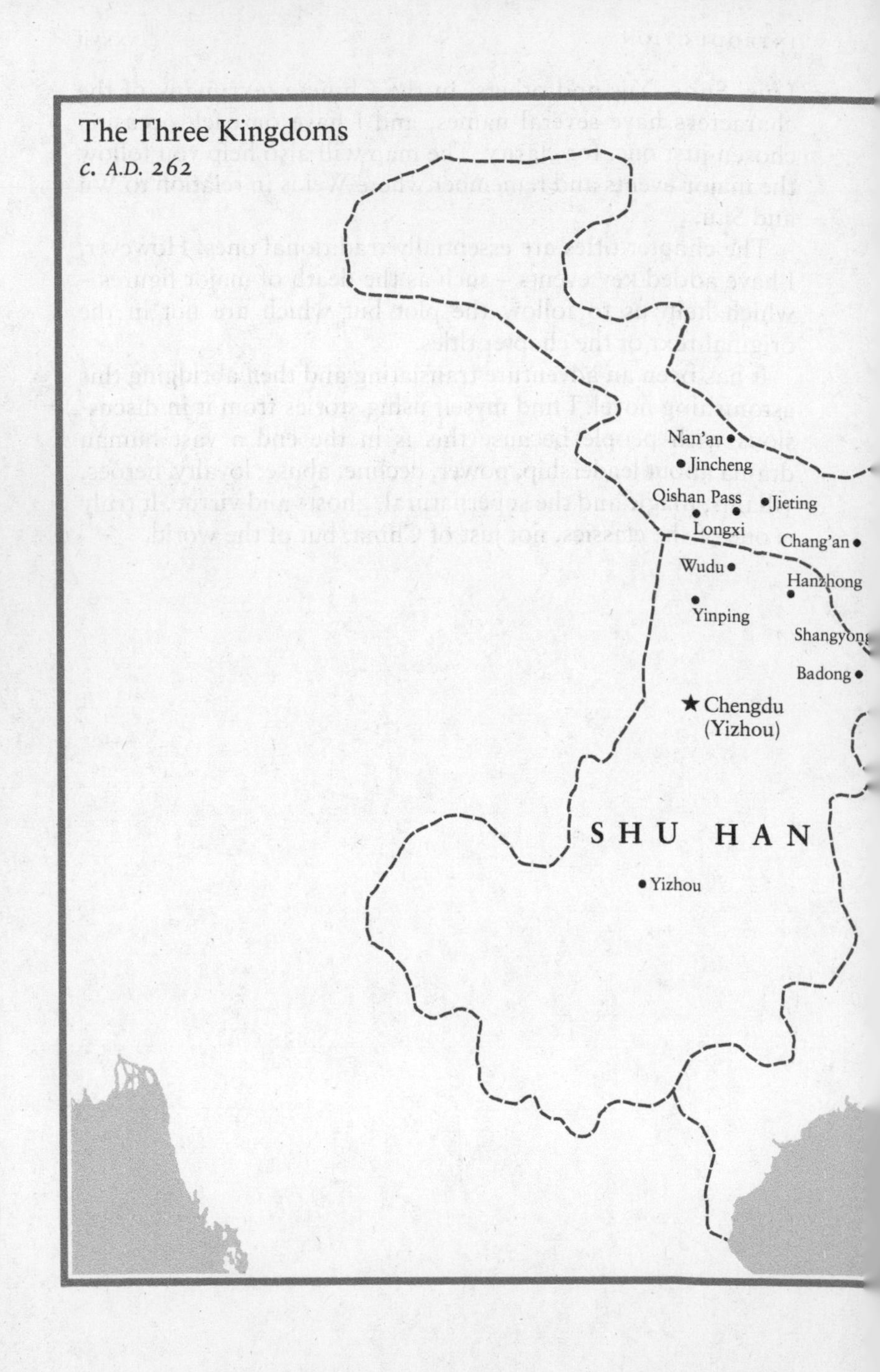

The Three Kingdoms
c. A.D. 262
Nan'an
Jincheng
Qishan Pass
Jieting
Longxi
Chang'an
Wudu
Hanzhong
Yinping
Shangyong
Badong
Chengdu
(Yizhou)
SHU HAN
Yizhou

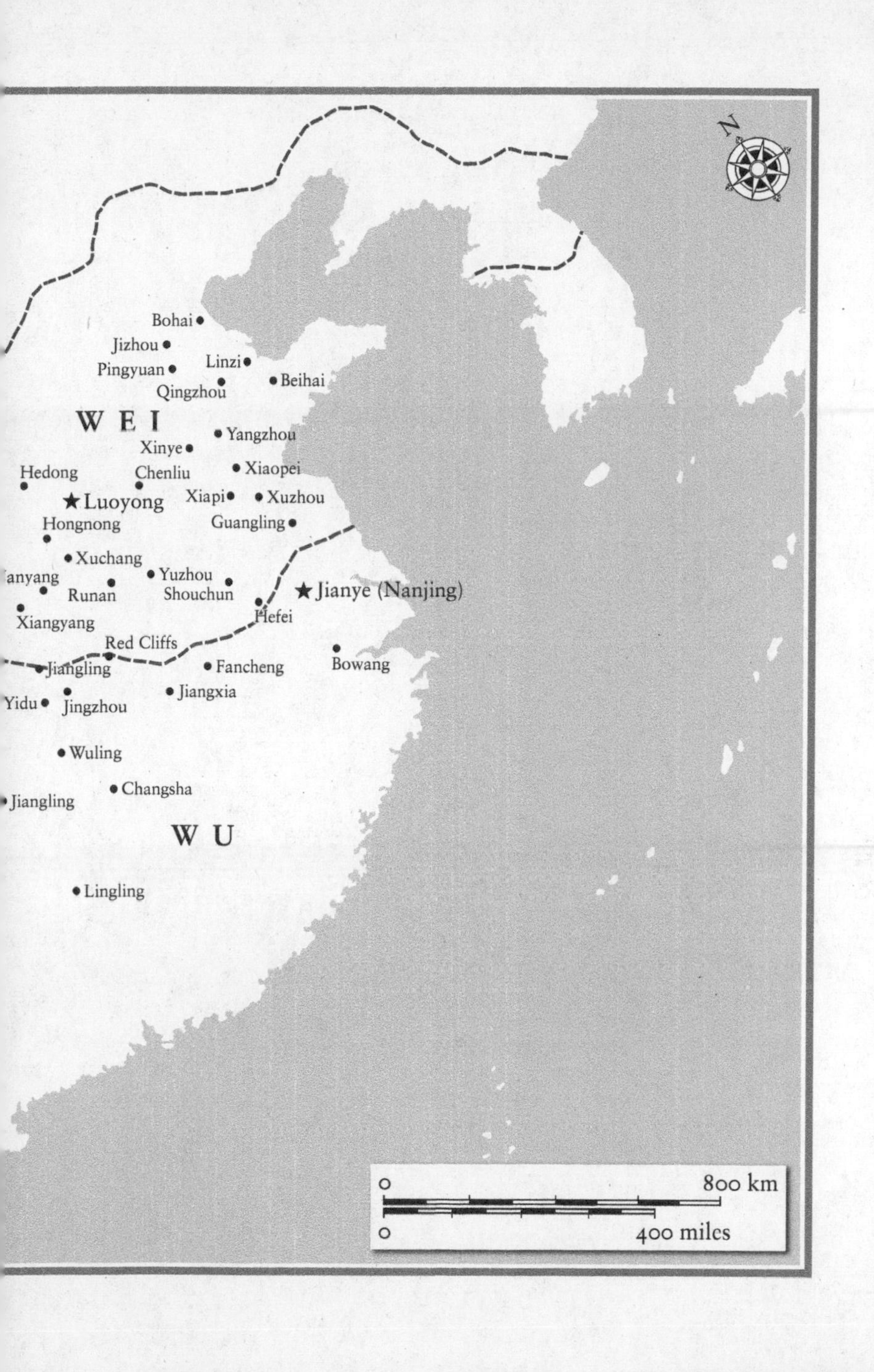
N
Bohai
Jizhou
Pingyuan
Linzi
Qingzhou
Beihai
WEI
Yangzhou
Xinye
Hedong
Chenliu
Xiaopei
Luoyong
Xiapi
Xuzhou
Hongnong
Guangling
Xuchang
Yuzhou
Runan
Shouchun
Jianye (Nanjing)
Hefei
Xiangyang
Red Cliffs
Jiangling
Fancheng
Bowang
Yidu
Jingzhou
Jiangxia
Wuling
Changsha
Jiangling
WU
Lingling
0
800 km
0
400 miles

List of Main Characters

Cai Mao: brother of Lady Cai, the wife of Liu Biao, and his bitter rival.

Cao Cao: one of the founders of the Three Kingdoms, namely the kingdom of Wei, whose son Cao Pi dismisses the last Han emperor and founds the Wei dynasty. The main enemy of Xuande. Posthumously declared First Emperor.

Cao Fang: adopted grandson of Cao Cao and the third emperor of the Wei dynasty.

Cao Hong: cousin of Cao Cao and a senior commander of his army.

Cao Huan: fifth and last emperor of the Wei dynasty, who abdicates to Sima Yan.

Cao Mao: fourth emperor of the Wei dynasty, murdered by the Sima family.

Cao Pi: son of Cao Cao and first emperor of the Wei dynasty.

Cao Rui: second emperor of the Wei dynasty.

Cao Shuang: son of Cao Zhen and enemy of Sima Yi.

Cao Zhen: senior officer in the Wei army.

Cao Zhi: son of Cao Cao; set to one side so Cao Pi can be the heir apparent. A famous if dissolute poet.

Chen Deng: initially adviser to Lü Bu; later turns against him.

Chen Lin: senior adviser to Yuan Shao who goes over to Cao Cao.

Deng Ai: heroic Wei general who resists the attacks of the Shu and eventually is central to the overthrow of the Shu army and dynasty.

Deng Zhi: masterful diplomat sent to restore relations between the Shu and Wu.

Dian Wei: Cao Cao's most loyal bodyguard and hero of many a battle.

Diao Chan: the dancing, singing servant girl who helps Wang Yun set Dong Zhou and his adopted son Lü Bu against each other.

Ding Feng: senior commander of the Wu army.

Dong Cheng: unwitting recipient of the secret message from the emperor to organize the murder of Cao Cao.

Dong Zhuo: one of the main villains of the story: removes the legitimate emperor and installs his own puppet emperor and then rules ruthlessly, fatally weakening the Han. He orders the destruction of the capital Luoyang.

Emperor Shao: (Liu Bian) legitimate heir to Emperor Ling; he is deposed and then murdered by Dong Zhuo and whose younger brother is made emperor instead.

Emperor Xian (Liu Xie): placed on the throne by Dong Zhuo, who has deposed Emperor Shao. The last and increasingly embattled and feeble Han emperor.

Empress Dong: foster mother of Emperor Xian; she uses her position to gain power and control.

Empress He: mother of Emperor Shao; she is murdered along with her son by Dong Zhuo.

Fa Zheng: adviser in the court of Liu Zhang who supports and enables Xuande's conquest of Shu.

Gan Ning: naval expert of Wu who deserts Liu Biao.

Gongsun Zan: close military friend of Xuande; dies after defeat by Yuan Shao.

Guan Xing: son of Guan Yu who avenges his father's betrayal and death. Becomes one of Xuande's most successful military officers.

Guan Yu: one of the three brothers of the peach orchard. Heroic, loyal and faithful.

Guo Jia: long-standing adviser to Cao Cao.

Guo Si: along with Li Jue takes over the capital after the death of Dong Zhuo and Wang Yun. Ruthless exploiter of the chaos and the power vacuum.

Huang Gai: senior commander of the Wu whose fake defection to Cao Cao brings defeat for Cao Cao.

Huang Zhong: veteran warrior who joins Xuande and whose exploits put the younger commanders to shame.

Hua Xin: an adviser to Cao Pi and the one who forces Emperor Xian to abdicate, thus ending the Han dynasty.

Jia Xu: wise military adviser to many of the most powerful warlords, especially Cao Cao.

Jiang Wei: Shu commander whose obsession with conquering Wei ultimately destroys Shu.

Ji Ping: court physician whose involvement in a plot to assassinate Cao Cao goes horribly wrong.

Kong Ming: Daoist adept and master military adviser to Xuande who becomes prime minister under Xuande's successor. Also known as Zhuge Liang.

Lady Cai: sister of Cai Mao, wife of Liu Biao, mother of Liu Zong. Fierce opponent of Xuande.

Lady Gan: wife of Xuande, mother of Liu Shan.

Lady Mi: sister of Mi Zhu, wife of Xuande, who dies in flight to save her son.

Lady Sun: sister of Sun Quan, warrior wife of Xuande.

Liu Bei: family name of the first of the three brothers of the peach orchard, also known as Xuande, the name used throughout this translation.

Liu Bian: family name of Emperor Shao.

Liu Biao: governor of Jingzhou who gives refuge to Xuande. Husband of Lady Cai, a fierce opponent of Xuande.

Liu Feng: adopted son of Xuande.

Liu Qi: heir of Liu Biao, hated and opposed by his stepmother Lady Cai.

Liu Shan (Ah Dou): eldest son of Xuande and second emperor or ruler of Shu.

Liu Zhang: governor of what became the kingdom of Shu; removed by his clansman Xuande.

Liu Zong: son of Lady Cai and Liu Biao, murdered by Cao Cao.

Lu Su: diplomat from Wei who tries to work with Xuande and Kong Ming.

Lu Xun: son-in-law of Sun Ce who defends Wu against the attacks of Xuande.

Lu Zhi: teacher of Xuande and commander against the Yellow Headbands revolt.

Lü Bu: originally an opponent of Dong Zhuo, later his adopted son; turns against him because of romance with Diao Chan.

Lü Meng: Wu commander who captures Guan Yu.

Ma Chao: one of Xuande's Five Tiger Generals.

Mi Fang: brother of Lady Mi who fails to rescue Guan Yu and is killed on Xuande's orders.

Mi Zhu: Supporter and brother-in-law of Xuande.

Pang De: supports Cao Cao but is slain by Guan Yu. Carried his own coffin into battle.

Pang Tong: adviser to Xuande and teacher of Kong Ming.

Shan Fu: Daoist name of Xu Shu, adviser to Xuande, tricked into joining Cao Cao and denounced by his mother.

Sima Shi: son of Sima Yi and a major participant in the overthrow of the Cao family in Wei.

Sima Yan: overthrower of the Wei dynasty, first emperor of the Jin dynasty and grandson of Sima Yi.

Sima Yi: outstanding general under the Wei who sets in motion the eventual collapse of the Wei and the rise of his own family as the Jin dynasty.

Sima Zhao: son of Sima Yi who overthrows the Shu dynasty.

Sun Ce: eldest son of Sun Jian and brother of Sun Quan.

Sun Jian: founder of the kingdom of Wu.

Sun Qian: senior adviser and supporter of Xuande.

Sun Quan: second son of Sun Jian and brother to Sun Ce; declares himself the first emperor of Wu.

Taishi Ci: opponent of, and then adviser to, Sun Ce.

Tao Qian: governor of Xuzhou who offers Xuande refuge and then his post, which Xuande refuses.

Wang Yun: senior Han adviser; designs the plot with Diao Chan to set Dong Zhuo and Lü Bu against each other.

Wei Yan: senior commander of Xuande's army, then commander of Hanzhong but never trusted by Kong Ming.

Xiahou Dun: warrior in Cao Cao's army.

Xuande: The first of the three brothers of the peach orchard; founded the kingdom of Shu. Referred to as Xuande throughout this translation, but also known by his family and given name of Liu Bei.

Xu Huang: commander in Cao Cao's army.

Xu Shu: *see* Shan Fu.

Yu Ji: Daoist master who after his murder returns to haunt Sun Ce.

Yuan Shao: head of the initial military confederation against Cao Cao.

Yuan Shu: weak brother of Yuan Shan who betrays Sun Ce.

Yuan Tan: eldest son of Yuan Shao.

Yue Jin: senior adviser to Cao Cao.

Zhang Bao: son of Zhang Fei and brother-in-arms to Guan Xing.

Zhang Fei: the third of the three brothers of the peach orchard. Loyal but prone to violent outbursts which eventually lead to his murder.

Zhang He: commander in the army of Cao Cao.

Zhang Liao: starts serving Lü Bu but surrenders to Cao Cao.

Zhang Lu: governor of Hanzhong; overthrown by Cao Cao.

Zhang Song: Shu emissary sent to Xuande who joins his side and helps overthrow Liu Zhang.

Zhang Zhao: adviser to Sun Quan and advocate of peace deals.

Zhao Zilong: loyal commander under Xuande and fearless warrior.

Zhong Hui: commander of Wei who leads the final attack on Shu.

Zhou Tai: senior commander of Sun Quan.

Zhou Yu: adviser to Sun Quan and head of war party.

Zhuge Jin: brother of Kong Ming (Zhuge Liang), and adviser to Sun Quan, often caught up in conflicts between Kong Ming and Sun Quan.

Zhuge Liang: *see* Kong Ming.

Zhuge Zhan: son of Kong Ming (Zhuge Liang), Shu commander who opposed surrender to Wei.

Zhu Ran: Wu commander.

Zhu Zhi: senior Wu commander.

CHAPTER 1

Three heroes, Xuande, Guan Yu and Zhang Fei, bind themselves by the vow of the peach orchard. They triumph against the Yellow Headband rebels.

Empires arise from chaos and empires collapse back into chaos. This we have known since time began.

The Zhou dynasty collapsed when seven kingdoms tore apart the empire by fighting among themselves, until eventually the Qin kingdom conquered all of the other kingdoms. But the Qin did not last long, and after them came the competing forces of Chu and Han. They also fought among themselves until the Han triumphed, uniting all under Heaven into one empire again. Many years later, the empire was divided by an uprising, but unity was restored by Emperor Guang Wu, and all was well again – until, that is, the reign of Emperor Xian, when the empire split into three kingdoms. It was brought about by two previous bad emperors: Emperor Huan, who favoured eunuchs over men of distinction and integrity, and Emperor Ling, his successor, who failed to support a palace conspiracy against the eunuchs, and the instigators were executed. From that time on the eunuchs were in complete control, and nobody could stop them.

From early in the second year of his reign[1] the Emperor Ling was troubled by omens of bad fortune. There was a green snake which appeared and wrapped itself around the throne during a great ceremony; in later years a terrible thunderstorm which destroyed many buildings; and an earthquake which struck at the heart of the capital Luoyang, while floods crashed in on the coast. Reports arrived of hens turning into cocks; strange dark clouds filled the Hall of Gentle Virtue, while a rainbow appeared in the Jade Chamber. The cliff-face of a mountain collapsed. All these omens, and there were many others, were too numerous to be dismissed as simply isolated incidents.

Despite warnings by loyal ministers, the emperor retreated into his palace, and a gang of eunuchs, called the Ten Imperial Attendants, took over. They were led by Zhang Rang, who was the emperor's favourite. Things became so bad that across the empire people's hearts and minds turned to thoughts of rebellion, and outlaws swarmed over the land like wasps . . .

One of the rebellions is led by three brothers, Zhang Jue, Zhang Bao and Zhang Liang. Zhang Jue failed his imperial exam and in despair took himself off to find solace and healing in the mountains. One day he meets an old man – a master of secret knowledge. He leads Zhang Jue into a cave and there presents him with a divinely inspired book in three volumes. The old master says, 'This is known as *The Peaceful Way for the Future*. Heaven has chosen you to be its messenger, spreading its teachings throughout the land for this whole generation. But you must practise compassion. If you do otherwise, ill fortune will befall you.'

Zhang Jue wants to know who this old master is.

'I am the Old Immortal from the sacred mountain of Hua Shan,' he replies and, with that, disappears from sight.

Zhang Jue applies himself to the study of the texts and soon, through the magic arts he acquires, such as being able to call up the wind and rain, he becomes known as the Peaceful Master of the Way. In the last year of Emperor Ling's reign[2] the plague strikes. The amulets and spells Zhang Jue distributes to the people are so successful that his fame spreads far and wide, and soon he has hundreds of thousands of followers. A song starts to be sung at this time:

The Blue Heaven is dying
The Yellow Heaven arising
A new cycle is beginning
Bringing good fortune for all.

Zhang Jue gives himself the title of Great and Esteemed Leader. He decides to seize the moment and overthrow the dynasty. He has yellow banners made, agrees an auspicious date for the uprising and sends one of his trusted disciples to the capital, where there are already supporters within the palace itself. He meets a senior contact within the palace and informs him about the planned uprising. But the disciple betrays him: all conspirators at the court are arrested, and the whole gang of rebels within the palace is imprisoned.

With his plot uncovered, in desperation, Zhang Jue summons his troops. Calling himself Heaven's Commander, he announces to his followers that a great sage will soon appear, and a new era will begin. From across the empire, hundreds of thousands of people respond to his call. They wear yellow cloth wrapped around their heads, and the sheer force of their rebellion causes the imperial troops to scatter as if blown away by the wind.

Zhang Jue's army invades the area where the governor is a man called Liu Yan, a distant member of the imperial family. He is advised to urgently issue a written proclamation in order to recruit an army of volunteers.

The proclamation is posted up in Zhuo County, where one man, a true hero, sees it. While he is not a scholar, he is a good man: generous, reserved and modest. His greatest aspiration is to befriend the worthiest men of the empire. He is a tall man, with arms that reach down below his knees. He has long earlobes, and his eyes are so wide apart he can actually see his own ears. His face is as pure as jade, while his lips are bright-red.

This man is called Xuande, meaning Mystic Virtue. His family surname is Liu, and his given name Bei. His father died when he was young, leaving him and his mother in poverty despite being descendants of the imperial family. In order to survive, he wove mats and sandals which he then sold. They lived in a village named after its huge mulberry tree, two storeys high, which looked like a canopy for an imperial carriage. Once a fortune-teller foretold that a man of significance would emerge from this village. And one day, when he was a young child, playing under the canopy of the tree, Xuande said, 'When I am the Son of Heaven, my carriage will have a canopy just like this.' His uncle, Liu Yuanqi, who took care of the poor family and often supported his nephew, commented that this was no ordinary child. At the age of fifteen Xuande's mother sent him away to school.

Xuande is twenty-eight years old when he reads the proclamation posted by Governor Liu. As he is reading it, he sighs deeply. Then, suddenly, a voice behind him asks rather sharply,

'Why such deep sighs? Surely a true man will serve the emperor at times of such danger.'

Turning round, Xuande finds a man a little taller than him. His forehead is flattened like that of a panther, he has great round eyes, the heavy jowls of a swallow, a great hairy beard and moustache, a voice like thunder and the energy of a prancing horse.

'Who are you?' Xuande asks, with a mixture of fear and astonishment.

'My name,' he says, 'is Zhang Fei. For generations we've lived here on our farm, trading wine and pork. Now I'm looking for men of true spirit to join me, and when I heard you sighing in front of this proclamation, I decided to have words with you.'

'Actually,' Xuande replies, 'my name is Xuande, family name Liu, so I'm related to the emperor. When I heard about all the trouble the Yellow Headband rebels were causing, I decided to go and help attack them and protect the people. I was sighing just then because I was worried about whether I could really help. And then you challenged me.'

'I've contacts that could be used to recruit men from around here,' says Zhang Fei. 'So why don't we work together for this great cause? Now don't you think that's a good idea?'

Xuande is delighted, and to celebrate the two go off to an inn. While they are drinking they see an athletic-looking man pushing a wheelbarrow. He stops to rest at the inn.

'I'm off to volunteer,' he announces, after brusquely demanding some wine. Xuande studies him with great interest. He is huge, with a two-foot beard and red cheeks. His lips shine, and his eyes are slanted like those of the crimson phoenix, while his bushy eyebrows look like silkworms. With his size and his fearful bearing he is clearly a fighter, and it is no time before

Xuande invites him to join them at their table and to tell them who he is.

'My name is Guan Yu and I'm from Jieliang in Hedong,' the newcomer says. 'However, I had to leave there in a hurry after I killed a bully who was terrorizing the local people. I've been travelling for about five or six years now. And after I heard about the call to arms I decided to come to join up.' Xuande fills him in on his own plans, and Guan Yu is delighted. Zhang Fei invites them to leave the inn and go to his manor house nearby to make plans.

When they get there, Zhang Fei tells them that there is a peach orchard behind the house. 'It's in full flower at the moment,' he says. 'Why don't the three of us go there tomorrow and make sacrifices to Heaven and Earth. We can bind ourselves to each other so that we can fulfil our destiny together and fight side by side in our great adventure.' Xuande and Guan Yu agree completely with his plan. 'Yes!' they both say, as if with one voice.

The following day the three go to the peach orchard. They prepare among various other offerings a black bull and a white horse. Then in the midst of the smoke from the incense the three men make their vow, one to the other.

'We, Xuande, Guan Yu and Zhang Fei,
Even though we come from separate families,
We vow to stand by each other
And be blood brothers for ever.
Let us agree to protect the people of our homeland!

When we're in trouble, we'll rescue each other,
When we're in danger we'll be there for each other,
So even though we weren't born in the same year, month, day,
On the same day and month in the same year,
May we die . . .

We pray that Heaven above
And the Earth below that nurtures everything

Will hear this plea from our hearts.
And if we fail to do what is right,
If we fail to do what is gracious,
Then may Heaven and the people bring us down.'

Having sworn their mutual allegiance, they agree that Xuande will henceforth be considered the elder brother, Guan Yu the second and Zhang Fei the third. Having vowed this before Heaven and Earth, they cook the meat and share out the wine and invite the three hundred or so who have agreed to join them from the surrounding area to feast and drink with them in the middle of the peach orchard.

Over the next few days everyone is busy gathering weapons, finding enough horses and getting special armour made. Xuande has two double-edged swords fashioned, Guan Yu has a curved sword called Cold Wonder forged, while Zhang Fei orders a long spear.

By now some five hundred young men have joined. Together they all march off and report for duty to Liu Yan, the governor whose call to arms was the original spur to action. Needless to say, he is delighted, not least when, just a few days later, a Yellow Headband army of around fifty thousand men attacks the Zhuo district.

Xuande leads his men forward. Flanked by Guan Yu on his left and Zhang Fei to his right, he challenges the rebels, crying, 'You traitors, surrender now!' In the battle that follows, Zhang Fei slays the enemy champion with his giant spear, while Guan Yu slices the champion's companion in two. The rebels flee; many are taken prisoner. This valiant effort is honoured by a poem:

What courage on this auspicious day.
One with his spear, another with his sword.
In their first encounter, their bravery shines.
A land split three ways will always sing of their success.

But the very next day an urgent request for help comes from the governor of the besieged city of Qingzhou. Xuande and his brothers-in-arms, now with five thousand men, march there to help. But they are driven back by the rebels.

'There are too many of them,' Xuande says to Guan Yu and Zhang Fei. 'The only solution is to surprise them.'

Which is why they plan an ambush.

Xuande and the bulk of the army march forward, making as much noise as possible, while the other two take a thousand men each and hide on either side of a mountain. The rebels attack, and Xuande's men fall back as if they are retreating. Suddenly the war gongs ring out, and from either side of the mountain pass soldiers surge down, while Xuande's men turn and attack their pursuers. The rebels flee back to the camp outside the besieged Qingzhou, from where the governor leads out his people to the attack. The rebels are overwhelmed by this pincer movement. Many of them die that day. So it is that Qingzhou is saved.

News now reaches the three men that the rebel leader Zhang Jue is attacking the neighbouring city of Guangzong, and that the city is defended by Xuande's old teacher, Lu Zhi. So off the three brothers-in-arms go, with their five hundred men, and my goodness is Lu Zhi delighted to see them! However, he tells them that the real struggle is further afield, at the city of Yingchuan, where the two brothers of the rebel chief are locked in combat with imperial forces, so at dead of night Xuande and his troops ride to Yingchuan.

The rebels have set up a temporary fort in the countryside, and that night they are attacked in an unexpected way. The commanders on the emperor's side have ordered each of their soldiers to carry a straw torch. As the night wind rises, the soldiers set fire to the fields all around the rebel encampment. As the flames soar high into the night sky, the troops attack, and the rebels flee in panic.

The two brothers of the chief rebel, Zhang Liang and Zhang Bao, race through the night with their men. As dawn breaks they run straight into a new troop of soldiers. They are led by a cavalryman of modest height, with sharp eyes and a long beard.

His name is Cao Cao. He is a schemer and dedicated to the chase and to partying. When he was young, one of his uncles complained about him to his father, leading his father to punish him. So the next time Cao met that uncle he fell down as if he was having an epileptic fit. Horrified, the uncle rushed to fetch his father, who, when he came running, found Cao perfectly well. Cao's father couldn't understand what was going on and asked his son if he was all right.

'I'm fine. Nothing happened, but this is typical of the lies my uncle tries to tell to alienate you from me,' Cao said. This trick turned the father against the uncle, so no matter what complaints were made thereafter, Cao was free to behave just as he wished.

When the first Yellow Headband revolt broke out many people spoke of Cao Cao as being the one who could save the dynasty. One fortune-teller said:

'You're wise enough to rule the world and perverse enough to destroy the world.'

'Oh good,' Cao Cao thought.

Running into Zhang Liang and Zhang Bao fleeing with their men, he attacks them with the five thousand troops under his command. Although the two Zhang brothers manage to escape once again, Cao's men kill ten thousand of the rebels and capture their train of wagons with all their goods. Then Cao sets off after the two fleeing brothers.

Back at Yingchuan, Xuande and his two brothers arrive to find the rebels already in disarray. There they are told that the scattered remnants of the rebel army are heading for Guangzong, the city where Xuande's old master Lu Zhi is governor. So they turn around and hurry back. But as they are travelling back they come upon a prison wagon, surrounded by soldiers. To their astonishment, who is inside but Lu Zhi?

'What on earth is going on?' they ask.

'I almost captured that rebel Zhang Jue,' Lu Zhi says bitterly. 'But he used magic and escaped. The court sent a corrupt official to investigate who wanted me to pay him off so he would report back to the court in my favour. But we had exhausted all our resources fighting the rebels, so even if I had wanted to – which I didn't – I coudn't bribe him. So he told the court that the failure to capture Zhang Jue was my fault because I was frightened to go on the offensive. The court then sent Dong Zhuo to take my place and have ordered me back to the court for trial.'

Zhang Fei, whose fury is never far from the surface, wants to kill the guards and free the prisoner, but Xuande stops him.

'We should trust the court and let justice be done,' he says.

'With Lu arrested we don't have anywhere to go except back to Zhuo,' Guan Yu says. And it is agreed that this is exactly what they will do.

It is two days later, back in Zhuo County, that they hear the sounds of a battle nearby. Climbing a hill, they see a host of Yellow Headband rebels overrunning an imperial army. In the midst of the rebels, who are clearly winning, they see a banner declaring the troops are led by 'Heaven's Commander'. They know this must be Zhang Jue, in person.

'Let's attack!' cries Xuande, and the three brothers sweep down the hill with their troops, falling upon the rebels. They are just in time, because Zhang Jue is on the point of defeating the imperial commander Dong Zhuo, who has been sent to take Lu Zhi's place after he was arrested. The battle is long and hard, but eventually Zhang Jue retreats. The three brothers rescue Dong Zhuo and escort him back to their camp. When Dong Zhuo discovers his rescuers are not officers, just ordinary men who have taken command, he dismisses them. He rejects any idea that they might have helped him and he sends them out of the camp.

Zhang Fei is furious. He vows to get revenge on this worthless man whom they have just rescued.

'He must die!' Zhang Fei shouts. He draws his sword and rushes back to the imperial forces' camp, intent on killing Dong Zhuo.

Will Dong Zhuo survive?

This will soon be revealed.

CHAPTER 2

A furious Zhang Fei punishes a pompous official. At court He Jin plots to destroy the eunuchs. Cao Cao joins the plot.

Dong Zhuo is the governor of Hedong and he is incredibly overbearing and rude. It is this rudeness which so provoked Zhang Fei, but Xuande and Guan Yu just about manage to stop him.

'Dong Zhuo is an official, and it would be madness just to try and strike him down,' they say.

'Unless we deal with him now he'll be ordering us about for evermore, and I won't stand for that,' snarls Zhang Fei. 'You two can stay if you want, but I'm leaving.'

'The three of us have sworn to stick together through thick and thin,' says Xuande. 'We can't be separated, so let's go together.'

'Well,' snaps Zhang Fei, 'we're off, then. That's good.'

They decide to go with their men to the camp of Zhu Jun, an imperial officer struggling against the rebel Zhang Bao. Soon after they unite with Zhu Jun the armies clash. Zhang Bao, who is on horseback, unbinds his hair, and with his sword in his hand begins to chant magical spells. A thunderstorm breaks over Xuande's troops, and a dark cloud descends on them from Heaven. In the middle of the dark cloud innumerable horses and men appear. The imperial troops flee in panic, and Xuande rushes back to report all this to Zhu Jun.

'So he uses occult powers,' comments Zhu Jun. 'Then tomorrow we'll sacrifice a pig, a goat and a dog. We'll make sure all the blood and entrails and excrement are collected together. Then when the rebels attack we'll throw this mess down upon them and then watch the occult forces evaporate!'

The very next day Zhang Bao appears again with his troops and invokes a great raging storm, filling the air with rocks and stones. The black cloud descends again, full of the same spectral horses and men. Xuande pretends to flee, drawing the rebels and their ghostly forces in pursuit, when suddenly from the hillside the appalling mixture of blood and entrails rains down. Instantly the storm dies away; the cloud disperses; the paper men and straw horses collapse, and the rocks and pebbles fall to the ground. Zhang Bao and his men break and run.

Zhang Bao is badly wounded and takes refuge in the city of Yangcheng. Zhu Jun responds by besieging the city. During the siege news comes that Zhang Jue, the original leader of the rebellion, has died and that his son has been killed in battle. This news pushes Zhang Bao's own men to revolt. One of his own men kills him and carries his leader's severed head with him when he surrenders to the imperial forces.

Three other rebel leaders emerge from the chaos, seeking revenge for the collapse of Zhang Jue's revolt. They set up their headquarters in the city of Wancheng. Here they are besieged by an army led by Zhu Jun and the three brothers in arms. The siege swings this way and that, until the imperial forces have to retreat.

Zhu Jun retreats ten miles from Wancheng and is surprised if not a little alarmed to suddenly see a troop of men and horses approaching from the east. They are led by a man whose face is broad and open. He is fit as a tiger, and his body is as strong as a bear's. His name is Sun Jian, and he is a descendant of the famous military writer Sun Zi, who wrote *The Art of War*. When Sun Jian was seventeen and out walking with his father they saw a gang of pirates attack a merchant and then start to divide up his goods. 'Come on, we can capture these pirates!' the young Sun Jian had said to his father and, drawing his sword, he rushed on them, shouting to left and right as if commanding followers to attack. This so frightened the pirates that they panicked and ran, but not before Sun Jian had cut one of them down dead. Locally he became famous for this feat. When, many years later, a rebel arose who claimed he was the Yang Ming emperor, Sun Jian helped defeat his massive army, numbered in tens of thousands. When this was reported to the emperor, Sun Jian was made an official mandarin.

So it was that, when the Yellow Headband revolt broke out, Sun Jian recruited fifteen hundred men from the lands around the Rivers Huai and Si and marched off to help Zhu Jun in his struggles at Wancheng. Boosted by the new troops, Zhu Jun orders a full-out attack on the city. Sun Jian is the first to break through, killing twenty men by his hand alone.

The revolt collapses; tens of thousands of rebels are executed, and the region is pacified. When they return in triumph to the capital city, Zhu Jun is rewarded for his courage. Sun Jian and Xuande are mentioned in despatches, and, as a result, because he has family connections, Sun Jian is promoted. However, nothing is offered to Xuande. He becomes very disillusioned by this treatment.

One day the three brothers are wandering around the capital when an official notices them and asks who they are. Xuande tells him about his victories, and how he hasn't been given any reward. The official asks permission to see the emperor and points out that, due to the interference of the Ten Eunuchs who control the court, only their cronies are being appointed, and good men are ignored. This is the reason why rebellion is rife.

'Cut the eunuchs' heads off and expose them on the gates,' the official advises the emperor. But the eunuchs outmanoeuvre him, and he is expelled from the court. However, this does alert the eunuchs to the dangers of bypassing worthy men, and in the ensuing rash of minor appointments, Xuande is made the magistrate of Anxi County. His two brothers-in-arms accompany him and join him in his duties and responsibilities. Xuande's justice is so honest and forthright that, within just one month, crime has ceased.

However, this peaceful and successful life does not last.

A few months later an inspector comes to Anxi. Although Xuande greets him with all due formalities, the inspector barely acknowledges him. He then quizzes Xuande on his claims about being descended from the imperial family, which the inspector proceeds to rubbish. It soon becomes clear that, unless the inspector is bribed, Xuande will be dismissed as a 'corrupt official'. But as Xuande has never extorted even a single grain of rice from anybody, he cannot pay him off even if he wanted to. Soon Xuande is banned from even entering the court.

One day, not long after the inspector has taken over, Zhang Fei rides up. He is already drunk and disgruntled and discovers some old people weeping outside the court. When he asks why they are so troubled, they say, 'This inspector is forcing false statements out of people. He wants to destroy your master, and we want to plead his case. But they won't even let us inside to be heard!'

Hearing from these old people about the corrupt practices of the inspector, Zhang Fei loses his temper. Leaping down from his horse, he smashes his way in. Confronting the inspector, he roars, 'Do you know who I am?' and before the terrified man can speak Zhang grabs him by the hair and drags him outside. There, he ties him to a hitching post. Breaking branches from a willow tree, he lashes the inspector until his whips have broken into many pieces. Yet not that even this stops Zhang Fei from continuing to lash the man.

Xuande hears the shouts and cries and when he learns it is Zhang Fei he comes rushing.

'Stop!' he shouts. But Zhang Fei's anger is still raging, and he shouts back, 'Such a louse as this needs to be squashed or what else will he get up to?' Xuande, being a gentle person, tries again to stop Zhang Fei. Then Guan Yu turns up. He too feels the inspector should die but he also points out to Xuande that the position the court has given him is barely worth his time, and that this pompous inspector has simply confirmed that he is destined for greater things.

'Brother!' says Guan Yu, using an old proverb. 'Does a glorious phoenix belong in a mere prickly bush? Let's finish him off and get out of here.'

Xuande removes his seal of office and hangs it around the inspector's neck. He tells him that because of his corruption, and the terrible damage this does to the ordinary people, they should kill him. 'But we'll spare you, so take this back to the court!' he says. Then he and his two brothers in arms mount their horses and, turning their backs on the inspector, ride away.

Needless to say, when the inspector returns to his superior, he tells him what has happened, and orders for the arrest of the three brothers are sent out. But by this time the three are long gone and have taken refuge with friends.

Back at the imperial court the Ten Eunuchs continue to get rid of anyone who stands in their way. The least worthy men are promoted, and this leads to rebellions breaking out across the land. Yet the Ten act as if nothing is wrong. Brave men still try to open the emperor's eyes to the evils the Ten are bringing upon the country, but the Ten claim they are the most loyal of subjects. And behind the emperor's back they are murdering everyone who stands in their way.

Xuande is quietly recommended to help in the suppression of another revolt and he is so successful that his offence against the inspector is forgotten. At last he is given a major post worthy of his talents and is made magistrate of Pingyuan County.

Not long after, Emperor Ling falls into a terminal illness. This causes a major crisis. Who is to succeed him? The Empress He has a son called Prince Bian. She has already poisoned the second consort, Wang the Beautiful, whose son, Prince Xie, was left to be raised by his grandmother, the emperor's mother, Empress Dong.

He Jin, the grand administrator, is a man of humble origins. He is also the brother of the empress and the uncle of Prince Bian. He finds himself caught between the conflicting claims to the throne. Plot upon plot is hatched, until one man dares to speak out during a meeting of the Council.

'We've been under the control of eunuchs since the Emperors Chong and Zhi over fifty years ago,' he says. 'We must get rid of them. But how can we plan to kill them all without them discovering this and killing us and all our families? We have to be so very careful.'

The speaker is Cao Cao, who is by then a commander in the military. He Jin is just starting to respond when news comes that the emperor has died. Furthermore, the messenger says, 'The eunuchs are planning to keep this a secret until they have secured the succession for their own candidate, the young Prince Xie.'

Cao Cao immediately nominates He Jin's nephew, Prince

Bian, as the heir, and he is joined in this declaration by Yuan Shao, who commands the troops of the capital.

'Give me five thousand soldiers,' General Yuan Shao says, 'and I'll storm the palace!' He promises to place Prince Bian on the throne, kill the eunuchs, cleanse the court and restore harmony under Heaven again.

Inspired by this, they storm into the palace and in front of the coffin of the dead emperor they place Prince Bian on the throne and declare him the new Emperor Shao. Emboldened, they decide to wipe out all the eunuchs, but they have already fled to the protection of Empress He, who, elated by the elevation of her son to emperor, promises to protect them. In the confusion Empress Dong, the dead emperor's mother, tries to reassert her power but fails, because the Ten Eunuchs do not support her. She is sent off to the countryside, where she is murdered six months later.

Yuan Shao still wants to exact revenge on the eunuchs, but Grand Administrator He Jin opposes this for the simple reason that the new emperor's mother, Empress He, his sister, is against it.

'Who cares?' shouts General Yuan Shao. 'Let's summon the brave men of the land and storm the capital, killing those eunuchs!' This time Grand Administrator He Jin is swayed by Yuan Shao's enthusiasm and sends forth the order to summon the troops.

And the person who supports him, while others stand against him, is Cao Cao, who says something that changes the tide of the destiny of the Han dynasty.

As the saying goes, 'Wise advice can counter the influence of treacherous officials, if and when it is heeded.'

So what is it that Cao Cao said?

Let's find out.

CHAPTER 3

Warlord Dong Zhuo usurps the throne, opposes Ding Yuan and aided by his sidekick Li Su bribes the hero Lü Bu to join his army

What Cao Cao has to say is this:

'These eunuchs have been a curse since antiquity,' he pronounces. 'We must strike at the leaders and we must do so stealthily with a small, dedicated force so that nobody finds out what we're doing. Bringing in troops and trying to kill them all will fail, because the others will know what is happening and they'll stop us.'

'I have my own plans,' He Jin retorts. 'And they involve summoning troops from across the land.' Annoyed at being ignored, Cao Cao walks out, but not before saying to others:

'He Jin will bring disaster on all beneath Heaven if he doesn't take care.'

One of the leaders who responds to He Jin's call to arms is none other than Dong Zhuo, who had so spectacularly failed to suppress the Yellow Headband rebels. He sends an advance petition to the capital Luoyang, asking to be allowed into the city and claiming he wants to protect the dynasty. He Jin agrees, but many others warn him of the dangers.

'Dong Zhuo hides the viciousness of a wolf under the guise of innocence. Let him in, and disaster will result,' says Lu Zhi, the former teacher of Xuande, who has been released from prison after his good name has been cleared following appeals made to the emperor. 'Keep him out, and order will be maintained.' But once again He Jin ignores good advice.

Dong Zhuo's arrival creates turmoil. Yuan Shao and Cao Cao want to attack the palace and wipe out the Ten Eunuchs, but He Jin once again misreads the situation. Responding to a command from his sister, the Empress He, to visit her in the court, he enters the inner court alone while Yuan Shao and Cao Cao are forced to wait outside. It is a trap. No sooner has He Jin entered than he is cut in half by the supporters of the Ten Eunuchs. When Yuan Shao calls out to see if he is ready to leave, he is answered by having He Jin's head thrown over the palace gate.

Furious at this turn of events, Yuan Shao and Cao Cao storm the palace gates and break in. They slaughter four of the Ten Eunuchs, while in the ensuing chaos the palace itself catches fire. Attempts by some of the surviving Ten Eunuchs to use the emperor, his brother Prince Xie and the empress as a shield fail, and these eunuchs are killed.

The leading eunuch, Zhang Rang, and another of the Ten, Duan Gui, have seized the fifteen-year-old Emperor Shao and his nine-year-old brother Prince Xie and smuggled them out of the palace. They manage to reach the nearby hills but here they are surprised by a troop of soldiers. Zhang Rang is recognized, and the leader of the troop calls out, 'Stop, you traitors.' Realizing his time has come, Zhang Rang throws himself into a stream and drowns, while Duan Gui is seized. The emperor and his brother, bewildered and frightened, hide, not sure who is on their side and who wishes them dead. Lying in a wet ditch, they evade discovery and through the cold night they lie wrapped in each other's arms to try to keep warm. Sadness overwhelms them, but they dare not cry for fear they will be heard. Towards the end of the night they also know they must now move on, so, tying themselves together, they scramble out of the ditch, pushing through thorn bushes and nettles. It is still dark, and at first they cannot see a path, let alone decide which way to go. Suddenly a swarm of fireflies appears, lighting the way and leading them to safety. 'Heaven has come to our aid,' cries the emperor. So they follow the fireflies.

Meanwhile, in a nearby farmhouse the master has had a dream. In his dream he saw two red suns falling from Heaven and landing behind his farm. Waking, he looks out and sees that two red lights are shining up into the dark night from behind one of his haystacks and when he goes to investigate he finds the two boys. 'Whose family do you belong to?' asks the startled master. The emperor, frightened, cannot speak, but Prince Xie responds, 'This is his imperial majesty, the emperor, and I'm his younger brother. We escaped from the chaos in the palace and from the evil eunuchs.' The master, astonished, kowtows and then leads the boys to his house, where they are warmed, fed and comforted.

Meanwhile, the leader of the troop of soldiers has questioned Duan Gui, demanding to know where the emperor is. Duan Gui confesses he has no idea and is summarily executed by the soldier, who hangs the head on his horse's neck and sets off to find the boys. Eventually the boys are found, and the news conveyed back to the loyal ministers in the capital. Soon fresh horses are brought, and ministers in full array come to escort the emperor and the prince back to the city.

As they approach the city, a huge, terrifying army appears in front of them. Heading this vast force is none other than Dong Zhuo, who demands to know where the emperor is. Once again the emperor is frozen with fear and cannot speak. But Prince Xie rides forward and says, 'And who are you?' 'I'm Dong Zhuo,' he replies and he is challenged again by the young prince: 'Have you come to protect his imperial majesty or to capture him?' 'I'm here to protect him,' replies Dong Zhuo. 'Then get off your horse,' demands the prince, 'and show proper respect. Here is the emperor.'

Dong Zhuo is impressed by how calm Prince Xie is in comparison to the panicking emperor. When the emperor is reunited with the Empress He, all seems well, but already, deep in the devious mind of Dong Zhuo, a plan is forming to depose the emperor and replace him with Prince Xie.

There is one thing that worries him after the palace coup. Where is the jade seal which the emperor needs in order to be able to issue commands? It is nowhere to be found.

Meanwhile, Dong Zhuo's troops run riot in the capital. Their destruction is terrible to behold; the city is devastated. Dong Zhuo comes and goes in the palace with no regard for the proper protocol. Dong Zhuo's assistant is Li Ru, and it is not long before Dong Zhuo speaks in secret to him, whispering that he is planning to remove the current emperor and put Prince Xie on the throne instead. Li Ru agrees with him and comes up with a plan as to how this should be done.

The very next day, at a grand feast and in the presence of the key nobles, Dong Zhuo springs his surprise. 'We know that the emperor, as Son of Heaven, is lord of everything that is below Heaven,' he says. 'But if he is without gravitas, he cannot fulfil everything that is demanded of him by his ancestors. Our current emperor does not have this gravitas, but his brother Prince Xie most definitely does. So I propose to depose the current emperor and place his brother on the throne. Do any of you here have anything to say?'

Only one person, Ding Yuan, speaks out. 'This is absolutely wrong!' he shouts.

Dong Zhuo wants to kill him there and then but is restrained by his assistant Li Ru.

Ding Yuan flees in order to save his life and to gather his troops. Meanwhile, Dong Zhuo once again demands if anyone has anything to say, and this time it is the old teacher Lu Zhi who speaks out against this. Once again Dong Zhuo is only just restrained from killing him.

The next morning things really start to unravel. Ding Yuan has drawn up his troops outside the city, and Dong Zhuo leads out his men to do battle. Facing him in Ding Yuan's army is a young man called Lü Bu. He has a golden crown in his hair and is wearing a fabulously coloured robe; his sword is decorated with lions and snakes.

As soon as the armies meet, Lü Bu charges straight at Dong Zhuo, and Dong Zhuo turns and runs. Ding Yuan's army overwhelm their opponents, and Dong Zhuo retreats and sets up camp.

'What a fighter,' Dong Zhuo says of Lü Bu. 'Imagine if he was on our side.'

At this, a man named Li Su steps forward. 'I could turn him, my lord, as I come from the same village as him. Let me offer him your fabled horse Red Hare, plus gold and pearls, and I will get him to betray Ding Yuan and join you.'

And indeed this is what happens.
A poet later described Red Hare:

Surging and soaring he travels over a thousand miles
Shaking the dust off his feet in a cloud.
Fording rivers and galloping at mountains
Even the very skies part when he comes!
Shaking his reins and his gem-studded harness
He's like a fiery dragon
Coming down from Heaven itself.

Making his way stealthily into the enemy camp, Li Su finds Lü Bu and says to him, 'You deserve a fine master. The wise bird carefully chooses its branch; the wise servant likewise is careful in the choice of his master.' And so with silken words and treasures such as Red Hare, Li Su brings Lü Bu over to Dong Zhuo's side.

That night Lü Bu creeps into Ding Yuan's tent. Ding Yuan is quietly reading but on hearing Lü Bu he looks up and says, 'What brings you here, my son?' To this Lü Bu says, 'I'm a man of great importance, so why on earth would I want to be known as your son?' Bewildered Ding Yuan asks, 'What has happened to make you say this?' Lü Bu gives no answer. He simply raises his sword and with one blow cuts off Ding Yuan's head. At this most of Ding Yuan's soldiers fade away into the night.

The next day Lü Bu brings the head to Dong Zhuo. Dong Zhuo is so delighted he bows to the young man. 'Your arrival is like dew to parched grass.' Lü Bu bowing down before him asks to be accepted into his army. Dong Zhuo is delighted with such a new recruit and presents him with many gifts of great value.

Emboldened by Lü Bu's presence, Dong Zhuo and Li Ru decide to press ahead with the forced abdication of the emperor and with raising his brother to the imperial throne. At a grand banquet, with the whole court in attendance, he sets out his proposals, citing ancient precedents from former dynasties and once again threatening death on anyone present who wants to oppose him.

It is Yuan Shao who rises, sword in hand, and opposes him. Dong Zhuo is outraged. He draws his sword and advances upon the resolute Yuan Shao.

And what happens next to Yuan Shao?

You will find out.

CHAPTER 4

Dong Zhuo overthrows the Emperor Shao and installs Shao's brother as emperor. Cao Cao tries to assassinate Dong Zhuo with a bejewelled dagger.

Dong Zhuo leaps towards Yuan Shao but at the last moment is wisely restrained by Li Ru, his adviser. 'Don't act like this when all still hangs in the balance,' he says. Yuan Shao, firmly gripping his sword, is thus able to leave, honour intact. Piling up his official papers publicly at the gate as a sign of his disdain for the rule of Dong Zhuo, he takes refuge in the provinces. Realizing he has overstepped the mark, Dong Zhuo's councillors recommend that, to pacify Yuan Shao, Dong Zhuo make him the governor of Bohai District. This he does.

In late summer of AD 189[3] in the Hall of Worthy Virtue, in the presence of the fifteen-year-old Emperor Shao, Dong Zhuo unveils his plan. With his sword in his hand, Dong Zhuo addresses the greatest and most powerful men in the land.

'This Son of Heaven is weak and untrustworthy and is not worthy to reign over those of us who live under Heaven,' he declares. 'Today I have ordered a proclamation to be published and announced concerning the future.'

Li Ru then reads out the proclamation. It tells how, at the death of the late emperor, people had held high hopes for the young Prince Bian as new emperor, but these soon faded. His mother the empress had also failed to show the wisdom everyone had hoped for, and the tragic death of the Empress Dong had shocked the people. Heaven and Earth were in distress at all this. 'In contrast,' he reads, 'Prince Xie is saintly, virtuous and wise, conducting himself with dignity from the period of mourning onwards. Everyone under Heaven knows this, and this is why the emperor will now be deposed and made Prince of Hongnong; his mother relieved of all responsibilities and Prince Xie enthroned.'

And so it is. Only one man opposes this, and he is beheaded there and then. Prince Xie is enthroned, and the former emperor, his mother and his consort are all shut away in the Palace of Perpetual Harmony, where no one is allowed to visit them. The young former emperor reigned only from the fourth month to the beginning of the ninth month.

The new emperor takes the reign title of Xian and he is just nine years old. Dong Zhuo becomes the prime minister, though it is noted that he displays none of the customary respect towards his emperor.

Life for the deposed emperor, his mother and his consort goes from bad to worse. They are half starved and weep without ceasing. One day, when the former emperor sees a pair of swallows flying past the window, he writes this poem:

At dawn, the grass itself is fresh and awake.
Swallows soar into the sky, weaving their delicate pattern.
Beyond lies the River Luo, dark at the horizon.
People are moved by this wondrous sight.
But not us. For beyond that horizon
Are the palaces and courts which are no longer ours.
At such a time, who is loyal, who is honourable?
Who can lift this heavy burden from my heart?

These words are reported back to Dong Zhuo, who immediately orders Li Ru to murder the former emperor, his consort and his mother. Li Ru arrives at their home where they are imprisoned and offers them poisoned wine to drink. Knowing what it is, and that they are going to die, the former emperor sings this sad song:

Earth is greater than Heaven now;
The sun and moon change places.
Once I ruled over everything,
Now I live on the edges.

My life is abbreviated,
Seized by others.
This disaster is great,
And I grieve in vain.

To this his consort replies:

The star of Heaven falls,
The earth itself declines.
Married to this man, the emperor,
I go where he goes.
Life and death divide,
Each goes its separate way.
It's so quick –
My heart of hearts breaks.

Li Ru is furious. He flings the former emperor's mother out of the upper window. He has the former emperor's consort strangled before his horrified eyes. And he forces the poisoned wine down the former emperor's throat.

With them dead, Dong Zhuo knows no constraints. For example, one day he takes his troops to a nearby village where the people are in the midst of holding a festival. Surrounding the village, he has more than a thousand men beheaded and then he enslaves the women and children. The heads are displayed on the sides of the wagons bringing the women back to Luoyang. Dong Zhuo claims he has won a famous victory over rebels and then he sells the women and children to his troops.

Word of these brutalities travels as far as Yuan Shao, who is in the provinces. Writing to his friend the minister of the home office, Wang Yun, he urges him to organize the overthrow of Dong Zhuo. When he receives the letter, Wang Yun invites a group of men whom he suspects also want the removal of the corrupt Dong Zhuo. Under cover of a birthday party they discuss the terrible state of affairs. It is at this point that Cao Cao steps forward. If he could be given Wang Yun's seven-jewelled dagger as the implement and inducement, he says he will stab

Dong Zhuo to death. The jewelled dagger is handed over, and everyone present nervously but hopefully drinks to the success of Cao Cao's plan.

Armed with the precious dagger, Cao Cao makes his way to Dong Zhuo's palace, where he finds Dong Zhuo. He is now so fat he has to lie reclining on a couch. Asked why he is so late, Cao Cao replies that his horse is unfit for travel, whereupon Dong Zhuo orders Lü Bu – his golden recruit from Ding Yuan's army, and the new owner of Red Hare – to go and find him a fine new one. Now that he is left alone with Dong Zhuo, Cao Cao draws his dagger and moves towards him. But Dong Zhuo catches sight of him in a mirror and turns.

'What are you doing?' he calls out. In terror, Cao Cao drops to his knees. Thinking quickly, he offers up the beautiful dagger with both hands.

'This is a present for your honour,' he mutters. Dong Zhuo appears delighted with such a gift. At just this moment Lü Bu returns, having found a horse. Dong Zhuo and Cao Cao go outside to view the horse. Expressing huge gratitude, Cao Cao asks if he might try the gift horse out. As soon as the saddle and reins have been put on, Cao Cao springs upon its back and without a backward glance rides at full tilt out of the palace gate.

Watching him go, Lü Bu and Dong Zhuo find that they agree. They both suspect that, rather than wanting to present the dagger as a gift, Cao Cao meant to murder Dong Zhuo. Summoning Li Ru, they discuss what to do and decide to send soldiers to track him down. The soldiers don't find him, but guards at the eastern gate report that he fled the city at a mad gallop, claiming he was on a special mission for Dong Zhuo.

Realizing he has narrowly avoided an assassination plot, Dong Zhuo is incandescent with rage. A huge reward is offered for the capture of Cao Cao, and his portrait is circulated far and wide.

Cao Cao rides pell-mell towards his home region of Qiao. Passing through Zhongmu County, he is recognized and arrested by the local magistrate, Chen Gong. However, the magistrate has no intention of sending his captive back to the palace. Instead he asks why he is in such a hurry. Expecting to be sent for execution the next day, Cao Cao simply tells the truth.

'I no longer wish to serve a tyrant like Dong Zhuo,' he says. 'And I was returning to my home to rally men to overthrow him.' Hearing this, Chen Gong frees Cao Cao and offers to come with him. They set out together in disguise.

They travel for three days until they come to the area of Chenggao.

'One of my father's sworn companions lives near here,' Cao Cao says. 'His name is Lü Boshe. He's like an uncle to me. He'll give us somewhere safe to stay.'

And, sure enough, when the two men turn up, Lü Boshe makes them welcome. He tells Cao Cao that the court has sent soldiers to intimidate his father into revealing where Cao Cao is hiding. Making his guests comfortable, Lü Boshe realizes that he has run out of wine. So he tells them he is going to ride over to the next village to buy some, but that they should just rest.

Not long after he has left, the two men overhear voices in the back yard of the house. What alarms them most is the sound of knives being sharpened.

'You know, he isn't a blood relative,' whispers Cao Cao anxiously. 'So perhaps this is all a trick and he's gone off to betray us.'

So saying, the two men creep around the side of the house and listen.

'Let's bind first and then kill,' says a voice, confirming Cao Cao and Chen Gong's worst fears. Without hesitation they rush round the corner with their swords drawn. They kill everyone there – eight people, men and women alike. Only when they search the house do they discover to their horror a pig trussed up, ready to be slaughtered.

'Cao Cao, we've murdered innocent people!' Chen Gong says, aghast. Distraught, they flee from the house and have only gone about half a mile when they meet their host, Lü Boshe, riding back from his expedition to the village to buy wine. Surprised to see his guests already leaving, he implores them to stay, saying he has ordered a pig to be slaughtered to feed them, and even if hunted men cannot rest long anywhere, they would be safe tonight at least. But Cao Cao brushes past, not saying a word, while the astonished man calls out to him to turn back. Suddenly Cao Cao does exactly that. He turns back, draws his sword and before the terrified old man can say a word, Cao Cao cuts him down. He falls dead from his mount.

Chen Gong is horrified. 'What happened back at the house was a terrible accident, but this – this was cold-blooded murder. Why, why?' he asks.

'Don't you understand?' Cao Cao answers. 'Once he got home and saw what had happened, he would have set up a hue and cry. A mob would have come after us and they would have killed us.'

'But to murder an innocent man is wrong,' Chen Gong remonstrates.

'I would rather defeat the world than have the world defeat me!' Cao Cao snarls back.

Chen Gong says nothing but broods upon what has happened. Later that night he says to himself, 'I thought Cao Cao was a good man but now I realize he's as vicious as a wild beast. If I don't kill him, he'll go on to bring more misfortune to others.' And this is why he draws his sword.

Can Cao Cao survive?

Read on, and find out.

CHAPTER 5

With a forged imperial edict Cao Cao summons leaders to oppose Dong Zhuo, and the three brothers battle Lü Bu. The opponents are led by Yuan Shao.

Standing ready to kill Cao Cao, Chen Gong thinks about why he followed this man in the first place. He did it for the good of the country.

'If I kill him, I will just be adding to the sum of wrong deeds,' he reflects. 'So perhaps the only honourable way is to simply abandon him.'

When Cao Cao awakes it is to find that Chen Gong has gone. He muses ruefully on the impact his words must have had on him. 'My high-handed comments and selfishness must have made him think I am a thug. I must be more careful.' So he sets off for his family home at great speed.

At last he arrives at his father's house. He asks his father to raise funds to hire troops. His father lacks the wherewithal, but a local notable is persuaded to raise the money. Sending out a fake edict claiming to come from the emperor, Cao Cao soon has a growing army of volunteers. He gathers them together under a white banner emblazoned with the two words 'Loyalty' and 'Integrity'.

Copies of the fake edict travel as far as Yuan Shao, who responds by bringing his own army of thirty thousand to join Cao Cao. Emboldened, Cao Cao sends out a proclamation urging others to join them in wiping out Dong Zhuo for his crimes of murdering the emperor, usurping the palace and harming the ordinary people. From across the land people respond. A total of seventeen military leaders rally to the call and head for the capital.

One of these is Gongsun Zan, the governor of Beiping. He is en route to the capital with fifteen thousand men when he sees

Xuande, his two brothers-in-arms and his troops riding towards him. Xuande has come as the local magistrate to pay his respect but is swiftly persuaded to join the uprising against Dong Zhuo.

'I'd like to be given the honour of killing Dong Zhuo,' Xuande says. To this Zhang Fei retorts, 'Why didn't you let me kill him last time? Then we wouldn't have to be put to all this effort.' But Guan Yu simply says, 'Come on. Put up with it! Let's gather our things and get going.'

Yuan Shao is chosen as the leader of the whole expedition and, having made sacrifices, he vows to the emperor of Heaven, the empress of Earth and to the ancestors that everyone gathered there will protect the imperial family and their shrines from the evil deeds of Dong Zhuo. He gives responsibility for the supplies to his brother Yuan Shu. Meanwhile Sun Jian has also joined, and he offers to form the advance party heading to the pass: this is happily accepted by one and all.

The news of this swiftly reaches the capital, though Dong Zhuo is so sunk in debauchery he barely pays any attention. Li Ru, however, takes it very seriously and he summons the council in response.

Dong Zhuo's adopted son Lü Bu tells him, 'Father, don't worry. These are just straws in the wind, and I'll deal with them.' But someone else challenges him in a dismissive way and says, 'A butcher's knife just to kill a chicken!' The one who spoke is Hua Xiong, a huge man, built like a tiger and as swift as a wolf, with a forehead like a panther and arms like a monkey. Dong Zhuo loves both this comment and the man's self-assurance, so Hua Xiong is sent off that very night with fifty thousand troops to stop the enemy at the pass.

The armies of Sun Jian and Hua Xiong clash violently at the pass, and Sun Jian is forced to retreat. He urgently sends a message to Yuan Shu, the quartermaster, asking for additional supplies, but these do not come. Someone has muttered in Yuan Shu's ear: 'Sun Jian is like a tiger from the east, and if he overthrows Dong Zhuo and captures the capital, then we'll have replaced a wolf with a tiger. Better, therefore, that by not sending supplies, Sun Jian's army should fail and be destroyed.'

Yuan Shu follows this advice, so no supplies are sent. The lack of supplies leads to rioting in Sun Jian's camp, and word of this soon reaches Dong Zhuo.

Summoning Hua Xiong, he commands him to attack that very night. At midnight, by the light of a bright moon and with a strong wind blowing, they attack, and in the complete confusion, Sun Jian's troops are routed. All of Sun Jian's commanders, except for one whose name is Zu Mao, abandon Sun Jian. Together they flee for their lives, pursued by Hua Xiong. Sun Jian's bright-red cloak is so conspicuous that Zu Mao tells him to take it off and give it to him, so he can wear it and provide a diversion to the pursuing soldiers.

Sun Jian escapes, and Zu Mao hangs the cloak on a tree to fool the soldiers. Having tricked them into believing the cloak is being worn by Sun Jian, he attacks them when they least expect it but is brought down by a single blow from Hua Xiong.

The slaughtering of Sun Jian's defeated infantry goes on until daybreak, and Sun Jian and his surviving foot soldiers straggle back to the main camp of the rebels. Here a council of war is being held by a deeply distressed Yuan Shao, who proclaims that the army's morale has been severely diminished by the disastrous campaign.

'What should we do next?' he asks. This is met by a guilty silence. It is at this point that he sees three odd-looking characters grinning at the back of the room. When he asks who they are, he is informed that the senior one is Xuande, who destroyed the Yellow Headband revolt, and that he is also a descendant of the imperial family. He invites Xuande to join the war council, and his two brothers-in-arms take up protective positions behind him.

By this time, Hua Xiong has advanced to the edge of the camp and is challenging anyone who wants to try him in mortal combat. Two great warriors come forward, but Hua Xiong kills both of them. The war council is in despair, and Yuan Shao asks who else is available to fight Hua Xiong. At this Guan Yu offers, but when Yuan Shao asks who he is and is told he is 'just an archer', Yuan Shao is furious at what he sees as an insult to the military leaders. However, Cao Cao speaks up for Guan Yu and suggests they have nothing to lose if he tries.

Cao Cao orders warmed rice wine for Guan Yu to drink before the battle. 'Keep it warm and ready. I'll be back soon,' Guan Yu says.

Riding swiftly and drawing his sword, he disappears in the direction of the enemy. All that the war council can hear is the sound of the war drums and shouting so loud it seems Heaven would split, the Earth crack open, the very hills and mountains collapse. Guan Yu returns before the wine has had a chance to cool. He contemptuously throws the severed head of Hua Xiong at the feet of the astonished leaders. As a poet would write many years later:

He was the greatest among men,
At the very gates of the camp,
The thunderous roll of the drums could be heard.
Guan Yu set the wine cup to one side,
Keen to show his courage.
With the wine still warm
When Hua Xiong was no more.

While everyone else cheers, Yuan Shu broods.

In revenge for the death of Hua Xiong, Dong Zhuo orders the murder of every member of Yuan Shao's family in the capital. Then the might of Dong Zhuo's forces is sent against the rebels – two hundred thousand men march out to confront Yuan Shao and his troops and to guard Tiger Cage Pass, some fifty miles from the capital of Luoyang.

On the front line, Lü Bu rides forth to challenge any warrior who dares. He is arrayed in rich robes embroidered with flowers, while on his head he wears a triple-layered headdress of pure gold. His body armour is a snarling head of a wild beast, while his belt is clasped by a lion's head. With his arrows, his halberd and his two-edged sword, he rides the war horse Red Hare, whose every neigh sounds like a raging storm. Not only is Lü Bu the chief among warriors, but Red Hare is the first among horses.

Challenger after challenger goes forward from Yuan Shao's forces, only to be killed almost at once by the wrath of Lü Bu. Only one champion, a man with the name of Gongsun Zan, escapes with his life. He is racing back, hotly pursued by Lü Bu on the magnificent Red Hare. And then just in time he is saved by a cry from one side.

'Come on, you pompous upstart, claiming titles you've got no right to!' shouts the voice. 'My name is Zhang Fei!' it continues. And with this, Zhang Fei surges forward towards the charging Lü Bu, diverting him from his pursuit of Gongsun Zan. For fifty rounds they go at each other, but neither has the upper hand. Guan Yu charges in to support his sworn brother, and they fight many more rounds, but still Lü Bu is undefeated.

However, Lü Bu is getting tired. At last he makes a feint, pretending to attack and then turning and charging off with the two brothers in hot pursuit. With a roar, the troops of the rebels sweep forward, while Lü Bu's men stampede and flee. They head for the pass, chased by Xuande and his brothers and their whole army.

As the three brothers-in-arms gallop towards the pass they see the vast blue canopy of Dong Zhuo blowing in the western breeze.

'Why bother with Lü Bu when we could get the main culprit and so wipe out this evil root and branch?' cries Zhang Fei. And, charging forward, the three brothers head straight towards Dong Zhuo.

And what is the outcome of this battle?

Read on and find out.

CHAPTER 6

Dong Zhuo destroys the capital and moves the court to Chang'an, but Sun Jian, hiding the imperial seal, betrays the leaders opposed to Dong Zhuo.

Zhang Fei's headlong charge brings him swiftly to the pass, but he is halted by a barrage of missiles hurled at him and is unable to reach Dong Zhuo. However, the battle has been won anyway, and the lords congratulate Zhang Fei on his role in their success.

That night Sun Jian comes to see Yuan Shu.

'You know I've no personal feelings against Dong Zhuo, but I've given my all in this great struggle because the country needs to be freed. He's a tyrant,' he says. 'But you, you've listened to someone who slandered me and that's why you failed to deliver the grain I needed. And that led to my defeat. Why? Tell me why!'

Yuan Shu, of course, has no answer. His only option is to have the slanderer killed.

Later that same night Sun Jian has a visitor. It is a supporter of Dong Zhuo named Li Jue, sent by Dong to try to persuade Sun Jian to desert and come and join him. Li Jue says, 'Dong Zhuo greatly admires you. He wants to offer his daughter to you as a bride for your son.'

'How dare he!' exclaims Sun Jian, in a fury of indignation. 'He no longer follows the Way of Heaven and he's conniving to take the throne. I will destroy his lineage to the ninth generation!'

Li Jue sees that his plan is bound to fail and he escapes and returns to Dong Zhuo with the bad news.

The disaster at the pass coupled with Sun Jian's rejection so infuriates Dong Zhuo that it sends him spiralling into depression. His adviser Li Ru comes up with an outrageous plan. He bases it on a children's ditty that is being sung at the time. The ditty goes like this:

> There first was a Han in the west,
> Then a Han over there in the east.
> If the deer flees to Chang'an,
> He'll find he's able to breathe without distress.

Li Ru interprets this as follows:

'The Han in the west was the original dynasty founded by the Supreme Ancestor, where twelve emperors reigned in Chang'an. The Han in the east refers to the twelve emperors who came after Guang Wu, the emperor who moved the capital to Luoyang. Now the cycle of Heaven has come full circle, and the court should return to Chang'an, and then there will be nothing to fear.'

And so Dong Zhuo decides to move the capital to Chang'an. Summoning all the officials, he announces that after two centuries of rule in Luoyang the imperial family have been drained of inspiration and drive, but by moving them to Chang'an this can be revived. Some oppose him, including two officers who try to stop him as he leaves the city gate. For their temerity in opposing him he has them beheaded there and then.

Li Ru is aware of how much money will be needed to rebuild the virtually deserted Chang'an, left desolate after a rebellion two hundred years ago. Li Ru therefore proposes the following.

'Anyone in Luoyang we can associate with the rebel Yuan Shao will be rich, so let's kill them and take their goods.'

As a direct consequence of this evil plan, five thousand troops are sent into the city. They murder thousands, not only the leading nobles and wealthy merchants, but also their entire families. Millions of the city's citizens are then driven out on the long march towards Chang'an. But many of them die en route, while the soldiers rape and pillage at will until the cries of the oppressed touch both Heaven and Earth.

Finally, as Dong Zhuo is about to leave he commands that the whole city – including the ancestral shrines and palaces – should be burned to the ground. The imperial tombs are smashed open on his command, and the treasures of the emperors and empresses are scattered while the soldiers break into the tombs of the nobility and the rich.

At last Xuande, his brothers-in-arms, and their men break through the pass, and Sun Jian gallops towards Luoyang. Yet for hundreds of miles nothing but desecration meets their gaze. Not a bird or animal can be seen or heard, nor any human being.

Cao Cao is all for chasing after the retreating forces, but Yuan Shao disagrees, and so Cao Cao takes ten thousand men of his own and sets off in hot pursuit.

By now Dong Zhuo has reached Xingyang, midway to Chang'an. Li Ru, aware of the risk of attack, plans an ambush for any pursuing troops. When Cao Cao and his men sweep in for the attack, they fall into the trap. Cao Cao is heavily outnumbered. He has no option but to wheel his horse and flee.

An arrow pierces his shoulder. Then his horse is killed beneath him. As the triumphant enemy troops are closing in, his friend Cao Hong comes to his rescue. He hands Cao Cao his horse, saying, 'The world can do without me, but not without you.' They set off, Cao Cao riding and Cao Hong walking. Cao Hong toils behind the horse for many miles, pursued relentlessly by the enemy. They manage to escape by the skin of their teeth, even when Cao Hong has to carry the wounded Cao Cao on his back across a river with arrows raining down. Soon other survivors of the defeated army arrive, while elsewhere Dong Zhuo continues safely on his way to Chang'an.

Arriving in the midst the devastated city of Luoyang, Sun Jian orders the fires extinguished, the palaces cleared, the imperial tombs sealed and offerings made to the ancestors. When the ritual is over, Sun Jian stands and looks up to the night sky. Even as he watches, he sees a pale mist shroud the stars of one of the constellations. 'The imperial star is no longer bright,' he sighs and, mourning the destruction of the dynasty and the capital city, he falls to his knees and weeps.

As he sits wrapped in melancholy a soldier points out five strange lights emanating from a well. When Sun Jian orders the well to be explored, they find the body of a woman, still intact; around her courtly neck hangs an embroidered pouch.

Inside the pouch is a beautiful box some four inches across, with a golden clasp. Inside this box is a jade seal, its top carved with five dragons wrapped around each other. One of the corners has been broken and repaired with gold in antiquity, while at its base are carved eight characters in the ancient seal script which read: 'Receive the Mandate of Heaven: now you will have long life and eternal prosperity.'

When Sun Jian shows the treasure to his adviser Cheng Pu, he instantly knows what it is. 'This is the seal of the emperors,' he says and relates its long history. 'Once there was a phoenix spotted sitting on a stone on the Jian mountain. This apparition caused the stone to be noticed and removed. When it was cut open in front of King Wen of Chu[4] its heart was found to be jade. Hundreds of years later, in the twenty-sixth year of the reign of the first emperor, the very year he unified all China, the first emperor ordered the jade to be cut. His prime minister, Li Si, composed the eight characters for it. Just two years later, during a terrible storm on Lake Dongting, the emperor hurled the jade overboard to pacify the waves. Then, eight years later, when the emperor was on a long journey, an old man stepped forward. He presented the jade to the emperor, then he disappeared. After the first emperor died the seal was taken by the founder of the Han dynasty. Two hundred years later, during the Wang Mang rebellion, the queen mother of the overthrown emperor used the seal to hit two of the rebels over the head. She chipped the corner, which later was repaired with gold. The emperor who restored the Han after the rebellion found the seal, and ever since that time it has passed from emperor to emperor. When the troubles with the Ten Eunuchs broke out it was lost. Now you've found it, which must mean you're destined to rule. But don't stay here in the north: you must head southeast to our homeland and begin your kingly preparations.'

Sun Jian is more than happy to agree. He says that the next day he will plead sickness and then he will steal away.

However, word gets out. Yuan Shao hears about the seal, and when Sun Jian comes to see him, saying that due to ill health he will go home to Changsha, Yuan Shao says he knows what the ailment is – a bad case of imperial seal! Despite Yuan Shao's best efforts he cannot persuade Sun Jian to even admit he has found the seal. Deeply offended and frightened, Sun Jian does not hesitate but rides off, taking his entire army with him.

Yuan Shao's desire for the seal causes the alliance to start to fall apart. Cao Cao departs as well, taking his troops to Yangzhou. Gongsun Zan, along with the three brothers-in-arms, is also left feeling Yuan Shao has no prospects. Passing through the town of Pingyuan, he asks Xuande to remain there and defend it.

Sun Jian is heading south when he passes through a district where the governor is Liu Biao, a member of a well-known group of intellectuals called the Eight Gentlemen of Jiangxia. Having received a letter from Yuan Shao, ordering him to take an army to stop Sun Jian, Liu Biao appoints two of his top commanders, Kuai Yue and Cai Mao, to lead it.

'Why is the road blocked?' demands Sun Jian when the two armies meet. 'And why are you escaping with the imperial jade seal?' Commander Kuai Yue demands in return. To settle the matter, each army selects a champion to fight on its behalf. Sun Jian chooses Huang Gai, while Liu Biao's chooses Cai Mao.

After a few brief bouts Huang Gai lashes Cai Mao with a whip on his chest. Cai Mao panics and flees, which encourages Sun Jian's men to surge forward. The soldiers have not gone far when the beat of war drums resounds throughout the valley. From behind a hill Liu Biao himself emerges at the head of his troops. 'Why are you blocking my way? asks Sun Jian once again. 'And why are you escaping with the imperial seal?' comes the response once again. Sun Jian claims, 'I do not have it.' 'Well, then, you won't mind if I search your bags, will you?' retorts Liu Biao. Sun Jian challenges Liu Biao to a fight but Liu Biao retreats, drawing Sun's troops into a trap. Kuai Yue and Cai Mao, the two commanders, close in from behind, and Sun Jian is trapped.

Does Sun Jian escape?

We will find out.

CHAPTER 7

At the River Pan battle, Yuan Shao fights Gongsun Zan. Sun Jian attacks Liu Biao at the Great River.

By sheer determination and courage Sun Jian and his men fight their way through. But at a heavy cost. Three of his closest commanders die, as do more than half of his army. At last, exhausted and hunted, they ford the Yellow River and escape safely to the south. But from that day on Sun Jian and Liu Biao are sworn enemies.

Meanwhile, Yuan Shao has, through sheer cunning, seized control of Jizhou. This is how he did it. He began by suggesting to Gongsun Zan that they attack Jizhou together. He then informed Han Fu, the governor of Jizhou, of the threat Gongsun Zan posed and then offered to join forces with Han Fu to protect the city! Some of Han Fu's advisers saw this for what it was – a plot to seize the city – but most thought he would ensure their freedom. When Yuan Shao arrived with his army and took over Jizhou, two of the advisers tried to assassinate him, but they were easily overwhelmed and slain by his guard. Han Fu was given an impressive but meaningless title and shunted out of the way, and Yuan Shao established himself and his army in Jizhou. Only then does Han Fu realize how foolish he has been and takes refuge in Chenliu.

Gongsun Zan is naturally outraged at this treachery and goes on the offensive. His army meets Yuan Shao's army at a bridge crossing the River Pan. One army stands to the east of the bridge and one army stands to the west of the bridge. 'Traitor!' shouts Gongsun Zan.

'What's this got to do with you?' retorts Yuan Shao. 'Han Fu surrendered to me because I'm his superior, so I ask again: what has this got to do with you!' Gongsun Zan replies, 'Once,

Yuan Shao, you were called the rightful leader of the uprising but now you have shown yourself to be no better than a beast.'

'Attack!' shouts an enraged Yuan Shao. The struggle is so fierce that soon Gongsun Zan is in full retreat, galloping flat out for the mountains. He is chased by Wen Chou, one of Yuan Shao's champions. Bareheaded, exhausted, without weapons to defend himself, Gongsun Zan rides for his life, but his horse stumbles and throws him to the ground. Wen Chou is closing in for the kill, spear raised, when out of nowhere a young man charges down the hill and clashes with him, holding him off while Gongsun Zan rolls down the hill to try to escape. The young warrior holds Wen Chou back long enough for a group of Gongsun Zan's men to ride up. Wen Chou has no option but to retreat.

The young man is tall, with large eyes under bushy eyebrows, an open face and heavy jowls. His family name is Zhao, and he has become known as Zilong, meaning son of the dragon. Having originally served under Yuan Shao, he grew disillusioned and was coming to join Gongsun Zan and is as surprised as he is that they have met this way. Side by side with Zhao Zilong, Gongsun Zan returns to his camp and begins to reassemble his forces.

The battle once again returns to the bridge. Gongsun Zan's main strength is his cavalry, while Yuan Shao relies on his force of crossbowmen. With a thousand crossbowmen split into two wings, plus a further eight hundred bowmen and fifteen thousand infantry behind, he places himself right at the centre.

Gongsun Zan has his huge war banner embroidered with the word 'Commander' planted before the bridge. As the artillery begin their bombardment, his forces attack, only to be driven back by Yuan Shao's bowmen. Emboldened by this, Yuan Shao's infantry attack, cutting down the banner and forcing Gongsun Zan to abandon the bridge. Had it not been for Zhao Zilong once again coming to his defence and killing the attacking general, all would have been lost for Gongsun Zan.

Fired up by this, Zhao Zilong singlehandedly launches a counter-attack, slashing his way through the troops of Yuan Shao. He is soon joined by Gongsun and his men. They drive in close to where Yuan Shao is fighting and nearly break through. But Yuan Shao rallies his troops and turns the tide of the battle once again, forcing Gongsun to retreat.

Just as Yuan Shao feels confident of final victory, a great cry is heard and into the fray, as if from nowhere, rushes Xuande, Zhang Fei and Guan Yu, leading their men. Yuan Shao drops his sword in fright and only just makes it back to the safety of his own camp. He loses many men who die in the river or in the counter-attack of Gongsun's troops.

Back at Gongsun's camp, the three brothers-in-arms meet Zhao Zilong for the first time, and Xuande and Zilong swiftly become the firmest of friends.

The battles of the bridge result in a stand-off between the armies of Yuan Shao and Gongsun Zan. It lasts for a month. Neither side giving way. Back in Chang'an, Li Ru hears about this and advises Dong Zhuo to mediate between Yuan Shao and Gongsun Zan so that these two will once again be on Dong Zhuo's side. This strategy is surprisingly successful, and the betrayal of their cause by the two leaders profoundly horrifies both Xuande and Zilong.

Meanwhile, the enmity between Sun Jian and Liu Biao is further fuelled by Yuan Shao's despicable and greedy brother Yuan Shu. This selfish man is thwarted from obtaining the horses and grain he wants, because his brother gives orders that he is not to be helped.

So Yuan Shu tries to get hold of the goods from Liu Biao, but is again refused, as no one really trusts him.

As a result the frustrated and embittered Yuan Shu suggests to Sun Jian that they work together. Yuan Shu's plan is that they plot against both Liu Biao and Yuan Shao. They agree that Sun Jian will capture Jingzhou while Yuan Shu captures Jizhou.

When news of the plot reaches Liu Biao he starts to prepare for the attack, relying on the defensive strength of the Yellow River as a natural barrier. As Sun Jian is about to set out, his eldest son Sun Ce asks to be taken with him, and so it is that Sun Ce joined the war.

Huang Zu is the frontline general of Liu Biao's defence. He

has placed archers all along the river. As Sun Jian's boats approach, Huang Zu orders the archers to open fire. For three days the boats draw near, but not a shot comes from them. Instead the soldiers hunker down behind their shields, while the arrows fall on them. On the fourth day, with a huge supply of the arrows that had been salvaged from those stuck in the shields and boat, Sun Jian's men fire back on their enemy – who have by now run out of arrows! Landing on the riverbank, his troops confront Huang Zu and his men. Battle rages, but Huang Zu's men are no match for Sun Jian's. As his enemies close in upon him Huang Zu panics, tears off his helmet and, jumping from his horse, hides himself among the ordinary soldiers, and so is able to escape. Sun Jian, triumphant, captures the land right up to the Han River – while Huang Zu retreats and advises Liu Biao that they cannot hold off Sun Jian.

Now seeming unstoppable, Sun Jian lays siege to the city of Xiangyang. Yet during a storm the pole of his banner snaps in two – a bad omen. Inside the city, another portent has been sighted. Liu Biao is informed that a star has fallen to earth behind the enemy lines and that this foretells the death of a great general – Sun Jian.

As a result of this it is agreed that a letter should be sent to Yuan Shao urging collaboration in order to get rid of Sun Jian once and for all. Lü Gong, a volunteer, comes forward offering to be the messenger and he is given five hundred soldiers to help him escape. He is advised to use the soldiers to set an ambush for any of the enemy who come after him. The location for the ambush is a nearby hill. His troops are instructed to pile up stones to use in an attack and if he is successful he should signal back to the city. Then the besieged army will come out and attack. If he is not stopped, then Lü Gong is to ride on to Yuan Shao with the letter.

So, come nightfall, the east gate is quietly opened, and Lü Gong and his men slip out. Even so, Sun Jian hears them and, gathering only thirty horsemen about him, he gives chase. Sun Jian rides straight into the ambush. Stones rain down, and one of them strikes Sun Jian on the head, killing him instantly.

Sun Jian was only thirty-seven years old when he died. All

thirty of his men are killed. Then Lü Gong signals to the city, and out pour Liu Biao's troops. In the ferocious battle that follows, fortunes sway backwards and forwards between the opposing armies. Lü Gong is slain while Huang Zu is captured and brought back as a prisoner to the besieger's camp. As day breaks, each side retreats.

It is then that Sun Ce learns that his father has been killed and his body has been captured and taken into the city. It is agreed that an envoy, Huan Jie, should go to speak with Liu Biao and offer the return of Huang Zu if Liu Biao will send back the body of Sun Jian. Liu Biao agrees, but on the condition that the invading troops withdraw and promise never to attack again. Just as the envoy is about to return to Sun Ce, one of Liu Biao's advisers shouts out, 'No! I believe we can wipe out this enemy once and for all, but to do this we must kill this messenger.'

As it is said:

> Sun Jian died pursuing his enemies;
> Huan Jie in the quest for peace risked his life.

What fate awaits Huan Jie?

Let's find out.

CHAPTER 8

Imperial official Wang Yun plots with his serving girl to destroy Dong Zhuo and Lü Bu. The plot succeeds, and the two men dramatically fall out.

The adviser says, 'Sun Jian is gone, and his sons' voices haven't even broken, so their lands lie open to us if we attack now. Make peace and you will only encourage them to grow stronger and become a major danger to us.'

But Liu Biao will not sacrifice his friend Huang Zu. And so the coffin is sent, and the life of the envoy spared. The body of Sun Jian, already placed in a fine coffin by Liu Biao, is sent into the care of his son, who in turn releases Huang Zu.

Sun Ce returns to his home city to bury his father, and soon the fame of his wise judgement and humility spreads. This brings many a talented person to his court.

Needless to say, Dong Zhuo, way off in Chang'an, is delighted to hear of the death of Sun Jian. When he is told that Sun Ce is only seventeen years old, he feels he has nothing more to fear from that quarter. This encourages him to become even more outrageous in his behaviour. He insists on being called 'The Most Venerable Father' and acts as if he is indeed the emperor. Some way outside Chang'an he has a vast palace created, forcing over a quarter of a million serfs to labour on it. Once finished, he fills it with eight hundred of the most beautiful women to be his personal attendants. The palace is stuffed full of plunder – gold, jade and many other treasures.

His terrible abuse of power knows no limits. On one occasion, during a feast, he has a large number of rebels who have surrendered brought in. While the guests eat, he has the arms and legs of the rebels hacked off, their eyes gouged out, tongues cut out and even has some boiled alive. The terrified screams shake the guests to the core, but Dong Zhuo eats on as if nothing untoward is happening.

At another feast he has one of the top officials who is attending the feast arrested for conspiracy. Seized, he is taken away to be killed, and his head is brought back in on a platter and placed in front of all the officials.

Returning from this particular dreadful event, the minister Wang Yun is in despair. It is the late evening, and he wanders into his garden, hoping to find there some peace and so to restore his spirits. He raises his eyes to Heaven and weeps. Then suddenly he hears a sound nearby. It is a deep, heartfelt sigh of distress. Approaching, he finds it is a young woman called Diao Chan who has grown up as a singing girl in his house. She is both beautiful and bright and he considers her almost as a daughter.

'What have you done wrong, young lady?' he asks.

'I would never do anything wrong,' Diao Chan replies, startled to see him.

'So why are you so distressed?' Wang Yun asks.

'Let me tell you the truth from the very bottom of my heart,' she replies. 'You've looked after me and had me tutored in the arts of music and dancing and have always been generous to me. Nothing I can do could ever repay you. But I've noticed recently that you seem unhappy – I can see it in your face. Yet who am I to ask you what's troubling you? Then tonight I saw you in the garden and this made me sigh . . . never for a moment thinking you'd hear me. If there is anything I can do to help, I would be prepared to embrace death itself over and over again.'

Wang Yun is speechless for a moment and then says, 'The whole Han dynasty is about to be destroyed. But, you, I really think you could be the one to save it. Come.' And the bewildered young woman follows him to his own chambers. Dismissing the other servants, he sits her down on a chair and then prostrates himself before her. 'What are you doing, my lord?' Diao Chan cries, and in return she prostrates herself before him, asking, 'What is going on?'

In tears, Wang Yun asks, 'Can you have pity on the people of our land and for the Han dynasty?'

'I am willing to undergo any number of deaths if I can be of service,' she replies.

'Listen, the truth is,' says Wang Yun still kneeling on the ground before her, 'that the people are in grave danger but you could be the one who will save us all! It's now crystal clear that Dong Zhuo plans to usurp the throne, and there's no one who can stand up to him. Dong Zhuo has an adopted son, Lü Bu, a great warrior, and, like his father, he loves beautiful women. My plan is to set a trap for them both by promising you in marriage to Lü Bu. Once he is caught in this engagement then I'll offer you to Dong Zhuo as well. This will mean you can set them against each other. If you can incite Lü Bu to kill Dong Zhuo you can end this terrible evil, and then the sacred order of our land will be restored. I'm sure you can do this . . . But it is very dangerous. Are you willing?'

Diao Chan replies immediately, 'I'm willing to die ten thousand deaths. Just say the word, and I will be ready to go and meet them. Then just leave it to me!'

'Nothing of this must leak out,' says Wang Yun lowering his voice, 'or we'll all be killed.'

'Have no fear,' Diao Chan reassures him. 'Not even a thousand knives could prise this secret from me.'

'Thank you, thank you, thank you,' says Wang Yun.

So the next day Wang Yun gathers together gold and wonderful pearls from his family heirlooms and commissions a skilled craftsman to create a magnificent crown. When this is finished he has it delivered to Lü Bu, who is so delighted he comes to thank Wang Yun personally. When he arrives at Wang Yun's house it is Wang Yun himself who meets him at the doorway and escorts him inside. Laid out on the table are bowls of expensive delicacies. Lü Bu is overwhelmed and says so. 'I'm but a simple person within the prime minister's team, but you are a great minister. I really don't think I'm worthy of such kindness.'

'My lord, throughout the land there is no one today who is your equal in courage,' Wang Yun says. 'So I'm offering my respect not to the office you hold but to your heroic fame.'

This fills Lü Bu with joy. And Wang Yun continues to laud

him, drinking to his health and heaping praise on the virtue of both Dong Zhuo and Lü Bu, while Lü Bu drinks heavily and roars with delight.

Wang Yun dismisses most of the servants, just keeping those who are plying his guest with alcohol. Soon Lü Bu is seriously drunk, and at this point Wang Yun orders the servants to fetch 'my daughter'. So Diao Chan is brought in. She is dressed to kill, so elegantly and so alluringly.

Lü Bu is astonished. He seems to sober up immediately. 'Who is this?' he asks in wonder.

'She is my little daughter, Diao Chan,' Wang Yun replies. 'I hoped that in the light of how touchingly friendly you've been to me, you might like to meet her.' So saying, he orders Diao Chan to offer Lü Bu a cup of wine, and as she does so, she makes sure she catches his eye. She makes it clear to him that she finds him very attractive.

From that moment on Lü Bu's eyes never leave Diao Chan, and she is commanded to sit beside him. Yet more wine is drunk. It is then that Wang Yun suddenly says, 'If I were to offer her to you as your concubine, would you be willing to accept?'

Lü Bu is stunned. 'Of course. Of course I would love this. I would be bound to you for ever. Trust me, I would be as loyal as a horse. Or a dog!' To this outpouring, Wang Yun replies:

'Then we will find an auspicious day and she will be sent to the palace.'

Lü Bu is over the moon and cannot tear his eyes away from her, while she reciprocates with amorous glances. Eventually he leaves but only after thanking his host over and over again.

A few days later, and after making sure Lü Bu is nowhere to be seen, Wang Yun kowtows before Dong Zhuo and invites him to dine 'at my humble home'. Dong Zhuo graciously accepts.

An array of delicacies is again prepared and set out in the main hall. No expense has been spared to make the scene as luxurious as possible. At midday Dong Zhuo arrives and is met by his host dressed in his best finery. Dong Zhuo enters with a swarm of armed guards and takes the seat of honour.

He beckons Wang Yun to come and sit beside him. Wang effusively expresses his gratitude.

'Your Excellency, your virtue towers above all others – greater by far than Yi Yin or even the duke of Zhou!'[5] Needless to say this pleases Dong Zhuo greatly, and while the wine is served and the music begins to play, Wang Yun continues to praise his guest in the most fulsome terms. As dusk draws on, and the wine begins to work its magic, Wang Yun invites his guest into the private quarters of the house. The guards are dismissed, and Wang Yun offers his guest another cup of wine. 'Ever since my youth I've studied astrology,' he confides. 'So I could not help but notice that Heaven is telling us that the days of the House of Han are numbered because of the outstanding reputation for virtue you have throughout the world. It is as if we were in the time of the Emperor Shun, when he made way for his virtuous prime minister Yu, and both Heaven's and humanity's wishes were fulfilled.'

Dong Zhuo is taken aback by this prediction that he might become emperor and professes his astonishment. Wang Yun continues:

'Since the beginning of time, those who follow the Way have succeeded those who have lost the Way. Those who have lost their virtue have been succeeded by those who are guided by virtue. In my experience this is a truth beyond doubt.'

'Well!' Dong Zhuo exclaims. 'If this is indeed what Heaven wants, to bestow upon me the Mandate of Heaven to rule the land, then, Wang Yun, you will be acclaimed as having been the first to discern it!'

At this point Wang Yun moves to the next stage of his plan for the evening.

'No ordinary musicians are good enough for such a worthy guest as you, my lord,' he says. 'This is why I've chosen the most outstanding performer in my entire household.' And with this Diao Chan appears and she begins her dance. Poets ever since that time have sought to describe her beauty. They have compared her to a swallow in her gracefulness and her movements to the most exquisite perfume from a flower.

As planned, Dong Zhuo is completely enamoured of the dancer.

'Who is she?' he asks.

'She is our singing girl and she's called Diao Chan,' Wang Yun replies.

On hearing she can sing, Dong Zhuo is even more fascinated, and then, accompanied by the percussion of castanets, she sings. A poet has described the song of Diao Chan to Dong Zhuo:

You, seemingly so delicate with your bright cherry lips,
Finest pearl-teeth and breath like a perfumed passion . . .
Ah, but your tongue's hidden like a sword –
And it's this that will prove deadly to this worthless lord.

Overcome, Dong Zhuo asks how old she is.

'Sixteen,' is the answer.

'She's like an immortal spirit come to grace the earth,' he says. This is the moment Wang Yun has been waiting for and, getting to his feet, he says:

'If you will not be offended, I would like to offer you this young girl!'

And naturally Dong Zhuo is more than happy to accept.

Straight away a coach is summoned, and Diao Chan is sent on ahead to the prime minister's home. Dong Zhuo and Wang Yun travel there together so Wang Yun can say his farewells once his guest has reached home.

Later, as he is returning home, Wang Yun suddenly finds the roadway blocked. In front of him are two lines of red lanterns, and there stands Lü Bu, armed to the teeth. He seizes Wang Yun roughly. 'You promised Diao Chan to me,' he snarls. 'Now you've given her to the prime minister! What kind of game are you playing?'

'We cannot discuss this here,' Wang Yun replies hurriedly. 'Come back with me to my home.'

When they are ensconced in Wang Yun's private quarters, Wang Yun says, 'Why do you say this about me, general?'

'I was told,' replies Lü Bu, 'that you had Diao Chan sent to the prime minister's house in a special coach. Why? What's going on?'

'You've no idea what has been going on!' Wang Yun exclaims as if with astonishment and weariness. 'Yesterday, the prime minister told me he wanted to come and see me to discuss something confidential. When he came he said, "I have heard of this beautiful young woman called Diao Chan whom you've given to my son. I wanted to come and see her for myself and to find out if this is true." I could hardly refuse now, could I?' says Wang Yun.

'So I had her come and offer due respect. Then to my surprise he said he would take her back to the palace and present her to you! As you can well imagine, I had no option but to agree. Tomorrow I'll send her bags to your palace.'

Lü Bu falls for this. 'It is I who should apologize to you for having misunderstood the situation,' he says. And so Lü Bu goes off, but not before he has apologized and offered his thanks time and time again.

However, when Lü Bu calls the next day at Dong Zhuo's palace, he is told by the maids that the master came home last night with a new woman, and they have not yet risen from their bed. Lü Bu's heart is clogged with anger, and he creeps round to peer in through the bedroom window. Diao Chan is combing her hair when she spots him. Immediately she feigns an expression of terrible distress and sadness, dabbing at her eyes over and over as if she is crying. Lü Bu watches for quite some time and then strides into the main hall of the palace to 'offer his morning greeting' to Dong Zhuo.

'Is everything all right?' Dong Zhuo asks, concerned by his adopted son's expression.

'Of course! Everything is fine,' Lü Bu curtly replies. But he then notices the figure of a young woman moving around behind the curtain and glimpses Diao Chan peering out and looking passionately at him. Lü Bu cannot hide his emotion, and Dong Zhuo guesses why he is distracted and dismisses him abruptly.

Over the next month, Dong Zhuo becomes entirely besotted with Diao Chan, so much so that he ignores his official work. When he falls ill, Diao Chan sits beside him night and day to minister to him. One day when Lü Bu comes in to see how he is, he finds Dong Zhuo asleep and Diao Chan, spotting him, silently makes it clear that she is in distress and has eyes only for him. Lü Bu is deeply moved and at just that moment Dong Zhuo awakes and sees that Lü Bu is staring fixedly at a spot behind the bed. Turning round quickly, he sees Diao Chan standing there. 'Are you trying to seduce my lover?' he cries and he has Lü Bu thrown out.

Now Lü Bu is really enraged. On his way home he runs into Adviser Li Ru and tells him what has happened. Immediately Li Ru rushes off to see Dong Zhuo and pleads with him to make amends with Lü Bu.

'Otherwise such a split will spell disaster for us all,' he says.

'So what do you recommend?' asks Dong Zhuo.

'I suggest you call him back tomorrow and shower him with expensive gifts and sing his praises.'

The next day Dong Zhuo summons Lü Bu, apologizes and plies him with presents. However, although Lü Bu thanks him, from that day on, while his body might be at the service of Dong Zhuo, his heart is with Diao Chan.

One day, Lü Bu, clad in his armour and on guard duty, notices that Dong Zhuo is having an audience with the emperor. And so he takes the opportunity to slip out and ride off to the prime minister's palace. Tying his horse to the front hitching post and carrying his halberd, he makes his way to Diao Chan's apartment.

'Leave straight away,' she whispers urgently. 'But go to the Phoenix Garden, where I will meet you.'

Faithfully he goes there. He rests his halberd against one of the pillars in the garden and awaits his lover.

He waits for a long time but eventually is rewarded by seeing her coming towards him. Moving gracefully through the willows and flowers, she truly looks like an immortal descending from the palace of the Moon. With tears in her eyes, she comes to him beside the pool and says:

'Even though I'm not his natural daughter, Minister Wang Yun has always treated me as if I were. So when he gave me to you it was as if all my dreams had come true. Can you imagine my horror at the way in which the prime minister just came and seized me? Now I am in despair. I am in torment. I just want to kill myself; I'm only holding on so that there might come a moment when I could say goodbye to you. Now I have seen you, I know I'm no longer worthy to be with such a hero as you. So I'll die in front of you to show you how much I honour you and how little I'm worthy of you.' And saying this, she makes as if to jump into the pool and drown herself.

Lü Bu leaps forward and sweeps her up into his arms. Tears are pouring down his face as he holds her tight against him. 'I knew it was me you really loved,' he sobs. 'But we've never been able to talk.'

Clasping Lü Bu to her, she whispers, 'If it's not possible to be your wife in this life, I shall meet you again in the next.'

'If I cannot marry you in this life, then what kind of a hero am I?' he answers.

'Please rescue me!' groans Diao Chan.

Lü Bu suddenly realizes he might be missed by Dong Zhuo at any moment and is alarmed. Diao Chan clings even more tightly to him.

'If you're so afraid of that old villain, then I'll never see another day rise. All is lost!' she sobs as if in despair.

Lü Bu is bewildered and asks her to give him a moment to think this through.

'In the women's quarter they were talking about how you were the greatest hero,' she says. 'I could never have imagined that you would be one to be ruled by a lesser man than you!' Now she weeps openly. Lü Bu, moved beyond reason, sweeps her again into his arms, speaking words of comfort as they cling together, swaying with emotion, she unable to speak further.

Back at the palace, Dong Zhuo has noticed that Lü Bu is absent. And so, quickly taking his leave of the emperor, he sets off home. When he arrives he sees Lü Bu's horse tied up outside and upon questioning the servants hears that his adopted son is inside. Unable to find him, he calls out for Diao Chan.

'She's in the Phoenix Garden,' a maid tells him. Rushing into the garden, Dong Zhuo sees to his horror the two of them locked in an embrace together. He lets out a terrifying roar.

Lü Bu spins round when he hears the noise and, seeing it is Dong Zhuo, runs. Dong Zhuo spots the halberd in a corner and hurls it after him. Lü Bu dodges the weapon and keeps running. Dong Zhuo tries to race after him but he is too fat and slow, and Lü Bu is long gone by the time Dong Zhuo charges out of the garden gate and collides with someone who is running into the garden the opposite way.

Who on earth can this be?

All will be revealed.

CHAPTER 9

The result is that Lü Bu, urged on by Wang Yun, kills Dong Zhuo. The capital is captured by Li Jue and Guo Si.

It is Li Ru who has bowled Dong Zhuo over. Picking themselves up, they turn back into the grounds and retire to the library. Dong Zhuo wants to know what on earth Li Ru is doing charging through the gate.

'I was passing the garden gate when I heard you in the garden with your son,' says Li Ru, 'and then suddenly Lü Bu came rushing out, crying that you were after him! I rushed towards the gate to see if you were all right and now I've only made things worse by knocking you over. I'm so sorry – I can only say I deserve to die, I deserve to die!'

'How dare he!' cries Dong Zhuo. 'That wretched boy was flirting with my true love. He must die for this.'

Thoughtfully, Li Ru replies: 'My Lord, you're in danger of making a mistake. Remember the story of King Zhuang of Chu and the tassel.[6] The king didn't make a fuss about what had happened to his wife, and it was Jiang Xiong who later saved the king when in the midst of battle he was surrounded by his enemies. Let's be honest, Diao Chan is just another woman, but Lü Bu is your most trusted commander and dearest friend. If you were to give him this woman, he in return would without hesitation give his life for you. I beg you to think about this.'

'All right,' says Dong Zhuo, 'I agree I need to think about this properly.'

Going into his private chambers, he asks Diao Chan bluntly: 'Are you having an affair with Lü Bu?' Bursting into tears, she says, 'I was in the garden simply enjoying the flowers when he attacked me. I was so frightened I tried to run away.

He shouted: "What are you doing rejecting the Prime Minister's son?" He chased me all the way to the Phoenix Pavilion with that great big halberd of his in his hand. I was terrified because I was sure he would rape me. So I tried to throw myself into the pool. Then he grabbed me, and there was nothing I could do! Thank goodness you came along at that precise moment.'

'And to think I was wondering whether to give you to him!' says Dong Zhuo. 'Can you believe that?'

'Having been yours,' she cries aloud, 'can I even imagine being a slave? Never. I would rather die.' So saying, she grabs a dagger hanging on the wall as if to kill herself, but Dong Zhuo seizes the dagger and clasps her to him, saying, 'I was only teasing you!' Resting her head upon his chest, she sobs bitterly, saying, 'This is the work of Li Ru. He is in league with Lü Bu, and I'm sure it was his suggestion, wasn't it? He has no concern for your reputation or my life. I would like to devour him alive!'

Dong Zhuo replies, 'Do you imagine, my love, that I could lose you?'

'I know you love me,' she replies, 'but you must understand that I cannot stay here. Lü Bu will seek to harm me. I'm terrified of him!'

Dong Zhuo promises to take her away from the city the very next day to his new palace at Meiwu, where they can be happy together, free from any anxieties. So, she dries her eyes and expresses her immense gratitude.

The very next day Li Ru comes to see Dong Zhuo, saying, 'This is the day to send Diao Chan to Lü Bu, as it's an auspicious day according to the astrological calendar.'

'We're like father and son,' says Dong Zhuo, 'so I really have no need to do this. But you can reassure him that I will not mention this again. Go and calm him down.'

'Has that woman got you under her spell?' demands Li Ru, at which Dong Zhuo reddens and replies sternly, 'Tell me. Would you want to give your wife to someone else? Do not mention this again. It would be to your distinct advantage to remember that.'

At this Li Ru departs but when he is out of sight he raises his eyes to Heaven and says, 'We are all doomed. This girl will be the death of us all.'

A poet has written about this:

> Simply bring in a woman and strategies will succeed.
> There's no need for soldiers or weapons.
> Bloody battles were fought,
> Heroic deeds performed. But it was in a wooden
> summer house
> That victory was won.

As the cavalcade is getting ready to depart for Meiwu, Diao Chan spots Lü Bu. Immediately she casts her eyes down, and sadness seems to overwhelm her. As he watches her carriage disappear over the hill, Lü Bu is in the depths of despair.

Suddenly a voice asks, 'Why aren't you going as well instead of staying here sighing?' Looking around, he sees it is Wang Yun, who says, 'I have been ill for a few days but am feeling better now. So I decided to come to see the prime minister off.' And he asks again, 'What is the matter with you?'

'It's because of that young woman of yours,' replies Lü Bu.

'Do you mean to tell me, she still hasn't been given to you?' says Wang. To this Lü Bu replies, 'That wretched old man has fallen in love with her himself.'

'This cannot be true!' exclaims Wang Yun, so Lü Bu tells him everything. When he has finished, Wang Yu expresses his disgust at Dong Zhuo's behaviour. Appearing to take pity on the young man, Wang Yun invites him to his house to talk this through.

There in the private quarters they talk about the events that have led up to the present situation.

'He's corrupted my little girl,' exclaims Wang Yun, 'and the one who should be your wife. The world will mock us. People will see us as shameful, and we'll be held up to ridicule. People won't mock him – oh no, not the mighty Dong Zhuo. No, they will mock you and me! Ah me! I'm old and useless, but you, you are a famous warrior. The greatest in the land. And yet you have to put up with such awful treatment!'

Lü Bu becomes increasingly furious and he cries out in rage and frustration. His host tries to calm him down. But Lü Bu bursts out: 'I'll kill the wretch, I swear before Heaven and Earth. There is no other way to be rid of my shame.' Wang Yun again appears to try to calm him, saying, 'This will only bring disaster on both of us.' But Lü Bu counters, saying, 'How can it be possible that one as mighty and brave as myself can ever be content to remain under the dominion of such a vile person as Dong Zhuo?' To this Wang Yun comments that Dong Zhuo is not a worthy man to have such dominion over someone as great as Lü Bu.

'I would kill the old bastard now,' says Lü Bu, 'even though we are related. But I fear the judgement of history.'

Wang Yun replies, 'Your family name is Lü. His is Dong. And where's his paternal care for you when he threw that halberd at you?' Seeing that this has disturbed Lü Bu, Wang Yun continues:

'If you were to be responsible for the restoration of the Han dynasty, why, you would be famous and your name would be praised for a hundred generations. But if you continue to support the traitor Dong Zhuo, then your name will stink for ten thousand years!'

'I've made up my mind,' says Lü Bu, 'have no fear.'

And he takes a dagger and cuts his arm, vowing by the blood that flows: 'I will do what has to be done, have no fear.'

Wang Yun falls to his knees and gives thanks that the Han and their ancestors will not be abandoned and that Lü Bu will be their saviour. 'But,' says Wang Yun, 'this must remain our secret. When everything is ready I'll explain how this plot can unfold.'

So Lü Bu takes his leave.

Wang then confers with two friends, and they finalize the plot. The emperor has been ill but has recovered. They decide to send a messenger to tell Dong Zhuo to come to the palace for a meeting. The plan is that Dong Zhuo will be murdered as soon as he enters the palace gate.

The next task is to find someone willing to go to Meiwu and deliver the fake imperial decree ordering Dong Zhuo to come back. They decide this should be Li Su. It was Li Su who had fooled Lü Bu into killing his former benefactor and joining Dong Zhuo. Lü Bu is delighted by the opportunity this gives him to revenge his former master and the chance to humiliate Li Su. If he fails, Lü Bu swears he will kill Li Su. When Li Su arrives, Lü Bu tells him that the trick of making him kill his former master has meant that Dong Zhuo has grown more and more evil and ambitious and a greater and greater burden on the people. 'He's hated,' Lü Bu says, 'not only by the people but also by the gods. Go and lure him to come to the palace, where we will kill him.' Li Su swears that he too wishes Dong Zhuo dead. The very next day Li Su leaves for Meiwu with the fake imperial decree.

When Li Su comes before Dong Zhuo he is asked what this decree is about. 'The emperor,' says Li Su, 'having recovered from his illness, now wants to discuss with his cabinet his abdication in favour of your honourable self, sir.'

Now it so happens that Dong Zhuo has had a dream the night before. 'I dreamed,' says Dong Zhuo, 'that a dragon had coiled itself around me and now I receive this auspicious message. I will set off as soon as possible.'

Before he leaves he goes to see his ninety-year-old mother. 'Where are you going, my son?' she asks. 'To accept the abdication of the last Han ruler and to become emperor!' he replies. 'This means you will become the queen mother.' She is blunt with him. 'I've a very bad feeling about this. I've not felt well for days. I believe this is a bad omen.'

'Given you are shortly going to be the mother of the nation, it is not surprising that you should feel apprehension.' And so saying, he leaves her. Before he departs for the palace he tells Diao Chan that soon she will be his first imperial lady. Bowing, she appears to be delighted and honoured but in her heart she knows what is going to happen next.

On the long journey to the palace a whole series of ominous events takes place. The wheel of his carriage breaks, and he has to continue on horseback. Then the horse rears up, breaking the reins. Alarmed by these omens, Dong Zhuo asks Li Su what they mean. He tells Dong Zhuo that they are auspicious. 'You will soon be emperor, exchanging an ordinary carriage for a bejewelled carriage and an ordinary saddle for a golden one.'

On the second day of the journey a great storm breaks upon them, and they are surrounded by a dense fog. Once again Li Su is there to comfort him. 'You are a mighty yang dragon about to mount the throne, surrounded now, as is appropriate, by the yin of clouds and mist. See how it's all lit by the bright light of Heaven.' All of this puts Dong Zhuo's heart at ease.

When he arrives in the capital he goes first to his own palace. Lü Bu comes to meet him, and Dong Zhuo tells him that as soon as he becomes the emperor, Lü Bu will be made commander of all the armies.

That night Dong Zhuo hears children nearby singing a strange song: 'The grass in the meadow looks green and fresh. Wait ten days and not a blade will remain.' Li Su again has an easy answer to Dong's concerns. 'This means the Han will disappear, and the Dongs will take their place.'

En route to the palace, a Daoist monk suddenly appears, wearing a black robe and a white turban. He carries a tall staff to which is attached a white banner, and at each end of the banner is drawn a mouth. Dong Zhuo is alarmed and asks Li Su what this means.

Li Su replies that the monk is simply mad and has him driven away.

Arriving at the entrance to the palace, Dong Zhuo finds all the officials in their finery waiting for him. Li Su, for ceremonial reasons, draws his sword and walks beside Dong Zhuo's sedan chair, as if protecting him. Standing at the entrance to the Reception Hall is Wang Yun with a group of supporters, and Dong Zhuo notices to his surprise and alarm that they are all armed. 'What is the meaning of all this?' he asks, but no answer comes back from Li Su, and the sedan chair moves further in. Suddenly Wang Yun shouts, 'The traitor has arrived! Where are the executioners?'

From the wings leap armed men, who fall upon Dong Zhuo. He has forgotten to put on his breastplate and as the blows bring him to his knees he cries out, 'Where is my son?' Lü Bu appears beside him and shouts, 'Here I am with a decree to kill the traitor.' And so saying, he strikes his 'father' with a halberd, sinking it deep into Dong Zhuo's throat. Then, hacking off Dong Zhuo's head, Li Su triumphantly holds it high. Lü Bu draws from inside his jacket the 'decree', saying, 'This ordered Dong Zhuo's death. No one else is to suffer.'

Greatly relieved, the entire group of officials and sycophants who have surrounded Dong Zhuo enthusiastically shout, 'Long live the emperor!'

The murder of Dong Zhuo unleashes pent-up fury, and soon Li Ru too is executed. Dong Zhuo's head is put on display in the marketplace. Here passers-by throw stones at his head and stamp on his grossly fat body with their feet.

Led by Lü Bu, an armed group sets off for Meiwu. When they arrive there, Lü Bu 'rescues' Diao Chan and then slaughters every member of Dong's family – not even sparing his old mother. Hidden away in Meiwu the soldiers find many young women from noble families who have been held as captives. These they free. The vast collection of stolen treasures is seized.

On their return Wang Yun lays on a great celebration feast, but all is far from well. The power seems to go to Wang Yun's head. When news comes that someone has been heard mourning over the corpse of Dong Zhuo, he is hunted down. It is found to be a very senior official, Cai Yong, who is writing the official history of the dynasty. When asked why he dares mourn such a traitor to the Han, he replies robustly, 'Once Dong Zhuo treated me kindly, so it was only right that I mourn him.' Deeply alarmed by his arrest, he pleads, 'As the recorder of the Han History I am, of course, concerned deeply for the well-being of the Han, but kindness cannot just be ignored. I beg you, brand me, or cut off my feet, but let me live to continue writing the history.'

But Wang Yun fears that, just as Sima Qian[7] wrote false stories about the Han, so this man might do the same. So, despite many pleas for clemency, Wang Yun orders his murder.

The land is now in uproar. Rebellions break out everywhere. Former generals under Dong Zhuo, fearing for their lives, seek forgiveness from Wang Yun. But he rejects their pleas and in so doing he turns them into enemies. The generals, led by Li Jue and Guo Si, advance towards the capital, and Lü Bu rides out with Li Su to confront them. Li Su is sent ahead to hold the rebels back, but he fails abysmally. Furious at this failure, Lü Bu has Li Su executed and his head impaled above the entrance to the camp. But this does nothing to improve the situation. Lü Bu's impetuous nature is exploited by Li Jue and Guo Si, who attack and then withdraw, then attack again until Lü Bu is exhausted. He is still deep in the countryside, trying to chase the rebels, when word is brought to him that the capital itself is now under attack. He immediately turns his army around and heads as fast as possible to the capital.

He cannot get through. The city is surrounded and besieged by the rebels. At the same time, an uprising takes place, led by Dong Zhuo's surviving supporters inside the city itself. Lü Bu despatches messengers, pleading with Wang Yun to escape and join him. Wang Yun replies that he hopes to restore peace in the city, but if he fails then his body would be his final sacrifice. He recommends that Lü Bu go east to join Yuan Shu and his troops, who also wish to restore the Han.

Then the insurgents inside open the city gates to the rebel army, who pour in. And so Lü Bu, left outside, has to flee, leaving his family to their mercy. The rebels under their commanders Li Jue and Guo Si are given free licence to loot and destroy, and many of the officials and ministers are murdered.

Only when the emperor himself appears on the palace wall do the leaders try to halt the rampage of their soldiers. Seeing the emperor, the rebels call out for Wang Yun to be given to them to avenge the murder of Dong Zhuo. The emperor doesn't know what to do, but Wang Yun steps forward on the palace wall and says:

'All that was done was for the well-being of the throne. However, from this nothing but turmoil has resulted, so I assume Your Majesty will not mind losing me. I'm responsible for this evil, so I will surrender myself to these rebels.'

So saying, he jumps from the wall, only to be seized by the rebel leaders. 'Why was Dong Zhuo killed?' they cry.

'We all rejoiced the day he died,' replies Wang Yun, 'because his crimes were so terrible they cried out to both Heaven and Earth.'

Hearing this, the leaders murder Wang Yun there and then at the base of the palace wall.

A historian has written:

> Wang Yun conceived a cunning plot,
> That brought Dong Zhuo to his demise.
> Moved by compassion for the people,
> Catalysed to action by the ruler's distress.
> Oh, his courage rises with the wind –
> His spirit sojourns with the stars.
> His souls remain here, in the ether,
> Sensed for ever in the Phoenix Tower.

Breaking into his home, they slaughter every single member of his family. Such terrible acts cast a pall of sadness and distress across the whole land.

Emboldened by their success, the rebels Li Jue and Guo Si then said to each other, 'Why don't we go the whole way and get rid of the emperor and so create our own dynasty?'

Do they succeed?

Find out!

CHAPTER 10

Ma Teng rises up to defend the emperor.
Cao Cao in fury prepares to attack those
he believes murdered his family.

The two key rebel leaders, Li Jue and Guo Si, want to murder the emperor straight away and seize the throne. However, two other leaders, Zhang Ji and Fan Chou, point out, 'The people won't stand for it. They will see us simply as the ones who overthrew the dynasty and killed the emperor. So, instead, let's pretend we support the emperor, seize power within the palace and get rid of any who support him. Then and only then will it be safe to kill the emperor.' Grudgingly recognizing the strategic wisdom of this, Li Jue and Guo Si agree.

The emperor is forced by the rebel leaders to 'reward' them with official titles. Frankly he has no other option. Emboldened by their successes, they decide to give Dong Zhuo an honourable and official burial. However, so few bits of his body can be found that in the end they have to have a wooden effigy made of him to lay in the coffin. They decide to bury him at Meiwu. Choosing an auspicious day, they begin to perform the imperial burial rituals.

But as they bury the coffin in the ground a terrible thunderstorm erupts. So torrential is the downpour that it floods the site, causing the coffin to float out of the ground on a surge of water. The coffin is smashed into pieces. Despite this, they try again. However, during the night the coffin is once again washed out of the ground, as thunder peals and lightning flashes all around. A third time they try to bury him, only for the same thing to happen yet again. By now nothing remains of him, not a fragment of bone or flesh, for the lightning has destroyed what the floods have not washed away. In this way Heaven makes plain its anger, its real fury, against Dong Zhuo.

Rebellion arises everywhere. A rebel army of one hundred thousand march on the capital, but they are defeated and driven off. The Yellow Headband rebels rise once again with hundreds of thousands of men in armed gangs. When the rebels Li Jue and Guo Si wonder who can tackle this uprising they are recommended to call upon Cao Cao.

Within a short period of time Cao Cao has defeated the rebels and has received the surrender of over three hundred thousand former Yellow Headband rebels. From among them he chooses the best to join his own army. Basing himself in Yanzhou, away from the capital, he in effect builds up his own court, drawing into his service many wise and worthy individuals.

Now that he has become so powerful, he decides to bring his father and the whole of his family to Yanzhou so they can see how important he is. Thus it is that the whole family – over forty members, around one hundred servants and over one hundred wagons piled high with their goods – set out on the long journey to Yanzhou. They pass through Xuzhou, where the imperial governor is Tao Qian. He is a genuinely good man, who meets them as they enter his territory and hosts them in the city. He then gives a former Yellow Headband rebel leader, Zhang Kai, and his men the task of escorting Cao Cao's family to the border.

En route a fierce storm lashes them with rain. They are all soaked through and take shelter in an old temple. While the family are given reasonable quarters by the resident monks, the soldiers have to make do with the chilly, windy corridors. Wet and cold, they start to complain. Hearing this, Zhang Kai summons his lieutenants. 'As former Yellow Headband rebels we've gained almost nothing by surrendering. But in the wagons and chariots of the Cao family there's enough treasure to make us all rich. In the middle of the night let's kill the whole family and take off with the wagons. What do you think?' His men greedily agree.

So that night, while the storm rages, the rebels slaughter the entire family, hunting them down as they hide in places like the toilet or as they try to clamber over the walls to escape. Not a single one of them survives. Then the treacherous rebels burn the temple down and flee to Huainan.

When Cao Cao hears the terrible news he collapses, weeping. Believing that this was a plot by Tao Qian, he swears revenge and orders an invasion of Xuzhou. He gives instructions that, when the city falls, everyone is to be murdered. Ministers and courtiers try to plead with Cao Cao, but he will not be swayed. Blinded by anger and hatred, he presses ahead with the invasion. Soon the province is terrorized by his soldiers' brutal massacres. Not even the graves of the dead are respected but are looted, and bodies desecrated.

Tao Qian rides out at the head of his army to meet Cao Cao's vast horde. He tries desperately to reason with Cao Cao, pointing out that they were both betrayed by Zhang Kai, but Cao Cao is deaf to his pleas. Returning to the city, Tao Qian speaks with his advisers and declares that, as it is his fault this invasion has occurred, he will offer himself up to Cao Cao to try to stop any more violence.

But someone comes forward and says that the city is well defended. 'I have a plan,' says this man, 'which will mean Cao Cao will die somewhere where not even he can have a decent burial.'

Who is this man and what is his plan?

We will find out.

CHAPTER 11

Xuande rescues Kong Rong at Beihai.
Lü Bu defeats Cao Cao.

The man with the plan is Mi Zhu, renowned for his generosity. Many years ago, while travelling home to Luoyang, he offered a ride to a beautiful woman who was walking slowly in the same direction. He got out of his carriage to make room for her and walked alongside. But she insisted they share. He behaved with absolute propriety. After a few miles the woman dismounted and as she left she said, 'I am the southern manifestation of the deity of the Virtuous Fire Planet. I was sent down to destroy your house. But your kindness has moved me, so I give you this warning. Get home now and remove all your valuables before I descend upon your house tonight.'

Mi Zhu raced home and did as instructed. Sure enough, that night a fire broke out and destroyed the house. Mi Zhu was deeply affected by this, so that his natural generosity grew and he became renowned for his kindness and his desire to help any in need. This is why he is in the court of Tao Qian and why people listen to him.

He recommends creating alliances with two other local governors, Kong Rong at Beihai and Tian Kai in Qingzhou. He himself goes to plead for help from Kong Rong, a twentieth-generation descendant of Kong Fu Zi.[8] Kong Rong had been a child prodigy, having started his rise to power at the age of ten!

Kong Rong is uncertain whether to come to Tao Qian's help. He has no personal animosity towards Cao Cao but knows him to be a dangerous enemy to have. As he is wondering what to do, a large Yellow Headband army appears before the city, ravaging the area and demanding food or they will sack the city. The rebels lay siege to the city, cutting it off from all help.

Kong Rong watches the siege with growing despair, until one day out of the blue a lone rider slashes his way through the rebels until he reaches the city gate. The gate is hastily thrown open, and the warrior rides in. This hero is called Taishi Ci. When Kong Rong asks who he is and why he has come, he replies, 'My mother has often received kindness from you, sir. When she heard of the siege she immediately ordered me to come to your aid. This is her way of saying thank you. So here I am.'

He is just what Kong Rong needs. While Taishi Ci wants to take a force of a thousand men and attack the rebels, Kong Rong has a better idea. 'I hear that Xuande is a great hero and not far away. If we can get a message to him he could come to our help.'

'Write the letter, sir,' says Taishi Ci, 'and I'll take it to him immediately.' As he charges out of the city and races towards Xuande at his base at Pingyuan, the rebels chase after him. Taishi Ci slays many of them until the rest give up the chase.

On receiving the appeal from Kong Rong, Xuande, Zhang Fei and Guan Yu, accompanied by three thousand warriors, set off for Beihai.

The rebels don't stand a chance. Even though they have many, many times more men than Xuande, Guan Yu, Zhang Fei and Taishi Ci charge forward, slashing their way through to the city gate. Meanwhile Xuande attacks the rest of the rebel army with the main divisions of his army, creating chaos among the rebels and sending them fleeing. The siege is lifted.

Once inside the city, Xuande is asked by Kong Rong to join him in coming to the assistance of Tao Qian and oppose Cao Cao's murderous assault on the province. As Kong Rong had done, Xuande raises the fact that he has no quarrel personally with Cao Cao. But Kong Rong, now convinced they must resist Cao Cao's devastating invasion, persuades him to come to the beleaguered province's assistance. Having given his word that he will join Kong Rong, Xuande returns to his base to recruit more men. Among those he asks to join him is Zhao Zilong.

When Xuande joins the others at Xuzhou, he suggests that he try one last attempt at appealing to Cao Cao to understand that the murder of Cao's family had nothing to do with Tao Qian.

He writes a personal letter to Cao Cao. 'I rejoice that we are in touch again, for I have admired all that you have done. I am profoundly shocked that your father has been killed by the rebel Zhang Kai. This had nothing whatsoever to do with Governor Tao Qian. With rebels rising on all sides, and henchmen of Dong Zhuo controlling the court, surely the sensible thing would be for all loyal supporters of the Han to unite. Let us place the needs of the Han before personal quests. Withdraw from Xuzhou and let us concentrate on defending the empire.' But when the letter is delivered to Cao Cao, he roars with anger, executes the messenger and orders a full-out attack on the city.

It is at exactly this time that a messenger comes to Cao Cao bearing terrible news. Lü Bu, in league with various rebels, has attacked Yanzhou and seized most of Cao Cao's own province. Deeply troubled that he is about to lose his only base, Cao Cao agrees to respond to Xuande's letter. Leaving for Yanzhou, he abandons the siege.

In honour of the success that Xuande has appeared to achieve in removing Cao Cao from the area, Tao Qian twice offers him the governorship of Xuzhou. Twice he refuses, concerned that people will believe he had manipulated the situation to his own advantage.

As Cao Cao races back to Yanzhou, he is informed that Lü Bu's army has grown hugely and is now a serious threat. But Cao Cao dismisses this and in so doing gravely underestimates the danger. It is near Puyang that the two armies meet. When Cao Cao attacks, Lü Bu's men easily drive off the enemy. Then Cao Cao leads a night attack on Lü Bu's camp. While at first this night attack is successful, it is driven off by a concerted defence by all Lü Bu's generals. So determined is this counterattack that Cao Cao's attack collapses, and his men flee. Cao Cao is forced to try to escape, but every way he turns he is confronted by Lü Bu's men. Trapped, he cries out, 'Who will come and save me?' Gallant Dian Wei responds. Dismounting and arming himself with throwing axes, he advances on foot, telling his followers to shout when the enemy soldiers are within ten paces of him. The shout goes up: 'Ten paces, sir', to which Dian Wei replies that they must now tell him when the enemy is within five paces. 'Five paces, sir,' cry his desperate followers, and at this point Dian Wei hurls the hand axes left and right, killing all those attacking him.

So ferocious is Dian Wei's attack that he breaks the enemy assault and is just able to rescue Cao Cao.

But their troubles are not over. Just as they struggle back to their camp a shout of triumph is heard. 'Cao, you bastard, stop!' It is Lü Bu! Exhausted, Cao's men are ready to cut and run.

Is this the end of Cao Cao?

Let's find out.

CHAPTER 12

Tao Qian tries to hand over governorship to Xuande three times. Cao Cao battles Lü Bu.

It is the warrior Xiahou Dun who comes to Cao's rescue. Gathering a troop about him, he charges at Lü Bu. The battle rages until a heavy storm brings the fighting to an end, and each side retreats to its own camp. Frustrated and embittered, Lü Bu is determined to finish off Cao Cao. He has a letter written and sent to Cao Cao as if it were a secret message. It claims to come from one of the most influential citizens of Puyang and says that Lü Bu and his forces have left, and the city is ready to be taken.

Fooled by this letter, Cao Cao is lured into what appears to be an almost empty city. But no sooner is he well inside than the trap is sprung. From every direction, from north and south, from east and west, Lü Bu's men emerge from hiding and bear down upon the enemy troops. In desperation, as his army is annihilated around him, Cao Cao dashes from to gate to gate, trying to escape. No matter which of the city gates, north or south, he tries, Lü Bu's men drive him back. Realizing what is happening, Cao's generals try to break through to rescue him but are driven back. Now in utter despair Cao Cao tries once more to escape by slipping through the north gate. As he approaches, who should ride up but Lü Bu. Covering his face, Cao Cao hopes he will not be spotted. Imagine his horror when Lü Bu actually rides up and bangs him on his helmet with his halberd and asks where Cao Cao is! Cao Cao points to a horse and rider disappearing into the distance and says, 'That's him up there, sir'. Lü Bu rides off in hot pursuit, and Cao Cao turns and rides for his life towards the east gate.

As he approaches the east gate, Dian Wei appears beside him

and slashes a pathway through the soldiers, creating utter chaos. But just as Cao Cao is riding under the gate a burning wooden beam crashes down upon his horse. Cao Cao tries to fend off the burning beam with his arm but is badly burned in the process. In real pain and shock, he seems about to fall. Once again he is rescued by Dian Wei, who takes control of Cao's horse, and through the gate they charge to safety. By stages, moving as stealthily as possible, they get beyond the battle scene until at last they are able to make their way back to their camp. In the light of such a disaster and such a trick, Cao Cao discusses with his staff what to do next. It is decided that they will resort to such tricks of their own.

Cao Cao's men spread the rumour that Cao Cao has died. Assuming that this will mean Cao's men will be in chaos and distress at such a turn of events, Lü Bu decides to attack. This time it is Lü Bu who is caught in a trap, and his men are overwhelmed. Lü Bu barely escapes with his life! Neither side has gained the upper hand. It is in effect a stalemate. And so it is that a truce is declared between them.

Meanwhile, back in Xuzhou, Tao Qian is on his deathbed and once again asks Xuande to take over as governor. Once again he refuses, even when Tao Qian dies pleading with him with his last breath. It is only when the people of the city come themselves and beg him that he agrees. However, he only agrees to do so on a temporary basis.

With the threat from Lü Bu contained, Cao Cao returns to his consuming desire to try to capture Xuzhou, in order to punish those whom he believes have murdered his family. But he is persuaded that the time is not right. So instead he attacks and wipes out a rebel army of Yellow Headbands and then suddenly advances upon Puyang and drives out Lü Bu. He goes on to capture most of the northeast. But Lü Bu is not finished.

Or is he?

Read on!

CHAPTER 13

Li Jue and Guo Si fall out, while Yang Feng and Dong Cheng rescue the emperor. They return him to the old capital at Luoyang.

In desperation Lü Bu turns for help first to Yuan Shao, but he refuses and instead goes to support Cao Cao. So Lü Bu turns to Xuande. As it was Lü Bu's attack on Cao Cao's army that caused the siege of Xuzhou to be lifted, Xuande offers him sanctuary. Not that this pleases Zhang Fei, to put it mildly.

In fact, during a banquet that Lü Bu holds to thank Xuande, Zhang Fei takes violent offence at the way Lü Bu addresses Xuande. Arising from his seat and roaring with anger, Zhang Fei challenges Lü Bu to a duel 'of three hundred rounds'. Xuande commands him to hold his tongue, and Guan Yu shoves him roughly out of the room. Undeterred, Zhang Fei later again challenges Lü Bu. A furious Xuande has to personally go and reprimand him. Not that Zhang Fei shows the slightest remorse, for he hates Lü Bu with a vengeance.

When the triumphant Cao Cao reports his victories over Lü Bu to the imperial court at Chang'an he is rewarded and honoured with various new titles and roles. But the imperial court is not in good shape. The rebel leaders Li Jue and Guo Si are ruthlessly exploiting the power they have seized. The whole court lives in fear of them. The emperor is in despair. Not even the suggestion that Cao Cao as a famous hero could attack the rebels can console the emperor.

Such is the state of affairs when Yang Biao, one of the ministers, comes up with a plan. Knowing that Guo Si's wife is very jealous, he decides to exploit this. He also knows that most evenings Li Jue and Guo Si dine together to discuss matters, often drinking and talking late into the evening. He sets out to cause a rupture in the relationship between them.

Yang Biao's plan is to send his wife, the Lady Yang, to visit the wife of Guo Si, Lady Guo, and to sow the seeds of distrust. During the conversation Lady Yang lets slip that she understands that Guo Si is having an affair with the wife of Li Jue. 'Imagine, my lady,' says Lady Yang, 'if Li finds out! You must do all in your power to stop your husband having this affair.'

Needless to say, Lady Guo is furious. 'So that is where he is in the evenings! Rest assured', she says, 'I'll deal with this!'

It is a few days later, in the early evening, when Guo Si is getting ready to visit Li Jue for their usual planning meeting that Lady Guo tries to stop him. 'You cannot trust Li Jue,' she says. 'Is there really space at the top for two ambitious men? What if he were to murder you? What would become of me?' Swayed by her concern, he is persuaded to stay home that evening.

However, Li Jue sends over the dinner that had been prepared for Guo. Lady Guo, determined to undermine what she believes is an affair, slips some poison into the food, and just as Guo is about to eat it she cries, 'No. We cannot trust this food sent from outside.' So saying, she gives a little of the food to their pet dog, who convulses in agony and dies before their very eyes. From that day forward, Guo Si never trusts Li Jue again.

Another time, Li Jue and Guo Si have been drinking to excess, and this gives Guo Si indigestion. Lady Guo is able to persuade him that he has been poisoned by Li Jue. In revenge he plans to launch his branch of the rebel army in an attack on Li Jue. When word of this reaches Li Jue he decides to strike first.

In the mayhem that ensues when the two groups of soldiers clash, Li Jue orders his nephew Li Xian to break off and secretly capture the emperor and the empress. Taking everyone in the palace by surprise, the young man is successful. He seizes the emperor and empress, and takes them to Li Jue's camp. When, as a result of the fighting, Guo Si captures the palace, he discovers this added betrayal. He imprisons the remaining court officials and in his fury he burns the palace to the ground.

Li Xian takes the imperial couple to the palace at Meiwu. Here he dismisses almost all their staff and reduces the imperial pair to living in poverty. So bad do things become that they have barely enough food to keep them alive.

For two months, Guo's and Li's men battle with each other. Despite various attempts at mediation, not least in order to secure the release of the imperial couple, nothing results but endless, futile bloodshed.

By various means the emperor's supporters weaken Li Jue's hold: for example, telling the various troops of tribal soldiers that they have the emperor's permission to go home. Li Jue is a great fan of women shamans. Invited to the palace, they go into mystical trances and offer him advice as if from the gods themselves. His generals feel that no matter what military successes they might achieve, credit is always given to the shamans, and this too feeds resentment within his army. However, attempts at assassination fail, most dramatically that of Yang Feng and Song Guo. They have helped Li Jue in his various campaigns. But they have also watched as the Qiang tribesmen troops started to slip away, disenchanted by Li Jue's leadership and reassured that the emperor had given them permission to go. They resent the fact that the women shamans are given all the credit and so they decide to kill Li Jue and rescue the emperor. But they are overheard. Song Guo, inside the city, is seized and beheaded, while Yang Feng, waiting with his men outside the city for the signal to attack, is suddenly confronted by a furious Li Jue and his men but manages to escape.

Into this chaos rides Zhang Ji from Shaanxi with a huge army, determined to end this war and reconcile the two sides. By now Li Jue's army has largely faded away, and Guo Si's position is so weak he is unable to exert any real influence. Through Zhang Ji's diplomacy at long last the warfare ends. As a result Zhang Ji is able to present a memorial to the emperor. Zhang Ji argues that the emperor will be much safer if he moves to the eastern capital of Hongnong. The emperor is delighted with this proposal. Zhang Ji negotiates a compromise between the two rebel leaders. Li Jue will organize the carriages to convey the imperial couple to Hongnong with a couple of hundred guards, while Guo Si releases the imprisoned court officials.

But all is not as it seems. Guo Si goes back on his word. An order from him to hold up the imperial entourage at the Baling bridge is foiled when his own guards let the emperor cross. Furious at this disobedience, Guo Si decides personally to stop the emperor and sets off after him with an armed force.

Just as the convoy reaches Huayin County, Guo Si rides up, demanding that the convoy be brought to a halt. The emperor is beside himself with fear, saying, 'Alas! Out of the wolf's lair and now into the tiger's mouth!'

When it seems to the desperate emperor that there is no hope left, and as Guo Si's men draw closer, a thunderous roll of drums is heard. Onto the scene rides another armed force with a banner unfurled, proclaiming that this troop are men of 'Yang Feng the Mighty Han'. Having survived fleeing from Li Jue, he has taken up refuge in the hills of the Zhongnan mountains and has come to help protect his emperor. Riding to the attack, Yang Feng's men drive Guo Si and his men off.

The emperor, upon being introduced to his champion, says, 'It's the greatest of services that you have performed for us. We owe you our lives.' Yang Feng kowtows and thanks the emperor for his gracious words.

Guo Si tries one final time to attack and capture the emperor but is once again defeated by Yang Feng. He in turn is assisted by yet another surprise arrival, Dong Cheng, a relative of the emperor.

Undaunted, Guo Si now teams up with Li Jue for fear that with Zhang Ji in charge at Chang'an and Yang Feng en route to Hongnong, the two rebels could soon find themselves powerless and facing destruction. So they decide to ride for Hongnong in order to murder the emperor. They cut a path of utter devastation on the way to Hongnong and overtake Yang Feng, Dong Cheng and the imperial convoy, who are resting in the city of Dongjian. The loyal troops are overwhelmed by the rebel army, and it becomes clear that they cannot hold them back and that they will seize the city itself. Yang Feng and Dong Cheng are barely able to get the imperial couple safely out of the city before it is overrun. The rest of the imperial convoy is captured by Li Jue and Guo Si. Dongjian is looted and destroyed, and it is a miracle that the emperor is able to escape to Shanbei. But close behind come Li Jue and Guo Si.

In desperation, Yang and Dong try to both pacify Li and Guo and at the same time raise an army to fight back. To do this they have to approach a splinter movement of the Yellow Headbands known as the White Wave. Among their leaders is one Li Yue, through whose inspired leadership many rebels come forward to join the defence of the emperor.

Despite this new army, Li Jue and Guo Si push on, defeating the White Wave troops and seizing Hongnong. There they slaughter the old and the weak and force the healthy men to join their army. The fall of Hongnong forces the emperor to flee once again, this time to the north. It is Li Yue who on the banks of the Yellow River finds a small boat to ferry the emperor and empress across to safety. This leaves the emperor with but a handful of servants and Li Yue and Yang Feng, who tries his best to care for the imperial couple. Commandeering a farm wagon, he manages to get the couple to the town of Dayang, but there is nothing there for them to eat. Pressing on, they spend the night in a rough farm hut, and though the local peasants offer them food it is so coarse they cannot eat it.

Eventually the sad procession arrives in Anyi, but here there are no grand buildings, just simple, one-storey huts. It is in one of these that the imperial couple at last rest. It is at this point that Li Yue shows his true nature and begins to bully everyone, attacking the courtiers and denouncing people before the throne for no reason whatsoever. The food and drink he gives to the emperor is deliberately of poor quality, and he forces the emperor to appoint other White Wave leaders to positions of authority. The court has reached its lowest ebb yet.

However, the mission to reconcile Li Jue and Guo Si in order to protect the emperor is eventually successful. At last governors from across China are able to send supplies to the imperial couple. But it is a time of terrible famine.

Yang Feng and Dong Cheng have decided to return the emperor to the original capital of Luoyang, a move opposed by Li Yue. Despite this, Yang Feng and Dong Cheng set off with the emperor for Luoyang. It is now that Li Yue turns traitor.

He has decided to collaborate with Li Jue and Guo Si and seize the emperor as he travels. Hearing of the plot, Yang Feng and Dong Cheng race ahead with the imperial couple, forcing Li Yue to attack on his own without the support of the other rebels. At night, at the Ji Guan mountain pass, he overtakes the emperor, shouting, 'No further! Here are Li Jue and Guo Si!'

The emperor is terrified, quivering with fear as torches descend into the pass, lighting up the night.

> The rebels, once divided in two,
> Were now three joined in union.

What is to become of the emperor?

CHAPTER 14

Cao Cao is brought to defend the emperor but moves him to Xuchang. Worried by Lü Bu and Xuande, he tries to set them against each other.

The emperor falls for Li Yue's lie that he is backed by the other two rebel chiefs. But Yang Feng does not. 'There are no others, just Li Yue,' he says. Li Yue's bluff is called. Yang Feng can see that the rebel is now of little importance and he sends the champion Xu Huang out to challenge him. In a swift encounter Li Yue is killed, and the White Wave army scatters. The road to the old capital is now clear.

So it is that the emperor returns to his former capital of Luoyang. The emperor is horrified by the ruined state of the capital. All the palaces and halls have been burned to the ground. The streets are overgrown with weeds. Brambles smother the ruins. Of the palaces and courts, all that remains are collapsed roofs and crumbling walls. One building is still partially intact, and it is in this small, humble place that the emperor lives. But the court actually meets in the overgrown ruins surrounding it.

And there is no food. It is yet another year of famine. Even the few hundred families still in Luoyang have to survive on bark and roots. So bad is it that people just lie down and die beside the ruins of their homes.

To secure the safety of the emperor, Yang Biao suggests summoning Cao Cao as he has the strongest army. With the consent of the emperor a messenger is sent to summon Cao Cao to Luoyang. Cao Cao immediately starts to put his affairs in order and prepares to set off on the long march to the capital.

Before news of Cao Cao's preparations reach the troubled emperor, rumours spread that Li Jue and Guo Si are advancing on Luoyang. In despair, the court begins to retreat from the capital. The cavalcade has only just started out of the city gate when Cao Cao's troops appear over the horizon. Joyfully the emperor returns to the palace in Luoyang while in a series of swift manoeuvres Cao Cao's army confront and rout the rebels Li Jue and Guo Si. They flee for refuge into the mountains.

Once Cao Cao has settled into quarters in the capital the emperor sends a messenger called Dong Zhao to summon Cao Cao. Cao Cao is impressed by his forthrightness and vigour. For example, he sees that Dong Zhao looks well fed, whereas the others in the city look half starved. 'How come you look so fit and well?' asks Cao Cao. 'This is simply the fruits of a simple lifestyle,' he replies. 'I've been a soldier for thirty years. You learn a thing or two.' It is Dong Zhao who suggests to Cao Cao that the emperor be moved to Xuchang in order that only Cao Cao will be in control, squeezing out others such as Yang Feng, who fear Cao Cao. Together they plan how to extract the emperor without upsetting the other commanders. 'Just say there is more food in Xuchang,' advises Dong Zhao. 'That will placate everyone.' The emperor has the plan put to him and, frankly unable to disagree with such a strong man as Cao Cao, he gives his assent.

En route to Xuchang, Yang Feng, alarmed at his loss of control over the emperor, tries to stop the procession by placing his army across the pathway. His champion is the mighty Xu Huang. However, Cao Cao manages to bring Xu Huang to his side. His envoy quietly points out that a hero like Xu Huang deserves to serve another hero, not a good-for-nothing like Yang Feng. 'You know the proverb,' the envoy says. 'The wise bird chooses its own branch; the thoughtful servant chooses his master.' Xu Huang finds himself agreeing and decides to come over to Cao Cao's side. But when the envoy suggests that Xu might kill Yang Feng and bring his head as a goodwill offering, Xu refuses, earning the admiration of the envoy. When Yang Feng discovers that his champion has gone, he retreats and takes refuge with Yuan Shu.

Once settled in Xuchang, Cao Cao has increasing control over the emperor. But he is troubled by Xuande and Lü Bu. 'Xuande has taken up residence in Xuzhou and has the province in his power,' he says, 'and now Lü Bu has gone to join him and has taken up residence in Xiaopei. My concern is what will we do if they combine in attacking us.' It is his adviser Xun Wenruo who comes up with a way forward. He suggests a divide-and-rule policy or, as the saying goes, 'two tigers fighting over food'. 'Tell the emperor to promote Xuande,' says Xun Wenruo, 'to a high official position. But tell him secretly that it is conditional on his killing Lü Bu. If he succeeds, all is well. If he fails, then Lü Bu will kill him. This is my two tigers plot!'

Delighted with this suggestion, Cao Cao arranges for the emperor's commission to be sent along with the secret orders to Xuande in Xuzhou.

Xuande receives the envoy and is, of course, pleased to be promoted but troubled by the secret orders. Not so Zhang Fei, who has always hated Lü Bu. When Lü Bu comes to congratulate Xuande on his promotion, Zhang Fei charges in with a drawn sword and bursts out that Xuande has orders to kill Lü Bu. Having driven Zhang Fei out of the room, Xuande reassures Lü Bu that he has no intention of doing as the secret orders have commanded.

It is some time later that Guan Yu and Zhang Fei confront Xuande and demand to know why he would not obey the secret orders. But Xuande has seen through the plot and explains it to his two friends. While Guan Yu understands, Zhang Fei does not, declaring that he is more than ever ready to kill Lü Bu.

When Cao Cao is informed by the envoy that Xuande has no intention of killing Lü Bu, Xun Wenruo comes up with another saying. 'The tiger attacks the wolf. Let Yuan Shu know,' says Xun Wenruo, 'that Xuande has secretly asked permission to attack him and seize his district. This will lead Yuan Shu to attack Xuande, and then you can officially sanction Xuande to attack back. Seeing Xuande and Yuan Shu at each other's throats, Lü Bu will no longer be sure whom to follow or trust.'

When the envoy brings the second secret message to Xuande, Mi Zhu his adviser points out that this is yet another trick. 'I do understand, but, as this is an imperial command, I cannot refuse.' As he prepares to follow the orders to attack Yuan Shu he has to decide whom he will leave in charge of Xuzhou. Because Guan Yu is needed by Xuande for the attack, Zhang Fei volunteers, but Xuande rounds on him. 'You!' he says. 'I can't trust Xuzhou to you! You're usually drunk and when you are you attack people! On top of that you always ignore good advice, even when I give it! Do you honestly think I would sleep easy if you were in charge?'

'From now on I'll never drink nor beat anyone,' swears Zhang Fei. Xuande doesn't trust him and leaves his commander Chen Deng in charge with orders to keep an eye on Zhang Fei and his drinking.

When the two armies meet, Yuan Shu with one hundred thousand men and Xuande with a much smaller army, the clash is brief and goes against Yuan Shu, who has to retreat.

Back in Xuzhou all is far from well!

Zhang Fei has decided to host a feast, claiming that this is to be his last drinking day. At the feast he insists that everyone accept a toast from him. Coming to the commander Cao Bao, he proposes a toast, but Cao Bao says, 'I've never drunk alcohol.' Mocked by Zhang Fei for not being a proper soldier, Cao Bao is forced to drink. When Zhang Fei comes round again, now very drunk, Cao Bao this time says, 'No, I won't.' 'Why?' demands Zhang Fei. 'You did last time.' But Cao Bao persists in refusing. Zhang Fei flies into a rage. 'How dare you refuse an order from me! Guards, seize him and give him a hundred lashes.'

At this point Chen Deng rises and says, 'This is exactly what Xuande warned you about.' Zhang Fei tells him to mind his own bureaucratic business and at this point Cao Bao begs, 'Please have mercy upon me for the sake of my son-in-law, Lü Bu.' Mention of his arch-enemy only enrages Zhang Fei even more, and he beats Cao Bao fifty times until others at the dinner manage to calm him down.

As you can imagine, Cao Bao now truly hates Zhang Fei. This drives him to send a message to Lü Bu, saying that if he attacks Xuzhou now, the city can be taken, because Zhang Fei is drunk.

Riding through the night with five hundred horsemen, Lü Bu

easily takes the city, and Zhang Fei is forced to flee for his life. Most shameful of all is that in doing so he abandons Xuande's family to their fate. They are rounded up by Lü Bu and locked away.

Reaching Xuande and Guan Yu, Zhang Fei has to tell the awful truth. 'Where are our sisters-in-law?' asks an astonished Guan Yu – referring to the wives of Xuande. 'Still in Xuzhou,' replies a mortified Zhang Fei. 'You idiot!' says Guan Yu. 'What did we say to you before we left? What did we caution you about? What on earth are we going to do now with them trapped there?'

Full of remorse, Zhang Fei draws his sword and is about to cut his own throat.

Is this the end for Zhang Fei?

Let's find out.

CHAPTER 15

Sun Ce clashes with Taishi Ci.
He moves south to create his own kingdom.

Zhang Fei is about to slit his own throat, but Xuande grabs the sword from him and throws it away, crying out, 'There's an ancient saying, "Brothers are like one's own hands and feet, whereas family are like the clothes you wear." Clothes can be repaired, but who can replace a missing limb? We three swore an oath in the peach orchard that we would seek to die side by side on the same day, never mind what life threw at us. Today, it's true, the city is lost, and my family as well. But this won't stop us from journeying together along the path we have chosen, right to the very end. Let's be frank, the city was never really mine, and Lü Bu won't harm my family. Indeed, he'll protect them. I won't let you throw away your life because of one mistake.'

So saying, he wept, and so too did Guan and Zhang.

Meanwhile the world is full of conspiracies. Hearing about Lü Bu's success in capturing Xuzhou, Yuan Shu offers fabulous gifts to encourage Lü Bu to attack Xuande. Just in time Xuande hears about the plot and escapes, fleeing to Guangling, which he besieges. To the fury of Lü Bu, Yuan Shu refuses to send the promised gifts. 'Xuande is still free,' says Yuan Shu. 'The gifts will come when Xuande is not free but your prisoner.' At this, Lü Bu, angry and disillusioned, decides to team up with Xuande instead!

Yuan Shu's troops have converged on Guangling and have inflicted heavy losses on Xuande's men after besieging the town. Having had to abandon the siege Xuande is grateful for the offer of support from Lü Bu, but this generous view is not shared by his two brothers. Despite their opposition Xuande returns to Xuzhou and en route he meets his wives, whom Lü Bu has freed and sent to him as a sign of good faith. Even though they report that Lü Bu has protected them and looked after them, Zhang Fei's loathing of Lü Bu does not abate one iota. Indeed, it increases.

One of those who comes to visit Yuan Shu's court is Sun Ce, whose own court has grown even more famous as a place of learning and statesmanship. Yuan Shu throws a great celebration for him and comments, 'If I had a son like him I could die happy.'

However, despite such a compliment, all is not well. Sun Ce feels Yuan Shu has slighted him with his patronizing airs and attitudes during the celebration. That night he is pacing up and down in the pale moonlight. In truth he feels he is a lesser man than his murdered heroic father. Troubled by this, he sighs out loud. 'What's the problem?' asks a man who has just walked on to the terrace. 'When troubled, your father often asked for my advice.' The speaker is Zhu Zhi, one of Yuan Shu's commanders. Just as they start talking, another man joins them, Lü Fan. He is one of Yuan Shu's advisers. They gently persuade him to assert himself, independent of Yuan Shu, and between them hatch a plot.

The next day Sun Ce goes to talk with Yuan Shu. Using the imperial seal, which Sun Ce still holds, he persuades Yuan Shu to lend him three thousand men and five hundred cavalry. 'My father's murder has yet to be avenged,' he says. 'And I'm worried about the safety of my mother and family held now by Liu Yao. I can protect them against the enemy with these troops and to show my gratitude I will leave the imperial seal with you as a token of trust.' Yuan Shu has long wanted control of the imperial seal but, pretending it is of little interest to him, he takes it and gives Sun Ce the required troops. Leaving the seal with Yuan Shu, Sun Ce sets off with the troops.

En route he is joined by his childhood companion and friend Zhou Yu, who comes with his own army. He also brings the recommendation that in planning the attack they should seek the assistance of a pair of brothers who could read the auspicious and ill-fated auguries of Heaven and Earth.

Meanwhile the prefect Liu Yao, a member of the imperial family, hears that news of his ill treatment of Sun Ce's family has reached Sun Ce. Then news comes that he is on his way with an army. So Liu Yao plans his defences. He sends men to protect the river crossing of Niuzhu, but there they are defeated with huge loss of life. Sun Ce is able to advance and to directly confront Liu Yao and his main army.

That night Sun Ce has a dream. In the dream he hears the founder of the Later Han summoning him to a temple dedicated to his memory. When morning comes he asks his advisers where this temple might be. When he is told it is to the south, close to where Liu Yao is encamped, they advise him not to go there. But he is insistent, saying, 'I want to pray to him, and the gods will protect me. Why should I be afraid?' So saying, and taking just twelve guards, he rides to the temple and prays for success.

As his men feared, he is spotted by the enemy. However, Liu Yao is convinced that this sudden exposure of his enemy so close by must be a trap. 'He is trying to get us to come out into the open and then will ambush us.' But Taishi Ci, the great warrior, is dying for a fight. Ignoring Liu Yao's pleas to stop, and with only one other, rather minor commander joining him, Taishi Ci rides out to fight Sun Ce. He and Sun Ce go fifty rounds without either gaining the upper hand. Given that Sun Ce has twelve guards with him and Taishi Ci only one, he lures Sun Ce away from his guards by feigning flight. When Taishi Ci turns, the fight starts again, only it grows more and more desperate. Blow after blow rains down until they are both knocked from their horses. But still they fight, struggling on the ground. The fight only stops when soldiers from both sides ride up and separate them.

This bitter feud shapes the encounters between the two armies as the battles rage across the countryside. Subterfuge is employed by both sides until at last Taishi Ci is captured and brought before Sun Ce. Sun Ce greets him as a true hero, and this deeply moves Taishi Ci.

'If you had captured me when we fought by the temple,' asks Sun Ce, 'would you have killed me?' To this Taishi replies, 'I really don't know!' Laughing at this, Sun Ce invites him to dine with him. Moved by this virtuous man, Taishi Ci says, 'Liu Yao's troops are disheartened and divided. If you'll trust me, I can go and bring them over to your side.'

And sure enough, Sun Ce does trust him, and Taishi Ci recruits thousands of the enemy troops to join Sun Ce.

Moving across the river into the south, Sun Ce's army at first spreads panic and chaos, but soon people see that this army never steals anything, nor harms any of the ordinary folk. So grateful are the people that they themselves bring food and drink to the camp.

Moving further south, Sun Ce comes up against various conspirators, thugs, rebels and bandits, all of whom want to try to ride on his coat-tails and seize part of the south. Sun Ce's response is always swift and severe, and battle after battle is won by him, aided now by Taishi Ci. Between them they capture the cities of Jiaxing, Wucheng and Wujun among others.

While all this is going on, Sun Ce's brother Sun Quan and his companion Zhou Tai are guarding Xuancheng. Out of the blue they are suddenly attacked at dead of night by robbers who have holed up in the mountains. The attack is so unexpected and sudden that Zhou Tai is in bed when the sound of battle reaches him. With no time to dress and therefore naked, Zhou Tai fights with astonishing bravery and even manages to rescue Sun Quan. Severely wounded, Zhou Tai is barely alive when he is brought at last to Sun Ce's camp. Deeply concerned for the well-being of such a hero, Sun Ce orders a search for the best possible doctor. He is recommended to Hua Tuo. What a man! It is as if he is already an immortal, so profound is his knowledge. He examines Zhou Tai and declares that this is not a difficult case. Using herbal remedies and medicines he has healed Zhou Tai within a month.

Enraged by the attack on Sun Quan and Zhou Tai, Sun Ce sets out to destroy the mountain robbers. In a swift campaign he eradicates the thugs of the mountain. With that achievement under his belt he goes on to strengthen his hold on key places, reporting to the court on his triumphs, making contact with Cao Cao and finally demanding that Yuan Shu return the imperial seal.

This Yuan Shu has no intention of doing. He plans to seize the imperial throne himself, and possession of the imperial seal is, of course, of immense significance. He also feels Sun Ce is in his debt for his having lent the original troops, which have made all Sun Ce's conquests possible. He deeply resents what he sees as Sun Ce's lack of gratitude. Yuan Shu is determined to have his revenge and asks the advice of his council. The advice is that Sun Ce is far too strong for him at present. Instead, adviser Yang Dajiang suggests attacking Xuande. 'I have a plan that will ensure the fall of Xuande, and then we can attack Sun Ce.' Is this wise? As the poem says:

> Instead of attacking the tiger in the east,
> He decided to attack the dragon in the north!

So what is this grand plan that is recommended to Yuan Shu?

Read on and find out.

CHAPTER 16

Lü Bu uses a feat of archery to reconcile enemies. Cao Cao loses at the battle of the river.

The plan is to divide and rule. They will send the grain that he has long requested to Lü Bu. However, not the gold, silk and horses he has demanded. These they will hold back so that Lü Bu will not come to the rescue of Xuande when they attack. 'Let us give him the grain along with secret instructions,' says Yang Dajiang, 'in order to win back his favour and prevent him going to the aid of Xuande. After we have defeated Xuande we can easily take out Lü Bu.'

But Lü Bu is no fool. He sees through this ruse when the gifts and a secret letter arrive. Instead he plans his own solution to the problem of the three rivals.

Lü Bu brings his troops to the field where Yuan Shu's commander, Ji Ling, is camped facing Xuande's troops. Secretly he invites the two commanders, Xuande and Ji Ling, to a banquet without telling either of them that the other is also invited. As each believes Lü Bu is on his side, they both come. Imagine Ji Ling's astonishment when he enters Lü Bu's tent and finds Xuande seated there!

'Do you plan to kill me?' asks Ji Ling, to which Lü Bu replies, 'Certainly not.'

'So,' says Ji Ling, 'you plan to kill old Long Ears over there,' pointing at Xuande.

'Certainly not,' replies Lü Bu.

Completely befuddled now, Ji Ling asks, 'So what's this all about?'

'Xuande and I are brothers,' replies Lü Bu, 'and you're planning to attack him, so I've come to save him.'

Now really alarmed Ji Ling cries, 'Then you really do mean to kill me!'

'No,' replies Lü Bu. 'I've always advocated resolving conflicts rather than fighting, and this is what I'll now do.'

Still alarmed, Ji Ling asks, 'But how will you do this?' to which Lü Bu answers, 'I have a plan, which is that we seek the Will of Heaven.'

Then he calls for food and drink and makes the two foes sit on either side of him.

When after a few rounds of drinks the two are still eyeing each other suspiciously, Lü Bu tells them off. 'Will you two stop this and listen to what I propose, please!'

Then Lü Bu reveals his plan. Calling for his halberd, he says, 'I'll have my halberd planted one hundred and fifty paces away from the entrance to my tent. If with one arrow I can hit the smaller of the two blades then you must call off your warfare. If I miss, then you're free to return to your camps and prepare for war. But if either one of you refuses to abide by this, then I and my men will join with the other side to fight you.'

They readily agree. Ji Ling is convinced that it is impossible for Lü Bu to hit the small blade, and then his role in Yuan Shu's plot can be carried out. However Xuande, ever the virtuous one, prays that he will hit the target and so end the risk of bloodshed – but he is very doubtful that the target can be hit.

Imagine their astonishment – and, for Xuande at least, delight – when Lü Bu does indeed hit the small blade. 'So Heaven decrees that you stop,' he says.

While Xuande is mightily relieved, Ji Ling knows his master will never understand. But Lü Bu offers to write to Yuan Shu, explaining what has happened.

When Ji Ling reports back to Yuan Shu he is furious, but en route Ji Ling has thought of another ploy. He suggests that Yuan Shu offer his son to be wed to Lü Bu's daughter, thereby making it a family issue that Lü Bu must kill Xuande because, as the old saying goes, 'Family comes before strangers.'

However, this ploy doesn't work either. Lü Bu eventually sees through the trick and cancels the marriage.

Lü Bu's relationship with Xuande and with Zhang Fei, who truly hates Lü Bu, is put to the test again when Zhang Fei steals horses belonging to Lü Bu. Even when Xuande offers to return them, Lü Bu is so furious he attacks Xuande ensconced in the city of Xiaopei. Forced to retreat, Xuande, with his two brothers, leaves at dead of night, heading to Cao Cao to offer to join him.

Cao Cao is advised by many to use this opportunity to kill Xuande. But as one of his advisers puts it, 'You've promised to support the legitimate dynasty of the Han and free the people from fear. Because of this you're held in great respect, which is why men come to serve you. If you kill a hero like Xuande because he is vulnerable at this moment, then you'll be notorious for such an unworthy act, and men of virtue will no longer seek you out. How, then, will you be able to restore the empire?' This response pleases Cao Cao, and so instead of killing Xuande he offers him additional troops as a sign of friendship.

Not long after, romance diverts Cao Cao. Cao Cao's determination to fight Lü Bu is seriously undermined by a love affair. Cao Cao is swept away with lust for the woman Lady Zou, the widow of Zhang Ji. In fact she is also the aunt of one of Cao Cao's commanders, Zhang Xiu. Positioning guards outside his tent, day after day, night after night, Cao Cao gives himself over to the delights of Lady Zou, forgetting all else. This tangle of emotions and families leads to disaster for Cao Cao. Zhang Xiu is deeply offended by the love affair and, using Cao Cao's distraction by the beautiful woman, attacks Cao Cao's camp at dead of night.

His personal guard, Dian Wei, once again comes to his rescue. With no weapon or armour, he seems an easy target for the attackers. But, grabbing a sword from one of the soldiers, he fights back, killing twenty men straight away. As enemy swords slash him, he fights on until his sword shatters. Then he simply picks up two of the bodies of the dead enemy and, using them as weapons, slays many more. In the end it takes archers and an attack from behind with spears to bring him down. Collapsing, he gives a great cry and dies. Although wounded with an arrow in his shoulder, Cao Cao manages to escape the trap. Mounted upon his swift Fergana horse and escorted by his son Cao Ang, he dashes for the river. The great horse, already wounded by an arrow, brings him to the riverbank. Hesitating for a moment, the great horse then plunges into the river and swims to the other side. As the horse scrambles up the bank, a final arrow brings the heroic beast down. Without a moment's thought, Cao Ang gives his father his horse, and Cao Cao escapes. But before Cao Ang can escape he is slain by a hail of arrows.

Cao Cao regroups his men and realizes that they are still superior to the forces of Zhang Xiu. His men are ready when he attacks again. Zhang Xiu is soon defeated and flees, seeking refuge with Liu Biao.

Lü Bu, meanwhile, has broken off all negotiations with Yuan Shu and scotched his idea of a marriage alliance. Cao Cao is only too aware that dealing with Lü Bu means trusting someone who is not trustworthy. He uses Lü Bu's old adviser and friend Chen Deng to try and lure him into an alliance. The upshot of all this is that a furious Yuan Shu decides to attack Lü Bu. The size of the invading army both shocks and alarms Lü Bu.

Can he survive?

Read on and find out.

CHAPTER 17

Yuan Shu despatches seven divisions to attack the east. Cao Cao unites three forces to combat Yuan Shu.

With the imperial seal in his possession, Yuan Shu becomes more and more arrogant. He makes no secret of his intention to destroy the House of Han and make himself emperor. He even claims that it is clear to him that the Mandate of Heaven has been removed from the Han and placed in the hands of the Yuan clan. When advisers argue against this impetuous move, Yuan Shu cites oracles and sayings based on the Five Elements,[9] which to his ears at least confirm that he is destined to be emperor. Soon he is performing all the imperial rituals and has established an 'imperial court'.

Determined to destroy Lü Bu, he simultaneously launches seven vast armies to attack Xuzhou. However, one of the seven commanders, Han Xian, is brought over to Lü Bu's side. He was one of those who helped the true emperor escape from Chang'an. Therefore his first loyalty is to the Han dynasty. Working upon this, he is turned by Lü Bu's men. He in turn brings on board another of the seven commanders, Yang Feng. At the crucial moment these two betray Yuan Shu, who flees, almost falling into the hands of Guan Yu, who is supporting Lü Bu's army. Few, indeed, out of Yuan Shu's vast armies make it home.

Meanwhile, Cao Cao has ensured that Sun Ce is ready to attack Yuan Shu. He needs little encouragement, for he is still furious with Yuan Shu. It is possession of the imperial seal, which Sun Ce feels is his, that has given Yuan Shu imperial ambitions. As a result, Sun Ce is more than keen to attack Yuan Shu. Having aligned all his alliances, Cao Cao agrees to coordinate his attack on Yuan Shu with Lü Bu and Sun Ce. As he besieges Shouchun, dissent arises within his troops. Cao Cao uses brutal but ultimately successful tactics to suppress such troubles: for example, executing an innocent officer and blaming him for all the problems the army was experiencing and then killing any who did not make every effort to overwhelm the city. The city falls, and Cao Cao executes all of the members of Yuan Shu's court whom he can catch and burns to the ground the newly created imperial palace.

His new partnerships with Xuande, Sun Ce and Lü Bu are confirmed by new titles and honours, but in confidence Cao Cao tells Xuande to watch out for Lü Bu and to be prepared to help overcome him in the future.

Returning to Xuchang, Cao Cao discovers to his delight that loyal officers have taken affairs into their own hands. At long last the two rebels, Li Jue and Guo Si, have been murdered and their families rounded up and imprisoned. Cao Cao then executes all two hundred members of the Li family outside the city gates and has their heads impaled on the top of the gates. This is greeted with rejoicing by the ordinary people, and Emperor Xian hosts a huge celebration. This takes place in the year AD 198.

Zhang Xiu has now teamed up with Liu Biao, and Cao Cao starts to pay them attention, defeating Zhang Xiu in open battle. Zhang Xiu retreats to his city of Nanyang and shuts himself up. Surrounded by Cao Cao's men, who look set to break in, all seems doomed for Zhang Xiu. Then his adviser Jia Xu comes forward with plans for trapping Cao Cao.

Can Jia Xu fool Cao Cao?

Read on.

CHAPTER 18

Jia Xu wins a great victory.
Guo Jia gives Cao Cao ten reasons for victory.

Jia Xu has noticed something. He has been watching Cao Cao's activities. He notices that he is beginning to pay attention to one particular section of the city wall. 'He knows,' says Jia Xu, 'that the southeastern part of the city wall is weakest. The earth ramparts are crumbling, and the wall is really just wooden stakes. However, he's also pretending not to have noticed. This is why he has piled up wood and other materials on the northwest side to make it look as if he is planning to attack there.'

'So what can we do?' asks a troubled Zhang Xiu.

'We can play the same trick on him,' says Jia Xu. 'Move your crack troops to the southeast wall and have them hide out of sight, inside houses, down lanes and alleys. Then dress up ordinary folk in armour and have them crowd onto the wall on the northwest side. When Cao Cao attacks what he thinks is the weakest part of the wall on the southeast side and breaks through, we can trap him and his men and annihilate them.'

The trick works. Cao Cao's men report increased troop activities on the northwest wall, and so Cao Cao orders the attack that night on the southeast wall. At dead of night the men scale the crumbling walls, pull down the wooden stakes and rush in. Then the ambush is sprung. It is a massacre. The triumph of Zhang Xiu's men is total. It is said that Cao Cao lost fifty thousand soldiers that day.

As Cao Cao retreats, Zhang Xiu sends a messenger to Liu Biao, urging him to attack the retreating army and prevent their escape.

From then on there is a vicious game of cat and mouse as

Zhang Xiu and Liu Biao track Cao Cao's retreating army, attacking whenever they can. Progress is slow for the retreating army until word comes that Yuan Shao is planning to attack Cao Cao's base at the capital. At this news Cao Cao rushes his army homewards. He is retreating but also advancing to the attack!

Securing the capital and the emperor, Cao Cao is astonished to receive a letter from Yuan Shao suggesting that they work together and that he will go to fight Gongsun Zan. Cao Cao turns to his adviser Guo Jia and asks, 'Can't we teach him a lesson! Are we strong enough to defeat Yuan Shao?'

To this question Guo Jia replies: 'Yuan Shao has ten faults while you have ten strengths, so the size of his army is not relevant.

'Yuan Shao rules through a myriad petty rules. Your way is simple and straightforward. So as regards governance you come out on top.

'Yuan Shao has no legal basis for his actions. You have the imperial authority to act. Your position is one of honour and truth.

'For years the court has been out of control, and he's only made it more so. You're disciplined and therefore you're the better administrator.

'Yuan Shao makes an outward show of being generous. But in reality he's jealous and selfish. You're outwardly demanding but inwardly you've a profound understanding of the real ability of those you choose. So you win in terms of judgement.

'He is ambitious but indecisive. You're strategic and action-orientated. So you win in terms of policy.

'He chooses men who make him look good. You choose those who are sincere. So as regards virtue you excel.

'Yuan Shao is generous to those close to him, but disregards others less close. You care about everyone, so you win in terms of culture.

'He listens to gossip. You do not. So you excel in wisdom.

'He cannot tell the difference between right and wrong. You follow strict moral codes of ruling and so you win in terms of knowing how to run a country.

'Finally, Yuan Shao will fantasize about his military strength but has no grasp of warfare. You through your military skills win even when outnumbered. So you are the supreme warrior and fighter.

'Because of these ten points, you need have no fear of overcoming Yuan Shao.'

'I really don't think I can claim all this, to be honest!' says a somewhat astonished and deeply moved Cao Cao. But others agree with Guo Jia and, encouraged, Cao Cao and his team make their plans. Yuan Shao is given authority from the emperor to tackle Gongsun Zan. 'We can take care of Yuan Shao after he has defeated Gongsun Zan,' say the advisers. 'Our current problem is dealing with the threat from Lü Bu. This is where we need to team up with Xuande.'

Letters are sent, and Xuande writes back to say he is ready to attack Lü Bu. But disaster strikes. One of Lü Bu's most trusted advisers, Chen Gong, is out hunting. He is deeply troubled by the way Chen Deng, the friend of Xuande now in Lü Bu's court, is egging him on to ideas of supremacy, as if trying to encourage him to overstretch and make serious tactical mistakes. Chen Gong has gone hunting to try to ease his mind. He spots a messenger travelling fast along the road near where he is hunting and has the man stopped. 'Where are you going, and whose message are you carrying?' he demands. The terrified messenger says, 'I took a message to Xuande from Cao Cao and I'm returning with his answer. But what it says I've no idea!'

Chen Gong has the letter seized and takes it to Lü Bu. He reads it and discovers that Xuande has agreed to Cao Cao's plot and will join in attacking Lü Bu.

'How dare Xuande do this!' exclaims a furious Lü Bu. The poor messenger is executed, and Lü Bu starts to plan for war. Three armies are sent out: one to seize Xiaopei from Xuande, one to seize Runan and Yingchuan and one to join up with rebels camped on Tai mountain. Lü Bu himself leads a support army, which heads first to besiege Xiaopei.

When news comes of Lü Bu's attack on Xiaopei and Xuande, Cao Cao moves to the defence of Xuande. But his army is decisively beaten by Lü Bu's commander Gao Shun, who comes back from defeating Cao Cao to reinforce the attack on Xuande. Then Lü Bu and his men arrive.

Can Xuande survive?

Read on and see.

CHAPTER 19

Cao Cao gathers the army at Xiapi.
Lü Bu is killed in battle.

To defend Xiaopei, Xuande, Zhang Fei and Guan Yu have set up camps beyond the city to protect the approach to thc city itself. In a pincer movement, Gao Shun attacks Guan Yu's camp, while Lü Bu, intent on personal revenge, attacks Zhang Fei's camp. Both camps are overrun, and Xuande's own men are crushed as the pincer movement rolls forward. Desperate, Xuande tries to flee back to the safety of the city. But so close behind him comes Lü Bu that the soldiers on the city walls cannot protect Xuande, and even as the drawbridge comes down to let him in, Xuande swerves away, and instead it is Lü Bu and his men who swarm across the bridge and capture the city. And still inside the city is Xuande's family.

As the triumphant Lü Bu comes to Xuande's house, Mi Zhu warns him, 'A truly gallant man doesn't harm a man's family. Now there's only one person under Heaven with whom you've to struggle: Cao Cao. Xuande will always recall how he was protected by your actions at the gate. He'll never forget this. He had no option but to follow Cao Cao, so we must remember this.'

Lü Bu replies, 'We are committed to each other, so how could I even think of harming his family?'

So saying, he sends Xuande's family to safety in Xuzhou.

Xuande is now effectively a refugee seeking to make his way to Cao Cao to try to continue the alliance. Yet, desperate as he is, whenever he enters a village, the local people are virtually competing with each other to find provisions for him. Such devotion sadly leads to a terrible incident.

Xuande and his companion Sun Qian seek shelter in a

hunter's home. The hunter is called Liu An, and he immediately offers to go and hunt for fresh meat for them to eat. To his distress, he cannot find any game. Desperate to keep his word, he kills his wife and serves up flesh from her body. When Xuande asks what meat they are eating, Liu An replies, 'Wolf.'

It is only as they depart the next day that the two companions see the dead body of a young woman in the kitchen. The flesh from her arms has been cut away. This extraordinary action draws tears from Xuande when he realizes to what lengths Liu An has gone to keep his promise.

Xuande joins up with Cao Cao. Soon they are on the warpath again, heading for Lü Bu. Back in Xuzhou, Lü Bu is kept informed of developments against him and he places much of his trust in Chen Deng. This is a great mistake, as will be revealed.

On Chen Deng's recommendation, Lü Bu moves his reserves and his own family to Xiapi as a safe haven should Xuzhou fall.

But Chen Deng has realized that Lü Bu's cause is doomed and has already decided to betray him. Through secret messages, Chen Deng keeps Cao Cao informed of Lü Bu's intentions. This enables Cao Cao's men to thwart all attempts by Lü Bu to gain the upper hand in the skirmishes and battles that follow. Through such treachery Xuzhou falls. It is Chen Deng's plotting which leads to Xiaopei falling into Cao Cao's hands. Chen Deng persuades the bulk of Lü Bu's commanders that Lü Bu has sent urgent messages asking them to ride to his assistance. When they leave, Chen Deng opens the gates to Cao Cao's cousin Cao Ren. When Lü Bu retreats to what he thinks is the safety of Xiaopei, having been defeated by Cao Cao's men, he finds the city in enemy hands. With nowhere else to go and with Zhang Fei closing in on him, Lü Bu has no option but to escape to his fallback city of Xiapi.

Trapped there and besieged, Lü Bu wants to strike out from the city to attack his enemies. But he is persuaded by the fearful tears of his wife and concubine not to leave them. Distraught and depressed, he sinks into alcoholism.

It is in these circumstances that his advisers Xu Si and Wang Kai revive the idea of an alliance with Yuan Shu through the marriage of Lü Bu's daughter to Yuan Shu's son. With great bravery, Xu Si and Wang Kai make their way through enemy lines to Yuan Shu. Despite his initial anger – remember Lü Bu had executed Yuan Shu's envoy when had come to discuss the marriage previously – he agrees. But on the way back one of the envoys of Lü Bu is captured by Zhang Fei, and the plans are revealed to Cao Cao. The stranglehold of the siege is increased to prevent Lü Bu and his daughter escaping to Yuan Shu.

So desperate is Lü Bu that he decides to make a break for it, even though the odds are seriously stacked against him. An auspicious date is chosen, and at dead of night he prepares to break out. His young daughter is wrapped in protective cotton and then a suit of armour. She mounts behind her father on his famous steed Red Hare, and they attempt to get out of the city and break through the besieging troops. Under cover of darkness they slip out of a small gate, but, as they approach the outskirts of Xuande's camp, their flight is discovered. The three brothers-in-arms rush to attack, pushing back Lü Bu's armed escort. No one is braver than Lü Bu, but he will not put his daughter's life at risk. Instead, he is forced to retreat back into Xiapi with his daughter.

This failure drives Lü Bu deeper into drink and despair.

The siege is getting nowhere, and Cao Cao is ready to give up, when his advisers Xun You and Guo Jia come up with a plan. They divert the Rivers Yi and Si and flood the city. Inside the city, discontent with Lü Bu is mounting among his own men. From drunkenness he has swung to abstinence and banned all alcohol. When one of his greatest generals breaks this to celebrate a small victory, Lü Bu condemns him to death and is only just persuaded to mitigate this to fifty lashes. This greatly disturbs the other generals. Plots begin to take shape and one of them results in Red Hare, Lü Bu's amazing horse, being stolen and delivered to Cao Cao.

The next day, a massive assault on the city takes place, and during this long attack Lü Bu, exhausted, falls asleep in one of the towers. Two of his men decide to take things into their own hands. Song Xian seizes the opportunity to steal away Lü Bu's famous halberd and, with Wei Xu he binds Lü Bu, who suddenly wakes to find himself a prisoner of his own men. Wei Xu then shouts down to Cao Cao that Lü Bu is now their prisoner and opens the city gates. The city is swiftly seized by Cao Cao's men. Chen Gong, a former ally of Cao Cao, is also captured.

Once order has been restored, Cao Cao, with Xuande, sits to judge the prisoners. When Chen Gong is brought in, Cao Cao asks how he has been since they last met, to which Chen Gong responds bitterly, 'You're a man of deceit – this is why I abandoned you.'

Cao Cao retorts angrily, 'So is that why you left me to go serve Lü Bu?'

'He may have been a fool,' snaps Chen Gong, 'but he's not like you, full of deceit.'

'Well,' replies Cao Cao, 'you may be clever, but that doesn't help you much today, does it?'

Chen Gong shouts back that he expects nothing but death, and when Cao Cao asks what should become of Chen Gong's family – his wife and mother and children – Chen Gong replies, 'It is said that those who rule by the laws of filial piety will never harm another man's family. One who is benevolent will never curtail the sacrifices appropriate to a man's tomb. My family are at your mercy. I just ask for a swift death.'

Cao Cao gives instructions that Chen Gong's family are to be taken to the capital and cared for all their lives. There is hardly a dry eye in the hall when Chen Gong bows his head and is executed. As a poet has written:

> To him, life and death were undivided.
> What a charismatic figure he cut!
> Alas, his lord didn't value his words;
> A man like that can't understand such qualities.
> Despite it, he was constant in his support.
> Our hearts are moved
> by his parting words to his family.
> At the White Gate he gave his life like this:
> Tell me, who is not in awe of Chen Gong?

Then Lü Bu is brought in. Cao Cao sentences him to death by strangulation. In desperation Lü Bu appeals to Xuande: 'Have you forgotten that I saved your life with the shot of one arrow?' At this, one of his men, Zhang Liao, shouts, 'Die like a hero, Lü Bu! What are you afraid of?' And so it is that the sentence is carried out, and Lü Bu is no more.

As a poet has said:

As the waters flood his city,
Lü Bu's own men restrain him:
No longer can his thousand-mile horse
Or his slashing halberd save him.
Once cowed, even a tiger yowls for mercy,
But you'd never give a hunting falcon all it asks for.
Stupidly, he allows Chen Gong's warning to be ignored,
Preferring his women's gossip.
So no point in him now
Blaming the example of Xuande.

When Zhang Liao is brought before Cao Cao, Cao Cao recognizes him. Zhang Liao says that they met in battle at Puyang and that he regrets now that he did not kill him then. Furious at these words, Cao Cao raises his sword to kill Zhang Liao, but he is restrained by someone seizing his arm, while another kneels before him, pleading for Zhang Liao's life. It is true to say that:

Lü Bu's request for mercy failed:
Zhang Liao's defiance saved his life.

So who is it who saves him?

Let us find out.

CHAPTER 20

Cao Cao and the emperor go hunting. Dong Cheng is given a secret edict by the emperor

It is Xuande who holds back Cao Cao's sword arm and Guan Yu who kneels to plead for Zhang Liao's life. 'He has a pure heart,' says Xuande. 'We need men like him.' Throwing the sword aside, Cao Cao smiles and says, 'I was just joking!' He himself frees the prisoner and wraps his own cloak around him. From that day on Zhang Liao becomes one of Cao Cao's most ardent supporters.

When Cao Cao and his men at last return to the capital, they are given a grand ceremonial welcome by the emperor. Hearing that Xuande is of the imperial lineage, he names him imperial uncle and takes him into his confidence.

Basking in his glory as the saviour of the imperial house, Cao Cao grows more and more arrogant. The careers of those who displease him he destroys. But when his adviser Cheng Yu suggests that he might take the throne for himself, Cao Cao warns that there are too many loyal ministers who would oppose this right now. His plan is to be more subtle: to encroach upon imperial powers in such a way that few will notice and those who do would be powerless to stop him. His first step is to propose an imperial hunt – and then to subvert it.

Going on a hunt is not something the emperor wants to do. But he has found it increasingly difficult to say no to Cao Cao. So, against his better judgement, the emperor agrees, and the date is set. The whole event is planned by Cao Cao, so although the court officials accompany the emperor, it is Cao's men who staff the hunt.

The emperor is escorted to the hunt by Cao Cao. The emperor carries the imperial jewelled bow and the imperial gold-tipped arrows. The three brothers-in-arms accompany the emperor as bodyguards. However, with Cao Cao riding beside the emperor and Cao Cao's men massed behind, the courtiers and ministers are forced to the rear. This is completely contrary to traditional protocol.

Suddenly a stag is disturbed and breaks cover. The emperor fires three times with his bow but misses each time. 'Now you try!' cries the emperor to Cao Cao, who takes hold of the imperial bow and arrows and with one shot brings the stag down.

Seeing the imperial arrow strike the stag, all the courtiers and ministers assume the emperor fired it himself. They break into sycophantic applause, pressing forward to congratulate the emperor, crying, 'May the emperor live for ten thousand years!'

But it is Cao Cao, not the emperor, who acknowledges the praise. Praise reserved for an emperor! Shocked, the courtiers and ministers visibly pale, wondering what this could mean for the future. Guan Yu is so furious that his great eyebrows rise in anger, and his piercing eyes glare. Urging on his horse, he charges forward, his great sword drawn, determined to slay the upstart Cao Cao. Just in time, Xuande catches his eye and hastily signals that he must not attack. Furious, but obedient to his elder brother, Guan Yu reins in and sullenly puts his sword back in its sheath.

Xuande faces Cao Cao and congratulates him on such a great shot. But Cao Cao, laughing, says, 'It is only possible because of the blessing of the emperor', and so saying he rides over to the emperor to express his congratulations. But he does not return the imperial bow. Instead, he hangs it over his own shoulder.

After they have all returned to the court, Guan Yu demands an answer from Xuande. 'Why? Why did you stop me? That man is a traitor, and I could've saved the emperor from him.'

Xuande says, 'I did it to protect both the emperor and you from the violence that Cao Cao's followers would have unleashed.'

'If we don't deal with him now, then he'll be a plague by tomorrow,' retorts Guan Yu.

'Discretion now, my friend,' says Xuande. 'This requires serious discussion but not now.'

On his return to the empress, the emperor breaks down and tells her of his fears.

'Ever since I ascended the throne, I've been surrounded by vicious ministers. First it was the awful Dong Zhuo; then the rebellion of Li Jue and Guo Si. You and I've had to suffer such sorrows, more than anyone could imagine. And now we have Cao Cao pretending to defend our honour but actually usurping it. Today, in the hunt he tricked my ministers and officials into giving him praise – which was really meant for me! I fear that he is planning to lead a rebellion. I don't think we are fated to die natural deaths!'

At this point they are joined by her father, Fu Wan. 'I know how to get rid of this man,' he says.

'So you saw what he did?' replies the emperor.

'Impossible to miss. But we have to be careful. The court is full of his cronies,' says Fu Wan. 'But I believe I've a solution. Let's ask Dong Cheng, the brother of the imperial concubine, to assist us. But beware! All your staff are in the pay of Cao Cao, so we must do this in great secrecy. This is why I've a plan. Have a special robe and jade belt made for Dong Cheng and present it to him formally. But, within the jade belt, create a hidden pouch, and there hide a secret formal imperial decree. This he will discover when he gets home and examines the gift. The decree will give him authority to take whatever actions he deems necessary. Then he can act, and not even the deities above or the ghosts below will know anything about this.'

So the emperor writes the secret decree. Biting the tip of his finger, he writes it with his own blood. No more powerful sign of his serious intent can be imagined. And it is the empress herself who sews the secret message into the secret pocket.

Summoning Dong Cheng, he takes him to visit the temple of the Han ancestors. They walk side by side through the imperial gallery, where the portraits of the former emperors hang. Walking from portrait to portrait, the emperor reflects upon the fortunes of the former rulers and bemoans his own weakness. Dong Cheng is confused and alarmed, especially when the emperor starts to point out pictures of those who supported or came to the aid of former emperors. Turning to Dong Cheng, the emperor bluntly says, 'Now we need you to protect us just as these heroes did in the past!'

'But I don't have the ability of these great ones. How could I possibly serve you as they did?' says Dong Cheng, to which the emperor replies, 'I remember well how you rescued us when the western capital fell. No reward is enough to express our thanks to you for such bravery.' Then he gives Dong Cheng the special robe and belt. 'Examine this belt well when you return home,' whispers the emperor. Dong Cheng, understanding only too well what he means, nods his agreement.

However! Cao Cao is waiting for Dong Cheng just outside the palace gate. 'Why are you here? What brings the imperial relative to visit?' asks Cao Cao.

'His imperial majesty wished to give me a gift of this robe and belt,' replies a thoroughly alarmed Dong Cheng.

'Indeed,' says Cao Cao, 'and why would that be?'

'Because I helped to save him when the western capital fell,' replies Dong Cheng.

'Let me see this belt,' demands Cao Cao. When a very frightened Dong Cheng hesitates, Cao Cao has him stripped, and the robe and belt handed over. Cao Cao asks Dong Cheng, 'Would the imperial relative like to present me with the robe and belt?' A terrified Dong Cheng has to use all his diplomatic skills to ensure that Cao Cao returns them. 'As you know, sir, a gift given by the emperor cannot be passed on to anyone else.' Frustrated, Cao Cao says, 'These gifts – they're part of some plot, aren't they?'

'Of course not!' replies Dong Cheng. 'Who would dare do such a thing? But if you really want to be sure, please take them.'

'As you have pointed out,' replies a reassured Cao Cao, 'these imperial gifts cannot be given away.' And so saying, he hands back the robe and belt to a hugely relieved Dong Cheng.

At last Dong Cheng reaches the safety of his home. Here he puzzles over the emperor's words and examines the belt in detail. But he cannot see any hidden secret compartment. After long hours worrying about this, he falls asleep. As he sleeps a spark falls from the candle and burns a hole in the lining. Smelling the burning material, he wakes up with a start. Then and only then does Dong Cheng sees that beneath the lining is a document.

Pulling it out, he stares with astonishment at this document written in the emperor's own blood. It commands him to create a group of patriots who will rid the empire of the rebels gathered around Cao Cao and restore the dignity of the dynasty. It is the year AD 199.

The infamous incident during the hunt has outraged many. Soon Dong Cheng has literally signed up on a long piece of white silk as co-conspirators the following courageous men:

Wang Zifu;
Chong Ji;
Wu Shi;
Wu Zilan;
Ma Teng.

Inspired by the high status of these five, Ma Teng determines to advance the plot. He recommends that they go and see the most powerful person he knows. One who could help this conspiracy to succeed.

And who is this?

Let's find out.

CHAPTER 21

Cao Cao discusses heroes with Xuande.
Yuan Shu dies, and Guan Yu kills
Che Zhou to capture Xuzhou.

'Xuande,' says Ma Teng to the surprise of the others.

'Really? I mean,' says Dong Cheng, 'he is related to the imperial family but he is also a close ally of Cao Cao himself. He won't take the risk.'

'I saw what happened during the hunt. Guan Yu would have slain Cao Cao but for Xuande's intervention. Xuande could see that they were outnumbered. But given the chance to succeed, I'm sure he will jump at the opportunity.'

So it is agreed that Dong Cheng will quietly probe to see if Xuande will join the conspiracy. At first, the interview doesn't seem to be going the way Dong Cheng had hoped. When he mentions Guan Yu's actions at the hunt, Xuande seems to defend Cao Cao. But slowly, little by little, the two men begin to open up to each other until Xuande finally concedes that he has been testing Dong Cheng, worried that he has been sent by Cao Cao to check on his loyalty.

Finally he too signs his name on the white silk sheet and commits himself to the overthrow of Cao Cao.

Xuande is only too aware of the dangers of attracting Cao Cao's suspicions and so he buries himself in working in his garden, apparently having no interest in the affairs of state.

Imagine, then, his horror on being invited to visit Cao Cao in his home.

A smiling Cao Cao greets him, and warmed wine and delicacies are set before them as they sit in Cao Cao's garden pavilion.

Everything Cao Cao says seems to the frightened Xuande to be loaded with inauspicious meaning, as if Cao Cao already knows about the plot. At one point Cao Cao spots a dark cloud formation which looks like a dragon. As they lean on a balustrade in Cao's garden watching the cloud, Cao Cao asks, 'What do you know about dragons?'

'Not a lot,' confesses Xuande.

'Dragons, you know,' says Cao Cao, 'can be any size, either large or small. They can fly in the sky or disappear into the depths. Large, they can create clouds and pour forth mists. Small, they can disappear from sight altogether. Soaring up, they reach Heaven itself. Sinking down, they lie at the very bottom of the sea. This is now springtime. This is the season when dragons rise to the occasion. Like a man who wants to rule the whole world. These dragons are the greatest – just as heroes in any age are the greatest. Now, you are well travelled. Who are the greatest heroes of our age?'

Xuande knows he has to answer this very, very carefully so as not to stir up the anger or resentment of Cao Cao.

'Yuan Shu?' he says cautiously. Laughing, Cao Cao replies, 'Just old bones in a grave!'

'Yuan Shao?' to which Cao Cao responds, 'Fierce, it's true, but weak. He likes plotting but hates making a decision. He wants to win but will never take the risks involved. But offer him something of minor significance and he will go all out for it! So I don't think he really is hero material, do you?'

So Xuande asks about Liu Biao. 'A person with no reputation,' snaps Cao Cao.

'Sun Ce?' asks Xuande. 'He just relies on his father's greater reputation,' replies Cao Cao.

'Liu Zhang?' ventures Xuande, only to be told that, 'Although of the royal family, he's just a dog guarding the gate.'

Then, in despair, Xuande rattles off a list of others, to which Cao Cao dismissively replies that they are of no significance at all.

Finally Xuande has to admit, 'There's no one else I can think of.'

Smiling, Cao Cao leans forward and says:

'There are only two heroes alive today – you and me!'

This puts Xuande into such a state of almost total panic that he drops his chopsticks.

Suddenly into the garden burst two heavily armed soldiers. Shoving aside Cao's own men, they come tearing across the garden towards Cao Cao and Xuande. It is, of course, Zhang Fei and Guan Yu. Having just heard that Xuande had been summoned to see Cao Cao, they have rushed over to make sure he is all right. So imagine their surprise to find the two men calmly sitting, talking and drinking! Needless to say, they have to be careful not to arouse Cao Cao's suspicions. However, when they arrived they were clearly gripping the hilts of their swords with their hands! So they claim they have come to perform a sword dance in honour of the two men. Cao Cao makes a joke about how an assassination attempt had once been made hundreds of years ago under the guise of a sword dance and that therefore he would prefer it if they didn't do a dance! Not long after, taking advantage of the disruption these two brothers have caused, Xuande is able to leave.

The next day, Xuande is once again with Cao Cao when news arrives which alarms Cao Cao. Yuan Shao has besieged and killed Gongsun Zan. This is despite Gongsun Zan having built a huge defensive tower and having ample supplies. Yuan Shao had a tunnel dug under the tower and set on fire. The tower collapsed, and there was no escape for Gongsun Zan. In despair he killed his wife and children and then committed suicide.

While Xuande is deeply saddened at the death of a dear friend, Cao Cao is concerned that as a result Yuan Shao is a much stronger foe than before. News also comes about Yuan Shao's brother Yuan Shu and the imperial seal. Yuan Shu is now a drunk – and he knows it. He is therefore bringing the imperial seal that he has stolen to Yuan Shao, as he feels his brother is the better man to use such a powerful symbol of imperial authority. Cao Cao realizes that the two brothers united with the imperial seal will be a very formidable foe.

Xuande is also worried as to what has happened to his friend Zhao Zilong. He is desperate to escape the claustrophobic atmosphere of Cao Cao's court, so he volunteers to lead a force against Yuan Shu.

As a result, and with an imperial commission, Xuande departs with fifty thousand soldiers. On hearing this, Dong Cheng hastens to visit Xuande. 'Please don't worry,' says Xuande. 'I will not forget the emperor's command.'

As he rides side by side with his two brothers, they ask him why he was so keen to leave. 'Here I feel like a bird caught in a cage or a fish caught in a net. Now I'm able to escape into the sea or like a bird soar into the air free of any cage or net.'

Xuande clashes with Yuan Shu's forces and utterly routs them. As a result a short time after that Yuan Shu is deserted by many of his men and cut off from any possibility of further support. With less than a thousand soldiers left, he is attacked by bandits, abandoned with almost no food and with many, including members of his family, dying of starvation. Yuan Shu could not be in a more desperate state. Everything has failed. There is no hope left. Unable to eat the coarse food that is all that is left, he asks for some warm water with honey to ease the dryness of his throat. On being told there is none, he collapses and dies. It is the year AD 199. Later someone wrote this poem:

At the Han's end, war erupted throughout the land,
And Yuan Shu (fool that he was) had no honour left.
He gave no thought at all to all his family had given,
Instead, insanely, he thought *he* could be emperor!

Stealing the imperial seal, he thought *he* was the chosen One,
Even believing Heaven itself had decreed it!
In the end, not even able to drink water and honey,
He died alone, blood flowing like a river from his mouth.

As his coffin is borne back for formal burial, the entourage is attacked and the imperial seal seized. It is triumphantly brought to Cao Cao in Xuchang.

It is, of course, Xuande the victor who reports the defeat and death of Yuan Shu to the emperor. Cao Cao is now more and more alarmed at the popularity of Xuande. He orders the governor of Xuzhou, Che Zhou, to conspire against Xuande and to trap him in an ambush as Xuande returns to his city. Forewarned, Xuande and his two brothers spring their own trap, and in the ensuing mêlée Che Zhou is slain by a ferocious and furious Guan Yu. After the brothers have gained entry to Xuzhou, Zhang Fei, angry at what he sees as the betrayal by Che Zhou, slays the whole of Che Zhou's family.

This impetuous act of Zhang Fei deeply alarms Xuande. He knows that Cao Cao will seek revenge for these actions against his governor. At this point Chen Deng comes forward with another of his plans. Having succeeded in capturing Lü Bu, Chen Deng now believes he can save Xuande from Cao Cao.

How?

Well, let's find out.

CHAPTER 22

Yuan Shao and Cao Cao go to war. Guan Yu and Zhang Fei capture two enemy agents.

Chen Deng suggests to Xuande: 'Write to the one person Cao Cao really fears – Yuan Shao. Ask him for help. He has a million-strong army.'

'I have never had any dealings with him and now I have just defeated his brother Yuan Shu. So why on earth would he help me?'

'You don't need to write yourself,' replies Chen Deng. 'There is a family here with links to the Yuan family going back generations.'

'And who is this?' asks Xuande. Chen Deng reveals that it is the renowned scholar and former imperial secretary Zheng Xuan. Xuande himself had once been one of his students. Zheng Xuan is famous for his knowledge and love of the *Shi Jing* – the *Book of Songs*. If such a man as this would help, Xuande feels there is some hope. And Zheng Xuan is happy to oblige. The letter suggesting an alliance to attack Cao Cao is written, and Sun Qian is sent to deliver it to Yuan Shao.

When Yuan Shao reads the letter he is deeply troubled. He is naturally upset that Xuande caused the death of his brother. But he also deeply respects the former imperial secretary. In the end it is his adviser Tian Feng who suggests there is something in this proposal, but recommends a cautious approach. 'Let's go and tell the emperor of our victory over Gongsun Zan. If Cao Cao's people refuse us admittance to the imperial presence, then we can lodge a formal protest and prepare ourselves for conflict. We can pull back to Liyang, strengthen the fleet on the Yellow River and prepare for war. Within three years I believe we can defeat Cao Cao and seize power.'

Others advocate an immediate attack on Cao Cao and yet others that no such action should be taken at all!

In the end Yuan Shao is persuaded to take up Xuande's offer and go to war against Cao Cao. To strengthen the moral case for his attack and the virtue of his cause, he has a long formal document drafted by Chen Lin, a renowned scholar and writer. The document opens by citing historical examples of what happened when people did not speak out against corruption. Then comes a detailed list of the crimes of which Cao Cao is guilty. Mocking Cao Cao's grandfather as a eunuch who committed terrible crimes, and accusing his father of avarice and manipulation, the document paints a picture of a depraved Cao Cao and lists his many crimes. For example, moving the capital; murdering officials who disagreed with him; looting the imperial tomb of Prince Xiao, a member of the founding clique of the Zhou dynasty; aiding rebels; and effectively imprisoning the emperor within his own palace by posting his own men around the buildings.

The document is copied and distributed around the country until eventually, of course, it reaches Cao Cao. He is ill in bed with a migraine but on reading the document he leaps from bed, shaking with anger, and demands to know who has written this. When told it is the scholar Chen Lin he laughs out loud and says, 'Without an army what is the use of even a great scholar's pen? Can Chen Lin's skills in writing make up for Yuan Shao's weakness in battle?'

But the incident spurs on his resolution to deal finally with Yuan Shao.

After much debate and disagreement it is decided to attack Xuande and Yuan Shao at the same time, not because it is expected they could defeat Xuande but to divide and rule. Cao Cao sets off to attack Yuan Shao, while his commanders Liu Dai and Wang Zhong set off to attack Xuande. In order to spread confusion, Liu Dai and Wang Zhong bring with them the war banner of Cao Cao. Xuande's spies therefore report back to him that it seems that Cao Cao himself has come to attack Xuande.

In Xuzhou the three brothers plan how to deal with this.

Both Zhang Fei and Guan Yu offer to venture out to find out what really is going on. They are both itching to go into battle. Xuande turns down Zhang Fei's offer. 'You're too impetuous,' says Xuande. It is Guan Yu who rides out first. He challenges Wang Zhong to single combat, captures him, scatters the enemy troops and brings him back a prisoner to Xuzhou. Desperate to have a go, Zhang Fei is allowed to go out to try to capture Liu Dai. For days he tries to taunt Liu Dai to attack but without success. So Zhang Fei plans a trick. Seizing a perfectly innocent soldier from his own ranks, he has him beaten. Then he declares that the man will be sacrificed the next day to bring good fortune on the army. This is in order that the army can attack Liu Dai's camp the following day. He even spells out how the attack will take place as the poor soldier is being beaten. To add to a sense of chaos, he pretends to be drunk. To the enemy this gives the impression of an army out of control. But secretly Zhang Fei has the soldier released, and of course he flees to the opposing army and tells them of the 'impending attack'. The information he brought is, of course, false, even though the poor soldier doesn't know this. It works. It misleads Liu Dai and his men so they take up station outside the camp to ambush the attack they expect. But Zhang Fei attacks from three different directions at once, capturing not only Liu Dai but most of his men as well.

Zhang Fei rides back to Xuande and reports his success. Xuande says, 'It seems our brother has grown less impetuous!' Zhang Fei boasts, 'So, do you still think I am too violent?' to which Xuande replies, 'If I had not goaded you, you would never have bothered to rise to this level of sophistication!' At which Zhang Fei roars with delight.

The very next day, Xuande releases Wang Zhong and Liu Dai, asking them to tell Cao Cao that he bears no grudge against Cao Cao. The two commanders willingly agree to do so. They have not gone far when Zhang Fei gallops at them in a rage. His attack is only prevented when out of the blue Guan Yu also gallops up to stop him. Zhang Fei is furious that the commanders have been released, but Guan Yu insists that their brother has decreed this and so it must be.

But back in Xuzhou the three brothers-in-arms discuss how vulnerable they are in that city, and so it is decided that Guan Yu will travel with Xuande's wives to the security of Xiapi, while Xuande and Zhang Fei fortify Xiaopei.

Cao Cao is incandescent with rage at the two commanders and in his anger orders that they be taken out and executed. As a poet has said:

What possible use is a dog or pig when a tiger is fighting,
Can a shrimp or minnow take on a dragon under the sea?

Will he kill the two commanders?

Let's find out.

CHAPTER 23

Mi Heng the eccentric strips at a feast and abuses Cao Cao. Doctor Ji Ping is tortured for trying to poison Cao Cao, and the 'secret edict' plot fails.

Their lives are saved by Kong Rong. He points out to Cao Cao that executing the two generals will seriously undermine the confidence of the whole army. Reluctantly, but recognizing the truth of what Kong Rong said, Cao Cao has them cashiered and reduced to the ranks.

Cao Cao and Kong Rong now start to plan to overthrow Xuande when spring comes and the fighting season can start. They agree that if Zhang Xiu and Liu Biao could be persuaded to join them they could all attack Xuande at Xuzhou.

An envoy is sent to Zhang Xiu's adviser Jia Xu, who listens to the plan in outline and presents the envoy to Zhang Xiu the next day. Imagine everyone's surprise when, as the envoy is explaining Cao Cao's proposal, another envoy arrives – this one from Yuan Shao. This envoy is also seeking Zhang Xiu's assistance.

Jia Xu dismisses the envoy of Yuan Shao: 'Tell your master that, given he couldn't even unite with his own brother, why should he expect that he can do so with the chief men of the state!' And he tears up the letter from Yuan Shao.

Zhang Xiu questions this: 'Yuan Shao is stronger and Cao Cao has been a sworn enemy of mine.' Jia Xu points out three reasons why they should unite with Cao Cao and ignore Yuan Shao.

'To start with, Cao Cao controls the imperial proclamations and so can claim authority for his actions wherever and whenever he wishes. Secondly, while Yuan Shao is currently the stronger, he will be far less interested in your modest contribution, while Cao Cao will be very grateful. Finally, Cao Cao wants to be the supreme ruler. He has to show that he is so virtuous he can rise above the petty intrigues of court life. He will be easier to manage as a result.'

And so it is that Zhang Xiu goes to Cao Cao and agrees to join him.

Cao Cao then asks him to write as a friend to Liu Biao to persuade him to also join them. Noting that Liu Biao likes to be flattered by scholars and literary types, it is proposed that a friend of Kong Rong's by the name of Mi Heng should be asked by the emperor to pen a formal letter to Liu Biao. To ensure this happens, Kong Rong writes a long and flowery letter to the emperor extolling the virtues of Mi Heng as one young in years – just twenty-four – but steeped in the knowledge and skills of literature. He suggests that the emperor choose this young man to write to Liu Biao to seek an alliance.

The emperor naturally passes this responsibility on to Cao Cao, who summons Mi Heng to come and see him. It is not exactly a successful first encounter.

It doesn't begin very well. Cao Cao, being rather dismissive of so-called scholars, especially such young ones, doesn't offer Mi Heng a seat. So Mi Heng stands sighing and looking up to Heaven and says, 'Despite the vastness of the universe, it has yet to produce a real man!'

Cao Cao is taken aback by such rudeness. He fires back that he has scores of such men at his command.

'Really?' says Mi Heng. 'Name them, then!'

Cao Cao rattles off a long list of his most worthy men. Mi Heng is supremely dismissive. 'I am sorry to say I disagree,' he replies. 'I know these men – in fact I know them only too well!' He then launches into a dismissal of each and every one. He says, for example, that one was only fit to attend funerals, another to be a gatekeeper, while another was fine as a butcher of pigs and dogs and yet another known best as the Greedy Commander!

Furious, Cao Cao asks, 'And you? What are you good at?' To which Mi Heng replies, 'I know everything about Heaven and Earth. I've mastered the Three Teachings and the Nine Philosophies. I can make a prince as wise as Yao and Shun because I've the combined virtue of Kong Fu Zi and his disciple Yan Yuan. Given all this, you, you dare to compare me to the petty folk you cited! Hah!'

Mi Heng is almost killed then and there by Cao Cao's guard. But instead, and to humble him, Mi Heng is appointed as a drummer to the court. Cao Cao is aware that Mi Heng is supposedly brilliant but he really isn't sure what on earth to do with him!

A few days later Cao Cao holds a grand feast at the palace and orders Mi Heng to play. Despite being told to get new, clean clothes, Mi Heng turns up in some terrible old, grubby clothes. However, his playing is so superb he holds everyone spellbound. As the performance goes on, one of the servants of Cao Cao shouts at Mi Heng, telling him off for not wearing new clothes to such an important event. Whereupon Mi Heng takes off all his clothes and stands naked before everyone, still playing the drum. Having ensured that everyone is now truly embarrassed and is trying to look somewhere else, Mi Heng then leisurely puts his clothes back on.

Cao Cao roars with rage, 'How dare you behave so rudely in the palace!' This simply provokes Mi Heng into a virulent retort:

'Rude! I'll tell you what's outrageously rude. To fool a ruler. My body is as pure as the day I was born, but you, you cannot even spot the difference between the wise and foolish, because your eyes are corrupt. You have never read the books of poetry or history, so what comes from your mouth is corrupt. You don't listen to words of truth, so your ears are corrupt. You can't learn from the past to shape the present, which means you're utterly corrupt. Your disdain of the other nobles shows your very stomach is corrupt. Your plans to oust the emperor show your mind is corrupt. And you've the audacity to make a famous scholar like me a drummer! Can you act like this and honestly expect you can become the most respected man, the leader, among all the nobles?'

Kong Rong, who had recommended Mi Heng in the first place, is mortified and fears for the man's life. But Cao Cao resists the urge to have him killed and instead sends him to Liu

Biao. 'You will be my envoy to Liu Biao and, if you bring him to join us, you will be rewarded with honours and titles.' Yet Mi Heng resists and is incredibly rude to the petty officials sent to ensure he leaves. When he is summoned for his formal farewell dinner, Mi Heng arrives but lets out a deep sigh. 'What is that all about?' asks Xun Wenruo, the official in charge.

'I am here among men who are already dead, corpses – so why shouldn't I mourn?' is his reply.

Furious, the others shout out that, if they are dead, then he is nothing more than a headless devil!

'I have my own head – not like you lot serving in Cao's little gang!'

He is almost killed at this point, but Xun Wenruo shouts, 'Don't bother killing what is really just a rat!'

'I may be a rat,' shouts back Mi Heng, 'but at least I have a human soul. You lot, well, you're just parasites!'

At last, and against his will, Mi Heng is despatched to Jingzhou to see Liu Biao. Here his behaviour is no better! In praising Liu Biao, he actually manages to insult and humiliate him. One of Liu Biao's advisers says, 'Kill him! He has insulted you.'

Liu Biao is no fool. 'Cao Cao was also insulted but didn't kill him. He knows how bad this'll look – to kill a famous scholar. That's why he sent him here – for me to do his dirty work for him. However, I'm going to send him to Huang Zu. That'll show Cao Cao that I too can play this game!' And so Mi Heng is despatched to Huang Zu.

While this is going on, Yuan Shao's envoy turns up, also proposing an alliance. Uncertain what to do, Liu Biao equivocates, first going one way then another.

Soon news comes of Mi Heng's fate. Huang Zu and Mi Heng get drunk together, and then Huang Zu makes the mistake of asking Mi Heng what he thinks of him. He is told he is a wooden statue in a temple, pretty but useless. Furious and with no fear of Cao Cao, Huang Zu has him killed then and there.

It has to be noted, however, that Liu Biao does honour him and has his body properly buried on Yingwu island. Cao Cao's only comment is: 'A rotten little worm, cut down by his own sharp tongue!'

Cao Cao's advisers now recommend that he first attack Yuan Shao and Xuande and then turn his attack on Liu Biao. He agrees with this, and so the scene is set for the next bout of warfare.

Now back to the plotters of Cao Cao's assassination. With Xuande no longer in the capital, the others of the 'silk roll' conspiracy meet regularly and grow more and more offended and distressed by Cao Cao's arrogance.

One night Dong Cheng falls asleep after some heavy drinking with his friend Ji Ping the physician and dreams that he and his co-conspirators have succeeded in murdering Cao Cao. Waking in a fright, and still calling out about murdering Cao Cao, he is alarmed to see his physician Ji Ping still there, clearly having overheard what he was saying.

'Do you really intend to kill Cao Cao?' Ji Ping asks, and Dong Cheng is terrified that he will be betrayed. But Ji Ping swiftly reassures him, saying that as a loyal servant of the Han he too wants to get rid of Cao Cao, even if it means his whole clan would be wiped out in reprisals. And to show the seriousness of his intent, he bites off the tip of one of his fingers. Reassured, Dong Cheng shows Ji Ping the edict from the emperor. Ji Ping then reveals that when Cao Cao suffers from his crippling migraines it is he who treats him. He declares that he plans to poison Cao Cao the next time he is summoned.

After Ji Ping has left, Dong Cheng walks out of his room only to find a slave, Qin Qingtong, chatting up one of his concubines. Furious at this, he orders their death. However, his wife persuades him not to do this. Instead, he orders that they both be beaten forty times, and the slave be locked into a cell. That night, burning with resentment, the slave Qin Qingtong escapes and makes his way to the palace of Cao Cao. There he relates all that he has heard about the plot to assassinate the prime minister, including the latest plot involving Ji Ping.

The next day Cao Cao claims he is suffering from a migraine and summons Ji Ping. Ji Ping is elated that now he can end the rule of this traitor and he brings with him a poison to add to the usual medicine. However, Cao Cao of course knows what is planned, and when Ji Ping takes the 'medicine' to him, Cao Cao says,

'You are well read in the Classics and so you know what they say. It is the role of the servant to test the medicine for his master; the role of the son to test for the father. You are like a son as well as being a servant to me, so you should try this medicine first, then I will take it.'

Realizing he has been discovered, Ji Ping grabs hold of Cao Cao and tries to force the poison down his throat. But Cao Cao is too strong and throws the medicine onto the floor, where it spills and cracks the tiles. Ji Ping is seized by Cao Cao's guards, who wrestle him away. Cao Cao orders that he be tortured. Sitting on a bench, watching the torture, Cao Cao offers him release if he will betray the others involved. Ji Ping denies anyone else is involved and claims he was acting on his own. Despite the most horrific torture, Ji Ping refuses to name anyone, and even Cao Cao can see that any more torture will kill him. He has plans to use Ji Ping later, so the torture is stopped – not least because there is no part of Ji Ping's body that has not already been beaten and abused.

The very next day Cao Cao holds a feast for all his officials, and, with the exception of Dong Cheng, who says he is unwell, the other conspirators are in attendance. Just as everyone is relaxing, Cao Cao calls for 'entertainment', and at this point Ji Ping is brought in, dragged by no less than twenty guards. Cao Cao then speaks:

'Unbeknown to you, my officials, this man was part of a plot to overthrow the court and to murder me. But Heaven has thwarted their evil plans, as you'll now hear from the prisoner.'

So saying, he orders the guards to beat Ji Ping. The treatment is so rough he collapses. Brought round by having water thrown in his face, he shouts out, 'You traitor, Cao Cao! Why don't you just finish me off?'

'There were six original conspirators, weren't there?' says Cao Cao. 'And you became the seventh.' But Ji Ping continues to deny this, while the four conspirators in the room stare with horror and deepening fear.

Despite continued beatings, Ji Ping holds to his statement that he is alone in this, and eventually Cao Cao has him dragged away. Dismissing the other officials, he orders just the four conspirators to stay behind. Imagine their terror!

Then the slave Qin Qingtong is brought in. Wang Zifu tries to discredit the slave by pointing out that he is a runaway and therefore unreliable. But Cao Cao points out that the slave told him about Ji Ping, and this has proved to be true. So saying, he gives orders for the imprisonment of the four officials.

The next day Cao Cao, surrounded by his bodyguards, goes to Dong Cheng's house.

'Why didn't you come for the feast last night?' asks Cao Cao. Dong Cheng says that he had a sickness. Cao Cao replies, 'Could it be that you had a touch of anxiety about the Han?' As Dong Cheng takes on board what this means, Cao Cao continues, 'I expect you heard all about the Ji Ping affair? No? Well, I'm surprised.'

At this point Cao Cao orders Ji Ping to be brought in – so as to 'cure the imperial brother-in-law's illness'!

Once again Cao Cao orders Ji Ping to say who has instigated this revolt, and once again Ji Ping claims he acted alone. So yet again Ji Ping is beaten. Dong Cheng feels his heart break with sadness and terror.

'I note that you have lost the tip of one of your fingers,' observes Cao Cao. 'Why is that?' And when Ji Ping says it is as a sign that he is committed to killing Cao Cao, Cao Cao takes a knife and cuts off all of Ji Ping's fingers.

'Hah!' exclaims Ji Ping, 'I still have a tongue to curse a traitor', and when Cao Cao gives orders that his tongue be cut out, Ji Ping appears to break down. 'OK, I will tell you everything. Just release me from my ropes.'

No sooner is that done than Ji Ping faces towards the imperial palace and says, 'It's Heaven's will that I not succeed', and so saying he smashes his head on to the stone steps and dies.

As a well-known historian has written:

> In the dismal days of the decline of the Han
> There lived a simple doctor, no warrior he.

He risked his life
To save his emperor.
Sad to relate, he failed,
But he will be honoured for ever.
He had no fear of death,
Those ten bloody stumps
Mean his name will be revered for eternity.

With Ji Ping dead, Cao Cao brings in the slave Qin Qingtong and asks Dong Cheng, 'Do you know this man?' to which Dong Cheng replies that of course he does and he is glad to have this runaway back, and he should be executed for his crimes.

When Cao Cao tells him of the accusations, Dong Cheng tries valiantly to defend himself by disparaging the words of a slave. But it is pointless. The house is searched and the imperial decree is found inside the belt and the roll of silk as well. Cao Cao orders Dong Cheng and his entire household to be seized. Armed with the evidence, Cao Cao now proposes to depose the emperor and put another on the throne.

What now will befall the emperor?

Let's find out.

CHAPTER 24

Cao Cao murders the emperor's concubine Lady Dong. Xuande unites with Yuan Shao to attack Cao Cao.

Dong Cheng, the other four conspirators and their entire families and clans are publicly executed at the city gates – over seven hundred people in all. At first Cao Cao thinks that this would be the perfect time to depose the emperor and seize the throne. But he is advised not to push things too far, because at this time it could lead to civil war.

This poem was written later:

A secret decree hidden in a belt,
Written in imperial Heavenly vermilion.
Addressed to Dong, the determined defender,
Who had rescued his emperor once before.
While he was in deep anxiety about the throne
One day his dreams revealed his plan.
His loyalty will be celebrated for a thousand years.
Successful? Death came – but his fidelity remains.

Cao Cao still seeks revenge, and his chosen victim is none other than the emperor's concubine, the sister of Dong Cheng. The emperor is just discussing with his empress that he has heard nothing yet from Dong Cheng about how the plot is going when in bursts Cao Cao with his sword drawn. When confronted with news of the plot and of the discovery of the edict written in blood, the emperor is speechless.

Cao Cao orders the concubine to be brought in and, despite the pleas of the emperor that she is in the fifth month of her pregnancy, he orders her death. Even when the empress offers to take her place, Cao Cao is unmoved. She is forced out of the hall and strangled. He then orders the sealing off of the imperial family and posts three thousand of his own guards to ensure no one but he has access to the emperor.

This leaves only Ma Teng and Xuande from the original group of rebels. Initially it is planned to lure Ma Teng back to the capital and kill him. But Xuande with his army poses a graver problem. Given Xuande's troubles and difficult situation, it is decided to attack him straight away. As a consequence, a force of two hundred thousand soldiers is sent out to capture Xuzhou and Xuande.

Informed by spies of the troop manoeuvres, Sun Qian speeds to Guan Yu in Xiapi and then on to Xuande in Xiaopei to discuss what should be done next. It is decided that help should be sought from Yuan Shao, and so messengers are despatched to his camp. Sadly, no help is forthcoming. Yuan Shao is deep in depression, as his favourite son is dangerously ill, and he refuses to leave while the boy is in such a desperate state. Not even the desperate pleas for help which Sun Qian presents can make him change his mind.

Deeply troubled by this, Sun Qian rides through the day and night to bring this message back to Xuande. He has to tell Xuande that no help is on its way. This news profoundly alarms Xuande. Then to his and everyone else's surprise it is Zhang Fei who comes up with a plan. Zhang Fei – better known for just fighting, not planning! His proposal is to attack Cao Cao's troops at night as soon as they arrive. They will be tired after such long journey, eager just to set up camp and rest. As a result they will not be as vigilant as usual.

En route, Cao Cao himself is deeply troubled – by an omen. A standard pole breaks in the wind. The fall of his banner clearly signals to Cao Cao that something is wrong. He asks Xun Wenruo, who is renowned for being able to read the auguries. He declares that this foretells a night raid by their enemy. Forewarned as a result, Cao Cao sets a trap for those who thought they were going to be the trap!

With Sun Qian remaining behind to guard Xiaopei, Xuande and Zhang Fei move out that night to attack Cao Cao's camp. Zhang Fei charges in first, only to find the camp virtually deserted. As it dawns on him that he has fallen into a trap, fires break out all around him, trapping him. No matter which way he turns he is confronted by the might of Cao Cao's senior commanders closing in for the kill. His own men, only recently captured by him from Cao Cao's own troops, desert him, and he finds himself fighting almost alone on all fronts. Through sheer bravado he slashes his way through the surrounding warriors and makes good his escape. Finding the road to Xiaopei cut off and fearing that the ways to Xiapi and Xuzhou would also be closed to him, he races for the safety of the Mang Dang hills.

Meanwhile, Xuande is unaware of what is happening and is also ambushed. He loses touch with half his men, who are cut off by an attack from the rear. Before him appear Xiahou Dun and his men. They clash, many of Xuande's men dying in the battle. With only around thirty men, Xuande manages to escape. But Xiaopei is on fire, so there is no safety there. The road to Xiapi is blocked by the enemy and the route to Xuzhou likewise cut. In despair, Xuande heads north for Qingzhou and Yuan Shao. In the turmoil and chaos, he manages to escape. But all his men are captured.

He rides hard for day after day, covering hundreds of miles. When he arrives at the gates of Qingzhou, Yuan Tan, Yuan Shao's oldest son, comes to greet him. Yuan Tan is a fan of Xuande and his heroic acts and is delighted to meet him at last. From Qingzhou Xuande is escorted to Pingyuan, where Yuan Shao greets him with due ceremony. He also apologizes for having failed to come to his assistance due to his other son's grave illness. Far from bearing a grudge, Xuande offers to join Yuan Shao's forces – an offer gladly received.

Back to the night of the raid: Cao Cao has captured Xiaopei and attacked Xuzhou. With no alternative, Chen Deng has to surrender Xuzhou. Then Cao Cao and his advisers set about planning the capture of Xiapi. It is Xun Wenruo who points out: 'Guan Yu is in command there and protects Xuande's family. There's no way he'll give up the city. He'll fight to the death.' But Xun Wenruo also warns, 'If we don't attack first, then Yuan Shao will.'

Cao Cao is delighted at the opportunity of encountering this hero whom he so admires. 'I would love to have Guan Yu in my service,' muses Cao Cao. 'Is there anyone who could bring him to our side?' While most express grave doubts that this is possible, one man comes forward and says he would like to try, as Guan Yu is a friend of his. This is Zhang Liao. 'I know Zhang Liao and Guan Yu are friends,' says Cheng Yu, 'but I know Guan Yu. Words will not be enough to bring him over. But let's put him in an impossible situation, trap him and then let Zhang Liao talk him round.'

Now that Xuande is defeated, how will Guan Yu react?

Let's find out.

CHAPTER 25

Guan Yu is captured by Cao Cao's men but sets three conditions. Cao Cao breaks the siege of Baima.

Cheng Yu's plan is to use subterfuge. In their ranks are some former soldiers of Guan Yu. They will be granted their freedom if they agree to be part of a trick. They are to go back, pretending to have escaped. This will mean they will be allowed into Xiapi. Once inside, they are to betray the city by opening the gates. Sad to say, Guan Yu is fooled and welcomes the men back into the city.

The attack on Xiapi commences under the command of Xiahou Dun. Time and time again he tries to lure Guan Yu to come out and fight. Only when he sends a lowly soldier to shout abuse does Guan Yu react. Incandescent with rage, he charges out, supported by three thousand men, to personally challenge Xiahou Dun. Feigning panic, Xiahou Dun turns his horse and flees, drawing Guan Yu away from the city. Suddenly aware that his impetuous actions have put the city at risk, Guan Yu turns, only to find every pathway back closed to him as the enemy close in from all sides. Unable to reach Xiapi, Guan Yu and his remaining troops fight their way to the top of a hill. This they can defend and so they stand their ground.

Cao Cao's men seal off the hill. In the distance Guan Yu can see from the flames and smoke that Xiapi has fallen. As the dawn comes up the next day, Guan Yu is preparing a suicide attack down the hill when a lone rider is spotted, spurring his way up the hill. It is Zhang Liao. When he and Guan Yu meet, Zhang Liao speaks warmly of the time Guan Yu saved his life, and that this is why he is here now, to try to do the same for Guan Yu. Guan Yu thinks this means he has brought troops to join Guan Yu in his struggle, but Zhang Liao has to disillusion him. 'So why are you here, then?' asks a confused Guan Yu.

'We've no idea what has happened to Xuande. The same is true for Zhang Fei. What is known is that last night Cao Cao took Xiapi and that he has placed a special guard over Xuande's family to protect them.'

'If this is meant to impress me,' says Guan Yu, 'it doesn't. I would rather die than surrender, for death would be a homecoming for me. Go now, because shortly I will ride into battle.'

Zhang Liao bursts out laughing. 'Do you want to be mocked by the entire empire?'

Guan Yu replies, 'As I'll die doing my duty, I think the world won't see this as much of a joke.'

'But if you die here,' says Zhang Liao, 'you'll have committed three errors.'

'And what exactly would those be?' queries a troubled Guan Yu.

'Firstly, you promised your brothers that you would die together when you made your joint vow. Your brother, it is true, has been defeated, but you plan to go and be killed! What if Xuande survives and wants your help? What use will your vow be then! Secondly, his family was placed in your care. If you die now, then his wives will be unprotected, and you'll have betrayed him. Thirdly, you're not just a warrior but also steeped in the Classics. You all swore to protect the Han dynasty, yet you seem willing to throw this away in order to die! How does that help anyone? These are your three errors.'

Guan Yu questions Zhang Liao: 'So those are your three errors. Now what do you want me to do about that?'

'Submit,' says Zhang Liao. 'You are surrounded. If you submit you'll have three advantages. You can protect Xuande's ladies; you will be faithful to the vow you made in the peach orchard; and finally you will still be alive!'

'You have given your three advantages, now I have three conditions. Firstly, as a defender of the Han, I will only surrender to the emperor, not to Cao Cao. Secondly, I must have total control over how my sisters-in-law are to be protected. Thirdly, whenever I find out where Xuande is, I will be free to go to him.'

When Zhang Liao reports back to Cao Cao, he doesn't want to agree to the third condition. But Zhang Liao points out that if Cao Cao can prove to be even more honourable than Xuande, he might win Guan Yu's loyalty. So the deal is done.

When the army moves out of Xiapi back to the capital, Guan Yu takes charge of the transport for Xuande's wives, riding alongside their carriage. Cao Cao decides to test his loyalty and virtue. The first night they stop he allocates only one room to the ladies and Guan Yu. But Guan Yu simply stands outside the room all night on guard. Cao Cao is suitably impressed.

When they arrive at the capital, Guan Yu ensures that the women have their own quarters while he takes the front room to be on guard.

From the day they arrive Cao Cao tries to subvert him by holding feasts in his honour, piling gifts of gold, silver and silks upon him and sending beautiful women to serve him. All these gifts he immediately hands over to his sisters-in-law. This impresses Cao Cao even more.

One day he notices the somewhat decrepit state of Guan Yu's overcoat and orders a beautiful one to be made for him. To his surprise, Guan Yu puts it on and then puts the old one on top. When asked why, he says that, as Xuande gave him the old one, it reminds him of his brother. While this again impresses Cao Cao, it also alarms him, as it is clear his strategy to win Guan Yu over is not working.

In the midst of all the plotting and scheming of Cao Cao's court, Guan Yu tries to keep up the spirits of his sisters-in-law. One day they have similar dreams, which convinces them that Xuande is dead. Not just dead but in Hell. Guan Yu reassures them: 'Dreams don't show the truth. Have no fear.'

A little while later, Cao Cao notices that Guan Yu's horse is almost skeletal, showing signs of near collapse. 'This is because I have got fatter,' says Guan Yu, 'and I have worn the poor beast out.' So Cao Cao presents him with a horse, but not just any horse. The gift he is given is the former horse of Lü Bu, the magnificent Red Hare. This time Guan Yu expresses his thanks fulsomely.

'Well, now!' says Cao Cao. 'I've given you beautiful women, treasures such as gold and silks, and you never once thanked me. Yet I give you a horse, and you haven't stopped thanking me. Are animals of greater importance to you than women?'

'Because this horse can cover a thousand miles in one day,' Guan Yu replies, 'it means that, when I know where he is, I can reach my brother in just one day.' Cao Cao once again has to recognize his loyalty even if he now rather regrets the gift!

At Cao Cao's earnest request, Zhang Liao goes to see Guan Yu to ask why he is so determined never to abandon Xuande. Guan Yu reminds him of the vow the three have made and when asked, 'What if Xuande is dead?' says he would then go to the underworld to serve him. However, he does say that he owes Cao Cao one great service to thank him for his generosity and kindness.

When Cao Cao hears this reported back, he once again acknowledges the true virtue of Guan Yu and notes, however, with interest that Guan Yu feels obliged to do one last deed for him.

Meanwhile, Xuande is safe with Yuan Shao but in great distress. He is desperately worried about what might have happened to his two brothers. And having had no news other than their capture by Cao Cao, he is also anxious about the well-being of his family.

When spring comes the two leaders agree it is time to go to war. They decide to attack the capital despite some speaking-out against this and predicting doom and failure. The army has as their primary target the city of Baima. As soon as word reaches Cao Cao, he sets out with a force of one hundred and fifty thousand men. The commander of Yuan Shao's troops is Yan Liang, and, seeing him in the distance, Cao Cao orders Song Xian, a former associate of Lü Bu, to go out and challenge him. No sooner has he done so than Yan Liang cuts Song Xian down with one stroke, earning the grudging admiration of Cao Cao. Furious at the death of his friend, Wei Xu asks permission to challenge Yan Liang. But he lasts no longer than it takes for Yan Liang's sword to rise and fall. One further challenger, Xu Huang, rides forward, and though he manages to battle Yan Liang for twenty rounds he too fails to kill Yan Liang and retires to his lines. All this deeply troubles the commanders of Cao Cao's army.

Cao Cao realizes only one warrior could possibly overthrow Yan Liang – Guan Yu. Cheng Yu sees this as the opportunity to turn Guan Yu to Cao Cao's side.

'Look,' he says. 'If Xuande is still alive he is with Yuan Shao. If Guan Yu kills Yuan Shao's commander, this will turn him against Xuande, and he will be executed. Then Guan Yu will have no option except to stay and serve you.'

So Guan Yu is summoned. Riding the mighty horse Red Hare and wielding his sword, the Green Dragon, he arrives. Cao Cao takes him to the top of the hill and points out Yan Liang to him. Without further ado, Guan Yu leaps on to Red Hare and gallops down the hill. As he rushes forward, the enemy army parts like a river, and Guan Yu, unchallenged, rides straight at Yan Liang, who is completely unprepared for such a dramatic attack. With one thrust of Guan Yu's sword Yan Liang is killed. While the astonished and shocked army watch helplessly, Guan Yu leaps from his horse, cuts off Yan Liang's head, leaps back on Red Hare, brandishing his great sword, and, with Yan Liang's head tied to his reins, gallops back to Cao Cao.

Realizing that the enemy is paralysed with terror and astonishment, Cao Cao's army attack and rout the northern army, killing huge numbers and seizing vast quantities of loot.

When Guan Yu presents the head to Cao Cao, the latter says, 'This is beyond anything a mere mortal could do!' Whereupon Guan Yu says, 'This is nothing. My brother Zhang Fei could kill a commander of an army of ten times a hundred thousand men.' Alarmed by this, Cao Cao makes his commanders take note of this warning – even making them write it down on their collars.

As predicted, when Yuan Shao hears that his army had been defeated by the actions of Guan Yu, he turns against Xuande, convinced that Xuande must have plotted this. Calling for the executioner, he has Xuande seized ready to be executed there and then.

Is this the end of Xuande?

Let's find out.

CHAPTER 26

Yuan Shao is defeated and Guan Yu slays his best generals. Guan Yu learns where Xuande is and leaves with the wives and returns almost all of Cao Cao's gifts.

Xuande remains calm and says to Yuan Shao, 'This claim that I plotted this and Guan Yu executed it is just a rumour. Many people look like Guan Yu, so why assume it was him? Let's see if it is true first.' Yuan Shao, who is always easily swayed, agrees, reprimanding the official who had told him it was Guan Yu.

All are agreed that the death of Yan Liang has to be avenged. This unites everyone in the desire to attack Cao Cao as soon as possible. Yan Liang's friend Wen Chou steps forward, eager to lead the attack. When Xuande asks to join the expedition in order to find out what has happened to Guan Yu, Wen Chou is far from happy.

'Xuande has lost battle after battle,' he says, 'and will therefore bring bad luck.' But Yuan Shao insists, so Wen Chou puts Xuande at the rear with thirty thousand men while he leads the main force of seventy thousand.

Cao Cao rides out with his troops to confront the northern army. He has devised a very unusual plan. Noting that his enemy likes to attack his supply wagons, he orders them to be put at the front of the army, not at the back. This bewilders his own men, who cannot understand such a strange move. Hardly able to believe their luck, Wen Chou's men attack and easily capture the baggage train with all the supplies. Cao Cao's men retreat and then, at his command, they release the hundreds of war horses. The opportunity of seizing such prizes is too much for Wen Chou's troops. Soon they are rushing about trying to grab as many of the horses as possible. This is the moment Cao Cao has been waiting for and into the midst of the chaos and disorganized enemy he charges. It works. The enemy are scattered. Spotting Wen Chou, Cao Cao orders two warriors, Zhang Liao and Xu Huang, to attack. Their attempts fail, but just as Wen Chou thinks he has escaped, Guan Yu rides to the attack. Within minutes Guan Yu has slain Wen Chou.

The death of their commander throws Wen Chou's army into even greater chaos. Cao Cao seizes the moment and attacks in full force, destroying the enemy and regaining the baggage and all the horses whose release caused the initial breakdown of discipline in the enemy forces.

On the edge of the battle Xuande is told that a red-faced, long-bearded warrior has killed Wen Chou. Riding forward, he sees the banner of Guan Yu. Thanking Heaven and Earth for the survival of his brother, he tries to reach him but is swept back by Cao Cao's army.

In the aftermath of the battle, Yuan Shao is once again and very understandably furious that Guan Yu has slain his commander in chief. Yuan Shao again seizes Xuande in order to execute him. But Xuande points out that this is exactly why Cao Cao used Guan Yu to kill the commanders. He is trying to sow discord between Xuande and Yuan Shao. Once again Yuan Shao changes his mind and invites Xuande to dine with him as an honoured guest.

Meanwhile, during the celebrations of this victory, Cao Cao is informed of a new Yellow Headband army ravaging Runan. Guan Yu offers to lead the attack on the rebels and is given permission and troops to do so. The very day Guan Yu arrives ready for battle, two spies are captured and brought to Guan Yu's tent. To his surprise and delight he sees that one of them is Xuande's adviser Sun Qian. Dismissing his men, Guan Yu asks, 'What are you doing here?' to which Sun Qian replies, 'It's by pure chance that I'm here. I was given refuge by Liu Pi. But what has happened to you? Why are you on Cao Cao's side? Where are Xuande's wives?' Swiftly Guan Yu brings him up to date, reassuring him that the ladies are all right.

'Xuande is with Yuan Shao, I've been told,' says Sun Qian. 'It's my intention to join him, but that hasn't been possible until now. The two leaders of the Yellow Headbands, Liu Pi and Gong Du, actually want to join Yuan Shao to fight against Cao Cao. I've come to tell you that tomorrow they'll pretend to be defeated and will turn away, drawing you after them. You can then capture the city, and then from that base you can come over to our side with the ladies to join Yuan Shao and Xuande.'

So the plot is set in motion. Pretending to be defeated, the Yellow Headband leaders and their men flee, and Guan Yu captures Runan. In triumph, Guan Yu returns to Cao Cao in the capital.

Upon his return, Guan Yu goes to pay a formal visit to the two wives. 'Have you found out anything about our lord?' they ask. 'No news yet,' he replies. But the wives find out that Xuande is with Yuan Shao and challenge him: 'Is it because you have decided to join Cao Cao that you have apparently decided to forget all about our lord?'

'You're right,' replies a contrite Guan Yu. 'He's alive and with Yuan Shao. But we have to keep this a secret, so that I can plan how we escape.' But for the life of him he cannot work out how to achieve this.

His anxiety is increased when a smuggled letter from Xuande is brought to him. In the letter Xuande asks why he has apparently abandoned the vow the three of them made in the peach orchard. Weeping, Guan Yu decides to simply go to Cao Cao and remind him that he has agreed that Guan Yu could go to Xuande when he knew where he was. Guan Yu then composes a letter to Xuande, explaining that in order to protect his two sisters-in-law he has had no option but to take up service under Cao Cao. He then tells him that, now he knows Xuande is alive and where he is, he is about to set off to bring the two ladies back to Xuande.

That very day Guan Yu goes to call upon Cao Cao to remind him of the promise. But Cao Cao knows that this is coming. When Guan Yu arrives at the prime minister's gate he is told Cao Cao is not at home so he has to turn back.

The same thing happens the next day, and again and again until Guan Yu realizes this is part of a strategy to deny him the right to leave. So instead Guan Yu writes a letter of farewell and leaves it at the prime minister's gate. He also packs up all the gifts Cao Cao has given him so they can be left behind, and he cannot be accused of stealing anything.

Mounted upon Red Hare, brandishing his Green Dragon sword, Guan Yu escorts the two wives in their carriage, breaking out of the city via the north gate. The gatekeeper rushes to inform Cao Cao, while others arrive to say Guan Yu has taken none of the gifts.

'Give me three thousand men, and I will capture him,' cries Commander Cai Yang. As it has been said:

Guan Yu swopped the dragon's den
For a pack of wolves in hot pursuit!

What will happen next?

CHAPTER 27

Guan Yu escorts Xuande's wives over four hundred miles. He kills six officials en route at five passes.

Cao Cao, keen to be seen by Guan Yu as a man of virtue and honour, also recognizes that Cai Yang has never liked Guan Yu. He therefore responds to Cai Yang's offer by exclaiming that Guan Yu is a man of honour and they should try one more time to appeal to that honour. So he sends Guan Yu's friend Zhang Liao racing after him to ask him to stop while Cao Cao follows up behind to talk with him.

Zhang Liao soon catches up with Guan Yu because the ladies' carriage moves quite slowly. When he sees Zhang Liao racing towards him he fears that his friend has come to fight him. He orders his staff to go on ahead as fast as possible with the ladies to keep them safe. He takes up a defensive position on a bridge. Then he sees Cao Cao and his attendants arriving, and none of them is armed. He relaxes. Cao Cao asks him, 'Why have you left so quickly – and without saying goodbye?' But Guan Yu points out, 'I've tried to see you to express my thanks and to say goodbye, but you were never at home! I must leave, as I now know where my lord is. You will recall we agreed this.'

Cao Cao again tries to offer him extravagant gifts of gold and fine clothes. He says, 'I worry that you have enough to cover the costs and wear and tear of such a long journey.' And again Guan Yu declines, saying, 'I've done nothing to earn such generosity.' However, he does decide to accept a gorgeous silk robe. Then Guan Yu turns his horse and continues to head north.

Deeply disappointed but also acutely aware of how honourable Guan Yu is, Cao Cao returns empty-handed to the capital.

After his encounter with Cao Cao, Guan Yu dashes off to catch up with the carriage with the two ladies inside. But after riding pell-mell for thirty miles he can find no trace of them or the escort. Suddenly a group of wild-looking horsemen led by a young man in rich clothes sweeps down upon him. What alarms Guan Yu most is that the young man has a human head hanging from his reins. Without warning, the young man leaps from his horse and prostrates himself in front of Guan Yu. Startled but also a little bit relieved, Guan Yu enquires who he is and what is going on.

'I am Liao Hua and I've had to become a highwayman. My five hundred men and I survive by robbery. My colleague in crime seized the two ladies by mistake. Once I discovered they were the wives of Imperial Uncle Xuande and protected by you, I wanted to set them free immediately so they could go back to you. But my colleague was against this and spoke in such insulting terms about them that I killed him and have brought his head to you in the hope that you will pardon this dreadful act of ours.'

Guan Yu demands to know where the ladies are now, to which Liao Hua replies that they are safe on the hill above. At Guan Yu's orders they are brought to him.

Humbly, almost kowtowing with respect, Guan Yu approaches the carriage. Anxiously he asks, 'Did these dreadful robbers frighten you?' The ladies reply, 'Had it not been for the courage of Liao Hua we would have been assaulted by the other leader, Du Yuan.'

'What happened?' asks a deeply troubled Guan Yu.

'The other leader,' reply the servants of the ladies, 'wanted to make one of the ladies his wife and offer the other to Liao Hua. But as soon as Liao Hua found out who they were and Du Yuan's plans he killed him and was most attentive to the needs and comfort of the ladies.'

Having thanked Liao Hua, Guan Yu gets the convoy going again.

They stop late that night at a small manor-house farm. The farm is owned by Hu Hua, who used to be an adviser to the Emperor Huan. Having ended his time at court, he retired to the farm. The next morning, hearing who his guests are, he asks Guan Yu to take a letter. It is for his son Hu Ban, who is serving with Cao Cao's troops in the area through which Guan Yu will be passing. Guan Yu, of course, agrees, little realizing how important this kindness will be.

That same morning Guan Yu and the convoy set off for Luoyang.

When they reach the borders of Cao Cao's territory at the Dongling pass, they are stopped. The commander there has five hundred men on guard duty and he wants to know where the party are going. He expresses considerable surprise on hearing that they are heading north over the river.

'That's Yuan Shao's territory. Our enemy,' says the commander. 'I assume you have written permission to go there?'

'We had to leave at very short notice. There was no time for such formalities,' replies Guan Yu.

'Well, I'm sorry,' says the commander, 'but you'll have to wait until written permission has been obtained.'

'Such a wait is not possible.'

'I have no option,' says the commander. 'That is what the army orders command.'

'So you're saying we cannot leave?'

'Only if you leave the ladies behind as security.'

'I cannot allow such a delay,' says Guan Yu and he draws his sword. The commander withdraws only to return shortly with his men all armed and ready. 'Try and get past me!' shouts the commander, and Guan Yu charges. With one swift blow he slays the commander. The troops, terrified, bowed down to Guan Yu, who pardons them, and the convoy goes through the pass, heading for Luoyang.

As they enter the next district, Han Fu, the governor, hears of their progress and is seriously alarmed.

'If he has no papers, then he's a fugitive, and we must stop him or we'll be punished.' Knowing of Guan Yu's fierce reputation, the governor and his adviser think their only hope is to try to trick him, making it possible for them to then kill him. The adviser says, 'Let's build a barrier of branches and stakes. When he arrives, I'll attack him, drawing him into combat.

But then I'll pretend to run away, and when Guan Yu pursues me, I can lead him into a trap. You, governor, will be hiding and as he passes you can fell him with an arrow.'

So the plot is laid. Governor Han Fu with a thousand men blocks the road and gets ready with his bow and arrow. Again Guan Yu is asked for his papers and once again says he has none. At this point Han Fu declares that, as a fugitive, he must be arrested. When Guan Yu reminds him that he has already killed one official who tried to stop him, Han Fu cries out, 'Who will stop him?' and at this signal the adviser charges out with two drawn swords and makes straight for Guan Yu. After a brief clash of swords, the adviser turns as if fleeing. But before he can draw Guan Yu far enough away, Guan Yu has caught up with him and slain him. Nevertheless Han Fu fires his arrow, and this fails to kill Guan Yu. It has enough force, however, to hit his arm. Despite the pain, Guan Yu pulls the arrow out with his teeth and dashes off in pursuit of Han Fu. Swiftly overtaking him, he kills him, and once again the soldiers flee. Guan Yu and the convoy pass through and continue on their way to Luoyang again, with Guan Yu bandaging his arm as he rides.

Yet again they come up against a guarded pass. Here the commander, Bian Xi, is much more cunning. He lays a plan to invite Guan Yu for drinks in the Zhenguo temple, and at a given signal – tapping his wine cup – two hundred guards will rush out and overpower Guan Yu.

So it is a surprise for Guan Yu when, instead of challenging him, Commander Bian Xi welcomes him. 'Your fame goes before you, sir,' says Bian Xi. 'I fully appreciate the bonds of loyalty which lead you to depart for Yuan Shao's lands. Before you go I would like to invite you for a drink at the nearby Buddhist temple.' Guan Yu is more than happy to agree!

However, one of the monks, called Pujing, is from Guan Yu's home town and has found out about the plot. Through quiet subterfuge and signals which Guan Yu picks up, Pujing warns Guan Yu of the impending attack. Spotting the waiting ambush, Guan Yu denounces Bian Xi. 'I thought you an honest man!' Bian Xi, realizing all is up, shouts for his men to attack. Guan Yu draws his mighty sword and sweeps in to attack, slaying Commander Bian Xi and once again scattering the troops. He cuts down the soldiers who are surrounding the ladies' carriage and then profusely thanks the monk who has saved their lives.

'I must leave here now,' says the monk, 'so I will collect my robe and my alms bowl and set out to wander like a cloud through this world. But we two will meet again, and, until then, take care.'

So on the convoy goes and once again they come to a pass and once again there is trouble. The governor of Yingyang, Wang Zhi, is a relative of the murdered Han Fu, the commander at the second pass. So he too decides to confront Guan Yu. Once again the plot is to feign delight at seeing Guan Yu and to offer the exhausted ladies rest and refuge in the city as the guests of Wang Zhi himself. Trusting Wang Zhi, Guan Yu makes sure the ladies are comfortable and then removes his heavy armour and lies down to get some rest.

This time a thousand soldiers are detailed to surround the building where Guan Yu and the ladies are staying. At the appointed time a signal will be given to burn it down.

However, the commander of the troops is none other than Hu Ban. This is the son of Hu Hua. Guan Yu, of course, has a letter to give Hu Ban from his father. Once Hu Ban has put his troops in place ready for the signal, Hu Ban creeps forward to try to get a look at this famous warrior. Peering through a window, he sees Guan Yu sitting, stroking his long beard and reading. 'He really does look like a god!' he says, louder than he intended. Guan Yu calls out, 'Who's there?' When he hears it is Hu Ban, he asks him to come in. Guan Yu presents the letter to him. Realizing, from his father's letter, that Guan Yu is a man of honour, he tells him of the plot to burn him and the ladies to death. Telling him to hurry up and get the ladies into the carriage, he goes secretly and opens the city gate so the convoy can escape.

Once the party are safely beyond the city walls, Hu Ban sets fire to the lodgings they have just left. But Wang Zhi has not been fooled. Charging after Guan Yu with his men trailing him, he commands Guan Yu to stop. But as Wang Zhi charges at him, Guan Yu swings his mighty sword and literally cuts him in two, leaving his dead body by the roadside, and rides on. And once again the others run away as soon as they see what has befallen their commander.

Quietly giving thanks for the help Hu Ban has given, Guan Yu leads the convoy on until they reach the border at Huazhou. Here he meets an old friend, Liu Yan, who warns him that the river crossing is guarded by Qin Qi, a deputy governor under the Governor Xiahou Dun. 'I fear it is very unlikely that he will let you cross,' says Liu Yan. 'Lend me a boat so I can escape the border crossing,' says Guan Yu, but Liu Yan is too afraid of the power of Qin Qi and refuses. Frustrated, and knowing he can gain nothing more from such a weak man, Guan Yu presses on.

At the river crossing, once again Guan Yu is asked to provide the papers that show he has the prime minister's permission to leave. 'I don't need such papers,' says Guan Yu.

'Without papers, not even wings will enable you to cross over!' states Qin Qi defiantly.

'I've already killed others who have tried to stop me,' says Guan Yu.

'Try and kill me then,' shouts Qin Qi impetuously. So saying, he attacks Guan Yu, but with one swift stroke Guan Yu strikes off Qin Qi's head. Guan Yu then tells the soldiers guarding the crossing that he has nothing against them so would they now please ferry the convoy across the river. The men hasten to obey.

At last as they landed on the far shore, they are in the land of Yuan Shao. Guan Yu has forced his way through five places and killed six officials. He truly regrets that this has been necessary and realizes that Cao Cao will inevitably feel betrayed by his actions.

Just at that moment a lone horseman rides towards him from the north. It is Sun Qian come to warn him not to go on to the court of Yuan Shao. Sun Qian has grown frustrated by the indecision of Yuan Shao. He has persuaded Xuande to move out and go and join Liu Pi in Runan. Realizing the danger

Guan Yu would be in if he had ridden to Yuan Shao, Liu Pi has sent Sun Qian to warn him.

So Guan Yu and the two ladies set out for Runan, but they have barely started when thundering up behind them comes a troop of horsemen led by Xiahou Dun. 'Stop!' he shouts.

Can Guan Yu escape?

Let's find out.

CHAPTER 28

Guan Yu kills Cai Yang to show Zhang Fei he is no traitor. The three brothers are united again.

Xiahou Dun is furious at the deaths Guan Yu has caused, not least because among those killed was one of his officers. 'I've come to capture you,' he shouts and levels his spear at Guan Yu, ready to charge. At that precise moment another horseman rides up at a gallop, shouting out, 'Stop! Stop now! You mustn't fight Guan Yu!'

The rider thunders up and presents an official paper. 'The prime minister,' the messenger says, 'admiring the honour and virtue of Guan Yu, has granted him permission to travel freely.'

This, however, does not impress Xiahou Dun. 'Guan Yu has killed several officers, and I don't think the prime minister is aware of this – is he?' he asks. To which the messenger says, 'I don't think so.'

So Xiahou Dun declares that therefore he will arrest Guan Yu and take him for trial before Cao Cao.

This makes Guan Yu furious. 'Do you think I'm frightened of you?' And he charges with his spear levelled at Xiahou Dun, who likewise charges with his spear levelled. Ten rounds they go, when yet another horseman gallops up shouting, 'Wait, wait!'

Yet again, the messenger declares that the prime minister, moved by Guan Yu's loyalty, grants him permission to leave.

Again Xiahou Dun asks if the prime minister knows of the murdered officers and, when he is told no, he once again prepares to charge Guan Yu, and Guan Yu draws his mighty sword as Xiahou Dun's men close in.

At this point yet another horseman – the third one now – charges up shouting, 'Do not attack!' This time the messenger is none other than Zhang Liao.

'The prime minister has heard about the deaths of the officers and, worried that this might lead to difficulties, he's sent me to say Guan Yu is still free to leave.'

When Xiahou Dun raises the fact that one of the dead was Qin Qi, Cai Yang's nephew, whom he was supposed to protect, Zhang Liao dismisses this. 'I will explain what happened,' says Zhang Liao, 'when next I see Cai Yang.'

In the light of so many messages from Cao Cao, and with Zhang Liao's personal assurance, Xiahou Dun has no option but to give in. So he departs with Zhang Liao, but empty-handed.

Guan Yu and the two ladies travel on for many days. At one point they are confronted by a gang of robbers – former Yellow Headband rebels who have turned to crime. But when their leader, Zhou Cang, realizes who the warrior leading the convoy is, he leaps from his horse, kneels and begs to be allowed to join Guan Yu.

It is a few days after this that they see in the distance a city called Gucheng. Local people tell them that a few months back a ferocious warrior appeared, expelled the governor and took over the city. He has now recruited a large army, secured provisions and has the whole area in awe of him. When they ask who this 'fierce warrior' is, they discover it is none other than Zhang Fei!

Guan Yu, confident of a warm reception, sends Sun Qian into the city to announce that his brother is outside and that his sisters-in-law are with him.

When Guan Yu sees his brother Zhang Fei riding out of the city leading a thousand horsemen, he sets aside his great sword and rides forward to greet him. But imagine his astonishment when Zhang Fei suddenly gives a roar of anger and charges straight at him with his spear levelled for the kill.

Deeply shocked, Guan Yu cries out, 'Brother, what are you doing? Have you already forgotten the peach orchard?'

'You traitor!' roars Zhang Fei. 'It's you who betrayed our brother by surrendering to Cao Cao, taking a place in his court and receiving his gifts. I'm going to kill you!'

When the two ladies hear the noise, they pull aside the curtains and look out. 'What on earth is going on?' they demand of Zhang Fei, who reins in, in the midst of his charge, to pay his respects.

'Don't you worry, little sisters. I'm going to kill this traitor and then escort you into the safety of the city,' declares Zhang Fei.

'But Guan Yu had no idea where either you or Xuande were,' they say. 'We had to stay with Cao Cao. As soon as he found out that Xuande was at Runan, we left. He's seen us through such terrible times on our journey and defended us so gallantly! Please don't be angry with him!'

'You've been fooled by him,' retorts Zhang Fei, 'and the truth is that a truly loyal man would rather die than be dishonoured. No one who is virtuous can serve two masters.'

'Dear brother,' says Guan Yu, 'you're seriously misjudging me.'

'Trust me,' says Sun Qian, 'Guan Yu has been looking for you, and that search is why he is here now!'

But Zhang Fei shouts back, 'Rubbish! You've come here to capture me!'

'But,' replies a shocked Guan Yu, 'if I'd wanted to capture you, surely I'd have come with an armed force.'

'Which is exactly,' says a furious and equally shocked Zhang Fei, 'what you've done.' And he points behind Guan Yu.

Guan Yu turns and to his astonishment sees a huge cloud of dust kicked up by what has to be an immense military force. The banners flying high above the horde declare that this is the army of Cao Cao.

'So,' says Zhang Fei, 'are there any other tricks of yours to try to persuade me?' And so saying he charges at Guan Yu.

'Stop, brother!' shouts Guan Yu. 'To prove to you I'm telling the truth let me go and kill the leader of the troops.'

'If you can do this in the time it takes for three rolls of the war drums, then I'll believe you,' replies Zhang Fei.

Soon the army's leader comes into clear view, and it is none other than Cai Yang, who, the moment he sees Guan Yu, shouts, 'Found you, you murderer. You killed my nephew. The prime minister has ordered your arrest.'

Zhang Fei picks up the drumsticks. Guan Yu utters not a word but charges forward. Before Zhang Fei can complete a single roll of the drums, Guan Yu's mighty sword has risen and fallen, and Cai Yang's head rolls to the ground. At this sight the troops panic and start to flee. When a junior officer is captured and questioned it is revealed that Cao Cao has not ordered the capture of Guan Yu, but an attack on Runan. The meeting with Guan Yu was an accident which Cai Yang tried to turn to his own advantage. Zhang Fei interrogates the prisoner thoroughly until at last he is convinced that his brother has told the truth.

Together, they all enter the city. They spend the day celebrating and telling each other of their adventures and exploits since they were last together. It is then decided that Guan Yu and Sun Qian will travel to Runan to see Xuande. Meanwhile, Zhang Fei will stay in the city and look after the two ladies.

However, when Guan Yu and Sun Qian arrive at Runan it is only to find Xuande has left sometime ago. He has gone back to consult with Yuan Shao. So they return disappointed to Gucheng. It is agreed once again that Guan Yu and Sun Qian should go to find Xuande while Zhang Fei guards the city and the ladies. The danger, of course, is that, in entering the territory of Yuan Shao, Guan Yu will be a wanted man for having killed Yuan Shao's two best commanders. Secrecy has to be paramount.

When Sun Qian and Guan Yu arrive at the river border, Sun Qian persuades Guan Yu to seek shelter at a nearby farm while he rides on into Yuan Shao's territory to find Xuande.

While Guan Yu takes refuge in the farm, Sun Qian makes it safely into the city of Jizhou and finds Xuande. He tells him of the reunion of his two other brothers. Calling in his adviser, Jian Yong, Xuande and Sun Qian plot how they can all escape from under Yuan Shao's nose. It is Jian Yong who comes up with the plan. The heart of the plot is that Xuande will suggest that he go to Jingzhou to consult with Liu Biao. He will propose that Liu Biao join their alliance against Cao Cao.

'That will help us escape,' says Xuande, 'but what about you Jian Yong?'

'Don't worry about me. I've my own plans up my sleeve.'

At the meeting with Yuan Shao the following day Xuande

suggests that he should go to speak with Liu Biao to see if he will agree to a joint attack on Cao Cao. Yuan Shao agrees, and just as Xuande is leaving says, 'I gather that Guan Yu has left Cao Cao and is somewhere near here. If he comes I'll kill him in revenge for the deaths of Yan Liang and Wen Chou.'

Highly alarmed, Xuande tries to reason with him only to be told by Yuan Shao that he is just joking.

To complete the plot, Jian Yong comes to Yuan Shao and says he thinks he ought to keep an eye on Xuande. So Yuan Shao gives him permission to depart as his personal spy.

Soon Xuande and Guan Yu are reunited. Guan Yu has been given hospitality by the farmer, whose family name is also Guan. The farmer's son, Guan Ping, asks permission to join Guan Yu, and Guan Yu agrees. From now on Guan Ping treats Guan Yu as his father and Xuande as his uncle. Then the party departs swiftly before they are discovered.

En route back to Zhang Fei, they are suddenly attacked by a ferocious warrior and his men who charge downhill at them. Just as they think they are doomed, the attackers pull up sharply. Xuande cries in delight. 'It's Zhao Zilong!'

'My lord!' says Zhao Zilong. 'After leaving you, I joined Gongsun Zan again. But he wouldn't listen to any advice. In the end Yuan Shao not only defeated him but caused his death by burning. Despite many offers from Yuan Shao I could see he was a weak man. I tried to find you and then heard that Guan Yu had betrayed you and joined Cao Cao. When I heard you were with Yuan Shao I was tempted to come. But in the end I didn't and have been wandering ever since. When I heard Zhang Fei was at Gucheng I decided to go to him. I can't believe my luck in now finding you!'

'I'd always hoped you would join us,' says Xuande.

'And I've always wanted to join you!' says Zhao Zilong. Kowtowing, Zhao Zilong and his band of warriors join with Xuande, and together they ride for Gucheng.

Arriving back at Gucheng, Xuande is greeted by Zhang Fei with joy and each of the brothers tells the story of the adventures he has been through. They sacrifice to Heaven and Earth with an ox and a horse and they celebrate. The addition of

Zhao Zilong and Guan Ping is also a cause for great rejoicing among them.

As a poet later said:

> For a time, the men were scattered like severed limbs;
> Rumours, whispers, but nothing to confirm what was happening.
> Today, they're reunited – brothers once again,
> Dragon and Tiger combined, like a roaring wind.

Xuande now decides that with their combined force of around five thousand they should march to defend Runan, and at just that moment Liu Pi and Gong Du ask for their help. So off the band of brothers go, strengthening their army along the way with new recruits.

Once Yuan Shao realizes he has been tricked into letting Xuande and Jian Yong go, he is determined to have his revenge. But his counsellor Guo Tu, who advised against letting either Xuande or Jian Yong go, now advises him to ignore Xuande. 'You need now to focus on the greater threat of Cao Cao. To overcome him, I suggest that you create a new alliance. This time with Sun Ce to the south of the Great River, in the southlands of the Three Rivers with its six districts. Join with him to attack Cao Cao,' says Guo Tu, and, following his advice, Yuan Shao sends Chen Zhen to speak for him.

> The warrior from the north has gone;
> The warrior from the south is now sought.

And what comes of this?

Let's find out.

CHAPTER 29

Sun Ce kills Yu Ji. He dies, and Sun Quan takes over the south – Wu.

Sun Ce by the year AD 199 is the ruler of the south. So strong has he become that Cao Cao is now seriously worried by him. 'There is no way we can confront this lion directly,' he says, 'so why don't we instead bind him to us by marriage?' So Cao Ren's daughter is married to Sun Ce's brother, Sun Kuang.

All is well until Sun Ce petitions the emperor for a high-status post, which Cao Cao refuses to give him. In his anger, Sun Ce declares he will attack the capital. Hearing of this, one of his city governors, Xu Gong, secretly writes a letter to be taken to Cao Cao, warning of the plot. The messenger is captured and brought before Sun Ce. On reading the letter, he executes the messenger and summons Xu Gong to his court. Here, the poor man is murdered on Sun Ce's orders.

What Sun Ce has not expected is that loyal followers of Xu Gong would seek revenge. One day he is out hunting when three assassins jump him. He is alone and he fights back as hard as he can. His sword breaks, and all he has left to defend himself with is his bow. The attackers spear, shoot and slash him in their desperate bid to kill him. At last his own men come to the rescue and slay the three assassins. But by then he is very badly wounded.

So serious are his wounds that he sends for a renowned healer. He is unable to come but sends his disciple. Because the arrow was tipped with poison he is told he must rest for a hundred days, or the wounds will prove fatal.

Now Sun Ce is not a restful man. Far from it. He is always wanting to leap into action and has a terrible temper. For twenty days he manages to rest. Then news comes that Cao

Cao has been told by his adviser Guo Jia not to worry about Sun Ce. It is reported that Guo Jia said, 'He's foolish, never prepares properly and fails to plan in advance.' Sun Ce is incensed by this and swears again that he will storm the capital. Rising from his rest, he starts frantically to plan the attack. Then Chen Zhen arrives from Yuan Shao, offering to combine forces to attack Cao Cao. This delights Sun Ce, who orders a grand feast to celebrate.

Imagine, then, his surprise when, during the feast, men start slipping away, while others whisper to each other. When he asks what is going on, he is told, 'The Immortal Yu is in the marketplace below. Everyone is going out to honour him.'

Looking out of the window, Sun Ce sees a Daoist monk wearing a cloak of crane feathers and resting on a walking stick. All around, people are bowing down, lighting incense and worshipping him. Furious, Sun Ce orders that the priest be brought to him.

His attendants are worried. 'He is very famous and a renowned healer. He is an immortal. Please treat him well.'

'I don't care,' exclaims Sun Ce. 'Seize him and bring him to me.'

When the monk is brought before Sun Ce, he says, 'You fake! You fool people and exploit their ignorance.'

To this Yu the Daoist replies, 'I'm just a poor Daoist monk, that's all. Except, back in the reign of Emperor Shun,[10] I found a sacred book called *Finding the Way of Peace for a Thousand Years*. In fact, it was one hundred volumes in total. And every page taught me how to cure illnesses. Ever since, I have travelled the land healing but have never received anything as a reward.'

'Then where,' asks Sun Ce, 'did you get those clothes? This sounds like the seditious rubbish spouted by Zhang Jue and the Yellow Headbands rebels. You'll therefore be executed.'

Adviser Zhang Zhao immediately springs to the priest's defence. 'He has been active for decades, and no one has had a bad word to say about him. You can't just kill him!'

'I'll kill any of these sorcerers I can, just you watch me!'

Almost every member of his court pleads with Sun Ce to

spare the priest. In the end Sun Ce has him put in prison while he decides what to do.

Even his mother pleads with him, but he ignores her.

Mocking his courtiers as a bunch of fools, he intends to press ahead with the execution. However, someone suggests that they hold a trial of Immortal Yu's powers. 'It is said that Yu can summon rain. We have a drought at the moment. Let's see if he can call down rain from Heaven.'

'Well, all right,' says Sun Ce, and so Yu is brought out from the prison.

The trial is set up the next day. Yu mounts an altar and says, 'By noon I will summon three feet of rain for the benefit of the people.' But he also says he believes that he will still die. 'My time is up,' he says, to the distress of his followers.

When Sun Ce arrives, he orders that if Yu fails he is to be burned to death there and then. Just before noon Sun Ce orders the pyre to be lit, and the flames leap up around Yu. But at that moment a black vapour rises, thunder crashes and lightning flashes. Torrential rain descends, and within minutes the water is indeed three feet deep everywhere. Too much water, in fact! So Yu cries aloud, and the rain stops. All around the pyre, people fall to their knees in veneration and awe. This only inflames Sun Ce's anger even more. 'This is just a fluke. Just good luck that he prayed when it was about to rain. Cut off his head,' he says to a soldier. And without any further ado the soldier's sword flashes, and Yu is immediately beheaded. His body is left, on Sun Ce's orders, to rot in the marketplace as a warning to others.

In the morning, after a stormy night, the body has disappeared. Sun Ce is about to order the execution of the soldiers who were on guard that night when Sun Ce sees Yu walking boldly in front of the main hall. Overcome, Sun Ce collapses and is borne off to his bed. His mother tries to appeal to him to repent, pointing out that his killing of Yu was a terrible crime. But he will not listen and grows even more desperate in his determination to ridicule and dismiss all such spiritual ideas. Eventually he does agree to his mother's plea to go to offer prayers and incense at the local temple. He goes, burns the incense but refuses to pray. Suddenly Yu appears, sitting on top of the incense smoke. Retreating from the temple, Sun Ce suddenly finds Yu in front of him at the gate. Grasping a sword, he hurls it at the ghost. Flying through the air, it hits a soldier, who is killed instantly. This, it turns out, was the soldier who struck off Yu's head the day before.

Sun Ce encounters Yu's spirit again beside the temple so he orders the entire place to be burned to the ground. As the flames leap up, Yu is seen sitting in the midst of them. Time and time again the spirit appears, until Sun Ce is screaming with fear; the experience has left him looking haggard. The final straw is when his mother says he looks terrible. He takes up a mirror, but it is the face of Yu that looks back. With a terrible cry he collapses, and all his wounds open up again.

It is now clear even to Sun Ce that he is dying. Summoning his adviser Zhang Zhao and his younger brother, Sun Quan, he hands over the seal of office to Sun Quan as his heir. 'If there's any internal issues that need resolving,' he advises his mother and brother, 'ask Zhang Zhao. As for external affairs, ask Zhou Yu.' Zhou Yu is not present at this point. Having set his affairs in order, Sun Ce dies. He is twenty-six years old. As a poet has said:

> Ruler of everything to the south,
> Known ironically as 'the little Ruler',
> Crouching like a tiger,
> Poised for flight as a hunting eagle –
> He dominated the land of the Three Rivers,
> His name known and dreaded everywhere.
> However, prevented from finishing his agenda,
> He had to hand over to Zhou Yu.

When Zhou Yu arrives at court he is deeply touched by the role Sun Ce has set for him but hastens to say that he feels he is not worthy of such trust. He recommends that someone he has met recently who has helped provide grain free of charge to the army be invited. This man is Lu Su, renowned for his honesty and virtue. 'I recommend that you invite him immediately to come and join the court and handle affairs. He is a brilliant thinker, planner and military mind. He is also cunning. His father has died, but he attends to his mother with true filial piety. The family is rich but renowned for their generosity to the poor.' So Lu Su is brought to the court.

One night Sun Quan and Lu Su are deep in discussion. 'When I look around me,' says Sun Quan, 'I see the Han are on the brink of complete collapse. I would love to be the one, like the heroes of old, who protects and restores the dynasty. What do you suggest I do?'

To this Lu Su replies, 'The Han's time is over. Cao Cao is in control. You need to strengthen your hold on the south until you can move out and take over the rest of the country. You must plan to create a new dynasty – your own!'

These words excite and delight Sun Quan.

Another adviser joins the court – Zhuge Jin. Following his advice, Sun Quan turns down Yuan Shao's suggestion of an alliance against Cao Cao. Instead he decides to work alongside Cao Cao – but cautiously.

When Cao Cao hears of the death of Sun Ce, his first instinct is to plan an invasion. But he is dissuaded from this when it is pointed out how disreputable this would appear throughout the land. Instead, the recommendation is that Cao Cao ask the emperor to raise the official status of Sun Quan in order to make the new ruler a friend, not a foe.

Chen Zhen returns empty-handed to Yuan Shao. Yuan Shao's response is to summon his army and to plan to attack Xuchang.

So, who is going to win? Cao Cao or Yuan Shao?

Let's find out!

CHAPTER 30

Yuan Shao runs out of food and is defeated.
Cao Cao burns down the granary.

It is a huge army that Yuan Shao leads out and heads towards Guandu. In response Cao Cao can only muster about one-tenth the number, but he sets out too. When news of the scale of Yuan Shao's army reaches Cao Cao his adviser Xun You urges immediate action. 'Our men are veterans and can take on ten of theirs, but our supplies are very limited and will run out quickly if this is a prolonged campaign. Attack now,' he says. Cao Cao concurs with this and so he advances upon Yuan Shao's army.

Confronting each other, Cao Cao and Yuan Shao trade abuse. 'I had the Son of Heaven make you a supreme commander – and now you have turned rebel!' shouts Cao Cao.

'You might pretend to be the prime minister,' replies Yuan Shao, 'but you are nothing but a traitor to the Han. The stink of your crimes even reaches Heaven and you claim I'm the traitor!'

'I have the imperial authority to punish you,' cries Cao Cao, to which Yuan Shao replies, 'And I have the secret imperial command that was hidden in the belt as my authority!'

So battle commences. Champions ride out, but none triumphs, and then the armies clash head on. It is Cao Cao who breaks first and retreats, defeated by the sheer number of the enemy's arrows. He and his men return to camp outside Guandu. In response, Yuan Shao moves his camp to confront them. Here stalemate ensues, despite all sorts of military tactics such as trying to tunnel under Cao Cao's camp and blow them up. This is thwarted by Cao Cao's men digging a deep moat around their camp and thus foiling the enemy plan. The confrontation goes on for month after month.[11] The situation grows more and more desperate, and supplies of food begin to run out on both sides.

One day, Cao Cao's men capture a spy and find out from him that Yuan Shao is expecting a huge convoy of grain wagons within the next few days, led by Commander Han Meng. The decision to attack and destroy this convoy is made, and Xu Huang is given command of the small elite attack force. The surprise attack is a complete success. Han Meng flees, and Xu Huang is able to destroy the entire convoy.

Yuan Shao now becomes seriously concerned about his main supply base at Wuchao. Twenty thousand men are sent under the command of Chunyu Qiong to protect this vital resource. But Chunyu Qiong is a bad choice. He is an alcoholic whose drink-fuelled rages terrify his own men. From the moment he arrives in Wuchao he is drunk.

Now, in a reverse of what happened earlier, one of Cao Cao's messengers is captured by Yuan Shao's men. The letter he carries reveals that Cao Cao is running desperately short of food. It is an old friend of Cao Cao, now on the staff of Yuan Shao, who brings the letter to Yuan Shao. Xu You is his name, and he urges his lord to attack Cao Cao's capital at Xuchang and at the same time attack Cao Cao's camp outside Guandu. 'He is almost out of food, and this is the time to strike.'

But Yuan Shao, ever cautious, suspects a plot. 'Cao Cao is so cunning. I think this letter is a trick.' 'But', says an exasperated Xu You, 'unless we attack now we'll lose this golden opportunity.'

However, Yuan Shao is equally suspicious of Xu You and his past links with Cao Cao. 'You,' he shouts, 'you're part of Cao Cao's plot! I could have you executed now. But instead just get out. Get out!'

Xu You is in despair, viewing Yuan Shao as little more than a fool, and in his anguish he takes up his sword meaning to kill himself. He is restrained by his own men and they say, 'As

Yuan Shao is now doomed to failure, why not cross over and rejoin Cao Cao?'

And this is exactly what he does. So delighted is Cao Cao to hear that his old friend Xu You has come, he rushes out to greet him, not even waiting to put his shoes on. 'Tell me, my old friend, how can we defeat Yuan Shao?'

'First tell me,' says Xu You, 'how much grain do you have?'

'At least a year,' says Cao Cao, whereupon Xu You says, 'Really?'

'Well perhaps more like six months,' confesses Cao Cao, at which Xu You rises, ready to depart, saying, 'I came to you and never expected you would lie to me.'

'I'm sorry, old friend,' says Cao Cao, 'honestly – just three months.'

Xu You smiles and says, 'The world calls you a liar and thief, and now I see why.'

'Ahh,' says Cao Cao, 'warfare is all about subterfuge! We've about a month's worth of supplies.'

'Cut this out!' says Xu You. 'You've actually run out, haven't you?'

'How on earth did you know that?' demands Cao Cao, whereupon Xu You shows the captured letter.

'So what can I do now?' asks Cao Cao.

'Yuan Shao's supplies are all at Wuchao, and that old drunkard Chunyu Qiong is in charge. Lead a crack troop of your men down there. Pretend you are Jiang Qi, who has just been commissioned to protect the supplies. Get inside and destroy the grain. Within three days Yuan Shao's army will have collapsed.'

Dressed in the armour and colours of the enemy, Cao Cao leads his men to Wuchao and attacks in the middle of the night. Chunyu Qiong is, of course, drunk and asleep and is swiftly seized, and the entire supply of grain burned to the ground. Chunyu Qiong's nose, ears and fingers are cut off and he is tied to his horse and despatched back to Yuan Shao as a dreadful warning.

When news of the disaster reaches Yuan Shao, he calls his advisers together. It is Zhang He who offers to go to recapture

Wuchao. But Yuan Shao so fears Cao Cao that he won't order a direct attack. Instead, believing he is still at Wuchao, he orders an attack on the enemy camp at Guandu. Zhang He disagrees, pointing out that Cao Cao is too cunning to leave Guandu unprotected. But Yuan Shao won't listen. So Zhang He is sent with a small force to attack Guandu while Jiang Qi is sent with a larger force to recover the stolen grain.

Jiang Qi and his men are wiped out by Cao Cao's men, but Cao sends a fake report to Yuan Shao, saying that Jiang Qi has triumphed. This leads Yuan Shao to think the grain is secure and to direct his men to attack Guandu alone. Cao Cao has set up a trap. With his men in the camp attacking from the front, he comes up from the rear and catches Zhang He and his men and the additional troops sent by Yuan Shao in a pincer movement.

Zhang He is left deeply disillusioned by Yuan Shao's obstinacy. He is also aware that enemies within Yuan Shao's court are slandering him, saying he has sided with Cao Cao and helped him in his attacks. Given he has nothing to return to at Yuan Shao's camp, he decides to transfer his allegiance and join Cao Cao.

As Xu You notes to Cao Cao, Yuan Shao has lost him and now one of his greatest commanders – Zhang He. 'Now is the time to strike. His men are troubled and fearful.'

Spreading rumours of where they might launch their assault, they make Yuan Shao divide his army and scatter his forces widely in preparation for the supposed attacks. Then Cao Cao drives straight at the main camp. Yuan Shao's men panic and flee. Yuan Shao doesn't even have enough time to put on his armour. Leaping on his horse and abandoning everything, he escapes with his youngest son, Yuan Shang. It is said that upwards of eighty thousand of his men are killed that day. The soil turns red with the blood. Untold numbers drown.

In among the papers abandoned by Yuan Shao, Cao Cao finds many letters from men in his own capital city who were in secret communication with Yuan Shao. Urged by some to kill them all, he says, 'No. To be frank, when Yuan Shao seemed to be the strongest, I wasn't sure whether I would survive. So I can't blame others for hedging their bets.' So he has the letters destroyed, and nothing more is done.

Now Cao Cao orders an all-out attack on Jizhou.

> Overconfident in his strength, he lost;
> Weaker but with better planning he won.

So who will triumph now?

Let's find out.

CHAPTER 31

Cao Cao defeats Yuan Shao. Xuande is in despair but finds refuge with Liu Biao.

Yuan Shao eventually manages to escape from the enemy troops, and soon his shattered forces are regrouping ready to march home to Jizhou.

One night en route to Jizhou, Yuan Shao is disturbed by the sounds of men in distress. Wandering out, he overhears so many men in his army bemoaning the loss of friends, of brothers or fathers and uncles slain in the battle. Deeply touched and troubled, he becomes aware of the suffering of his own men, and even when he reaches safety in Jizhou his heart is distressed. Is there any point in going on?

Soon, however, he is heartened when fresh troops start to arrive from across his domain. At the same time, Cao Cao arrives with his invading army and camps along the river. Somewhat to his surprise, the local people greet him as a hero. When he asks some of the oldest folk in the village near where the camp is why this is, they tell him a strange tale. 'Back in the days of Emperor Huan a yellow star appeared, hovering just above this place here,' they say. 'A well-known astrologer was passing through and told us that this meant that in fifty years' time there would come a worthy man. That was fifty years ago. Sir, we have suffered long under the taxes of Yuan Shao. But you, sir, are known for your benevolence. You bring down the mighty. The defeat of Yuan Shao at Guandu fulfils the astrologer's predictions. So now we, the ordinary people, can look forward to a time of peace.'

Deeply moved by this, Cao Cao says, 'Can I even dare to hope that this might be me?' and he gives orders that the villagers are to be protected. Anyone stealing anything from them is to be executed. While his men are surprised by this order, they obey. This earns Cao Cao and his army the blessing and thanks of the local people.

News comes that Yuan Shao has brought his army of two to three hundred thousand to Cangting. So Cao Cao marches to confront him. After hurling insults at each other the two armies clash, and terrible loss of life ensues. But it is inconclusive. Frustrated by this, Cao Cao and his advisers plan to use a complex set of ambushes – no less than ten in total – to fool and then destroy Yuan Shao's army. They will attack at midnight and draw the enemy into a series of ambushes. Central to this is that most of Cao Cao's men will end up backed up against the river. The plan works well, and as dawn rises Cao Cao shouts to his men who are backed up against the river, 'There's no way out of here! Let every man fight to save his life!' With desperate energy, his men surge forward. As Yuan Shao falls back, ambush after ambush springs into action to confront him. Soon most of his army lie dead on the battlefield or have fled. In despair, Yuan Shao too races away, eventually escaping all the ambushes and pursuits only to collapse upon reaching safety. All he can do now is to send his few remaining commanders to defend the borders of his own land.

Cao Cao rests after his victory, but his respite is short-lived. News reaches him that Xuande is advancing on the capital. He has no option but to head for Xuchang.

Xuande and Cao Cao come face to face at Rang mountain.

Seeing Xuande, Cao Cao shouts, 'You were once my guest and treated with great honour. Is this how you repay such friendship?'

'You say you are the prime minister,' retorts Xuande, 'but you are nothing more to the Han than a traitor. I, being of imperial blood, have been given the order to crush you.' And Xuande then reads aloud from the 'secret belt' decree.

Infuriated by this, Cao Cao gives the order to attack. But it is the attack by Guan Yu and Zhang Fei that settles the outcome. The very ground trembles as the two brothers and their men ride into battle. Cao Cao's men, already tired by their long march, are terrified, and soon the army are fleeing from the battleground back into their fortified camp.

However, Xuande's triumph is short-lived. Despite many attempts to draw the enemy out of their camp, they resolutely remain behind its protecting walls. Worse is to follow. News comes that Runan has been taken by Cao Cao's commander Xiahou Dun. Meanwhile, Zhang Fei, who has been sent to intercept an enemy supply column, is trapped. Xuande finds himself as a result being advanced upon from the front and from the rear. In the chaos that ensues Xuande's men are forced to retreat, and many lose their lives that day. Xuande escapes, but only just. Just as they think they are safe, they round a hill and are confronted by enemy soldiers advancing from many different sides, an ambush set by Zhang He. With less than a thousand men left, with his own family who have been rescued, and fearing that Guan Yu has been captured, Xuande is in despair. He even cries aloud to Heaven and tries to cut his throat, but is prevented by his own men. It is fortunate that they do, for just as all seems lost, Zhao Zilong appears, leading his men. Charging into battle, Zhao Zilong slays men left and right, but even he is soon surrounded and hemmed in by Zhang He's men. At this crucial moment Guan Yu, Guan Ping and Zhou Cang emerge from the hills and attack. Zhang He is forced to retreat, and at last Xuande and his men are able to rest. Guan Yu rides to rescue Zhang Fei from attack, and soon the three brothers are united again.

But bad news continues to come. Cao Cao is hunting for Xuande and is determined to trap him. Hearing this, Xuande orders Sun Qian to take his family to safety while he and his men lead Cao Cao's troops away on what proves in the end to be a wild goose chase for Cao Cao. Xuande has escaped after all.

Resting, Xuande decides that he must speak openly and clearly to his men. 'Dear friends. You all deserve to be the confidants of a mighty ruler. But following me you've ended up here with nothing but sadness. I've nothing. Not even this bit of land where I stand today. You've been misled by me. Go. Go and find a better, more worthy lord to serve.'

His men do not know where to look, they are so embarrassed and saddened.

'Brother,' says Guan Yu, 'don't speak like this. Remember

how the founder of the Han lost battle after battle. But in the end he won and founded a dynasty which has lasted four hundred years. Defeats – victories – these are the natural course of warfare. Don't let this bring you down.'

Sun Qian adds, 'There is a time for victory and a time for defeat, so don't give up. Near here is Jingzhou, and Liu Biao. He too is related to the Han emperor, like you. Why don't we go to him and take refuge there?'

'Why would he want to protect me?' asks Xuande

'Well, let me go and see if he will,' says Sun Qian – and soon he is on his way.

When Sun Qian meets Liu Biao he soon convinces him to offer a fellow defender of the Han refuge. However, not everyone is happy at the decision. His brother-in-law Cai Mao points out that Xuande started serving under Lü Bu; then Cao Cao; then Yuan Shao. 'None of these has he stayed with for long. What does that tell us about him? Bring him here, and Cao Cao will attack us. Instead, execute this messenger and send his head to Cao Cao as a sign of your friendship.'

But Liu Biao refuses and reprimands Cai Mao in front of everyone else. Cai Mao is left nursing a grudge for this humiliation. Soon Xuande is being formally welcomed by Liu Biao, and together they enter the city.

Cao Cao is all for attacking Jingzhou straight away. But his advisers urge him to wait until spring. So it is that in the early months of AD 202 he is ready for war once again. His first target is Yuan Shao. He has now recovered from his collapse after the last great battle and is in turn planning to advance on the capital. When news comes of Cao Cao's own advance and threatened attack on Yuan Shao's capital at Jizhou, Yuan Shao's son Yuan Shang takes command of the army and rides out to confront Cao Cao.

Who is going to win?

Let's find out.

CHAPTER 32

Yuan Shao dies, and Yuan Shang struggles to take Jizhou. Cao Cao plans to flood the river and so capture the north.

Yuan Shao's son Yuan Shang is arrogant and overconfident. As he heads towards Cao Cao's army with his vast horde of soldiers, this arrogance results in a cataclysmic defeat for Yuan Shang outside Jizhou. He only just escapes, and when the news is brought to his father, the shock causes Yuan Shao to collapse with blood pouring from his mouth. With his last breath he makes it clear that his successor is to be this selfsame son Yuan Shang. Then, with blood streaming from his mouth, he dies. A poet has written:

> Descendant of an ancient noble family,
> Proud and falsely confident from his youth,
> Clicking his fingers for heroes to join his botched
>   adventure
> – three thousand of them swelling under his banner.
> No triumph for him, this lamb in a tiger's skin.
> Nothing more than a chicken in phoenix-plume drag!
> And what was the worst thing of all?
> That his was a cursed household, divided by two
>   brothers.

As soon as he is dead, his widow has her son Yuan Shang installed as ruler. She murders her husband's five concubines, even going so far as to mutilate their dead bodies so they cannot follow him into the Underworld. Yuan Shang's only serious rival is his brother Yuan Tan. Fearful of him, when his brother asks for reinforcements to fight Cao Cao, Yuan Shang sends such a pathetically small force it is swiftly wiped out by Cao

Cao's men. Yuan Shang's strategy is to ensure that it is Cao Cao who will kill Yuan Tan.

In the early months of AD 203 Cao Cao goes on the attack again. However, he is unable to take Jizhou and, frustrated, he withdraws. It is then that Guo Jia, his adviser, comes up with a simple but deadly plan. If they can get the two brothers Yuan Shang and his older brother Yuan Tan to really fall out, then this divide and rule would work to their benefit. Yuan Tan is already deeply resentful that he, as the older son, has been passed over by their father on his deathbed. As a result Yuan Tan is easily drawn into conspiracy with Cao Cao.

Yuan Tan is now seeking counsel from his father's adviser, Guo Tu. He recommends inviting his brother Yuan Shang to a banquet. 'Launch your men at his while the feast is going on and kill him!' advises Guo Tu. Against this advice stand others who point out that brothers are like the two arms of a body. 'If you are fighting someone else, you don't cut off one of your arms, now, do you!'

But when Yuan Shang turns up for the banquet it is with fifty thousand men. Realizing his plot has been discovered, Yuan Tan rides out to fight his brother. He is beaten and flees for sanctuary to Pingyuan. Despite gathering more troops to him and attacking his brother once more, Yuan Tan is again defeated and retreats back to Pingyuan. It is at this point that Guo Tu advises him to formally approach Cao Cao for help. This is readily accepted. Cao Cao has realized that the north, the land ruled by the Yuans, is ripe for conquest. The people resent the Yuans; the family is divided and, unlike in the Jingzhou region, the ruling family has no support.

The deal is done. Cao Cao advances, and when Yuan Shang withdraws from besieging Pingyuan, Yuan Tan comes out to give chase, harrying him from behind. But deceit and conspiracy are in the air. Cao Cao and Yuan Tan plot against each other until Cao Cao decides that Yuan Tan's usefulness is at an end. Meanwhile, the struggle for the north sways backwards and forwards between Yuan Shang and Cao Cao. Cities fall and armies are routed until once again Cao Cao stands before the closed gates of Jizhou. Determined not to be stopped again, he turns to a simple strategy. He diverts the River Zhang and floods the city. However, he gives strict instructions that no members of the Yuan clan are to be hurt. The city falls.

Cao Cao's eighteen-year-old son Cao Pi is part of the invading army. At his birth a purple cloud surrounded him, and this was interpreted as meaning he would be an emperor. At eight he was skilled in composing literary works. Now eighteen, he is renowned for his widespread knowledge of things ancient and modern, for being a skilled horseman and sword fighter.

Cao Pi arrives at the home of Yuan Shao and, despite the best efforts of the guards set there to protect the family, he pushes his way in. There are two women clinging to each other and weeping, and Cao Pi decides he will kill them both.

What will become of them?

Let's find out.

CHAPTER 33

Cao Pi seizes his moment to find a wife.
Yuan Tan is killed.

With his sword drawn, he advances upon the two women, but suddenly a bright light flashes before his eyes. Stunned, he asks:

'Who are you?'

'I was the wife of Yuan Shao,' replies Lady Liu.

'And who is this?' demands Cao Pi.

'This is Lady Zhen,' says Lady Liu, 'wife of Yuan Shao's second son, Yuan Xi.'

Cao Pi lifts the distraught woman up and, brushing her hair away from her face, he sees that she is of extraordinary beauty. Her face is like jade, her skin like a newly blooming flower – a beauty which could overthrow kingdoms.

Amazed by her beauty, he immediately offers to protect her, and in honour of his protecting them, his father agrees that this beautiful woman is ideal for his son. With his approval they marry shortly afterwards.

Cao Cao proves to be a benevolent ruler of Jizhou. He honours the tombs and shrines of the Yuan family and relieves the people all across Hebei Province of paying taxes for a whole year. He says it is because they have suffered so much during the wars. He also tries to bring in the best advisers to help him run the region.

It doesn't take long for Yuan Tan to prove as unreliable to Cao Cao as he was to his own brother, Yuan Shang. Yuan Tan has rallied his brother's men and is preparing for war against Cao Cao. Meanwhile Yuan Shang, shocked by his own failure, has no heart for battle and takes refuge with his other brother, Yuan Xi. Cao Cao advances against Yuan Tan, who in desperation seeks to create an alliance with Liu Biao. Liu Biao has no great desire to be supporting what is clearly a collapsing Yuan family against the rising power of Cao Cao. At the suggestion of Xuande, Liu Biao uses Cao Cao's own trick of divide and rule. Through an exchange of fake letters, Yuan Tan is encouraged to be reconciled with his brother while Yuan Shang is told that he needs his brother's support to oppose Cao Cao. Cao Cao is furious with what he sees as the betrayal of Yuan Tan and besieges him in the city of Nanpi. In an attempt to escape, Guo Tu advises Yuan Tan to force the civilian population out and to then ride through them to safety. But he is cut down by one of Cao Cao's cousins, Cao Hong, while Guo Tu is also spotted and killed.

After the fall of the city, Cao Cao has Yuan Tan's head cut off and exposed. He gives orders that no one should mourn his death. However, one man does. When he is arrested and questioned he says he served under Yuan Tan when he was in charge of Qingzhou. He left Yuan Tan's service because he told him publicly that he disapproved of the way he ran things. But he still feels that he should pay his respects. Cao Cao has ordered that anyone disobeying his order not to mourn should be executed. But moved by the true sense of loyalty and honour that this man shows, he pardons him and even gives him a post in his new administration.

With Yuan Tan dead and buried, it is not long before the other brothers, Yuan Shang and Yuan Xi, are tracked down. They have escaped to the desert in a desperate bid for freedom. Cao Cao is determined to go after them, even though it means entering such barren lands and encountering hostile local tribes. This becomes even worse when, with war still raging in this hostile environment, winter comes.

Meanwhile the two Yuan brothers have taken refuge even further into this strange land and have come to the prefect of Liaodong for sanctuary. He, alarmed at the thought of becoming Cao Cao's enemy, has the two brothers murdered and their heads sent to Cao Cao.

So it is that the rule of the Yuans ends for ever.

Having conquered the north, Cao Cao can now start to plan his assault on the south.

One night, standing in a tower on the wall of Jizhou with Xun You beside him, he sees a golden light shining out of the ground. 'That can only mean treasure is buried there,' says Xun You. Cao Cao gives orders for the spot to be excavated.

So what is it that is found?

Let's find out.

CHAPTER 34

Lady Cai eavesdrops on a secret.
Xuande and horse leap a river.

It is a bronze statue of a bird. Xun You comments, 'In time past the miraculous appearance of a bird statue was always an auspicious sign.' Very pleased with such a Heavenly signal of his rise to power, Cao Cao orders a special tower to be built on the site – to be known as the Bronze Bird Tower. On the advice of his son, the poet Cao Zhi, three towers are built. The one on the left is called Jade Dragon, the one on the right Golden Phoenix, and the tower in the middle is called the Bronze Bird. This, Cao Cao decides, is where he will spend his later years.

Xuande, his two brothers and Zhao Zilong join up with the forces of Liu Biao at Jingzhou, and there they help him quash a local rebellion. The three brothers even offer to help defeat invaders from further south such as the Viets and to ward off attacks from Zhang Lu in the west and from Sun Quan. However, Lady Cai's brother Cai Mao in particular resents Xuande's rising status and power. Going to his sister, Liu Biao's wife, Lady Cai, he persuades her to whisper rumours about the loyalty of Xuande and his friends into the ear of her husband. As a result of these doubts, Liu Biao decides to remove Xuande and his men from the city. Instead he offers Xuande command of the city and region around Xinye.

Xuande agrees to go to defend the city of Xinye, and it is here that his son Liu Shan is born to his wife, Lady Gan, in the spring of AD 207. Auspicious signs herald the birth of Liu Shan. On the night of his birth, a white crane lands on the roof and sings before flying west. And Lady Gan dreams that she has swallowed the stars of the Northern Dipper, and that this is why she conceived.

To Xuande's great frustration, Liu Biao refuses to exploit Cao Cao's attention being taken up with battles in the north. 'We could easily capture his capital,' says Xuande. But Liu Biao replies, 'I am happy with the lands I have. What would I do with more?' Then he turns to Xuande, saying, 'I've something troubling me. I would like your opinion.' But before he can unburden himself, Lady Cai appears, and the conversation stops.

Late in the year, in deep winter, Xuande is summoned to Jingzhou to see Liu Biao. He now regrets that he ignored Xuande's advice. 'I should have attacked Cao Cao's capital when I had the chance. That's gone now, and I'm sorry not to have listened to you.'

'Trust me,' says Xuande, 'the whole country is falling apart. There will be many other opportunities. What we need to do is seize the moment, not dwell on regrets.' And so they sit, get drunk and start to share confidences. Liu Biao asks Xuande's advice about his two sons, offspring of different wives. Xuande warns Liu Biao to simply follow ancient precedent and make the elder of the two his heir, even though he is the weaker of them. To this Liu Biao raises the problem of the clan of his second son and his ambitious mother.

Xuande recommends gradually cutting back the power of the clan of Lady Cai so they are no longer able to seize power. Unfortunately Lady Cai is eavesdropping and hears all this, and a terrible anger against Xuande arises within her. She starts to seriously undermine Liu Biao's confidence in Xuande while at the same time urging her brother Cai Mao to go and kill Xuande. Forewarned, Xuande rides out before the break of day and returns to Xinye.

Cai Mao, furious that Xuande has escaped, fakes a slanderous poem, which he writes on the wall of Xuande's room. He then claims it was written by Xuande. This seditious poem is enough to seriously trouble Liu Biao into wondering if Xuande is a traitor. So incensed is he that he shouts, 'I'll kill him!' The poem says:

Why have I spent so bloody long wasting my time away?
Gazing out day after day at the same view.

A dragon should never be trapped in a pond,
He should be riding to Heaven on the air-waves of thunder.

However, Liu Biao pauses. He cannot recall Xuande ever writing poetry so is suddenly much more cautious. As a result, he holds back from authorizing the murder of Xuande.

However, undaunted by the failure of his poem plot, Cai Mao plans to bring Xuande back to Jingzhou in order to kill him. He is to be lured back by suggesting a celebration of the good harvests that have taken place. When the invitation arrives, Xuande agrees to go, despite the warnings of Zhao Zilong and Sun Qian.

At the banquet he is secretly warned to flee as Cai Mao plans to kill him that very evening. Saying he has to go to the toilet, Xuande slips away, mounts his horse and dashes through the city gate and away. As soon as Cai Mao hears this, he sets off in pursuit with five hundred men.

Xuande is riding hard but comes up against a broad, fast-flowing river, the Tan. Turning around, he sees the cloud of dust raised by the pursuing troops. In despair Xuande has no option but to trust to his horse to ford the river. This horse, whom many have claimed was cursed because of strange markings on his face, is able to heroically leap through the waters, struggle out of the grip of the mud on the far side and bring Xuande safely to the far bank.

The poet Su Dong Po wrote this poem:

I'm growing old, the leaves drift from the trees;
I journey, on official business, by the Tan river.
Halting my carriage, I get out and walk beside it.
Catkins glisten, stirred by the wind:
I see the dying virtue of the Great Yang!
How dragon fought tiger; and tiger, dragon.
At Xiangyang, the nobles gathered round their king,
And among them Xuande, as if doomed to die.
But he rides for his life out of the western gate,
Escaping, but soon he is, pursued with a vengeance.
He's stopped by water, the water of the Tan.
The enemy ploughs on, intent on his death:

'Go!' he shouts at his faithful horse –
Heaven's whip-like golden wind urging him on.
The sound of a thousand horsemen clattering behind him.
And into the thick of it, these two dash like dragons:

The one, born to rule the west,
The other, for this dragon horse to bear him.
The Tan's waters race, streaming eastwards . . .
Dragon horse and brave warrior, ah, where are they now?
I'm standing by the riverbank, perplexed,
As the sun's last rays light on the hills.
Was it just a dream, these Three Kingdoms?
What will it be for the future . . . just a dissolving memory?

On the other side of the river, Cai Mao rides up and shouts, 'My lord, why did you leave us so suddenly?'

'Why did you want to kill me?' answers Xuande.

'A misunderstanding. That's all,' replies Cai Mao.

Then Xuande notices that as he speaks Cai Mao is reaching for his bow and arrow. Turning his horse, Xuande rides off swiftly. It is then that Cai Mao hears the sound of thundering horses drawing near. It is Zhao Zilong, racing towards him with three hundred men.

Will Cai Mao survive?

Let's find out.

秦瓊

CHAPTER 35

Xuande encounters a hermit.
Xuande starts to search for a master.

Zhao Zilong is searching for his lord and as yet has no idea of the tricks Cai Mao has tried to play. Riding up to Cai Mao, he asks him where Xuande is. Cai Mao says he has no idea and in fact has ridden out to try to find him. Zhao Zilong rides to the edge of the river and can see the marks where a horse has tried to cross. He cannot believe that Xuande has actually managed to jump such a vast and swift-flowing river. But enough unanswered questions arise in Zhao Zilong that, despite the best efforts of Cai Mao to reassure him, he takes his men away from the city and back to Xinye.

Convinced that it was by the Will of Heaven that he escaped, Xuande rides on, deeply troubled by all that has happened. As the evening draws on, he comes upon a young ox-herder riding an ox and playing a flute. Such a simple, peaceful scene moves Xuande deeply.

'How I wish my life was like this!' he muses as the young lad brings the ox to a halt and stares at Xuande.

'I think you're General Xuande, who defeated the Yellow Headband rebels!' he says, to which Xuande replies, 'How's it possible that a young country dweller like you knows who I am?'

The boy tells him that while looking after his master's guests they often talk about Xuande and what he looks like – that is how he knew who he is.

'And who is your master?' enquires Xuande.

'He is Sima Hui Decao and goes by the Daoist name of Master Tranquil Water,' replies the boy. Xuande asks to meet him, and together they go the two miles to a farm.

The sound of someone playing a flute greets them as they

ride in. Master Tranquil Water senses through a change in the music that some great warrior has arrived and stops playing his flute to come and greet him. Xuande is astonished when Master Tranquil Water mentions that Xuande has just had a lucky escape and invites the weary Xuande inside.

What a place of tranquillity! Inspired and at ease, Xuande pours out his troubles to the master.

'Your problem,' says the master, 'is that you've yet to find the right kind of men to help you.'

To this Xuande replies, 'I do appreciate that I'm far from worthy, but I've lots of good men to help me. Men like Sun Qian, Mi Zhu, Jian Yong and soldiers like Guan Yu, Zhang Fei and Zhao Zilong. These are all good men.'

'Very true,' Master Tranquil Water replies. 'These are indeed fine warriors, but you have no one who can help you make best use of them. And the bureaucrats that surround you are useless, incapable of dealing with the sheer complexity of modern life in these difficult times.'

'I do realize I need a more worthy person to assist me, but so far I have had no luck in finding one,' replies Xuande.

'Do not forget what Kong Fu Zi says,' comments the master, 'that even in a hamlet of just ten households you'll still manage to find one person who is loyal. Don't give up hope. Heaven's Mandate is given when the time is right, and the dragon trapped in mud is able to soar to Heaven again. That's you, general.'

'Can I even think of such a thing?' asks a troubled Xuande.

To which the master replies that in this region there are the greatest experts to be found anywhere in the country and that Xuande should go searching for them.

'But where do I go to find them?' asks a perplexed Xuande.

The master replies, 'They are called Hidden Dragon and Youthful Phoenix, and either of them could help you to run the country and re-establish peace.' Xuande, still troubled, asks again, 'But where can I find them, and who exactly are they?'

'Excellent, very good indeed,' replies the master to the total confusion of Xuande. 'We can discuss this further in the morning,' he continues, and with that they all retire for the night.

Late that night, Xuande awakes, disturbed by the sound of

a visitor to the master. He hears the two of them discussing why the visitor has given up trying to collaborate with Liu Biao.

'I'd heard,' says the visitor, 'that Liu Biao was a man of discernment, treating both the virtuous and the false as they justly deserve. But I'm sorry to say this is not so. It's true he favours the virtuous but he never makes real use of them to govern. Meanwhile, he may be able to discern the false but somehow he never actually gets rid of them. So I gave up and have come here.'

'You have such talent,' Xuande hears the master say. 'Don't waste it on a no-hoper like Liu Biao. Now we happen to have a real leader here with us tonight!' And with that the conversation fades away, and Xuande is unable to overhear anything further. Xuande thinks to himself that this must be either Hidden Dragon or Youthful Phoenix, but, being too polite to interrupt, he goes back to sleep.

The next morning Xuande asks who the visitor was the previous night, but Master Tranquil Water simply says again, 'Excellent, very good indeed.' And when Xuande asks the master to come and work with him, the master gives him short shrift: 'I'm happy to be without worries, and there are many people who're ten times better than me!' When Xuande asks who they might be, the master simply says again, 'Excellent, very good indeed!'

While they are talking, Zhao Zilong and his troop clatter into the courtyard of the farm. They have been looking everywhere for Xuande after the near-disaster of the dinner. In the midst of a happy reunion, Zhao Zilong tells Xuande that he must hurry back to Xinye, as fighting is about to erupt there. Taking a fond farewell of the master, they ride off and en route to their delight meet up with Guan Yu and Zhang Fei.

Soon after getting back to Xinye and being reunited with his band of warriors, Xuande is passing through the marketplace and hears a man dressed in simple clothes singing this song:

> Heaven and Earth are upside down – oh my god!
> The heat has gone out of the fire.

A great house is shaken . . . heavens!
One spring beam alone can't sustain it.

Somewhere in the valley is a man who can help – my goodness,
waiting for the right leader to appear.

But the one who's looking doesn't know him – do you see?
He doesn't even know me!

Convinced that this man must be one of the two masters he has just heard about, he stops him and asks his name. 'I am Shan Fu,' replies the strange man, 'and I've come seeking you but didn't know how to attract your attention – hence the song!'

Soon the two are boon companions, and Shan Fu is deeply impressed by the virtuous way Xuande rules and his real compassion for the ordinary people. When Cao Cao decides to attack Xuande and sends his cousin Cao Ren to oversee taking Xinye and capturing Xuande, it is Shan Fu whose advice Xuande follows.

Despite being foiled time and time again, Cao Ren decides to mount a major invasion across the River Yu in order to seize Xinye.

So who is going to win?

Let's find out.

CHAPTER 36

Xuande plots to seize Fancheng.
Xu Shu reads a fake letter and leaves,
but suggests Kong Ming to Xuande.

Cao Ren has decided to match the military skills of Xuande by using a highly specialized military tactic: the Eight Gates. This very complex attack-and-defend system is the pride of Cao Ren's strategy. So much so, he even challenges Xuande to look at how clever he is!

However, he has not taken into account Shan Fu. He is able to advise Xuande on how to foil the clever strategy of the Eight Gates by attacking from a specific angle. Zhao Zilong, leading five hundred picked warriors, carries out this out, and Cao Ren is soon fleeing from the battle. Too late he realizes that Xuande has found a formidable military genius to join his forces. He decides on a night attack to try to seize the initiative. But Shan Fu has already guessed he might try this, and so, when Cao Ren and his men attack, they are ambushed, and Cao Ren only just escapes with his life. He struggles back to Xuchang having lost most of his army. As a result, Xuande captures the enemy city of Fan.

When the defeated Cao Ren comes before Cao Cao, they discuss who this military genius might be. Cheng Yu says, 'He is known as Shan Fu, but that's not his real name. When young he was a skilled fencer, but one day many years ago he killed someone – to right a wrong – and he had to flee. When he was captured he refused to give his name. His captors even had him tied up and paraded through the streets to ask if anyone knew who he was. But not a soul answered! Not long after, his friends freed him, and he again fled. He became a scholar and travelled the land, visiting the great masters. His real name is Xu Shu.'

'This Shan Fu. Is he any good – say, in comparison to you?' asks Cao Cao.

'Ten times better, frankly.'

Cao Cao then to decides to lure Shan Fu over to his side.

'I know what we can do,' says Cheng Yu. 'His mother, to whom he is devoted, lives all alone – she only has Shan Fu. Let's bring her here and fool her into writing to Shan Fu to come and join her. So filial is he, he will come straight away!'

So Cao Cao has her brought to the capital and effectively placed under house arrest. She is fiery and scornful of Cao Cao, once even hitting him with an ink stone. He very nearly has her killed there and then, but Cheng Yu persuades him to spare her. 'She is just trying to be killed so that you become for ever a wicked man!' he says. 'Kill her, and her son will be your enemy for ever. Look after her, and he must come to see her soon.'

Swallowing his pride, Cao Cao pretends to dote on the old woman and by these means is able to secure a few examples of her handwriting. Then he has a letter forged and sent to Shan Fu. The letter claims to come from his distressed mother. The fake letter does the trick, for when Shan Fu reads the sad letter he immediately knows he has to leave Xuande and go to care for her.

Xuande is in despair at the loss of his invaluable adviser. But because it is for good, filial reasons he can't challenge it. Just before Shan Fu rides off he advises Xuande that there is someone ten times greater than he is, who could be Xuande's adviser. However, he warns Xuande that this man is not the kind of person who can be easily summoned.

'In terms of his wisdom and virtue, what is he like in comparison to you?' asks Xuande, to which Shan Fu replies, 'Can you compare a plodding carthorse to a qilin[12] or a crow to a phoenix? This man can measure Heaven itself and encompass the earth. There is simply no one else like him anywhere in the world.'

'And his name is . . . ?'

'He comes from Yangdu in Langye. His family name is Zhuge, and his given name Liang. However, he is known as Kong Ming,' Shan Fu tells him. 'He came to this area of Jingzhou because his uncle was a friend of Liu Biao. But the uncle died, so he and his younger brother Jun moved to a farm near Nanyang. He likes to write poetry in the style of the "Poem of Liangfu Mountain". On their farm there is a hill called Sleeping Dragon, and this is why he has now named himself Master Sleeping Dragon! Go and see him immediately and if you're lucky enough to have him join you, you need never worry again!'

As he rides away from Xuande on the long road to the capital, Shan Fu suddenly realizes that he may have been a bit forward in suggesting Kong Ming to Xuande without consulting him. So he calls on his friend en route to the capital.

When Kong Ming hears what Shan Fu has done, he is indignant.

'What am I? Some kind of sacrifice for the altar?' Greatly upset, he turns and walks away. Shan Fu climbs back on to his horse and leaves, deeply embarrassed and worried about what he might have done.

Troubled in his heart, Shan Fu rides on to the capital, uncertain of what the future might bring.

So what will happen next?

Let's find out.

CHAPTER 37

Sima Hui recommends Kong Ming.
Xuande tries to see him three times.

When Shan Fu arrives at the capital, he goes immediately to see Cao Cao, who assures him that he can have whatever he needs to care for his mother. However, when Shan Fu appears before his mother she is incandescent with rage and without pity vents her anger upon her son.

'You wretched, worthless son!' she cries. 'You spent years just wandering around, and I'd hoped this might mean you'd learned something! But truth be told, you're stupider than before. Have you read nothing? Don't you know that loyalty and filial piety are often in opposition?' Exasperated, she says, 'Surely even you can see that Cao Cao is a traitor? He scorns not only the emperor but everyone around him, whereas Xuande is a man of virtue. The whole world knows this! As a member of the Han family he was someone worthy of your service. Yet all it took was a forged document, and here you are having made no attempt whatsoever to find out if it was true or not. As a result you have left the light and descended into darkness. You're a disgrace. What a fool. I'm so ashamed I can't even bear to look at you. You've ruined the good name of your family, and I wish you had never been born.'

At this Shan Fu falls to the ground and lies at her feet in a position of complete submission. But she leaves, and Shan Fu is left utterly humiliated. He lies stretched out in supplication upon the floor, unable to rise. It is only when a servant rushes in distraught that he looks up. 'Sir, you mother has hanged herself!' Overwhelmed with fear and dread, he rushes to her room, but it is too late. The heroic old lady is dead.

Back in his city, Xuande is feeling the lack of an adviser. He remembers Shan Fu's recommendation, and decides to track down this Kong Ming, the Sleeping Dragon. So with his two brothers to escort him he sets off towards the Sleeping Dragon hill he has been told about. And as they draw near they hear some peasants in the fields singing a song:

So azure the vault of heaven,
The earth mapped like a chessboard.

Generations pass here;
Some they rise, some fall.

The winners have all they need,
The losers, nothing but trouble.

Hidden in Nanyang is a man
who sleeps safe and sound – or does he?

The three brothers ask the singers who this song is about. 'It's Master Sleeping Dragon, of course!' says one. And when they ask where he is to be found, the peasants point south.

At last they come upon the hill and its valley. Both seem as if they are wrapped in a mystic air of great beauty. They ride up to the door of a simple rural hut, and a young man appears in the doorway.

'Who are you?' asks the young man, to which Xuande replies, giving all his formal titles: 'I am Liu Bei Xuande, general commander of the Han empire, lord of Yicheng, prefect of Yuzhou, uncle of his majesty the emperor and I have come to greet your master.'

'Well,' says the young man, 'there is no way I can remember all that lot.'

Humbled, Xuande says, 'Then just say to the master that Xuande came calling.'

'He went away this morning,' replies the young man.

'When do you expect him back?'

'Who knows? Maybe in three days or maybe five days,' he says. 'Or possibly ten.'

Xuande is deeply disappointed and asks the young man to tell Master Sleeping Dragon that Xuande has called and, mounting his horse, he rides off. But before he leaves this peaceful scene completely, he turns back to look at it once more. The little hut in the wood; the hills, small but delightful; the streams modest but as clear as crystal; the landscape not grand but graceful and flowing; and the woods likewise simple, but glorious. Here, he thinks, all creatures live in harmony. It is a scene of perfect peace.

Then Xuande sees a man walking down towards them and riding up asks if this man might be Master Sleeping Dragon?

He is not.

But while he is not Master Sleeping Dragon, it turns out he is a friend of the master. He is Cui Zhou Ping and naturally he asks who Xuande is and why he wants to see the master.

After Xuande introduces himself, he tells the stranger that he wants to seek the help of Master Sleeping Dragon because the empire is torn apart by trouble and he wishes to bring peace and order to the land.

'You're a thoughtful and kind man,' says Cui Zhou Ping, 'seeking to bring peace and order to the land, but let's be frank. Ever since time began, the world has swung between order and chaos. Just think,' he adds. 'Ever since the uprising which overthrew the evil Qin dynasty and the Han dynasty emerged, it has been order replacing chaos. For two hundred years all was well until Wang Mang rebelled, and the world descended into chaos. The overthrow of Wang Mang brought order once again. Now that another two hundred years of peace have passed, it's inevitable that chaos is going to come once again.'

Sighing he continues. 'We're living right now in the time of great transition when order breaks down and chaos arises. Warfare is erupting in all four quarters of the world. You just have to bear with this. To think you can restore peace at a time like this – well it's nothing more than an illusion. The time isn't yet right. So now you're seeking Kong Ming, hoping to persuade him to reform and repair time and the very seasons. You're probably even hoping that he's going to rebalance the universe! But you have to be aware that this is not possible, and to try to do so will just wear you out. As you know, those who go with the flow of Heaven will find all works well for them. Those who struggle against it have no rest. Whatever fate has in store will be – there is nothing that can stop that!'

'What you say isn't just true but wise as well,' replies Xuande, 'but I'm of the House of Han, and therefore my destiny is that I must struggle to restore the dynasty regardless of what fate might finally decide.'

'I'm only a simple country bumpkin with little knowledge of the affairs of state,' replies Cui Zhou Ping. 'Perhaps I should have remained silent.'

'Not at all,' says Xuande. 'But I don't suppose you know where Master Sleeping Dragon is right now?'

When it becomes clear that Cui does not know, the three brothers mount their horses once again and ride off. Zhang Fei is less than impressed, pointing out that not only did they not find Kong Ming but they had to listen to the wild ranting of a lunatic!

A few days later, news comes that Kong Ming has returned, and so once again Xuande sets off with his two friends. Zhang Fei asks why on earth Xuande doesn't just order this chap to come to him. But he is silenced by Xuande, who more profoundly understands the nature of the person they are dealing with.

By now the weather has taken a turn for the worse, and it is bitterly cold. Just before dusk it starts to snow. This does nothing to improve Zhang Fei's mood. 'This isn't even weather for warfare, yet here we are heading into the storm to see some useless fellow. This is pointless, so why don't we just get back to the warmth of the city?'

But Xuande is determined, so, despite the terrible weather, they ride on.

At long last they arrive at the simple hut, and when Xuande asks if the master has returned, imagine his delight to be told he is reading in his room.

However, he is to be disappointed once again, for this is not Kong Ming. Instead it is his brother, Zhuge Jun. There are three brothers, of whom the eldest, Zhuge Jin, is working with

Sun Quan; Zhuge Liang – Kong Ming – is the second brother and Zhuge Jun is the third and youngest.

Zhang Fei is once again less than impressed, to put it mildly, and urges Xuande to leave now to get back to the warmth of the city. But, before leaving, Xuande writes a letter for Kong Ming. In this he politely points out that twice now he has tried to see him in the hope that he will help him restore the honour of the House of Han. He then says that he will try one more time to see him.

So the three brothers return to Xinye, and it is many months before they can travel out again on this quest – almost springtime in fact. Selecting an auspicious day, and after ritually fasting for three days and bathing, Xuande gets ready to go. His two brothers decide they must try to persuade him not to bother.

Are they successful?

Let's find out.

CHAPTER 38

Kong Ming reveals the truth about the three kingdoms. Sun Quan prepares to avenge his father.

Try as they might to dissuade Xuande, he recites precedent after precedent from history to show that the greatest heroes of China's past have gone humbly, often many times, before being able to speak to great sages. The disgust of Zhang Fei in particular at all this sentimental rubbish is clear, but Xuande warns him to be on his best behaviour.

So they go off and before long stand once again in front of the door of the simple hut. Imagine Xuande's delight to be told that Kong Ming is asleep within. He enters the hut and stands deferentially at the foot of the bed. Kong Ming sleeps on hour after hour, while Zhang Fei in particular grows more and more annoyed, even threatening to set fire to the back of the hut to wake the sleeper up! But Xuande silences him.

At long last Kong Ming awakes and from his sleepy state mutters:

Does anyone have any idea what fate has in store?
But I know, and have known all my life
That there will come a day when all this will be left behind
And I will leave this refuge . . . for trouble and strife.

Turning to his assistant, Kong Ming says, 'While I slept, have there been any visitors?' to which the lad replies that Xuande, the uncle of the emperor, came and has been waiting for quite some time. 'Why didn't you wake me?' retorts an annoyed Kong Ming. 'He is very important, so I must go and change into appropriate clothes.'

When Kong Ming appears, Xuande is truly impressed

because he looks like such a gentleman. He is tall, with a complexion like jade, and is dressed in a long cloak of crane feathers; his head is bound with a silk scarf. To be honest, he looks like a god or an immortal. Bowing deeply, Xuande says, 'I'm one of the last surviving members of the House of Han, a nobody, but I've heard tell of your fame for so long. I've in fact tried to see you on two previous occasions, but without success. Last time I left a message for you. Did you by any chance see that?'

Kong Ming apologizes profusely and then reveals he has indeed read Xuande's note. 'I do so appreciate the depth of your passion for the country and its people,' he says, 'but I'm young and ignorant – so really not the kind of person you need.' Even when Xuande points out that wise sages have recommended Kong Ming, he replies that he is nothing more than a farmer. 'Why come to me, just a little ordinary stone, when you have already found the jade?'

To this Xuande replies, 'I'm sorry but I really cannot believe that you want to spend the rest of your life hidden away when everything under Heaven needs the wisdom of your guidance. Please help me. Teach me.'

When Kong Ming asks what he really wants, Xuande replies, 'The Han are collapsing; their authority has been usurped by evil ministers. Although I'm weak, I want the land to be ruled by justice. But through my own fault, I've failed thus far. You, sir, can help me – teach me. There is nothing greater that I desire.'

'The rot started with that appalling rebel Dong Zhuo,' says Kong Ming. 'Now, in the north there is Cao Cao. True, not as strong as Yuan Shao but by cunning he's overcome him. He not only has a vast army of over a million but control over the Son of Heaven, the emperor. With that comes the allegiance of many nobles. He, you cannot oppose.

'To the south of the river we've Sun Quan, whose family have ruled there for three generations. While not so strong, he does have the support of the people, and therefore you should view him as a potential ally, not as a foe.

'Now, it's Jingzhou ruled by Liu Biao that you need to focus on. This is the place where the future will be decided. I've nothing against the current ruler, but the Will of Heaven has decreed that it's yours for the taking, even if you have failed to recognize this or act upon it.

'Turning to Yizhou, we find another key territory, vast and bounteous, a favourite of Heaven, and let's not forget that it was from here that the founder of the Han came. Its ruler, Liu Zhang, is not only stupid but also weak, for despite the wealth and skills of his people he's no idea whatsoever how to control them, and they in return long for a wise ruler. With your reputation as a member of the imperial family, your proven valour and the many heroes who've flocked to your banner as well as your honouring of the sages, you should find it easy to take this city.'

Kong Ming then sets out with whom, where and through which alliances Xuande needs to plan in order to take control across the land. He tells him that, in doing so, 'You'll be the hero of the ordinary people.' Using a map, he points out how Xuande needs to make Jingzhou his base in order to move forward with his plans.

Xuande expresses his profound gratitude. But while he is grateful for all this advice, he has to raise the fact that there is a fundamental problem. Both Liu Biao in Jingzhou and Liu Zhang in Yizhou are also members of the imperial house of Han. As they are kin – he cannot attack or usurp them. But Kong Ming assures him that Liu Biao has not long to live – his fortune is in the stars. As for Liu Zhang, he is not ambitious so will be willing to work under Xuande.

After hearing this advice and wisdom, Xuande again pleads with Kong Ming to come and work with him. Once again Kong Ming refuses, saying he likes his rural solitude. At this Xuande bursts into tears and asks, 'But what will become of the people?' and tears rolled down his face. Confronted with such sincerity, Kong Ming gives in and agrees to join Xuande.

The first piece of advice he gives Xuande is that, as Cao Cao is training his men in naval warfare, he must be preparing an invasion of the south by river.

In the south, Sun Quan is busy consolidating his position

even as Cao Cao makes demands such as that Sun Quan's son should come to the imperial court to 'serve' the emperor – in fact to be a hostage in the grip of Cao Cao. Sun Quan refuses, and the path to war is opened.

So what happens next?

Let's find out.

CHAPTER 39

Liu Qi asks three times for help. Kong Ming commands his first battle at Bowang.

Sun Quan's first objective is to avenge his father by attacking Huang Zu, whose warfare led to Sun Jian's death. He also plans to take Xiakou. The battle is hard fought, but it soon becomes clear that Xiakou will fall. This forces Huang Zu to flee. He has not gone far when he finds the road blocked. Gan Ning bars his way. 'I was kind to you in the past, so why are you attacking me now?' asks Huang Zu.

'I worked hard for you, but you treated me as if I were a thief,' replies Gan Ning.

Huang Zu suddenly turns and flees, and Gan Ning rides after him. Fitting an arrow to his bow he shoots Huang Zu, bringing him down from his horse. Dismounting, Gan Ning cuts off Huang Zu's head. This he brings in a box as a trophy to Sun Quan, who has it taken and offered at the tomb of his father.

Knowing that Liu Biao will come to avenge the death of Huang Zu, Sun Quan consolidates his forces to the north. It is vital now to prepare for the attack on the south from Cao Cao.

Back at Xuande's base, news is brought of the death of Huang Zu. 'I am not surprised,' says Kong Ming, 'for he was a harsh master, and his men didn't trust him.'

As he is speaking, Liu Qi, the eldest son of Liu Biao, arrives and asks to speak with Kong Ming and Xuande.

'My life is in danger,' he says. 'My stepmother Lady Cai wants to kill me. Please, Imperial Uncle, can you help me?'

After this first, frankly rather embarrassing meeting with its unexpected and unwelcome request, both Xuande and Kong Ming try to avoid either meeting or helping the young man.

But his sheer persistence overcomes them, and eventually Kong Ming gives him the following advice. 'Get away from your stepmother and from her son. Ask to be sent to Jiangxia to take over protecting the area now Huang Zu is dead. That way, you will be beyond the evil reach of your stepmother.'

When Liu Biao asks Xuande's advice as to whether to let his eldest son go to Jiangxia, he, of course, says he thinks it is a very good idea. And so Liu Qi escapes the machinations of the court.

Now, it is no secret that Guan Yu and Zhang Fei are very unhappy at Xuande choosing Kong Ming as his adviser. This troubles Kong Ming, who asks Xuande to give him the insignia of authority – a sword and seal. This will show that Kong Ming has the authority to command. Cao Cao's army of over one hundred thousand soldiers are advancing upon Xinye, and this is going to be the first test of Kong Ming's skills. Zhang Fei and Guan Yu reluctantly agree to collaborate with him, just to see if he is any good. To be honest, they rather hope he will fail!

Kong Ming issues his orders, sending Guan Yu to hide his troops in the hills around Bowang with orders to let the invaders pass. When he sees flames rising he is to attack the rearguard and the supply train. Zhang Fei is to hide in the valleys behind the forest and to watch also for the flames and then attack the army stores at Bowang. Two commanders are told to collect firewood ready to start a fire on either side of the ravine through which the enemy must advance, while Zhao Zilong is summoned to lead the advance party but is told to pretend to run away as soon as he encounters Cao Cao's men.

Zhang Fei and Guan Yu are dismissive of these plans and especially of the fact that Kong Ming is not going to be anywhere near the actual fighting. But Xuande reprimands them sharply, and in a sulk the two brothers leave to see just how badly all this will actually work out.

Even Xuande is troubled when Kong Ming orders him to abandon the camp when the enemy arrive the next day, but when he sees the flames to turn back and attack. However, so confident is Kong Ming that he orders Sun Qian and Jian Yong to prepare the victory celebrations!

Cao Cao's advance troops are commanded by Xiahou Dun, supported by Commander Yu Jin, and as they approach Bowang they split their forces into half to go forward and half to hold back to guard the supply wagons. When Zhao Zilong appears with his small force, Xiahou Dun laughs out loud and charges forward, confident of a quick victory. Zhao Zilong does as ordered by Kong Ming and, after a brief skirmish, retreats, drawing Xiahou after him. It is at this point that another of Cao Cao's commanders spurs his horse forward and warns Xiahou Dun that he is clearly being lured into an ambush, only to be brusquely dismissed by Xiahou Dun.

Xuande joins the fray and also begins to retreat, drawing Xiahou Dun and his men deeper and deeper into a narrowing ravine. And still Xiahou Dun cannot see that he is riding into an ambush.

It is only when Yu Jin realizes that they could be caught by fires set on either side and rushes to warn Xiahou Dun that the commander sees the danger. But it is too late. Fires erupt on each side, causing utter confusion, and many are killed trying to escape. Then Zhao Zilong attacks the trapped troops, slaying many, and Xiahou Dun only just manages to escape. Guan Yu and Zhang Fei between them tackle the troops guarding the supplies. They are completely successful in destroying the supply wagons. This spells final disaster for Cao Cao's men. Bodies lie everywhere, and the land runs with rivers of blood. As the celebration poem says:

> He waged war at Bowang with fire;
> Inspirational in strategy, everyone wants him.
> Even Cao Cao trembles at his example:
> A novice who has never fought, can still win!

Needless to say, Guan Yu and Zhang Fei are suitably impressed, and when they come upon Kong Ming's humble carriage they dismount and bow to acknowledge his skills.

They return triumphantly to Xinye but they all know that this is just the start. Cao Cao will soon come seeking revenge and with a huge army.

When Xuande asks what to do next, Kong Ming says, 'I have a plan.'

And what is this plan?

Let's find out.

CHAPTER 40

Lady Cai plots to hand over Jingzhou to Cao Cao. Liu Biao dies, and his sons fight, and Kong Ming burns Xinye.

What Kong Ming knows is that Liu Biao is dying and that instead of trying to defend a small place like Xinye they should move immediately to Jingzhou.

At the same time Cao Cao prepares to invade the south and appoints five commanders to oversee his vast half a million strong army. Only one man speaks out against the impending war and that is the imperial teacher Kong Rong. He opposes the war because it is against members of the imperial family. But palace intrigue soon brings about his downfall, and he and his entire family are executed. And so the war machine rolls out of the imperial capital, heading south.

Meanwhile, in Jingzhou, Liu Biao lies dying.

Hearing that Cao Cao is on his way, he calls for Xuande and hands over responsibility to him and passes to his eldest son from his first wife, Liu Qi, the right to rule. The Lady Cai, his second wife, is furious. She has plans for her own son and hates her stepson. She orders her henchmen to close the city gates to prevent Liu Qi entering.

Liu Qi, hearing his father is dying, leaves his command post at Jiangxia and arrives before the city gate at Jingzhou only to find his arch-enemy Cai Mao, the brother of Lady Cai, blocking his entry.

'Dear boy,' says Cai Mao, 'you were told to protect Jiangxia. By what authority have you abandoned it? What if it is attacked? You coming here like this will only upset your father and make his illness even worse. This is most thoughtless of you, and I strongly recommend that you return to your post immediately.'

This stops Liu Qi in his tracks, and, helpless, he waits outside the gate. Weeping, he hopes to hear that, despite all that Cai Mao has said, he will be admitted to his father's side. But eventually he gives up and, burdened by sadness, returns to his post.

In the city, his father waits for him. But he does not come, and no one tells him why. This is the final blow. Liu Biao is so distraught by this it fatally weakens him. This blow is the end. He dies in part from a broken heart. A poet has said the following.

To the north of the Yellow River were the Yuans;
Holding the middle was Liu Biao.
That was until listening to women brought them both down.
And today there is no trace whatsoever of them.

No sooner is Liu Biao dead than Lady Cai, Cai Mao and Zhang Yun forge a will and claim it is his last wish that Lady Cai's son Liu Zong become the successor. They bury Liu Biao near Xiangyang but do not invite Liu Qi to come for the rituals. Settling into the city, they make it their base, only to discover that now they are directly in the path of Cao Cao's invading army.

What happens next is a terrible betrayal – a massive shock! Liu Zong's advisers gather to decide what to do. One of them, Fu Xuan, says, 'We're in danger not just from Cao Cao. You've excluded your elder brother Liu Qi and Xuande from the rituals. If they gang up against us, we're doomed and we'll lose Jingzhou.'

'So what can we do?' asks a very troubled and frightened Liu Zong.

'Let's write to Cao Cao,' says Fu Xuan, 'and offer him our lands. I'm sure he'll give you a senior post and protect you.'

'I can't believe this!' cries a bewildered Liu Zong. 'I have only just become ruler, and now you want me to give it away!'

'Fu Xuan is right,' says Kuai Yue. 'Cao Cao is strong – we're not. You, sir, have only just taken up your position, and there is no evidence that you have the loyal following of our people at this point. The people are terrified of Cao Cao's advancing army and show no desire to resist.'

Liu Zong is gradually convinced that there is no other option, and a messenger is sent to Cao Cao offering the surrender of the lands.

Cao Cao is delighted to hear this and agrees. But in his reply message he insists that Liu Zong must come out and formally welcome him in front of the gates of Jingzhou.

However, when travelling back to say the offer has been accepted, the messenger is captured by none other than Guan Yu. Brought before Xuande, the captured messenger confesses all, showing Xuande the letter. This reduces Xuande to tears at such a betrayal.

Following Kong Ming's advice, Xuande decides to retreat to the city of Fan. Xuande is a man of honour and virtue. He realizes that he cannot simply abandon the people who have followed him or the people in Xinye who rely upon him for protection. He decides he must move all the ordinary folk, who have faithfully followed him, out of Xinye and across the river to the safety of Fan. This is a huge undertaking and makes them all vulnerable to attack. So Xuande and Kong Ming sit down to plan how to hold back the army of Cao Cao, which is almost upon them, encamped at Bowang nearby, while the people are helped to escape.

Guan Yu is told to take a thousand men to the upper waters of the White River and to dam it. At a given time the next day, they are to destroy the dam and release the floods, the force of which will wipe out most of the enemy. Zhang Fei is told to take a thousand men and hide down by the Boling river crossing, at a point where the flow of the river is sluggish. This is where any of the enemy seeking to escape will go.

Zhao Zilong is to take three thousand men, divided into four companies, and to put one group close to each of the four gates, north, south, east and west, of the city of Xinye. They are to have sulphur with them and saltpetre. These they are to haul up onto the roofs of the houses.

'When Cao Cao's men take the city,' says Kong Ming, 'they'll be worn out and want to rest in the houses. Tomorrow evening the wind will rise and blow, and at that point have archers fire flaming arrows into the town from three of the gates, but leave the east gate open for the enemy to rush to in order to try and escape. Then you can attack them at that gate. Guan Yu and Zhang Fei can ride to your assistance after they have completed their tasks.'

Kong Ming turns to commanders Mi Fang and Liu Feng and tells them: 'Put two thousand men at Xi Wei slope, a thousand each under a blue and red banner. When the enemy appears, they should each run away but in opposite directions which will seriously confuse the enemy and delay pursuit. Once you see the flames rising from Xinye, prepare an ambush and descend upon the enemy. When you've finished there, come to the upper waters and help us.'

Having given their instructions and despatched their men, Xuande and Kong Ming leave and climb up an observation tower to observe the battle.

In sweep the enemy, led by an elite force of three thousand iron-clad warriors commanded by Xu Chu. Behind them come a hundred thousand men led by Cao Ren and Cao Hong. Reaching Xi Wei slope, they see the two troops under their red and blue flags. As arranged, as soon as they are attacked, these troops move in different directions. Such actions lead Xu Chu to fear an ambush. He rides back to the main force and informs Cao Ren that he suspects this is a plan to lure them into an ambush. But Cao Ren disregards this advice and pushes forward.

Frustrated, Xu Chu returns to his crack force of three thousand and soon they reach a small wood. As there is no one there, they halt. It is late in the day – the sun is setting in the west. All of a sudden the hills around echo with the sound of trumpets and drums. Looking up to a small hill, Xu Chu can see Xuande and Kong Ming sitting calmly having a drink beneath the shade of two umbrellas. Incensed, Xu Chu and his men try to scale the hill but are driven back by a barrage of stones and logs. Everything seems to be in chaos, and this sense is only increased when they hear the sound of an army attacking from somewhere behind. Desperately Xu Chu tries to marshal his men, but night is now closing in.

Cao Ren has now arrived outside Xinye ready to fight but finds to his astonishment that the city gates are wide open and the city itself deserted. Riding into the deserted city, he gives orders for his men to rest so they can be ready for the fray tomorrow.

That night, as the army sleeps, the fires break out. When news of this reaches Cao Ren he at first dismisses it as insignificant. Only when he is told that three of the four city gates are ablaze does he realize how serious this is. Cao Ren is really alarmed. It is clear they have been fooled and are trapped. He dashes back and forth, trying to see if they can escape through any of the gates, until word comes that the east gate is open and not on fire. Men rush towards the gate, trampling the weak beneath them, and dash through the opening only to be confronted by Zhao Zilong charging at them. Many are slain there and then, but Cao Ren manages to struggle through and out into what he hopes is freedom. But another wave of attack, led by Liu Feng, overwhelms him and his men. Yet again, through sheer determination and courage, Cao Ren escapes.

The survivors make it to the Bai River, where, grateful for the cooling water, they drink and wade across the shallows. But on the upper river Guan Yu has seen the flames and remembers his orders. The dam is broken and the flood waters rush downstream, sweeping men and horses away.

Only a very few escape with Cao Ren and they head for Boling, where they know there is a ford. Just as they think they are safe Zhang Fei rises up before them and confronts Cao Ren.

Is it possible for Cao Ren to survive?

Let's find out.

CHAPTER 41

Xuande leads his people to safety. Zhao Zilong rescues the heir apparent of Xuande.

As Zhang Fei charges forward, it is Xu Chu who rides out to defend Cao Ren. But Xu Chu has little energy left for such a battle and soon he flees. However, he has given Cao Ren the chance to escape, and soon Cao Ren has found safety ironically in the ruins of Xinye, where he draws together the remnants of his army. With the power of Cao Ren's army broken Zhang Fei, Xuande and Kong Ming are now able to start ferrying the people across the river to Fan.

Once safely across, they burn the boats. There is no going back.

When Cao Cao learns of the tricks Kong Ming has played and the cost to his men, his fury knows no bounds. He now turns the full force of his vast army against his enemy, intent on attacking and seizing Fan. His immediate fury and desire to destroy are curbed by his adviser Liu Ye. He suggests that diplomacy be tried first and that an offer be made to Xuande to surrender so as to spare the suffering of the ordinary people. He knows this will appeal to Xuande's sense of honour and virtue. He also suggests that Xuande's old friend Shan Fu be the messenger bearing this proposal. So Shan Fu sets off to visit Xuande.

Shan Fu, Xuande and Kong Ming make the most of having the opportunity to be together again, and in confidence Shan Fu tells Xuande not to pay any attention to this seemingly humanitarian offer from Cao Cao. 'It's just designed to make him seem humane and to gain popularity. He has eight armies and has filled in the riverbed ready to attack across it. My concern is, to speak frankly, that this city is indefensible. You must get out as soon as possible. I just wish I could stay but I must return to honour this role of messenger. But believe me, my mother's death is seared into my very heart! While I'll honour my pledge to stay with Cao Cao, I'll never, ever help him to develop a plan of attack. Now you've Sleeping Dragon with you, all will be well.' So saying, he makes his farewells and departs.

Shan Fu returns to Cao Cao and informs him that Xuande will not surrender.

Back with Xuande and Kong Ming, the dilemma is that, now that they have rejected Cao Cao's supposedly generous offer, they know he will throw the entire might of his army against them. They will have to move again, as Fan is not defendable. This raises once again the issue of what do to about the ordinary folk of now both Xinye and Fan. The two men agree that there is no question of abandoning them and that they should ask the people what they want to do. When they ask, everyone cries out that they want to go with Xuande. So once again Xuande has to plan for an exodus of the people who look to him as their protector.

The retreat starts straight away. In tears the young help the elderly; parents their children; men take care of the women, while on all sides rise cries of deep distress.

All this touches Xuande to the very heart. 'This is my fault,' he says. 'Why, since I have caused so much distress, should I go on living?' And he tries to commit suicide by throwing himself into the river. Only the timely and desperate intervention of his closest commanders prevents him.

At last they arrive at Xiangyang, only to be denied entrance and safety by a terrified Liu Zong. This cowardly younger son of Liu Biao, now supposed to be the ruler, is horrified at the thought of the vengeance that Cao Cao will exact if he gives sanctuary to Xuande. This despite the obvious suffering of the masses of ordinary people gathered outside the city walls. Cao Mao and Zhang Yun even order the archers on the walls to fire at those gathered before the gate.

Suddenly there is a terrible commotion inside the city. A fierce-looking warrior, with a couple of hundred men behind him, roars, 'You two traitors! Lord Xuande is a man of virtue!'

And so saying, the warrior Wei Yan slashes his way to the gate, swings it open and lowers the drawbridge, crying out, 'Come on in and let's kill these traitors.'

But no sooner does Wei Yan do this than another warrior, Wen Ping, bursts forth and attacks him. Chaos ensues inside the city.

Watching the violence unfold, Kong Ming turns and recommends to Xuande that they abandon trying to enter Xiangyang. They decide instead to head for Jiangling. By now those travelling with Xuande are a vast crowd of over one hundred thousand. Stopping to offer prayers at the tomb of Liu Biao, Xuande weeps over the disasters that surround him. Here news comes that Cao Cao is already at the river, preparing to cross. His officers try to persuade Xuande to head immediately to Jiangling, even if this means abandoning the people. This Xuande refuses to do, even though this means progress will be very slow indeed. And that his own life will be in serious danger.

As a poet has said:

> Even now his heart is moved by people's suffering,
> He steps into the boat in tears.
> To this day, when visiting the riverside,
> The older folk are entranced by his compassion.

Back in Xiangyang, Cao Mao and Zhang Yun persuade Liu Zong to surrender to Cao Cao. Despite Liu Zong's uncertainty and the advice of other ministers, the two traitors take themselves off to Fancheng and negotiate the terms of surrender. In return Cao Cao makes them both senior honorary officials, puts them in charge of the naval troops and promises that Liu Zong will be given a region to rule in perpetuity. Delighted with all this, the two traitors return to their city to finalize the surrender. After they have gone, Xun You enquires of Cao Cao why, given these two are completely untrustworthy, he has flattered them so much. Cao Cao points out that he needs men with naval experience but that he is under no illusions as to their real nature. 'I will deal with them later,' he says.

When the news of the deal reaches Liu Zong, he and his mother, delighted by this development, cross the river to personally thank Cao Cao and to hand over the symbols of authority. Mother and son are received with appropriate honours. However, this will not last.

The following day, Cao Cao enters Xiangyang and takes control. To the dismay of Liu Zong and his mother, far from being given a post of real importance they are told to go to the remote north, where Liu Zong is to be made governor of a city. In vain Liu Zong asks to be kept near the city, and soon mother and son are on their way. Not long after, Cao Cao sends one of his trusted officers after them. When he catches up with them, he tells them to surrender now as he has orders to kill them both, mother and son, so there is no point in resisting. Clinging to each other they cry out, but in vain, and soon their bloodied corpses lie beside the road.

Other officials are sent to Kong Ming's home village with orders to kill every member of his extended family. But they are too late. Foreseeing this, Kong Ming has moved them out, and they are safe, beyond Cao Cao's reach.

Cao Cao now turns his sights and his fury on Xuande and despatches a crack force of five thousand warriors to overtake and destroy Xuande, who by this time is just over a hundred miles ahead.

Meanwhile, as Xuande advances with the people, protected by Zhang Fei and Zhao Zilong, he sends Guan Yu to seek reinforcements from Liu Qi in Jiangxia. One day, as they are travelling, a sudden gust of wind blows up in front of Xuande. The dust cloud is so dense it blots out the sun, and Xuande knows this is not an auspicious omen. Quite the reverse. He consults Jian Yong, who is skilled in the reading of auguries and omens, and he tells Xuande that this is a very bad sign indeed and that a terrible fate awaits them that very night. Jian Yong tries to persuade Xuande to flee in order to save his life and that he must abandon the people. But once again Xuande refuses. Instead, they take up defensive positions on a nearby hill and await what the night will bring.

It is a bitterly cold winter night, and in the early hours of the morning, before the sun comes up, Cao Cao's men attack. Soon the night air is rent with terrible shrieks and cries. Despite his most gallant efforts, Xuande is unable to hold them back and he is almost slain in the midst of this chaos, but Zhang Fei arrives just in time to rescue him, cutting his way through the attackers to rescue his beloved brother. Turning east, they run into Wen Ping, who is now on Cao Cao's side since the surrender of Jiangyang and the deaths of Liu Zong and his mother.

'You traitor!' cries Xuande. 'How dare you even look at me?' Wen Ping is overcome with shame and turns his men away, allowing Xuande and Zhang Fei to escape. But their path is far from clear. Other enemy commanders come to the attack. Zhang Fei slashes left and right, cutting a path through the enemy troops for Xuande as they flee, until dawn at last appears.

Xuande looks around in the pale dawn light and sees just about a hundred of his men left. Of the whereabouts of his family or his people he has no idea. 'Untold numbers of lives,' he cries, 'are undergoing terrible suffering because of me. And all because they wouldn't leave me. My family, my staff, all gone. So overwhelming is this sorrow that even if I was made of wood or brick I would be weeping right now.'

Looking up, he sees Mi Fang, arrows stuck in his face, come staggering up the hill. 'Zhao Zilong has joined the enemy!' he shouts, but Xuande swiftly silences him, saying, 'Zilong is one of my oldest friends. He wouldn't betray me.' But Zhang Fei joins in: 'Seeing we've lost, maybe he's decided to look to his own fortune first!'

'He's been with me without self-regard through all our adventures and disasters,' says Xuande. 'He stands as firm as a rock. No offer of power will ever sway him!'

'But I saw him heading in Cao Cao's direction,' says Mi Fang, to which Zhang Fei says, 'Let me go searching for him, because if I find him I'll kill him!'

Despite Xuande's continued defence of Zhao Zilong, Zhang Fei sets off with twenty men. He heads for the bridge over which any attack will come, intent on catching and slaying Zilong. As he draws near to the bridge, he passes a small wood and has an idea. Telling his men to cut branches from the trees, he has them tie them to their horses' tails. 'Now charge up to the bridge. The dust storm this creates will make the enemy think a huge army is heading their way, and that should scare them off.' He then takes up a defensive position on the bridge and waits.

On the battlefield, Zilong has been fighting through the night until dawn comes, desperately seeking his lord and, especially, his family. Distraught, because Xuande has left his family in his care, he decides to go into battle. It is an apparently hopeless plan – a suicide attack because, having failed so badly, he has nothing to live for. There is no point in living now – unless he can find Xuande's family and especially his son and heir. With a handful of followers he charges into the fray. His hope is that he can find the two wives of Xuande. All around him are the pitiful cries of the people. Such sadness would move even Heaven and Earth to pity.

As he rides, he sees a man by the roadside whom he recognizes as Jian Yong. Zilong cries out, 'Have you seen the two ladies?'

Jian Yong replies, 'The two ladies abandoned their carriage, taking the child with them, and ran. I chased after them uphill but was attacked and wounded and thrown from my horse. Unable to fight any more, I've ended up here.'

Zhao Zilong sends the man off to be cared for and despatches a messenger to Xuande, saying, 'I'll search for the two women and the child, going to Heaven or throughout the earth in pursuit, through good or evil, if I have to, and failure will only happen if I die in the attempt.'

Further along the road, he hears that Lady Gan is walking, barefoot and ragged, with a crowd of other women. Zilong urges his horse on until he sees in the distance a crowd of over two hundred, both men and women. Crying out, he asks, 'Is Lady Gan here?' and from the rear of the column a cry goes up – it is Lady Gan. Zilong leaps from his horse, tears flowing, and admits that it is his fault that all this has happened. 'But where,' he asks, 'where is Lady Mi and the child?'

'She and I had to abandon our carriage and travel along with the people. But then in the crush and chaos when a group of soldiers appeared we became separated. I've no idea where they are now.'

Suddenly a cry goes up from among the people. A band of soldiers has ridden into view, and in their midst is a prisoner. Zilong realizes this is none other than Mi Zhu, Lady Mi's brother. Rushing to the attack, he scatters the troop and rescues Mi Zhu and captures two horses. With Lady Gan on one and Mi Zhu on the other, they all ride off to find Xuande.

As they approach the bridge, Zhang Fei, who is standing guard there, shouts out, 'Why have you betrayed my brother?' to which Zilong replies that he has been looking for the ladies and the child and that he has no idea what Zhang Fei is talking about! Grudgingly Zhang Fei has to confess that he has heard about this from Jian Yong, but only because of that will he believe Zilong!

Zilong hands over Lady Gan to Mi Zhu with orders to take her to Xuande, while he himself turns about and heads back into the battle to try to find Lady Mi and the child.

By now Zilong is travelling alone and he dashes here and there searching for Lady Mi and the child. Everyone he meets is asked the same question, 'Have you seen Lady Mi and the child?' but no answer comes until at long last someone says, 'She's been wounded in the thigh and cannot walk. She and the child are over there, taking refuge.'

The man points to a ruined and burned-out wreck of a house. When Zilong bursts through the shattered front door, he finds the lady and the child. Zilong falls to his knees before her.

'Now I know the child will live,' says Lady Mi. 'Take him to his father, for now I can die in peace.'

Zilong is stunned and urges her to come up onto his horse and he will take them both to Xuande.

'No!' Lady Mi cries. 'Without a horse you cannot protect the child. My wound is so bad I know I'll not survive. Get going, I beg you, and don't worry about me.'

The sound of shouting echoes around the ruin, and Zilong says, 'But the enemy are coming. We must flee now.'

But Lady Mi is adamant. 'I'm dying, but if you stay both lives will be lost.' And so saying, she thrust the child into his arms. Zilong tries time and time again to persuade her, handing the child back, but to no avail. Finally he says, 'But imagine what will happen when the soldiers find you.'

To his horror, she puts the child on the ground, rises and staggers to the mouth of a dry well. Turning, she throws herself into it and dies. A poet has honoured her self-sacrifice with this poem:

> A fighter needs his horse's power to give him strength.
> He'd never be able to protect the child on foot.
> What a mother, to die for her husband's heir!
> This woman was truly heroic, so adamant and brave!

To protect her from any abuse, a distraught Zilong topples a crumbling wall onto the well to hide her body. Picking up the child, he loosens his breastplate and places him gently inside. Mounting his horse, he turns and rides hell for leather towards Xuande.

Almost immediately he has to fight off attackers. These he despatches swiftly, but soon he confronts a more ferocious foe, Zhang He. Normally Zilong could have taken him with ease but, clutching the child to his chest to protect him, he cannot fight as he usually would. Eventually he has to turn and flee, only to be pursued by Zhang He. He would have got clear away but for a disaster. Rider, horse and child suddenly crash into a pit dug in the road, and at this sight Zhang He rides up, spear held ready to kill. Then, from nowhere, there comes a flash of intense bright light surging up from within the pit, bringing with it horse, rider and child, who are catapulted into the sky and fall back to firm ground again. Terrified, Zhang He turns and escapes from this supernatural force, while Zilong and the child ride on.

Again he is attacked, this time by four men, but swinging his mighty sword in his fury, he kills them all and rides on again. From a hill Cao Cao watches, filled with admiration for this heroic warrior. He gives orders that Zilong must be taken alive. Many men try, but none succeed. The dead lie all around him as he battles on until suddenly his way is blocked by troops led by the brothers Zhong, one armed with a huge axe and the other with a massive halberd.

Can Zilong escape?

All will be revealed.

CHAPTER 42

Zhang Fei wreaks havoc at the bridge.
Xuande retreats in defeat.

So the two brothers think they can stop Zilong! Well, one falls from his horse dead as a stone when Zilong attacks, enabling him to make a bid for freedom. He is hotly pursued by the other brother. He rides so fast and furiously that he is able to touch the tail of Zilong's horse. Zilong turns and with one swing of his sword kills his pursuer; then, facing forward again, he rides as if devils themselves were after him, towards the bridge and the hill where Xuande awaits him.

But his troubles are not over yet, for streaming after him comes Wen Ping and his troops, crying out for vengeance.

His horse is almost dead on its feet when Zilong at last reaches the bridge, and he cries out for Zhang Fei to help him. 'Get yourself across quickly,' shouts Zhang Fei. 'I'll deal with this lot.'

So on Zilong rides until at long last he reaches Xuande. Weeping, he dismounts and bows before Xuande.

'I've failed, and my punishment should be death,' he gasps. 'Lady Mi was so badly wounded she was unable to ride and instead threw herself down a well. She died, and all I could manage was to quickly cover up the well by pushing over a ruined wall. So I placed the child here inside my breastplate and battled my way through the enemy. He must be a sacred and divinely protected child because through his grace I've made it through. I hope he is protected by the gods because he cried when we set out but I've heard nothing for a while and now am fearful that he didn't make it through after all.'

So saying, Zilong opens his armour and to his delight discovers the child is fast asleep. 'Thank goodness your son is alright,' he says as he hands the child to his father.

Imagine his astonishment when Xuande throws the child to the ground. He is furious and cries out, 'To protect this child I very nearly lost my greatest commander!' Zilong lifts the child from the ground as he kowtows before Xuande, declaring that even if he were to die he could not do more to prove his loyalty to Xuande.

Back at the bridge, Wen Ping arrives to find Zhang Fei in command and behind him dust rising in huge clouds. Wen Ping is thus convinced Zhang Fei has command of a formidable force of men. So ferocious is Zhang Fei's glare and shouts of defiance that no one dares attack. Everyone is convinced that Kong Ming has set yet another cunning trap. Even when Cao Cao himself rides up, not even he dare attack. Zhang Fei constantly shouts challenges and threats at the enemy, calling them cowards and daring them to attack him. Fear sweeps through the enemy forces, and even Cao Cao feels the force of it. So much so that he turns tail and flees, his horse panicking, and rides pell-mell until he is slowed and brought to a stop by his commanders.

When Zhang Fei sees this full-scale retreat and confusion, he takes the opportunity to destroy the bridge and tells his men to cut loose the branches tied to their horses' tails. Then he rides back to tell Xuande of all that has taken place.

Annoyed, Xuande has to point out to Zhang Fei that, while he might be a mighty and brave warrior, he is no strategist. Cao Cao will interpret the destruction of the bridge as a sign of weakness. If the bridge had been left, then fear of a trap would have kept Cao Cao at bay. Now he will know that there is no such trap and that Xuande is frightened of attack. So he will now go on the offensive. So saying, Xuande and his men start to retreat towards the river.

And, as Xuande predicted, Cao Cao sees the destruction of the bridge as a sign of exactly that weakness, and pontoon bridges are created that very night to ferry the vast army across the bridgeless river. Soon the advance guard is across the river and heading for Xuande and his men when out of the blue a warrior with a troop of ten thousand men bursts onto the scene. It is none other than Guan Yu.

Convinced this is indeed part of a Kong Ming trap, Cao Cao and his men turn and retreat while Guan Yu protects his brother's retreat to the banks of the further river.

At the river, embarkation is well under way when from the south side of the river drums are heard. Looking down-river Xuande sees an armada of ships bearing down upon them in full sail. Initial terror turns to relief when Xuande sees that the fleet is led by none other than Liu Qi, who, upon landing, kowtows to Xuande and offers his support to his imperial uncle.

But then a new fleet of warships is spotted coming from the southwest. Convinced this must be the fleet of Cao Cao's navy, Xuande's men are in fear of defeat when suddenly they espy a familiar figure in the bow of the lead ship. It is Kong Ming in his habitual Daoist robes, and with him Sun Qian.

A war council is held, and it is agreed that the main force will head for Jiangxia, while Guan Yu will stay behind to defend Xiakou with just five thousand men. This deters Cao Cao, who turns aside to take the surrender of Jingzhou, and here he prepares for his main attack. His troops number eight hundred and thirty thousand – which Cao Cao rounds up by claiming he has a million men bearing arms. The scale of this army is almost unimaginable. The soldiers' camps alone stretch for hundreds of miles along the Great River.

Back at Sun Quan's headquarters, in the capital of the state of Wu, news of Cao Cao's advance has reached them, and the taking of Jingzhou right up against their border deeply alarms Sun Quan's advisers.

It is decided to send Lu Su to Xuande to suggest an alliance against Cao Cao. At the same time, Kong Ming is persuading Xuande to form exactly such an alliance. He has realized the perilous state of Wu now that Cao Cao is up against their own borders. In response they are very likely to turn to Xuande for assistance. This way, as Kong Ming points out, 'If the south wins, then that is the end of Cao Cao. If the north wins, we are there and can take over much of Wu.'

Kong Ming is therefore delighted when Lu Su arrives offering precisely such a partnership. However, Kong Ming advises Xuande to be deliberately vague about not only how strong

Cao Cao is but also about whether such an alliance is really in his best interests.

In the end, this strategy results in Lu Su inviting Kong Ming to come to see his brother, who is an adviser to Sun Quan, and to discuss a possible alliance.

What this leads to we will now find out.

CHAPTER 43

Kong Ming debates with the advisers of Wu.
Lu Su goes against the majority opinion.

When they arrive at Chaisang, Kong Ming is given rooms in which to rest while Lu Su goes to see Sun Quan. He has just received a letter from Cao Cao, which, using the most formal imperial language of command, suggests – really almost orders – that Sun Quan join Cao Cao in attacking Xuande. Sun Quan is uncertain what to do and, despite the forthright opinion of his adviser Zhang Zhao, who strongly supports the idea of taking up Cao Cao's offer, he remains silent.

It is only when he is alone with Lu Su that he speaks, asking him what he thinks. Lu Su advises against such an alliance and then tells him that Kong Ming has come back with him. Sun Quan is surprised and delighted.

The next day Kong Ming is brought to meet some twenty of Sun Quan's advisers, led by Zhang Zhao. What follows is nothing less than an inquisition of Kong Ming by the advisers.

Zhang Zhao goes first, asking why, if Xuande is so pleased to have secured Kong Ming's services, he has lost all the lands around Jingzhou and Xiangyang.

Kong Ming knows that Zhang Zhao is the most important of Sun Quan's advisers and that unless he can convince him all is lost. He replies carefully, only to have Zhang Zhao accuse him of being nothing more than an irrelevant hermit, before whose arrival Xuande was seen as the great hero. Now he is in flight, unable to protect his lands.

Using the metaphor of treating a man who is seriously ill, Kong Ming rebukes Zhang Zhao:

'How can a simple bird understand the roc, who can fly ten thousand miles without tiring? When someone is ill, you first have to build up his strength with simple, plain food and medicine. Then you give him meat and more powerful drugs to bring him back to full health. Too much too soon will harm the patient.

'Yes, Xuande was defeated at Runan and had to find sanctuary with Liu Biao because he had so few soldiers – in fact just three officers. Xinye was a stopping place, basic and without resources. But from there we destroyed Cao Cao's camps at Bowang, then we flooded his army at the river and finally we scared off his key generals. Not bad really!

'Xuande didn't know about Liu Zong's disgraceful surrender and was far too honourable to take advantage of that. He is, as you know, followed by a vast crowd of ordinary folk whom he refuses to abandon, even though it makes things far, far more difficult. What an example of his virtue!

'Remember, the founder of the Han dynasty, Gao Zu, was defeated many times but eventually he overcame his great foe, aided by his adviser Han Xin. It's true Gao Zu and Han Xin weren't always successful. But then real success relies upon a grand vision and plan, not the usual nonsense that overconfident armchair generals and pompous academics spout who can't actually deal with the realities on the ground!'

That shuts Zhang Zhao up!

But after him, one adviser after another rises to question Kong Ming. For example, adviser Xue Zong raises the question of what Kong Ming thinks of Cao Cao. When Kong Ming replies that he is a traitor to the Han, Xue Zong retorts that the time of the Han is fast drawing to its end and that, despite having been passed down the generations, it is now clear that Heaven's Mandate is being withdrawn. Cao Cao is in charge of most of the empire, and Xuande's resistance is like an egg being thrown against a rock.

To this Kong Ming replies sharply:

'You would spurn both your king and your father! Loyalty and filial piety are what should shape a man's life in his time here between Heaven and Earth. You, you're a servant of the Han and if you see that someone is abusing his powers you must help to remove him. Cao Cao has turned from the kindness his ancestors received from the Han and the respect he therefore owes to the dynasty and has become nothing more than a rebel. This has infuriated everyone, yet you, you suggest that Heaven has now decided he will be the ruler. In so doing you betray your father and your king and are no longer fit for the company of loyal men.'

That shuts Xue Zong up.

At long last, Kong Ming has dealt firmly with all the objections and is rescued from the petty interrogation by Lu Su, who takes him off to meet Sun Quan. On the way they bump into Zhuge Jin, Kong Ming's brother, who is delighted and welcomes him to the south. But Zhuge Jin does want to know why King Ming has not been to see him yet. Saying that his public duties override personal ones, he promises to come and see him as soon as possible.

As Lu Su and Kong Ming go in to see Sun Quan, Lu Su says, 'Don't frighten him by reminding him how strong Cao Cao's army is.'

'Of course not,' says Kong Ming.

Sun Quan, after the opening formal greetings, goes straight to the heart of the matter and asks Kong Ming how strong Cao Cao really is in terms of his military forces. To Lu Su's astonishment, Kong Ming says, 'If you add up cavalry, infantry and naval, well over a million men!'

Horrified, Sun Quan asks whether this is not an exaggeration, so Kong Ming tallics all the troops. 'Actually it is nearer one and a half million but I deliberately understated so as not to scare your lordship!' says Kong Ming. Lu Su is completely bewildered by this change of what he thought was an agreed tactic.

Kong Ming continues, 'He's heading this way so what other plans could he have than to conquer the south? If you want my opinion – though you may find you don't like it – I believe you should abandon any thought of an alliance with Cao Cao even though I know your advisers suggest otherwise. They, I know, just want you to face north and surrender.'

Overcome with indecision and anxiety, Sun Quan leaves in a flurry, and Lu Su rounds on Kong Ming: 'Why on earth did you have to upset Sun Quan with such dismissive words?'

'To be honest,' says Kong Ming, 'I have a plan to destroy Cao Cao, but as Sun Quan never asked me, how could I share it with him!'

'If you have such a plan,' says Lu Su, 'then I'll tell Sun Quan.' This he does, but Sun Quan is so furious with Kong Ming that he at first rejects any idea of listening to him, but he is eventually brought round by Lu Su. The two men, Kong Ming and Sun Quan, quietly apologize to each other and, going into Sun's private quarters, they start to talk in earnest.

'There were six foes of Cao Cao,' says Sun Quan. 'Lü Bu, Liu Biao, Yuan Shao, Yuan Shu, Xuande and myself. The first four are now dead, and really only Xuande can tackle Cao Cao, yet his current track record is not great, given so many defeats. Can he really resist?'

'Guan Yu still has ten thousand men, and Liu Qi's men are about the same number,' replies Kong Ming. 'Cao Cao's men are exhausted – they have travelled vast distances and moreover have no experience of naval warfare. Add to this that they've all been conscripted and so have no heart for this either. Your linking up with Xuande will further undermine such a demoralized force. You will then create a tripod, a three-legged vessel of the state, with the south, Jingzhou and the north.'

At these words, all Sun Quan's doubts disappear, and he finally agrees to join Xuande in confronting Cao Cao.

But his advisers are horrified and, led by Zhang Zhao, they argue furiously that such a course would be disastrous. Once again Sun Quan finds himself in a quandary of indecision. Despite Lu Su's efforts, Sun Quan is unable to make up his mind. Troubled, he visits his mother, who reminds him of her older sister's dying words.

What are these words?

Read on!

CHAPTER 44

Kong Ming pushes Zhou Yu into action. Sun Quan finally decides to attack Cao Cao.

What his mother reminds him of is the advice that her sister heard from the lips of the dying Sun Ce: that on domestic affairs, Sun Quan should listen to Zhang Zhao but he should listen to Zhou Yu on external affairs. So it is decided to consult Zhou Yu, who at that time is at the Poyang lakes, where he is conducting naval exercises.

Lu Su sets off straight away and is reassured by Zhou Yu that he will support him the moment Kong Ming comes as well. But then a delegation led by Zhang Zhao arrives and argues in favour of surrendering to Cao Cao – and Zhou Yu appears to agree with them! Then the military leaders turn up, urging resistance to Cao Cao – and Zhou Yu seems to side with them!

After this comes a delegation of bureaucrats led by Kong Ming's brother Zhuge Jin, who makes the comment that 'Surrendering certainly means a sort of security while war – well who can tell what that will lead to?'

Again Zhou Yu plays safe and says he will give a decision the next day.

They are followed by yet another group, who debate back and forth among themselves in front of Zhou Yu until eventually he says he will definitely decide tomorrow, and they all leave.

Now Lu Su brings Kong Ming to see him. Lu Su informs Kong Ming that his master is unable to make up his mind as to what to do. Imagine his shock when Zhou Yu says that he has decided to recommend surrendering to Cao Cao. 'Cao Cao represents the Son of Heaven,' says Zhou Yu. 'To fight him is to court disaster. Surrender will prove the best form of safety.

Understanding this, I'll inform our master to make the offer to surrender.'

Lu Su tries to argue against this, as a betrayal of three generations of lordship over the south, but Zhou Yu points out that there are a vast number of ordinary people living in the south, and war would bring disaster upon them, and the leaders such as he would rightly be blamed. Undeterred, Lu Su argues back, and the two men continue in this fashion, while a smiling Kong Ming sits back and watches.

Challenged by both Zhou Yu and Lu Su as to why he is smiling, Kong Ming answers them. Having initially seemed to agree with Zhou Yu about surrendering, given that only Xuande is left to confront Cao Cao, Kong Ming then springs his surprise.

'No need to have relays of offerings. Indeed no need even for us to cross the river. It can be done with just one person so long as that one person can take two other people over the river to Cao Cao! If Cao Cao has these two then his vast million-strong army will pack up and go home.'

Zhou Yu cannot hide his astonishment and asks, 'Is that right? Who are these two people?'

'Sending these two,' replies Kong Ming, 'will be like the fall of a leaf from a great tree or a grain store losing a few grains. But if Cao Cao can have these two, then he will leave a happy man.'

An even more annoyed Zhou Yu asks, 'Yes, but who are they?'

'I've heard,' says Kong Ming, 'that Cao Cao is building a tower to be known as the Bronze Bird Tower and that in this tower he'll house all the most beautiful women of the land. In particular, he has designs on the two daughters of the Qiao family of the south, women so beautiful that birds fly down to see them, fish drown for shame of not being as beautiful, the moon hides, and flowers are outdone by their beauty. Cao Cao's plan is to create his own empire, to seize the two Qiao sisters and thus be able to spend his time indulging himself with them and die happy! All that army? Just a ploy to get these two women. Go and ask their father if he'll sell you his daughters and then give them to Cao Cao and all will be well.'

Zhou Yu wants to know how this desire of Cao Cao's can be proved to be true, to which Kong Ming replies that Cao Cao's own son, Zhi, a noted writer and poet, was commissioned to write a poem which is now known as the 'Bronze Bird Tower Poem'. He proceeds to recite the poem as if from memory:

It's good to walk in the footsteps of a wise king seeking delight:
I climb the tower's levels in my heart's joy
To see the vast expanse of this new realm
And the regions this great man rules.

The noble gates lift, hill-high
The towers rise up into the blue . . .
This amazing work sits in the midst of heaven.
From here he can see the western settlements,
Gazing down on the River Zhang and its swirling waters,
While his gardens are visibly full of fruit.

The twin towers rise either side,
One called Jade Dragon, the other Golden Phoenix.
It's here he plans to trap the gorgeous Qiao girls from the southeast,
Carousing morning and night in their company.

From here he observes the imperial city's splendours,
Noting the swirling clouds around, like the waters.
He rejoices in the glamorous literati around him,
Dreaming, like King Wen did, of auspicious signs.

Look up, for here's the harmony of springtime;
Listen, and your ear is rinsed by birdsong.
Heaven itself stands like a guardian above.
The dynasty has fulfilled its twin goals.
His benevolence fills the universe,
His capital is filled with honour –
So much so that all former emperors' glory
Pales into insignificance!

What success, what splendour!
See how this kindly considerateness ripples out.
Everyone wishes our house well,
May this spread throughout the world.
It's only limit – the edges of Heaven and Earth,
Illuminating everything, like the sun and moon combined.

For ever true, for ever sustained
(He will live as long as the eastern emperor)
His dragon banner is carried to the ends of the earth,
While his phoenix chariot comes home triumphantly.

His blessing spreads out to the four seas,
The state is prosperous and the people content.
My hope is that these towers last for ever
And that this happiness, likewise, remains.

On hearing this poem, Zhou Yu explodes with anger. He rises up and points his finger to the north, roaring, 'You old traitor. This insult goes too far!'

Pretending confusion, Kong Ming asks him what is so difficult in letting two women go if this will sort things out.

'Clearly you have no idea what you are talking about,' retorts Zhou Yu. 'The older sister is the wife of the late commander Sun Ce, while the younger sister is none other than my own wife!'

'Oh, dear me!' says an apparently embarrassed Kong Ming. 'I'd no idea.'

'I cannot live on this earth with that man,' roars Zhou Yu, to which Kong Ming recommends restraint and careful thought, but to no avail.'

'Ha!' says Zhou Yu. 'I was only pretending when I appeared to support surrender. Tomorrow I'll recommend action to Sun Quan.'

The next day dawns, and Sun Quan assembles in the Hall, on his right his military officials and on his left his civil officials. The atmosphere is fraught with tension. Into this scene strides Zhou Yu. Bowing to Sun Quan, he asks to see the letter from Cao Cao in which he proposes an alliance. Snorting with disdain at the letter, Zhou Yu asks what Sun Quan is thinking of replying, to which Sun Quan says that, having asked for advice, he still cannot make up his mind.

Zhou Yu speaks his mind, reminding Sun Quan that he is the third-generation ruler of these lands and has a sacred trust from his ancestors. He then outlines four reasons why Cao Cao is far from being as strong or formidable as those arguing for an alliance are suggesting.

'He has advanced south when his northern flank is far from secure from attack. That is his first mistake. Secondly, he has moved from land warfare, at which he excels, to naval engagement, which his men do not understand. Thirdly, he is attacking in winter, when forage will be scarce. Finally, he has brought his men to strange lands and unknown diseases. This is why he will be defeated, never mind how many men he has now! Give me one hundred and fifty thousand tried and tested soldiers, and I will destroy him.'

Rising and brandishing his sword, Sun Quan gives Zhou Yu command over his forces and appoints Cheng Pu and Lu Su to be his seconds in command.

Returning to his rooms, Zhou Yu informs Kong Ming of the decision by Sun and is very surprised to see a look of concern on Kong Ming's face. When he asks why, Kong Ming says, 'Your Lord still has not finally made up his mind and until he does there is no point in making plans!'

Zhou Yu is astonished. 'What on earth do you mean, he "has not finally made up his mind"?'

To this Kong Ming replies that Sun Quan is still terrified by the apparent disparity in the number of troops available, convinced that Cao Cao has so many he can easily destroy Sun's troops. 'Before you can make any plans you must reassure him, and the only way to do this is to go through the numbers and types of troops at Cao Cao's command.'

Convinced by this, Zhou Yu returns to Sun's quarters and discovers that Kong Ming is absolutely right about Sun's anxieties, so he lays out for his lord the realities involved.

'It is said that Cao Cao has a million-strong army. Well, let's examine that. His own northern troops actually number around 150,000, and they are exhausted. The troops who were with Yuan Shao and were forcibly conscripted into his army number about 80,000 and have no commitment to Cao Cao. Because of this, with 50,000 men I can break them.'

Sun Quan thanks his commander and says he is now without fear, so let battle commence, 'And if necessary I will face Cao Cao man to man in battle!'

Zhou Yu leaves, happy that this is now resolved, but also deeply disturbed. What troubles Zhou Yu is that Kong Ming has clearly got a better understanding not only of strategy but also of the very mind of Sun Quan. He can see that Kong Ming's brilliance could spell real trouble for him in the future. So he starts to think about how to remove him – how to have him killed. That evening, he shares this with a shocked Lu Su, who replies that this would certainly be a terrible mistake while the struggle with Cao Cao remains. Instead, he suggests that they ask Kong Ming's brother Zhuge Jin to try to win Kong Ming away from Xuande and into the service of Sun Quan. Calmer now, Zhou Yu agrees.

The next day, Zhou Yu gives his orders. Even Cheng Pu, who has been upset at not being made overall commander, realizes that Zhou Yu knows what he is doing. Having been ordered that under no circumstances are the ordinary people to be harmed by their actions, the officers depart to take up their positions for war at the Three Rivers.

It is the next day that Zhou Yu asks Zhuge Jin to try to persuade his brother to join them. However, in the ensuing discussion it is Kong Ming who nearly persuades his brother to change sides and join him in serving Xuande! This is what Zhuge Jin reports back to Zhou Yu. Once Zhou Yu has ensured that Zhuge Jin will remain faithful to Sun, he says that he knows a way to bring Kong Ming on board.

Can he?

Let's find out.

CHAPTER 45

Cao Cao is defeated at the Three Rivers.
Jiang Gan is fooled by a fake letter.

Zhou Yu's plan is simple. He suggests that Kong Ming, along with Guan Yu, Zhang Fei, Zhao Zilong and a thousand men, should penetrate deep behind the enemy lines and destroy their supplies. Kong Ming realizes that this is in truth a suicide mission, designed primarily to ensure his death, but, unable to immediately think of a way out, he has to agree. When later Lu Su challenges Zhou Yu as to the reason for this mission, Zhou Yu is honest enough to admit he wants Cao Cao's soldiers to kill Kong Ming and thus not have the blame fall upon himself.

Lu Su reports this back to Kong Ming, who is busy getting ready to go on the mission – or so it appears! When Lu Su asks why he is doing this, Kong Ming repeats a rhyme that he says is going the rounds among the local children:

> To lay an ambush or defend a pass,
> Lu Su is your man.
>
> When the battle's to be on water,
> It's Zhou Yu!

'So,' says Kong Ming, 'clearly neither of you is any good at this kind of mission, so I have to go instead.' When this is reported back to Zhou Yu, he is furious and announces that, to show how wrong Kong Ming is, he will personally lead the mission with ten thousand men! This, of course, is exactly what Kong Ming hoped would happen.

When he hears this, he says, 'You see it was just a plot to have Cao Cao kill me. That is why I taunted him with that comment! But let's be sensible now. What we need is for Xuande and Sun Quan to collaborate. We must stop this plotting against each other, otherwise we'll be outmanoeuvred by the plots of Cao Cao. If Zhou Yu does lead this ridiculous mission he'll be killed. He is far too important for that. Can you gently help him see this?'

And, sure enough, Lu Su manages to dissuade Zhou Yu from the folly of his own proposed suicide mission. However, when Zhou Yu realizes he has been tricked once again by Kong Ming, he is even more determined to kill him. But Lu Su persuades him to at least wait until they have defeated Cao Cao. Again reluctantly Zhou Yu agrees.

Back at Jiangxia, Xuande prepares himself to go down to Xiakou and the forthcoming battle. He orders that Liu Qi be left in charge of the city but is worried that nothing has been heard from Kong Ming. Xuande sends Mi Zhu to go to Zhou Yu's camp to find out what is going on.

Mi Zhu is received with due honour by Zhou Yu, who earnestly requests him to inform Xuande that he longs to see him. When Lu Su questions Zhou Yu about this invitation, Zhou admits that his plan is to assassinate Xuande, and, despite Lu Su's best efforts to dissuade him, he will not be shifted from this devious plot. Instead, he gives instructions that if Xuande comes, fifty armed men are to hide behind screens at the welcome banquet. 'When I drop my wine cup,' he says, 'that will be the signal to kill him.'

When the invitation reaches Xuande, he agrees to go. 'Zhou Yu is renowned for deceit,' says Guan Yu. 'And we have heard nothing from Kong Ming. Don't go!'

'I have to,' says Xuande. 'We are supposed to be allies.'

'If you must go, then I come too,' says Guan Yu. Xuande agrees to take Guan Yu with him but seems oblivious of the plot being hatched.

When Xuande arrives, Zhou gives orders for a banquet to be set and then secretly orders the armed men to hide behind the screens. They are to wait for his signal to strike: when he throws a wine cup to the floor.

What Zhou Yu did not expect is that Guan Yu, famous for

his skills with his great sword, would stand guard behind Xuande throughout the banquet. So terrified is Zhou Yu by the presence of this great warrior that he abandons the plot. It is with huge relief that a deeply worried Kong Ming finds Xuande and Guan Yu down by the riverside after the banquet, ready to return to their own army. Suddenly realizing the danger he has been in, Xuande is anxious to have Kong Ming return with him. But Kong Ming replies that ironically he is safer inside the tiger's mouth than anywhere else!

Not long after Xuande leaves, a messenger comes from Cao Cao to deliver a letter to Zhou Yu. On the envelope are the words: 'The prime minister of the Han grants permission to General Zhou Yu to open this letter.' The patronizing tone of this absolutely infuriates Zhou Yu, and, without even bothering to read the letter, he rips it into pieces. He then orders that the messenger be beheaded; the head is then given to the poor man's servant to carry back to Cao Cao. Lu Su is horrified at this breach of protocol and protests strongly. 'This shows them,' says Zhou Yu, 'that we know we can win.' Now Zhou makes the final preparations for the attack and commands that Gan Ning lead the assault on Cao Cao.

Enraged by the murder of his envoy, Cao Cao sets in motion preparations for the battle. Command of his army is given to Cai Mao, and the troops are put on board the battleships ready to attack. Soon they see the massed flotilla of Zhou Yu's navy approaching, led by Gan Ning, who shouts, 'Here I come – and who will stop me?' Cai Mao's younger brother, Cai Xun, is sent to attack him, but just one shot from Gan Ning's bow slays him. Gan Ning's southern troops then open fire from their boats, creating utter chaos among the northerners. They simply are not used to naval conflict, and thousands fall as the arrows rain down upon them as they huddle, seasick, in the boats. Gan Ning inflicts a crushing defeat on the soldiers of Cao Cao, but Zhou Yu, worried by the superior numbers of Cao Cao's army, pulls his men back before they can utterly crush the northerners.

The humiliation stirs Cao Cao into ordering that Cai Mao and Zhang Yun, who are, of course, experienced in naval warfare, should establish a training centre where the land-lubber soldiers can be trained to fight on water. The sheer industrial and training scale of this undertaking and the size of the army mean that at night the sky is bright with the furnaces, fires and lights of the northern army. Deeply troubled by this, Zhou Yu decides to get as close as possible to spy out what is happening. In a small boat he is rowed at dead of night towards the enemy encampment. Here he sees for himself the developments and is duly impressed and troubled by how far the enemy has come in preparing for naval combat. Suddenly there is action all along the enemy bank of the river. News has reached Cao Cao of Zhou Yu's spying expedition, and orders are given for boats to race out and capture his vessel. But the southern rowers are stronger and more skilled than those of the north, and Zhou Yu is soon back in his own camp.

Incandescent with rage, Cao Cao asks how Zhou can be defeated.

'I'm an old school friend of Zhou Yu. Let me go and see if through friendship I can win him over. I really do think I can.' The speaker is Jiang Gan, one of Cao Cao's advisers.

'You know Zhou Yu?' asks a surprised Cao Cao.

'Have no fears,' says Jiang Gan. 'I will succeed.'

So it is agreed. Jiang Gan will go to see Zhou Yu.

When Jiang Gan arrives, Zhou Yu throws a great party for him, which all the military commanders are ordered to attend – to bring home to Jiang Gan just how powerful Zhou's forces are. Jiang Gan is also invited to stay the night. This is all part of Zhou Yu's plan to use this visit for his own ends.

Poor Jiang Gan! He is paraded around to see the military might of Zhou and the formidable preparations for war until he is suitably cowed. Together, the old friends drink heavily, and Zhou's behaviour becomes more and more eccentric, more and more like someone who is so drunk he has no idea what is going on!

As the evening draws to a close, Zhou Yu, now apparently the worse for wear through drink, invites Jiang Gan to come and sleep in his tent. But his apparent drunken state is a ruse. Pretending to be sleeping deeply, Zhou Yu snores reassuringly. This encourages Jiang Gan, who has quickly realized during the evening that he has no hope of persuading Zhou Yu to change sides. So he takes the opportunity to explore what is lying around in the tent. He soon discovers a letter which appears to come from Cai Mao and Zhang Yun. In the letter they say they were forced into serving Cao Cao. However, as a result and through deceit and cunning, they are now within reach of striking and killing Cao Cao, whose head they will deliver to Zhou Yu.

Jiang Gan steals the letter, realizing that, even if he will not be forgiven for failing to bring Zhou Yu over to Cao Cao's side, this letter with its explosive revelations will gain him Cao Cao's approval.

After a fraught night of anxiety, fearful that Zhou Yu will wake or notice that the letter has gone, Jiang Gan slips away in the early morning and makes good his escape.

Arriving back at Cao Cao's camp, he goes directly to Cao Cao, where he has to confess that Zhou Yu will not change sides. Cao Cao explodes with fury, but Jiang Gan says that he has discovered something of greater importance but that he can only confide this to Cao Cao alone.

So the room is cleared. Then and only then does Jiang Gan show Cao Cao the supposed letter of betrayal by Cai Mao and Zhang Yun. Roaring with rage, Cao Cao orders the immediate execution of the two commanders.

It is only when the heads are brought in that Cao Cao comes to his senses and realizes that he has been fooled, but, unable to bear the ignominy, he refuses to acknowledge this. This is despite the fact that he has just murdered the two commanders who understood marine warfare. His other commanders are appalled.

When the news reaches Zhou Yu, he smiles with relief, for it was those two who worried him most. Yet he is also anxious to know if Kong Ming has worked out what has happened. Lu Su offers to go and see.

Can he sort things out?

Let's see.

CHAPTER 46

Kong Ming 'borrows' arrows through a clever plot. Huang Gai agrees to be punished to help a secret plan.

It is very clear to Lu Su that Kong Ming knows perfectly well what kind of trick Zhou Yu has pulled on Cao Cao. When, despite Kong Ming asking him not to tell Zhou Yu that he knows, Lu Su blurts this out to Zhou Yu, once again Zhou is determined to destroy Kong Ming.

So it is that, the very next day, Zhou Yu summons all his commanders and asks Kong Ming to join them.

'Obviously,' says Zhou Yu, 'we will need to fight Cao Cao on the Great River with bows and arrows, yet we haven't enough arrows to be able to do this.' And turning to Kong Ming, Zhou Yu says, 'I wonder if you would be so kind as to provide them for us? We will need one hundred thousand.'

To this outrageous suggestion Kong Ming mildly replies that he is of course happy to help in any way, and by when would Zhou like his one hundred thousand arrows to be ready?

Zhou smiles and suggests that ten days would be very convenient. So imagine his astonishment when Kong Ming replies, 'I think we will be attacked before then, so ten days is too long. I suggest three days instead.'

'Do not make fun of me,' barks Zhou Yu, to which Kong Ming quietly replies, 'I wouldn't dream of doing so. If I fail to do this within three days, then, binding myself under military law, I'll take my punishment as due.'

A delighted Zhou Yu thinks that he has trapped Kong Ming, for failure under military law means execution. Kong Ming says, 'In three days' time send five hundred men to collect the arrows down by the river.' And after drinking a few cups of wine to honour the deal, Kong Ming departs.

Deeply troubled and distressed, Lu Su goes after Kong Ming and finds him lamenting his fate. 'I told you not to say anything to Zhou Yu,' says Kong Ming, 'and now he is even more determined to kill me. That's why he made me fall into this trap! How on earth am I going to produce one hundred thousand arrows in such a short time! You must help me!'

Lu Su says, 'Well, frankly, it's your own fault, but tell me, what can I do to help?'

'Lend me twenty boats with thirty men to each boat. I want a thousand straw bales covered with black cloth. If my plan works we'll have all the arrows ready by the third day. But not a word to Zhou Yu! Otherwise this won't work.'

So a somewhat bewildered Lu Su returns and tells Zhou Yu that Kong Ming doesn't seem to need any raw materials for making the arrows. This leaves Zhou even more confused than before.

Even though Lu Su provides the boats and other materials he has asked for, Kong Ming does nothing on the first day. Nor on the second day either. It is at the fourth watch of the third night that Lu Su is summoned by Kong Ming.

'Why am I here?' asks Lu Su, to which Kong Ming replies, 'To help me get the arrows, of course!'

'But where do we get them from?' asks a bewildered Lu Su.

'Just follow me and don't ask any questions,' replies Kong Ming.

So they board one of the thirty boats with their strange cargo of the bales of straw and set off for the enemy encampment on the north shore of the great river.

Now this night there is a dense fog, so dense it is impossible to see someone standing right in front of you. And it is into this dense fog that the boats sail at Kong Ming's command.

By the time of the fifth watch, the boats are nearing the north shore, and it is now that Kong Ming orders the sailors to beat the drums and shout out loud as if they are a huge invading force. Lu Su is horrified. 'What if the enemy attack us?' But Kong Ming points out that no one is going to venture out into a fog this bad.

Meanwhile, on shore, Cao Cao hears of what is going on

and orders his men to fire into the fog to ward off the apparent attack. Indeed, so eager is he for the firepower of crossbows and bows to inflict the severest possible damage on the enemy that he orders all the crossbowmen to join in the defence, firing into the fog in the direction of all the noise. Soon there are ten thousand archers and crossbowmen firing into the fog, hoping to prevent what they imagine is a surprise landing by the enemy. So intense is the action it is as if the arrows were falling like a great rainstorm.

Back on the boats, Kong Ming urges his sailors to sail as close as they can to the north shore. Arrow after arrow thuds into the barriers of the bales of black-wrapped straw as the sailors keep up the cacophony of sound. As the sun rises and the fog begins to dissolve, Kong Ming orders the boats to turn around and head home. By now each and every one of the thousand bales of straw is bristling with arrows. As they depart, Kong Ming shouts out, 'Thank you, Prime Minister, for sending us the arrows!' and by the time Cao Cao's men try to launch a counter-attack, Kong Ming and his arrows are far, far away. Cao Cao has to face the fact that yet again he has been fooled.

Turning to Lu Su, Kong Ming says, 'Well, each boat has collected around five to six thousand arrows and by my calculations and without any cost to the south, we have more than the one hundred thousand arrows required. So tomorrow we will return them to the enemy!'

Lu Su is, of course, delighted as well as astonished.

'How did you know about the fog?' he asks.

Kong Ming replies, 'A truly great commander must understand the patterns in Heaven, and those on Earth. He must understand how the gates open and comprehend the flow of yin and yang. He must know how to read and understand a map and have a profound brilliance in planning the disposition of his forces. Three days ago I was able to calculate that there would be such a fog, which is why I told Zhou three days when he offered ten! Given that Zhou offered no practical help whatsoever, it was clear he meant to do away with me. But I'm protected by the Mandate of Heaven, so there is nothing that Zhou Yu can do to overthrow that!'

As the boats arrive at the shore, so do the five hundred men that Kong Ming has asked to be ready. And thus the one hundred thousand arrows are delivered to Zhou Yu. Here, Lu Su tells him all about the ploy Kong Ming devised and its success. All Zhou Yu can do is sigh with a combination of admiration and regret!

As a poet has said:

> One day the fog shrouds the river,
> It's impossible to demarcate near and far.
> The arrows pour down like rain!
> Today Kong Ming is the absolute winner.

Swallowing his pride, Zhou Yu greets Kong Ming with appropriate praise and invites him to come and discuss strategy with him. Zhou Yu starts by outlining the problems and issues and conflicting advice he has received until Kong Ming asks him to stop talking for a moment and instead suggests that they each write on their own hand the word that would best sum up what each of them thinks will be the best strategy. Taking up brushes dipped in ink, they secretly write down a single character each. Then, shuffling close together at the same moment, they show each other what they wrote. To their surprise and delight, each has written 'fire'.

Back on the northern side, Cao Cao is fuming about his setbacks and longing to retaliate. He and Xun You decide to infiltrate spies into the south's camp. They agree to send men who claim to be deserting and choose Cai Zhong and Cai He, members of the Cai clan. As they are related to the recently executed Cai Mao, this will make it more plausible that they might desert and go to join Zhou Yu.

So the two agree to go and shortly afterwards they approach the south shore and 'defect'. Zhou Yu, however, is not fooled. He notes that they have not come with their families, who are still under Cao Cao's guard, and therefore he knows this is a ruse. However, he can see that they could be used in reverse, to feed false information to Cao Cao. Zhou Yu keeps this to himself and even fools Lu Su into believing he has been taken in.

But when Lu Su shares this concern with Kong Ming, he only smiles and tells him that this is all part of Zhou Yu's trick.

What Zhou Yu needs to complete the trick is a volunteer from his own side who will appear to defect and to provide that man with a plausible reason to do so.

One night Huang Gai secretly comes to see Zhou Yu, advocating the use of fire to destroy the enemy's fleet. Zhou Yu asks him if he is willing to undertake a dangerous exploit to help overcome Cao Cao, and Huang Gai is adamant that he will do anything he can. So Zhou Yu explains that he needs someone to 'desert' and join Cao Cao. But for this to be believable, especially to the two spies Cao Cao has sent, that person must have a powerful grudge to motivate such an action. Huang Gai says he is willing to give his life, so it is agreed that on the morrow he will be flogged for some fabricated reason and this will provide the justification for his desire to desert.

The next day, Zhou Yu summons all his commanders to attend a council of war. As he starts speaking about the need to have three months of rations laid up for the expected duration of the war, Huang Gai bursts out in an apparent rage.

'Three months! More likely this'll take thirty months, so why waste time? Let's attack now and get it over with in one month. Either that or we just surrender!'

Zhou Yu dramatically explodes with fury and orders Huang Gai's execution for the insult.

'I have served your worthy father up and down this land, so who are you to speak to me like this!' says Huang. This makes Zhou Yu order his immediate execution.

'My Lord,' says Gan Ning, 'Huang Gai is one of our most important commanders. Please, forgive him.'

'And if I do, who will obey my orders in future.'

At this the whole council of officers kneel and implore Zhou Yu to relent. Eventually he agrees that, instead of execution, Huang Gai be given a hundred lashes. This is duly carried out, leaving Huang Gai with deep cuts across his back and barely able to walk. Everyone except Zhou Yu is shocked and offers what help they can to the poor man.

When Lu Su discusses all this with Kong Ming, he is in a

state of deep distress. 'We could do nothing to help Huang Gai. But why did you just stand by? You're a guest, so you could have asked for mercy and it would probably have been given.'

'Don't you realize this is all a trick?' says Kong Ming. 'This is to fool Cao Cao when Huang Gai "defects". It has to look genuine if the two spies Cai Zhong and Cai He are to believe it and report this to Cao Cao. Then Cao Cao will believe in this "defection". Now, you must promise me not to tell Zhou Yu that I know this. Do you understand?'

A bit wiser now, when Lu Su discusses this all with Zhou Yu, and Zhou Yu tells him it is a trick, Lu Su keeps his counsel and simply wonders again at the brilliance of Kong Ming.

Later that night, as Huang Gai lies recovering in his tent, Kan Ze, one of the military advisers, comes to see him and tells how he too has realized this is all a trick. When Huang Gai asks for Kan Ze's help in carrying out the ruse, he is only too happy to help. What Huang Gai needs is someone to take his letter offering to defect to Cao Cao. Kan Ze readily agrees.

So what happens next?

All will be revealed.

CHAPTER 47

Kan Ze delivers a fake letter.
Pang Tong cons Cao Cao into linking his ships.

Now this Kan Ze is from a poor family, but he loved to study and in return for doing chores he was allowed by wealthy families to borrow books. He only needs to read a book once and he can remember it all. And he is famous for his eloquence. He is also a man of rare courage. So it is that he agrees to carry the letter, and Huang Gai has it prepared and hands it to him.

That night, disguised as a fisherman, he ferries himself across the river, where, upon landing, he is immediately arrested, and news of his capture and his letter is brought to Cao Cao. To be honest, Cao Cao is sure he is a plant, a spy, but he agrees to meet him. 'You claim you are Kan Ze,' says Cao Cao, 'yet you have come here. Why?'

'Poor Huang Gai,' cries Kan Ze, 'you have made another mistake! You, sir, are supposed to be magnanimous and searching for men of true courage and virtue. But your question shows this is not the case. Poor Huang Gai! You have made the same mistake again!'

'I am fighting Sun Quan,' replies Cao Cao, 'and suddenly you turn up. That is why I have to ask – why?'

Then Kan Ze tells the story of the humiliation and beating of Huang Gai. 'This is why I bear a letter to you from him,' says Kan Ze.

'Give me this letter,' demands Cao Cao.

In the letter Cao Cao reads of Huang Gai's service and loyalty to the Sun family for many years. But now he can see that their time is up. Everyone, he claims, at the top of the army can see that resistance to the great northern army is foolish except for that idiot Zhou Yu. He has such an exaggerated sense of his own importance he thinks he can smash a stone with an egg! In his arrogant foolishness he has punished the faultless and disregarded those worthy of promotion. 'I, Huang, have been humiliated and, knowing that you wish to have men of excellence, I have decided to come over to you with all my men.'

Cao Cao studies the letter over and over and then suddenly flares up.

'This is the old trick of a flogging followed by an apparent desertion,' he cries, and he orders the execution of Kan Ze. As he is about to be dragged away to be killed, Kan Ze suddenly laughs. Surprised by this, Cao Cao orders him brought back. 'I know what you are up to, so why are you laughing?'

'I am not laughing at you,' replies Kan Ze, 'but at poor Huang Gai, who thinks he understands men. Just get on with the execution, will you, please, and stop asking questions!'

'You can't fool me,' replies Cao Cao. 'I have studied the books of warfare and know this old trick when I see it.'

'What trick?' asks Kan Ze. 'Where in this letter do you find this "trick" – show me!'

'Huang Gai doesn't say a date or time when he will desert. If he was really wanting to come over he would have set a time.'

'You claim to know the books of war,' says Kan Ze, 'but really you know nothing! Don't you know the old saying that there is no set time for betraying your lord? What if he had said a day and time but for unforeseen circumstances was unable to be there on time. Then the whole venture might collapse. You can't fix a time to slip away. Really, you are a fool!'

This all makes Cao Cao stop and reflect. 'I'm sorry,' he says.

'You see, both Huang Gai and I want to come over to you,' says Kan Ze confidently.

It is at this point that a messenger comes in and whispers in Cao Cao's ear. It is clear to Kan Ze that this must be the report from Cao Cao's two spies, the Cais, that will confirm Huang's letter. And so it is, finally convincing Cao Cao of the sincerity of Huang's letter. However, somewhat to Kan Ze's consternation, Cao Cao asks him to return to the south in order to finalize the practical arrangements for Huang Gai's desertion. Reluctantly he agrees and sails back down the river.

He informs Huang Gai of his success thus far and then goes to see Gan Ning in order to find out what the two Cais are up to.

Arriving at Gan Ning's tent, Kan Ze says, 'I was appalled to see how you were insulted yesterday by Zhou Yu simply because you wanted to protect Huang Gai.' Gan Ning smiles but says nothing, and almost immediately the two Cais enter. Kan Ze flicks a look at Gan Ning, who catches the significance of this and explodes with righteous anger, saying, 'Zhou Yu's far too cocky and has no regard for others. He humiliated me, disgraced me in front of my peers.' And with that he grits his teeth, smashes his fist down on the table and roars with fury. In an apparent act of co-conspiracy, Kan Ze bends down and whispers in Gan Ning's ear.

Sensing momentous events are afoot, the two Cais ask, 'General, what's so upset you? And you, sir, what's this insult you have suffered?'

'You cannot even guess how bitter we are,' says Kan Ze, to which Cai He responds, 'Is it possible you want to leave Sun Quan and come over to Cao Cao?'

Hearing this, Kan Ze visibly pales, and Gan Ning rises up, draws his sword and in feigned horror shouts, 'We're discovered. We must kill them or we'll be betrayed.' Greatly alarmed, the two Cais rapidly reassure them, saying, 'There's nothing to fear here. In fact, we have something to tell you.'

Gan Ning looks at them sternly and asks, 'Well, what is it?' to which Cai He confesses that they are in fact spies sent by Cao Cao and that if they would like to come over to his side they would be only too happy to make the arrangements.

'Is this true?' asks Gan Ning, to which the Cais reply, 'Are we likely to invent something like this?'

'Heaven has indeed sent you,' says an apparently grateful Gan Ning. To this the Cais reply that the plight of both Huang Gai and Gan Ning has already been communicated to Cao Cao. Kan Ze tells how he has delivered a letter of surrender to Cao Cao from Huang Gai and that he is here today to try to persuade Gan Ning to desert as well.

The con is completed by Gan Ning proclaiming, 'If a man of decisive action meets a truly wise lord he should offer himself to him without hesitation.' Greatly encouraged by this, the four of them drink to the success of their decisions.

Immediately afterwards the two Cais write to Cao Cao to tell him of this great news while Kan Ze also writes secretly to Cao Cao, saying that Huang Gai will now desert and that he will sail across in a boat with a green flag in its prow.

However, despite the two letters which corroborate each other, Cao Cao is still not convinced this isn't a trick. So he decides to send a spy into the enemy camp. At the request for a volunteer, it is once again Jiang Gan who offers, saying that he is still embarrassed by his first attempt and consequent failure to lure Zhou Yu to join Cao Cao.

Zhou Yu is delighted when news comes of Jiang Gan's return, as he realizes he is about to fool Cao Cao once again. As part of his plan he calls for Pang Tong to come and attend him. Now Pang Tong, also known as Master Young Phoenix, is himself an exile from the north and its troubles. Known as a strategist, he has already offered advice to Lu Su, who has shared this with Zhou Yu. Pang Tong has advocated the use of fire but has also pointed out that if each ship is independent of the others then the moment a fire starts on one ship the others will simply slip away. The answer is to get them all tied together – then success will be assured.

Zhou Yu orders Jiang Gan brought to him, but Jiang is troubled that Zhou doesn't come down to meet him. So he hides his boat in a quiet location on the river, ready for a swift getaway.

When Jiang Gan comes before Zhou Yu, Zhou pretends to be very angry indeed and reprimands him for his treachery the last time he came to visit. The theft of the letter has, claims Zhou, been a disaster for his plans because Cai Mao and Zhang Yun have been executed! To show him that as a result their friendship is over, he sends Jiang off to stay at the Western Hills monastery as his guest until he has defeated Cao Cao.

Jiang Gan thus finds himself in a lonely, rather run-down setting and he becomes quite depressed.

When darkness comes, he wanders out to look at the stars and as he walks he hears in the distance someone reciting from a book. Drawing near, he sees a man reading by lamplight and to his astonishment he sees that the book is Sun Zi's *Art of War*. Introducing himself, he discovers that this man is called Pang Tong, whom Jiang has heard of as Master Young Phoenix and whom he has wanted to meet for a long time.

'But why are you stuck out here?' asks Jiang, to which Pang Tong replies, 'Zhou Yu is so full of himself he thinks there is no need for anyone else with skills, so I have retreated out here. And who exactly are you?'

'I am Jiang Gan.' And the two men fall into conversation, during which Jiang Gan, spotting a great opportunity, says, 'Your skills will win fame wherever you go, so why not come and serve Cao Cao? It would be my honour to introduce you.'

'Oh, you've no idea,' says Pang Tong, 'how I've longed to escape from here. But we must move swiftly, before Zhou Yu finds out.'

And so they set off straight away, climb into Jiang's hidden boat, swiftly cross the river and arrive at Cao Cao's camp. Cao Cao is delighted to hear that Master Young Phoenix has come, and soon they are talking away.

'That stripling Zhou Yu,' says Cao Cao, 'is a fool to disregard his own staff and their talents. I've heard about you for so long and am delighted you have come to join us. I would very much appreciate your advice.'

'Well,' says Pang Tong, 'I've heard so many times that you're a master of military affairs so I would very much like to see how you order your forces.'

And so off they go on a grand tour of the layout and disposal of Cao Cao's forces. At every place, Pang Tong praises Cao Cao's strategic thinking, and Cao Cao preens himself hearing such praise.

Returning to Cao Cao's camp, the two men continue their conversation, but Cao Cao is suddenly caught unawares when Pang Tong says, 'I hope you have lots of doctors.'

Needless to say, Cao Cao is intrigued but also confused to hear this. In fact, there has been an outbreak of illness among his men, and this has worried him.

'The problem is,' says Pang Tong, 'that your men on the boats are at risk, but there's a way of preventing this.'

Cao Cao, of course, wants to know what that could be, so Pang Tong tells him.

'It's all down to how you've set up your naval depots. The river is a turbulent one, and this constant movement is making your landlubber men sick. Now, if you were to tie up your various ships in groups of, say, between thirty and fifty and linked them with broad walkways, then this would stabilize them and keep them still even in a storm.'

Cao Cao leaps up with delight and thanks Pang Tong.

Within hours, the blacksmiths are ordered to create huge chains and fixtures to link the ships together.

Pang Tong, meanwhile, offers to go back to the south to try to persuade more men to come over. But before he leaves Cao Cao, he asks him to write an order of protection for his family and to be magnanimous when he crosses the river and spare the ordinary people.

'I fulfil the Will of Heaven,' says Cao Cao, 'so the people will not be harmed.' And so saying, he presents Pang Tong with a decree promising protection to his family in the case of attack.

Having taken his leave, Pang Tong goes down to the river to sail across to the south, when suddenly he is grabbed from behind. Turning, he sees a man in a Daoist robe with a bamboo hat, who says, 'You're brave, aren't you! Huang Gai plays the old torture trick, while Kan Ze plays the old letter of submission trick. Now you have added to this by suggesting the disastrous plan of chaining the ships together in order that fire can leap from ship to ship. You may have fooled Cao Cao, but you don't fool me!'

Pang Tong is so terrified his three souls flee, and his seven spirits desert him.

So who is this speaker?

Who indeed.

CHAPTER 48

Cao Cao holds a banquet on the river and sings a song. The north attacks the south with chained ships.

With huge relief Pang Tong realizes the speaker is none other than his old friend Xu Shu! 'Please don't tell anyone – think of the fate of all the people of the counties in the south,' says Pang Tong.

'Ah yes,' says Xu Shu, 'but what about the hundreds of thousands of northerners?'

'Are you going to destroy my plan?'

'No,' says Xu Shu. 'I'll never forget Xuande's kindness and I've also vowed to have my revenge on Cao Cao for the death of my mother. But I also run the risk of being trapped here, and when defeat comes for Cao Cao death will come to all, whether good or bad. Can you suggest a way I can escape this? If so, then I'll say nothing to anyone about your plot.'

So Pang Tong leans in and whispers in Xu Shu's ear. Xu Shu smiles, and Pang Tong at last departs for the south shore.

Xu Shu returns to the camp and begins his plot. He starts to spread rumours that Generals Han Sui and Ma Teng are advancing from the north on the capital. These rumours soon spread like wildfire among the troops until they reach the ears of Cao Cao himself. This is the only anxiety Cao Cao has had about coming south to attack Wu. At a hastily summoned meeting of his advisers, he asks for suggestions. This is when Xu Shu stands up and volunteers to take a force to defend their rear position at the San pass. 'If there is any crisis I will be able to report this to you straight away,' he says. Cao Cao is delighted and agrees to this with alacrity. Pan Tong's plan has worked! Xu Shu has Cao Cao's permission to leave and to place a great distance between himself and the battlefront.

Cao Cao surges south, but behind him
Always the fear of being attacked from behind.
Xu Shu follows Pang Tong's advice,
And so the fish dances aside from the hook!

With Xu Shu supposedly guarding his rear, Cao Cao's confidence returns, and he hosts a huge party for all his commanders on the largest of his ships. He is now ready to invade.

But at the party he drinks too much and soon is in a belligerent and drunken mood. Right from the start of the party there are inauspicious auguries, such as a raven calling in the middle of the night. But this just seemed to increase Cao Cao's bravado, and, sticking his great spear into the prow of the ship, he declares that just as this spear disposed of the Yellow Headbands, Lü Bu, Yuan Shu and Yuan Shao, so it means he is an invincible hero who will overcome all. Now very drunk indeed, he sings a song full of reminiscences of heroes, the wonders of nature, the delight of friends and the triumphs of past heroes such as the duke of Zhou.

Everyone cheers – they are almost all drunk too! But one man does not cheer. He challenges Cao Cao, saying that he has ignored inauspicious auguries and indeed has even talked of some in his song. Furious at being scolded, Cao Cao turns on the speaker, who is Liu Fu, the governor of Yangzhou, and in a moment of drunken madness spears him to death there and then.

The party ends abruptly. People scurry away, and there is a sense of great foreboding.

The next day, when Liu Fu's son comes to collect the body, Cao Cao apologizes profusely, admitting he had been drunk.

By now the fleet is ready for action. Cao Cao seats himself in the largest ship in the centre of his flotilla and gives the order to attack. It fills Cao Cao's heart to bursting point to see his magnificent fleet move out, steady as a rock thanks to Pang Tong's advice about linking all the ships. Even when Cheng Yu suggests that this might put the ships at risk of contagious fire, Cao Cao dismisses this, pointing out that the wind is blowing in the wrong direction because it is that time of the year.

The sound of the war drums reaches Zhou Yu and his men

on the south bank, and they prepare for action. Watching the huge armada sailing down upon them, Zhou Yu's commanders ask him how they are to confront such a vast horde. Suddenly they are all pointing at the great ship in which Cao Cao is sailing. The huge yellow banner's pole has snapped, and the great flag comes crashing down. Not a good sign, as they all agree, but then something else unexpected happens. A strong wind arises and whips Zhou Yu's standard into his face. A foreboding comes into his mind, and with a loud cry he collapses, blood pouring from his mouth. His men rush to him, but he is unconscious.

Will he survive?

Let's find out.

CHAPTER 49

Kong Ming prays for an eastern wind at the Altar of the Seven Stars. At the Red Cliffs, Zhou Yu uses fire to destroy Cao Cao's navy.

You can imagine the dismay that Zhou Yu's collapse causes. With a million-strong army descending upon them, what are the men of the south to do? Lu Su rushes off to inform Kong Ming of this disaster.

'What is your reading of this?' asks Kong Ming, to which Lu Su replies that it is good for Cao Cao but disastrous for the south.

'I can cure Zhou Yu,' says Kong Ming, which of course is music to Lu Su's ears. So off they go to see Zhou Yu.

Zhou Yu is laid out in bed, and when Kong Ming asks how he is feeling he says that his heart is in pain and that he feels faint. Asked if he has taken medicine, he says he cannot get any down because of nausea.

'I have missed you in the last few days,' says Kong Ming. 'Why have you fallen ill?'

'Unexpected fortune or lack of fortune can come upon us at any time. Indeed, no one can be safe.'

Smiling, Kong Ming replies, 'And what of sudden winds from Heaven? Indeed, no one can predict.'

At this Zhou Yu pales and groans, and Kong Ming adds, 'Are you feeling deeply troubled? Does it feel as if your heart is heavy with anxieties?' to which Zhou Yu manages to gasp, 'Yes.' 'Then you need something cool to rid you of this,' says Kong Ming. 'Clearly your qi is out of balance, and once we balance it you'll be fine.'

Zhou Yu knows Kong Ming is talking in riddles, so he asks, 'What do you recommend?' to which Kong Ming asks for pen and paper and writes something down. He then shows this to

Zhou Yu, who reads, 'To defeat Cao Cao fire is our best solution. But what can we do if the wind does not blow from the east?'

Zhou Yu is once again astonished and fearful of the unerring powers of Kong Ming and says, 'So you know what troubles me. What remedy can you offer, and quickly too?'

'I've little in the way of skills,' says Kong Ming, 'but I did learn from some magic books how to command the winds and call down rain. If we're going to need a southeasterly wind I'll need a special altar built – the Altar of the Seven Stars – and this must be built on Nanping mountain, nine feet high, with three levels and surrounded by one hundred and twenty men carrying banners. With this I should be able to create a wind that will blow for three days and nights. Will that do?'

And Zhou Yu agrees that this will more than do but it must happen quickly. He then rises, his sickness cured, and orders that Kong Ming be supplied with whatever he needs.

So Kong Ming travels with his workforce of five hundred men and the one hundred and twenty banner carriers, and with Lu Su he starts work on creating the altar on Nanping mountain. He selects a site with the best feng shui and has red earth brought. Swiftly the altar arises – two hundred and forty feet in circumference, nine feet high, with each level being three feet high. The symbols of the twenty-eight constellations are placed on the lowest level – to the east, the symbol of a green dragon; to the north, the symbol of the black turtle; to the west, the symbol of the white tiger, and to the south, the symbol of the red bird.

On the second level he has the symbols of the sixty-four hexagrams, while on the top level he places four men clothed in Daoist costume. One of them holds a pole with feathers at the top to detect the direction of the wind. One holds a pole with a belt with the symbols of the seven stars, again to detect the wind direction. The third man holds his sword and the fourth holds the incense burner.

When all is ready, Kong Ming fasts, bathes and then mounts the altar barefoot and with his hair falling upon his shoulders. Turning to Lu Su, he says, 'I will do my best, but don't blame me if it doesn't work!' Lighting the incense and sprinkling water, he stands and prays silently. Then he goes and rests. Three times he does this, and yet nothing happens.

Back at the camp, Zhou Yu, Lu Su and others wait for the promised wind, and messengers are sent to Sun Quan to alert him to the plans and asking for reinforcements. The fire ships are ready, stuffed full of kindling soaked in fish oil and covered with sulphur, saltpetre and just about anything else that will burst into flames. News comes that Sun Quan is moored with his fleet awaiting developments, and yet no wind arises.

It is at the time of the third watch in the night that the wind begins to blow. Within minutes a full-scale southeasterly is blowing. To this Zhou Yu reacts with yet another bout of his paranoia. 'Kong Ming is clearly in league with dark powers, with ghosts and evil spirits, if he is able to do this,' he says. 'He is a threat to us all. He shouldn't be allowed to live.' He summons two of his officers, Ding Feng and Xu Sheng, and orders them to go immediately to Nanping mountain, one by river the other by land, and to bring back the head of Kong Ming.

Riding hard, Ding Feng and his cavalry arrive first but can find no sign of Kong Ming. Discovering that he has left, Ding Feng rushes down the hill, where he finds Xu Sheng just landing from his boat. There they discover that Kong Ming has been seen setting sail in a boat that arrived commanded by Zhao Zilong. So off they go in pursuit by land and by water. Xu Sheng orders every sail to be unfurled, and soon he sees the little boat ahead of him and, calling out, he tries to persuade Kong Ming to return 'to go and see our commander'.

Kong Ming just laughs and shouts back, 'Tell Zhou Yu to be careful how he advances. I am going back to Xiakou, but we'll meet again!'

Xu Sheng tries to persuade him again to stay, but Kong Ming shouts, 'I knew Zhou Yu would not want me to live, which is why Zhao Zilong came to collect me. So don't bother to chase after me.'

However, Xu Sheng is not that easily put off. Given his superior craft and the sails he has hoisted, he is sure he can easily overtake the little boat. But he has not reckoned on Zhao Zilong! As Xu Sheng's boat draws closer and closer, Zhao Zilong stands up and notches an arrow to his bow.

'I am Zhao Zilong,' he shouts, 'and I've come on express orders to bring our adviser home. Why are you chasing him? Myself, I would like to kill you, but that might do damage to the relationship between our two leaders. But I'll show you what I can do.'

And so saying, he lets fly the arrow. Swiftly it cuts through the air and then slices through the rope holding up the main sail. Down it comes, crashing into the water, and the hapless vessel begins to swing round and round as Zhao Zilong and Kong Ming disappear in their little boat, far beyond sight.

Returning to Zhou Yu, Xu Sheng reports their failure, and it takes Lu Su's common sense to calm things down by pointing out that they should wait until after defeating Cao Cao to deal with Kong Ming.

Now it is time to launch the attack.

Zhou Yu sends Gan Ning with Cai Zhong to destroy the grain supply of Cao Cao, telling them to go flying the banners of the north to fool the enemy. Taishi Ci is sent to Huangzhou to be ready to cut off Cao Cao's men in Hefei. 'Watch for a red banner,' said Zhou Yu. 'That will be the sign that our Lord Sun Quan's troops have arrived.

Lü Meng is sent to assist Gan Ning and to burn the main camp of Cao Cao; another detachment is sent to Yiling ready for action, while yet another detachment is sent to take Hanyang. From there they are to attack the enemy along the river.

Once they are on their way, Huang Gai readies his fireboats and then sends a letter to Cao Cao announcing that he will desert that very night. Four fleets, each of three hundred ships, are ready, with fireboats in the van. News comes from Sun Quan that he has despatched troops towards Qizhou and Huangzhou. Hearing that, Zhou Yu sends men to the Western hills with fire bombs and to raise the battle banner on Nanping mountain.

Now all that remains is to wait for dusk to fall and for the battle to commence.

So while we wait, let's return to Xuande. Anxiously he has

waited for Kong Ming's return so he is delighted when the little boat comes into sight. Soon Kong Ming, Xuande, Liu Qi, Zhao Zilong and the two brothers are in conference. The time for action has come.

Kong Ming sends Zilong to cross the river at Wulin and prepare an ambush because he knows that Cao Cao will retreat that way. 'Wait until half his force has gone past then set fire to the undergrowth. We may not catch Cao Cao, but at least half his detachment will die.'

Next, he sends Zhang Fei to cross the river and block the roads to Yiling. Here he can catch Cao Cao if he heads to North Yiling. 'He'll stop to cook food, and as soon as you see the smoke, set fire to the hill. You probably won't catch Cao Cao, but this'll be of great assistance anyway.'

Next, he sends Mi Zhu, Mi Fang and Liu Feng to attack the enemy on the river and to seize all the weapons they can.

Liu Qi is sent to Wuchang because Cao Cao's men will probably try to escape that way. 'But do not under any circumstances leave the city,' warns Kong Ming.

Finally, he says to Xuande, 'Go to Fankou and from there watch how Zhou Yu leads his men into battle.'

Standing to one side throughout this has been Guan Yu, to whom no task has been assigned. Unable to stand this any longer, he erupts, 'I've never been left out before while my brothers go into battle. What's going on?'

'Cao Cao once treated you most kindly, and this means you're sure to feel that you must repay him. My concern is that this will mean you will let him pass if you are sent to block his path along a road. That is why I haven't assigned you a role.'

'What!' exclaims Guan Yu. 'That is why you don't trust me? I've repaid Cao Cao many times, killing Yuan Shao's commander Yan Liang; executing Wen Chou; breaking through the siege at Baima. Do you really think I would let him go now?'

'Yes, but what if you did?' says Kong Ming, pushing Guan Yu hard.

'Then let military law for treason be my judge!'

'Alright, but put that down in writing,' says Kong Ming, unwilling to let him off the hook.

So Guan Yu is given command of the ambush on the road to Huarong. He is to lure Cao Cao that way by setting fire to the brush wood. This will make Cao Cao think an ambush has already been sprung and encourage him to try to force his way through.

It is only when Gua Yu has left that Xuande confesses he fears Guan Yu's sense of honour will mean he will let Cao Cao escape. To this Kong Ming replies that he has studied the stars, and Cao Cao is not due to die tomorrow. So he has put Guan Yu there to perform an act of kindness which will greatly enhance Guan Yu and make no difference to the fate of Cao Cao!

Back now to Cao Cao, who is waiting for confirmation that Huang Gai has abandoned Zhou Yu and is on his way. Even though the wind has shifted to the southeast, Cao Cao is blasé about it. The letter from Huang Gai arrives, and Cao Cao reads that not only is he planning to come over to Cao Cao but he will also capture the grain ships which are coming to supply Zhou Yu and the southern army. These he will bring as a tribute to Cao Cao.

Back again to the south side, and Zhou Yu has ordered Cai He to be brought to his tent. Bound and terrified, he is thrown at the feet of Zhou, where he pleads that he has committed no crime.

'Really?' says Zhou Yu. 'You think you can come over here pretending to join us and we won't guess this is a trick? Well we did, and today you'll be the sacrifice needed to consecrate our banners.' At this, Cai He is marched down to the riverbank and there executed, his blood poured as a libation to the banner. Then and only then do the ships set sail.

Leading the attack and heading for the area known as the Red Cliffs is Huang Gai in full battle armour and with a huge banner on his vessel proudly declaring that he is 'Vanguard Huang Gai'. Cao Cao, already gloating over his impending victory, looks out over the waters and sees coming towards him, just as promised, a boat with the standard of Huang Gai. 'Truly this is a sign of the Will of Heaven,' says Cao Cao, but his smug reflections are suddenly punctured by Cheng Yu's desperate cry. 'It's a trick! They mustn't come near us!'

'What are you talking about?' demands Cao Cao.

'If he was bringing grain in these vessels, they would be much, much lower in the water. Instead these boats are so light they are flying down the river, aided by the wind. There's no stopping them!'

In an instant Cao Cao sees he has been fooled and in desperation asks for someone to try to stop the attack. Wen Ping volunteers and with a flotilla of a dozen or so small ships tries to head off the armada. But no sooner does he get near than an arrow takes him out, and the flotilla flees in disarray.

Now, with the raising of his sword, Huang Gai gives the signal to fire the boats. Sped on by the wind, the flames race across the boats as they bear down on Cao Cao's navy. Twenty fireboats crash into the chained ships, and, as there is no escape, the flames tear across from ship to ship to ship in an instant. From the south shore, catapults hurl huge missiles to add to the confusion, death and destruction. Every surface of the junction of the three rivers seems to be on fire, so intense is the conflagration.

Cao Cao looks about him, seeking how to escape. Huang Gai spots him, jumps into a skiff and sets off after him. Zhang Liao drives through to rescue him in a small boat, and Cao Cao leaps in, and now it is a race to see who lands first.

'Stop, you traitor,' roars Huang Gai, waving his sword. 'Huang Gai has indeed come!' But these are his last words of defiance to Cao Cao. Zhang Liao fires an arrow, which takes Huang Gai full in the armpit, and, felled by this blow, he falls into the river.

With the fires of fate roaring, he too met his fate by water;
While beating with wood had healed,
It is an iron arrow that toppled him.

Can he survive to enjoy the victory he has helped make?

Let's find out.

CHAPTER 50

Kong Ming predicts Cao Cao will try to escape via Huarong. Guan Yu lets Cao Cao escape because of friendship.

Zhang Liao's arrow shot gives him the advantage needed to rescue Cao Cao. He hauls him onto dry land, and they then mount upon horseback and flee even as the whole army descends into chaos.

Meanwhile, Han Dang, one of the commanders from the south, is steering to the attack on Cao Cao's naval yard, trying to find his way through the smoke and flames, when one of his men says, 'There is someone being dragged along, clutching at the rudder and calling your name!' Han Dang stands still and listens carefully and sure enough he hears a voice crying, 'Dang, save me!' Realizing that this is Huang Gai, he has him pulled up out of the water. With his teeth he yanks the arrow shaft out, but the head of the arrow is left behind. Taking his sword, he digs out the arrowhead and then binds up the wound with his own cloak. Having done this, he has Huang Gai transported back to camp, where he recovers, for, as he is a sailor, the fall into the water has not been fatal despite the cold and the weight of his armour.

On this day fire rolls across the river in waves, and the earth itself shakes with the sound of warfare. Attacks come from all sides. What the fire does not destroy the soldiers do and vice versa. Either by spears or arrows, by fire or by drowning, men beyond number are lost to Cao Cao on that day of the dreadful battle of the Red Cliffs. As a poet has said:

> Wei and Wu fight for control,
> The ships all smashed at the Red Cliffs.
> Roaring flames flare on the river –
> Zhou Yu the victor; Cao Cao the vanquished.

While this terrible onslaught is taking place on the river, back on land Gan Ning has penetrated deep inside Cao Cao's camp. He has tricked Cai Zhong into believing he is going to desert and so fooled everyone. Once inside the camp he slays Cai Zhong with one blow, and the traitor falls dead from his horse. Immediately Gan Ning sets fire to undergrowth. This is the signal southern commander Lü Meng has been waiting for, and he lights his fires as well. Then Pan Zhang and Dong Xi follow suit, while all the soldiers roar their battle cry and beat their war drums in every direction.

Cao Cao and his stalwart Zhang Liao have only a few men left, and they flee through the blazing countryside even though they cannot see where to go through the flames and smoke. When Cao Cao demands that they find a way through, Zhang Liao points out the only way is through the nearby forest.

No sooner have they taken that path than a cry rings out from the enemy. Lü Meng has caught up with them, crying, 'Halt, you traitor.' Cao Cao plunges on with his small troop, leaving Zhang Liao to fight Lü Meng. Cao Cao has barely gone any distance before yet another cry rings out from his enemies. It is Ling Tong, charging down the valley towards him! Cao Cao's nerves begin to fail him, and he is sick to the stomach with fear. Then yet another group of soldiers crashes through the forest towards him, but this time the cry is one of encouragement, because this troop is led by his friend Xu Huang. The men of Ling Tong and of Xu Huang clash, charging at each other. In the mêlée Cao Cao makes good his escape to the north, where to his relief he comes across three thousand northern troops, who, seeing the chaos, have held back, unsure what to do next.

Cao Cao sends a thousand to clear the road ahead while he keeps the rest to protect him as he goes forward. But there is more to come. They have not gone more than a few miles when yet another cry rends the air, and charging towards them comes Gan Ning. He strikes down the lead commanders with single blows, and men rush back to tell Cao Cao of this latest disaster. Cao Cao is still holding out hope that reinforcements will arrive from Hefei. But the net is closing, for Sun Quan, seeing the fires, knows that the south is triumphant and signals this to Taishi Ci and Lu Xun, who then lead their men into the attack. This forces Cao Cao to now turn towards Yiling.

It is around the fifth watch that Cao Cao stops and asks where they are. The reply is west of the forest and north of Yidu. To everyone's astonishment Cao Cao roars with laughter, and when his men ask him why he says, 'I'm laughing at Zhou Yu and Kong Ming, who simply aren't that bright! This is where they should have set an ambush, as I would, because there's no way of escape from here.'

No sooner does he say this than war drums thunder out and flames roar up around them. Out of the smoke and chaos comes the voice of the enemy commander. 'I am Zhao Zilong, sent to await you by order, and I've had to wait a long time for you!' Xu Huang and Zhang He charge forward to battle with Zhao Zilong, and Cao Cao makes good his escape again in the mêlée.

Then the heavens open, and torrential rain falls upon them all. By now the men with Cao Cao are exhausted and starving. Realizing this, Cao Cao sends scavenging parties out to loot local villages of food, and soon a fire is burning to cook the food. Here they are joined by a few more men led by Xu Chu and Li Dian. When it is time to move on, Cao asks where they are and is told they are at a fork in the road. One leads to South Yiling and the other, over the mountain, leads to North Yiling. Following advice, he leads his party off towards Hulukou – the pass on the way to North Yiling. Reaching the pass, and realizing how exhausted his men and horses are, Cao Cao orders a rest break. Fires start, food is cooked and the horses are turned loose while the men try to dry their sodden clothes. Suddenly Cao Cao bursts out laughing again. Deeply troubled, the men say, 'Last time you laughed at Zhou Yu and Kong Ming this brought disaster, and Zhao Zilong attacked us. So what're you laughing about now?'

'Well,' says Cao Cao, 'to tell the truth, at the foolishness of Zhou Yu and Kong Ming, because this is a perfect place for an ambush, especially of men who are exhausted.'

Once again, no sooner has he said this than war cries erupt

all around them! This time Cao Cao in panic throws aside his armour and leaps on his horse to escape once again, but most of his men have no time to mount. They are soon surrounded by the attackers, who are led by none other than Zhang Fei. He questions some of the men who are captured and tries to discover where Cao Cao is or has gone. But soon he is caught up in a fight against Zhang Liao and Xu Huang. They deliberately block him until Cao Cao has made good his escape. But then Zhang Fei breaks free and sets off on the trail of Cao Cao.

Cao Cao pauses in his flight, and one of the soldiers asks which of the two roads ahead they should take. 'Which one is shorter?' barks Cao Cao and is told that the main road is easier but longer while the road towards Huarong is shorter but much, much harder. Cao Cao's men notice that smoke is rising from a number of places along that road but that the main road is clear, and so it is to everyone's surprise that Cao Cao decides to take the road to Huarong. When he is questioned as to why, Cao Cao replies, 'Remember what Sun Zi tells us in *The Art of War*: "When you are weak, pretend to be strong; when you are strong, pretend to be weak!" Kong Ming is full of tricks and he has had fires lit along that route to scare us off so we will walk into his trap on the main road. Well, I'm not falling for that trick!' And so, disastrously, they turn off and head along the narrow road to Huarong.

This is now a beleaguered, exhausted and worn-out band of men. Racked by hunger, weeping wounds, burns, almost unable to walk unaided, they drag themselves along, weighed down by sodden clothes and heavy hearts. It is the middle of winter, and the cold bites into them. Imagine their distress.

Suddenly all movement stops, and when Cao Cao enquires why, he is told that the path is overgrown and narrow and the horses have become stuck in the thick mud caused by the torrential rain. Furious, Cao Cao lambasts his men. 'Leave the old, feeble and sick to fend for themselves. The rest of you cover the mud with branches and undergrowth so we can get through. We go on regardless. Anyone who complains or disobeys will be executed!'

So, grudgingly, the soldiers cut branches and start to cover the mud, while Cao Cao orders a hundred of the remaining horsemen to patrol, ready to execute anyone who does not obey. When they are ready, Cao Cao urges them on, even though this means trampling upon not just the branches but upon the bodies of the fallen. So many are dying, and the air is rent by cries of distress of the survivors. Cao Cao rages against them, shouting, 'The Will of Heaven decides life or death. So why are you crying? The next one to do so will be killed!'

The men have divided into three by now; one third stagger on as best they can; one third work to cover the mud and clear the path; and one third escort Cao Cao. By the time they get past the worst of the mud, Cao Cao has only got about three hundred soldiers left. Despite pleas to stop and rest, Cao Cao insists they press on.

Suddenly Cao Cao laughs out loud again and on being questioned by his anxious men says, 'So Zhou Yu and Kong Ming are supposed to be brilliant plotters! But they've failed to set a trap here, where we would have no option but to surrender!'

Suddenly the air is rent with explosions, and five hundred swordsmen block the road. At their head, wielding his Green Dragon sword and mounted upon Red Hare, is Guan Yu. Utter despair sweeps over Cao Cao's men, and Cao Cao says with a sigh, 'So this is it. The last battle.' But his officers say the men are not able to fight. Then Cheng Yu says, 'Look, Guan Yu is famous for his virtue, noble to the weak and hard on the strong. He understands the difference between duty and anger. He is renowned for his righteousness and honour. You, my lord, showed him such kindness in the past. If you make a personal appeal, we might be saved.'

Cao Cao sees the wisdom of this and, riding slowly forward, head bowed in deference, he addresses Guan Yu.

'I hope you have been well,' says Cao Cao, 'since we last met.'

Bowing, Guan Yu says, 'I've orders from my commander and have waited long for you to come.'

'I come before you today,' says Cao Cao, 'a beaten man and with a beaten army. I've nowhere to go, but I hope, sir, that in honour of our past friendship you'll think kindly of me.'

'It is true that you were kind in the past, but I repaid that by killing the two enemy commanders and relieving the siege at Baima. Today I must not set aside my duty for purely personal reasons.'

But Cao Cao has a clever answer. 'Have you forgotten that you killed my own officers at the five passes as you escaped? A truly great man considers both righteousness and honour, as our ancient texts tell us. Remember the story of the student Yugong, who was sent to hunt down his erstwhile master, Zizhuo Ruzi. He let him go, unable to use what he had learned from his master to destroy the same man!'

And this touches Guan Yu. He cannot lightly dismiss Cao Cao's past kindnesses or the fact of the deaths of the officers at the passes. Looking upon the terrible state of Cao Cao and his men, his heart is moved by pity.

'Spread out along the road,' he commands his troop, turning his horse away from Cao Cao as he speaks. Seizing their opportunity, Cao Cao and his officers dash through the gap created and ride off into the distance. Guan Yu turns back and addresses the remainder of Cao Cao's men. He roars at them, and they fall to the ground. But Guan Yu's heart is touched once again and when his old friend Zhang Liao rides forward Guan Yu relents and lets every man go free.

> Cao Cao, defeated, retreats to Huarong
> Only to meet Guan Yu on the path.
> Heart-moved by memory of past kindness,
> Guan Yu lets the dragon escape.

As he rides pell-mell out of the valley, Cao Cao looks back and realizes there are only twenty-seven men still with him. At last, as the fateful day fades, they find sanctuary at Nanjun, where shortly afterwards Zhang Liao also arrives with his men to tell of the further compassion of Guan Yu.

The next day Cao Cao sets off for the capital to raise another army for revenge. But before he leaves he calls Cao Ren to come to see him. Handing him a letter, he says, 'You are to protect this place. I am leaving this secret letter with you. Do not open it except if you are in a real crisis and then you must do exactly as the letter says. This will protect you from Zhou Yu.'

He also spells out how he would protect Xiangyang, Jingzhou and Hefei, but, if any crisis emerges for any of them, Cao Ren is to notify him immediately.

Let us now return to Guan Yu. He has made his way back to the victorious army's camp, where the leaders are celebrating their triumphs and trophies of victory. He alone has returned with nothing. Kong Ming rubs this in. Hearing Guan Yu has returned, he goes out to meet him and says, 'Congratulations! You have got rid of the worst enemy and we should've prepared a proper Triumph for you on your return.'

To this, Guan Yu says nothing – there is nothing to say.

So Kong Ming continues in a similar vein of faux congratulations until Guan Yu barks out, 'I've come back to die.'

'Why?' asks Kong Ming. 'Didn't Cao Cao come that way in the end?'

'He did, but I was foolish enough to let him go.'

'So who did you capture? Where are they?' asks Kong Ming.

'No one.'

'So you mean to tell me that you deliberately let him go because he has been kind to you in the past? You know the consequences. You signed this agreement, and we'll now have to enforce it.' And so saying, he calls for the guards to come and execute Guan Yu!

Guan Yu has risked his life to honour kindness.
This is why his name is spoken with pride to this day.

Cao Cao has escaped with his life.

Can Guan Yu?

CHAPTER 51

In a tremendous battle between north and south, Zhou Yu is wounded. Kong Ming provokes Zhou Yu to fury for the first time.

Kong Ming appears to be ready to execute Guan Yu when Xuande arrives and forbids this. 'We brothers made a pledge that we would live and die together. This former pledge overrides the commitment he made under martial law. Just record that he was wrong and broke the code and let him show in future that he has repented.'

So Guan Yu lives to fight another day.

Meanwhile Zhou Yu, triumphant after his victory, is thinking through what to do next. News is brought to him that Xuande has moved his force to the mouth of the River You and that Kong Ming is with him.

This causes Zhou Yu to be deeply alarmed. He is convinced this means that Xuande is planning to seize the city of Nanjun – the very city Zhou Yu plans to capture. Determined to find out if this is Xuande's plan, he sets off with Lu Su to visit Xuande.

It is a very tense meeting in an atmosphere of distrust on both sides. Xuande has been warned by Kong Ming that Nanjun is the bone of contention. He has briefed Xuande on how to answer Zhou Yu's questions.

After Zhou Yu has said he understands Xuande is planning to take Nanjun and Xuande has countered by saying he understands that is Zhou Yu's plan, Zhou says, 'If we fail, you're very welcome to try.'

Immediately, as advised by Kong Ming, Xuande says, 'We've witnesses here – Lu Su and Kong Ming – who will vouch that you said this, and so you'll not be able to go back on that commitment.' To which Zhou Yu replies, 'Do you not think I am a man of honour? Of course I will not renege on that.'

When Zhou Yu leaves, Xuande asks Kong Ming what this is all about. Kong Ming says, 'Let Zhou do the fighting. We will be sitting inside Nanjun before long!'

As far as Zhou Yu is concerned, his promise is meaningless, as he is now determined to be the one to take Nanjun.

So the struggle for the city begins. Zhou Yu sends an advanced party, which is roundly defeated by Cao Ren's men. It swiftly becomes clear that the town of Yiling is strategically important in the defence of Nanjun, and Cao Ren sends men to defend it. However, as the southern commander Gan Ning advances upon Yiling, Cao Ren's men come out to attack and are driven off so successfully that Gan Ning enters the safety of the town only to then find himself almost immediately besieged by the northern forces. News of this reaches Zhou Yu, who sets out to raise the siege. The combined forces of Zhou Yu's main army and Gan Ning's men inflict a crushing defeat on the northern army. Leaving Yiling to turn back to attack Nanjun, Zhou Yu runs into the relieving force that Cao Ren has sent to aid the northern army at Yiling. Battle commences, but without resolution. In the end, worn out and incapable of any further struggle, Cao Ren returns to Nanjun and Zhou Yu to his camp.

With the loss of Yiling, Cao Ren and his men are in fact in an increasingly desperate state, and Cao Ren decides this is the time to open Cao Cao's secret letter. The result? He orders his men to be prepared to abandon Nanjun when dawn breaks, while placing his banners on the walls as if the army is still in full command.

The two forces face each other that dawn, and soon battle commences, with Zhou Yu splitting his army into two, one section of which he is going to lead into the city and take control. Cao Ren leads the northern attack, but soon the northern army is faltering under the combined attack of the two flanks of the southern army. However, to Zhou Yu's surprise, instead of seeking refuge in the city, Cao Ren retreats north in apparent disarray. As a result Zhou Yu rides swiftly into the city through the outer wall gate and heads for the inner wall gate.

Hidden up in the tower over the inner gate, Chen Jiao

marvels at Cao Cao's secret letter and its wisdom as he gives orders for the massed ranks of archers to open fire. It is as if it were raining arrows and crossbow bolts! The enemy fall in huge numbers, and a bolt from a crossbow strikes Zhou Yu himself as he desperately tries to escape. Had it not been for the bravery of Xu Sheng and Ding Feng, he would have been captured.

Cao Cao's army now turns back to attack the soldiers as they run from the city. But for a courageous charge by Ling Tong, who manages to confront and halt the attack of the northerners, it would have been a complete disaster for Zhou Yu and his men. Cao Ren is able to re-enter the city, while Zhou Yu's men limp back to their camp. There, Zhou Yu lies seriously ill and in great pain. Without their leader, Cheng Pu decides that the army should just rest and not respond to any provocation. However, one of Cao Ren's commanders can't resist riding out each day to hurl insults and taunts at the enemy.

On one of these days, Zhou Yu asks what all the fuss is – knowing full well that his men are being challenged. His men try to lie to him, saying the noise is his own men in training, but he tells them to call Cheng Pu to come to see him.

'Why have you done nothing about this abuse and challenge?' asks Zhou Yu.

'The doctor says you need to rest,' replies Cheng Pu, 'and that you mustn't be upset. That's why I haven't told you about this.'

'But why,' persists Zhou Yu, 'have you refused to fight?'

'Your officers feel we should retreat south and wait until you've recovered before we attack again,' says Cheng Pu.

Furious at this reply, Zhou struggles up from his sickbed and says, 'Any man worthy of the name will wish to die in the service of his lord and to be brought home wrapped in horsehide as a hero. Don't fail our cause and claim you do this for me! Standing up, he dons his armour and calls for his horse, which he mounts, leaving his officers stunned.

Followed by hundreds of horsemen, Zhou Yu rides to the front of the camp, where Cao Cao's men are waiting. Cao Ren himself is there and, seeing the enemy advancing, he cries out, 'Zhou Yu! You baby! So fate has caught up with you, and you're such a coward you dare not face me!'

At this Zhou Yu charges forward, shouting, 'Cao Ren, you worthless creature! Can you see me now?'

The sight of Zhou Yu terrifies the enemy. To rally them, Cao Ren calls upon his men to hurl abuse at Zhou Yu.

In response, Zhou Yu sends his champion to fight, but before even a single blow is given, Zhou Yu slumps forward, crying out loudly, and falls from his horse, blood pouring from his mouth. Seeing this, Cao Ren urges his men to the attack, and battle commences. No one is quite sure what is happening, and confusion reigns. Meanwhile, in the chaos, his officers rescue Zhou Yu and carry him back to the safety of his tent.

Anxiously Cheng Pu asks how he is feeling, to which Zhou mutters, 'It's a trick that I've played! I'm not really that ill but I wanted the enemy to believe that I'm dying. Send some men who will pretend to desert and let them tell the enemy that I've died. Tonight they'll attack, thinking that you'll all be in mourning. But in reality we'll ambush them when they attack.'

So it is that soon the sound of mourning arises from the tent and then from the whole camp.

Back in Nanjun, Cao Ren is sure that Zhou Yu is on the brink of death. When the 'deserters' turn up saying that Zhou Yu has died and they have absconded because no one has confidence in Cheng Pu, Cao Ren starts to plan his night raid. He intends seizing the dead body of Zhou Yu so he can cut off his head and send it to Cao Cao in the capital as well as inflicting a crushing blow on the enemy.

Leaving just Chen Jiao to guard the city with a few men, Cao Ren sets out under cover of darkness. They steal up to the gate of the camp but find it open and the camp apparently empty. Suddenly fearing that this might be a trap, they start to retreat. But it is too late. The enemy attack begins with a bombardment and then a ferocious assault from every direction. Cao Ren's army is destroyed. Only Cao Ren and Cao Hong and their guards escape the onslaught. Dashing back towards Nanjun, they are attacked by a column of men led by Ling Tong. Turning aside, they try to flee but are attacked by Gan Ning and his men, who destroy most of the rest of the troop. Cao Ren manages to escape and rides hell for leather to Xiangyang.

Triumphant, Zhou Yu and Cheng Pu gather their army together and advance on Nanjun. Imagine their astonishment when they arrive to see banners flying from the towers and someone calling out to them from the wall.

'I'm sorry to say,' says the voice, 'that on orders from above, I, Zhao Zilong have taken this city.'

Zhou Yu's fury knows no bounds, and he immediately orders an attack, but a torrent of arrows drives his men from the walls. Zhou consults with his men, and they agree to send a troop to capture Gong'an and another to take Xiangyang, thereby cutting off Zhao Zilong's supplies. Then they can prepare for the major assault on Nanjun. But Kong Ming has outwitted them again! News comes flooding in to Zhou Yu: the soldiers at Jingzhou were fooled into believing they were needed and left the city, which Zhang Fei then seized; the same trick was played on the men guarding Xiangyang, and Guan Yu has now captured it.

On hearing this dreadful news, Zhou Yu gives a terrible cry, and his wound bursts open.

The struggle between Sun Quan and Xuande has taken a dramatic turn.

What will happen now?

What indeed!

CHAPTER 52

Kong Ming justifies capturing three cities. Zhao Zilong uses a clever plot to capture Guiyang.

The loss of Nanjun and Xiangyang to Kong Ming is too much for Zhou Yu. It causes his wound to reopen, and he collapses. When he comes round, his officers try to pacify him, but he exclaims, 'Nothing but the death of that country bumpkin Kong Ming will do!' He later tries to persuade Lu Su to join him in an attack on Xuande and Kong Ming, but Lu Su is blunt and to the point. 'Absolutely not!' he declares. Eventually Zhou Yu agrees that, rather than fight them, Lu Su will go as an ambassador and see if he can patch things up between the two leaders.

Arriving at Kong Ming's headquarters in Gong'an, Lu Su has to confess to himself that he is really rather impressed by Kong Ming's skills and the appearance of his army.

When Lu Su lays before Kong Ming the south's view that he and Xuande have usurped their land and that they have no right to take it, Kong Ming is quite shocked.

'I'm sorry, but on what legal basis do you make this claim?' he asks. 'Surely we all agree that "things belong to their proper owner" and these lands we've taken never belonged to the south. They belonged to Liu Biao – of whom my lord Xuande is an uncle. Liu Biao may be dead, but his son lives, and what uncle would not care for the well-being of his nephew?'

To this Lu Su tries a riposte, 'That would be the case if the son was here, but he is not. He's in Jiangxia.'

'Well, perhaps you would like to meet him!' says Kong Ming, and he summons Liu Qi. As he emerges from behind a screen, Lu Su is shocked to see how ill he appears. He has to be helped by two assistants. 'I'm so sorry,' says Liu Qi, 'but my ill-health means I am unable to offer you the proper greetings due to an honoured guest.' Soon after, he is helped away.

'What if the son were to die?' asks Lu Su.

'Well, of course, in that case,' replies Kong Ming, 'we could discuss what happens next.'

'It would be my belief that if he dies the land reverts to the south.'

'Indeed, you are probably right,' says Kong Ming and then to celebrate this understanding he orders a banquet to be prepared.

When later that night Lu Su reports back to Zhou Yu, his master is far from impressed. 'But surely,' says Zhou Yu, 'Liu Qi is but a youth with many, many years to live?'

'Believe me,' says Lu Su, 'if you'd met him you'd have seen how his dissolute lifestyle, women and drink, has sapped his qi. He looks weak and wasted. His breathing is laboured. I give him six months at the most. Once he is dead, I'll go and claim Jingzhou by rights, for Xuande will have no excuses left!'

Zhou Yu is still troubled, but this is soon put into context, for a messenger comes announcing that Sun Quan is besieging Hefei and requests more troops. After his collapse Zhou Yu needs to rest and recover in Chaisang, so he sends Cheng Pu to the aid of Sun Quan at Hefei.

Back again to Xuande. His problem is how to retain his recent gains. His friend Yi Ji, who saved his life from Cai Mao's plot, suggests that there are highly prized scholars in the area who could help. They are the five brothers of the Ma family, renowned for their skills and wisdom. The foremost is Ma Liang, and Xuande sends for him.

'My advice,' says Ma Liang, 'is that you need to secure Jingzhou by increasing the status of Liu Qi. Ask the emperor to make him imperial governor of Jingzhou, surround him with former leaders of the province and let the young man recover his health while controlling, through his family reputation, the city. The local people will be happy with this. Then you'll be free to march south to take Wuling, Changsha, Guiyang and Lingling. There you'll have a much more secure base, with money and food aplenty. My suggestion is that you take Lingling first, then

Wuling. Then go east of the river and take Guiyang and finally Changsha.'

Xuande is delighted with this advice and sends Zhang Fei to attack Lingling. Foolishly the governor of Lingling, urged on by his son Liu Xian, places his trust in a mighty warrior called Xing Daorong. The governor believes that Xing Daorong can defeat anyone who comes up against him. Zhang Fei's army arrives, and Xing Daorong rides out to confront them. 'Traitors,' he shouts, 'go from my country!' To his surprise he sees coming out of the massed troops a carriage in which sits none other than Kong Ming, dressed in his Daoist robes.

'I've defeated a million-strong army, so you are nothing. My advice to you? Surrender now and save your life.'

'You didn't win the battle of the Red Cliffs,' shouts Xing Daorong, 'so don't come trying to intimidate me!' And as he speaks he charges towards Kong Ming. Kong Ming has the carriage turned about and disappears into the ranks of the army. Xing charges on regardless, convinced he can reach Kong Ming and slay him. But instead of Kong Ming he suddenly finds himself confronting a furious Zhang Fei. After trying to hold him off, Xing turns and flees, only to then be challenged by Zhao Zilong. Knowing he is defeated, Xing surrenders and, bound, he is brought before Xuande.

Xuande is all for executing him there and then, but Kong Ming stops him. Xing Daorong is offered his life if he will help them capture Liu Xian. Xing eagerly agrees, and a plot is hatched. He will be released and make his way back to the enemy camp. 'Attack tonight,' he says, 'and I'll work from within to help you. Once you have his son, the governor of Lingling will surrender.'

However, no sooner has Xing Daorong returned to his camp than he tells Liu Xian everything. Together, they plan to turn the trick back upon Kong Ming and his men by ambushing them.

At dead of night the enemy approach Liu Xian's camp and swiftly set fire to the undergrowth. In response, Xing and Liu attack and drive them off. So excited are they, they chase them for some distance until suddenly there is no one there to chase! Seized with foreboding, they wheel round and dash back to their own camp, only to find Zhang Fei coming out of the camp, roaring at them.

'Why don't we turn the tables and raid their camp?' says Liu Xian, and they wheel round again but have not gone far before encountering Zhao Zilong and his troop. With a single thrust Zhao kills Xing, and even though Liu Xian tries to flee he is swiftly taken and brought bound before Kong Ming.

In desperation Liu Xian pleads with Kong Ming: 'I was fooled into doing this by Xing Daorong!' To his surprise, Kong Ming orders him set free. He is given fresh clothes and wine to calm him down. Then Kong Ming sends him back to his father, the governor. He is to tell him how well he has been treated and to persuade the governor to surrender.

Liu Xian does exactly as instructed, and his father, seeing the wisdom in all this, surrenders the city. In recognition of this action, the governor is left as governor, and Liu Xian is sent to join the army of Xuande stationed at Gong'an. The ordinary people rejoice that, for once, a city has changed hands but they have been left unharmed.

Now Xuande has to plan for the capture of Guiyang and he calls for a volunteer. Zhao Zilong immediately offers, but Zhang Fei somewhat brusquely says he wants to go. This creates considerable tension and disagreement between the two warriors until Kong Ming says that, as Zhao Zilong volunteered first, he is the chosen one. Zhang Fei furiously rejects this, so Kong Ming has them choose lots, and once again fate determines that it will be Zilong. Zhang Fei tries one more time by saying that he could capture the city with just three thousand men, to which Zilong retorts, 'Well, so can I.'

So it is that Zilong departs – to Kong Ming's delight – with just three thousand men. Xuande tells Zhang Fei in no uncertain terms to shut up and retire with at least some semblance of grace.

As Zilong advances upon Guiyang, the governor, Zhao Fan, knowing his reputation, decides to surrender. However, a young firebrand, Chen Ying, argues that he should be allowed to at least try to defend the city, pointing out that, if he fails, the governor can always surrender afterwards.

It is a bold Chen Ying who with three thousand men rides out to the battle. But it takes Zilong only a short time to rout Chen Ying's men and put them to flight. Zilong spots Chen Ying fleeing on horseback and hunts him down, until he is captured and brought back to the camp. 'Did you honestly think you could defeat me? Well, I've decided to spare your life,' says Zilong, 'simply because I want you to go back to Zhao Fan and persuade him to surrender.'

As this was always Zhao Fan's intention, he, of course, welcomes this news. He rides out to Zhao Zilong's camp to surrender in person. Over the initial celebration wine, Zhao Fan notes that he and Zhao Zilong belong to the same family, come from the same town of Zhending and that five hundred years ago they were one family. So they dedicate themselves as sworn brothers one to the other.

When Zilong rides into the city to take over, people are so relieved that there has been so little fighting they line the road offering incense, and Zilong assures them of their safety. Zhao Fan has prepared a banquet, and the two get quite drunk. Afterwards, Zhao Fan invites Zhao Zilong back to his own chambers, where, without warning, a beautiful woman dressed in formal mourning clothes of exquisite silk brings him wine. Her beauty is of the kind that overthrows empires!

Needless to say, Zhao Zilong asks who she is. 'She is my sister-in-law,' says Zhao Fan, and Zilong bows graciously to this family member. Although Zhao Fan suggests that the woman join them, Zilong feels uncomfortable, and so the lady retires.

Now a little troubled by what has happened, Zilong asks his new brother, 'Why did you have your sister-in-law bring me my drink?'

'Ahh!' says Zhao Fan. 'I've a good reason. Her husband, my older brother, died three years ago. I've tried to suggest she should remarry, but to no avail. She's set three criteria for any man she will marry. Firstly, he must be famous for both his literary and military accomplishments. Secondly, he must be good-looking and well thought of. And thirdly, he must have the same family name as her late husband. Now where on earth am I going to find someone like that? You, however, respected brother, meet all three criteria! So why don't you marry her, even if she is plain-looking, and I will give her a dowry so she can be at your service and link our families for generations to come. Now, what do you say to that? Eh!'

Zilong is furious and he gets to his feet and lambasts his new brother. 'We've sworn to be brothers, so your sister-in-law is also my sister-in-law! How on earth can you imagine I would want to confound that with such outrageously immodest behaviour!'

Zhao Fan is totally nonplussed and pleads that he meant no harm by the suggestion. 'There really is no need to be so rude,' he says and he looks towards his guards, indicating that they should kill Zilong. But Zilong catches the look. He hits Zhao Fan so hard he falls over and then he marches out, mounts his horse and rides out of the city.

Deeply troubled by the anger he has provoked, Zhao Fan calls in his two bravest commanders, Chen Ying and his friend Bao Ling. They offer to pretend to desert so they can get inside Zhao Zilong's camp. With five hundred men who will also seem to have deserted, they will seize Zhao Zilong when Zhao Fan attacks.

Arriving at Zilong's camp, the two officers claim that Zhao Fan was planning to get Zilong so drunk that night that he could then kill him and send his head to Cao Cao. 'That is the sort of violent man he is, which is why we decided to desert,' they say.

But Zilong is not fooled. He gets them so drunk they are easily overpowered, and one of their servants is made to confess their plan. Calling in the five hundred other men, Zilong presents them with wine and food and tells them that none of this was their fault and that, if they will assist him in a plot, then, far from being killed, they will be rewarded. Needless to say, they agree with alacrity.

As for Chen Ying and Bao Ling, Zilong has them executed straight away.

The five hundred soldiers return to Guiyang that same night and convince the guards to let them in, saying that Chen Ying and Bao Long have captured and executed Zhao Zilong. Hearing this, Zhao Fan rushes to the gate to meet the soldiers. They immediately seize him and swing open the gates to the enemy. For the second time Zhao Zilong enters the city and immediately seeks to reassure the common folk that all will be well.

When Xuande and Kong Ming come to the captured city, Kong Ming interrogates Zhao Fan and discovers the story of the offer of a wife to Zhao Zilong. He teases Zilong about the offer of a wife, but Zilong is truly appalled that he was offered someone who was effectively his sister-in-law and resolutely refuses to marry her – or indeed to even think about marrying anyone!

'There is no shortage of women in the world,' he declares, 'but I want fame, not a wife!'

Xuande frees Zhao Fan and restores him to his post, while Zilong is awarded great riches.

This victory of Zhao Zilong only stirs Zhang Fei's anger even more! 'Just give me three thousand warriors and I will take Wuling and you will have the governor Jin Xuan in front of you before you know it!' he says. Kong Ming, delighted with this offer, agrees but he says, 'You must promise to do one thing for me.'

What is that one thing?

Let's find out.

CHAPTER 53

Guan Yu frees Huang Zhong in honour of his virtue. Sun Quan fights against Zhang Liao.

What Kong Ming wants is for Zhang Fei to agree to the same military law contract that Zhao Zilong has made – the law that makes him culpable if he fails. As Zhang Fei has no problem with that, he signs and soon is on his way to Wuling with his three thousand soldiers. When news of the impending attack by such a famous warrior as Zhang Fei reaches Wuling, the governor calls his officers to him and starts to discuss the plans for an attack. Only one officer, Gong Zhi, argues that this is pointless and that they should submit. The governor is all for executing him on the spot but is dissuaded by others of his officers. It is agreed that the attack will be led by the governor himself.

The attack by the governor of Wuling is an abysmal failure, and when the governor flees back to his city gate he finds that Gong Zhi has taken over. 'You brought down the wrath of Heaven upon yourself,' calls down Gong Zhi. 'We the people have decided to join Xuande!' Arrows rain down on the governor and his retreating troops until one arrow strikes the governor in the face and throws him from his horse. His men cut off his head and bring it to Zhang Fei to win their reprieve. They are followed by Gong Zhi, who surrenders the city. In recognition of his role he is made governor by Xuande. Once again Xuande reassures the population of a captured city that they will not be harmed.

When Guan Yu hears that Zilong has taken Guiyang and Zhang Fei has taken Wuling, he writes back that he wants to now go and take Changsha. Guan Yu comes to discuss the attack with Kong Ming.

'The governor of Changsha, Han Xuan, is no problem, but beware of General Huang Zhong from Nanyang. He's almost sixty, but do not underestimate him. To win you'll need more than the three thousand troops Zilong and Zhang Fei had . . .' but Guan Yu interrupts him. 'Why are you trying to discourage me when you praise others? This old soldier doesn't worry me. I won't need the three thousand. I'll take my own band of five hundred fighters and shortly I'll bring you the heads of Huang Zhong and Han Xuan.'

After he has gone, Kong Ming tells Xuande that he fears Guan Yu will fail and suggests that they set off after him to offer support, should that be needed. And so it is that Xuande and Kong Ming also head for Changsha.

Now the governor of Changsha, Han Xuan, is a vile man, loathed by everyone, not least for his sudden rages, during which he would have people killed or even kill them himself without warning. When news of the attack is brought to him, he calls in General Huang Zhong. He reassures the governor that he will be able to deal with this threat without any trouble. 'You see this sword and bow? Well, if a thousand men come, a thousand men will die!'

When Guan Yu and his men arrive, Huang Zhong rides out to confront him. Challenging him, Guan Yu says, 'So, this must be General Huang Zhong', to which he replies, 'If you know who I am, what are you doing invading my lands?' 'I've come for your head,' replies Guan Yu, and battle commences. Round after round they fight, but neither one gains an edge. After one hundred sallies against each other, Han Xuan calls Huang Zhong back, fearful that his general will eventually be defeated. Guan Yu acknowledges that Huang Zhong's reputation is well deserved. 'I think the only way I can defeat him is the old trailing sword trick.'

The next day they battle again. After some fifty to sixty bouts, Guan Yu turns as if to flee, 'trailing his sword', as the saying goes, and pursued by Huang Zhong. Just as Guan Yu prepares to spring his surprise attack by turning round, he hears the sound of someone falling. Looking back, he sees that Huang Zhong has fallen from his horse. Raising his mighty sword high, he rides towards the fallen warrior and the shouts out, 'I spare you. Find yourself another horse, and we will meet again to finish this once and for all!'

Huang Zhong collects his horse and gallops back to Wuling. The governor, Han Xuan, is confounded by this, but Huang Zhong says it is the fault of the horse, who is unused to such intense warfare. 'But you're a superb archer,' says Han Xuan. 'Why didn't you just shoot him?' So Huang Zhong agrees to try to lure Guan Yu back to the city walls and then kill him with an arrow. Mounted on a new horse given especially by the governor, Huang Zhong prepares for the next day but deep down he is troubled. 'Is there another man who would have acted as honourably as Guan Yu did today? Can I really use such a trick to shoot the man who gave me back my life? On the other side, can I refuse an order from my superior?' That night he tosses and turns, unable to resolve this conflict of loyalty and honour.

The next day they ride out again and clash dramatically. After thirty inconclusive bouts Huang Zhong turns and flees, and Guan Yu follows closely behind, intent this time on seizing victory. At the crucial moment when Huang is supposed to shoot Guan Yu, he still cannot resolve his moral dilemma and so first of all just twangs the bowstring, which at least causes Guan Yu to duck. Huang does this again, and again Guan Yu ducks, thinking, 'Well, he's not much of a shot.' The third time Huang notches an arrow and lets fly. The arrow strikes the top notch of Guan Yu's helmet, and this sufficiently alarms Guan Yu that he turns and retreats while from the walls the soldiers cheer and jeer. Only when he looks carefully at where the arrow has lodged does Guan Yu realize that Huang Zhong has acted virtuously, as he, Guan Yu, acted the day before. In the light of such mutual respect, Guan Yu orders his men to raise the siege.

However, all is far from well inside the city, for, the moment Huang Zhong returns, Han Xuan arrests him. 'Why are you doing this,' roars the old general. 'What have I done wrong?'

'For three days I've watched what you've been doing. Do you think I'm an idiot?' shouts Han Xuan. 'On the first day you didn't really try. On the second day, when your horse fell, you were spared – which makes me think you have some sort of deal going with Guan Yu. And today, today you fake two shots and then fire one which just sticks in his helmet! The only explanation is that you're in league with him, and, if I don't have you executed now, you'll betray me.'

So saying, he summons his guards and orders the execution to take place in front of the city gate for all to see, saying, 'Anyone who opposes me will also die!'

Huang Zhong has been led outside the city gate, and the executioner has his sword raised ready to strike the fatal blow, when, as if from nowhere, a warrior charges forward. Slaying the executioner, he rescues Huang Zhong and cries out in defiance of the governor, 'This man is the protector of Changsha, in contrast to that villain Han Xuan. What a violent, vindictive, worthless man! He rejects the wise and dishonours the worthy! Let's all go now and kill him! Who's with me?' The astonished crowd strains to see who is saying all this. The hero's name is Wei Yan of Yiyang. He has heard of the valiant struggle of Xuande to protect the Han and is on his way to offer his services. He has been unable to locate him so has offered his services to Han Xuan. Han Xuan thought him a lazy, pointless fellow and basically ignored him, making Wei Yan deeply frustrated and angry.

The momentum he has unleashed takes its full toll the next day when, despite Huang Zhong's best efforts, Wei Yan leads a mob who storm the city. Catching Han Xuan, he slays him by cutting him in half with a single blow. He takes the governor's head and goes out to offer this to Guan Yu and to surrender the city.

When Xuande and Kong Ming arrive in the city, they are told of the events and go immediately to greet Huang Zhong. However, when Wei Yan comes in, to everyone's astonishment Kong Ming orders his death.

Greatly troubled by this, Xuande questions why he wants to do such a thing. Kong Ming says that a man who will betray his overlord is simply not to be trusted. 'If we don't kill him now we'll regret it later on, I can tell you,' says Kong Ming, but

Xuande will not permit this. 'If we kill him, why would anyone ever surrender to us again?'

So Wei Yan lives to fight another day.

And Xuande, now lord of four new districts rich in resources and with good men on his side, is securely established at last.

Meanwhile, Zhou Yu is recovering from his wound while Cheng Pu is sent to assist Sun Quan, who is besieging, rather unsuccessfully, the city of Hefei. Hearing that Cheng Pu has arrived, Zhang Liao sends a formal challenge, which Sun Quan takes as a personal insult. He decides to go, without any assistance from Cheng Pu and his newly arrived troops, to fight Zhang Liao with his own troops.

It is a good decision by Zhang Liao. When the two armies meet he makes straight for Sun Quan, but Taishi Ci rides to protect him. A side attack on Sun Quan nearly succeeds but is held off by the loyal officers surrounding Sun Quan. When Taishi Ci retreats after a long but ineffectual struggle with Zhang Liao, Zhang charges forward, and the southern army scatters in disarray. Zhang very nearly captures Sun Quan, and if it had not been for the timely intervention of Cheng Pu he would have succeeded.

Satisfied with his defence of Hefei, Zhang Liao returns to the city while Sun Quan retreats and watches as the remnants of his defeated army struggle back. His officers remonstrate with him and make him promise not to be so rash again.

Not long after, Taishi Ci comes to see Sun Quan with news. A groom called Ge Ding has a blood brother in Zhang Liao's army who hates Zhang Liao because he feels he has been unjustly punished for some offence. He is willing to kill Zhang Liao and will signal that night when he has killed him so that Sun Quan's men can then swarm into the city and take it.

Delighted with this, Sun Quan agrees that Taishi should have five thousand men to go with him. When the signal is given, they should force their way into the city. One adviser does suggest that this could well be a trap, but Sun Quan is having none of it.

However, what no one expected is that Zhang Liao orders his men to stay fully alert in case of a night attack by the enemy. When questioned by his own men, Zhang says that such an attack is highly likely and reiterates his orders.

No sooner has he said this than a fire breaks out, and a cry of 'uprising' is heard. Some of the officers are convinced that this is a real revolt, but Zhang says, 'Can the whole city have suddenly decided to revolt? I don't think so. This is some sort of enemy plot.' His men start to scour the city, looking for those responsible for the fire.

Almost immediately, Ge Ding and his blood brother are captured, and when the nature of their plot is revealed they are beheaded. Suddenly the sound of war gongs and drums sounds outside the city gate, and Zhang Liao realizes this is part of the plot. So he decides to turn the plot back on his enemy. 'Set fire to rubbish beside the main gate and cry "revolution" and then open the gate,' he cries.

When Taishi Ci sees the fire and then hears the shouting and watches as the gate swings open, he rushes in, believing the plot has succeeded. Bombs and arrows rain down on the southern troops. Taishi is seriously wounded, and half of the men die as the northerners hunt them down. It is only when reinforcements rush out from Sun Quan's camp that Taishi is rescued and the surviving troops are saved.

Sun Quan and his men have really no option now but to abandon the attack and retreat back to their own lands. There, Taishi Ci dies of his wounds, mourned by all, and Sun Quan adopts Taishi's son, Taishi Heng.

The news of Sun Quan's defeat gets back to Xuande, and he discusses this with Kong Ming. The latter relates to Xuande that the previous night he saw a shooting star fall to earth in the northwest, which he takes to mean a member of the imperial family has died. The very next moment a messenger brings news of the death of Liu Qi. Xuande is overcome with grief and weeps uncontrollably. Kong Ming seeks to reassure him. 'Both life and death are determined by fate. What we need to do now is to plan the funeral and send someone to take control of the city.' They decide that Guan Yu should take over Xiangyang, and Xuande raises the thorny issue that, now the legitimate heir to the city is dead, the southerners can come to claim the city as they have discussed with Kong Ming.

'Don't worry,' says Kong Ming, 'I know how to handle this.' And so it is that, two weeks later, Lu Su comes as an ambassador from Zhou Yu.

> Now the plan is prepared
> The ambassador will return home empty-handed.

So what exactly is Kong Ming's plan?

Well, read on.

世興局
敬德

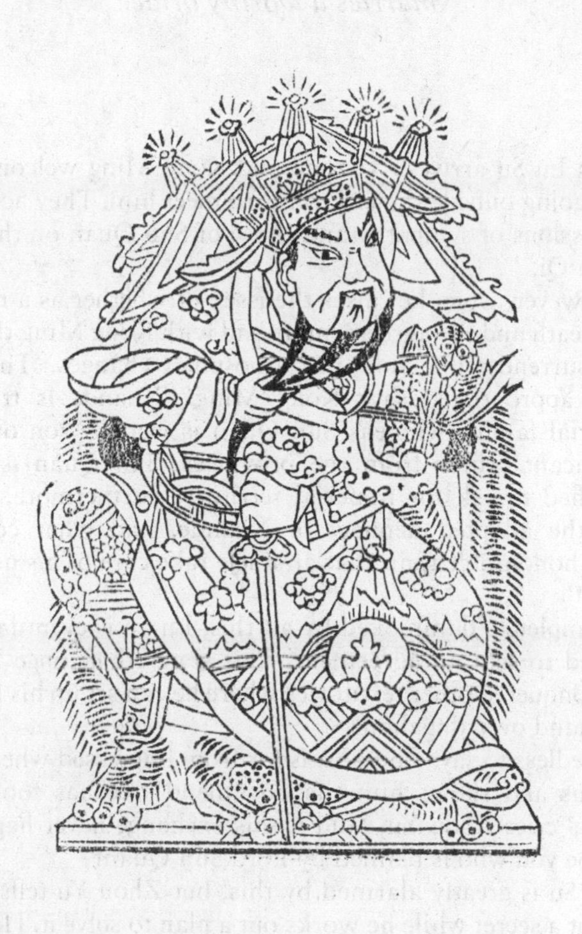

CHAPTER 54

Dowager Empress Wu meets her future son-in-law in a temple. Xuande marries a worthy bride.

When Lu Su arrives, Xuande and Kong Ming welcome him, even going outside the city walls to meet him. They accept his expressions of sympathy and those of Sun Quan on the death of Liu Qi.

However, when he raises the issue of whether as a result of this death and the agreement he had with Kong Ming they will now surrender Jingzhou, the atmosphere changes. 'This is far from appropriate,' says Kong Ming. 'Xuande is from the imperial family, whereas Sun Quan is just the son of an insignificant officer from the provinces. Sun Quan is hardly qualified to ask for imperial territory. Furthermore, Liu Qi was the adopted nephew of Xuande, and what could be more honourable than that an uncle take care of his nephew's lands!'

Completely flummoxed by all this, Lu Su is eventually persuaded to sign an agreement. This states that, once Xuande has conquered other territories where he can set up his base, he will hand over Jingzhou!

Needless to say, Zhou Yu is far from impressed when Lu Su returns and shows him the document! 'He has fooled you again,' cries Zhou Yu, 'and if this exchange never happens it will be you who is blamed by Lord Sun Quan!'

Lu Su is greatly alarmed by this, but Zhou Yu tells him to keep it a secret while he works out a plan to solve it. He is also awaiting news from his spies. They return, telling him that Xuande has ordered a new tomb to be constructed on the outskirts of the city. Everyone is in mourning because Xuande's wife Lady Gan has died. 'Now I know what to do,' says a very pleased Zhou Yu. 'Soon you will see Xuande captured, and then we can sort out Jingzhou!'

'But what exactly,' asks a troubled Lu Su, 'is your plan?'

'Xuande needs a new wife,' says Zhou Yu, 'and our lord has a sister, a real warrior woman with hundreds of armed fighting women guards. We will ask Sun Quan to send an emissary to suggest this marriage and then, when he comes for the wedding, we will seize Xuande and demand Jingzhou back as ransom!'

A day or so later he gives Lu Su the document from Xuande and a letter to deliver to Sun Quan and sends him by fast boat to Nanxu. When Lu Su presents Sun Quan with the document outlining the 'agreement', Sun Quan erupts in anger. 'What kind of an idiot are you to agree to this?' roars Sun Quan. Then Lu Su presents the letter from Zhou Yu. Having read the outline of the secret plot Zhou Yu is proposing, Sun Quan smiles and begins to think of who would be best to carry out this plan. He needs an emissary to go to Xuande to propose the marriage. His thoughts turn to his assistant, Lü Fan.

'Lü Fan,' says Sun Quan, 'I want you to go to Xuande and propose a marriage between himself and my sister so that our two families and armies will be united. Then we can be comrades in arms against Cao Cao. I've selected you for this auspicious task.'

Xuande, meanwhile, has been deeply affected by the death of his wife and is certainly not himself, so great is his distress. When Lü Fan arrives, Xuande is discussing issues with Kong Ming. Hearing that the emissary wants to discuss something with Xuande, Kong Ming hides himself behind a screen to listen in, convinced that this is yet another plot by Zhou Yu.

Lü Fan conveys Sun Quan's condolences to Xuande and then says that he brings news of a possible new marriage.

'Losing one's wife in middle age,' says Xuande, 'is a real sadness, but while her body is barely cold in the grave I can't even consider a new match.'

'But a man without a wife is like a house without its beam,' says Lü Fan, and he proceeds to outline why a marriage with the beautiful and skilled sister of Sun Quan would be good for

Xuande and good for the country – especially in opposing Cao Cao.

Despite Xuande's commenting that he is fifty and she is a young woman in her prime, Lü Fan persists in extolling her virtues. 'She thinks and acts like a man and has said quite categorically that she is only interested in marrying a hero! The only issue to be solved is the queen mother, Lady Wu, who adores her daughter and will need to be personally convinced you are the right one. This is why we hope you will come to the south to meet her and her daughter so you can decide for yourself.'

Xuande asks Lü Fan to retire while he considers this.

Kong Ming tells Xuande that he knew this would be a plot. However, he has consulted *The Book of Changes*, the *Yi Jing*, and the reading is very auspicious. 'This will play out to our advantage,' he says. 'I recommend that you go ahead with the plans for the wedding.' Xuande is far from certain, convinced as he is that Zhou Yu plans to have him killed. But Kong Ming reassures him that he can easily outwit Zhou Yu. Nevertheless, Xuande is still far from comfortable with all this.

Kong Ming arranges for Sun Qian to go back with Lü Fan and to negotiate the details of the marriage. Sun Quan says how much they want Xuande to come in person to be married, and this message Sun Qian brings back to Xuande and Kong Ming.

Xuande is still very unhappy about all this. But Kong Ming again assures him that he has worked out the three stages of his strategy, and that the only man capable of carrying them out is Zhao Zilong. Xuande reluctantly agrees to go, and, just before they depart, Kong Ming takes Zilong on one side and gives him three small embroidered bags with three documents inside. 'Use them in this particular order,' says Kong Ming, indicating each one, 'when the need arises.' So Zilong hides the little bags inside his clothes and sets out.

It is late in the year AD 209 when Xuande, accompanied by Zhao Zilong and Sun Qian, sails with five hundred soldiers to Nanxu in the lands of the south. And Xuande is still far from happy.

As the boats pull into the port, Zilong decides it is time to open the first of the three bags. He reads the secret message and immediately sends the soldiers into the city with orders to do as he says. Then he says to Xuande that they should go and pay their respects to Elder Statesman Qiao. He is the father of the two beauties whom Cao Cao has so lusted after – the wives of Sun Quan and Zhou Yu. Their visit is deeply appreciated, and during the meeting they talk happily about the forthcoming nuptials and the invaluable role Lü Fan has played.

Meanwhile, the five hundred soldiers are out on the town, buying up all the goods necessary to celebrate a grand wedding. They are telling everyone they meet that this is because their lord, Xuande, is to marry the sister of Sun Quan. Soon everyone is gossiping about this!

Elder Statesman Qiao goes immediately to convey his congratulations to the queen mother. 'What exactly,' asks a rather surprised queen mother, 'is it that you wish to congratulate me upon?'

'Why, the engagement of your dear daughter to Xuande, of course,' says an equally surprised Elder Statesman Qiao.

'Are you trying to make a fool of me? I know nothing about this!'

And so saying, she summons her son to come immediately to see her.

While she awaits his arrival, one of her servants has come back to report that the rumour is true. 'There are soldiers of Lord Xuande everywhere buying things for the wedding. Lü Fan negotiated this, and Xuande and Sun Qian are resting in the state guest house.'

When Sun Quan arrives it is to find his mother beating her breast and weeping.

'What's the matter, Mother?' asks a worried Sun Quan.

'What's the matter? Is this how you treat me, as if I'm a person of no consequence? Have you already forgotten the last words of my older sister?'

A very troubled Sun Quan replies, 'What are you talking about, Mother? Please just tell me frankly why you're so upset!'

'It's of course natural that a man should marry a woman. So

it's been since time immemorial. In case you've forgotten, I'm your mother and I should have been asked for my approval first. How could you not tell me your sister is to marry Xuande. Is she not also my daughter?'

'Where did you hear this?' asks a now very worried Sun Quan.

'Are you claiming you know nothing about this? The whole city knows about it, but you forgot to tell me, your mother – her mother!'

Elder Statesman Qiao chips in, saying, 'Indeed, I heard about this sometime ago and came simply to convey my congratulations!'

'No, no,' cries a very agitated Sun Quan. 'You've got it all wrong. This is a plot by Zhou Yu to get back Jingzhou. By pretending there'll be a wedding, we've fooled Xuande into coming so we can hold him as a prisoner until he's ransomed by giving us back Jingzhou. If that doesn't happen, then we can kill him. It's just a plot. We never intended that there would be an actual wedding!'

Far from calming his mother, this only infuriates her even more. She takes out her wrath on Zhou Yu, saying, 'So despite being head of the army he cannot work out how to get Jingzhou back? His only weapon is to use my daughter as a foil! Can you imagine anyone wanting to marry her after this scandal breaks? You will ruin her!'

Elder Statesman Qiao adds his pennyworth by saying, 'Even if this worked, imagine how ridiculous we would appear to the whole world! It'll never work.'

Sun Quan sits in deep depression while his mother continues to vent her wrath upon him. Eventually, Elder Statesman Qiao suggests the only way out of this mess is if Xuande actually does marry her daughter, whereupon the queen mother insists that she must meet this prospective son-in-law. 'If I don't like him, do what you want. If I do, then I will personally ensure the marriage goes ahead! Arrange for him to come and meet me in Sweet Dew Temple tomorrow.'

Sun Quan, the filial son, has no option but to accede. However, on Lü Fan's advice he commands Jia Hua to go to the temple early with three hundred men in case the queen mother rejects Xuande and they need to kill him.

When Xuande is informed of the forthcoming meeting, Zhao Zilong is truly worried and promises to come with the soldiers in case anything goes wrong.

So it is that, when the queen mother and Elder Statesman Qiao have seated themselves and Xuande is summoned, he puts on a lightweight breastplate and covers it with his ceremonial clothes, while all those attending him come bearing swords. The whole entourage of Xuande and his officers and the five hundred men are greeted by Sun Quan at the doorway to the temple. The moment the queen mother sets eyes upon him, she declares, 'This is the son-in-law for me!' and Qiao says, 'He has the appearance of the dragon and phoenix and the glow as of Heaven's sun! He is renowned throughout the world for his benevolence and virtue. Congratulations on acquiring such a splendid son-in-law!'

Invited to join the banquet that has been set out, Xuande takes his place. Zhao Zilong appears and whispers that the corridor is full of men armed to the teeth. 'You should alert the queen mother to this.'

So Xuande falls at the feet of the queen mother and, with tears in his eyes, cries, 'If it is my death you seek, then do it now!'

'What on earth are you talking about?' says a startled queen mother.

'The temple is crawling with assassins. Why else would they be here?'

The queen mother vents her fury upon her son: 'Now he's my son-in-law, Xuande is my son. So why are there murderers lurking here? Answer me!'

Sun Quan denies any knowledge and calls for Lü Fan, who in turn blames Jia Hua. The queen mother would have had him executed if Xuande had not pleaded – as her new son-in-law – that she show mercy so that their relationship does not start off on an inauspicious note. Jia Hua slinks away with his terrified men.

Later, Xuande is walking in the temple grounds when he

sees a large rock. Asking for a sword, he looks up to Heaven and says, 'If my fate is to return to Jingzhou and succeed in becoming king, let this sword split this rock. If my fate is to die here, let the stone survive intact.' With that he strikes the stone a mighty blow, and it splits in two.

Sun Quan has been watching all this. He steps forward and asks, 'Lord Xuande, what exactly have you got against this stone?'

'I am nearly fifty but I've failed in my task of ridding the country of traitors, and this distresses me greatly. But now, honoured by the queen mother in being invited to be her son-in-law, I feel this is an auspicious moment. So I asked Heaven that if indeed my time has come to destroy Cao Cao and revive the Han dynasty, then let me split the rock – and it has happened!'

Not to be outdone, Sun Quan also implores Heaven openly if he too will be given help to destroy Cao Cao but secretly he asks that if he is to regain Jingzhou and his lands are to prosper that the rock split again. Bringing his sword down, he too splits the rock. To this day the rock remains with the cross cuts in it, and is known as the Rock of Hatred.

A poet visiting this site has written as follows:

The swords slash down, and the mountain rock's split;
Metal rings out, and sparks fizz.
The creation of two Houses Heaven decrees
And from now on, there will be three.

Returning to the hall hand in hand, they retake their seats. After a little more drinking, Sun Quan glances at Xuande, who says, 'My apologies. The wine is too much for me. Allow me to retire.' Sun Quan walks with him out of the hall, and they stand on the veranda and contemplate the view.

'This truly is the best view in the world,' says Xuande, and still today you can see the stele carved with those very words.

Xuande sighs gently and says, 'Southerners are sailors and northerners are horsemen.'

Thinking that Xuande is mocking his ability to ride, Sun Quan orders his horse brought. He leaps on it, charges down hill and then comes tearing back up. 'So,' says Sun Quan, 'southerners are not horsemen, eh!' In response Xuande leaps onto his horse and tears down the hill and comes galloping back up. Roaring with laughter at their exploits, the two men sit atop the hill, which to this day is still known as 'The Hill where the Horses Stopped'. Then, still laughing, the two men return to the city. The local people of Nanxu watch these antics and smile, for this all seems very auspicious.

On their return, Sun Qian urges Xuande to go and see Elder Statesman Qiao in order to ensure the wedding takes place very soon, before any other plots can bring disaster. This Xuande does, and Qiao says to have no worries and assures them he will take care of this.

The queen mother invites Xuande and his entire troop to be her guests until the day of the wedding, which is held but a few days later.

The night of the wedding, after the guests have left them alone, Xuande makes his way to the bridal chamber. Walking down the long corridors, he cannot but help noticing the vast array of weapons and the women guards with their swords. He is so overcome with fright that he feels as if his very soul is fleeing from his body!

Is this another plot to kill him?

We must find out.

CHAPTER 55

Xuande convinces his wife to flee Wu, and her cunning saves them. Kong Ming drives Zhou Yu to fury for the second time.

Seeing Xuande turning pale with fright, the housekeeper reassures him that he has nothing to fear. 'Not very ladylike, is it, though!' comments Xuande. When this is reported to Lady Sun, she laughs and wonders why a man who has spent half his life in battles would be frightened of weapons. But to put him at ease she has the majority removed and tells her women guards to put aside their swords. And the couple spend that night in a passionate embrace.

Needless to say, news of the disastrous outcome of their plot – an actual wedding – is sent by Sun Quan to Zhou Yu. Sun asks him for advice on what on earth to do next. After a long time of contemplation, Zhou Yu writes to Sun Quan with a new plan. In his letter he basically points out that they need to tame this man of action and that the best way to do this is to make his life at Nanxu so delightful and so sensual that he will forget all about the affairs of state.

Sun Quan immediately sets to work and has the palace redecorated and the gardens landscaped. Women musicians are despatched to the palace, along with many rich gifts of gold, jade and silk. The queen mother, thinking that this shows how well the whole family is getting on, is delighted. As for Xuande he frankly just sinks into this life of luxury. After so many years of hardship he enjoys himself, and all thought of returning to Jingzhou soon fades.

While this is going on, Zhao Zilong and his men fill their time with sports, entertainments, wine, women and song. However, as month extends into month and the end of the year draws near, Zilong remembers what Kong Ming said. 'When that happens, open the second bag.' No sooner has he read the second document than he goes to see Xuande.

'My lord,' says Zilong, 'this morning news came from Kong Ming that Cao Cao, bent upon revenge, has set off with five hundred thousand men to take Jingzhou. Kong Ming asks that you return at once.'

'Well, I'll go and discuss this with my wife,' replies Xuande, whereupon Zilong says if he does she is bound to tell him not to go! 'We need to leave immediately.' But Xuande will not be dissuaded.

Entering Lady Sun's room, Xuande weeps and falls down before her and pretends that he has suddenly realized he has failed to pay due respect and regard to his parents and to make the ritual sacrifices to his ancestors. 'With the New Year almost upon us, I'm overwhelmed with distress at this,' he claims.

'Don't try and fool me!' replies Lady Sun. 'I know perfectly well what this is all about. Zhao Zilong has told you that Jingzhou is about to be taken. You're being called back, and this frankly was just a poor excuse in order for me to let you go.'

With no option left, Xuande says, 'Let me speak honestly. If I stay here, and Jingzhou is lost, I'll be a laughing stock. But I don't want to leave you! This is my dilemma.'

'I'm your wife and I'll go where my lord goes.'

'This may be how you see things, but I cannot believe that your mother or brother will agree. Just have compassion on me and let me go for a brief time.'

Lady Sun tells him to pull himself together, as she will ask her mother's permission, but Xuande says her brother won't agree to her leaving. Then Lady Sun comes up with an idea:

'When we go to offer the New Year sacrifices, I'll say you wish to pay your respects to your ancestors, and that we'll go to the river to do this. Then we can escape from there with no one watching. What do you think?'

Kneeling before her, Xuande says emotionally, 'If you will do this for me, I will never ever forget it, whether I am dead or alive. But we must keep this absolutely secret.'

Xuande tells Zhao Zilong to lead his men to the main road on New Year's Day and be ready to leave.

So it is that on New Year's Day AD 210 Sun Quan hosts a huge celebration. Lady Sun and Xuande enter and kowtow before the queen mother. Lady Sun says that her husband's parents and ancestors lie buried in the north in Zhuo County and that being unable to get there has caused him much grief. 'Today he wishes to go to the river and face the north to offer his prayers for that holy place. We have come to let you know.'

The queen mother is deeply touched by such filial piety. 'I know you never had the chance to meet your parents-in-law, so you should accompany him, for this is fitting.' And so, kowtowing once more, the pair make their escape.

With Lady Sun travelling in her carriage and Xuande riding alongside, they meet up with Zhao Zilong and his men and set off as fast as they can.

It is later that evening that Sun Quan realizes they have escaped. He orders Chen Wu and Pan Zhang to set off immediately with five hundred elite warriors to catch them. But not long after they have left, Cheng Pu and Zhang Zhao point out how in awe of her all the commanders are for her knowledge of martial arts. They suggest that others with a sure sign of his authority are sent to finish the job.

So, giving his official sword to Jiang Qin and Zhou Tai, he orders them to stop the runaways and cut off their heads – or they will be executed instead. These two set off in pursuit with a thousand men.

Ahead of them Xuande and Lady Sun are racing forward, barely resting their horses or men. They are almost at the border with Chaisang when they can see rising up behind them the clouds of dust from their pursuers. Zilong urges them to go on and he will form a rearguard. But at that precise moment, they find their path blocked. Zhou Yu suspected a plot and sent Xu Sheng and Ding Feng with three thousand men to block the road. With troops in front and troops behind, all appears lost. But at this point Zhao Zilong remembers the third bag with its secret document and opens it. He passes it to Xuande, who reads it and then runs to Lady Sun's carriage.

'My lady, I've something to tell you in confidence.'

'Whatever it is, keep nothing back,' says the lady.

'The idea of our marriage was just a plot originally by Zhou Yu and your brother to trap me so they could take Jingzhou. If that failed then they were going to murder me. You were just bait to catch me. I came because of your fame but have fallen in love with you. Yesterday I was told of a new threat so I made up the excuse of needing to go to Jingzhou. How lucky and blessed am I that you chose to come with me! Now the troops are hunting us and closing in, and the only person who can save me is you. But if you will not do this, then I will die here before you to honour your kindness in coming with me.'

Lady Sun is furious at this and rails against her brother, whom she says she never wants to see again. 'Now, leave this to me,' she says.

So saying, she has her carriage moved to the front line and, looking out, she calls out to the two officers sent to block the way by Zhou Yu – Xu Sheng and Ding Feng – to attend her.

'So, are you rebels now?'

Meekly the two stand before her, their weapons laid upon the ground. 'Not at all. We've our orders from General Zhou to be here to prevent Xuande leaving.'

'That worthless rebel Zhou! What has our family ever done to deserve such treatment! Not only is Xuande a member of the imperial family, but he is also my husband. My brother and mother know we are going to Jingzhou. So why are you here? To rob us!'

The two browbeaten officers profess that they are not rebels or thieves, and that this is not their plan. They are just following orders.

This does not impress Lady Sun, who retorts, 'So you fear the general more than me! Let me tell you that he may hold you in fear of your life, but I hold that same power over him!' She rages on for some time against Zhou. The end result is that the cowed officers agree to let her pass.

Not long after they have moved off, two other officers, those sent initially by Sun Quan, Chen Wu and Pan Zhang, ride up. They tell an alarmed Xu Sheng and Ding Feng that they have explicit orders to prevent the escape of Xuande and Lady Sun. Horrified at their mistake, Xu Sheng and Ding Feng with the other two gallop off after the fast-disappearing troop and carriage.

Xuande soon notices the clouds of dust and realizes the pursuit is on again. And once again Lady Sun takes control. She tells him to ride on for the river with three hundred of his men while she and Zhao Zilong deal with this new threat.

No sooner do the four officers see Lady Sun than they leap from their horses and bow deeply. Lady Sun barks, 'Chen Wu, Pan Zhang. What are you doing here?'

'We've been instructed by Lord Sun to ensure you both return.'

For a moment, Lady Sun looks at them in distasteful silence. Then, sighing, she says, 'It is the fault of people like you that problems have arisen between my brother and me. It's not as if this is an elopement – I'm after all married to Lord Xuande. My mother has agreed to this trip – as indeed has my brother. We're simply fulfilling our ritual and filial duties! So why do you have these weapons? Is it your plan to kill us?'

This speech just leaves the four generals shamefaced and also contemplating the fact that, whatever else happened, Lady Sun and Lord Sun would always be sister and brother; that this trip is sanctioned by the queen mother and that Lord Sun, filial son that he is, would never gainsay his own mother! What if tomorrow he repents and changes his mind? Guess who would get the blame then! It might be best to just show some kindness now.

So the four bow deeply and quietly retreat.

A little while after this, the four see riding towards them at a furious pace the second troop sent by Sun Quan, commanded by Jiang Qin and Zhou Tai. Crying out, 'Have you seen Xuande?' the four reply that they passed them this very morning. When they are challenged as to why they did not detain them, the four relate their encounter with Lady Sun. The two newcomers tell of the sword and special commission Sun Quan has given them to execute the pair, and the other officers say that the couple are already well on their way.

The six officers decide that Xu Sheng and Ding Feng will ride back to Zhou Yu and tell him what has happened. They will request the fastest boats possible to race after them. The other four will chase the fugitives along roads and try to catch them. 'Whatever you do,' says Jiang Qin, 'don't let them speak! Kill them before they can argue.'

Meanwhile, Xuande, Zhao Zilong and Lady Sun have reached the edge of the river. But not a single boat is to be found to ferry them over to safety. 'Don't worry,' says Zilong, 'I am sure Kong Ming will have thought of something.'

But this does little to reassure Xuande. He finds his thoughts drifting back to his recent life of luxury and he gently weeps.

As a poet has said about this couple:

Here on these shores, east and west wed.
Comforts and luxury were theirs for the taking.
Who could have foreseen the drastic choice she would make,
Choosing noble Xuande and undoing plots?

The sound of the pursuing troops comes clear on the air, and Xuande's heart grows heavier and heavier. Suddenly, coming down the river are twenty ships, and Zilong shouts with relief that this is the gift of grace they needed to escape. Only when they and the five hundred have all swiftly embarked do they spot someone dressed like an ordinary Daoist with a headband in one of the boats. It is Kong Ming!

When the four generals arrive breathless at the riverbank, Kong Ming laughs and shouts, 'I planned all this ages ago, so you go back and tell Zhou Yu – no more seduction plots!' And so saying, despite arrows being fired at the retreating ships, they sail safely away.

Or do they? For suddenly the air is rent by a great cry, and round the bend in the river comes Zhou Yu with his navy, sailing as fast as they can. Kong Ming urges his oarsmen on to renewed effort, and they land on the north shore just ahead of the southern navy landing as well. Xuande, Lady Sun and all those who are with them, including Kong Ming, leap onto horseback and charge off into the woods. Close behind comes Zhou Yu and his men. Just as it seems they will overtake the fugitives, Guan Yu bursts out of the woods at the head of his men. It is, of course, one of Kong Ming's traps. Zhou Yu and his men turn in horror and flee back to their boats and just manage to escape.

'I have failed again,' bemoans Zhou Yu. 'What am I going to say to Lord Sun?' His distress makes him collapse unconscious on the boat deck, and his wound opens up again.

Will he survive?

Who knows!

CHAPTER 56

Cao Cao hosts a banquet at the Bronze Bird Tower. Kong Ming drives Zhou Yu to fury a third time.

Carried away downstream by his men Zhou Yu is able to rest and survive this new shock. Deeply conscious of the mess he has helped create, he writes from his sickbed to Sun Quan. He wants revenge on Xuande at almost any cost. But Zhang Zhao once again urges caution on Sun Quan, pointing out that Cao Cao is only held at bay by the fear generated by the union of Sun's and Xuande's armies.

It is Gu Yong who comes up with the idea of sending an emissary to the emperor recommending that Xuande be appointed imperial governor of Jingzhou. This is because such an appointment would pitch Cao Cao against Xuande. Cao Cao will resent and fear Xuande's new authority and power but will not be able to countermand an imperial appointment.

Meanwhile, by the spring of AD 210 Cao Cao has completed his Bronze Bird Tower. This astonishing building – with its three tall towers, lined by walkways and decorated with glittering gold and jewel decorations – is his pride and joy, and to celebrate its completion he hosts a festival.

At the celebration banquet, poets are invited to compete with each other to see who can write the most flattering ode. When they have finished, Cao Cao delivers a mockingly self-effacing speech. 'I'm but a simple, ordinary man. All I've ever really wanted is to live quietly in a humble cottage in the countryside, but our turbulent times have meant I've been exalted by being made a military commander and have had to come to the rescue of the emperor. All I ever want to be remembered for can be best summed up by what I hope might be written on my tomb. "Here lies Lord Cao Cao, the Han general who quelled the west". Never forget, it was I who got rid of Dong Zhuo; crushed the Yellow Headbands; destroyed Yuan Shu; defeated Lü Bu; exterminated Yuan Shao; conquered Liu Biao and so brought peace to the empire. I'm the most important of all his imperial majesty's servants, and without me – who knows – many might have tried to seize the throne for themselves! I always hold dear those words of Kong Fu Zi about King Wen and his "perfect virtue" and if I could I would give up all this power and retire. But this is sadly not possible at the moment. If I were to retire, someone would probably try to kill me, and then what would become of the Han dynasty? You clearly have no real depth of understanding of my position.'

This self-congratulatory prose causes all the officials present to kowtow and proclaim how immensely wise he is, unequalled by any of the great ministers of the past, not even those historic heroes Yi Yin and the duke of Zhou.

It is at this precise moment that the emissary Hua Xin arrives with the petition from Sun Quan and the request that Xuande be made the governor of Jingzhou. This shatters Cao Cao's aplomb, and he erupts with fury. Asked by Cheng Yu why this news so upsets him, Cao Cao says, 'Xuande is truly a dragon standing in the midst of everyone else. However, he's not until now been able to find his true destiny. Now he's like a dragon released into the ocean. That's why I am troubled!'

Cheng Yu says, 'All this is a plot by Sun Quan to get you to attack Xuande, because he too fears Xuande. He wants you to take him on so he can win by divide and rule. But I've a plan to outwit them both and turn Sun and Xuande upon each other.'

His plot is to have Zhou Yu given a senior appointment as governor of Nanjun, elevate Cheng Pu as governor of Jiangxia and give Hua Xin a post of honour at court. 'That will set Zhou Yu against Xuande as his greatest rival and we can sit back and watch them destroy each other. How about that for an idea?'

And so it comes to pass.

As Cheng Yu foresaw, the appointment hardens Zhou Yu's desire for revenge on Xuande and Kong Ming. After heated discussions which also involve Sun Quan, Lu Su once again proposes that, rather than war, he will try diplomacy in order to regain Jingzhou and once again he sets off for Xuande's base.

When news comes of his arrival, Xuande asks Kong Ming what he should do. Kong Ming says, 'Act dramatically as one deeply offended, and then I will step in to be the voice of reason.'

Lu Su is ushered into the presence of Xuande and as diplomatically as possible raises the issue that Jingzhou really belongs to Sun Quan, and when might they expect Xuande to hand it over?

Xuande bursts into tears and seems inconsolable. Lu Su is taken aback, and at this precise moment in comes Kong Ming.

'Do you know why my lord is so distressed?' he says. 'Yes, he agreed to hand back Jingzhou when he took the western Riverlands. However, the ruler there is Liu Zhang. He, like my lord, is a member of the imperial family so he cannot attack him, for he would rightly be criticized for such inappropriate behaviour. So if he were at this stage to hand over Jingzhou, where exactly would he live? And in not handing it over, he of course understands that he is not behaving appropriately to his now new brother-in-law. Can you see the awful dilemma he is in and why he weeps so uncontrollably?'

Just to pile the pressure on even more, Xuande's weeping rises to a new level of intensity and emotion.

So it is that Lu Su is persuaded by Kong Ming to return to Sun Quan to describe the touching scene he has just witnessed and to ask for more time, especially now that Sun Quan is a brother-in-law. What could be more honourable or natural?

So Lu Su returns to Chaisang and Zhou Yu, and delivers the message. Zhou Yu is incandescent with rage and bluntly tells Lu Su, 'He has fooled you again!'

However, after giving the matter some thought, Zhou Yu comes up with his own plot. He sends Lu Su back with the message that his brother-in-law, in order to honour their being now one family, will invade the western Riverlands of Shu. He will do this on behalf of them both and once he has seized those lands he will of course hand them over as a sort of dowry and then take back Jingzhou in return. However, Zhou Yu also confides to Lu Su that he has no intention of invading the western Riverlands. His plan is to appear to set off to invade the west but en route suddenly turn and attack Jingzhou. So off goes Lu Su once again.

And once again, before Lu Su is ushered in, Xuande and Kong Ming consult. 'If I nod, agree to whatever Lu Su says,' says Kong Ming.

Lu Su enters and after the usual courtesies outlines the proposal and says, 'When we pass by, we would of course expect that you will help us with funds and resources.' Kong Ming nods, so Xuande agrees. Kong Ming adds, 'When these brave men come by we'll do all in our power to entertain and support them.'

After Lu Su has left, Xuande asks Kong Ming what that was all about. 'It is the old ploy of passing by but really going to attack,' says Kong Ming. 'If you go out of the city to greet them, they'll kidnap you and take the city.'

'So what do we do?' asks Xuande.

'Don't you worry. I have a plan. By the time we finish with Zhou Yu he will be as good as dead.' And, calling for Zhao Zilong, he gives him explicit instructions.

As a later poem says:

Zhou Yu schemes the fall of Jingzhou,
His enemy, from history, knows what will happen first.
The lands-over-the-river trick seems good to Yu,
But what he doesn't get is that he's the one to be fooled!

Lu Su reports back to Zhou Yu, telling him of the apparent success of his mission. Zhou Yu, confident that this time, at last, he has fooled Kong Ming, sets out in his fleet with some fifty thousand men for Jingzhou.

They soon reach Xiakou, where Mi Zhu is waiting for him to tell him that Xuande has indeed made preparations for their arrival. 'So where exactly is Lord Xuande?' asks Zhou Yu. 'Waiting outside the city gates of Gong'an to greet you,' says Mi Zhu.

So on the fleet presses but when they reach Gong'an there is no sign of anyone waiting to greet them. They press on further, and news comes when they are almost in sight of Jingzhou that the city has two white flags flying, but no one seems to be there at all!

Troubled by all this, Zhou Yu disembarks and rides to the city gate with three thousand of his crack troops led by Gan Ning, Xu Sheng and Ding Feng. When a call is made announcing that Zhou Yu has come, suddenly the walls are alive with heavily armed men, and Zhao Zilong stands forward and asks, 'What are you doing here, general?'

'We have come to take the western Riverlands for you,' shouts Zhou Yu. 'I'd have thought you knew this.'

'Well, actually,' shouts back Zilong, 'what we know is that you're using the old trick of marching past in order to attack, and that is why I'm here to prevent that. For, as you know, my lord is related to Liu Zhang, as both are members of the imperial family. How could he sanction such an attack? The disgrace would mean he'd have to give up all his dignity and authority and live in seclusion in the countryside, such would be the shame this would bring upon his head.'

Realizing that his plot has been foiled, Zhou Yu starts to turn back. But then news comes that a vast horde of soldiers is advancing on all sides, led by Guan Yu and Zhang Fei, by Huang Zhong and Wei Yan. 'They are beyond counting,' says the messenger, 'and all chant that they want to seize you!'

The shock is so great that Zhou Yu falls with a terrible cry from his horse, and again his wound bursts open.

What now will be Zhou Yu's destiny?

All will be revealed.

CHAPTER 57

Zhou Yu dies, and Kong Ming comes to mourn him. Pang Tong is shunted off to govern at Leiyang.

As Zhou Yu is carried to his ship, insult is added to injury when it is reported to him that Xuande and Kong Ming have watched the whole affair from a nearby hill, where they were seen drinking and laughing. Despite a last-minute attempt by Sun Quan's brother Sun Yu to continue the expedition, it comes to nothing, blocked as they are by Xuande's troops.

Not long after, Zhou Yu receives a letter from Kong Ming. In it he sternly reprimands Zhou Yu for his foolish plans. For the danger he has put his own men in and the real risk that, if Zhou Yu did go off to conquer the western Riverlands, Cao Cao would use the opportunity to invade and destroy Wu. 'I do wish,' finishes the letter, 'that you would be so kind as to pay attention to what I am saying and the real dangers you face.'

This all proves too much for Zhou Yu. Knowing he is dying, he writes a final letter to Sun Quan. Then, looking up to Heaven, he says, 'Having made me, why did you have to make Kong Ming?' And with that he dies. He is only thirty-six years old.

> The battle of Red Cliffs made him famous;
> Even in his youth he was renowned.
> His singing made manifest his integrity,
> Partying, he thanked his many friends.
> Through courtesy he secured food for his men,
> One hundred thousand men were at his command.
> Baqiu was where fate overtook him,
> With what sorrow is he still mourned.

When the news reaches Sun Quan he weeps openly. Zhou Yu's final letter urges him to offer the post of supreme commander to Lu Su, for 'Lu Su is a man of utmost loyalty, thorough in his planning and worthy to take my place,' wrote Zhou Yu. And so Lu Su is appointed.

Far away, Kong Ming sees in the night sky a 'general's star' fall to earth and knows that Zhou Yu has died. He also sees that there is a congregation of stars signifying that many skilled men are gathering in the east and so he sets off to join them, pretending he is coming to pay his respects to Zhou Yu's coffin.

Taking Zhao Zilong and five hundred warriors with him, he is able to fend off any plots to kill him and instead finds himself eventually kneeling before Zhou Yu's coffin. There, he pours forth a quite extraordinary eulogy. 'I'm heartbroken,' he says, 'when I recall your youth. You were a man of virtue and you soared upon wings like a roc. I recall when you befriended Sun Ce. I wonder at how you created the state of Wu. I remember your triumphs over Liu Biao and your unfaltering support for Sun Quan. And what of your marriage to Lady Qiao? How happy you were! You will always be honoured for your stance against the demands of Cao Cao.' He speaks of what a capable man he was and declares his grief at a life cut short after only thirty-six years, recalling 'our fight side by side against Cao Cao'. 'Sadly,' he concludes, 'the living and the dead cannot meet. But your fame will live for ever.'

Everyone is frankly astonished! And even Lu Su has to note that Kong Ming seems a bigger person than Zhou Yu ever was.

But as Kong Ming is preparing to board his ship to travel home, someone comes up dressed in the dishevelled clothes of a Daoist and says bluntly, 'You literally drove Zhou Yu to his death! And now you've the cheek to come here and pretend you're a mourner. This is nothing less than an insult to Wu. As if you were telling them there is no one with any talent left here at all!'

Initially he is somewhat shocked, but his anxiety soon turns to delight when he sees it is none other than his old friend Pang

Tong – Young Phoenix. They talk together for a while, and then Kong Ming gives him a letter he has written and says that if he finds his skills unappreciated here, he is to come to Xuande and offer his services.

Now after Zhou Yu has been buried, Lu Su comes to see Sun Quan and says that he is not worthy of the new appointment but he knows of one who is. 'Zhou Yu listened to him, as did Kong Ming,' he says.

So it is that Pang Tong – for it is he – is invited to the palace. However, Sun Quan is really put off by his appearance, and, when he seems to make a rather dismissive comment about the late Zhou Yu, Sun Quan's heart is set against him.

Dismissed, he wanders off, but Lu Su catches up with him and asks what his plans are now. 'I will go and join Cao Cao,' he says, to which Lu Su reacts with horror and suggests that he really should join Xuande and gives him a letter of recommendation.

So Pang Tong arrives at the court of Xuande. But Kong Ming is away and not able to make the introductions. Xuande also finds Pang Tong's appearance and manner off-putting. As a result he only offers him a very minor post as magistrate in a country town called Leiyang, miles away from the city. Deeply annoyed by this, Pang Tong almost rejects it out of hand but he realizes that, without Kong Ming being there to speak for him, this is all he can expect at the moment, so he takes the post.

It is not long before stories begin to circulate about the fact that he does no work whatsoever and is essentially drunk most of the time! Furious at this further indication of this man's off-hand manner, Xuande sends Zhang Fei to investigate, along with Sun Qian, to ensure Zhang Fei doesn't go off the deep end.

The pair arrive and ask where the magistrate is, only to be told that he is sleeping off a very drunken night before. Zhang Fei is furious at this and is all for dragging the man out of bed, but Sun Qian reminds him that this is no ordinary man and they should wait. Their patience is rewarded – well sort of – when a little while later a dishevelled and clearly hung-over Pang Tong strolls in.

'You were given responsibilities by my brother,' says Zhang Fei, 'and you've treated them with nothing less than wanton neglect.'

'What precisely,' answers Pang Tong, 'have I neglected?'

'Why, you've been here for a hundred days and have done nothing but get drunk! How can you possibly govern in that state?'

'To be honest,' replies Pang Tong, 'this is a very small place with not much going on, and even that requires very little action. However, wait here, and I'll deal with that.'

All the cases that have piled up during his hundred days are brought before him – supplicants, defendants and so forth. Within the space of half a day he not only deals with them all but does so to the outright approval of all. Even Zhang Fei has to admit he is impressed. Only then, to Zhang Fei's astonishment, does Pang Tong bring out the letter of recommendation from Lu Su.

Returning to Xuande, they report on what has happened and show the letter from Lu Su. Xuande begins to realize that his judging by appearances has very nearly lost him a great man. When Kong Ming returns from his travels he asks what high position Xuande has given to Pang Tong, and a shamefaced Xuande has to confess his mistake. But Kong Ming smiles and asks if Pang Tong has shown them the letter he, Kong Ming, wrote. Again, surprise all around that Pang Tong has not used this to gain favour.

And so it is that Pang Tong is brought back to Jingzhou and is made Kong Ming's assistant. He is given a high military role, and the two of them start to work side by side preparing for the next battle against the north.

Back in the capital, this information reaches Cao Cao, in particular news of their planned joint attack on the north. Cao Cao starts to plot his attack first but is deeply worried that the tribal leader Ma Teng from the remote western regions might use the opportunity of their being deep down south to attack. It is suggested that if he were to offer Ma Teng a formal title and ask for his help in attacking the south this might lure him to come to the capital, and then they could kill him and thus curtail this risk.

But Ma Teng is no fool. He knows when the invitation and offer come that this could well be a trap. Taking his eldest son Ma Chao on one side, he orders him to hold their home base. He also tells him that once he was part of a plot to bring about the death of Cao Cao. This was, of course, the infamous 'secret message in the belt' conspiracy. 'That plot failed,' says Ma Teng, 'and now I am summoned by Cao Cao. What do you think I should do?' His son says, 'You have to go because Cao Cao controls the emperor, and to refuse could mean you are charged with treason. Take this advantage and see if as a result you can finally achieve your long-held desire to get rid of Cao Cao.'

So he comes to the capital but brings with him five thousand tribal warriors as protection. Cao Cao commands one of his officials by the name of Huang Kui to oversee his arrival and comfort but with instructions that he must reduce his own army as Cao Cao will supply him with his own men, and there is not enough food for all of them at the moment.

When Huang Kui and Ma Teng have drunk deeply, Huang Kui inadvertently blurts out his hatred of Cao Cao for having usurped the imperial prerogatives. Although Ma Teng is at first suspicious and will not confess his hatred of the man as well, Huang Kui goes on to mention the plot involving the secret message hidden in the belt. With this Ma Teng knows he really means what he says, and together they plot to murder Cao Cao. It is agreed that they will lure Cao Cao out of the city to inspect the troops, and then Ma Teng will kill him.

And this might have worked.

But that night Huang Kui returns very disturbed and agitated. Unable to tell his wife about the assassination plot, he does confide in his concubine Li Chunxiang. However, she is having an affair with his own brother-in-law, Miao Ze, who desperately wants her for himself and would, as it turns out, do anything to have her. She tells Miao Ze about this plot, and he suddenly sees a way to get rid of his brother-in-law and have Li Chunxiang for himself. He goes immediately and tells Cao Cao, who accordingly summons his commanders and lays a counter plot.

The next morning Ma Teng and his sons and troops parade before the city walls, and out of the gate come a collection of banners. Thinking this is where Cao Cao is, Ma Teng and his sons charge at them, only for the banners to part and archers and crossbowmen to start firing. Trying to flee, they turn to find Cao Cao's men attacking them from all sides. One son dies there and then defending his father, and the other son and Ma Teng, seriously wounded, are captured. Together with Huang Kui, they are brought as prisoners before Cao Cao.

Ma Teng and his son are immediately condemned to death and taken out and executed. Then Miao Ze sidles up to Cao Cao and in a self-effacing way says, 'All I want as my reward is to marry Li Chunxiang. No need for anything more.'

Laughing out loud, Cao Cao speaks: 'For the sake of gaining a woman you have brought down destruction on your brother-in-law. Such a person doesn't deserve to live.' And he gives orders that Miao Ze, Li Chunxiang and Huang Kui along with his entire family are to be executed in public. Those who watch are moved by this tale of treachery, and a poet has said:

> Lust-led, Miao Ze damns a good man.
> Nothing gained, she dies too!
> The one they helped is pitiless –
> While this petty man's actions gain him
> nothing but death.

After this, Cao Cao moves forward with his plans with even more determination. Then news comes that Xuande is planning to invade the western Riverlands of Shu. This alarms Cao Cao, as it could mean that Xuande's territory would expand hugely and he would be unable to be contained. At this point there comes forward someone who claims he can break the alliance between Sun and Xuande, thereby helping Cao Cao to seize all the lands.

And who exactly is this?

Let's find out.

CHAPTER 58

Ma Chao raises an army for revenge.
Cao Cao not only shaves his beard but
sheds his cloak to escape capture.

The speaker is Chen Qun, a minor official, who points out that Sun Quan and Xuande are now as close 'as lips and teeth'. What is needed is to drive a wedge between them. If Cao were to attack Hefei and Sun Quan, this would create a dilemma for Xuande. 'He wants to go west for his own gain,' says Chen Qun, 'but Sun Quan would expect him to drop everything and come to his rescue. But Xuande won't. It's quite simple. Sun without Xuande will fold quickly, and then we can take care of Xuande after that.'

So Cao Cao sends an army of three hundred thousand south to the attack.

When the news reaches Sun Quan, he, of course, asks Lu Su to speak to Xuande and to create a joint front. Lu Su writes to Xuande proposing this, and Xuande consults Kong Ming. 'Don't lose sleep over these northerners,' says Kong Ming. 'I have a plan which means they'll never get as far as invading the south.'

After the messenger leaves, Xuande asks what exactly this plan is that will protect Hefei from over three hundred thousand soldiers. 'Cao Cao's greatest fear is attack by the western tribal soldiers,' Kong Ming replies. 'Now that he's killed Ma Teng, his son Ma Chao has taken control of the Xiliang tribal warriors. Write to him suggesting an alliance, because he'll be dying to revenge his father. If he attacks the north, then they can't attack us.' The message is duly sent.

When news reaches Ma Chao of the death of his father and brothers, he vows revenge, and at just that moment Xuande's message reaches him. Without hesitating, Ma Chao responds, saying he will attack Cao Cao from the west, as the letter suggests, if Xuande will attack from the south. After gathering support from others in the region, over two hundred thousand tribal warriors march towards the capital Chang'an. The governor Zhong Yao urgently sends news of this attack to Cao Cao. Then, taking his own troops, he advances to meet the enemy. The first engagement ends in defeat for the governor, who flees back into the safety of Chang'an, while Ma Chao and his men lay siege to the ancient capital.

Ten days of siege go by without success for Ma Chao. It is then that Pang De, one of Ma Chao's commanders, suggests a ruse. 'Things will be pretty desperate inside the city now. Why don't we retreat so that the people can come out and refurbish their supplies,. Many will come and go and . . . well. I have this idea.' Ma Chao listens and agrees heartily with what he hears. So the besiegers lift the siege and melt away into the distant hills.

As soon as Zhong Yao is certain they are far off, he opens the gates and, sure enough, people pour out – and pour back in again – plus some people who have never been in the city in the first place! This goes on for five days until the enemy forces are sighted moving back down to the attack, and the gates are hastily closed.

Late that night, a fire breaks out by the west gate. Riding to investigate is the commander of that gate, Zhong Jin, the brother of the governor. Suddenly out of the darkness comes a shout as a man strides towards him. 'I'm Pang De', and so saying he cuts down Zhong Jin. Soon the gate is thrown open, and the Xiliang troops pour in. Governor Zhong Yao flees and takes up a defensive position at the Tong pass, while word is sent as fast as possible to Cao Cao.

The fall of Chang'an does exactly what Kong Ming planned, and the southern campaign is abandoned. Cao Cao, realizing the strategic importance of holding the pass, sends a crack force of ten thousand under the command of Cao Hong and Xu Huang to help guard it. Ma Chao has brought his troops to below the pass and daily taunts the defenders to come out and fight. Cao Hong is desperate to do so, but Xu Huang knows better than that and restrains him. But on the ninth day Cao Hong sees the troops below are resting and with a force of three thousand he descends upon them, catching them unawares and scattering them.

When Xu Huang finds out what has happened, he charges down after Cao Hong to restrain him, calling for him to return. But no sooner have they joined up than Ma Chao suddenly charges at them, with Pang De attacking from the other side. Half of Cao Hong's men go down under the assault, and Cao Hong himself has to flee for his life, hotly pursued by Pang De. As a result, Ma Chao seizes control of the pass.

You can imagine Cao Cao's fury when the defeated commanders Cao Hong and Xu Huang arrive to tell of the disaster. He is all for executing Cao Hong but is eventually dissuaded.

Cao Cao now sets off for the pass and establishes his camp below, ready for battle. The very next day the armies clash, and the Xiliang troops break the northern army almost immediately, with Ma Chao and Pang De charging into the mêlée, determined to capture Cao Cao. In terror Cao Cao turns and flees but he hears behind him someone cry, 'Cao is the one in the red robe', and on hearing this he rips it off and casts it aside. Then he hears a cry, 'Cao is the one with the long beard!' As he rides, he hacks at his beard with his dagger. Then he hears another cry, 'Cao's the one with the ragged short beard', and this time he veils his face with his battle flag, but to no avail. Ma Chao is catching up with him. A dramatic thrust with his spear nearly stabs Cao Cao, but the spear strikes a tree, and, while Ma Chao struggles to pull the spear clear, Cao Cao is able to escape. By the time Ma Chao catches up with Cao Cao he is being defended by none other than Cao Hong, who holds Ma Chao at bay until more men arrive to protect Cao Cao and Ma Chao retreats.

It does not pass Cao Cao's notice that, if he had executed Cao Hong, he himself would have died, and he rewards him handsomely.

From now on Cao Cao holds back from any attack. News comes that Ma Chao has received twenty thousand Qiang tribesmen to reinforce his army, and Cao Cao, to the astonishment of his commander, smiles. Three days later comes news of more reinforcements for Ma Chao, and again Cao Cao smiles.

Shortly after this, Xu Huang and Cao Cao agree on the following strategy. Because Ma Chao has all his troops stationed at the pass, the west bank of the River Wei is undefended. They decide to send a task force to seize the bank so they can cut off any retreat by Ma Chao's men and then they will attack the enemy from the north of the River Wei.

It doesn't take long before Ma Chao realizes what is happening and moves to the attack to thwart Cao Cao as he manoeuvres his men into place. The confrontation takes place just after dawn on the bank of the Yellow River, when Ma Chao attacks as Cao's men are trying to embark for the other bank. Chaos ensues, though throughout it Cao Cao sits blankly and calmly as if not noticing anything is wrong. Then from behind him comes another attack, led by Ma Chao himself. When Ma Chao is less than a hundred yards from Cao Cao, Xu Chu realizes the seriousness of the situation. 'We are surrounded, my lord,' he says. 'Let's get to the boat.'

'So what?' replies Cao Cao. So Xu Chu simply lifts Cao Cao up and, carrying him on his shoulder, runs for the nearest boat. He pushes the boat off, but others who are trying to flee and are struggling in the river try to grab hold and climb aboard. Xu Chu slashes at them, cutting their hands off to stop them overturning the frail little boat.

But danger is still all around. From the bank Ma Chao directs archers to fire on the boat, and Xu Chu has to protect Cao Cao by holding his saddle as a shield. The archers pick off the rowers one by one until Xu Chu is the only one left. He has to steer the boat, push with his oar and protect Cao Cao, who is cowering in the bottom of the boat.

All seems to be up for Xu Chu and Cao Cao, but a local official, Ding Fei, spots what is happening and orders the grazing cattle to be driven down onto the flood plains. This diverts the attention of the tribal warriors, who rush off after them to seize them as bounty. This enables Xu Chu and Cao Cao to be swept on down the river out of harm's way.

Recovering from his failure of nerve, Cao Cao now takes stock and orders his troops to prepare defences on this northern shore, including digging pits and covering them with branches so that any cavalry charge can be brought crashing down. Now they are ready to carry out their plan to attack Ma Chao from the north.

In return, Ma Chao realizes that he should try and attack first and he orders Pang De and Han Sui to advance with fifty thousand men.

The trick of covering the pits works well. Pang De's cavalry charge crashes down into the pits, and few escape. But Pang De by a mighty effort is able to ride back out. Dragging Han Sui also to safety, he flees, pursued by Cao Cao's men. But then Ma Chao rides to the rescue and in the nick of time saves his army from defeat. Consulting with his generals, Ma Chao agrees that they should attack again that very night before the enemy can really dig in. Back at Cao Cao's camp, he tells his men to expect exactly such an attack and to lay an ambush.

It is not Ma Chao who comes at dead of night but Cheng Yi with just thirty men. As they ride into the camp, it appears to be deserted. Thinking that this is a major attack, Cao Cao's men spring the ambush but find they have trapped only thirty men. Cheng Yi is slain, but then, as if from nowhere, Ma Chao and the mass of his men charge in and launch a terrifying assault.

Who is going to win?

Let's find out.

CHAPTER 59

Xu Chu fights Ma Chao. Cao Cao sows distrust between Ma Chao and Han Sui.

It is inconclusive, and by morning both sides have had enough and withdraw. Despite various plans and strategies of Cao Cao, in the end Ma Chao's men take control of the mouth of the River Wei and Cao has to think defensively. He tries to have walls built, but the mud is too wet and they collapse. Then one night an old Daoist sage visits him and tells him to take note of the change in the weather. A bitingly cold wind is about to sweep down upon them, and this will mean that if they build the walls and wet them then the bitter cold will freeze them as solid as blocks of ice and make the walls firm. When Ma Chao sees what has happened he begins to wonder if Cao Cao has gained the support of the deities!

The next day he advances upon Cao Cao, and this swiftly turns into a personal challenge. Ma Chao can see that beside Cao Cao there is a mighty warrior whom he is sure is Xu Chu – known also as Lord Tiger. When challenged, Xu Chu shouts back that it is indeed him and the next day he sends a challenge back to Ma Chao for a one-to-one fight.

The ensuing struggle is a titanic one. Both men attack, and the first bout lasts a hundred rounds with neither man coming out on top. The second bout also goes to a hundred rounds, but again with no conclusion. The third bout ends with the two men struggling to batter each other to death with two pieces of a broken spear with which Ma Chao has nearly pierced Xu Chu. He grabbed hold of the spear with his bare hands and in the struggle the spear broke.

Again, neither one triumphs, but both sides, fearing for their champion, surge forward, and battle ensues. It is Cao Cao who loses and he is driven back into his fortified camp of the frozen walls. Another bout of sorties and counter-sorties a few days later results in Cao Cao being able to set up camp on the west bank and thus being in a position to attack Ma Chao from two directions. As a result, a number of Ma Chao's officers, including Han Sui, urge him to ask for a truce through the winter. So emissaries are sent to Cao Cao, who tells them to return for his answer the next day.

When Cao's adviser Jia Xu comes to discuss this with him, he suggests that they use this period of truce to sow discord between Ma Chao and Han Sui. When the emissaries return, Cao Cao agrees to the truce and makes it appear in the next few days as if he is pulling back. Not trusting Cao Cao, Ma Chao comes up with his own strategy for trying to keep an eye on what is really happening. He decides that he and Han Sui will take it in turns, day in day out, to face the different sections of Cao's army – one day Han Sui will observe Cao's fortifications and Ma Chao those of Xu Huang on the west bank, and then vice versa. This gives Cao Cao the opportunity for deception that he was hoping for.

One day, when Han Sui is opposite him, he rides out. He shouts out, 'You know I'm Cao Cao. I'm just an ordinary human being, not some terrible demon with four eyes or many mouths!' Then he sends a message to Han Sui, saying that he wants to meet him and talk.

So Han Sui too rides out, and together, with no one else there, the two men talk of times past, of their families and of growing old. It is harmless chatter, but Cao Cao makes a point of often laughing out loud. The talk goes on for a couple of hours, and then each man rides back to his own lines.

Of course, Ma Chao hears about this and, deeply suspicious, asks Han Sui what is going on. Han Sui tries to reassure him that it was harmless chatter about times past, but Ma Chao is very suspicious indeed.

Back in Cao's camp, Jia Xu suggests how they could dramatically increase the tension between the two. 'Write a letter to Han Sui, but cross out some words, scratch out others and write over them. When Ma Chao hears about this letter from you he'll demand to see it. He'll think that Han Sui made these changes, trying to hide the real message of the letter. That will sow distrust.'

This is exactly what happens. When the letter arrives Ma Chao is, of course, informed and comes to see Han Sui, demanding to be given the letter. Observing the crossings-out and the scratchings-out and rewriting, he accuses Han Sui of plotting to betray him. Han Sui vigorously denies this. To show his loyalty, he suggests that he help trap Cao Cao so Ma Chao can kill him. He will go out to talk with Cao Cao, and, at a signal, Ma Chao will charge out and kill him.

The next day Han Sui sends a message, asking Cao Cao to come over to continue the discussions. But before he comes himself, Cao Hong rides up and in a loud stage whisper says to Han Sui, 'The prime minister wants to reassure you after what you said last night that there will be no mistakes', and then he turns and rides back. Ma Chao overhears this, as he is meant to do, and in a fury rides out straight at Han Sui with his lance lowered. Others intervene and pull him away, while Han Sui professes his innocence. But Ma Chao rides off determined to have revenge.

Realizing that things have moved from difficult to impossible, Han Sui decides to go over to Cao Cao because, as his friends point out, Ma Chao will never trust him again.

So it is that Han Sui secretly enters Cao Cao's service while still living in Ma Chao's camp. He also agrees with the other five officers who have joined him in this betrayal that they will attack Ma Chao on a given signal.

However, Ma Chao already knows of their plot and the secret deal and with faithful men such as Pang De and Ma Dai he strides off to confront Han Sui. Quietly entering Han Sui's tent, he finds all the conspirators together. Roaring with anger, he launches himself at the men, cutting off Han Sui's hand when he raises it to protect himself. The fight spills out of the tent. Ma Chao cuts down two of the conspirators, while the other three flee. Returning to finish off Han Sui, he is thwarted because attendants have pulled Han Sui away to safety. Now Cao Cao's men rush to the attack, and chaos prevails, with discord among Ma Chao's own men as well as the attack by Cao Cao's troops.

Realizing the dangers, Ma Chao takes up a defensive position to guard the Wei bridge with a small troop of loyal men. Arrows rain down on him, and he survives, but despite brave attempts to charge forward, the sheer number of Cao's men forces him back. With no other option, Ma Chao turns and charges off to the north, leaving his men to their fate. But even this does not work, for a crossbow shot kills his horse, and the enemy troops close in for the kill.

Suddenly, as if from nowhere, Pang De and Ma Dai thunder to the rescue, catching Cao's men off guard and scattering them. Soon they race off, with Ma Chao mounted now on another horse. Cao Cao gives orders that every possible effort is made to catch him and offers a huge reward to whomsoever does that. Ma Chao rides like the devil, and soon only a handful of his men are still with him – Pang De and Ma Dai among them. They ride pell-mell to sanctuary in Lintao.

Cao Cao rewards Han Sui and the surviving conspirators and then returns with the army to Chang'an. Here, however, Yang Fu, one of the military advisers, strongly recommends that Ma Chao be dealt with before anything else takes place. Cao Cao agrees but points out how stretched he is, so Yang Fu is given the task of hunting down Ma Chao. Once he has left, Cao's commanders come to discuss the campaign with him. In particular they want to know why he smiled when he heard of the reinforcements that came to Ma Chao's assistance.

'Quite simple really,' says Cao Cao. 'When spread out, these tribal warrior groups are difficult to deal with and doing so would take months of campaigning. But when they all congregate together, then we can deal with them with one blow!'

So the northern army return to Xuchang, where the emperor himself honours them and bestows upon Cao Cao special honours. From that day on the fearsome reputation of Cao Cao grows and grows.

News of what has happened spreads far and wide and reaches to the west to Hanzhong, where the governor, Zhang Lu, is deeply troubled. He is the grandson of Zhang [Dao] Ling, a

Daoist master who went to meditate on Mount Huming in the western Riverlands of Shu. There, he wrote a book designed to fool the common folk into believing he had magical, even divine powers. The local people greatly respected him, and, after he died, his son Zhang Heng continued his tradition. Those wishing to study the Dao had to donate five bushels of rice. This earned him the nickname 'Rice Thief'. When Zhang Heng died, Zhang Lu continued the tradition.

Zhang Lu gave himself the title 'supreme ruler', while his followers were called 'ghost fighters'. The headman was called 'libationer' while those in charge of large forces were called 'lead healing libationer'. True sincerity was the core of this tradition; neither lying nor deception was permitted. If someone fell ill, an altar was created, and the sick person was brought to the Place of Silence, where they could reflect upon their sins which had caused this illness. Once this was articulated, prayers could be offered and overseen by the superintendent of libations. The prayers accompanied the written confession of the individual and three copies were made, entitled 'The Petition to the Three Officials'. One was then put on top of a hill to reach Heaven, one was buried in the ground to reach Earth and one was thrown into water to reach the officials of the Underworld. After this, if the patient recovered, he or she donated five bushels of rice as a thanksgiving.

Besides this, they also had public places where the poor could find free rice, meat and somewhere to cook. Everyone was allowed to take this for their honest needs, but any excess, it was believed, would bring down punishment from Heaven. Those who offended were given three pardons and after that they were punished. They had no officials, because everyone was governed by the libationers. In this way Hanzhong has been ruled for thirty years and has survived because they are too far away from the imperial court for anyone to particularly worry about them. Instead, the court simply gave Zhang Lu an imperial title of prefect and insisted that he send in the tax as usual.

On hearing that Cao Cao has triumphed over the western army and is beginning to throw his weight around, Zhang Lu calls together his advisers. 'With Ma Teng murdered and Ma

Chao in retreat, it's inevitable that Cao Cao will next come after us. To pre-empt this I'm going to announce that I'm now the prince of Hanning and head the resistance. What do you think?'

His adviser Yan Pu replies, 'The people of this region number more than one hundred thousand households. There's considerable wealth and more than enough grain. We're protected on four sides by natural defences. The defeat of Ma Chao has meant huge numbers of refugees have flooded into our area. In my honest opinion, Liu Zhang, governor of Yizhou, is a weak man. So I suggest we seize the forty-one departments of the western Riverlands and from there declare independence.' Pleased with what he hears, Zhang Lu commissions his brother Zhang Wei to summon the army.

It is not long before news of this uprising reaches the heartlands of Shu. The governor, Liu Zhang, is a long-time enemy of Zhang Lu and has in fact executed both his mother and brother. Knowing that this makes Zhang Lu a danger, he garrisoned Baxi, a town close to Hanzhong, and appointed Pang Xi as the commander. It is Pang Xi who first hears of the uprising and sends news to Liu Zhang. Deeply frightened, Liu Zhang assembles his advisers and asks what to do. In the midst of this a man stands up and says, 'Don't you worry. I'm a man of few skills but with this little tongue of mine I can make Zhang Lu so frightened that he'll not even look this way!'

So who is this man?

Let's find out.

CHAPTER 60

Zhang Song tries to convince Cao Cao
but is dismissed. Pang Tong convinces
Xuande to seize Shu.

Zhang Song is his name, and a very odd-looking man he is, with his pointed head, his bulging forehead, flattened nose and sticking-out teeth. He is also very short but with a deep voice like a great bell.

When asked what this plan is, he spells it out. He points out that Cao Cao is now without equal anywhere in the land. It is time to pay due respect to him with proper gifts and praise. If he could be persuaded to attack Hanzhong, Zhang Lu would not be able to invade their land of Shu. Liu Zhang likes this idea a great deal and begins to prepare the gold and pearls to be presented. Thus equipped, Zhang Song sets out for the capital, but not before secretly collecting maps of the land of Shu. His journey is noted far away by spies, who report all this to Kong Ming, and he sends them back to watch what happens next.

After arriving in Xuchang, Zhang Song tries day after day to gain an audience with Cao Cao, but to no avail. Cao Cao now sees himself as so important he doesn't bother with minor affairs. Eventually, by bribing Cao Cao's servants, Zhang Song does gain an audience. As Zhang Song kowtows, Cao Cao asks abruptly, 'Your master, Liu Zhang, has failed to submit any tribute for many years now. Why?'

'Well, you see,' replies Zhang Song, 'we've so many thieves and robbers the roads are unsafe, and so we can't send the tribute.'

'What thieves and robbers? I've made our country safe, so how can this be?'

To which Zhang Song replies, 'Well, in the south there is Sun Quan, in the north Zhang Lu, while to the west, of course, is Xuande. At the very least they each have over one hundred thousand men. In the light of all that, how on earth can you say the land is safe and at peace?'

Now Cao Cao already dislikes Zhang Song's appearance and this dislike is increased by his blunt comments. Without another word, Cao Cao rises and leaves the room. His servants lecture Zhang Song on how he should have behaved, but Zhang Song simply says, 'Sorry, but we Riverlanders from Shu in the west don't bend and scrape', and, so saying, he prepares to depart. At this someone speaks up, saying, 'You lot really have no idea how to flatter, do you?' The speaker is Yang Xiu, a first secretary to Cao Cao. Intrigued by Zhang Song, he invites him to join him for talks in his library.

Asked about the land of Shu, Zhang Song tells of the difficulties of access either by river or by road, and praises its productivity and its people. 'Nowhere else on earth is so productive,' he brags.

In answer to Yang Xiu's questions, he speaks about the men of fame that Shu has produced, the highly educated people at the court and their skills. He then questions Yang Xiu on why he holds what appears to him to be a lowly role, which makes Yang Xiu bristle: 'I have great responsibilities for the welfare of the army.'

Zhang Song says, 'I understand that Cao Cao is ignorant of the teachings of Kong Fu Zi and Meng Zi,[13] or the strategies for warfare of Sun Zi and Wu Qi. I gather it's said of him that his only interest is in self-aggrandizement. Surely, you can learn nothing from one like this!'

To try to show how wrong he is, Yang Xiu brings out a scroll with the text of a book called *New Book of Meng De*, claiming that this had been written by none other than Cao Cao himself and based on Sun Zi's famous Thirteen Strategies!

Zhang Song quickly reads all thirteen chapters and then, laughing, says, 'But this is nothing new! All the children in Shu know this old book – it was written centuries ago in the time of the Warring States.[14] Cao Cao has simply copied it!'

Challenged by Yang Xiu to prove this, Zhang Song immediately repeats the text word for word. Astonished by this feat,

Yang Xiu in admiration says, 'You learned it in just one reading? You really are astonishing.'

A poet has said of Zhang Song:

A very unusual-looking being,
Bright, honourable, but so strangely other.
His diction like a mountain stream . . .
One glance at a page, and he remembers it whole.

His courage exalted above the rest of Western Shu,
His understanding universal . . .
So well read in philosophy and sacred texts
He reads just once, then knows what's next.

Inspired by all this, Yang Xiu offers to intercede for him with Cao Cao. This he does by recounting Zhang Song's extraordinary skills of memory and the challenge he has thrown down to Cao Cao's book. 'I wonder,' says Cao Cao, 'whether in some way my writing has accorded with more ancient wisdom?' Interestingly, Cao Cao orders the book destroyed!

Cao Cao agrees to meet Zhang Song the next day while inspecting his troops.

So it is that, the following day, Zhang Song observes the military might and splendour of Cao Cao's troops. Asked if Shu has anything like this, Zhang Song answers, 'We've nothing like this because we rule by benevolence and justice.'

Stung by this rebuke and resorting to boasting, Cao Cao recounts how his troops are triumphant everywhere they go, to which Zhang Song then says, 'Indeed, your military triumphs are well known – such as your defeat at the Red Cliffs, cutting off your beard to escape at Tong pass or fleeing the archers at the River Wei!'

By now seething with rage, Cao Cao orders his immediate execution and is only dissuaded by Yang Xiu pointing out that Zhang is an emissary of another state.

But Zhang is expelled from the palace.

As he packs his bags, he suddenly thinks that in order to fulfil his mission he has one choice left – to go and visit Xuande, not least because he is inspired by what he had heard of him as a man of benevolence and justice.

Imagine his surprise and delight, then, when, as he and his escort cross the border into Xuande's lands, he is greeted by Zhao Zilong and an official escort of five hundred cavalrymen, sent to bring him with all due honour to Xuande's city of Jingzhou. When he reaches his hotel, he is even more delighted to find a hundred men lined up to greet him. Guan Yu himself comes to formally welcome him and has ordered a banquet to honour him.

The next day Zhang Song and Guan Yu ride to meet Xuande, who, when he and Kong Ming and Pang Tong see Zhang approaching, dismounts to greet him properly.

During the official banquet they discuss the somewhat temporary nature of Xuande's lordship in Jingzhou and the demands from Sun Quan for the return of the territory. Zhang Song, stressing Xuande's imperial lineage, asks if it is not possible that one day he might ascend to the throne as a legitimate heir, to which Xuande quietly defers.

Three days later, it is time to leave, and once again discussion turns to the perilous state of Xuande's lordship and control of a region. It is now that Zhang Song puts forward his idea:

'My lord, I am truly impressed by you and so I'll be honest with you also. Liu Zhang isn't worthy of the lordship of Yizhou. He's weak and fails to make use of either the wise or skilful people in his court. He's threatened by rebellion in the north from Zhang Lu, and so naturally people yearn for a better ruler. I was sent to seek help from Cao Cao but discovered him to be a traitor unable to work with the worthy or draw upon the wise. So I came to see you. Come, take the Riverlands, take Shu for yourself. Start by pretending at first to be heading for Hanzhong but then seize the whole land. Your place in the history books will be assured. If you're willing to do this, I'll do all in my power to assist. So, what do you say to that?'

Xuande repeats what he has said so often before about not attacking a member of the same imperial family. Zhang Song counters this by pointing out that others might get there before Xuande does and then he would be sorry!

Xuande, in one last attempt at diversion, says he understands the roads are terrible and the mountains impassable.

This is when Zhong Song produces the maps he has secretly taken. He shows Xuande how to advance into Shu and assures him of support from his friends.

'So long as the hills are always green and the rivers flow, I'll ensure you are rewarded,' says Xuande, to which Zhang Song replies, 'I desire no reward, for having met a wise and benevolent lord, I've done what was necessary.'

Back in Yizhou, Zhang Song shares his plans with his friends Fa Zheng and Meng Da. They agree wholeheartedly with his plan. They also plot to have Liu Zhang send them as emissaries to Jingzhou.

The next day, Zhang Song reports back to Liu Zhang. 'Cao Cao is a traitor and ambitious. He wants to take our land as well. I suggest, therefore, that we ask Imperial Uncle Xuande, a man of great virtue, to help us in our struggle not only against Cao Cao but also Zhang Lu. His very name strikes fear into others.'

Liu Zhang is delighted with this suggestion and agrees at once. When he asks whom he should send to Jingzhou as ambassadors, he is also happy with the suggestion of Fa Zheng and Meng Da.

Despite the desperate pleas of some of his other advisers, who foresee that Xuande will overrun the whole country, the plan is set in motion. Liu Zhang sends Fa Zheng as his ambassador straight away.

Fa Zheng brings to the court of Xuande a formal letter from Liu asking for his kinsman's help in destroying the threat from Zhang Lu. Over dinner that night Xuande comments, 'I find it so hard to even contemplate the idea of attacking someone who is from the same imperial family as me.'

'My lord,' Fa Zheng responds, 'Liu Zhang has every possible natural advantage yet he is incapable of ruling. If you do not come to the rescue others will seize the country from him. To be honest it is as if the land is being presented to you.' This calms Xuande's nerves.

Later that night, Pang Tong comes to him while he is wondering what the right course might be. Xuande points out that he is the complete opposite of Cao Cao. 'Where Cao uses aggression, I seek reflection,' he says. 'Where Cao is vicious, I am humane; where Cao is wily, I'm straightforward. It's these differences which have given me the moral high ground. But if I attack my kinsman, all that would be lost.'

Pang Tong argues, 'That is all well and fine in ordinary times. But these are extraordinary times. There is no clear "right path". You should follow the way of the ancient rulers – seize power but then maintain it with integrity. Give Liu a region to rule by himself but under you and what wrong will you have done? For if you do not take the land, then someone else certainly will.' Finally, this seems to put Xuande's heart at rest, and he agrees to go.

Dividing his forces, and leaving Kong Ming in charge at Jingzhou with Guan Yu, Zhang Fei and Zhao Zilong in case of attack, he takes Pang Tong, Huang Zhong and Wei Yan with him. So, with a combined force of fifty thousand men, they set off for Shu, having first informed Liu Zhang of their coming.

Liu Zhang decides to go and meet Xuande at Fucheng. This is strongly resisted by two of his advisers, so much so that one of them, Huang Quan, literally grips Liu's clothes in his teeth to try to prevent his going.

The final attempt to stop him is dramatic. Liu receives notice that Wang Lei, one of his advisers, has strung himself upside down above the city gate with a letter of protest in one hand and a sword in the other. He threatens to cut the rope and crash to his death if Liu does not turn back from his planned trip and welcome. Furious that he is being denounced in this manner when he sees himself as going to meet 'a benevolent and just man', Liu Zhang goes on his way. Wang Lei then cuts the rope and with a terrible cry falls to his death.

Meanwhile, Xuande has advanced into Shu territory and has given strict instructions that his men are not to seize any goods or harm any of the people. Fa Zheng confides in Pang Tong that Zhang Song has recommended attacking Liu Zhang at the first meeting, to be held at Fucheng.

Liu Zhang is very excited when he at last meets Xuande and in his enthusiasm casts all caution to one side. His advisers are much more cautious, warning that Xuande's velvet glove hides an iron fist – but Liu Zhang will hear nothing of this.

Following their joint banquet, Xuande retires, and Pang Tong comes to see him. 'I suggest we strike now. Have a hundred men hidden around the wall and invite Liu Zhang for another banquet. If you give us the signal – for example, dropping a cup – we'll spring into action and kill Liu Zhang. Then our entry into the capital Chengdu will be unopposed.'

To this Xuande replies, 'He's my kinsman, and were I to do this neither Heaven nor the people themselves would forgive me.' At this moment Fa Zheng arrives and adds his words to the argument: 'This is not done for our own glory but because it's the Mandate of Heaven.'

Again, Xuande argues that he cannot murder a kinsman, but Fa Zheng again disagrees, pointing out that if Xuande does not seize control then Zhang Lu will. Having come this far across difficult terrain, what would be the point now of turning round and going away? 'Seize the moment – both Heaven and the people want this,' urges Pang Tong.

> The lord holds to the true Way.
> His advisers push forward with scheming.

So what will Xuande do?

All will be revealed.

CHAPTER 61

Zhao Zilong rescues Ah Dou from the river.
Sun Quan uses a letter to deter Cao Cao.

Now Xuande is a man of honour and he steadfastly resists the blandishments and plots of his advisers. There is no way he will exploit the opportunity to kill Liu Zhang.

So the banquet goes ahead, with both men expressing their friendship and trust. Meanwhile, however, Pang Tong and Fa Zheng decide to take matters into their own hands. They agree that Wei Yan should step forward and perform the famous sword dance and, using this as a cover, murder Liu Zhang.

But their plot is almost immediately spotted by both sides. One by one, others from both sides join in the dance – those from Liu Zhang's side to protect him; those from Xuande's side to help further the plot, until, that is, Xuande, realizing what is going on, rises and says with great force, 'Drop your swords. Liu Zhang and I are friends. No weapons are needed here.' At this the plotters flee from the feast. After the feast, Xuande tears into Pang Tong for having risked disgracing him with such a plot.

Not long after, news comes that Zhang Lu has advanced to the attack at Jiameng pass. At Liu's request, Xuande agrees to advance to the pass with his men. The exemplary behaviour of Xuande's men soon wins the approval of all the local people, for they pay for all they take and treat the local people with respect.

Back in the land of Wu in the south, the events in Shu – the Riverlands – are, of course, reported by spies to Sun Quan. Gu Yong, seeing that this offers an opportunity to seize Jingzhou, recommends to Sun Quan that, with Xuande gone, they should attack. Before any further plans can be developed, however, someone shouts from behind a screen, 'This will mean the death of my daughter!', and out steps a furious queen mother.

'My only daughter is Xuande's wife. You attack, and what will become of her? Eh! Answer me. Go on! My son, you have the eighty-one regions of the south. Is this not enough? Must you put at risk your own flesh and blood?'

Mortified, and with no other alternative, Sun Quan apologizes time and time again for putting his sister at risk. So it seems the plan is over before it begins, but that night, when Sun Quan is reflecting on the day's events, Zhang Zhao comes to him with another plot:

'Give me five hundred men, and I'll get into Jingzhou and present Lady Sun with a letter. This will say her mother is dying and wishes more than anything to see her before she dies. I'll make sure that she leaves with her son – because Xuande will willingly surrender Jingzhou in return for his only heir.'

Sun Quan is delighted and readily agrees. Zhao Shan, a loyal man trusted by Lady Sun, is sent to carry out the scheme. The letter is forged and handed over to Zhao Shan. It is easy for Zhao Shan and his men to slip into Jingzhou disguised as traders. He quietly makes his way to Lady Sun and presents the fake letter to her.

Reading the letter, Lady Sun bursts into tears, and Zhao Shan, seeing his advantage, says how desperate the queen mother is to see her daughter and her grandson. But Lady Sun resists, saying that, as Xuande is away, she must seek permission from Kong Ming as her lord's representative. To this Zhao Shan replies that there is no time to waste and urges her to depart now before they can be stopped.

Confused by this distressing news, Lady Sun decides to act without delay. Collecting seven-year-old Ah Dou, Xuande's son, she is soon in her carriage and heading for the river and the boats waiting to carry her to the south. Just as they are about to push off from the shore, a loud shout stops them in their tracks – 'Wait. I must say goodbye to my lady' – and there, riding up to the shoreline, is Zhao Zilong. Returning from patrol, he has discovered her departure and, riding as fast as he can, he just reaches the shoreline in time. But Zhao Shan is not to be thwarted and orders the boats to set sail.

Still shouting out, Zhao Zilong gallops along the shoreline, demanding that he be allowed to speak to Lady Sun – to no avail, for Zhao Shan simply ignores him. Then, however, Zhao Zilong spots a fishing boat tied up. He grabs his spear, leaps aboard and pushes off in pursuit, with one of his men steering the boat.

As they draw nearer and nearer to the boats, Zhao Shan orders the archers to fire, but Zhao Zilong easily deflects them using his spear. Getting closer and closer, Zhao Zilong is stabbed at by Zhao Shan's men with their swords, but again he deflects them, drawing his own sword. As soon as the boats are close enough, he leaps aboard, driving the defenders back in astonishment and fear. Advancing with his sword drawn, to her horror, he forces his way into Lady Sun's cabin.

'How dare you!' she cries.

'Where are you going, my lady? Why have you not asked permission?'

'My mother is dying, and there is no time for such things.'

'But, my lady,' replies Zhao Zilong, 'why are you taking the young master with you?'

'Ah Dou is my child. I would never leave him to be cared for by who knows who.'

'I'm sorry, my lady,' replies Zhao Zilong, 'but he belongs to my master. I saved him from a battlefield filled with a million soldiers so I have to ask, why are you taking him?'

'You, sir, are an upstart with no rights over what I or my family do.'

'You, of course, may go. But the young master stays.'

'You rebel! How dare you jump onto my boat?' replies a furious Lady Sun.

'Unless you leave the child, I'll go through ten thousand deaths before I'll give up.'

In desperation, Lady Sun cries out for her maids to help, but Zhao Zilong simply brushes them aside and seizes the child, rushing out of the cabin onto the deck. But there he realizes he is stuck, for the shore is now far away, and Zhao Shan is heading resolutely for the south.

Suddenly ten boats swing out from a creek. At first Zilong thinks this is how he will die until he realizes that in the prow of the lead boat is Zhang Fei. His voice booms across the water: 'Sister-in-law – leave the boy.'

The boats crash into one another, and Zhang Fei leaps aboard, sword flying. Zhao Shan's head is struck from his body, and Zhang Fei throws it at the feet of Lady Sun.

'How dare you!' cries Lady Sun.

'How dare *you*!' replies Zhang Fei. 'How dare you sneak away without a moment's thought about my elder brother!'

'My mother is dying, and if I'd waited for my husband's permission I would be too late. If you stand in my way, I'll drown myself in the river.'

Turning to Zilong, Zhang Fei says, 'To force her to do that would be an act of great dishonour. Let's simply take Ah Dou and leave her.'

And so they grab the child. Leaping on to Zhang Fei's boat, clutching the boy, they steer their boats away. With no options left, Lady Sun's boat proceeds south.

When Lady Sun arrives at last at her brother's capital, she tells him of all that has befallen her. Seeing his opportunity, Sun Quan starts to plan his attack on Jingzhou. The attack is about to go ahead, but then news arrives of an impending assault by Cao Cao leading four hundred thousand men-at-arms. Immediately Sun Quan gives orders to build a wall at the mouth of the Ruxu as a first line of defence against the invasion from the land of Wei in the north.

It is the winter of AD 212 when Cao Cao sets off to conquer the south. Arriving as expected at Ruxu, Cao Cao is startled to find not just the wall that has been built but a mighty fleet anchored there, and seated confidently in the middle Sun Quan.

Suddenly a cacophony of noise erupts as the boats of the south attack, while from behind the wall emerge troops advancing on Cao Cao's position. The attack takes Cao Cao and his men completely by surprise, and to their astonishment Sun Quan is now leading the cavalry charge up the hill towards them. To put it simply, Cao Cao panics, and only the heroism of Xu Chu saves him from almost certain death.

Back at his camp, recovering from the shock, Cao Cao rewards Xu Chu but upbraids his other commanders for their cowardice. It is to prove of little use, for that night Wu's troops attack the camp and, pouring in, they inflict terrible losses on the Wei army. Leaping onto his horse, Cao Cao escapes and rides far off from the battle scene. Later, having found sanctuary, he is sitting disconsolate, passing the time reading manuals of warfare. Confronted by Cheng Yu, he is upbraided by him. He points out that, in taking so long in planning his advance, he has given Sun Quan ample opportunity to prepare his defences. He advises that in the circumstances they retreat, but Cao Cao will not hear of it.

After Cheng Yu leaves, Cao Cao, worn out, lays his head on the table. Suddenly a tidal wave of noise rushes over him, as if thousands upon thousands of horses are galloping towards him. Rushing outside, he sees rising from the middle of the river a fiery sun, so bright it hurts to look at it. Gazing up into Heaven, he sees two more suns shining down upon the other one. Without warning, from the heart of the river the sun rises and then falls to earth behind a hill on the edge of his camp. The noise it makes is horrendous, and this is what wakes Cao Cao from his dream.

He orders his horse be brought and with just fifty men he sets off to where he saw in his dream the sun drop down. And there he finds Sun Quan resplendent in shining helmet and silver armour. When Sun Quan sees his enemy, he shows no fear but instead denounces him, saying, 'You're in charge of the capital. You've achieved great heights of power and wealth. So why do you have to come after our lands as well?'

'You have disobeyed the emperor, and it is at his command that I come,' replies Cao Cao.

'Rubbish!' exclaims Sun Quan. 'You've made the emperor little more than your puppet – we all know this! That is why I'm going to seize hold of you and end this tyranny.' And so saying, he charges at Cao Cao. In response Cao Cao leads his men into the attack. But almost immediately the sound of war drums erupts from behind the hill, and out charge more Wu troops. Three thousand archers unleash a storm of arrows on Cao Cao and his men. Once again Cao Cao flees, and once again it falls to Xu Chu to protect him in his flight.

Reflecting later on all this, Cao Cao realizes that his dream has foretold that Sun Quan will become an emperor. The obvious conclusion is that Cao Cao should retreat back to Wei in the north, but his pride stands in the way. So for a month the two men and their armies have a stand-off, with each side making sorties but no real engagement taking place. By the start of the new year, torrential rain has made life for the soldiers a misery, so, out of compassion, Cao Cao orders a return to the capital.

Sun Quan and his advisers are triumphant and start to think that now is the time, with Xuande still away and a victorious army, to seize Jingzhou. But this is opposed by Zhang Zhao. 'This is not the time to attack. Instead, I have an idea which will mean that Xuande never returns to Jingzhou.'

So what is this plan?

Let's find out.

CHAPTER 62

Yang and Gao are killed at the fall of the Fu pass. Huang Zhong and Wei Yan compete to capture Luocheng.

Zhang Zhao's advice is to use subterfuge. 'Write two letters,' he says to Sun Quan. 'One to Liu Zhang, telling him that Xuande has joined with us in order to capture Shu, and the other to Zhang Lu, suggesting he attack Jingzhou in order to cut Xuande off from his resources. That way we will win back Jingzhou!'

To this Sun Quan gives his approval.

Xuande is now based at Jiameng pass. Here, his thoughtful and compassionate behaviour and that of his men have earned him support from the local people. However, when news comes of what has happened between Cao Cao and Sun Quan, he is troubled and he seeks advice. Pang Tong recommends, 'Write to Liu Zhang saying that Sun Quan needs your help against Cao Cao. This'll mean you can head back to support him. Also, say you need support yourself – let's say between thirty and forty thousand of his best soldiers and a hundred thousand bushels of grain to manage the march back. If Liu Zhang does as you ask, we can then move to the next step.'

So Xuande sends the letter by messenger. But when the messenger reaches the Fu pass, he is intercepted by General Yang Huai. As soon as he finds out what the letter is about, he decides to accompany the messenger to the capital. When the letter arrives in Chengdu, Liu Zhang reads it and is convinced of its value and truth. But Yang Huai says, 'Don't be fooled. Xuande has been doing all in his power to win over your people to his side. Now he wants your own troops! This man is dangerous, and you must refuse his request!' Others also press Yang Huai's case, and in the end, instead of sending the thirty to forty thousand crack troops, Liu Zhang offers four thousand elderly soldiers and just ten thousand bushels of grain.

When the letter arrives Xuande is incandescent with rage at such an insult, especially because of what he sees as his efforts on behalf of his kinsman. It is now that Pang Tong puts forward his plan. He outlines three alternative strategies. 'Attack Chengdu immediately,' he says, 'or draw away from Chengdu the two top generals who will guard it – Yang Huai and Gao Pei – and kill them by pretending to be returning to Jingzhou so they come to say farewell. Or just pack up and go home!'

'Your first proposal is too hasty,' says Xuande, 'your third too slow so I will go with the second plan.'

Xuande therefore writes again to Liu Zhang saying that he must return home.

When news of this letter spreads in the capital, Zhang Song hears of it and believes it is true. In great anxiety he prepares a letter to Xuande lamenting that after all his efforts Xuande is going home. He then offers to help seize the city if Xuande will only attack. Unfortunately, before he can send it he is interrupted by a visit from his brother. The letter is discovered, and, when Liu Zhang is told of it, Zhang Song and his entire family are executed in the public square.

> Here was a man unequalled in understanding,
> Little did he think his letter would be leaked,
> Before Xuande could be crowned as he wished,
> Instead, in Chengdu, he meets his bloody end.

Alarmed by the discovery of a real plot and threat against him, Liu Zhang orders the passes to be strongly guarded. He commands that no one from Jingzhou should be allowed in or out.

Meanwhile, Xuande has arrived at the Fu pass and invites the two commanders, Yang Huai and Gao Pei, to come and pay their respects as he departs. They, pretty sure he is planning something, decide to bring an armed guard with them and hide knifes in their clothes, intending to kill Xuande as soon as they meet him. With two hundred men they descend into the pass and come to see Xuande.

Xuande is forewarned of trouble, not least by a banner blowing over, which is interpreted by Pang Tong as meaning there is a plot to murder him. As soon as the two commanders come bearing gifts, Xuande welcomes them and then, pretending he has some great secret to share with them, orders their men out of the meeting. Immediately the two men are seized and the knives found on them. 'Kill them!' cries Pang Tong. But Xuande hesitates, not sure that this is right. It has to be forcibly presented to him that they planned to kill him and so deserve to die. Persuaded by this, he gives permission and the two men are executed there and then. As for the two hundred men, Xuande offers them freedom or the right to join his army and in return is cheered to the rafters.

It is then that Pang Tong springs the next step in his plan. He asks the two hundred if they will help capture the pass through subterfuge by leading Xuande's men into the fortification. The men are so delighted at not being executed they agree and they lead the way. When the men arrive at the gate they call out for entry. Peering down, the soldiers inside recognize them, and the gate is thrown open. In rush Xuande and his men, as well as the Shu turncoats. It is all over in a few minutes, for, realizing they are overwhelmed, the men of Shu all surrender. Not one drop of blood is spilt in the capture of the pass.

When the news of the deaths of Yang Huai and Gao Pei and the fall of the Fu pass reaches Liu Zhang, he is horrified. He is especially distressed that a kinsman should have done this. Huang Quan advises him to fortify Luocheng, as this will block any further advances by the enemy. And so he sends Liu Gui, Ling Bao, Zhang Ren and Deng Xian to guard the city with fifty thousand men.

Now when they are en route, Liu Gui says to the others that he knows of a Daoist called the Supreme Master of the Purple Void who lives in the nearby hills. 'He has the power to foretell life and death,' says Liu Gui, 'and all manner of things. Why don't we go and ask his advice?'

Zhang Ren dismisses this. 'Men of war do not go visiting hermits,' he says with great disdain.

'I totally disagree,' retorts Liu Gui. 'After all the Master[15] has said, 'Those who follow the Way know the future.' This Daoist may be able to give us some guidance.'

So the four men with their escort turn aside and ride up the mountain to the sage's hut. They are admitted to the Supreme Master's presence only to find they are initially ignored, and Liu Gui has to repeat his request a number of times before the Master picks up a brush and writes eight lines.

> To the left: dragon – to the right: phoenix,
> To the western rivers they fly.
>
> Young phoenix falls to earth,
> Sleeping dragon soars to sky.
>
> One makes it, the other fails.
> This is Heaven's decree.
>
> See that when the chance comes, you take it
> – or else you're landing in the Nine Springs of Hell.

Having delivered himself of this, the sage refuses to answer any more personal questions regarding their individual fates. As they return down the hill, Liu Gui says with some embarrassment, 'Well, I suppose you just have to listen to the words of these immortals.' But Zhang Ren retorts, 'He's nothing more than a mad old man, and what he said was nonsense.'

So on they ride on to Luocheng. As this is crucial for the defence of Chengdu, they decide to divide their forces. Ling Bao and Deng Xian set up two camps on the approaches to the city, while Liu Gui and Zhang Ren defend the city itself.

By now Xuande is approaching with his force, and a dispute breaks out as to who should lead the attack on the two outlying enemy camps. Huang Zhong has offered but is challenged by a young upstart by the name of Wei Yan on the grounds that Huang Zhong is too old. It almost comes to blows until Xuande stops them and simply says that they can each attack one of the two camps. This settled, Huang Zhong tells his men to rest and be ready to set off at the fourth watch of the night.

However, Pang Tong advises Xuande to follow them both with his own troops in case there is a further falling-out.

Wei Yan, having learned from his spies that Huang Zhong will depart at the fourth watch, sets off silently with his men at the third watch. Driven by jealousy, he decides that, having gained the time advantage, he will not only attack the camp he was given, that of Deng Xian, but start by taking Huang Zhong's target of the camp of Ling Bao.

It is a disaster. Ling Bao's men hear them coming and spring a counter-attack. In the end Deng Xian's men from the other camp also join the attack on the enemy. The foolish Wei Yan is about to be killed by Deng Xian himself when an arrow takes Deng Xian down, and the cry goes up, 'Old man Huang Zhong has come.' Riding into the fray, the old warrior attacks Ling Bao, who flees. Deng Xian is finished off, and the men of Shu are scattered.

When Ling Bao rushes for sanctuary into the other Shu camp, that of the now dead Deng Xian, it is to find it occupied by none other than Xuande! Ling Bao retreats rapidly and, taking only country paths, he believes he can make it safely back to Luocheng. But this is not to be. Wei Yan, realizing the trouble he is in because of his arrogance, has worked out where to place an ambush, and it is he who captures Ling Bao.

Standing before the troops who have surrendered, Xuande says, 'Men of Shu. You have families here. If you would like to join us, then do so. If not, then you're free to return to your homes.' This news is greeted with loud and sustained cheers by the men.

Only because he has captured Ling Bao is Wei Yan not cashiered. But he is made to publicly acknowledge his debt to Huang Zhong, who saved his life.

To Wei Yan's consternation, Xuande frees Ling Bao, who swears that he will go to Luocheng and try to bring the other two commanders over to Xuande's side. Wei Yan protests loudly, but Xuande replies, 'This is an act of benevolence and of mercy. He'll not betray me.'

However, when Ling Bao returns to Luocheng, he tells no one about his capture and release, claiming instead to have been a true hero who slew a dozen men and escaped. When news of the defeat reaches Chengdu, Liu Zhang is deeply troubled. His eldest son, Liu Xun, offers to defend Luocheng and, supported by other commanders, he sets off with his army.

On arrival at Luocheng they confer with Liu Gui, Zhang Ren and Ling Bao. It is Ling Bao who comes up with an idea: 'The River Fu flows by and is very swift. Their camp is in the plains below the hills. Give me five thousand men with spades and picks and I'll divert the river and wash away Xuande and his army.'

As this work proceeds, Xuande is informed of the apparent plot of Sun Quan to link up with Zhang Lu and encourage an attack on Jiameng pass. On Pang Tong's advice he sends reinforcements to the pass, because if this were to be captured, he would be stranded.

That night Pang Tong returns to his quarters only to be told that a stranger has come and is waiting for him in his rooms. What he finds is a tall, shabbily dressed man with badly cut hair. 'And who might you be, sir?' asks Pang Tong. But he gets no answer. Instead the man simply lies down on Pang Tong's bed! Again Pang Tong asks, 'Who are you?' to which the man says, 'Just wait a minute and then I'll tell you what fate is about to befall the world.' Stunned by this, Pang Tong meekly orders wine and food and the man wolfs it down. Then he falls asleep!

Now considerably annoyed, to put it mildly, Pang Tong asks for Fa Zheng to come and advise him. 'Could this possibly be Peng Yang?' asks Fa Zheng, and he goes to have a look. The stranger leaps up and says, 'Fa Zheng! I hope you are well?'

So who exactly is this stranger?

Who indeed!

CHAPTER 63

Kong Ming mourns the death of Pang Tong.
Zhang Fei frees Yan Yan.

Fa Zheng suddenly recognizes the stranger. 'Well, well! This is Peng Yang, he's famous in Shu. He once told Liu Zhang off very publicly – humiliated him, in fact. This so upset Liu Zhang he condemned him to slave labour. That's why he has the crude haircut. He had to wear a metal collar.' Pang Tong shakes hands but then asks why he's here.

'I've come to save the lives of thousands of your men,' he replies, 'and I'll tell you how just as soon as I meet Xuande.'

No sooner is he shown in to see Xuande than he points out how dangerous it is that they have placed their camp in the lowlands. 'If the river's diverted, thousands will die with no way of escape. You see the handle of the Dipper is to the west while Venus is low overhead? Well the stars show something's not right, so be very careful,' says Peng Yang. Immediately, Xuande takes action. Patrols are sent out along the river, led by Wei Yan and Huang Zhong.

Late that night, in the midst of a dramatic storm, Ling Bao and his troops head out along the river to cut the channel. They almost immediately run into Xuande's troops. Confused and thwarted, they decide to retreat. But it's too late. They are attacked, and in the battle Wei Yan captures Ling Bao and his men are put to the sword. Ling Bao is brought to Xuande. 'I was generous to you. I let you live! And this is how you repay me!' He orders Ling Bao's execution, and without any further ado he is beheaded there and then.

Not long after this, a message comes from Kong Ming, who has also seen the same astrological features as Peng Yang and wants to warn Xuande to be careful. The message deeply offends Pang Tong, who sees in it an attempt to belittle his own achievements. So he tells Xuande that he too has, of course, seen these signs but disagrees with Kong Ming. This is not an astrological warning to Xuande as he has pointed out before. 'These relate to your conquest of Shu and do not foreshadow disaster. Indeed, the warning was for Ling Bao, who has died as a result of these astrological signs. Now is therefore the time to attack!'

Xuande, however, is cautious, not least because he has had a disturbing dream, which he feels is a warning. 'I dreamed that a demon was hitting my right arm with a club. When I awoke, it actually felt painful. Surely this is a warning?' Commander Pang Tong scoffs and says, 'Kong Ming's tried to alarm you because he doesn't want me to gain fame through my successes. Let's forget all this and go into action.'

Early the next morning, en route to battle, Xuande notices that Pang Tong's horse is being very difficult and he swaps his grey for Pang Tong's unsettled horse.

Meanwhile, forewarned about the attack, the Shu commanders in Luocheng send out their men. Zheng Ren heads off to protect one road and in the distance sees someone riding a grey horse. 'That's Xuande's horse,' he is told and, now excited at the possibility of capturing Xuande, he prepares his ambush.

Pang Tong rides into the narrow valley. Something makes him really worried. 'Where are we?' he asks, and he is told that this is known as Fallen Phoenix valley. Now really alarmed, he cries, 'But my Daoist name is Young Phoenix – this can't be good!' and so saying, he orders a retreat. But it is too late. A hail of arrows and crossbow bolts descends upon him and his men, and he falls, dying alongside so many of his own men. He is but thirty-six years old.

At that time a children's song went like this:

Phoenix and dragon
Side by side,
Minister and commander
Arrive in Shu.

Just part way
Along the road to Luocheng
On the mountain side,
The phoenix dies.

Winds and rain,
Rains and wind.

As the Han rises again
The path to Shu is clear.
The way is open
And a dragon is there!

The battle that then ensues swings first this way towards Xuande's men and then back to the men of Shu. At one point Zheng Ren almost captures a cornered Xuande, but a timely intervention by thirty thousand of his troops saves him. Retreating back to their camp, Xuande hears that Pang Tong has died and, facing west, breaks down in tears. It is decided that what is needed now is Kong Ming. Messengers are sent to bring him from Jingzhou, and, even though Zhang Ren keeps riding up and taunting them to come to battle, Xuande forbids any such venture until Kong Ming arrives.

In Jingzhou, Kong Ming observes the night sky and sees a huge star fall to Earth. He knows this means Pang Tong has died, even though news of this does not arrive for a few more days. Kong Ming too weeps at this loss.

Having read the letter sent by Xuande asking him to come, he appoints Guan Yu to protect Jingzhou. Before leaving, he quizzes Guan Yu on what he would do if Cao Cao attacks and then what if Cao Cao and Sun Quan attack. As he departs, he gives Guan Yu eight words of advice:

'North – resist Cao Cao; east – reconcile Sun Quan.'

Kong Ming then divides his force into three columns. The first, led by Zhang Fei, is to go through the high country, while Zhao Zilong's will follow the river valley. Kong Ming will then follow them later. As they set off, Kong Ming warns Zhang Fei to ensure his troops behave in order to win the trust of the people.

At first Zhang Fei encounters no opposition, and all goes well. But when they come before the city of Bazhou, the governor, Yan Yan, will not surrender. He has long opposed the alliance with Xuande and now takes the opportunity to try to frustrate his plans.

Zhang Fei is astonished that he will not surrender and threatens reprisals. But Yan Yan's advisers recommend holding out because either Zhang Fei will soon run out of food and then have to retreat or he will erupt in anger and alienate his own troops, such that they can be encouraged to mutiny. Then Yan Yan can capture this famous if volatile general.

For three days Zhang Fei tries to draw Yan Yan and his men out by taunting them. And for three days nothing whatsoever happens, except that Zhang Fei grows more and more angry. He then orders three days of attacks, but again to no avail. At this point some men come forward and say they know of a secret path by which they could bypass Bazhou and go on their way to assist Xuande. However, spies within Zhang Fei's camp report this back to Yan Yan, who plans his own attack – an ambush along that very road.

That night both armies set off. Yan Yan's men settle in for the ambush, and about the third watch they see Zhang Fei coming, spear in hand, men following behind. Convinced they have him now, Yan Yan and his men charge to the attack. Suddenly a gong rings out, and from nowhere, it seems, warriors descend upon Yan Yan and his men. Leading the charge is none other than Zhang Fei, bellowing furiously. The man they all thought was Zhang Fei is a fake designed to flush them out. Yan Yan fights bravely but is soon overwhelmed and captured.

And so Bazhou falls to Zhang Fei, who brings his prisoner there.

'Why did you refuse to surrender?' roars Zhang Fei.

'You immoral raiders! I might lose my head but I will never give in!'

Zhang Fei, furious that he is still resisting, orders his execution.

'Oh go on, you thug! Take the head, but why this anger?'

Yan Yan's defiant stance catches Zhang Fei off guard, and he stops to consider this courageous man. He steps down and personally removes the chains, orders that he be given fresh clothes and brings him to sit beside him in a place of honour. Deeply moved by this, Yan Yan falls to his knees.

A poet has said:

> Heroic in capturing Yan Yan alive,
> Zhang Fei renounces killing; wins everyone over.
> For this he's honoured in shrines everywhere
> In the land of Shu, where daily offerings thrive.

Zhang Fei raises him and then asks him what is the best way to the land of Shu.

'Having been beaten, and then shown such generosity, I'll work ceaselessly to repay your kindness. Chengdu can be taken without any fighting.'

So what is the plan of Yan Yan?

Let's find out.

CHAPTER 64

Kong Ming plots to capture Zhang Ren.
Ma Chao's family are all murdered and
Yang Fu sets off to destroy Ma Chao.

Yan Yan's plan is very simple. Given his status and reputation and the fact that all the garrisons from Bazhou to the capital are under his command, he will order them to surrender to Zhang Fei!

And that is what happens. Every time they appear before a town or city, the garrison surrenders. If a garrison hesitates, Yan Yan says, 'I've surrendered – so what do you think you can do that is different?'

Back at the siege of Luocheng, Xuande has heard that Kong Ming and Zhang Fei are on their way. He decides to take the city, having bored the defenders by never responding to the taunts that Zhang Ren has thrown at him day after day. The very next day they launch an assault, but Zhang Ren is able to mount a counter-attack through one of the city gates that Xuande has not attacked. The result is a complete success for Zhang Ren, and his attack takes Xuande by surprise. Zhang Ren rides straight for Xuande and crashes through his men, scattering them. Xuande turns and flees. Zhang Ren, with just a few of his men, pursues him into the hills and draws closer and closer. Just as it seems inevitable that Xuande will be captured, round the corner comes a troop – led by Zhang Fei. The two Zhangs clash. But not long after Yan Yan arrives with the bulk of the army, and, seeing this, Zhang Ren turns and flees, with Zhang Fei in hot pursuit right up to the city wall. Zhang Ren makes it in through the city gate just in time.

Meanwhile Huang Zhong and Wei Yan have beaten another division of the enemy's troops and have accepted their surrender. This loss hits Zhang Ren hard. Together with his officers, he plans to trap and kill Zhang Fei by challenging him to a duel, then pretending to flee and leading him into an ambush. The next day this works so well that Zhang Fei finds himself in great danger. At the very last moment, and completely by good fortune, Zhao Zilong arrives and saves him.

By this time Kong Ming too has arrived, somewhat astonished that Zhang Fei is already there, and so many cities have submitted. He too decides upon the old trick of fighting, fleeing and then ambushing in order to finally deal with the resistance in Luocheng. He drives up to one of the main gates in his carriage, dressed in his Daoist robes and apparently without a care in the world. Behind him come a gaggle of deliberately shoddy-looking troops. This proves too tempting to Zhang Ren, who is lured out of the city. Drawn into the ambush set by Kong Ming and his men, he is captured.

He is brought before Xuande, who asks, 'Why did you hold out when everyone else has surrendered?'

'Do you think a loyal servant can have more than one master?' replies Zhang Ren, furious and fiery in his defiance.

'Submission means you live – that is the reality of the times we live in.'

'I might pretend to submit now but I will strike back later – so kill me!' says Zhang Ren.

Nothing that Xuande can do or say can soften this defiance, and in the end Zhang Ren is executed.

As a poet has said:

An authentic man can't serve two masters;
Through his loyalty, his death was like no death at all.
Like the heavenly moon, his honour still shines out,
Lighting up the whole city of Luocheng.

The army now move to the walls of Luocheng, and Xuande calls for the city to surrender. The gate is thrown open, and Xuande rides in to take his prize. As they enter the city by one gate, Liu Zhang's son Liu Xun flees through the opposite gate and takes the news to Chengdu. As he consults with his father, a letter arrives from Fa Zheng, who has suggested to Xuande that he try to persuade Liu Zhang to submit. The letter has somewhat the opposite result, as in his fury Liu Zhang tears up the letter and plans for the counter-attack. So desperate is he, he is even persuaded to write to his other arch-enemy, Zhang Lu, asking for help.

Far off in the northwest, Ma Chao has built up his own base among the Qiang tribes of Longxi. He has defeated the governor of Jicheng, taken over the city and then pardoned the governor for resisting. However, visiting relatives soon after, this governor, Yang Fu, breaks down and confesses he is ashamed that he betrayed the trust he was given to defend the city. There and then a plot is hatched, supported in particular by one relative, an eighty-two-year-old matriarch. Drawing Ma Chao to the attack before the city of Licheng, the plotters spring an ambush on Ma Chao, encouraged by the fact that Cao Cao has sent Xiahou Yuan to support the plot. Ma Chao's army is cut to pieces.

Ma Chao escapes but only just and rides hell for leather back to his city of Jicheng. But as soon as he arrives at the gate he is met by a hail of arrows. Two of the friends of Yang Fu who were pardoned at the same time have seized the city. They then drag his wife to the walls and slay her there before her husband's eyes, throwing her body down before him. Then his three infant sons are brought up and murdered – followed by more than a dozen other members of his family.

Ma Chao's grief and anger know no bounds, and he almost collapses from his horse. But Xiahou Yuan is fast coming up behind him, so he has to turn and fight his way through with a handful of followers. But he is not done for. Using the cover of darkness, Ma Chao and his men double back and arrive at the gate of Licheng. They fool the guards into thinking they are from the rebel group, and the gate is opened. The bloodshed and revenge that follow are horrific. Not even the eighty-two-year-old matriarch is spared – Ma Chao slays her himself. But there is no long-term safety here, so Ma Chao leaves the sacked city and flees west.

En route he is attacked again and again until eventually there are fewer than ten men riding with him. But on and on he rides, until he reaches Zhang Lu in Hanzhong, where he offers his services – which are gladly received. The new recruits give Zhang Lu the confidence to plan to seize Yizhou and to defy Cao Cao. Zhang Lu even contemplates making Ma Chao his son-in-law, but one of his advisers, Yang Bo, strongly resists this, pointing out that Ma Chao's actions have led to the death of his entire family, so this is not a good augury. When Ma Chao hears of this, he swears to exact revenge on Yang Bo, while Yang Bo swears to get rid of Ma Chao!

At this moment the letter from Liu Zhang arrives proposing an alliance against Xuande. Initially Zhang Lu refuses, but when a second letter arrives, his adviser Yang Song reads it and recommends that, seeing that Liu Zhang is offering to make over twenty cities to Zhang Lu, this is too good an offer to refuse. In the ensuing debate, the opinion goes this way and that until a man stands up and says, 'I've but little fame but I can capture Xuande and make Liu Zhang honour his promise of twenty cities. I just need a few soldiers.'

So who is this bold man?

All will be revealed.

CHAPTER 65

Ma Chao captures Jiameng pass, while Zhang Fei gets annoyed. Xuande takes over Shu.

It is Ma Chao who has spoken. 'Give me a troop of men, and I'll take Jiameng pass, capture Xuande and make sure Liu Zhang hands over the twenty cities.' So, first of all, Zhang Lu sends Huang Quan to Liu Zhang to say he will help. Then he gives Ma Chao twenty thousand soldiers and despatches him towards the pass. But he also sends Yang Bo to oversee manoeuvres.

Meanwhile Xuande is determined to seize Mianzhu. This is the gateway to capturing Chengdu. Huang Zhong and Wei Yan are sent to take the city. Initially resistance is offered by the champion Li Yan. He rides out and challenges Huang Zhong to single combat, but neither of them can overcome the other. Kong Ming therefore devises a plot to trap Li Yan. Huang Zhong rides out the next day to single combat but then turns and flees, luring Li Yan into following him. Li Yan rides straight into an ambush, and when Kong Ming calls upon him to surrender he does so immediately, and through this not a single man is wounded or dies.

Having surrendered, Li Yan offers to negotiate the surrender of Mianzhu, and this is swiftly achieved. As a result, no one is killed in the taking of the city. Then urgent news comes. A desperate message tells of the attack on the Jiameng pass by Ma Chao. This attack has caught the defenders off guard, and victory is within the grasp of Ma Chao.

Of course, Xuande immediately decides a relief column needs to be sent, and that Zhang Fei should lead it. But Kong Ming decides to play a game with Zhang Fei, to really get him geared up for action. 'Don't say anything about this commission to him when he comes in,' says Kong Ming to a somewhat bewildered Xuande.

Having heard that action was called for, Zhang Fei comes to see Xuande convinced that he will be chosen. Shouting out loudly and cheerfully, he says, 'Just coming to say goodbye before I go off and deal with this Ma Chao.'

Kong Ming acts as if Zhang Fei is not there and says, 'Ma Chao is attacking the pass, but I cannot think who could possibly take him on, except perhaps Guan Yu.'

'Excuse me,' says a cross Zhang Fei, 'do I count for nothing? I've defeated armies of one million – what's this Ma Chao to me!'

'You haven't always been that wise, and Ma Chao is renowned for his courage. Remember how Cao Cao had to cut his beard and try to disguise himself in order to escape Ma Chao. I'm not sure even Guan Yu could defeat him.'

'I will!' roars Zhang Fei. 'And should I fail, which I very much doubt, I'll take my punishment as martial law demands.'

'Well, so long as you are willing to take that vow, then you may lead,' says a smug Kong Ming.

Shortly after, Wei Yan is sent ahead with a small troop, with Zhang Fei behind and, following close behind him, Xuande. The battles are fierce – Wei Yan fights Yang Bo; then Ma Dai, Ma Chao's brother, wounds Wei Yan with an arrow and speeds after him; until Zhang Fei turns up and takes on Ma Dai, thinking it is Ma Chao himself; until he is restrained by Xuande. Chaos all round!

The next day Ma Chao challenges Zhang Fei to single combat, but Xuande initially refuses to allow him to go. Xuande has been immensely impressed by the bravado of Ma Chao as well as his dramatic dress – a helmet with a carved lion on top; white battle-gown and a belt covered in animal symbols.

Eventually, thinking he has the advantage, Xuande launches Zhang Fei and his troop. Now the two heroes fight, clashing over a hundred times but with no one gaining the upper hand. Pulled back once again by Xuande, Zhang Fei is furious. He so desperately wants to fight Ma Chao again. So when Ma Chao returns to the combat at night-time, the arena is filled with flaming torches so the two men can fight in the dark. But once again, despite many tricks and clashes, neither one prevails.

Yet again, when dawn breaks, Zhang Fei is up and ready for

combat. But before he can enter the fray, Kong Ming arrives, having heard of what is going on and very worried that the end result will be the death of Zhang Fei.

'I've a plan for bringing Ma Chao to our side,' says Kong Ming.

'I really admire Ma Chao's courage,' says Xuande, 'but do you really think you can get him?'

'As we know, Zhang Lu's ambition is to be the "king" of Hanning,' says Kong Ming. 'One of his senior advisers is a truly greedy little man by the name of Yang Song, who loves bribes. We send someone to Hanzhong to buy his friendship. Then we write to Zhang Lu, saying that your battle with Liu Zhang is because you want to avenge him and that, when you win, you will ask the emperor to make him king of Hanning. This will make him order Ma Chao to cease and retreat, and at that point we can turn Ma Chao to our side.'

So Sun Qian is despatched with the letter and enough gold and pearls to bribe Yang Song. As Kong Ming forecast, Yang Song is more than happy to be bribed. That done, Yang Song brings Sun Qian to meet Zhang Lu, who, because of Xuande's imperial family connections, believes his offer and accepts with delight. He immediately sends orders for Ma Chao to end the conflict and return.

But Ma Chao is having none of it. He sends back a terse note which simply says, 'Without merit; no return.' When Zhang Lu orders him again to cease, the same terse reply comes back. When for the third time Ma Chao refuses, Yang Song, having been primed by Sun Qian, says, 'I think this means Ma Chao is going to rebel', and soon he is circulating this rumour widely. Deeply troubled by this rumour, Zhang Lu turns for advice to Yang Song. He recommends that Ma Chao be given three conditions to comply with, otherwise he will be executed. 'First, he must seize the land of Shu; second, he must bring us Liu Zhang's head; and third, Xuande's troops must be removed. But in case he does rebel, reinforce our defences as well.'

To all this Zhang Lu agrees, and the demands are despatched. Ma Chao is profoundly confused and bewildered by all this but has no option but to stop the war and return. To make things worse, Yang Song actively spreads rumours that, on his return, Ma Chao will try to overthrow Zhang Lu. This leads to troops being despatched to prevent Ma Chao reaching Hanzhong. As a result Ma Chao is trapped. This is exactly what Kong Ming has hoped for. 'And now is the time,' he says, 'for someone to go and offer Ma Chao a way out. The messenger must tell him to come and join Xuande.' Right on cue, one of the former opponents of Xuande, Li Hui, from the court of Liu Zhang, turns up wanting to join Xuande because he has seen that he is a man of real virtue. It is he whom Kong Ming sends with the offer of help if Ma Chao will serve Xuande.

Off Li Hui goes and upon meeting Ma Chao points out the hopelessness of his situation. 'You are a mortal enemy of Cao Cao, a useless man to Liu Zhang, and Yang Song is poisoning the ear of Zhang Lu, so he doesn't want you either!' He then offers Xuande's proposal to join him. This is received with joy by Ma Chao. Within a few days he comes to offer his services to Xuande at the Jiameng pass. Then together they set out to conquer Chengdu.

A few of the men Ma Chao has taken with him desert him and make their way back to Liu Zhang and Chengdu and report on his switching sides. When Liu Zhang hears that the combined armies are heading for the gates of Chengdu, he has the city sealed and prepares for the worst. Ma Chao and his brother Ma Dai ride up to the gate and call for Liu Zhang to come up on the city wall and speak to them. When he hears from Ma Chao's own lips his account of joining Xuande, he realizes all is up. Moved by a genuine desire to spare the people any further suffering, he orders the gates to be opened. Some among his commanders still want to fight. But when a soothsayer appears and says that the stars show that a bright new ruler has appeared, this confirms Liu Zhang's desire to surrender to this bright new ruler. None other than Xuande.

Xuande's entrance into the city is greeted with rejoicing by the population. Xuande forbids any retribution on those like Huang Quan or Liu Ba who have opposed him. This is despite the fact that they still do oppose him. And moved by this, even those two surrender. At first Xuande wants to keep Liu Zhang in the city out of respect. But Kong Ming argues, 'There isn't enough room for two lords. And Liu Zhang's inability to decide has cost him his right to rule. Don't go all wimpish on me,' he tells Xuande. 'Seize the moment.' So Liu Zhang is sent to what is in effect comfortable house arrest in Jingzhou but given an honorific title to compensate him.

All those who have joined Xuande are rewarded with posts and titles and vast amounts of money, and treasures are sent to Guan Yu in Jingzhou. However, a plan to redistribute the land of the newly conquered territory to his followers is stoutly opposed by Zhao Zilong, who points out that the people have already suffered enough, and that generosity now will win support for the future. The land of Shu is now in Xuande's control.

The laws are overhauled; corrupt or over-rigorous local governors are held in check, and the land is settled. In the south in Wu, Sun Quan soon learns of Xuande's triumphs and, needless to say, immediately thinks of trying to seize disputed Jingzhou. Wise council from Zhang Zhao intervenes, and he says that what is most definitely not needed now in this moment of peace is more war. He goes on, 'I have a plan which will mean Xuande will restore Jingzhou to us and he will be humbled in the process.'

So what is this plan of Zhang Zhao?

Let's find out.

CHAPTER 66

Guan Yu goes to a dangerous feast – with his great sword. The empress tries to have Cao Cao murdered but is killed instead, and Cao Cao's daughter becomes empress.

Zhang Zhao's plot is simple: 'Xuande is dependent upon Kong Ming, and Kong Ming's brother, Zhuge Jin, is here in our own court. Let's seize the whole family and send him to Xuande with the message that unless we receive Jingzhou back, the family will be killed.'

To this, Sun Quan replies, 'But Zhuge Jin's an honest man. On what grounds could I do this?'

'Bring him in on the plot,' replies Zhang Zhao.

And that is what happens. Zhuge Jin's family is quietly hidden away, and off he goes.

When Zhuge Jin arrives at Chengdu, Kong Ming is only too aware of what is going on and of the whole plot. Taking his brother aside, he asks, as if really worried, what is troubling him. 'My family face death!' says Zhuge Jin.

'Oh no!' says Kong Ming. 'Surely not because of Jingzhou? This is terrible. I am so sorry. But, look, don't worry. I have a plan.' Reassured, Zhuge Jin is then led in to meet Xuande. Coming before Xuande, Zhuge Jin presents the message from Sun Quan that he will kill Jin's family unless Xuande surrenders Jingzhou. Furious, Xuande cries out, 'Not only have I lost my wife to Sun Quan, which is excuse enough to invade Wu, but now I am told to hand back Jingzhou!'

Suddenly Kong Ming throws himself on the ground, crying, 'I beg you, to save my family. Please return Jingzhou!' Seeming to be moved by this, Xuande agrees and says, 'Because you, my dear friend, have asked, I agree. I will hand back half the territory.'

'Thank you, sir,' says Kong Ming. 'Will you now write

formally to Guan Yu ordering this?' Xuande agrees. 'But, Zhuge Jin,' says Xuande, 'be very careful how you explain all this to Guan Yu. He can be very volatile, to put it mildly. Be very diplomatic in how you discuss this.'

So Zhuge Jin is given the letter and sent on his way.

The meeting between Guan Yu and Zhuge Jin is a disaster – which is exactly what Kong Ming planned. Guan Yu point blank refuses to surrender the territory, claiming that he is defending the imperial lands of the Han and that he swore a vow in the peach orchard with Xuande to uphold the Han.

Zhuge Jin scuttles back to Kong Ming in Chengdu, but he is away, so it is to Xuande that he makes his complaint.

'Tell you what,' says Xuande. 'Go back to Wu. Let me finish my conquests here in Shu, and then I will invite Guan Yu to come and govern them. At that point Jingzhou can be returned.'

Realizing he has been played and now utterly humiliated, Zhuge Jin has no option but to return to Sun Quan empty-handed. Sun Quan decides to act on the earlier promise of Xuande to return some parts of the land. He sends off a group of bureaucrats to try to simply take over the disputed part of the territory. They are no match for Guan Yu's fury, which soon sends them packing.

Deeply frustrated, Sun Quan summons Lu Su, who, of course, acted as guarantor of this whole deal. He sets forth a plot. 'Let me lure Guan Yu to a banquet at Lukou. I'll present our case carefully and thoroughly to him. If I can't persuade him to surrender the territory, then, well, I'll have him assassinated!'

Now, when the invitation arrives, Guan Yu agrees to go. But his son Guan Ping is deeply troubled. 'Why have you accepted this invitation? This is clearly a trap.'

'Not to go,' says Guan Yu, 'would see me marked as a coward.'

'At the very least,' says Guan Ping, 'let me follow behind you with some men in case of trouble.'

Eventually Guan Yu agrees that Guan Ping can follow behind quietly with an armed force, ready to attack if summoned.

So it is that Guan Yu arrives sailing down the river to meet Lu Su. But not alone. With him is his bodyguard, Zhou Cang, with a very large sword and a handful of other fierce-looking warriors to boot. Somewhat perturbed, Lu Su invites them into his tent for the banquet. Lu Su, conscious of his duplicitous role, cannot look Guan Yu in the eye, while Guan Yu acts as if there is nothing amiss whatsoever.

When Lu Su tries to raise the issue of the disputed territories, Guan Yu waves this aside by saying that banquets are not designed for state discussions. But Lu Su persists.

'Sun Quan only holds a modest amount of land in the south, and it was an act of kindness to lend you and your brother Jingzhou. Now you've conquered Shu and as a result Jingzhou should really be returned. Yet you won't even give us the half of the territory that Xuande has agreed should be handed over!'

Guan Yu points out the sacrifices, battles and risks that Xuande has taken in order to help Lu Su and Sun Quan against their enemies. 'Why should we have done so much and received so little?' asks Guan Yu.

'That simply is not true,' says Lu Su. 'When you were in trouble, Sun Quan was happy to help and give you a base from which to venture forth. But this kindness has not been reciprocated. Xuande has Shu but still holds on to Jingzhou. This is a dishonourable action and a scandal. Do you honestly not see this?'

'Sorry,' says Guan Yu, 'but this is Xuande's concern, not mine.'

At this Zhou Cang shouts from lower down the hall, 'This land should only belong to those who are virtuous – not just you lot from the south!'

Guan Yu rises and grabs the sword from Zhou Cang's hand, shouting, 'Silence! This is official business. What's this to do with you? Get out!' and Zhou Cang, catching the meaning of this, heads outside and summons Guan Ping and his armed troop.

Draping his left arm around Lu Su and holding the great sword in his right, Guan Yu stands as if drunk and informs a terrified Lu Su that in return for his hospitality he invites him to a banquet in Jingzhou, where they can continue the discussion. Lu Su is then half dragged, half escorted down to the riverbank.

His men cannot attack for fear of their lord being killed. Only when they reach the bank and Guan Yu steps into his boat does he release Lu Su. He can only watch helplessly as Guan Yu sails away downriver.

> He had little time for these men of the south,
> Travelling alone as he did to their banquet.
> He showed great bravery and spirit –
> Not even Xiangru could surpass him.

When Lu Su reports the failure of this plot to Sun Quan, he declares that he is determined now to go to war to seize Jingzhou. But then word comes that Cao Cao is preparing to attack with over three hundred thousand troops, and the plans for Jingzhou are put on hold while Wu prepares to face this new threat.

But the threat never materializes. Cao Cao is presented with a formal memorial by one of his advisers, Fu Gan. 'You're renowned, sir,' writes Fu Gan, 'for your success in suppressing rebels and bandits. You have complete control over much of the empire, with the exceptions of Shu and Wu. Of these Wu is guarded by the Great river and Shu by mountain ranges. Concentrate your efforts not on conquest but on good government. You should accept that the empire has been divided into three. Instead of war, encourage civil government, support learning. And bide your time!'

The memorial has the desired effect, and Cao Cao abandons his planned attack and instead starts to found schools and colleges and to recruit scholars. This almost imperial-like action encourages some of his flunkies to suggest that he should be given a new title – king of Wei. This is stoutly resisted by the chief of the imperial civil service. However, when he is taken on one side and told he will be murdered if he resists, he falls ill and dies shortly after.

Not long after, waving his sword, Cao Cao storms into the imperial palace. His arrival terrifies the emperor and empress. 'Sun Quan and Xuande', says Cao Cao, 'now rule their own territories and show no respect to the court. What are we to do?'

'Surely that is up to you, given your skills,' says the emperor, to which Cao Cao angrily replies, 'That makes it sound like it's my fault!'

'If you're willing to be of help to me, I will, of course, be very grateful. If not, then I would prefer to be simply left alone,' says the emperor. This infuriates Cao Cao even more, and he storms out.

Deeply disturbed by all this, servants of the emperor say they have heard that Cao Cao wants to be made a king, and that if the emperor is not careful Cao will usurp the throne. In tears, the empress says passionately, 'My father, Fu Wan, has long wished to get rid of Cao Cao. I'll write secretly to him and encourage him to plan for Cao Cao's assassination.'

'Don't forget what happened to Dong Cheng,' says the emperor. 'He was discovered and killed. If this is discovered, it'll be fatal for us.'

'This life is so full of fear already,' says the empress. 'It is like sitting on pins, so I would prefer to die than live another day like this.'

So they choose one of the very few people they believe they can trust to carry a letter to Fu Wan: the eunuch Mu Shun.

Hiding the letter in his hair, Mu Shun makes his way to Fu Wan's house.

On reading his daughter's appeal, Fu Wan realizes the scale of the task his daughter has set before him. 'To do this,' he says to Mu Shun, 'we will need the support of Xuande and Sun Quan and their armies.' In the letter he sends back with Mu Shun he urges the emperor and empress to write secret letters to both leaders, asking them to come and destroy the traitor.

Mu Shun again hides a letter in his topknot and is returning to the court when he is stopped by Cao Cao, who has learned of the plot.

'Where have you been?' asks Cao Cao.

'The empress is sick, so I've been to call her doctor,' says Mu Shun.

'And where is this doctor?' enquires Cao Cao.

'Coming, coming,' replies Mu Shun. But Cao Cao is not fooled.

Mu Shun is searched, and before long the letter is found. Yet, despite torture, Mu Shun will not betray the empress. But to no avail. That night Cao Cao arrests Fu Wan and the whole family. Then he orders Chi Lü of the Royal Guard to go and seize the imperial seal of the empress.

With three hundred armed men Chi Lü bursts into the imperial palace and, brushing aside the protests of the emperor, he orders the seal to be brought and handed over. Meanwhile, minister Hua Xin, leading five hundred soldiers, has also arrived and he demands that the empress be given over to him. She, meanwhile, has hidden herself behind a false wall in her quarters, but this cannot prevent what is going to happen. Ripping the wall down, Hua Xin hauls the empress out by her hair.

'Spare me!' she pleads.

'Ask the prime minister yourself!' he replies curtly. And at this, the empress is dragged out, barefoot, by two guards. Hua Xin enters the main hall as his guards struggle with the protesting empress. When the emperor sees her bound and held, he realizes that all is over for them now. But despite this he rushes to her and, holding her tight to him, bursts into tears.

'This is the end,' says the empress, to which the emperor replies, 'And I too have no idea when my end will come.' He watches helpless as the empress is dragged from the room. The emperor collapses weeping, while the empress is taken to see Cao Cao and to her fate.

'I've treated you both so well, and this is how you repay me! By planning my murder! Either I die or you do!' shouts Cao Cao.

And there and then she is mercilessly beaten to death by the soldiers.

Cao Cao's fury knows no bounds. Entering the palace, he has her two young sons seized and then poisoned. By the end of the day Fu Wan, Mu Shun and over two hundred members of their families have been executed in the public square. Fear spreads among all the officials in the court. This all happened in late AD 215.

As a poet has said:

> Cao Cao epitomizes cruelty,
> As Fu Wan symbolizes loyalty.
> Pity this imperial couple,
> How much better our ordinary lives!

The emperor does not eat for days after this. So Cao Cao goes to see him.

'Don't be upset! I've no plans to rebel. Indeed, my own daughter is already a member of your palace women and she's virtuous and a loyal woman. I suggest she takes the empress's place.' To this outrageous proposal the emperor has no option but to agree.

So just over a month later, on the first day of the new year, Cao Cao's daughter becomes the empress of Han, and not a voice is raised in opposition. As a result Cao Cao grows more and more powerful and he decides the time has come to conquer both Wu and Shu. He summons Cao Ren and Xiahou Dun to come and plan the war.

It is Xiahou Dun who suggests what should happen next. 'Forget attacking either Wu or Shu at this time. Instead attack Zhang Lu in Hanzhong, and then we can seize Shu.'

'That's exactly what I think,' says Cao Cao.

Can anything stop Cao Cao?

Let's find out.

CHAPTER 67

Cao Cao conquers Hanzhong.
Sun Quan escapes.

It is not long before Zhang Lu learns of Cao Cao's planned offensive. It is agreed by all his commanders to try to hold the enemy at the Yangping pass. Commanders Yang Ang and Yang Ren are sent to confront Cao Cao and his army. When Cao Cao's advance forces arrive after their long march, they are exhausted, which is why, on the very first night they camp opposite Zhang Lu's army, his men attack. Using fire to alarm the enemy and catching them still rising from their beds, they almost wipe out Cao Cao's men. Those who escape struggle back to tell Cao Cao of their defeat. When he comes in person to survey the pass, he is alarmed at the wild terrain and wonders why on earth he has come. On the following day, out trying to survey the scene, Cao Cao is almost trapped and captured by a surprise attack by Zhang Lu's commanders, Yang Ang and Yang Ren. Once again it is Xu Chu who saves the day by charging recklessly at the enemy commanders, who take fright and flee.

For fifty days there is an impasse, with neither side really making any significant move. In a final attempt to break through, Cao Cao orders what seems to be a retreat but really is a trick to lull the enemy into a false sense of security. Yang Ang is fooled and wishes to attack the retreating army, but Yang Ren is sure this is a plot by Cao Cao. However, nothing he can say convinces Yang Ang. He is headstrong and simply will not listen. Taking most of the troops, he sets off to chase the 'retreating' troops, only to plunge into such dense fog neither he nor his men can see where they are going. Eventually the fog lifts and Zhang He's and Yang Ang's troops fight, but Yang Ang is forced into retreat.

Wandering in the same fog is Cao Cao's commander Xiahou Yuan, who was sent off to be part of the attack when the ruse of an apparent retreat lured the enemy out. By pure good luck he stumbles upon the now almost empty enemy camps and overwhelms the few guards left. When the defeated Yang Ang tries to find safety in the camps, he discovers them occupied by the enemy and falls in battle, slain by Zhang He. And so Cao Cao takes possession of the pass and starts to plan the advance on Nanzheng.

Struggling back to Zhang Lu, the commanders report their failure. He unfairly blames Yang Ren. This tragically leads to his offering to go and attack the enemy. 'I will take on Cao Cao personally. And if I fail, then I'll bear the consequences.' Even before they reach their target, Yang Ren runs into Xiahou Yuan and his troop. They have been sent out by Cao Cao on a reconnoitre, and it is just bad luck for Yang Ren that they meet. Yang Ren immediately challenges Xiahou to single combat. At first it seems neither can overcome the other until Xiahou tricks Yang into chasing him in what looks like a retreat. But suddenly Xiahou turns and slays Yang Ren. Yang Ren's men flee back to their base.

Encouraged by this, Cao Cao advances on Nanzheng, the gateway to the capital. Here, his way is blocked by a foe he has encountered before – at the battle of the Wei bridge. When in despair Zhang Lu asks who can stop Cao Cao's advance, he is told to use Pang De. Summoning him, he gives him ten thousand men and offers huge rewards if he can break Cao Cao's advance. So it is that when Cao Cao and his men arrive before Nanzheng, they find Pang De shouting defiance. Cao Cao warns his men that Pang De is a formidable opponent. This doesn't stop all the main heroes trying their luck in single combat. But he remains unconquered – and they die. It becomes Cao Cao's greatest desire to get Pang De to defect to him, and when he discusses this with his officers, the name of that ambitious, greedy man Yang Song comes up. 'Give him gold and silk on the sly and he'll spread rumours about the loyalty of Pang De,' says Jia Xu. 'When Pang De comes out to attack tomorrow, run away and abandon the camp. Let Pang De take it but then counter-attack – he won't expect that. When he flees back to the city, have a spy slip in behind him as if he is one of Pang De's own men.'

The plan is that this spy will bribe Yang Song. The chosen soldier puts on a golden breastplate and then covers it with ordinary armour as if he were one of Pang De's men. Sure enough, the plan works, and Pang De, having first captured the camp, is then forced to run back to the safety of the city. As Pang De enters the city, the spy slides in behind him and makes his way to Yang Song's house. Here, he gives the traitor the gold breastplate and a letter proposing that when the time is right Yang Song should have the gates thrown open and let the enemy in.

Yang Song agrees and starts to spread rumours that Pang De has lost control of the enemy camp because he has been bribed by Cao Cao. Summoning Pang De, Zhang Lu rails at him and would have him executed there and then but for others interceding on his behalf. Deeply offended, upset and angry, Pang De withdraws to his own quarters.

The next day Xu Chu challenges Pang De and, at a crucial moment, turns and flees, leading Pang De on. Just as Pang De is thinking that he might even manage to capture Cao Cao, his horse plunges into a pit, and horse and rider are captured. When he is brought before Cao Cao, he is treated with the utmost respect, and when asked if he will surrender, he thinks back to Zhang Lu's anger with him, his false accusations and how near he came to being executed. It doesn't take him long to decide to accept Cao Cao's offer. And just to make sure Zhang Lu really does believe that Pang De betrayed him earlier, Cao Cao rides with Pang De in front of the city walls to show Zhang Lu how hopeless his cause now is.

It is then just a matter of time before the Cao Cao forces overwhelm the city and it falls, but not before Zhang Lu orders the grain warehouses and treasury to be sealed and protected. His reasoning is that these are the property of the Han dynasty and its people and not his own. Then he and his family, accompanied by Yang Song, flee to Bazhong.

Cao Cao is impressed by the honour of the man when he

discovers the warehouses protected. He sends a message to Bazhong asking Zhang Lu to surrender. He wants to, but his brother resists. Yang Song sends a message to say that if Cao Cao attacks, he will help him secure the city. Fooling Zhang Lu into going out of the city to attack Cao Cao's troops, Yang Song refuses him re-entry when he retreats from the battlefield, and there outside the city Zhang Lu has no option but to surrender to Cao Cao. He is received with great praise and honour.

As a consequence, the whole of the Hanzhong area is now in Cao Cao's hands, and all who have surrendered have been given new posts. But not the traitor Yang Song – Cao Cao has him publicly executed. As a poet wrote:

> Spoiler of good men, traitor to his lord,
> Greedy gatherer of gold and silver – to what end?
> An inglorious house; his death forlorn,
> From this day on, Yang Song's an object of scorn.

When news reaches Xuande in the west of Shu, he is convinced that Cao Cao will come for him next. Frankly he is really frightened. However, as usual, Kong Ming has a plan:

'Cao has an army at Hefei for fear of attack by Sun Quan. Well, if we give Sun back the half of the Jingzhou territory, that might encourage Wu to attack Hefei, and that would draw Cao Cao away.'

When the proposal is sent to Sun Quan, he accepts, even though some of his advisers are sceptical, to say the least. Lu Su is sent to take possession of the lands Xuande has given up, while Sun Quan, Ling Tong and others set off to attack Hefei. Capturing the border town of Hezhou, they set out for Huan. This is where Cao Cao's provisions are stored – a major rice-growing area. Cao Cao's troops in Hefei are supplied from Huan. In a surprise attack they seize the city. At the victory banquet that evening, a heated argument arises which nearly spills into bloodshed. Ling Tong sees Gan Ning, the man who killed his father, being praised. Unable to stand this, he gets to his feet, and within seconds both men are facing each other, armed and ready to fight. Only the intervention of Lü Meng and the reprimand of Sun Quan stop them attacking each other. Ling Tong takes the reprimand badly.

In Hefei, Cao Cao's men prepare for the attack of the one hundred thousand men Sun Quan is leading against them. Debate breaks out about whether to sally forth and do battle or stay inside the city walls and sit it out. A message from Cao Cao seems to suggest both. In the end, led by Zhang Liao's decision, they agree on an attack. A key to this is that they should destroy the Xiaoshi bridge.

The initial attack by Sun Quan's men is successful, but then, before he knows quite what is happening, Sun Quan is being attacked by Zhang Liao. Ling Tong is with him but has only about three hundred riders and is unable to withstand Zhang Liao's assault. 'My lord, cross the Xiaoshi bridge as fast as you can!' Ling Tong shouts to Sun Quan, as two thousand of the enemy cavalry bear down upon them. Sun Quan rides hell for leather to the bridge, only to find the far end already destroyed. He hesitates. One of his men sees his fear and shouts, 'Ride back and then charge forward and leap over the gap, my lord.' Riding back thirty paces, Sun Quan turns, urges his horse on and gallops towards the bridge. At the crucial moment the horse takes off and flies through the air, landing safely on the far bank.

Ling Tong loses all of his three hundred men but survives. Yet all over the battlefield the slaughter is terrible. So much so that the name of Zhang Liao is used for many years afterwards to frighten naughty children in Wu.

Sun Quan and his surviving men return to their camp and then pack up and make for the port at Ruxu to plan a fresh assault by sea and land. Reinforcements also have to be found.

Meanwhile, Zhang Liao, deeply concerned about a fresh attack, writes to Cao Cao asking for help. Cao Cao has to decide whether to press on and take western Shu or go south and defend Hefei and then take Wu. His advisers strongly recommend going to Hefei to assist Zhang Liao and then attack Wu. They feel that western Shu is too strongly defended at this time.

So Cao Cao summons all his troops and marches towards Ruxu to confront Sun Quan.

Will he succeed this time?

Let's find out.

CHAPTER 68

Gan Ning attacks Cao Cao's camp with just a hundred horsemen. Zuo Ci taunts Cao Cao with a flung cup.

News of Cao Cao's shift of all his main forces from Hanzhong to Hefei swiftly reaches Sun Quan. He is busy gathering his forces together at Ruxu. In response to the threat from Cao Cao, he has fifty warships made ready under the command of Dong Xi and Xu Sheng. Meanwhile, Chen Wu patrols the riverbanks.

Zhang Zhao points out that Cao Cao's men will have travelled great distances and so the best time to strike will be when they have just arrived, weary and tired. On hearing this, Ling Tong steps forward and offers to strike the first blow. 'How many men will you need?' asks Sun Quan.

'I can do this with just three thousand,' replies Ling Tong.

Suddenly his bitter rival Gan Ning speaks up: 'Three thousand?! Well, I can do this with just a hundred horsemen!'

This triggers the old rivalry between Ling Tong and Gan Ning, and they actually start to fight there and then in front of Sun Quan. He stops them and urges them not to underestimate the strength of Cao Cao. He agrees that Ling Tong should go with his three thousand men and search the area for any sign of Cao Cao's advance party. If he spots them, then he should engage with them. Arriving at the barrier at Ruxu, Cao Cao's army is soon spotted, and Ling Tong rides out to engage them. He personally challenges Zhang Liao, and they fight many rounds, but neither prevails. Ling Tong is ordered by Sun Quan to return – with little to show for his efforts.

Gan Ning, delighted by his foe's failure, asks Sun Quan for permission to attack with his one hundred men. 'If I lose even one man, then you can say I have failed,' he brags. In the middle of the night, Gan Ning and the one hundred set out, wearing white goose feathers in their helmets to identify themselves. Storming the barricades of the enemy camp, they create so much noise and confusion that Cao Cao's men think they are being attacked by thousands, not by a mere hundred. Slashing their way through the camp, they spread chaos and mayhem and then, as swiftly as they arrived, they gallop out by the south gate and return triumphantly home. Not a single man or horse has died. Great is the praise heaped upon Gan Ning by Sun Quan.

The following day Zhang Liao rides out and challenges the enemy. Ling Tong, spurred on by jealousy of Gan Ning's success the night before, responds by charging into single combat battle with Zhang Liao's companion Yue Jin. Their confrontation is heated, but after fifty bouts neither has gained the upper hand. Hearing of this confrontation, leaders on both sides come to watch the contest, and at a critical moment Cao Cao secretly orders Cao Xiu to fire an arrow at Ling Tong. The arrow brings down his horse, and Yue Jin races forward with his spear raised to slay Ling Tong. But at the crucial moment, in response, an arrow flies out from the southerners and hits Yue Jin in the face. In agony he falls from his horse. In the ensuing chaos men rush forward from both sides to rescue their own people and bring the battle to an end.

When Ling Tong comes to Sun Quan to apologize for having failed, he is quietly told that his life was saved by that arrow. To his astonishment he is told that it was fired by none other than Gan Ning. From that day on the old feud is forgotten, and they became bosom pals.

The next day, the war takes a much more dramatic turn. Cao Cao launches five separate forces against Ruxu. The fighting sways this way and that, Wu's troops sack one of the Wei camps; a storm sinks a Wu ship with one of the main commanders on board, and all perish; Pang De confronts Chen Wu in a maelstrom of fighting by the Ruxu wall; and Sun Quan rides out with Zhou Tai to help Chen Wu, only to find himself trapped between two of the Wei forces. Cao Cao spots the danger that Sun Quan is in and the possibility of killing or capturing him. He orders Xu Chu to attack immediately. The shock of his entry into the battle splits the Wu forces, leaving

Sun Quan dangerously exposed. Things are going very badly indeed for Sun Quan.

Zhou Tai, one of his most loyal commanders, has fought his way through to the riverbank but, realizing Sun Quan is not with him, he plunges back into the fray, crying, 'Where's our lord?', to which men shout back, 'There, in the thick of the enemy.' Charging into the mêlée, Zhou Tai reaches Sun Quan and cries, 'Follow me, my lord.' So saying, he turns and slashes his way back out again. But once again, when he reaches the shore, he finds Sun Quan is no longer with him. Undeterred, he once again plunges back into the fray, slashing his way through until he again reaches Sun Quan. 'There's no escape,' cries Sun Quan, as arrows and crossbow bolts rain down on them. 'You go first,' shouts Zhou Tai, 'and I'll follow.'

As Sun Quan surges forward, Zhou Tai fights left and right to defend him as warriors slash at him and arrows strike him. But at last he brings Sun Quan to the shore and gets him into a rescue boat.

'Without Zhou Tai coming back three times I would not have survived,' says Sun Quan to his men. 'But where's Xu Sheng? Is he still trapped?' Hearing this, Zhou Tai turns yet again and throws himself into the battle until he reaches Xu Sheng, who is surrounded by the enemy. Smashing his way through, he brings Xu Sheng to safety. Both of them are badly wounded and only just make it onto the rescue boat.

Just as it seems inevitable that Cao's men will overwhelm the southerners, Lu Xun, the son-in-law of Sun Ce, appears with one hundred thousand men and drives Cao's men back. The Wei suffer terrible losses, and thousands of their horses are seized by the triumphant Wu. However, great sadness descends upon Sun Quan when the body of Chen Wu is found lying upon the battlefield.

For a month there is an impasse, but finally a truce is declared. Now that peace has been restored Cao Cao withdraws to the capital while Sun Quan returns to his base at Moling.

Back at the imperial capital, the pressure to give Cao Cao the title 'king of Wei' grows and grows until Emperor Xian has no option but to agree. In the middle of AD 216, Cao Cao is enthroned as king of Wei. Cao Cao soon makes full use of his new kingly authority. He has heralds to clear the way as if he is the emperor and builds himself a grand palace at Yejun. All this is, of course, part of his designs to establish his own dynasty.

Planning for the establishment of his dynasty, he decides to name his heir apparent. His main wife, Lady Ding, is barren while his concubine Lady Liu lost her son Cao Ang during the war. So he initially choses Cao Zhi, famous as a poet and scholar, one of his four sons by his concubine Lady Bian. Removing Lady Ding, he makes Lady Bian his principal wife. Her eldest son, Cao Pi, is furious at being bypassed and asks Jia Xu's advice. As a result, he starts to turn up whenever his father goes out to fight, weeping and throwing himself on the floor as if deeply troubled at the risks his father is taking. In comparison, Cao Zhi writes long poems about his father's exploits. Cao Pi also uses bribery to get those close to Cao Cao to sing his praises. Over time, Cao Cao is persuaded that Cao Pi is a more loyal son. Cao Cao is now very unsure what to do, so he asks advice from Jia Xu. His advice is to choose Cao Pi, and so it is that he becomes the heir apparent.

When his palace is completed, Cao Cao wants to create an exotic garden and so sends men across the land to find rare plants. He also loves sweet oranges, and this brings his men to Wu and to visit Sun Quan. Now that a sort of peace has been established, he wishes to express his gratitude and so he has forty loads of these oranges prepared and sends them to Cao Cao's new palace.

En route the porters stop to rest at the base of a hill. Suddenly an old man, half blind and lame, wearing old and odd clothes, appears.

'Looks like you need some help,' he says. 'Can an old Daoist be of assistance?' And so saying, he heaves up one of the loads and goes some distance with them. When it comes time for him to leave, the others notice that their own loads seem to have become much lighter. As he departs, the old man says, 'This poor Daoist is known as Zuo Ci and has the Daoist name Master Blackhorn. He comes from the same village as your king of Wei. When you reach him, please give him my best wishes.' And with that he disappears.

The oranges arrive at Cao Cao's palace, and he eagerly takes one and peels it. To his surprise he finds nothing inside. Somewhat bewildered, he quizzes the head porter, who tells of the meeting with Zuo Ci. At that precise moment who should be announced as having arrived but Zuo Ci! Summoning him to his presence, Cao Cao demands, 'What kind of dark magic have you used to empty the oranges?'

'Really!' says Zuo Ci. 'What can have happened?' And, cutting open an orange, he shows that it is full and ripe. But no matter how many Cao Cao cuts open they are all dried up and empty.

Completely flummoxed, Cao Cao asks for an explanation, but before he begins Zuo Ci asks for food and drink. He then proceeds to eat huge quantities of food and drink vast amounts of wine. Despite the sheer quantity, this apparently has no ill effect upon him.

'So how do you do this?' demands Cao Cao.

Zuo Ci then tells his story. One day, when he was a student on Emei mountain in Shu, he heard someone calling his name. The voice came from inside a stone wall. Yet when he examined the wall he couldn't find anyone there. A clap of thunder made the wall break apart, and inside were three scrolls of sacred texts. Entitled 'Supreme Revelations of the Heavenly Texts', the three scrolls were named as one for Heaven, one for Earth and one for humanity.

Zuo Ci then tells of the magical arts each book teaches, such as riding upon the clouds and the winds, passing through mountains and how to change shape. 'Come and join me on Emei mountain,' he says to a bewildered Cao Cao, 'and become my student. Then I'll give you all three scrolls.'

'I would love to do so. To tell you the truth I've often thought about such a retreat. The problem is who could I trust to run the court?'

'Ah,' says Zuo Ci, 'why not Xuande, who is after all a member of the imperial family? Otherwise I may have to send a magic sword to cut off your head!'

This is too much for Cao Cao, who denounces him: 'He is in league with Xuande!' And he orders his arrest. A dozen guards rush to seize Zuo Ci and try to carry him off. But, no matter how hard they try, they cannot move him. Indeed he appears to be fast asleep. When they do get him to the cell, the chains fall off, and, although they refuse him food and drink for seven days, this has no adverse effect upon him whatsoever. Cao Cao has to admit he has no idea what to do with him.

Later that day he is hosting a banquet, when suddenly Zuo Ci appears, wooden clogs on his feet.

'Your mightiness,' says Zuo Ci, 'your table is overflowing with food, but is there anything missing? I will happily fetch it for you.'

'Dragon's liver, to make a stew. Can you fetch me that!' retorts a bemused Cao Cao.

'No problem,' says Zuo Ci, who draws a dragon on the wall and waves his sleeve, whereupon the dragon's body opens, and out falls a fresh, hot liver.

'You had that up your sleeve!' says Cao Cao dismissively.

'Now this is winter, and all nature is dead,' says Zuo Ci, 'is there a beautiful flower you would like?'

'A peony, that's all,' says Cao.

'Simple,' says Zuo Ci. At his command a flower bowl is brought, and he splashes water on it, and suddenly there is a fully grown peony with two flowers. After this astonishing feat he is, of course, invited to join the banquet.

When it comes time for the fish dish, Zuo Ci says, 'Of course, the best fish are from the River Song.'

'And how do you intend fetching them from so far away?' asks an incredulous Cao.

'So easy,' says Zuo Ci and, fishing in a pond below the window, he pulls out a couple of dozen large perch.

'These are just ordinary perch that were already there,' says Cao Cao, to which Zuo Ci replies, 'Everyone knows most perch have two pouches, but River Song ones have four.' Of course, these fish prove to have four.

'Now to cook them you need purple sprout ginger.' And of course, challenged by Cao Cao, he produces from a golden bowl exactly that kind of ginger. It is presented to Cao Cao, who notices a book nestling in the bowl and, taking it out, discovers it is called *The New Treatise of Meng De*. Glancing through it, he finds every word rings true to him.

Zuo Ci then takes a jade cup, which he fills with the best wine on the table. 'Drink this and you'll live to be thousand years old.'

Suspicious, Cao Cao says, 'You first.' Zuo Ci takes a jade pin from his hair, splits the wine in the cup down the middle and drinks one side. But Cao Cao refuses, and in disgust Zuo Ci throws the cup to the floor, where it becomes a white turtle dove, which flies around the hall. At this point Zuo Ci disappears.

Discovering that he has departed via the main gate and in a rage at what he sees as a dangerous maverick magician, Cao Cao orders Xu Chu and three hundred soldiers to race after him and capture him. Rushing out of the main gate, they see Zuo Ci wandering along without a care in the world just a little bit in front of them. But, try as they might, race as fast as they can, they cannot overtake him, even though he just continues to stroll along.

Climbing into the hills, Zuo Ci is suddenly in a flock of sheep. Xu Chu fires an arrow at him, but he simply disappears. Furious, Xu Chu slaughters all the sheep, leaving the shepherd boy in tears. To his astonishment one of the sheep heads suddenly speaks to him, telling him to put all the heads back on the sheep. Utterly terrified, the boy makes to escape, but another voice calls out, 'Don't worry. I'll do it and bring your sheep back to life.' When he looks round, he sees that Zuo Ci is doing exactly that. Then, with a twitch of his gown, he disappears.

News of this is reported by the lad's master, and Cao Cao has pictures drawn of Zuo Ci and circulated around the country with orders that he be arrested.

Three days later, hundreds of men who look exactly like Zuo Ci are herded into the capital. Chaos, of course, ensues so Cao Cao orders that they be sprinkled with pig and sheep's blood and taken outside the city walls. Here five hundred soldiers led by Cao Cao cut the heads off every one of them.

But suddenly from each severed head a thin, black mist rises. Swirling into the sky these mists merge together and there they become none other than Zuo Ci. Summoning a white crane, he seats himself upon it, claps his hands and says, 'The rats of the earth follow the golden tiger, but one day the evil one will be no more.' Cao Cao frantically orders his archers to fire, but a strong wind scatters everything. The executed men leap up and, clutching their severed heads, rush towards Cao Cao and his men. Cowering with terror and fainting with horror, the officials cover their faces.

> A powerful man can overthrow a whole country,
> But the powers of a Daoist immortal: far superior!

Is this the end for Cao Cao?

Let's find out.

CHAPTER 69

Guan Lu uses the Book of Changes *to work out what to do. Five brave men die for their country.*

Cao Cao watches in horror as the dead come back to life, and the shock makes him collapse. Then, just as quickly as it came, the wind disappears, and the bodies with it. He is carried back to his palace, but nothing seems to work to cure him of the shock.

Nothing, that is, until one of the imperial astrologers suggests that an astonishing diviner by name Guan Lu should be invited. Cao Cao is warned that this amazing man is not only ugly but also very rude and very fond of wine.

Born to a tribal family, even as a young man he showed an extraordinary interest in the stars – indeed his family found it very difficult to get him to go to bed at night because he just wanted to look at the stars!

As he grew, he took to studying the *Yi Jing*[16] and he developed a skill at physiognomy – reading people's fortunes from their faces.

Many are the stories told of the incredible skills of Guan Lu. He can out-debate any number of scholars on the meaning of the *Yi Jing*. And he is renowned as an exorcist. Once he was asked to help two brothers understand why they were both lame. Guan Lu discovered that there was a woman's ghost haunting the house. She was a relative murdered during a famine years before. The cause was a dispute over a few grains of rice. To hide her murder, her body was stuffed down a well. This revelation made the brothers confess to the murder.

Another time he was asked to help work out why a governor of Anping's wife was always fainting and her son had heart trouble. Guan Lu discovered that there were two corpses buried with their heads inside the wall of the hall and the rest of their bodies outside. One was holding a spear and the other a bow and arrow. Guan Lu realized that the spear was what caused the fainting and the arrows caused the heart problems. The bodies were dug up and reburied far away, and the troubles ceased.

Others liked to test his fame as someone who can tell what is hidden in a box or where a lost item might be. No matter what is hidden, Guan Lu knows what it is or where it is.

A famous story about him concerns a young man of nineteen. Guan Lu was walking in the countryside when he saw a young man ploughing a field. Asking the young man what his name was and how old he was, Guan Lu then announced that, having read his physiognomy, he knew that the young man was about to die in three days. The young man, called Zhao Yan, ran home and told his family. His father sought out Guan Lu and begged him to help his son. 'You cannot go against the Will of Heaven,' said Guan Lu. But the father and his son only increased their pleading.

Moved by this, Guan Lu recommended that Zhao Yan go the next day to try to find two men who would be playing chess under a large tree on the mountain, and facing south. 'They will be so absorbed in their game that they won't notice you but kneel down and offer them wine and meat – venison. When they have finished them, then you must plead for your life. They will answer your prayers, but for goodness' sake, don't mention me!'

The next day, Zhao Yan did exactly as he had been told and found the two men. So absorbed were they in their game that they drank the wine and ate the food without realizing it. Then they suddenly noticed that Zhao Yan was there, pleading for his life.

'You know,' said one of the men to the other, 'this has the feel of one of Guan Lu's tricks! Having taken the gifts, we have no option now but to help.' So saying, one of the men opened a ledger he had and, writing in it, extended Zhao Yan's life to ninety-nine years!

'Now, when you see Guan Lu,' said the other man, 'tell him to keep the secrets of Heaven to himself, or he knows what'll happen next!' And at that precise moment, a fragrant wind blew past, and the two men turned into white cranes and flew away. Returning home, Zhao Yan asked Guan Lu who these men were.

'The one in red was the Southern Dipper and the other was the Northern Dipper. The south marks life and the north death,' said Guan Lu. But from that day forth he was much more cautious about making such suggestions!

Having heard these stories, Cao Cao sends for him to help explain the horrifying events of the corpses. Guan Lu tells him not to be worried – that these were simple tricks of dark magic – and from that moment on Cao Cao revives. He then asks Guan Lu to cast the fortune for the empire, his own lineage and his own personal fortune. But Guan Lu is circumscribed in how much he foretells, not wishing to offend Heaven. On the empire he has this to say:

'Three and eight run across; a yellow pig meets the tiger; the expedition to the south loses you a limb.'

When he is asked to read the fortune for Shu and Wu, Guan Lu says, 'The south has lost its chief, and the west has gone on the attack.' Cao Cao doesn't believe him, but then news comes that Lu Su has died and that Xuande has sent Zhang Fei and Ma Chao to capture the pass at Xiabian. Infuriated by this, Cao Cao asks what he should do. Guan Lu urges caution. 'Not least,' says Guan Lu, 'because next spring there will be a terrible fire in the city.'

Cao Cao responds by staying put but sends Cao Hong to defend the east and increase the patrols in the city with an additional thirty thousand troops under Xiahou Dun. Wang Bi is given control of the royal troops – even though, as is pointed out, Wang Bi is prone to alcoholism.

It is early in AD 218 that a minor member of Cao Cao's staff, one Geng Ji, approaches Wei Huang, who is in charge of the protection of Cao Cao. Both have been horrified that Cao Cao has taken the title king. They decide that they can confide in Jin Yi, who also hates Cao Cao for his having usurped the imperial power. They also know that Jin Yi is a friend of Wang Bi, though this also makes them quite cautious. Having made sure he is on their side, together they hatch a plot to kill Wang Bi, bring the Royal Guard onto their side and then use them to kill

Cao Cao. They also recruit two others, sons of the imperial physician Ji Ping, whom Cao Cao had murdered years before. The two boys escaped but then secretly returned to the city.

They plan their attack for the night of the fifteenth day of the first month. This is the day for the annual lantern festival, which reflects and honours the first full moon of the new year. To start the attack, Geng Ji and Wei Huang will bring their armed staff to where Wang Bi has his camp for the Royal Guard. The instant they see fires in that camp they are to charge in. Once Wang Bi has died, they are to go directly with Jin Yi to the palace, where Jin Yi will ask the emperor to climb up into the Tower of Five Phoenixes, from where he will order the capture of Cao Cao. Meanwhile, the two sons of Ji will break into the city and start fires all over the place as a signal. They will then summon the ordinary, decent folk of the city to rise up, seize all traitors and defend the city against any counter-attack. Once the emperor has given his command for traitors to be seized, they will attack Yejun and capture Cao Cao, simultaneously calling on Xuande to come to the rescue of the imperial family.

In preparation, the staff of Geng Ji and Wei Huang, some four hundred or so, arm themselves. Another three hundred men come from the Ji family.

When night falls, out come the lanterns, and soon the city is ablaze with them. The soldiers enter into the spirit of the festival and are much more relaxed than they otherwise would have been. Wang Bi is dining with his officers when suddenly the cry goes up: 'Fire!' Wang Bi realizes that a coup is taking place and leaps on his horse to escape. Wounded by an arrow, he rides on, arriving just ahead of his pursuers at the entrance of Jin Yi's house, where he bangs in terror upon the closed door. All the male staff are of course out taking part in the revolt, so it is the women who answer. In fact, Jin Yi's wife, thinking it is her husband, calls out, 'Have you killed Wang Bi yet?' Wang Bi turns away and flees to Cao Xiu outside the city to tell him of the revolt. Cao Xiu summons a troop of some one thousand men and rides to the rescue.

The fires in the capital have run out of control. Even the Tower of the Five Phoenixes is burning, forcing the emperor to hide in the centre of the palace, while men loyal to Cao Cao hold the main gate against the rebels. Outside the city are thirty thousand soldiers, garrisoned there by Cao Cao after he heard the prophecy from Guan Lu and under the command of Xiahou Dun. With the arrival of Xiahou Dun and his men, the rebellion is doomed. By dawn it has collapsed, and the Ji brothers are dead. Geng Ji and Wei Huang are captured and more than a hundred of their followers lie dead.

Xiahou Dun's men put out the fires and arrest the extended families of the five plotters. Cao Cao orders the immediate execution in public of all the members of every guilty family. As he is led to his death, Geng Ji cries out that he will come back as a ghost to kill Cao Cao. To silence him, a sword is thrust into his mouth, and Geng Ji dies. Wei Huang kills himself by smashing his head against the paving stones. As a poet has written:

Geng Ji, truly dependable; Wei Huang, distinguished
Try to honour Heaven's choice with their own hands.
They didn't realize the Han's mandate was over –
Their grief goes down with them to the Nine Springs of Hell.

After the execution of the families, Xiahou Dun brings all the palace staff to Yejun, where Cao Cao has set up two flags – red to the left and white to the right. Then Cao Cao summons the officials. 'Those who came out to fight the fires stand by the red flag. Those who stayed at home and did nothing, stand by the white flag.' Two thirds of the officials, thinking that if they were assumed to have come out to help they will be rewarded, go to the red flag. The rest stand by the white flag and, to everyone's surprise, it is those by the red flag that Cao Cao orders arrested. Horrified at this, they protest, but Cao Cao replies, 'You didn't come out to help but to support the rebels', and he orders their immediate execution. Three hundred or more die that day. Those who chose the white flag are rewarded and return with relief to the city.

Wang Bi dies as a result of the arrow and is given a ceremonial funeral, while Cao Xiu is put in charge of the Royal Guard.

In response to all this, Cao Cao increases the size, splendour and authority of his court.

Cao Hong has arrived at Hanzhong and with Zhang He and Xiahou Yuan is ensuring it is well secured. As Ma Chao approaches, skirmishes take place, and one of his commanders is killed in battle with Cao Hong. Troubled by all this, Ma Chao takes refuge in Xiabian and refuses to be drawn out. Meanwhile, Cao Hong has retreated rather than push ahead. When Zhang He asks him why, Cao Hong confesses that he has been alarmed by Guan Lu's prophecy that a senior commander will die. Zhang He laughs at this and asks, 'How can a professional soldier with your experience take seriously the mutterings of a fortune teller? Let me go ahead and try to seize Baxi, and the rest will then fall into our hands.'

Cao Hong points out that Baxi is defended by none other than Zhang Fei, of whom everyone is scared. But Zhang He retorts that he is not afraid of a baby like Zhang Fei. Cao Hong makes him vow that if he fails he will accept the punishment decreed by the military law, and Zhang He happily agrees. And so he sets out to fight Zhang Fei.

Pride often goes before a fall;
Ill-prepared attacks usually fail.

So what happens next?

CHAPTER 70

Zhang Fei captures Wakou Pass by cunning. Old Huang Zhong captures the mountain by stealth.

Zhang He takes his thirty thousand men and creates three hill forts to defend their base and then advances with fifteen thousand men to the attack.

Realizing that the area is perfect for an ambush, Zhang Fei and General Lei Tong lay their plans. It is agreed that Zhang Fei will charge out to the attack, and when the enemy is distracted Lei Tong will quietly bring a surprise troop round to their rear.

The strategy is highly successful, and Zhang He's army is cut to pieces. Zhang He himself has to flee back to one of his camps, chased by both Zhang Fei and Lei Tong. Zhang He fortifies his main camp and for day after day resists the taunts of Zhang Fei to come out and fight like a man and stays safely behind his walls. Fifty days have gone by, and Zhang Fei now spends every day drunk, shouting abuse up at Zhang He.

To his distress Xuande is informed of Zhang Fei's drunkenness. So imagine his surprise when Kong Ming suggests sending fifty barrels of the best Chengdu wine.

'You know how destructive his drinking has been in the past, so why would you now send him such encouragement?' asks a bewildered Xuande.

Kong Ming replies, 'Zhang Fei knows what he is doing. He's fooling the enemy into thinking that he is losing the plot!'

When the barrels arrive, Zhang Fei distributes them and then sits and drinks heavily in full view of the enemy. Zhang He is by now so furious with this insolent behaviour that he decides to attack that very night, convinced Zhang Fei will be too drunk to resist. That night as they approach, he can see Zhang Fei sitting, surrounded by lamps and drinking. Charging into the camp, he makes straight for Zhang Fei and triumphantly stabs the drunk and incapacitated enemy leader with his spear. Or, to be more accurate, he spears a straw man made to look like Zhang Fei. Suddenly realizing this is all a trap, he turns to retreat, but bombardments erupt all around him and his men. And, coming straight at him out of the smoke, is the real Zhang Fei.

They fight long and hard, but Zhang He's plans are thrown into chaos. Hoping for support from his two other camps, he holds out as long as he can. But then he sees flames leaping up in each of them and realizes that they have been captured and his men routed. Eventually managing to fight his way free, Zhang He makes his way to the Wakou pass, having lost two thirds of his men. Not surprisingly Cao Hong is incandescent with rage at this disaster. He tells Zhang He to go back and fight. Ashamed, this is what he does the next day and runs straight into troops led by Lei Tong. In the ensuing mêlée, Lei Tong is lured into pursuing an apparently fleeing Zhang He, only for him to fall victim to that old trick. Zhang He suddenly turns and slays Lei Tong. When news of this reaches Zhang Fei, he rushes to the pass and challenges Zhang He. Zhang He tries to pull the same trick on Zhang Fei, but he doesn't fall for it. Their struggles over the next few days are inconclusive, despite each trying to outwit the other by such tricks and ambushes. Zhang He is now firmly ensconced in the camp guarding the Wakou pass.

Then one day Zhang Fei notices some traders travelling by a steep hillside path. Calling them to him, he finds out there is a very narrow pathway that means he can get behind the pass and attack from there. Wei Yan is sent with a hand-picked troop and takes up his position silently at the rear of the pass. Then Zhang Fei attacks. No sooner has Zhang He armed himself to confront the frontal attack than word comes of fires and attacks from the rear. The double attack is a complete success, and, of the men left after this battle, only ten escape with Zhang He and struggle back to Cao Hong's camp. Although Cao Hong wants to execute him, he is dissuaded by others and eventually reluctantly agrees to supply a further five thousand men for him to use to take Jiameng pass and hold Hanzhong.

When news of this advance on Jiameng pass reaches Xuande, he and Kong Ming hold a council to decide how to respond. 'We need Zhang Fei to go straight to Jiameng pass and confront Zhang He,' says Kong Ming.

'But he is vital for the defence of Wakou pass,' says another of the advisers.

'Let's be frank, Zhang He is the most fierce of opponents, and only Zhang Fei can bring him down,' says Kong Ming.

But just as it seems this has been agreed, up pipes Huang Zhong. 'Send me, and I will bring you Zhang He's head,' he says.

'I don't doubt your courage,' says Kong Ming, 'but aren't you too old at seventy to do this?'

Outraged by this, Huang Zhong grabs a sword hanging on the wall and swiftly shows his skill as a swordsman. He then takes down mighty bows from the wall and draws them until they snap in two. Kong Ming agrees to his going but only if he has a lieutenant to assist, whereupon Huang Zhong chooses the equally elderly but determined Yan Yan. 'If I fail, then you can strike this white-haired old head from my shoulders,' cries Huang Zhong. The other officers, led by Zhao Zilong, round on Kong Ming. 'Why are you doing this? What childish game is this?' asks Zhao Zilong. 'Zhang He is our most determined foe, and you send two elderly generals to fight him?'

'Do you know,' says Kong Ming, 'I am confident that it will be those "two elderly generals" who will capture Hanzhong for us!'

At this Zhao Zilong and the other generals smile knowingly and leave.

Arriving before Zhang He's forces, the two old generals are roundly abused and mocked by the defenders. Zhang He rides out to do battle with Huang Zhong, thinking this will be over swiftly. But the fight is fierce, and, unbeknown to Zhang He, that old veteran Yan Yan has used the diversion to take his men round behind Zhang He's men. Suddenly he attacks, and Zhang He is caught between the two generals and their men.

Zhang He is roundly defeated and forced to retreat many miles and regroup his shattered forces.

Once again Cao Hong is furious at yet another failure and sends reinforcements led by Xiahou Shang and Han Hao to assist Zhang He.

Now, while this is taking place, Huang Zhong's spies have reported back that Cao Cao has built his supply base at Tiandang mountain. They conclude that if they can cut that off, then Hanzhong will fall. So Yan Yan sets off to put into place his part of their new plan.

Huang Zhong then sets in place the other part of the plot. Challenging Xiahou Shang and Han Hao to battle, he then turns and flees, pursued by the enemy. He abandons one of his camps to them. The next day he again flees and again abandons another camp. Zhang He begins to be suspicious but is firmly put in his place by Xiahou Shang, who calls him a coward for having lost so many battles. 'Watch,' he says, 'as we show you how it is done and earn ourselves fame!'

The next day Huang Zhong once again retreats until at last he can go no further, as he is up against the pass. Kong Ming hears of this and reassures a troubled Xuande that this is all part of a plan to lull the enemy into false expectations.

And sure enough, in the middle of the next night, Huang Zhong attacks with five thousand of his men. Catching the enemy completely by surprise, he sweeps them before him, and by the time the sun rises he has regained all three camps and all the goods and chattels that the enemy have stored there. By pressing hard upon the enemy, Huang Zhong pushes the northern troops right to the banks of the Han River.

Zhang He realizes that the supply base at Tiandang is now under real threat and that if it falls then Hanzhong will fall. He and Xiahou Shang therefore take their men to Tiandang and join up with Xiahou De, who is already based there. Initially Xiahou De suggests they sally forth together and attack Huang Zhong. 'No,' replies Zhang He, 'we need to defend not attack at this time.' No sooner has this been said than the war drums of Huang Zhong resound around the hills, and the enemy is at the gates.

'What an old fool,' says Xiahou De, 'fancying going straight into an attack when his men must be worn out from their march.'

'Don't underestimate the old man,' replies Zhang He. 'Our strategy must be to defend, not attack.'

'Just let me attack with three thousand men,' says Han Hao, 'and I will triumph!' Against Zhang He's advice, Xiahou De details three thousand men, and Han Hao rides out to confront Huang Zhong.

Although exhausted, Huang Zhong tells his men to be ready to attack. When challenged by Liu Feng as to the wisdom of this with such weary troops, he replies, 'Heaven has presented us with an opportunity for victory. Not to take it would therefore offend Heaven!'

So into the attack they go, led by Huang Zhong. Han Hao falls almost immediately to Huang Zhong; Yan Yan takes out one of the north's main commanders, Xiahou De, brother of Xiahou Shang. The disasters force Zhang He and Xiahou Shang to abandon Tiandang camp and try to escape to another supply base on nearby Dingjun mountain. Meanwhile Huang Zhong and Yan Yan seize the supply depot at Tiandang, and the news of the triumph is sent back to a delighted Xuande in Chengdu.

It is agreed that Xuande himself should advance on Hanzhong. Now Zhao Zilong and Zhang Fei come with him in support. So it is that in the autumn of AD 218 Xuande's army arrives at Jiameng pass. Here, the old generals come to discuss the next steps. 'Thank you, Huang Zhong,' says Xuande. 'Even though some mocked you, Kong Ming had confidence in you, and you've done marvels. All our foes have left is Dingjun mountain. If we take that, then our way to Yangping is clear. Are you up for a further challenge?'

Even though Huang Zhong is keen, Kong Ming urges caution. 'Xiahou Yuan, who holds Dingjun, is no fool. Remember he defended Xiliang, defeated Ma Chao and has taken Hanzhong. I think we need to call for Guan Yu to come and take control.'

Huang Zhong is predictably furious: 'I will take my three

thousand best men and will bring you Xiahou Yuan's head.' Despite Kong Ming's continued opposition, in the end Huang Zhong wins but agrees that Kong Ming can choose the assistant to go with him.

So who does Kong Ming choose?

Let's find out.

CHAPTER 71

Huang Zhong scores another victory.
Zhao Zilong defeats a vast army.

Apparently grudgingly, Kong Ming has agreed that Huang Zhong should go, but he also sends others to assist him – Zhao Zilong, Liu Feng, Meng Da. 'The only way,' he says to Xuande, 'that you can fire up these old men is to appear to dismiss them!' It is also decided that Yan Yan will go to relieve Zhang Fei and Wei Yan so they can march to join the battle for Hanzhong.

When news of the fall of Tiandang mountain is brought to Cao Cao, he calls an urgent meeting to discuss how to save Hanzhong. The advice is that he will have to lead the troops himself. 'If Hanzhong falls, the whole of Wei will be at risk of collapse,' says Liu Ye.

So it is that, within a few days, Cao Cao rides out leading an army of four hundred thousand men. And what a grand sight they make! Cao Cao on his grey horse, wearing rich clothing, with a gilt saddle and covered by a glittering canopy of red silk. To either side of him, ritual symbols in gold and silver of his regal status. Around him ride a private escort of twenty-five thousand, all elaborately colour-coded to symbolize the power of the cosmos and seasons. A truly imperial-looking procession!

En route, Cao Cao realizes he is passing the home estate of an old friend, Cai Yong. The manor house is lived in now by his daughter Cai Yan and her husband, Dong Si. There is a touching story behind this friendship. In her youth, Cai Yong's daughter Yan had been married but during a raid by tribal people from the north she had been captured, raped and forced to bear two children by her captor. During her time in exile she had written a set of poems called 'Eighteen Compositions for

Foreign Music', which brought her renown. Cao Cao was deeply moved by her plight. He offered a ransom of a thousand ounces of gold. The chief of the Xiongnu tribe who had captured her was so in awe of Cao Cao that he sent her back. It was Cao Cao who arranged her subsequent marriage to Dong Si.

Arriving with just a small bodyguard at the front door, he is greeted by Cai Yan – her husband being away on business. On the way in, Cao Cao notices a stone rubbing and asks about it.

'It dates from the time of Emperor He[17] and is called the stele of Cao E. She was the daughter of a shaman. He was renowned for his ecstatic dances and singing and then one day when he was drunk he fell into the river and drowned. His daughter, Cao E, mourned by the riverside for seven days and nights and then threw herself into the river. Five days later, her body surfaced, holding her father in her arms. They were buried with due honour, and when the imperial court was told the story a stele was ordered and this story inscribed. The author was just thirteen years old when he wrote the text, and this made the stone even more famous. Years later, my father went to see it, and, even though it was almost dark, he was able to read the characters with his fingers. He then wrote eight characters in ink on the back, and these were later inscribed on the stele as well.'

Cao Cao reads the eight characters: 'Yellow silk; young woman; distaff grandchild; pounding mortar.'

'Does anyone understand what this means?' asks Cao Cao, to which comes the answer: 'No.' 'Even though my father wrote them,' says Cai Yan, 'I have no idea what they mean.'

After a pleasant but brief stay they are riding away, when Cao Cao laughs because he has worked it out. Yang Xiu, his adviser travelling with him, too has the answer, and Cao Cao tells him to spell it out.

'The character for colour – that's the yellow clue – and that for silk make the character for "absolutely". A young woman is both young and little, and the characters for young and little give the character "beautiful". A distaff grandchild is a daughter's son, and the characters for daughter and son give the character "good" or "worthy". Finally, pounding in a mortar is how to mix the five bitter herbs, and put the characters for bowl and bitter and you have the character for "tell". So the whole riddle means "Absolutely beautiful and worthy to be told."

Everyone delights in the skill involved in unravelling this riddle as they ride on to war.

Cao Cao and his army arrive at Nanzheng and set up camp. Meanwhile Dingjun mountain is now besieged by Huang Zhong. Xiahou Yuan and Zhang He wonder how to show Cao Cao that they are competent and worthy of his trust. It is decided that they will mount an attack led by Xiahou Yuan, who brags that he will capture Huang Zhong alive. Amused by this, Huang Zhong sends a minor officer, Chen Shi, to deal with the scouting party. However, he is decisively defeated by being drawn into an ambush and captured. Alarmed by this, Huang Zhong decides to build up the resolve of his men. This he does by giving them generous gifts and saying there is more to come. To loud cheers, the men set off and march forward, capturing sites as they go towards the mountain top. This strategy is known as 'turning the guest into the host', and Zhang He sees through it immediately. 'Don't be drawn into an attack,' he says. 'Instead, be defensive.' But Xiahou Yuan is so eager for battle he ignores Zhang He's pleas. He orders an attack party to ride out led by Xiahou Shang. As Zhang He foresaw, they are roundly defeated by Huang Zhong, and Xiahou Shang is captured.

A truce is called so that Chen Shi can be exchanged for Xiahou Shang. The exchange takes place the following day in an open valley. At the sound of drums rolling, the two prisoners dash for their own ranks. But just as Xiahou Shang is about to reach the northern troops, Huang Zhong shoots him in the back with an arrow. Outraged, Xiahou Yuan charges, which is exactly what Huang Zhong wants, and they clash over and over again. But neither is able to overcome the other, and at the sound of warning gongs Xiahou Yuan returns to his own side.

Meanwhile a mountain fort opposite the main supply camp at Dingjun mountain has been captured by the forces of Shu. Reviewing the scene from this vantage point, Huang Zhong can see how to trap and defeat his enemy. Once again it is the impetuousness of Xiahou Yuan that leads to disaster. Ignoring

Zhang He's advice, he surrounds the hill fort, calling on its defenders to come out and fight. On the recommendation of Fa Zheng the men wait. They make no response to the taunts. After a while the enemy grow bored, and it is at this point that Fa Zheng signals Huang Zhong to launch an attack. Suddenly, without warning, Huang Zhong attacks from a different direction than the fort and traps the enemy forces. In the fight Huang Zhong kills Xiahou Yuan with such a massive blow that he cuts off Xiahou's head and shoulders.

As a poet has written:

> Old he might be, but he fights his enemy,
> And what a mighty spirit he shows!
> Strong arms bend the bow,
> Like a great wind he rushes in.
> His roaring voice a tiger's,
> His horse's stride a dragon's flight.
> He gains victory, and all its rewards,
> And the kingdom of his lord expands.

The defeat opens the way for Liu Feng and Meng Da to capture Dingjun, and soon Zhang He and his remaining forces are in flight, not resting until they are able to camp beside the River Han. When Cao Cao learns of the defeat, he suddenly understands Guan Lu's predictions.

'Three and eight run across means this year, the twenty-fourth year of the Jian An era. The yellow pig meets a tiger was about Xiahou Yuan dying in the year of the pig. The expedition to the south is the defence of Dingjun and the loss of a limb is about my losing such a dear friend as Xiahou Yuan.'

In response Cao Cao launches an army of two hundred thousand towards Jiameng pass, determined to crush Xuande. When news reaches Xuande, he orders an assault on their camp and its supplies so as to cripple the attack. Huang Zhong is ordered to lead the troop and successfully overruns the supply camp. He is about to burn the supplies when suddenly Zhang He attacks them. Huang Zhong and his men are trapped. When Huang Zhong does not return, Zhao Zilong sets out to find him, leaving a small garrison behind under the command of Zhang Yi to watch over his camp.

Zhao Zilong soon runs into enemy troops, and ferocious battle ensues. Slashing his way through, he at last sees Zhang He and his men surrounding Huang Zhong. So terrifying is his attack that he smashes through the ring of soldiers, scattering them and creating chaos and confusion. So much so that Zhang He retreats, and Zhao Zilong is at last able to rescue Huang Zhong.

Returning to his camp, his second in command, Zhang Yi, spots the clouds raised by an advancing enemy. Together, they plan a surprise for the attacking troops. Zilong goes and stands at the main gate with his spear levelled. Meanwhile Zhang Yi positions archers and crossbowmen in hiding. Cao Cao himself is advancing with the troops when he sees Zhao Zilong standing defiant and alone. He spurs on his troops, but as they rush forward, Zilong's silent stance alarms them, and they halt. This is the moment when Zilong gives the signal, and the arrows and bolts fly through the air. Chaos reigns as the Wei soldiers, including Cao Cao, turn and flee in the face of the attacking Shu forces. Many are lost. The supplies are destroyed, and the whole Wei army retreats to Nanzheng in disarray.

Great is Xuande's praise for Zhao Zilong and his decisive actions. But news comes almost straight away that Cao Cao is advancing again towards the River Han. Command has been shared between Xu Huang and an unexpected secondary commander, Wang Ping, a local man with local knowledge.

Advancing to the banks of the river, Xu Huang prepares to cross. But Wang Ping strongly recommends that he doesn't, because how would he get back if disaster struck? But Xu Huang is not interested in this and, quoting historical precedent, he builds a bridge and crosses over.

So what happens next?

Let's find out.

CHAPTER 72

Kong Ming captures Hanzhong by cunning.
Cao Cao retreats.

As foreseen by Wang Ping, Xu Huang's adventure to the other side of the river is a disaster. Attacked on all sides by Xuande's troops, Xu Huang's men suffer catastrophic losses. In the end, as Wang Ping warned him, Xu Huang is forced to try to escape back across the river. Here many of his men drown.

You can therefore imagine Wang Ping's disgust when Xu Huang comes raging up to him saying it is Wang Ping's fault. 'You knew the danger, so why didn't you come and rescue us?'

'What!' exclaims Wang Ping. 'And put our base here in jeopardy! I warned you not to go.'

This simply puts Xu Huang into an even more intemperate rage. Frankly Wang Ping has had enough. That night, after setting fire to the camp, which forces Xu Huang to panic and desert the camp, Wang Ping crosses the river and surrenders to Zhao Zilong. Deeply angered by this betrayal, Cao Cao leads the advance to the bank of the river on the east side, where he faces off against Zhao Zilong on the west. Deadlock ensues, until Kong Ming takes things into his own hands. He sends Zilong with five hundred men to a secluded hillside beyond the enemy camp. He tells Zilong that when a given signal sounds, he is to get his men to make as much warlike, threatening noise as possible. Then Kong Ming watches as one by one the lights go out in the enemy camp opposite. Then, when all is quiet, he gives the signal, and over on the hillside Zilong's men set up a tremendous ruckus – banging war drums, blowing horns, shouting. Cao Cao's men leap up from their sleep, convinced they are about to be overwhelmed by the enemy – only to find no one there. This happens again the next night and the night after. Every night the sleep of Cao Cao's men is disrupted. By the third night the Wei troops are utterly exhausted and completely on edge – even Cao Cao – and so the next day they retreat from the riverbank.

On Kong Ming's advice, Xuande crosses the river and sets up camp with the river behind his men's backs. This unconventional move confuses Cao Cao, and he issues a challenge. Battle commences the next day, with Cao Cao denouncing Xuande as a traitor against the imperial court and Xuande replying that Cao Cao is the traitor for having murdered the empress, making himself king and having the audacity to use an imperial carriage. With that the armies engage, and almost immediately the army of Shu retreats, running back to the River Han, and leaving their camps and supplies for the enemy to seize. Just as it seems these will fall into the hands of the Wei troops, Cao Cao orders his men to pull back. Bewildered, his commanders ask why.

'My suspicions were first aroused by the fact that the enemy were backed up against the river. Then, that they abandoned so much stuff, horses and weapons. Pull back and don't touch anything!' he exclaims.

But they are too late. No sooner has the retreat started than Kong Ming gives the signal, and the trap he has prepared is sprung. With Xuande leading the central charge, Zhao Zilong the right and Huang Zhong the left, they soon have the enemy running for their lives. As Cao Cao tries to pull back, news comes that Wei Yan and Zhang Fei have seized Langzhong and then gone on to seize Nanzheng, cutting off his retreat. In disarray, Cao Cao retreats to the Yangping pass. Kong Ming's plot has worked, and Cao Cao is bottled up at the pass. In particular Kong Ming has sent Zhang Fei and Wei Yan to seize the grain convoy on its way to supply Cao Cao. Hearing of this, Cao Cao asks for a volunteer to go to protect the convoy, and Xu Chu puts himself forward. With a thousand men he rides off and soon, as night falls, meets up with the convoy. Relieved by the extra protection, the head of the convoy presents Xu Chu with meat and wine, which Xu Chu eats and drinks swiftly, becoming quite drunk. He then insists that they press on through the night, and even though the head of the convoy pleads with him not to, as it is too dangerous, Xu Chu insists. As they pass through a narrow defile they are suddenly attacked. Zhang Fei sweeps down and in single combat severely wounds Xu Chu, who in his drunken state is not able to hold his own. The northerners flee, and the convoy falls into the hands of the men of Shu.

This is the last straw for Cao Cao, who the next morning rides out to do battle once and for all with Xuande. It is a disaster for Cao Cao. Defeated, he tries to retreat to his camp at Yangping pass, and in the panic many of his men die trodden underfoot by other panic-ridden soldiers from their own side. Arriving at the pass, he tries to find safety there, only to be forced out by the enemy. Cao Cao flees, hotly pursued by Zhang Fei, Zhao Zilong and Huang Zhong. Riding hell for leather towards Ye valley, Cao Cao sees what appears to be yet more of the enemy coming towards him.

But relief overcomes him when he sees it is his son Cao Zhang. This aspiring warrior, determined since childhood to be a hero, has just defeated an uprising by the Wuhuan people. Hearing of his father's troubles, he has come marching to assist him. With these additional forces, Cao Cao defends the valley, and it is here that the armies fight again. The battle is indecisive, and for many days the enemies sit facing each other.

One night Cao Cao is having dinner when he is given a bowl of chicken soup, and floating in the soup is some chicken gristle. Asked at that moment to give the password for the night, he says, 'Chicken gristle'. When Yang Xiu, who is his primary secretary, hears this he tells his men to start packing up to go home. Challenged by Xiahou Dun as to why he has done this, Yang Xiu says because of the password. 'Chicken gristle has no meat on it, but it adds to the flavour. So this means we cannot advance, but to retreat will put us out of favour with others. So we have no option but to go home!'

Soon everyone is packing up, and when Cao Cao discovers what is going on he is furious. 'How dare you make up these stories!' he shouts at Yang Xiu and orders his immediate execution. Cao Cao and Yang Xiu have a long history of misunderstandings and of Yang Xiu being perhaps a little too clever for Cao Cao, who both admires and resents him. In particular, Yang Xiu's way of interpreting characters written by

Cao Cao to mean something different has both fascinated Cao Cao and annoyed him as well.

Cao Cao is also troubled by Yang Xiu's friendship with his third son, Cao Zhi. In the struggle to be named heir, the eldest son, Cao Pi, sought the help of Wu Zhi, one of the senior advisers. To prevent Cao Cao finding out, it was proposed to smuggle Wu Zhi into Cao Pi's quarters in a large container used for storing silk. Discovering this, Yang Xiu informed Cao Cao. But Cao Pi heard about this and so cancelled Wu Zhi's visit and had the container actually filled with silk rolls. When Cao Cao's police investigated, they found only the silk and reported this to Cao Cao. From that day on Cao Cao believed that Yang Xiu meant to harm his eldest son.

Many other instances of misunderstanding, mistrust and suspicion have created in Cao Cao's mind a desire to get rid of Yang Xiu, and the chicken gristle is the excuse he needs. Yang Xiu is thirty-four when he is executed and his head exposed at the entrance to the camp as a warning.

The next morning Cao Cao rides into battle. But no sooner has he ridden out than news comes that Ma Chao has attacked from behind. Turning to address this problem, Cao Cao suddenly finds himself attacked by a troop led by Wei Yan. Wei Yan manages to fire an arrow which knocks Cao Cao from his horse, and as Wei Yan closes in for the kill, it is only a dramatic charge by Pang De that saves Cao Cao. So powerful is Pang De's charge that Wei Yan has to retreat. Ma Chao has also been forced to retreat, so Cao Cao is carried safely back to his own camp. The arrow has knocked out two of his teeth. While undergoing treatment, Cao Cao recalls Yang Xiu's view that they should just go back home and he realizes how wise the adviser was. His body is exhumed and given full military honours for burial. And then Cao Cao sets off to return to the capital, with Pang De defending the rear. As they journey north, suddenly, without warning, there are fires on both sides of the valley, and an ambush is sprung.

Will Cao Cao survive?

Let's find out.

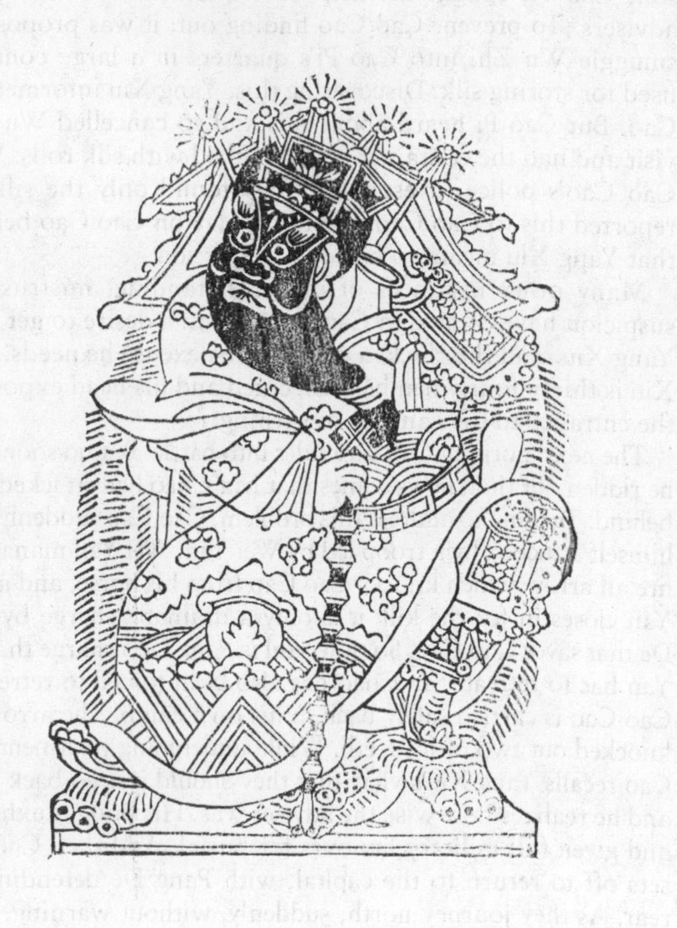

將軍

CHAPTER 73

Xuande becomes King of Hanzhong.
Guan Yu captures Xiangyang.

It is pretty clear to Kong Ming where Cao Cao will go when he has to retreat. As a result he sends Ma Chao to ensure as difficult a departure for Cao Cao as possible. Hounded by Ma Chao at every opportunity, the Wei troops suffer heavily, and morale collapses. Although he is in severe pain from his wound, Cao Cao has no option but to speed up the retreat. Only when he at last reaches Chang'an do he and his men feel safe and rest. Meanwhile, because of his retreat, the places around Hanzhong fall to Xuande's men, and others surrender once they know that Xuande will ensure peace and security to the ordinary people.

Following these successes, Xuande's commanders are keen for him to become emperor, and they raise this with Kong Ming. So Kong Ming comes to see Xuande and says, 'Cao Cao has seized so much power that the true ruler has been usurped. You're renowned for your benevolence and have brought peace back to these regions. You control the land of Shu. Now is the appropriate time to be obedient to the Will of Heaven and of the people and become the emperor. Then you can be a true blessing by righteously destroying the traitor. Do not hesitate: indeed chose the auspicious day!'

'Surely you're wrong!' exclaims Xuande. 'Although I'm of the lineage of the House of Han, I'm also just a denizen of the country. If I do this I'll be seen as a rebel!'

'That's not true,' says Kong Ming. 'The country is ripped apart by adventurers who seize what they can. Everywhere those who have been loyal, virtuous and brave have risked death trying to be honourable. They all long for a true emperor. They wish to be carried by the strength of a dragon, to fly with a phoenix and thus to have their own names honoured. If, for fear of being criticized, you turn aside, you'll lose the support of the people. Please, please, think again.'

'This I cannot do, so instead you need to think again.'

'If you continue to say no, the people's hearts will harden against you,' say those around him.

Then Kong Ming says, 'If taking the title of emperor is too much for a man of your virtue, then would you be prepared to have the title of king of Hanzhong, given you now control Jingzhou and Shu?'

'Only if the emperor will offer this. Otherwise this would still be rebellion,' says Xuande.

'Surely,' says Kong Ming, 'the point is that this is no ordinary time, and therefore to depart from convention is essential. Don't hold on to what is no longer useful.'

Into this discourse Zhang Fei suddenly breaks, shouting, 'You at least are a Han, but others who have no such name are trying to take over. Forget just being a king of Hanzhong. You deserve to be the emperor!'

'Enough,' snaps Xuande at Zhang Fei, 'you've said too much.'

'Look,' says Kong Ming, 'let's recognize where we are today. Take the title of king, and later we'll petition the emperor.'

So at last, after turning it down three times, as convention demands, Xuande agrees, and in late AD 219 he is crowned with full ritual, facing south, with the five directions marked on a specially created altar. He appoints his son Liu Shan as his heir, and Guan Yu, Zhang Fei, Zhao Zilong, Ma Chao and Huang Zhong are named the Five Tiger Generals. Wei Yan is made governor of Hanzhong.

Then Xuande writes to the emperor. In his long and dutiful letter he regrets his inability to overcome the forces that have set at naught the imperial family. Recalling the first such abuses by Dong Zhuo, he traces the ills that have befallen the imperial family back to that traitor. He recounts how he and others have risen to defend the throne often aided not just by their own efforts but by the Will of Heaven itself. Now all that remains is to take down Cao Cao, whose growing ambition has usurped the authority and power of the emperor. He writes about the plot that he and Dong Cheng hatched which failed through a breach in security. He points out that this left only him to fight on, having to flee from place to place. Because of this, Cao Cao was able to murder the empress unopposed and poison the heir apparent. Quoting from history, he argues that nothing is better or more appropriate for an imperial family than to promote and support its own members – even the most distant branches thereof. This, he argues, is especially necessary when someone as ambitious as Cao Cao is usurping and corrupting the court and seizing power. It is in the light of this that he, Xuande, as a member of the imperial family has agreed to the call by his own people to take up the mantle of family responsibility and become king of Hanzhong. He then talks about the pressure he has been under and how he has wrestled with his conscience. The key issue, however, is that the traitor Cao Cao has not been executed yet, and as a result the ancestral temple is in peril and the shrine for the well-being of the nation threatened. This could drive a man to despair, he says, but he has chosen to rise to the occasion by accepting the role of king. Now, though he trembles to think of the audacious act he has undertaken, he can as a result rally the people to him so that Heaven can bless him and the imperial family.

When Cao Cao hears that Xuande has been made king, his fury knows no bounds. 'That lowlife, straw sandal-maker. Now I'll destroy him!' And so saying, he orders an invasion force to be prepared to attack Shu. However, wiser heads intervene, and then one of those in the court previously unnoticed by Cao Cao steps forward. His name is Sima Yi. He says, 'Don't waste your energy on long-distance campaigns out of righteous anger. There's a simpler means of bringing Xuande down without firing a single arrow and it only requires one general.'

Amused but also intrigued, Cao Cao asks, 'And what is this plan?'

'There exists great enmity between Sun Quan and Xuande over the fate of Sun Quan's sister – the wife of Xuande – and over the contentious issue of Jingzhou,' Sima Yi says. 'Let's send a letter to Sun Quan suggesting he attacks and captures Jingzhou, which will mean Xuande will have to rush to its defence, and we can easily recapture Hanzhong.'

Cao Cao is much taken with this suggestion, and so it is agreed. Adviser Man Chong is chosen to take the letter to Sun Quan. Upon receipt of the proposal Sun Quan and his advisers decide that this is too good an offer to refuse. Man Chong returns with this news, while Sun Quan also decides to see what Guan Yu is up to in Jingzhou. He sends Kong Ming's brother Zhuge Jin to ask Guan Yu for the hand of his daughter in marriage to his son. The proposal is met with total horror by Guan Yu. 'Marry my tiger's child to a mere mongrel's offspring! Why, if it wasn't for the fact that your brother is Kong Ming I would have had you executed!' and with that Zhuge Jin is driven out of the city.

So plans are laid by Sun Quan and Cao Cao to attack, starting with Man Chong going to Fancheng to prepare for an assault on Jingzhou in partnership with Cao Ren. This is Sun Quan's ploy for using the troops of Cao Cao to soften up the enemy resistance.

When Xuande hears of the pact between Cao Cao and Sun Quan, he asks Kong Ming what to do next.

'Well, this isn't exactly a surprise,' says Kong Ming. 'And you can be sure that Sun Quan's advisers are behind the plan that Cao Ren attacks first. So let's send a messenger to Guan Yu and have him attack and capture Fancheng itself. That should put the cat among the pigeons and break up this alliance.'

Ordered to do this, Guan Yu begins to prepare and appoints two key officials to lead the attack, Fu Shiren and Mi Fang. But celebrating their promotion, these two get drunk. In their befuddled state they leave a fire smouldering. This bursts into flames, resulting in the loss of weapons, food and transport, while much of what is left is severely damaged. Furious with the two men, Guan Yu orders their execution. Persuaded that this would not be a good augury for this war, he instead has them whipped forty times and sends them to protect Nanjun and Gong'an. They go, but with terrible resentment burning in their hearts and a fear and loathing for Guan Yu. Meanwhile, Guan Yu is soon en route to Fancheng.

In Fancheng, Cao Ren is all for attack, while Man Chong, knowing of Guan Yu's skills, advocates defence. But Cao Ren has the greater authority and, leaving Man Chong in the city to defend it, he rides out to engage with Guan Yu.

Almost as soon as the first encounter takes place the Jingzhou men retreat, pursued by Cao Ren and his men. The same happens the next day until, fooled by this, Cao Ren suddenly finds himself caught up in an ambush. Seeing Guan Yu standing passively on the hillside, Cao Ren is struck with terror and rushes from the battle scene, back to the security of Fancheng. As a result Guan Yu is able to seize the city of Xiangyang.

However, Guan Yu is conscious that, while he will be away taking Fancheng, others might try to attack and seize Jingzhou. To prevent this, he establishes a long chain of beacons to alert him to any such attack.

Inside Fancheng, Man Chong and Cao Ren meet, with Cao Ren apologizing for his mistake and Man Chong recommending that they now just sit this out inside the city walls.

Despite this, one of Cao Ren's men is anxious to engage the enemy. 'Give me a couple of thousand men,' says Lü Chang, 'and I will challenge them by the river.' He denounces Man Chong's weakness in not going out to fight. 'Guan Yu and his men are only halfway across the river. If we attack now we can throw them back.' So, with two thousand men, Lü Chang goes out to attack. No sooner do the men see Guan Yu, riding confidently, sword resting in his arms, than panic breaks out. When Guan Yu charges, Lü Chang's men flee. Half of them died that day.

Seeing how desperate things are, Cao Ren sends urgent requests for help to Chang'an. Cao Cao chooses Yu Jin to go to the defence of Fancheng. He asks for a second in command, and a man stands up and says, 'I want to get rid of Guan Yu. I'll do whatever it takes.'

And who is this man?

Let's find out.

CHAPTER 74

Pang De takes his coffin on campaign with him. Guan Yu drowns seven enemy forces.

It is Pang De who volunteers to join Yu Jin. Cao Cao, pleased at this, then raises seven armies to go into the battle. Some of his commanders approach Yu Jin, questioning the wisdom of appointing Pang De. 'Pang De used to serve Ma Chao, and his own brother is also in the Shu army. How can we trust him?'

When Yu Jin raises this with Cao Cao, he summons Pang De and asks him to hand back his commission. Hurt by this, Pang De says, 'But tomorrow I will show you my loyalty. Why drop me now?'

'I have no problem with you, but others do. They doubt your loyalty, given that Ma Chao is with the Shu and your own brother as well.'

'I've never forgotten how generous you were to me when I surrendered. Not even my life could ever adequately repay you. As for my brother, we fell out many years ago. And Ma Chao? Well, he is certainly brave but he's also a fool!'

Moved by these testimonials, Cao Cao reappoints him and when questioned by Pang De confesses again that he has always believed in his loyalty, but that this needs to be proved to others. Going back to his home, Pang De decides to show his commitment. He has his coffin made and invites friends to come and see it at a banquet he hosts. His guests are somewhat taken aback and ask why, just before going into battle, he has had such an inauspicious thing made. 'I go to fight Guan Yu. If he's not killed by me then I'll have been killed by him. This coffin shows the degree of my determination.'

Later, taking his wife to one side, he tells her that he might well die. She is to bring up their son in order that he can avenge his father. Calling his five hundred men together, he tells them that either they will bring him home in this coffin, or he will use it to bring the head of Guan Yu to Cao Cao.

And then, with his coffin carried before him, he sets out.

When Guan Yu hears about the seven armies closing in on Fancheng, and about Pang De and his coffin, anger turns his face black, and his huge beard shakes with fury. 'The great heroes of our land fear me, so who exactly is this idiot?' to which his son Guan Ping says, 'Father, let me take him on, because it is unseemly that Tai mountain[18] should have to fight a little pebble!'

When the two forces take to the field, Pang De proudly flies his standard – a black flag with his title upon it and with his by now notorious coffins upright beside it. Guan Ping challenges Pang De, and, on hearing that this is Guan Yu's son, Pang De roars, 'I've the special commission of the king of Wei to take the head of your father. You pathetic little man, why, it's hardly worth my while fighting you! Go fetch your father.'

But, undaunted, Guan Ping rides forth, and the two men clash, fighting thirty rounds before both retire exhausted.

Hearing this, Guan Yu rushes to the front and shouts, 'Guan Yu, here. Time for you to die!' Pang De replies, 'I've the commission of the king of Wei to take your head back to Cao Cao, and if you doubt my word, well here is my coffin.'

'You pointless little man! Why would I even blunt my dragon sword on a rat like you?' cries Guan Yu and charges to the attack.

The two men fight over a hundred rounds, but neither prevails. Returning to their own sides, both confess that they have met their equal.

So the next day they ride out to fight again. But after fifty rounds, Pang De turns his horse and flees, with his sword dragging along the ground. Guan Yu pursues him, with his son riding close behind, fearing this is a trick. And it is. Pang De has hooked his sword into his belt, leaving both hands free, and, as he flees, he notches an arrow and, turning in the saddle, shoots Guan Yu, hitting him in the arm. Guan Ping dashes forward to rescue his wounded father. Suddenly Pang De turns to attack, but out of the blue the war gongs of his own side ring out, halting his attack and bringing him back.

Why? Why did Yu Jin stop him? Because of jealousy. He fears that if Pang De triumphs, his fame will far exceed his own. Meanwhile, back in his own camp, Guan Yu's wound is found to not be too serious, but the injury only increases Guan Yu's determination to destroy Pang De. However, his men persuade him to rest long enough for the wound to heal, and so, despite day after day of challenges coming from Pang De, he does not ride out.

After more than ten days of this, Pang De suggests to Yu Jin that this must mean Guan Yu is seriously wounded, and so this is the perfect time to attack the camp. But again, spurred on by jealousy, Yu Jin does the opposite and moves further away from the scene of battle. He even makes Pang De take up the humiliating rearguard position in the camp.

When Guan Yu comes to view the new site of the enemy encampment, he notes with interest that they are camped in low-lying land beside the rushing Xiang River. He is even more delighted to learn that the valley they have camped in is called Fishnet stream. 'This is a sign that we will win,' he says, 'because the fish has entered the trap.'

It is the late autumn of AD 219, and the rains are heavy. As a result the river is swollen. Guan Yu has boats made. He has the river dammed at a number of places and tells his men that by this strategy they will drown the enemy who foolishly have chosen a flood plain for their camp.

Meanwhile, in the rain-soaked camp of Yu Jin, dissent arises, and Cheng He actually goes to tell Yu Jin of the danger they are in from flooding but is dismissed. Confiding in Pang De, who agrees, they plot together.

That very night the assault happens. The released flood water rushes down into the valley. The tidal wave rises over ten feet high and sweeps away many. The leaders, Yu Jin and the others escape, leaving behind their armour and weapons, and climb up to higher ground. From there they see, as the dawn comes, Guan Yu's fleet sweep down the river. Completely overwhelmed, Yu Jin surrenders. Pang De, however, despite having no armour and with only some five hundred men, goes out to fight Guan Yu. Guan Yu, using his archers, pours arrows onto the group as they stand defiant before Guan Yu's army, and most of the men die there and then. Dong Heng and Dong Chao beg Pang De to surrender, but he simply slays both men, shouting his defiance.

Inspired and terrified in equal measure, his men rally to the fight, and the battle grows in intensity. Turning to Cheng He, Pang De says, 'Today I'll die. So let's make this worthwhile and fight to the death. Attack!'

Cheng He does and is almost immediately killed by an arrow fired by Guan Yu, while Pang De, riding on a raft, is knocked into the river and captured by Zhou Cang. As for the seven armies, they are wiped out. As a poet has said:

> It's midnight, and the war drums boom;
> At Fancheng, the dammed river releases.
> Guan Yu's plan defeats the enemy,
> His fame will last ten thousand generations.

When Yu Jin is brought grovelling before him, Guan Yu asks why he opposed him. 'I was just following orders,' says Yu Jin. 'It wasn't my idea. Please be merciful, and I'll serve you for the rest of my life.'

Roaring with laughter, Guan Yu says, 'Why even bother killing you! It would be like killing a dog or a pig. Why blunt a good axe? Take him away and put him in prison in Jingzhou. I'll deal with him later.'

Then Pang De is brought before him. Hatred is visible in every part of his face and body, and he refuses to kneel.

'Your brother is now in Hanzhong, and Ma Chao has been well rewarded, so why don't you surrender as well?'

'You'll have to kill me first,' shouts a defiant Pang De and he pours out curses and contempt at Guan Yu.

Yet, after Pang De is executed, Guan Yu gives him an honourable burial because he is touched by the sheer strength of Pang De's integrity.

The force of the flood has now undermined the walls of Fancheng, and, despite the heroic efforts of its citizens, they start to collapse. All but one of Cao Ren's advisers recommends retreat, fleeing the city before the walls finally cave in and Guan Yu triumphs. But Man Chong stands out against this, pointing out that this is a flash flood. 'Fancheng is the bulwark against which Guan Yu will crash. Let's stay to maintain this strength.'

Cao Ren agrees, making all his commanders swear to fight to the end, and urges on the repair of the walls. After ten days, the waters have indeed retreated.

Guan Yu, meanwhile, has sent his son Guan Xing to Xuande to inform him of the success in capturing Yu Jin. He divides his forces into two, sending one against Jiaxia; the other he leads in a mass attack on Fancheng. Riding up to the north gate, Guan Yu issues a challenge: 'The time has come to surrender, you vermin!' But Cao Ren from the watchtower notices that Guan Yu has only got his breastplate on and that his arms are unprotected. Summoning five hundred archers, he orders them to fire. As the rain of arrows descends upon him Guan Yu turns but not in time. An arrow hits him in the arm, and he tumbles from his horse.

> In the midst of the flood, seven armies fail;
> Yet one shot from the wall, and the leader tumbles.

Can Guan Yu recover?

Let's find out.

CHAPTER 75

Hua Tuo operates on Guan Yu's arm as he plays chess. Lü Meng sails to the capture of Jingzhou.

Seeing Guan Yu fall, Cao Ren charges out of the city, but too late. Guan Ping has come to the rescue of his father and defends him against further attacks until he is safely back in the camp. There, it is clear that the arrow was poisoned and that infection has spread rapidly. Being Guan Yu, he refuses both treatment and the proposal that they retreat so he can rest. Knowing that if Guan Yu dies, the troops will lose all hope, the best possible medical treatment is sought. But there is no one skilled enough to deal with such poison. Until, that is, out of the blue, a boat from the south sails in, and out of it steps Hua Tuo, the famous doctor.

By now Guan Yu is in real pain and only too aware that his death will undermine all that he has achieved. To keep his mind off the agony, he plays chess, and it is there that Hua Tuo finds him and examines the wound.

'I can save the arm but only if I operate on it. But you'll probably find the surgery too painful.'

'Look,' says Guan Yu, 'for me death is going home. Have no worries about me.'

'To operate successfully,' says Hua Tuo, 'I'll need a quiet room and a pillar with a looped rope through it through which you will place your arm so we can secure it. I'll also need to cover your head with a blanket. Then I will cut through the flesh until I hit the bone, scrape the infection off the bone and then sew the arm up. This will cure you, but I doubt if you can stand such pain.'

'That's it, is it?' says Guan Yu. 'Then get on with it here and now and forget about pillars and ropes and other such nonsense.'

So the operation takes place while Guan Yu continues his game of chess, eating and drinking as if nothing is happening. His own officers nearly faint when they hear the knife scraping the infection off the bone itself, but Guan Yu shows no emotion whatsoever. As soon as the wound is sewn up, Guan Yu stands up and, flexing his arm, says, 'Good as new! And what was all that about pain? I felt nothing! You, sir, are a wonderful doctor.'

'I have done many operations but never have I seen anything like this! You, sir, are frankly a superhuman!'

Hugely grateful, Guan Yu offers gold to Hua Tuo, who refuses, saying, 'I need no reward. I came because of your high reputation for virtue. But you should now rest for a hundred days, and here is a prescription for you to apply to the wound.' And so saying, he leaves. And as far as Guan Yu is concerned, he is ready for war again.

Meanwhile, Cao Cao is reeling from the defection of Yu Jin and the death of Pang De. Summoning his advisers, he asks them, given the recent bout of disasters, what he should do, even suggesting that they should abandon the capital.

Sima Yi says, 'Don't be too depressed by what has passed. There is conflict between Xuande and Sun Quan, and we need to exploit this. Send an emissary to Sun Quan offering him the whole of the south so that he'll move against Jingzhou behind Guan Yu's back. He'll have to turn back, and that way you save Fancheng.'

So it is agreed and having despatched the letter to Sun Quan he appoints Xu Huang as commander and Lü Jian as his second to go to oppose any further advances by Guan Yu.

When Sun Quan receives the letter, he summons his advisers. Zhang Zhao is deeply suspicious of Cao Cao's motives, pointing out that the Wei are faltering. 'Why, they are even discussing abandoning the capital,' he says. 'This is just a trick to divert us from attacking them and to get us instead to help them out by attacking Xuande.' Before Sun Quan can reply, news comes that Lü Meng has arrived from the city of Lukou. The news he brings is that Guan Yu is off attacking Fancheng and that therefore this is the perfect time to attack and take Jingzhou. That ends the discussion as far as Sun Quan is concerned. The decision is made to seize Jingzhou while Guan Yu is away. Lü Meng is given authorization to prepare the plan of attack, while Sun Quan will follow on soon with the rest of the army.

Arriving back at Lukou, Lü Meng is informed of the system of beacons that Guan Yu has established to give warning of exactly the sort of attack he is planning. He is also told that Jingzhou itself is well staffed and defended. The news profoundly alarms Lü Meng and, unable to imagine how to overcome such odds and fearful of having made promises to Sun Quan he cannot fulfil, he takes to his bed, pretending to be ill.

When news of Lü Meng's 'illness' reaches Sun Quan, he is naturally concerned. But Lu Xun tells him he is sure this is just an act and so he is sent to investigate. As he walks into Lü Meng's bedroom, he can see it is indeed just an act. He also knows that this is due to fear brought on because of the scale of the task of capturing Jingzhou. Lu Xun reassures him, telling him he knows how to cure this 'illness'. He has a plan for overcoming the beacons and for seizing Jingzhou. Overcome with joy at this news, Lü Meng asks Lu Xun to tell him his plan.

'We need to fool Guan Yu. His only concern is you, so we need to lull him into a false sense of security. Let it be known that you've resigned for reasons of ill health. Then we need to have someone appointed who'll appear to be in awe of Guan Yu and who loads him with gifts and praise, appealing to his pride and arrogance. This will make him feel secure and lure him into pulling back from any defence of Jingzhou. Then in we go and seize the prize.'

Having agreed the plan, Lu Xun apprises Sun Quan of the plot. Sun formally summons Lü Meng back to the court 'for health reasons' and appoints Lu Xun to be the flattering flunkey who will fool Guan Yu. Arriving in Lukou, Lu Xun writes a fulsome letter of praise to Guan Yu and despatches it with a surfeit of expensive gifts. When the letter and gifts are delivered to Guan Yu, he seems truly delighted, and this is duly reported back to a very pleased Lu Xun. His spies tell him that Guan Yu has indeed been fooled and has moved his troops to the siege of Fancheng. Here, he is biding his time until his wound has fully recovered before launching his assault. When news of this reaches Sun Quan, he commissions Lü Meng to lead the attack on Jingzhou. Taking with him thirty thousand soldiers and eighty attack ships, he sets off.

As his fleet approaches the area controlled by Guan Yu, he disguises some of his soldiers as merchants and hides the rest of his troops in the holds of the ships. Letters are sent to Cao Cao, advising him to attack Guan Yu, and to Lu Xun, to keep him abreast of the developments. Then the ships head for the Xunyang river, travelling night and day to get there as quickly as possible.

When they land on the north shore where the line of beacons starts, they are, of course, stopped by Guan Yu's men. But the latter are convinced they are just merchants and wave them through. That night, the troops hidden in the holds emerge and silently and very effectively overwhelm the men guarding the shore and the beacons. Not a soldier escapes. All are captured. Not a word is spoken. Not a single beacon is lit.

Sailing on down, they come close to Jiangling. As they approach, Lü Meng persuades the captured men to fall in with his plan and to be willing to fool their compatriots guarding the city gates into letting them in. Once inside, they are to set fires to cause maximum confusion and to act as a signal for the rest of the troops to attack.

Late at night, the men arrive at the gate and call up. They are recognized, and the gates are opened to them. Once inside, they set fires, and before dawn the city is in the hands of Lü Meng. To ensure the loyalty of the ordinary people, Lü Meng gives the strictest of instructions that nothing is to be taken from any of the citizens, nor are any to be harmed. Later, Lü Meng sees one of his soldiers wearing a rain cloak and hat which clearly have been stolen and, despite the pleas of the man that due to the terrible rain that day he just wanted to keep his armour dry, he is executed. His head is stuck on a pole for public display to instil fear and awe in the soldiers so that they kept to this strict discipline. Lü Meng does later give the man a decent burial and even weeps, but his point has been made.

Almost immediately after the city's capture, Sun Quan arrives with his vast army. With the Jingzhou region now in their control, they turn their thoughts to how to consolidate these triumphs and take Gong'an and Nanjun. Gong'an is controlled by Fu Shiren, and Nanjun by Mi Fang.

It is Yu Fan who offers the way forward, pointing out that neither man is enamoured of Guan Yu after their dramatic dressing down and punishment by him. Offer them escape from the control of Guan Yu and they might well jump at the opportunity.

When Fu Shiren receives the proposal that he surrender – by an arrow fired over his city walls – he thinks back to when he was disgraced by Guan Yu. In the light of that, he decides his future lies elsewhere. He opens the city gates and with Yu Fan takes the keys of the city to Sun Quan. Initially Sun Quan thinks to reappoint him as governor of Gong'an. But then wiser voices suggest that, if Guan Yu came back to attack the city, Fu Shiren might well betray his new master. Instead they send him off to Nanjun to persuade his old friend and fellow victim of Guan Yu's wrath, Mi Fang, to change sides.

Is he successful?

Well, let's find out.

CHAPTER 76

Xu Huang fights Guan Yu. Guan Yu retreats.

In Nanjun, the governor Mi Fang has heard all the disastrous news of the fall of Jiangling. What he does not expect is that his old friend Fu Shiren would turn up and tell him personally of his defection. 'I'm no traitor but I had no choice. The odds against me were too great. So I surrendered to Wu. I would urge you to consider doing the same.'

'I cannot betray the king of Hanzhong,' Mi Fang says.

'Guan Yu has hardly earned our undying loyalty,' Fu Shiren says, recalling his whipping of them. 'If he triumphs, then things will not go well for us – he is unlikely to forget or forgive.'

'But my brother and I, we have served the king for many years,' says Mi Fang, 'and I can't just stop being loyal.'

At that moment a messenger arrives from Guan Yu demanding that the two cities provide huge quantities of rice for the army. Fu Shiren immediately kills the messenger, to the horrified astonishment of Mi Fang.

'Why did you do that?' he demands.

'This is all a plot by Guan Yu to have us killed,' exclaims Fu Shiren. Suddenly they are informed that Lü Meng is advancing on the city. Fear of this finally persuades Mi Fang, who surrenders the city to a delighted Lü Meng.

Back in Xuchang, Cao Cao receives Sun Quan's letter outlining the attack on Jingzhou and asking for Cao Cao to join the attack on Guan Yu.

It is Dong Zhao who proposes that they let the defenders of Fancheng know they are coming and at the same time let Guan Yu find out that they are planning to attack Jingzhou. 'Guan

Yu will pull back for fear of losing Jingzhou and we send Xu Huang to take him out.'

Orders are sent, and Cao Cao himself sets out with a huge army.

No sooner has Xu Huang received his orders and been told that he should advance on Fancheng and confront Guan Yu than a spy reports in. 'Guan Ping is camped at Yancheng and Liao Hua is camped at Sizhong,' he says. 'Between them are twelve forts, which makes it very easy for them to communicate with each other.' Immediately Xu Huang despatches troops to confront Guan Ping at Yancheng. They are to fly his colours, making Guan Ping believe that Xu Huang is with them. Meanwhile, Xu Huang actually takes five hundred crack troops and moves towards Yancheng from the opposite direction.

The ploy works. Lured out to the attack, Guan Ping is drawn into a trap only to then see flames rising from Yancheng. Xu Huang himself rides to challenge Guan Ping, shouting out that Jingzhou has also fallen to the Wu. Their clash is brief, because it becomes clear to Guan Ping that Yancheng is about to fall. Having lost his base, he slashes a path through the enemy towards the second base at Sizhong. There, Liao Hua asks if it is true that Jingzhou has fallen. 'That is a lie. Execute anyone spreading such a rumour,' says Guan Ping. At that moment news comes that Xu Huang is attacking the camp to the north of Yancheng. 'If that falls, the forts will fall also,' says Guan Ping. 'This position, defended by the River Mian is safe, so let's go and relieve the northern camp.'

Sure that Sizhong is safe due to its formidable defences and leaving Liao Hua to hold it, Guan Ping sets off to rebuff the attack of Xu Huang on the northern camp.

When night falls, Guan Ping and his men attack the north camp – only to find not a soul there. Realizing too late that this is a trap, they are suddenly surprised by an attack by Xu Shang and Lü Jian. Guan Ping and his men flee, but many die in the conflict. Heading towards Sizhong, they are astonished and horrified to see that camp on fire and the whole encampment in the hands of the Wei army. Only by the skin of their teeth do Guan Ping and Liao Hua escape and make it back to where Guan Yu is based.

There, they report the collapse of their defence and the seizure of Yancheng and the camps. They also have to pass on the news that Cao Cao is advancing on Fancheng and that Lü Meng has taken Jingzhou. Guan Yu reacts angrily, denouncing the news about Jingzhou. 'That is nothing but a lie!' he roars. 'Lü Meng is ill, and this is just some inexperienced youth called Lu Xun. Nothing to worry about – do you understand?'

At that moment news comes that Xu Huang has arrived to confront him. Guan Yu calls for his horse.

'You're still too weak, father,' pleads Guan Ping, but to no avail. Guan Yu rides out to challenge Xu Huang.

'Where are you, Xu Huang?' shouts a fearsome-looking Guan Yu.

In response Xu Huang rides out and bows. 'My lord,' he says, 'it's been a long time since we last met. And your hair and beard have gone grey! Yet I do fondly remember our years of adventure together and what you taught me then. And now here we are again.'

Moved by these affectionate words, Guan Yu remonstrates with Xu Huang.

'Our friendship is indeed strong, so why have you attacked my son so violently?'

To this Xu Huang responds by turning to his commanders and saying, 'A thousand pieces of gold to the man who can bring me his head!'

'My friend, I can hardly believe that you would say this,' says an alarmed Guan Yu.

'Because today I'm here on official imperial business, not for sentimental personal reasons!' And so saying, Xu Huang swings into action, and the duel is on. For eighty bouts the two men fight, until Guan Yu begins to feel his right arm growing weak. Just as he starts to withdraw, a cacophony of sound erupts all around them. Cao Ren, knowing that his father is coming with a relief force, has charged out of the city and joined forces with Xu Huang. The result is a catastrophic defeat for Guan Yu and his men. Guan Yu only just manages to escape and, riding hell for leather, he heads towards Xiangyang, only to be told that Jiangling has fallen and that his whole family are now in the control of Lü Meng.

In a state of desperation, and realizing that Xiangyang is no longer viable as a place of refuge, he turns towards Gong'an, only to be told that Gong'an has been surrendered by Fu Shiren. This is immediately followed by news that the messenger he sent to Nanjun has been murdered, and Mi Fang has surrendered Nanjun to Cao Cao.

This final catastrophic piece of news is too much for Guan Yu, whose rage makes his wound burst open again. He collapses in a faint on the ground. After he has been revived, his trusted adviser Wang Fu, who advised against this course of action, urges that they send to Chengdu for reinforcements while they set out to try to take back Jiangling. Guan Yu agrees, and messengers are sent to Chengdu asking for help. Meanwhile, Guan Yu sets off for Jiangling with Guan Ping and Liao Hua to support him.

Cao Cao's arrival has lifted the siege of Fancheng. Cao Ren comes before his father, mortified that he has had to summon him. 'This is the destiny set by Heaven – not by you,' his father says.

By now Guan Yu has run out of places to find safety because he now knows Jiangling has fallen. He is caught between the Wei and Wu forces. He is advised to write urgently to Lü Meng, now ensconced in Jingzhou, reminding him that once they were on the same side in the struggle against Cao Cao and suggesting that they become allies again.

Back in Jingzhou, Lü Meng has given orders that the families of all the commanders under Guan Yu and of course Guan Yu's own family are to be treated with respect and taken good care of. When the letter arrives from Guan Yu, the families gather round the messenger, asking for information about their loved ones and handing over letters or sending messages back to the commanders saying all is well with them. Meanwhile, Lü Meng politely turns down the request from Guan Yu. When Guan Yu receives this news he roars with anger and frustration, vowing vengeance upon Lü Meng, and then gruffly dismisses the messenger. Going outside, the messenger is mobbed by men wanting to know how their families are. The letters and oral reports he gives move and trouble them. As a result, they begin to question why they should go on fighting.

Guan Yu blazes with anger and swears, 'I'll kill Lü Meng, either in this life or after I'm dead!' The news, however, begins to affect the army. As Guan Yu marches resolutely towards Jingzhou, whenever the opportunity arises, men slip away. When he realizes this is happening, Guan Yu's anger grows and grows. Skirmishes take place – all of which he loses. Eventually he is attacked in a valley into which he has been driven. Not only are his officers falling one by one to the combined assault, but, egged on by locals, the local Jingzhou troops desert him. Soon he is left with no more than three hundred men.

Just when there seems to be no hope left, a great cry goes up. Guan Ping and Liao Hua break through the encircling enemy and rescue Guan Yu. But the situation is still desperate. Chaos is all around; the men are deserting and running amok. The small band around Guan Yu retreats to the minor town of Maicheng. They seal the four gates and decide to send for reinforcements from Shangyong, where Liu Feng and Meng Da are based. As the enemy take up positions around Maicheng to besiege it, Liao Hua is able to slip through and ride hell for leather to Shangyong to get help.

'Guan Yu is trapped at Maicheng, and it'll be a long time before troops from Shu can arrive. This is why I've been sent to you. We need your help. Even the slightest hesitation on your behalf will spell doom for Guan Yu.'

After Liao Hua has gone to rest, Liu Feng and Meng Da sit down to discuss this.

'My uncle,' says Liu Feng, 'is seriously in trouble, so what should we do?'

To this Meng Da replies, 'The Wu have formidable armies and brave commanders, and now they hold all of Jingzhou, leaving Guan Yu with just little Maicheng. On top of this, Cao Cao is advancing with four to five hundred thousand men. What earthly use is our little army here, caught between two great enemy forces? I don't think we should take any risks.'

'Sound advice,' says Liu Feng, 'but he is my uncle. Seriously, I can't just do nothing.'

'Your uncle!' snorts Meng Da. 'You might think so, but he doesn't treat you as a nephew should be trusted, does he? Rumour has it that Guan Yu was very annoyed when you were adopted by Xuande. When Guan Yu was asked about this, he said he was opposed to an adopted son being made heir apparent and suggested you be sent off to rule somewhere remote and irrelevant. So why trouble yourself about him when this uncle-nephew thing doesn't seem to matter to him?'

'But how do I get out of this?'

'Simple,' says Meng Da. 'Say you've only just secured this town and that we cannot just rush off before we have gained the confidence of the locals.' And to this Liu Feng agrees.

So the next day they bring Liao Hua in to see them and inform him that they will not be sending any troops due to their own precarious position. Mortified, Liao Hua pleads, but to no avail.

'Even if we were to go, it would be like throwing a glass of water on a blazing wagon. You'll just have to wait until the Shu troops arrive.'

Seeing he is getting nowhere with these two, Liao Hua roars his disapproval and sets off for Chengdu instead.

Back in Maicheng, Guan Yu waits in vain for sight of the relief column. With so few men and so many wounded, the odds are stacked against him. Before the city gate appears Zhuge Jin, asking for an audience, and he is admitted.

'I come at the express command of Sun Quan,' he says to Guan Yu. 'You've lost everything except for this meagre place. It'll fall either tonight or tomorrow. So why don't you face reality and surrender to the lord of the south, and soon you'll be put back in control? This will save your family as well.'

'I'm but a simple warrior,' replies Guan Yu, 'but I had the fortune to become a brother of my lord. There is no way I can betray him. If the town falls, I die. Jade may break, but that it is white cannot be changed. Bamboo will burn, but the joints remain. A man may die, but his name will resound for generations. Go now. This will be finished between Sun Quan and myself.'

Zhuge Jin tries other means of persuasion, but this only causes Guan Ping to draw his sword and threaten to kill him. He is stopped by a wave of his hand by his father. Shortly after, Zhuge Jin is driven from the town.

Returning flushed with anger and embarrassment, Zhuge Jin informs Sun Quan that Guan Yu will not surrender.

'Well, that's real loyalty. So what do we do next?' asks Sun Quan.

Lü Fan recommends that they consult the *Yi Jing*, and this they do. The answer given is 'Master with the Earth above Water.' This is taken to mean an enemy will flee far, far away. 'If this is so,' says Sun Quan, 'how do we capture him?'

Lü Meng replies, 'This prediction is perfect. Guan Yu may have wings from Heaven, but we've nets to catch him!'

It is said:

A dragon down in a puddle can be teased by a shrimp;
A phoenix in a cage can be mocked by little birds.

So what is Lü Meng's plan to capture Guan Yu?

Let's find out.

CHAPTER 77

Guan Yu is executed, and his ghost visits Jade Spring Buddhist temple. Cao Cao and Xuande are both visited by Guan Yu's ghost, and Cao Cao collapses.

It is very simple. Lü Meng recommends to Sun Quan that they attack Maicheng on all sides except the north. This will mean that Guan Yu will try to escape through the north gate. All they need to do next is set two traps on the narrow country road that leads out of the north gate. So Zhu Ran takes up position with five thousand crack troops a few miles beyond the north gate. Meanwhile, a second trap is set up under the command of Pan Zhang a few miles further on with another five thousand. Having consulted the *Yi Jing* again, the hexagram says that the enemy will flee northwest, and so, assured of success, Sun Quan sets the plan in motion.

Back at Maicheng, Guan Yu is counting his forces. He has only about three hundred – that includes both cavalry and infantry. The food is running out, and men are still slipping away at night. Turning to his adviser Wang Fu, who had advised against this campaign, he bursts into tears, regretting deeply that he ignored his advice. 'With no help coming from Shangyong because of the betrayal of Liu Feng and Meng Da, there really is no other option but flight,' says his commander, Zhao Lei, with which Guan Yu concurs. Surveying the siege, he notices that the north gate is the obvious one to break out of. But Wang Fu points out, 'The road north is through mountain passes – perfect for ambushes.' But Guan Yu with bravado says, 'That doesn't scare me!' and prepares to charge forth, leaving just one hundred men with Wang Fu to hold the town until help can arrive.

So, with just two hundred men, Guan Yu, Guan Ping and Zhao Lei surge out of the north gate at the dead of night, ready for action. Having gone unchallenged for a few miles north, they are suddenly attacked by Zhu Ran. But when he is attacked by Guan Yu, he flees north, drawing the party on. Now Guan Yu has not gone far when more of Zhu Ran's men suddenly charge. Seeing no way forward, Guan Yu turns and gallops off down a minor road towards Linju. Zhu Ran overwhelms the rearguard and rides off after the fleeing Guan Yu.

Charging ahead, Guan Yu runs into the second ambush set by Pan Zhang. Guan Yu's valiant attacks soon force him to flee. But by now Guan Yu is exhausted. Riding hard, he is reunited with Guan Ping, who has been defending the rear. He has to report that Zhao Lei has been killed. Weary and worn down by sorrow, Guan Yu rides on with no more than a dozen men still with him.

It is as they enter a very narrow valley that the end comes. Overgrown with bushes and long grass, this desolate place is where, as dawn begins to appear, they are attacked for the third time. On this occasion, they are attacked with grappling hooks and nets set there by Ma Zhong. Guan Yu's mighty steed, Red Hare, is brought crashing down, and Guan Yu is thrown to the ground. Bravely Guan Ping rides to his father's rescue, but it's no good. He fights on until he has no strength left, desperately trying to reach and free his father. Exhausted at last, he too is captured. Both men, father and son, are now prisoners of the Wu.

When they are brought before Sun Quan, he says:

'I've for so long admired your outstanding virtues. You'll recall I tried to forge an alliance between us through marriage, so why did you reject this? For some reason you've believed you were irreplaceable. Yet here you are, now my prisoner. How is that, eh? Will you now surrender to me?'

'You foreigner-eyed bastard! You purple-bearded rat! My allegiance was given to my brothers in the peach orchard covenant. There we swore to support the Han dynasty, so why would I join a treacherous bunch of traitors like you? Yes, you've caught me – my fault. So now there is nothing left but to die. That is all there is to say.'

Sun Quan asks his assembled advisers what he should do. 'He is someone I have admired, a hero of our times. I think we should treat him well so that he'll eventually join us. But what do you all say?'

It is Zuo Xian who speaks. 'There is no point in trying that. Remember that Cao Cao piled honours upon him when he was his captive. He feasted him weekly, gave him gold and silver at every opportunity. And what happened? When Guan Yu left, he slew the guards at every pass, and Cao Cao is so frightened of him he is planning to abandon his capital and move somewhere beyond Guan Yu's reach. Kill him now, or who knows what will befall us?'

Sun Quan contemplates these words for a while and then orders the execution of both father and son. They are beheaded in the winter of AD 220. Guan Yu is fifty-eight years old. As the poet has said:

For a truly noble man, look no further than Jieliang,
For everyone there honours Guan Yu of the Han.
One day in the peach orchard he sealed his brother-bond,
For a thousand years now, imperial offerings are made.
Throughout the world, their fame spreads like a wind or
storm,
And shining like the sun or moon at midday.
Today shrines to this hero are everywhere,
Ancient the great trees; the home of countless crows.

Red Hare, his mighty horse, is captured at the same time and presented as a gift to Sun Quan. But that noble horse refuses to eat after the death of his master and within a few days has gone to join him.

The heads of the two Guans are borne to Maicheng and displayed to Wang Fu and Zhou Cang. As they stare down at the awful sight they are challenged to surrender the town. But, the night before, Wang Fu had a nightmare in which Guan Yu had appeared to him, covered in blood. Distraught beyond words, Wang Fu throws himself to his death from the walls, and Zhou Cang slits his own throat. So it comes to pass that Maicheng too falls to the forces of the south.

However, Guan Yu's tormented soul does not disperse. Instead, it drifts until it comes to rest on Jade Spring mountain in Jingmenzhou, in the County of Dangyang. Here an old Buddhist monk lives whose religious name is Pujing. He was once the abbot of an official state temple in Zhenguo, near the Si River gateway. He then wandered across the land until he came to the mountain. Its natural glory astonished him, and he built a simple dwelling there. Here, he meditates every day on the truth of the Dao. He has but one novice with him, and they survive on the food they are given as alms.

On the night Guan Yu dies, with a pale moon shining, there comes a cool breeze, and then in the depths of the night the monk hears a voice crying, 'Give me back my head!' Looking up, he sees a man riding a horse – Red Hare – and wielding a mighty sword – Green Dragon. Beside him are two other men, a general with a fair complexion and another with a very dark complexion and fearsome whiskers. All three descend, hovering above Jade Spring mountain. Pujing realizes that this must be Guan Yu and performs a ritual of protection. He then asks, 'Where is Guan Yu?'

The brave but tormented spirit of Guan Yu floats down to stand before Pujing. Bowing in the proper Buddhist way, he asks, 'What is your name, master, your Buddhist name?'

'My name is Pujing, and we met long ago at the Zhenguo temple.[19] Have you forgotten?'

'The memory of your kindness is indelibly marked on my memory,' replies the spirit of Guan Yu. 'A terrible disaster has come upon me, and I've been murdered. I need your wise words so that you can point out my way forward in this time of distress.'

To this, Pujing replies, 'What you did or didn't do in the past is now of no significance. The karma that has accrued through these actions will determine your fate. You now cry out for your head, but what of the heads of the many, many you have killed, such as the six guards at the passes. Who will find their heads?'

At these wise but tough words, the spirit bows in honour of the Buddha's teaching about karma and vanishes.

However, he often returns to Jade Spring mountain and takes to performing acts which help protect the ordinary folk of the area. As a result, the people, moved by such virtue, build a temple on the mountain. A poem is written on the walls of the temple.

> Ruddy face, reflecting a constant heart
> Faster than the wind on Red Hare!
> Always mindful of the Red emperor.
>
> By lamplight, studying the classic histories,
> In battle, bearing the Dragon Sword,
> His innermost thoughts as clear as the sky itself.

With Guan Yu out of the way, nothing now stands between Sun Quan and complete control of the Jingzhou region. To celebrate the main victory in the campaigns, he holds a feast and honours Lü Meng for his services. At the high point of the celebration he hands Lü Meng the cup of honour. Lü Meng takes it but then in a violent move dashes the cup to the ground. Lunging forward, he grabs hold of Sun Quan and cries out aloud, 'You foreigner-eyed bastard! You purple-bearded rat! Don't you know who I am?' Throwing Sun Quan to the ground, the possessed Lü Meng climbs on to the throne and shouts, 'Having fought my way across the land against the Yellow Headbands for thirty years, have I fought only to fall victim to your ambush? While alive, I was unable to devour you, Lü Meng, but your soul will find no peace in death, for I am Guan Yu!'

Stunned and terrified by this, Sun Quan and all the others present bow as in prayer, until suddenly Lü Meng falls to the ground dead, with blood pouring out of his mouth and nose. Horror and confusion overwhelm everyone, and even after the funeral, when things calm down, Sun Quan is deeply troubled at what he has done in having Guan Yu executed.

This is brought home even more when Zhang Zhao points out that, due to their oath taken in the peach orchard, Xuande is bound to seek revenge and that now he controls Shu he has a vast army at his command.

'This was a terrible mistake. What is to be done?' asks an agonized Sun Quan.

Zhang Zhao has a plan. He suggests divide and rule. 'Cao Cao has an army of a million, and if he unites with Xuande the south is doomed,' he says. 'But let us send the head of Guan Yu to Cao Cao, so that it will seem to Xuande that this was done at his express command. He'll then attack the north, and we can watch and see from the safety of the sidelines.'

So the plan is put into motion. Guan Yu's head is put in a special box and delivered to Cao Cao. Hearing of the death of Guan Yu, Cao Cao comments that he will now sleep well at night, but Sima Yi is not so sure he should be so sanguine.

'This is a trick to divert disaster from the south onto us,' he says.

'What on earth are you talking about?' asks Cao Cao.

'Xuande and his two brothers swore to live and die as one. Sun Quan now fears that his actions will draw the wrath of Xuande down upon him. So he sends you the head so that Xuande's fury will be diverted against you instead!'

'Well, well. Good point,' says Cao Cao. 'So what do we do?'

'Have a body created out of wood and put Guan Yu's head on it and give it full military honours and burial. This shifts the blame back to Sun Quan, so Xuande will attack Wu. Then we can wait and see. If Shu is winning, we attack Wu. If Wu is winning, we attack Shu!'

Cao Cao is delighted with this plan and orders the box be brought to him. Opening it, he sees that the face of Guan Yu looks exactly as it did in life. Teasingly he asks the head, 'I hope you've been keeping well since we last met!' But as he speaks the mouth opens, the eyes roll around, and the hair on the head and beard stands upright! Cao Cao collapses in a faint. 'Guan Yu's no mere mortal!' he says on coming round, and when he hears of what happened to Lü Meng he orders the grandest ceremony. With every official in the city attending, he buries Guan Yu outside the walls of Luoyang with the fullest of ritual observance.

Back in Shu, Xuande has remarried – a marriage that brings two more children – and the populace is at peace. The terrible news from the east comes through in dribs and drabs. First, the news that Wu has offered a marriage alliance to Guan

Yu – upon which Kong Ming comments, 'Jingzhou will fall.' Next, Guan Xing, Guan Yu's oldest son, arrives to tell of Guan Yu's triumph over the seven armies through the flooding trick. Then news comes of the establishment of the chain of beacons. This reassures Xuande that all is in order.

A few days later, Xuande is unable to sleep. Sitting in his inner room, he collapses in a faint on the table. The candle blows out and then relights itself as a cold wind blows through the room. Lifting his head up, Xuande can see the shape of a man in the light of the candle. 'Who are you that you dare come to my room in the middle of the night?' he demands. But answer comes there none. Suddenly Xuande realizes that it is Guan Yu, wandering back and forth. 'My dear brother, how have you been since we last met?' asks Xuande. 'There must be some trouble that brings you here like this in the middle of the night. Come, we are brothers, so why are you being evasive?'

Weeping, Guan Yu replies, 'My dear brother, I beg you to take an army and avenge me', and, so saying, he disappears. Horrified, Xuande summons Kong Ming, who tries to reassure him that this is simply because he is worried about Guan Yu.

As Kong Ming returns to his quarters, Xu Jing arrives to say that Lü Meng has taken Jingzhou and that Guan Yu is dead. 'Sadly I'm not surprised,' says Kong Ming, 'because I saw a military star fall over Jingzhou last night, and so I knew that Guan Yu was no more. But we must try to keep this from Xuande.' However, Xuande has overheard this and shouts, 'Why did you try to keep this terrible news from me?' 'But it could just be rumours,' replies a flustered Kong Ming. Then Ma Liang and Yi Ji arrive to report the fall of Jingzhou and Guan Yu's plea for help. But hot on their heels comes Liao Hua, who, with tears flowing, reports how Liu Feng and Meng Da refused to come to Guan Yu's aid.

Horrified, Xuande says, 'Then there is no hope for my brother.'

'Death is too good for such traitors,' says Kong Ming. 'Be reassured, my lord, I'll take an army and take back Jingzhou.'

But Xuande cannot be consoled, crying out that he cannot bear the thought of life without his brother and that he himself will lead the attack. A messenger is sent to inform the other brother, Zhang Fei, of what has happened.

As the day breaks the final round of news comes in. The fall of Jingzhou; Guan Yu's flight; his capture; his loyalty; and his death alongside his son. On hearing all this, Xuande cries aloud a keening cry and collapses.

What will happen next to Xuande?

Let's find out.

CHAPTER 78

Hua Tuo treats Cao Cao but is killed.
Cao Cao dies.

Xuande, overcome by sadness, collapses on the ground, and those around rush to help him. He is so racked by distress that it takes them some time to help him to his rooms, but eventually they get him there. 'My lord,' says Kong Ming, 'you must overcome your grief. As of old, the Way has always said, "Life and death are determined by fate." Guan Yu brought this upon himself by his arrogance. What you must do, my lord, is to protect your health and begin to plan revenge.'

'With Guan Yu and Zhang Fei I took an oath of loyalty in the peach orchard. We vowed to die together. Now he's gone, of what use is anything?'

Throughout the rest of the day, Xuande's distress causes him to collapse time and time again and to cry so violently that blood flows from his mouth. For three days he refuses to eat or drink.

'I vow that I will never live under the same sun or moon as the Wu.'

Kong Ming brings him the news as it comes in of the machinations of Sun Quan. Of how he sent the head of Guan Yu to Cao Cao, and how Cao Cao saw through this and provided full honours for the burial. 'So this means you need only seek vengeance on Sun Quan and Wu,' says Kong Ming.

'So let's prepare now to go and wreak our revenge on them,' says Xuande, to which Kong Ming says, 'Wait. Wait until you've held the funeral and watch to see if the partnership between north and south breaks down. Then it will be time to attack.'

Despite having performed all the appropriate rites, Cao Cao is still troubled by the spirit of Guan Yu. Seeking to understand why, he is told that the old palace is now haunted and that he should therefore build a new one. Plans are drawn up, but the scale of the new main hall requires trees of great length and strength, of which there appear to be none available. Not until someone mentions that beside the nearby Leaping Dragon Pool there is a temple, in front of which grows a huge pear tree over a hundred feet tall, which would do perfectly.

So men are sent off to cut it down, but, try as they will, using whatever tools they can, they can't even dent its trunk. Not believing their reports, Cao Cao leads a whole troop of men to cut the tree down, but, as they approach, local leaders come pleading that he spare the tree. 'It's many hundreds of years old, and a deity lives in it.'

'For over forty years no one – neither emperor nor commoner – has dared challenge me. So what is this deity that dares to do so?'

So saying, he slashes at the tree with his sword. To his astonishment, the sword bounces off with a sound of metal on metal, and from the wound blood spurts out onto Cao Cao, who throws his sword aside, leaps on his horse and flees in horror.

Later that night, Cao Cao cannot sleep. Suddenly there, standing before him, is a man, dressed in black, hair on end, holding a sword. He rushes at Cao Cao, shrieking, 'I am the deity of the pear tree. I know that you want to build a great hall as part of your plot to overthrow the dynasty. That's why you dare to attack a sacred tree. Your days are numbered, and I've come to kill you!'

Panic-stricken, Cao Cao calls desperately for his guards, but the black figure raises his sword and strikes him. With a terrified scream, Cao Cao awakes, an unbearable pain in his head. Doctors are summoned, but none can help.

Eventually, Hua Xin suggests calling in the famous doctor Hua Tuo, who cured Zhou Tai. He is summoned but in the process of telling Cao Cao his methods, and that to cure him he will need to cut open his skull, he mentions curing Guan Yu. This is disastrous for Hua Tuo, for Cao Cao is convinced that he has come to exact revenge for Guan Yu and has him imprisoned. Despite the kindly help of the prison warden, he dies shortly after.

It is said that Hua Tuo knew the cure for all illnesses and

wrote these down in a great book – *The Black Bag Book*. He had this brought and given as a gift to the warder who tried to help him. Sadly, the wife of this warder used the precious manuscript to light a fire, which is why almost none of his cures have come down to this day. As a poet said:

Hua Tuo was the greatest of physicians,
Able to discern the very spirit within a person.
What a tragedy his words were lost so casually,
The Black Bag Book is burned; we cannot get it back.

The death of Hua Tuo causes Cao Cao's sickness to worsen. A letter arrives from Sun Quan personally, full of flattery, and urging him to seize the throne. 'This is clearly the Will of Heaven and Earth. If you will attack Xuande,' says the letter, 'I will bring Wu in submission to Your Imperial Highness.'

Cao Cao laughs aloud at the presumption and pomposity of the letter and is all for dismissing it. But others add their voices, saying the Han rule is clearly at an end and that, 'with your being so renowned for virtue, everyone looks to you. Sun Quan's letter just confirms that all are awaiting your decision – all the signs point towards this. Be at one with the Will of Heaven and with what the people want.'

'I've been a loyal servant of the Han for years and through this the people have benefited,' reflects Cao Cao. 'Being made king of Wei was enough for me, but if the Mandate of Heaven is to come to me, then I must become like rulers of old such as King Wen of the Zhou.'[20]

But he grows steadily worse and worse as his illness advances.

One night, he dreams of three horses eating from the same trough. When he describes this dream to Jia Xu, he tells him that they are a sign of good luck.[21]

As a poet has said:

Three horses feed from the same trough, troubling him;
But he doesn't see the impending Jin dynasty.
What point is there now to Cao's triumphs?
From the centre of his world, Sima is rising.

Then comes a night of anguish. In the depths of the night he feels dizzy. He rises and goes to rest his head on a table, when suddenly a terrible sound makes him sit bolt upright. Coming towards him are the ghosts of the two queens he has murdered, Empress Fu and Lady Dong; the two imperial sons; and many, many others whom he has had killed. Dripping with blood, they cry out for his life. Grabbing his sword, he tries to cut them down, and at that moment the southwest corner of the hall collapses. Cao Cao collapses too.

The following night he hears nothing but the cries of men and women beyond the walls. When morning comes, he calls together his advisers and says, 'Through thirty years of warfare I've paid no attention to so-called supernatural events and beings. But what does this all mean now?'

It is suggested that a Daoist priest come and perform an exorcism, but Cao Cao says, 'As the sage said, "If you offend Heaven, then there is no one left to pray for you." My mandate from Heaven is exhausted, and nothing can be done.'

As morning breaks, Cao Cao's headache grows worse and worse. When Xiahuo Dun is summoned, he tries to approach but he too sees the ghosts and runs away terrified – and is never the same from that day on.

Cao Cao summons Cao Hong, Chen Qun, Jia Xu and Sima Yi to his bedside to impart his final will for the succession. They try to reassure him that he will recover, but he dismisses this.

'For thirty years I have conquered and slain so many brave men. Only Sun Quan and Xuande have evaded me, and now it's too late.' So saying, he discusses all his four sons and their strengths and weaknesses until finally he says, 'Only the oldest, Pi, is fit to take over. Please be sure to support him.'

He orders his women to come to his bedside and tells them to make sure that they perfect their needlework so they can make goods such as silk shoes to sell. This will make it possible for them to survive once he has gone and they are abandoned. Some he commands to offer prayers for him in the Bronze Bird Tower to assist his soul. Every day.

He orders seventy-two fake tombs to be constructed outside Jiangwu in Zhangde County to fool grave robbers.

Then, giving a great sigh, and with tears running down his face, he dies. He is sixty-six years old, and it is the year AD 220.

Cao Cao's body is placed in a gold coffin and set within a silver casket. Great mourning takes place throughout the land. When the heir apparent Cao Pi hears, he is beside himself with grief. But the situation is a dangerous one, and his adviser Sima Fu makes it abundantly clear to him that he must seize the reins of power. Chen Jiao, the minister for war, is equally adamant, pointing out that it would be disastrous if any of the other sons tries to usurp the kingdom. He threatens with death any who disagree.

Then Hua Xin, one of Cao Pi's closest associates, arrives, having ridden hell for leather from Xuchang, bringing with him an imperial decree which he has drawn up himself and forced the emperor to sign. This confirms Cao Pi as king of Wei, prime minister and governor of Jizhou.

It is in the midst of the feasting that follows his ascension that the news comes that his brother Cao Zhang is advancing at the head of an army of a hundred thousand men. Frightened, Cao Pi asks what he should do against such a ferocious warrior as Cao Zhang, when someone speaks up: 'Let me go and see him and I'll stop him.' Those around exclaim, 'It can only be done by one as great as you!'

As has been said:

> The two sons of Cao Cao are fighting,
> Just as Yuan Shao's sons did.

So who is this man?

The next chapter will tell us.

CHAPTER 79

Cao Pi, to trick his brother, commands him to create poems. Liu Feng is executed for failing to rescue Guan Yu.

The volunteer who is prepared to face down Cao Zhang is Jia Kui, and the offer is gladly received.

When Cao Zhang and Jia Kui meet, Cao Zhang immediately asks, 'Where is the late king's seal?'

To this, with stiff politeness, Jia Kui replies, 'Every House has an elder son; every country an heir apparent. Therefore such a question from your lordship is inappropriate.'

That silences Cao Zhang, and they ride on and into the city.

Upon arriving at the palace, Jia Kui asks politely, 'My lord, have you come to mourn your father at the funeral or to challenge your brother for the throne?'

'To attend the funeral, as I have no hostile plans.'

'So why, in that case,' asks Jia Kui, 'have you come with an army?'

In response to this polite but firm query, Cao Zhang has no option but to dismiss his men and go into the palace by himself. There, he embraces his brother, weeping, and hands over to him his armed forces. Then, following the orders of Cao Pi, he returns to Yanling to be commander there.

Cao Pi now starts to rule with full confidence. He makes Jia Kui his chief commander and Hua Xin his prime minister, and many others are given rewards. Cao Cao is named posthumously as King Wu.[22] He is buried at Gaoling in Ye.

Yu Jin is given responsibility for the tomb. However, when he reaches the site, he sees painted on the wall of the tomb a picture of the battle between Guan Yu and himself, complete with all the disasters that have befallen him – the loss of seven armies and his own capture. It even shows Pang De gloating, and himself prone on the ground. The fact is that Cao Pi despises him and no longer has any confidence in him. So shocked is Yu Jin by this deliberate and cruel insult that he falls ill and not long after he dies.

A poet has said:

Thirty years of fidelity
Trashed when a man turns traitor out of fear.
Can you ever know who anyone truly is?
If you want to paint a tiger, start with the skeleton.

While Cao Zhang has been tamed, two other brothers still live: one is Cao Xiong, but he commits suicide, having failed to attend the funeral. He is buried with due honour. The other is Cao Zhi, lord of Linzi, who with two well-known writers and drinkers – brothers by the name of Ding – is often drunk, even early in the morning. But Cao Zhi is also famous as a poet and initially refuses to respond to his brother the king's requests to come and pay homage.

An army of three thousand men attack and seize Cao Zhi and the Ding brothers. The brothers are immediately executed on Cao Pi's orders – a fact that brings sadness to many of the writers and thinkers at that time – while Cao Zhi is brought before his brother.

Now Cao Pi wants to kill his brother, but his mother pleads with him to be compassionate. So instead, Cao Pi sets his brother a task.

'You are renowned as a poet, so here is the task,' he says. 'Walk seven paces and by the end of that compose a poem based on this drawing of two bulls here on the wall. Do you see? One of them has died as a result of a fight and has fallen in a well. But you cannot say, "Two bulls fought beside a wall and one died in a well."'

Cao Zhi takes the seven steps and then recites the following brand-new poem:

Two beefsteaks are trundling along a lane,
A headdress of curving bone on each crown.
They meet each other at a mountain's base

And immediately clash, raging.
Both weighty enemies, but unequal.
One lies bleeding on the ground
Not because he had less strength,
But because his qi had all but drained away.

Everyone is astonished at this. Cao Pi sets him a similar task, only this time he has to capture the relationship between them but without using the word 'brother'. And again he triumphs:

Happily boiling beans on a beanstalk fire,
A voice is heard from the pot.
'Why, when we come from the same root,
Are you the one who now cooks me?'

So moved is Cao Pi by this, he bursts into tears. His mother pleads again to spare Cao Zhi. In order to show his concern for his brother and for his wastrel lifestyle, Cao Pi agrees but demotes him. Cao Zhi gratefully accepts a lower rank and leaves to take responsibility for governing Anxiang.

With no further sibling rivalry, Cao Pi is now in charge and as a result he starts to reshape the laws according to his own will. He also brings even more pressure upon the Han emperor than his father ever did, and word of this soon reaches Xuande.

Deeply alarmed by this turn of affairs, Xuande asks for advice from his officers, not least in the light of Sun Quan having acquiesced to the power and authority of the new king of Wei. Alongside these concerns, Xuande also wants to avenge Guan Yu and his son, and to do this it is suggested that Liu Feng and Meng Da should be punished for having failed to come to their rescue. It is decided to split them up and send Liu Feng to govern Mianzhu so they can't confer, and then they can be picked off one by one. This news alerts Meng Da to the fact that plots are afoot. When he receives official notice that Liu Feng is being despatched to Mianzhu on Kong Ming's orders, he decides to rebel. That very night he leaves with fifty riders and deserts to join the king of Wei. When the messenger who took the notice to Meng Da returns with the news and a carefully worded letter from Meng Da to Xuande arguing that out of loyalty he is deserting, Xuande is furious. It is Kong Ming who comes up with a plan to kill both Meng Da and Liu Feng: 'Send Liu Feng to fight Meng Da, given he is now a rebel. If he wins or loses we'll have resolved this problem.'

When Meng Da arrives at Cao Pi's capital, Cao Pi is convinced this is a plot. Hearing that Liu Feng, with an army of some fifty thousand men, is coming to seize Meng Da, Cao Pi tells him to go and do battle, and if he brings back the head of Liu Feng, then he will be believed.

Now the kingdom of Wei has already seized Xiangyang and is preparing to take Shangyong, and it is at Xiangyang that Meng Da confronts Liu Feng. But first he writes to Liu Feng, trying to lure him into deserting and joining him in serving Cao Pi. To this Liu Feng retorts, 'How dare you try to subvert the filial bond between uncle and nephew and between father and son?' And he rips the letter to shreds.

The next day they meet in single combat, and after a few bouts Meng Da turns and flees, closely followed by the furious Liu Feng. But this is a trap, and soon Liu Feng is attacked from left and right in an ambush. He just manages to escape and flees to Shangyong, only to find that the city has fallen to the Wei troops as the governor has surrendered. With the enemy closing in behind him, Liu Feng flees next to Fangling, only to see the flags of Wei fluttering on the battlements, for this city too has fallen.

With barely a hundred men, Liu Feng flees until eventually he staggers back into Chengdu, where he falls on the ground before Xuande, king of Hanzhong as he now is, and begs forgiveness. Xuande is so angry at this that, despite Liu Feng's attempts to explain why he failed to come to the defence of Guan Yu, he orders his adopted son executed. Only later does he hear that Liu Feng refused to betray his father by deserting to Wei. This news, combined with his profound mourning for Guan Yu, brings him low with sickness and depression and in response he retreats into himself.

Later in that fateful year of AD 220 many different auspicious signs appear: a phoenix, a unicorn, a yellow dragon. These are interpreted by the court astrologers and other high officials as signs that the authority of the Han dynasty is over, the Mandate of Heaven has been removed and the Han are about to be replaced by Wei. They request that a ceremonial event take place at which the Han emperor will resign and the new dynasty will take up the Mandate of Heaven.

As a direct result, a delegation led by Hua Xin goes to see Emperor Xian to officially ask him to resign and to hand over to Cao Pi.

And what is the emperor's response?

Let's find out.

CHAPTER 80

Emperor Xian is deposed by Cao Pi and he makes himself emperor. Xuande claims he is the only legitimate Han emperor.

Marching in with a delegation of officials, Hua Xin enters the imperial court and, ignoring imperial protocol, he speaks directly to Emperor Xian.

'It has been observed that since the enthronement of the king of Wei, the fame of his virtue has spread throughout the land. His benevolence has touched tens of thousands in ways not even equalled by those ancient great founders of dynasties, Tang and Yu. We members of the court have considered this and have come to the conclusion that the dynasty of the Han has run its course. We therefore petition Your Majesty to follow the example of Yao and Shun in handing over the lands and imperial shrines of the empire to a new king of a different lineage – namely the king of Wei. This would be in accord with the heart and mind of Heaven itself and of all the people here below. Such an action would ensure that Your Majesty could enjoy the fruits of freedom and be a cause of contentment to your ancestors and of all the souls here on earth. Having pondered upon this, we now come to present this request to you.'

So stunned and frightened is the emperor by all this he is at first unable to speak. Eventually he says, sobbing, 'I cannot but think back to the Supreme Ancestor and how through his actions he overcame Qin and defeated utterly the Chu and established this dynasty, which has passed from generation to generation down through the Liu family for four hundred years. Although I have little talent, what is it that I have done that is so wrong? So wrong that I have to surrender that which has been passed down to me from my ancestors? Go back and consider all this again.'

In response, Hua Xin brings forward two astrologers, who

describe the auspicious signs mentioned earlier and claim that this proves that Heaven has taken the mandate to rule from the Han and given it to the Wei.

However, the emperor dismisses these signs and interpretations without further consideration only to be confronted by another of Cao Cao's advisers, Wang Lang, who says:

'Ever since time began, what grows must also die. What has been successful must fail. Every dynasty ends, and every family falls. Your house has ruled for over four hundred years. It reaches its natural end with you, Your Majesty. Give way gracefully, or else who knows what might happen!'

To this the emperor simply responds by walking out, while the officials smile smugly at each other.

The very next day they are back and they send a eunuch to bring the emperor to them. But he refuses and is backed in his stance by his empress, the daughter of Cao Cao. Her uncle nevertheless eventually persuades the emperor to come to the Formal Hall. Here, Hua Xin confronts him again, saying, 'Be guided by what you heard yesterday, or who knows what troubles will ensue.'

'You,' cries the emperor, 'all of you have benefited from serving the Han. How can you, sons and grandsons of loyal servants, imagine committing this crime?'

'Your Majesty,' says Hua Xin, 'if you do not comply, as I have said before, who knows what will happen, and, in that case, you'll not be able to blame us for such a catastrophic collapse.'

'Who would dare to even think of killing me!' says the emperor, but this does nothing to stop the discussion. Hua Xin replies, 'The whole world knows that you no longer have the blessing of Heaven to rule and that therefore you are responsible for the terrible state of affairs we now find we are in. Indeed, had it not been for the king of Wei, Cao Cao, you would probably have been murdered well before now. Yet somehow you still cannot see his magnanimous actions in protecting you. Indeed, instead you seem bent upon bringing disaster upon yourself.'

At this the furious and terrified emperor rises, but Hua Xin grabs him by his dragon robe and furiously demands, 'Well, do you agree or not? Just one word will answer this!'

Speechless, the emperor stands aghast, so the keeper of the regalia, Zu Bi, is summoned, and Cao Hong, the new king's uncle, demands the imperial jade seal. But Zu Bi refuses, protesting loudly. His reward? He is taken away and murdered, continuing his protests right to the bitter end. As a poet has said:

Through betrayal, the Han dies.
The betrayers said it was like Yao passing on to Shun.
The court just a mob of men courting the Wei:
Only one man, defender of the seal, was loyal to death.

By now the emperor knows he has no options left and, facing the crowd of soldiers and officials with tears rolling down his face, he says, 'We will solemnly surrender the throne to the king of Wei and all that lies below Heaven. Please leave me to live out the last few years Heaven has accorded me.'

'No one will harm you, sir. The king will make sure of that,' says Hua Xin. 'Prepare the official abdication announcement so all may be reassured.'

The announcement is hastily written in the emperor's name and sent to Cao Pi. It says:

'Through the thirty-two years of my reign, our country has been in turmoil but the spirits of my ancestors have protected me. Today, however, I can see in the signs from Heaven and in the hearts of my people that the era of the Han fire has ended, and fortune has moved on to the Cao family. This is manifest in the late king's victories in war and the shining virtue of the king today. The Great Way teaches us that the empire does not belong to anyone, for it belongs to everyone. Because the Mighty Yao did not favour his own son, his name is for ever associated with fame. I seek to follow his example. Today, by abdicating to the prime minister, the king of Wei, I follow the example set by Yao and I hope that the king of Wei will not reject this.'

Cao Pi is, of course, delighted to receive this and is ready to accept but is advised by Sima Yi to go slowly and to initially refuse. Indeed Sima Yi persuades him to refuse again when the emperor 'writes' yet another appeal, once again citing historical precedents. Finally, Sima Yi manoeuvres the emperor into ordering an Altar of Abdication to be built and then brings Cao Pi to it to be officially if apparently reluctantly given the throne.

It is here that the emperor hands over his jade seal of authority before a vast concourse of officials and soldiers. Cao Pi accepts, and so begins the first year of his reign as emperor of Wei.

As for the former emperor, because, as Hua Xin succinctly put it, two suns cannot shine at the same time, he is demoted to governor of Shanyang and told to leave immediately.

As is customary, the new emperor prepares to worship Heaven and Earth. But no sooner has he knelt down than a violent storm erupts, with howling winds scattering dust and stones. The sky goes dark, and the ritual lanterns blow over on the altar. Terrified by this portent of Heaven's displeasure, Cao Pi collapses and has to be carried away swiftly by his attendants. He is in such a state that for a number of days he is incapable of any action. Eventually he appears but frankly he never recovers and indeed believes the very palace is haunted. So he orders work to start on a new one at Luoyang.

In Chengdu, the news of the emergence of the Wei dynasty is closely followed, as are the many rumours, such as that the former emperor has been assassinated. These make Xuande so unwell he hands over day-to-day management to Kong Ming. It is Kong Ming who comes up with the idea of opposing the new 'emperor' of the Wei by having Xuande crowned as the new Han emperor, thus continuing the lineage. As he is a descendant of the founder of the Han, this has a certain logic.

However, when Kong Ming and the other officials present the petition to Xuande, he is genuinely horrified and scandalized.

'How can you even suggest such a rebellious, disloyal action!' says Xuande, to which Kong Ming responds, 'But of course we are not suggesting rebellion. But let's face facts. Cao Pi has usurped the Han and seized the throne. You are a scion of the House of Liu, and it is your due and proper duty to take back control.'

Rising in his anger, Xuande retorts, 'You ask me to imitate the actions of a traitor!' and marches out.

Kong Ming leaves it for three days and then calls for a meeting with the king again.

'Cao Pi has had the emperor murdered, and unless Your Majesty takes the reins of power and goes to war against these traitors you'll surely have failed to be a loyal and faithful subject. The whole world wants you to rule and to thereby avenge the murder of the late Emperor Xian. If you fail to do so, well, frankly the people will be distraught with disappointment.'

But once again the king refuses, saying that, while he is a scion of Emperor Jing, he has nothing of the virtue of that great founder. Nothing seems able to make him change his mind.

But Kong Ming thinks of a plan to force him to act, and he departs for his home, telling everyone that he is very ill.

No sooner does Xuande hear this than he goes to visit Kong Ming.

Going straight in, Xuande asks, 'What is wrong with you?' to which Kong Ming replies, 'My heart is on fire, and I'm afraid I'll soon be dead.'

'What has brought this on?' asks Xuande, but Kong Ming makes no reply, no matter how often the king asks him. Kong Ming simply lies there looking worse and worse.

Eventually, Kong Ming sighs deeply and says, 'Ever since I left my humble little hut and came to serve you, you've trusted me. As a result, nothing but good fortune has come, and this is why you now control Shu. But now Cao Pi has usurped the throne, casting aside the rituals for the Han ancestors. Yet despite the pleas of all your officials and advisers, who want you to redeem the Liu and expel the Cao family, and for you to become the emperor, you just say no. This is ridiculous, but because of your stance the whole court will soon scatter, having lost hope. As a result Shu will be vulnerable to attack by Wei and Wu. These are the reasons why I am ill.'

Xuande replies, 'I refused genuinely. I'm not acting. Quite simply I fear the censure of history if I am seen to usurp the throne.'

'Remember what Kong Fu Zi said,' replies Kong Ming. '"The wrong words mean that truth is not aligned to reality." Understand this and you can see that you are of course entitled to act in this way. Do you not also recall the saying "That which Heaven wishes can be refused but only at great risk"?'

'Well, I see your point. All right, I suppose I must agree,' says Xuande. 'But there will be time enough to deal with this when you've recovered.'

Whereupon Kong Ming immediately leaps up from his sick-bed and, throwing aside a screen, reveals that gathered behind, listening to every word, are the court officials and commanders. Right on cue they prostrate themselves and shout, 'As you wish! Just let us now choose the coronation day!'

'You have tricked me,' cries the king, 'and what you ask is disreputable.'

Kong Ming replies, 'But, Your Majesty, you have now consented, so we must go and build the altar and choose the auspicious day for the rituals of coronation!'

And so it is fixed.

On the day a proclamation is read out in Xuande's name. It speaks of him as the August Emperor who is ensuring the unbroken lineage of the Han against the terrible deeds of the traitor Cao Cao and now his son Cao Pi. With no one else able to take up the challenge on behalf of the Han, it has fallen to Xuande to do so. It claims that he has sought the opinion of everyone, and they have all agreed that the Mandate of Heaven cannot be ignored even if he, Xuande, is shaking with fear and trepidation. Then, with a final prayer to the gods to bestow blessings upon this renewal and peace to the land, he takes the jade seal of authority, but not before three times again 'trying' to refuse.

As a result of the start of this new imperial reign, his whole family are elevated to imperial status, with his son Shan as the heir apparent. Kong Ming, of course, becomes prime minister, and great is the rejoicing in Shu at this news.

The very next day Xuande, as the new first ruler, announces that, because of the oath in the peach orchard, he is now duty bound to avenge the death of Guan Yu and attack Sun Quan. But just as everyone is buzzing with excitement, someone steps forward and says, 'No!' It is none other than Zhao Zilong. What is it that has moved him to make such a dramatic statement?

Let's find out.

CHAPTER 81

Zhang Fei is murdered. To avenge his two brothers Xuande goes to war.

Zhao Zilong's protest is that the real enemy is Wei, not Wu. Cao Pi has usurped the imperial throne and tried to destroy the Han dynasty. This is where Xuande – [the first ruler, as we must now call him as the first ruler of the New Han, the Shu Han] – should strike first. To attack Sun Quan and Wu is to risk being exposed to an attack from Wei when the troops of Shu[23] would be overstretched.

The first ruler is furious at this, saying he has a sacred obligation to Guan Yu to avenge him.

'Surely,' replies Zhao Zilong, 'this is a personal matter, whereas war against the Wei is a matter of honour and public duty.'

'What is the empire worth to me if I fail to avenge my brother?' So saying, he puts in motion preparations for the invasion of Wu. As part of this he elevates Zhang Fei to a supreme commander position and sends for an additional fifty thousand troops from the Qiang people.

Zhang Fei is based in Langzhong when the news is brought to him of the death of Guan Yu. For days he weeps and rages, blood mingling with his tears until his clothes are soaked. His officers try calming him with wine, but this simply increases his rage. So angry is he that he has many of those around him flogged for no reason – often so badly that they die.

His relief on being made the supreme commander for the revenge attack brings a degree of calmness, and yet he is still deeply unsettled to hear that in the first ruler's court many oppose this war in favour of first attacking Wei. Troubled by this, he sets off for Chengdu to see the new emperor, his brother.

Back in Chengdu, the first ruler has decided that he should lead the attack and goes daily to the army training grounds to oversee preparations. But Kong Ming and other officials advise against his taking this leadership role, as he has so recently become emperor – first ruler – and putting himself at risk so soon could be disastrous. But the first ruler constantly turns down the many requests, even though he is beginning to have some doubts about the wisdom of this himself.

Then the arrival of Zhang Fei puts an end to such doubt. His opening words are harsh.

'Today,' says Zhang Fei, 'you're the first ruler and yet the peach orchard oath is apparently already a thing of the past! Forgotten! How can you not go to avenge our brother?'

The first ruler replies, 'So many are against it, and I really don't think I can go against such advice.'

'Do they know the meaning of our oath?' roars Zhang Fei. 'Do they really? Well, if you won't go, I certainly will, regardless of the cost to me. If I fail, then I'll die and so never have to see you again!'

That did it.

'Then I'll go with you,' says a resolute first ruler. 'You set off from your base in Langzhong, and I'll come with a force of my own to meet you at Jiangzhou. Together we will fulfil our vow.'

Having agreed this, they are about to part, but the first ruler calls Zhang Fei back and warns him. 'When drunk, you become violent. You beat men and then foolishly make up for this by adding them to your personal escort. That's not a good idea and could lead to disaster for you. Try to behave better. Try to be more tolerant and compassionate.'

To this Zhang Fei simply bows and then leaves.

The first ruler's decision causes many to protest, but to no avail. With a combined force of seven hundred and fifty thousand men in late summer of AD 221 he sets out on his war of revenge.

Back at Langzhong, Zhang Fei gives orders for the troops to be ready within three days and to have all the banners and surcoats of the troops in white – the colour of mourning. The very next day two officers, Fan Jiang and Zhang Da, come and tell him that they can't possibly be ready in so few days. They and their men need more time. Aroused to a terrifying anger, Zhang Fei has the two men bound to a tree and each of them flogged fifty times.

'Everything, I say everything, will be ready by tomorrow or I'll execute you both!' he shrieks and he has them beaten again until the blood flows from their mouths.

Horrified and frightened, the two men stagger back to their tents and begin to plot how to escape from such a terrible fate. 'He's out of control, like a raging fire,' says one. 'We've no chance of completing the work in time. We're dead!' cries the other. 'So why don't we kill him before he can kill us?' says Zhang Da. 'And how exactly do we even get near him?' asks Fan Jiang. 'If our fate is to live, then he will be drunk. If our fate is sealed and we must die, he will be sober,' says Zhang Da, and on this basis they begin to prepare for the murder of Zhang Fei.

Unable to sleep because of his pent-up fury, Zhang Fei drinks heavily and soon falls down drunk. As soon as they discover that this is the case, the two murderers slip into his tent. Now Zhang Fei, a true soldier, has learned how to sleep with his eyes open. Seeing this, the two men freeze in horror until they hear a deep snore and realize he is asleep. Pulling out their daggers, they move in for the kill. Slowly they advance, silent until they are standing above the sleeping warrior. Glancing at each other, they signal they are ready. Then each one plunges his dagger into Zhang Fei's stomach. With but one cry, Zhang Fei convulses and within moments lies dead. He is fifty-five years old. A poet has said this about him:

He flogged the inspector at Anxi city;
Helped the Liu to defeat the Yellow Headbands.
At the famous pass his voice was loud and clear;
At the vital bridge he forced back Cao Cao's men.
Releasing Yan Yan, he won the Riverlands;
Fooling Zhang He, it was he who gained Hanzhong for
Xuande.
His death prior to the invasion of the south
Has been a cause of sadness ever since in Langzhong.

The two murderers cut off Zhang Fei's head and flee south to the Wu. By the time Zhang Fei's murder is discovered, it is too late to pursue them.

En route to meet his brother, the first ruler is unable to sleep at night. Standing watching the night sky, he sees a meteor blazing its way down to earth. Calling for Kong Ming, he asks him what this means. 'A great commander has died. News will reach us in three days.' This only unsettles the first ruler even more, and he halts the army.

When the news arrives of the murder of Zhang Fei, the first ruler collapses with grief. Then, the very next day, come two men galloping into the army camp at the head of different troops of soldiers. One is Zhang Bao, the son of Zhang Fei, while the other is Guan Xing, the son of Guan Yu. They have come to avenge their fathers and to stand side by side with their 'uncle', the first ruler. The sight of these two 'nephews' of his and the reminder of the oath he and their fathers have made is too much for the first ruler, who breaks down in tears again.

The two young men are desperate to avenge their fathers, which is why they have ridden to the emperor's camp. But when the first ruler hands over the seal of authority to lead the army to Zhang Bao, Guan Xing protests mightily. 'Give that to me!' he shouts.

'But I have been given the responsibility,' says Zhang Bao.

'Really? You really think you are worthy of this role? Me, I have trained as a warrior since I was a child. No arrow of mine ever misses the mark.' The row looks set to escalate, but the first ruler steps in and suggests that they display their relative skills in a contest. So a banner with a red target at its centre is placed a hundred yards away. In quick succession Zhang Bao fires three arrows. All three hit the target. In response, Guan Xing, seeing a flight of geese in the sky, says, 'I will take out the third one.' Sure enough, no sooner has the arrow left his bow than the third goose falls dead to the ground.

'Fight me for this honour,' shouts Zhang Bao, leaping onto his horse and seizing a huge spear. 'Happily,' roars back Guan Xing. 'You can have the spear, I have my sword.'

Seeing that this is getting seriously out of hand, the first ruler cries out, 'Enough! Enough, both of you!' Realizing they have overstepped the mark, the two lads throw themselves down before the first ruler. 'Long ago your fathers and I made a vow and bound ourselves together as brothers. So now you two must respect each other as brothers. Then you can side by side avenge your fathers.' As Zhang Bao is the older of the two, the first ruler orders that Guan Xing respect him as the elder brother.

With this apparently resolved, the vast army sets out again for Wu and for revenge.

While all this is happening, Fan Jiang and Zhang Da bring the head of Zhang Fei to Sun Quan. Turning to address his ministers, Sun Quan says, 'Having seized the imperial throne, Xuande is now advancing to attack us with over seven hundred thousand troops. What are we to do?' Fear shows on the faces of all the ministers, and then Zhuge Jin steps forward.

'I've always wished to fully serve my lord, so let me go regardless of the dangers to meet Xuande and try to persuade him to see that he should be friends with us so that we can together deal with this traitor Cao Pi.'

Needless to say, Sun Quan is delighted by this offer.

> A man went to meet the warriors,
> Peace lies in the gift of this messenger.

And what happens?

Let's find out.

CHAPTER 82

Sun Quan surrenders to Wei. Xuande rewards his men for the war against Wu but upsets Huang Zhong.

Zhuge Jin travels to Baidi, where the first ruler has settled his army, and asks for an audience with him. Initially the latter refuses to meet him, but he is persuaded by Huang Quan to change his mind, given Zhuge Jin is the brother of his own prime minister.

Zhuge's message is really quite simple. He spells out that when Guan Yu was in charge of Jingzhou, Lord Sun had made various offers of alliance, including offering his daughter in marriage to Guan Yu's son, but they were refused. Lord Sun also turned down suggested alliances with Cao Cao, and it was as an independent agent that Lü Meng attacked Guan Yu – certainly not with Lord Sun's approval.

'But now Lü Meng is dead, and Lady Sun wishes greatly to be reunited with her husband,' says Zhuge Jin. 'We wish also to restore Jingzhou to you as a sign of our friendship so that together we can destroy the traitor Cao Pi.'

But the first ruler is far from impressed and retorts that it was southerners who murdered his brother. But Zhuge Jin, to his credit, is not put off.

'If I may, let me examine the situation here,' he says. 'You are an imperial uncle of the Han. The Han emperor has been illegally deposed by Cao Pi. However, instead of focusing on extirpating this traitor, you chose to fail in your imperial duty for the sake of an oath with someone not even a blood relative! You set aside a sacred duty for a personal sense of obligation. The heart of the empire is the north, and Chang'an and Luoyang have ever been its capitals. But you are willing to abandon them for the sake of – what – Jingzhou! We all know that you could restore the Han if you really wanted to. So this is why I really do suggest that you attack Wei instead of Wu.'

This speech only enrages the first ruler even more, and Zhuge Jin leaves, having totally failed in his mission.

When Zhuge Jin returns to Sun Quan and reports the failure of his mission, Sun Quan is very disturbed at the prospect of the now almost certain invasion by the forces of Shu. But hope is offered by Zhao Zi, one of his officials, who advises that they should now seek help from Wei. 'If we offer to submit to Cao Pi as the emperor, we can also suggest that he attacks Xuande's city of Hanzhong, which will divert the Shu army.'

This is greeted with great excitement, and Zhao Zi is sent off to Xuchang to offer their submission. After some discussions and probing by Cao Pi about why Sun Quan would want to submit (Cao Pi is fully aware of the desire to deflect the Shu from invading Wu), Cao Pi sends back the formal papers for Sun Quan to submit and awards him the title of king of the south. Liu Ye, his senior adviser, is opposed, as he thinks letting Shu and Wu rip each other apart will be in the best interests of Wei, and he is against elevating such an ordinary soldier as Sun Quan to the status of king. But Cao Pi dismisses the latter point and reassures Liu Ye that he too has every intention of making sure Wu and Shu destroy each other!

Cao Pi sends his master of ceremonies Xing Zhen with Zhao Zi to convey the imperial appointment documents. Xing Zhen nearly ruins the submission by the haughty way he rides into the capital of Wu until the loud protests of the Wu officials humble him. When, realizing his mistake, he hastily descends from his horse to pay his respects to Sun Quan, someone shouts, 'Shame on us for accepting this title when we should be destroying Shu and Wei instead.' Alarmed, Xing Zhen looks around and sees this is the military commander Xu Sheng. Xing Zhen knows then that this submission will not last.

Sun Quan submits to Wei and accepts the title of king but this does not stop the Shu invasion. Far from it, and soon the vast army is at the kingdom's gates, and there is precious little sign of any help coming from the Wei emperor in Xuchang, despite Sun Quan now being a vassal king.

He is just bemoaning the lack of a Lu Su or Lü Meng to advise him when a young man steps forward and offers his services. This is Sun Huan, a nephew by adoption of the king, who says that if given thirty to fifty thousand troops he could bring the head of Xuande to Sun Quan assisted by his friends Li Yi and Xie Jing. The warrior Zhu Ran offers to go with them, and permission is given for fifty thousand troops to accompany them.

Wu Ban, leader of the forces of Shu, is astonished to hear that a stripling like Sun Huan has been sent against him. And the first ruler sends his two nephews, Guan Xing and Zhang Bao, to confront him but warns them to be careful. He can't bear the thought of losing them.

Confronting each other, the young men exchange insults, culminating in Sun Huan taunting Zhang Bao, saying, 'Your father is now a headless ghost, and soon you will be following him, you fool!'

This drives a furious Zhang Bao into action, and he charges at Sun Huan. His attack is halted by Xie Jing, whom he soon bests, only to then be attacked by Li Yi. Seeing neither side winning, Tan Xiong, another young commander, shoots an arrow at Zhang Bao, which misses him but hits his horse. The brave animal staggers back to the Shu forces but collapses just as they reach the front line. Zhang Bao is thrown to the ground. Seeing his opportunity, Li Yi charges forward to the kill. Seconds later his head is struck from his body. Guan Xing, seeing the danger to Zhang Bao, has charged forward and with one swipe of his great sword has killed Li Yi. Carried forward by his own momentum, Guan Xing sweeps into Sun Huan's army, followed by his troops. Sun Huan suffers a huge defeat that day.

The next day Sun Huan again taunts the two young men, and again they triumph. Charging forward, Zhang Bao slays Xie Jing, and the troops of Wu scatter, fleeing every which way. But at battle's end there is no sign of Guan Xing. Profoundly alarmed and shouting that he cannot live if Guan Xing does not, Zhang Bao goes in search of him and finds him holding captive the very man, Tan Xiong, who fired the arrow. Dragging him back to their camp, they execute him and pour his blood as a sacrifice to the spirit of the slain horse.

With the troops of Sun Huan demoralized and broken, the Shu commanders decide to attack their camp but they are aware that Zhu Ran's navy is untouched and powerful and fear an attack from the rear if they press forward too quickly. To prevent this, they plan an ambush and send men pretending to be deserters into Zhu Ran's encampment to lure him into the trap.

The plot works. Not only does Wu Ban successfully sack the camps but Zhang Bao and Guan Xing trap Cui Yu, whom Zhu Ran sent to relieve the camps. Sun Huan only just escapes with his life and flees to the fortified town of Yiling. Soon he is surrounded and when the first ruler executes Cui Yu, fear spreads throughout the south.

Sun Quan is devastated by the news of these defeats, and it is Zhang Zhao who suggests how they should now respond, recommending certain key commanders for various roles, and with an army of one hundred thousand they advance to confront Xuande.

The first ruler, meanwhile, is delighted by the performance of the two young men and says, perhaps a bit casually, 'My old commanders are frankly getting a bit past it, so I'm delighted to have such excellent new, young men to take their place.'

News comes of the advance of the troops of Wu, and also that Huang Zhong, that veritable old warrior, has deserted.

'No,' says the first ruler, 'I spoke without thinking about our older generals, and he has gone off in a huff to show us he is still the best!' But he sends Zhang Bao and Guan Xing after him to ensure the old fighter is all right.

So what has happened to Huang Zhong?

Let's find out.

CHAPTER 83

Xuande seizes his personal enemies at Xiaoting. Death of Gan Ning.

All this takes place in the spring of the year AD 222. When Huang Zhong hears that the first ruler has been dismissive of his older commanders, he is outraged. So much so that he takes up his sword, mounts his horse and sets off for battle!

Arriving at Wu Ban's camp, he is asked why he has come and tells them in no uncertain terms that he is fit enough and strong enough for war. When news comes that the troops of Wu are approaching, he swings himself back into the saddle and rides to battle. Wu Ban orders Feng Xi to follow him and to try to protect him.

The enemy forces are commanded by Pan Zhang. Seeing this, Huang Zhong challenges him to single combat. Pan Zhang is no match for the old warrior. Pan retreats, pursued by Huang Zhong. Having seen him off, Huang Zhong returns triumphantly to his own side to be met by Zhang Bao and Guan Xing. They tell him they have been ordered by the first ruler to bring him safely home. Huang Zhong simply ignores them!

The next day Pan Zhang rides out to challenge the old man again and again he rides into combat, only this time Pan Zhang turns and flees. But it is a trap. He leads the pursuing Huang Zhong into an ambush, where Ma Zhong shoots him in the armpit. Felled by this blow, he is almost captured by the Wu army. But at the very last moment, charging in as if from nowhere, he is rescued by Guan Xing and Zhang Bao.

But the wound in one as old as he is effectively a death sentence. The first ruler comes to comfort him.

'I'm just an old warrior,' Huang Zhong says. 'I've been fortunate enough to serve Your Majesty, and now at seventy-five my time has come. Please, Your Majesty, reserve your strength to fight the north.' And with these prophetic words, he dies. As a poet has said about this brave man:

This veteran was indeed the first among the warriors,
His conquest of Shu has won him great fame.
Tirelessly he put on his armour,
And his hands were strong upon the bow.
His strength, the north could speak of nothing else;
His success, held down the newly conquered lands.
White haired at the end,
Yet to the end, a truly brave warrior.

The first ruler mourns him with all the formal rituals and grandest ceremonies. Then he sets off for Xiaoting, where he gathers his troops and commanders.

The Wu commanders advance to confront him, and their armies clash. In one-to-one combat Zhang Bao fells Xia Xun, and Guan Xing fells Zhou Ping, and then they turn their attentions to the two supreme commanders. Confronted by such warriors, they retreat in confusion. The army of Shu descends upon the fleeing army of Wu, and so great is the slaughter of the Wu army that the very ground itself is buried under the bodies of the dead.

Gan Ning, who is resting from his wounds nearby, tries to come to the rescue. An arrow stikes him in the head and, though he rides on, it proves fatal, and he dies soon after. The tree under which he dies suddenly seems to release hundreds of crows, who rise and fly above his body. King Sun Quan honours the old warrior with a tomb and temple. A poet said of him:

Supreme among the warriors of Wu was Gan Ning.
With sails of silk he stopped the Yangzi River.
He served his lord with valour,
Making enemy into friend.
Leading his cavalry on the camp night raid,
He began by warming his men with wine.
Where he lay, the sacred crows revealed,
Incense will burn here for a thousand years.

Elated by his victory, the first ruler rides on to capture Xiaoting, while the troops of Wu scatter. But these triumphs are bitter for him. For it is found that Guan Xing is missing. He immediately despatches Zhang Bao to find him.

Where is he? In the heat of battle, Guan Xing suddenly comes across his greatest enemy, Pan Zhang. Realizing the danger he is in, Pan Zhang flees into a deep valley. Hunting for him as night falls, Guan Xing comes at last upon a farm. When in response to his fervent knocking the old farmer opens the door, Guan Xing finds a portrait of his father being venerated in the house. When he asks why there are offerings before the picture, he is told his father is revered and worshipped throughout the area as he was so respected when alive. 'His spirit is still revered here,' says the old man. 'Please stay and rest with us.' To this the exhausted Guan Xing happily agrees.

Imagine, therefore, Guan Xing's surprise when, deep into the night, there comes another knock on the farmer's door, and there stands Pan Zhang! As Guan Xing rises to confront him, a third man enters the room, blocking Pan Zhang's retreat. But this is no living man. It is none other than the spirit of Guan Yu. Seeing the spirit, Pan Zhang cries with horror and tries to flee. But Guan Xing springs forward and strikes him dead there and then. He then rips out his heart and sacrifices Pan Zhang's blood to his divine father. He picks up his father's sword, Green Dragon, which Pan Zhang had taken from the body of the slain Guan Yu. Hanging the head of his mortal enemy on his horse's neck, he rides off to return to camp.

He has not gone far when he is suddenly confronted by an enemy troop, led by one of Pan Zhang's officers, Ma Zhong. Seeing the head hanging there, he charges in fury at Guan Xing. Guan Xing, of course, recognizes his father's assassin and is filled with an anger that reaches to Heaven itself. He prepares to charge not just Ma Zhong but the three hundred men who ride with him. Just in time, another troop appears. Leading them is Zhang Bao, sent to find Guan Xing, and their arrival forces Ma Zhong to retreat. Guan Xing returns to the first ruler with Zhang Bao and presents the head of Pan Zhang to him. Great is the rejoicing.

Back at the camp of the shattered army of Wu, there is general despair. So great is this that the soldiers start to mutter and plot. They complain that they have been fooled into following Wu in the attack on Guan Yu. They decide that if they can kill the two traitors Mi Fang and Fu Shiren, then they might win the approval and forgiveness of the new first ruler.

Overhearing this, Mi Fang decides to pre-empt the plot, and he and Fu Shiren creep into Ma Zhong's tent late that night and murder him, cutting off his head. Then they make good their escape with a handful of followers, hoping to win the first ruler's approval and forgiveness for their crime.

But this is not to be. Brought before the first ruler, they say, 'We didn't mean to rebel. It was all Lü Meng's fault. He told us Guan Yu was already dead and tricked us into opening the gate and surrendering. So this is why we have come to you with the head of the traitor, so your revenge has been fulfilled, and we humbly beg your forgiveness.'

Incandescent with rage, the first ruler rises from his throne and says, 'So why didn't you come to me before now? You come now, full of your lies, because you're terrified for your lives. If I were to forgive you, to let you go free, how could I face the spirit of Guan Yu in the abode of the Nine Springs of Hell!'

So orders are given to prepare an altar with the image of Guan Yu upon it. The first ruler personally carries the head of Ma Zhong and offers it on the altar. Then he orders Guan Xing to strip Mi Fang and Fu Shiren and make then kneel down. There, before the altar to his father, Guan Xing cuts the two men into pieces as a sacrifice to his father.

This leaves Zhang Bao desperate to avenge his own father, and he asks when he too can have revenge. 'We will conquer the south,' declares the first ruler, 'and once we have killed all those dogs we will hunt down the two murderers, and you too will be able to cut them into pieces as a sacrifice to your father.'

So great is the fear created by the first ruler that Sun Quan is desperate to appease him. Therefore, he has the two murderers of Zhang Fei captured. He sends them, along with the head of Zhang Fei itself, with his ambassador, Cheng Bing, to the camp of the first ruler. Cheng Bing also brings a proposal that

Sun Quan should return the first ruler's wife, Lady Sun, and hand over Jingzhou as a sign of friendship.

The first ruler is profoundly moved by sight of the head of his old friend and brother and orders an altar be built. Here, Zhang Bao slices apart the two murderers as a sacrifice to his father's spirit.

But any hope Cheng Bing or Sun Quan might have had that this would turn the wrath of the first ruler away from Wu is swiftly shattered. He is still as determined as ever to destroy Wu and then go on to destroy Wei.

To counter this, and to almost everyone's surprise, Sun Quan appoints a young man, not a warrior but a scholar, to lead the fightback. This young man is called Lu Xun. His appointment is deeply unpopular with martial advisers such as Zhang Zhao. Indeed, when Lu Xun takes up his post, there is widespread mockery and disdain among the military officers. But despite this, Sun Quan gives him full authority on the battlefield.

His arrival at the front leads to even more mockery, but the officers have no option but to obey. They raise the issue of Sun Huan being trapped at Yiling and needing urgently to be rescued, but Lu Xun refuses to go to his aid, saying that he can look after himself until the western forces have been beaten. Dissent spills over into mutiny, and Lu Xun finds himself having to face down his own generals in heated argument over his plan to defend rather than attack. Lu Xun will not be drawn out to the attack and refuses to allow any others to go on the offensive.

While all this is happening, the first ruler has moved forward, establishing a string of forty camps along a vast front line of several hundred miles. Hearing that a mere stripling has been appointed in charge of the army of Wu, he laughs. But he is reminded that this was the one who masterminded the attack on Jingzhou and that he should not be underestimated. However, the first ruler is determined to capture him and defeat the army of Wu in revenge for Guan Yu's defeat and death and he pays scant attention to these warnings and moves forward to the attack.

Han Dang, in charge of the front line, summons Lu Xun

when the enemy comes into view, expecting to be given the order to attack. But once again Lu Xun holds back, refusing to go on the attack, much to Han Dang's chagrin. Lu Xun can see that with the full heat of summer now upon them and with Shu's supply lines overstretched, the enemy will soon start to suffer from lack of resources and fatigue. So, despite daily taunting from the Shu soldiers, he holds his restless men back.

Appreciating these dangers, the first ruler orders the vast majority of his men to move to the shelter of the woods and to wait until autumn brings cooler weather. He leaves ten thousand of the weaker troops on the plain and holds in reserve around himself eight thousand men ready to ambush any attack from the south. The plan is that if the weaker troops are attacked they will break and run, and this will lure the Wu troops into an ambush from the men hidden in the woods. On the advice of Ma Liang, a map is made showing the dispositions of the troops and sent to Kong Ming, who is protecting the east in case of an invasion by Wei.

When news of the move to shady woods reaches Han Dang and Zhou Tai, they go to see Lu Xun and say, 'Now is the ideal time to strike.'

And what is Lu Xun's response?

We can find out.

CHAPTER 84

Lu Xun burns down all his enemy's camps. Kong Ming uses the Eight Maze Puzzle but is defeated.

Despite the hopes of his commanders that he would give the order to attack, Lu Xun once again holds back. 'This is a trick to draw us into an ambush. I can see signs in the distance of other troops. Give it three days and you will see I am right.'

The commanders catch each other's eye and wink, still dismissive of Lu Xun as an amateur but having to obey his orders.

Three days later Lu Xun brings his commanders together, and sure enough there in the distance is troop movement. 'Watch,' he says. 'In a moment Xuande will appear with the ambush troops bored of waiting.' And right on cue the first ruler does indeed appear with his troops. 'Now we can attack and destroy their string of camps,' says Lu Xun. 'His men are vulnerable because they are bored, disillusioned and frustrated.'

Meanwhile, the first ruler has sent his navy downstream in order to create camps on both sides of the river. Huang Quan is troubled by this, pointing out that as a result they have overstretched their resources, and that could prove very dangerous if they have to retreat. But the first ruler brusquely dismisses any such talk. He gives command of the north side to Huang Quan, while he takes the south side. Camps are set up independently on both sides.

When the Wei emperor, Cao Pi, hears about these manoeuvres, he roars with laughter, saying that Xuande is a fool and that within ten days he will be defeated. He sends orders to his own front lines to be ready to attack Wu when the south is fully engaged in defeating the army of Shu.

The map showing the placement of the camps at last reaches Kong Ming, far away on the eastern border of Shu. Slamming his fist onto the table, he exclaims, 'Who the hell presented this idea to our lord? He should be executed!'

'None other than our lord himself,' replies Ma Liang, the messenger.

'Then the vitality of the Han is ending,' says Kong Ming.

'But why? asks Ma Liang.

'Because to lay out your forces like this goes against every rule in the book,' says Kong Ming. 'Get back as fast as possible and tell the Son of Heaven to move his camps closer together and away from such restrictive manoeuvring space, because being surrounded by woods and streams will be fatal if they are attacked. If you are too late, tell our lord to escape to Baidi. I've left ten thousand men there just in case.'

'But I travelled past there on my way here and saw no one,' says Ma Liang. 'Are you really telling the truth?'

'They're there, so don't worry.' And with that Kong Ming gives Ma Liang the urgent message, and he sets off immediately, riding pell-mell for the first ruler's camp.

Lu Xun can see that the troops of Shu are becoming lazy and forgetting to secure their camps properly. But to test how unprepared they are he sends out an expeditionary force to try to take one of the camps on the south. They are roundly defeated. This casts down the hopes of the commanders, but Lu Xun says, 'I needed to test the enemy. My plan can now roll out. It would never have fooled Kong Ming, but by the grace of Heaven, he is not here!'

He now issues his orders for battle. He orders Zhu Ran to advance by ship upstream. 'Fill your boats with straw. Han Dang is to attack the north shore and Zhou Tai the south. Every soldier must carry his weapons and a bundle of straw with explosive materials inside. As soon as you reach the enemy camps set fire to the bundles. Set fire to all forty of the camps. Make sure you have food enough for a couple of days and hunt the enemy down day after day until you capture Xuande.'

Back at the first ruler's camp, he is confident that the enemy cannot prevail but he is persuaded to issue orders to Zhang Bao and Guan Xing to go and see if there is any movement by the enemy. But before they can report back, fires break out in the camps either side of the first ruler. Suddenly troops of Wu soldiers are rushing up the hill, and chaos erupts. The first ruler leaps on his horse and dashes towards the safety of his commander Feng Xi. But the fires have already driven him away, and he is now trying to attack Xu Sheng and to stem the ferocious attack. However, Xu Sheng charges straight past Feng Xi and heads for the first ruler. He tries to escape but runs headlong into Ding Feng attacking from behind, and the first ruler is trapped. At the last moment a great cry goes up, and Zhang Bao breaks through, seizes the first ruler's horse and dashes off with the Royal Guard alongside to protect them. They take refuge on Ma An hill, while down below the hill is surrounded by the victorious southern troops. Looking out at nightfall, the first ruler sees nothing but destruction and the bodies of the slain men of his army.

The next morning the troops set fire to the hill, and the first ruler is only rescued by the courage of Guan Xing, who with a few others charges up the hill to join Zhang Bao and lead the first ruler away towards the safety of Baidi. When they are spotted by the Wu commanders, the chase is on, as the vast army spreads out across the plain in pursuit.

The first ruler and his escort throw away their armour, the better to ride hard for the city, but suddenly a cry goes up, and in front of them is Zhu Ran and his men. 'This is where I will die,' cries the first ruler, and despite the valour of Zhang Bao and Guan Xing, they are unable to break through, and the arrows raining down on them take a dreadful toll. All seems lost, but, as the sun rises, a great roar goes up. Before his eyes the first ruler sees Zhu Ran's men disappear as a troop slashes its way through, led by none other than Zhao Zilong. News of his arrival leads Lu Xun to cease the pursuit and to withdraw his men. In the mêlée Zhao Zilong slays Zhu Ran, rescues the first ruler and heads for safety to Baidi. By this stage, there are but a hundred or so men with the first ruler.

Protecting his retreat is Fu Tong, but he is swiftly overwhelmed by Wu troops led by Ding Feng, who lies, telling him Xuande is a prisoner. Fu Tong tries every way of escaping, but it is impossible. Realizing the hopelessness of his situation, he cries, 'No true Han commander would ever surrender to the dogs of Wu', and, charging with his spear levelled, he falls in battle. As a poet has said:

> At Yiling did Wu and Shu clash,
> When Lu Xun fought with fire.
> Fu Tong's dying words 'Dogs of Wu'!
> So died the faithful Han commander.

Many are the commanders of the Shu who fall that day – Cheng Ji takes his own life in despair, surrounded as he is; Wu Ban and Feng Xi, raising the siege of Yiling, are cut off and die at the hands of Sun Huan's army. The tribal leader Shamoke is slain by Zhou Tai, while commanders Du Lu and Liu Ning surrender. Thus all the provisions of the Shu fall into enemy hands. When Lady Sun hears of the destruction of the army of Shu and is told that her husband Xuande has died, she goes to the river and faces west in honour of her husband. Then she throws herself into the river and drowns herself. A temple has arisen there, and a poet has said:

> The queen flees to Baidi,
> The bad news brings her to suicide.
> Even now there's a stone by the water over there,
> Honouring her name for a thousand-year reign.

Drawing near to Baidi, Lu Xun is suddenly alarmed by strange apparitions. He halts the army and tries to work out what is happening. 'I think there must be an ambush,' he says and sends men to investigate. But they find nothing but eighty to ninety piles of rocks. But rising from them comes a strange mist. Questioning locals, Lu Xun is told that Kong Ming had these piles created, and ever since this strange mist has arisen. As they talk, a wind blows up, and soon the men are being bombarded by sand and rocks, and the rock piles are moving in terrifying patterns as if alive. 'We have been fooled by Kong Ming!' cries Lu Xun unable to retreat and desperate for his men's safety.

Out of the blue, an old man appears. He turns out to be Kong Ming's father-in-law and reveals to Lu Xun that these rocks are a magical spell called the Eight Maze Puzzle. The old man raises his stick and guides the terrified Lu Xun and his men to safety. The great poet Du Fu has written:

> Notorious above the tragedy of the divided land,
> The Eight Maze its signal achievement.
> Ming's stones stand by the river there
> Tribute to the magic that stopped Wu in his tracks.

So shocked is Lu Xun by this that, despite his triumph and the urging of his commanders, he orders retreat. 'It is not the rocks that frighten me. But I think Cao Pi will use this opportunity to attack.' And indeed, just two days later, news comes that hundreds of thousands of Wei troops have massed on the border. Smiling, Lu Xun says, 'I expected this, and my plans to stop them are already in motion.'

So what happens next?

Read on and you will find out.

CHAPTER 85

Xuande dies, leaving his son in the care of Kong Ming. Kong Ming disarms five armies.

It is in the summer of AD 222 when Lu Xun defeats the armies of the Shu. When Ma Liang arrives at Baidi, he is greatly upset to find the first ruler in refuge there. 'This was my fault,' he says, but the first ruler replies, 'Had I but listened to Kong Ming, none of this would have happened. How can I return to Chengdu after such a disastrous failure?' Instead of returning, he elevates the status of his quarters in Baidi and officially announces that they are to be known henceforth as the Palace of Eternal Peace.

News is brought that Huang Quan has deserted to the Wei, and advisers recommend the execution of his entire clan. But the first ruler knows that Huang Quan simply had no other option, as he was cut off from the rest of the army. 'If anyone betrayed anyone,' says the first ruler, 'it was I who betrayed him.'

Needless to say, Cao Pi is delighted to have Huang Quan brought before him and he offers him both position and authority. But he declines. 'The first ruler of Shu has always been generous to me – beyond anything I could have expected. That is why I was in charge of the forces to the north of the river. Then Lu Xun cut me off. I could not retreat to Shu and will not surrender to Wu. So that is why I am here. If you will spare my life, that will be enough. But I cannot serve you.'

Cao Pi is moved by this, but, despite many offers of a senior command, Huang Quan cannot be persuaded to accept.

Cao Pi himself is now determined to press home what he sees as his advantage by attacking the Wu while they rest on their laurels after defeating Xuande. This is despite the ardent advice of Jia Xu and Liu Ye to hold back. But Cao Pi chooses to ignore them, so sure is he of his own ability. With three armies already on the southern border, Cao Pi sets out to strengthen them. On the Wei side the armies are commanded by Cao Xiu, Cao Zhen and Cao Ren. Opposite them the Wu place Lü Fan, Zhuge Jin and the youthful Zhu Huan. None of this deters Cao Pi. But it should. Cao Pi has underestimated the skilled commanders facing his men. An attack by Cao Ren on Xianxi is skilfully defeated by Zhu Huan despite his youth – he is only twenty-seven. He easily traps the advance party led by Chang Diao, whom he personally slays on the battlefield, then trounces Cao Ren's own troop, seizing vast quantities of arms, horses and provisions.

No sooner has Cao Ren reported this to the Wei ruler than news also comes of the defeat of Cao Zhen, who was besieging Nanjun. He has been crushed between an attack from within led by Lu Xun and one from outside by Zhuge Jin. On top of this comes news that Cao Xiu has been defeated by Lü Fan. To add to the misery, as it is the height of summer, plague breaks out among his troops, and three quarters of the men collapse and die. Defeated and disillusioned, wishing he had listened to Jia Xu and Liu Ye, Cao Pi retreats back to Luoyang to lick his wounds.

Back at Baidi, in the confines of his Palace of Eternal Peace, the first ruler's strength declines rapidly, and he takes to his bed. It is the late spring of AD 223. Xuande knows that he is dying. The shock of what has happened to his two brothers has sapped his energy. He is no longer strong enough in body or mind to withstand sickness.

One night he lies awake, alone in his room. There are no attendants around him, for he has dismissed them. Suddenly he feels a cold wind moving through the room, making his candles gutter and then flare. In their light he sees two men and, upset at being disturbed, the first ruler says, 'I told you not to disturb me. Why are you here?' But the two men do not even move. Rising, the first ruler realizes to his astonishment that they are Guan Yu and Zhang Fei. 'Ahh!' he cries. 'You are alive!' 'No, we are no longer men,' replies Guan Yu. 'We are ghosts. The Supreme Lord knows that in our lives we remained faithful to our vow and as a result he has made us gods. Elder brother, you should know that soon we three shall be united once again.'

Stretching forth his hands to touch them, the first ruler jerks awake – and the ghosts disappear. Calling for his servants, he tells them that he has not long to live and that they must bring Kong Ming from Chengdu to see him immediately.

As soon as they can, Kong Ming, the first ruler's younger sons Liu Yong, king of Lu, and Liu Li, king of Liang, arrive. Left behind to hold Chengdu is the heir apparent, Liu Shan.

Speaking in confidence to Kong Ming, the first ruler says, 'You brought me success. So how could I have been such a fool as to ignore your advice and so bring this disaster upon us? I am dying. My heir – he's too weak to rule, so you must take over responsibility. That's why I place the kingdom into your hands.'

Kong Ming tries to persuade the first ruler that there is hope he might recover, but the first ruler knows this is not so. He warns Kong Ming about Ma Su, the younger brother of Ma Liang. 'What do you think of him?' asks the first ruler. 'I think he is one of our best men,' replies Kong Ming. 'Wrong,' says the first ruler. 'He is all hot air and nothing else. Don't promote him under any circumstances.' Then he dictates his last will and testament, officially handing responsibility for its execution to Kong Ming as his prime minister.

'We did our best to rid the world of that traitor Cao,' says the first ruler, 'and, in so doing, support the House of Han. I leave now with this still to be finished – not even halfway there to be honest. To you, Prime Minister, I entrust my heir. Teach him well. I am relying upon you for that.'

Kong Ming is overcome with grief, and his eyes fill with tears. The first ruler speaks again to Kong Ming. 'I'm about to die,' he says, 'and if my heir is unable to fulfil his duties and protect the kingdom, then you must take over. You must become the king instead.' Kong Ming is distraught and weeps, prostrating himself many times upon the floor.

Then the first ruler summons Liu Yong and Liu Li to come to his bedside and he commands them to serve Kong Ming as they would serve their own father.

Calling all his officials to him, he says the same thing to them, commanding them to support Kong Ming. Turning to his old comrade in arms Zhao Zilong, he says, 'We've survived a lot, you and I. I didn't think it would end like this. For the sake of our friendship, watch over my sons and honour what I have asked.' Zhao Zilong, weeping, promises to do exactly that.

Finally, he turns to all those assembled there and says, 'There are too many of you for me to speak personally to each of you, but I wish you all well. Look after yourselves and ensure you act in full accord with that which is best in you.'

He never speaks again.

He is sixty-three years old when he dies in the spring of AD 223. Du Fu wrote this poem in his honour:

The Shu king covets the Wu lands beyond the Three Gorges,
But in two years he's dying in the Palace of Eternal Peace.
His kingly thoughts reached beyond the mountains,
There were no salubrious rooms in this humble temple.
Ancient pines nearby his shrine house herons.
At certain times old people wander by at their ease.
His chief adviser's temple is just nearby;
Both are sacred – both men idolized.

Xuande's body is carried back to Chengdu. There, the formal rituals of mourning and of enthroning the new emperor, his son Liu Shan, as the second ruler take place so the Han lineage can continue without a break. Xuande is named as August Emperor Zhao Lie, meaning Reflected Glory, and he is buried at Huiling.

When Cao Pi hears of Xuande's death, he immediately wants to attack Shu to take advantage of the chaos such a death causes. Jia Xu warns him not to be too precipitous, but suddenly a voice rings out: 'We will never have such an opportunity again!' It is Sima Yi. When asked what he thinks should be done, Sima Yi suggests the following.

'We need five armies to vanquish Shu. That way there will be too many fronts on which Kong Ming will have to fight. The first army we recruit from the East Liao region by bribing their king with gifts of gold and silk to send a hundred thousand tribesmen to seize the Xiping pass. The second by recruiting from the Man people, requesting a hundred thousand men from south of Shu. The third from Wu, by offering land to Sun Quan in return for another hundred thousand – and for them to attack the three Gorges and Fucheng. The fourth to come from Meng Da, who has of course just surrendered to us. He is to attack to the west near Hanzhong. And that is where the final hundred thousand army, our regular army under Cao Zhen, will be. The plan is for them to move out from Jingzhao through the Yangping pass . . . into Shu.'

Cao Pi immediately agrees, and messengers are despatched straight away.

When reports come in to the second ruler of the five armies being mobilized, to say he is alarmed would be an understatement. Sending messengers to summon Kong Ming, he is surprised and frankly alarmed to hear that Kong Ming is too ill to obey. The next day, more senior officials are sent to ask Kong Ming to attend, and the second ruler's anxieties rise even higher when again he is informed that Kong Ming is too ill to attend. On the third day, officials wait all day in anticipation of the appearance of the prime minister, but to no avail. This is why the second ruler himself has eventually to go to see Kong Ming.

Finding Kong Ming standing leaning on a walking stick and looking into a fishpond, the second ruler surprises him, and he turns and apologizes profusely. When the second ruler chastises him gently for not helping him when the situation is so critical, Kong Ming smiles and says:

'I know all about these five armies. But don't worry about them. I've sorted it all out already.' He then tells the second ruler how, knowing where attacks will come and from whom, he has forestalled Cao Pi by getting in first. To the king of the Qiang he has sent Ma Chao, whom the tribes believe is blessed by Heaven itself, and with Ma Chao holding the Xiping pass, no Qiang man will dare attack. For the Man troops, a simple policy of having the army opposite moving about all the time has reduced these brave but simple folk to confusion, so they won't attack. 'Using trickery, I have fooled Meng Da into believing that his friend Li Yan has asked him to pretend to be too ill to come to Cao Pi's assistance. He is sorted out. As for Cao Zhen, Zhao Zilong is already there at my request and can easily defend the Yangping pass. To add to this, I have sent Zhang Bao and Guan Xing with thirty thousand troops apiece to help ensure that the pass is safe. As for the army of Wu, they're not going to attack if there are no others already engaged. But I need someone to go and persuade Sun Quan that his best interests lie with us. He hasn't forgotten what Cao Pi tried to do!'

A mightily relieved second ruler leaves Kong Ming. As he goes, Kong Ming notices one official, Deng Zhi, who seems to be amused. Kong Ming stops him leaving and invites him into his inner chamber.

'We now have three kingdoms,' says Kong Ming, 'Shu, Wei and Wu. My plan is to restore the Han dynasty by subduing both of the other kingdoms. Which one should I attack first?'

To this Deng Zhi replies, 'Wei's too strong at present. Our new ruler is young, and no one is yet sure about him. So let's not rush. Instead, let us mend fences with Wu and combine our efforts. After all, we no longer have to worry about the late ruler's quest for revenge. In the long run this will be to our advantage.'

Kong Ming is delighted and asks Deng Zhi if he is willing to go to Wu. Although he protests that he is not very experienced in such affairs, he is persuaded and the next day accepts the mission from the second ruler.

Will this work?

We can find out.

CHAPTER 86

Deng Zhi shows courage and convinces Sun Quan.
Xu Sheng destroys Cao Pi's army.

In the south, in Wu, Lu Xun's status has soared after his triumph over Wei. It is increased even more by his prediction that the four armies ordered by Cao Pi – to which he hoped Wu would contribute a fifth army – will fail. Sun Quan listened to him and so has not sent his army to join the ultimately futile attack planned by the Wei on Shu.

When Deng Zhi arrives as the envoy of Shu, the advisers of Sun Quan are convinced this is just another trick by Kong Ming. He is confronted by armed guards lining a walkway to a cauldron of boiling oil. To all appearances, it seems he is about to boiled alive. But Deng Zhi smiles at this pretence and when asked why says that this only shows how petty the people of Wu are! This calmness and bluntness impresses Sun Quan deeply. Deng Zhi soon convinces Sun Quan that his best interests lie in a partnership with Shu. Sun Quan sends one of his men back with Deng Zhi to negotiate the agreements.

Kong Ming agrees with the second ruler that if Deng Zhi returns with an envoy from Wu then they will forge an alliance against Wei. And so it comes to pass, and the alliance is signed.

In Wei, the emperor soon hears of these developments and is furious, knowing all too well that this spells trouble for his kingdom. Asking for advice, to his surprise he is told to wait ten years. During that time he should develop military agricultural colonies so the army will have enough food and resources of their own to fight such a battle.

This is not to the liking of Cao Pi at all. He orders immediate preparations put in hand for an invasion to be launched.

Ten 'dragon' boats are created, each more than two hundred feet long and each of them capable of carrying two thousand men. He also orders three thousand warships. By autumn AD 224 all is ready. The combined marine and land forces are over three hundred thousand men strong.

In Wu news of the enemy army's manoeuvres soon reaches the king of Wu. With Lu Xun defending Jingzhou, Sun Quan appoints Xu Sheng, an eager volunteer, to go on the defensive at the Great River. There he is joined by an impulsive and self-important young man by the name of Sun Shao, a nephew of the king. He demands the right to cross the river and bring the war into the lines of the enemy troops, but Xu Sheng forbids him to do so. 'I have three thousand men – let me go and attack!' Sun Shao demands time and time again, and Xu Sheng refuses him permission time and again. Eventually, and because of the threat to military order that such insistent questioning of his command highlights, Xu Sheng gives orders for his execution as a lesson to all.

But at the precise moment the executioner lifts his axe to cut off Sun Shao's head, the king rides into the camp and demands a halt.

Xu Sheng respectfully complains to Sun Quan about this, pointing out the dangers of a loss of martial spirit and discipline, but the king pleads for the young man's life. He does, however, allow Xu Sheng to dismiss Sun Shao from the army.

Infuriated by this snub, Sun Shao takes his three thousand men and crosses the river anyway. Hearing about this, Xu Sheng orders one of his commanders, Ding Feng, to also cross and to keep an eye on the impulsive young man.

By now the dragon boat bearing the Wei emperor Cao Pi has arrived at Guangling, where Cao Zhen is waiting for him.

'How many enemy troops are there on the other side?' asks Cao Pi. 'None at all, as far as we can see,' replies Cao Zhen. 'Then I'll go out and examine this for myself,' says Cao Pi, and his state barge, the great dragon boat, sails out into the middle of the river. It is bedecked with the full regalia of his imperial aspirations, flags bearing the dragon and phoenix; the sun and moon – all fluttering in the breeze.

'Why don't we cross?' asks Cao Pi, but Liu Ye warns him that precaution should come before rashness, and that it is best to wait and see.

At night, with a heavy fog, no light shows on the south bank. Cao Pi is told that this shows that fear of his presence has sent the enemy scurrying away.

But when the sun rises the next day and the thick fog is at last dispelled an astonishing sight greets them. For a hundred miles or so an immense wall has sprung up, guarded by a vast army. In fact this is all a fake, erected overnight at Xu Sheng's command, but the desired effect is achieved. The enemy are terrified by this sight.

'We may have a huge army,' says Cao Pi, 'but against such numbers and skills we're helpless. There's no point in attacking.' The rising wind also threatens to sink the imperial dragon boat and it is only through timely intervention by Wen Ping that Cao Pi is rescued.

At this moment bad news comes to the Wei ruler. Zhao Zilong and his men have surged out of the Yangping pass and are making for the Wei capital at Chang'an!

Cao Pi has no option but to order a retreat along the river to safeguard the capital. But as they retreat, they and their boats are attacked by Sun Shao, who nearly captures the Wei ruler – the latter loses half his men. Trying to move off the water and onto dry land, Cao Pi is suddenly confronted by a fierce fire created by burning reeds that have been soaked in oil. Blazing ferociously, they cut off his retreat. Then he is attacked by Ding Feng, and only through the bravery of Zhang Liao, who is badly wounded, and Xu Huang does Cao Pi eventually escape.

The scale of the defeat of the army of Wei is immense. Many men died, and the loot captured by the Wu army is beyond counting. Zhang Liao dies of his wounds, and Cao Pi gives him a full military funeral.

Over at the Yangping pass, Zhao Zilong is suddenly recalled by Kong Ming from his planned attack on Chang'an. Rebels led by Yong Kai and supported by the king of the Man people, Meng Huo, have attacked southern areas of the kingdom with over one hundred thousand men. Kong Ming has decided to go to deal with this himself and needs Zhao Zilong back in Chengdu to guard the capital.

And what is the result of all this?

Let's find out.

將軍

CHAPTER 87

Kong Ming goes to war against the Man people.
The king of the Man suffers his first defeat.

In Chengdu, capital city of Shu, Kong Ming has taken full responsibility for the affairs of state. As a result, the kingdom is at peace; everyone is happy and well fed; all are willing to shoulder their share of responsibilities.

In the year of AD 225 news comes of a revolt in the southern borderlands. Meng Huo, king of the Man tribes, has invaded with one hundred thousand men. Three local governors have joined the revolt: Yong Kai, governor of Jianning; Zhu Bao, governor of Zangge, and Gao Ding, governor of Yuesui. The city and governor of Yongchang are besieged, and the governor, Wang Kang, has sent an urgent appeal for help.

When the second ruler hears that Kong Ming himself wishes to go south to the borders to deal with this insurrection, he is far from happy. He is deeply concerned about the already existing threats – from Wei to the north and Wu to the south. But Kong Ming reassures him that he has put in place worthy commanders to protect the land.

So it is that shortly thereafter he sets forth for the south of the country, accompanied by trusted commanders such as Zhao Zilong, Wei Yan, Wang Ping and Zhang Yi. En route they meet the third son of Guan Yu, Guan Suo, whom Kong Ming appoints as head of the vanguard. The well-provisioned army proceeds on its way to battle.

When news of the advancing army reaches the three treacherous governors, they meet to confer and plot. Each of them has an army of some fifty to sixty thousand men. They send out an advanced party under E Huan, a giant of a man with an ugly face and the energy of many men. The armies meet on the border of Yizhou. Using cunning, Wei Yan pretends to flee after the initial battle. He is thus able to lure E Huan into a trap, and he is swiftly captured.

Imagine his surprise when, brought before Kong Ming, he is released and treated with great respect! Kong Ming enquires whose commander he was, and on being told that he served Gao Ding, says, 'Oh, I have heard of him. He is a loyal man who has been misled by Yong Kai. Go to Governor Gao Ding and tell him to surrender, and we will accept him back, otherwise ... well, let's just say it will not go well for him.'

You can imagine how moved Governor Gao Ding is by this news when E Huan returns. The next day, when rebel governor Yong Kai visits Gao Ding, he asks how E Huan has escaped. On being told of Kong Ming's leniency, he warns that this is simply a plot by Kong Ming to divide and rule.

Fearful now of losing prestige, Yong Kai moves to attack the Shu army. But this hasty attack fails, and his army is badly defeated. Undeterred, the very next day Yong Kai attacks again. But Kong Ming simply holds him off. A few days afterwards, this time in concert with Gao Ding, who has been persuaded to stand firm with the rebels, he attacks again. Once again the Shu army triumphs, and many men from both rebel groups are captured.

Kong Ming divides the captured soldiers into their two original groups. He has rumours spread that the men of Gao Ding will be spared while the men of Yong Kai will be executed. It is hardly surprising, then, that when Kong Ming calls for Yong Kai's men to be brought to him and he asks whom they served they all say, 'Gao Ding!' He lets them all go as he did with the real men of Gao Ding. However, he lets them know that someone has come to him from Yong Kai, offering to bring the heads of Gao Ding and Zhu Bao in order to obtain pardon.

This, of course, sets rumours running when the released soldiers return to the rebel camps. The rumours increase Gao Ding's fears. But he is still really uncertain about whether to surrender to Kong Ming. So he sends a spy into the Shu army camp.

The spy is captured, and in a further act of deception, Kong Ming pretends to believe that he is a messenger from Yong Kai.

'Where are the heads of Gao Ding and Zhu Bao that your master promised me?' demands Kong Ming. The spy, thoroughly confused but desperate to save his own life, mumbles vaguely and inaudibly. 'Take this letter to your master,' says Kong Ming, 'and tell him to act now before it is too late!'

Simply happy to escape, the spy kowtows and returns post haste to Gao Ding, to whom he presents the letter. The fake letter has exactly the effect Kong Ming hoped. Gao Ding decides to kill Yong Kai and surrender to Kong Ming. Together with E Huan, he plans the murder of Yong Kai. He invites him to a banquet, but, when he does not turn up, Gao Ding knows that there is a plot and so with E Huan he attacks Yong Kai's camp. As most of the men guarding the camp are the same as those released by Kong Ming, 'thinking' they were Gao Ding's men, they rally to Gao Ding's side. Although Yong Kai manages at first to escape, he is hunted down and killed by E Huan in an ambush.

Gao Ding turns up at Kong Ming's camp with the head of Yong Kai. With him come his own men and the men of Yong Kai. But Kong Ming has a further trick up his sleeve. 'Do you think you can fool me?' demands Kong Ming. 'Zhu Bao has sent a secret letter offering to surrender and warning me that you and Yong Kai are so close nothing will part you. So what treason is this that you kill him? I think you are lying and you have no intention of submitting.'

Completely baffled by this, Gao Ding replies, 'That's just a plot by Zhu Bao. Don't trust him an inch.' 'Well,' says Kong Ming, 'if you were to bring me the head of Zhu Bao I could of course then trust you.'

Gao Ding and E Huan take off to do exactly that. When they confront Zhu Bao, he is of course totally at a loss as to what they are talking about. With one swipe of E Huan's halberd, Zhu Bao is beheaded, and all his men submit.

Kong Ming is delighted when Gao Ding brings him Zhu Bao's head. The revolt of the governors is over, and Gao Ding is made governor of all three areas, and E Huan appointed as the commander of Gao Ding's troops.

News of the quelling of the revolt of the governors soon

reaches Meng Huo and his tribe. He calls together the chieftains of the three valleys and urges upon them the need to unite to defeat the Shu invasion. The three chieftains come with some fifty thousand men each – Jinhuansanjie to take the central position in the attack, Dongtuna the left flank and Ahuinan the right flank.

In planning how to confront them, Kong Ming plays games with the loyalty of his old martial allies Zhao Zilong and Wei Yan. He speaks as if he considers them too old and unfamiliar with the territory. So he appoints younger men – Wang Ping and Ma Zhong – to lead the main attacking troops. Disgruntled, the two older men take themselves off and, having captured some locals, from whom they gather information on the enemy, devise their own strategy for attacking the three armies in their various encampments.

Leading five thousand of the best fighters, Zhao Zilong and Wei Yan set out at the dead of night for the camp of Jinhuansanjie. They take the rebels completely by surprise, and Zhao Zilong slays the chieftain Jinhuansanjie, whereupon the Man troops scatter. Splitting their forces, Zhao Zilong heads for the camp of Ahuinan, while Wei Yan sets off for the camp of Dongtuna.

When Wei Yan attacks Dongtuna from the rear, unbeknown to Wei Yan, Wang Ping attacks from the front, and although Dongtuna escapes his army is defeated. Likewise, when Zhao Zilong attacks the rear of Ahuinan's camp, Ma Zhong is there attacking the front, and while Ahuinan escapes his troops are defeated.

The two chieftains are captured later. Kong Ming has not only foreseen the way of dealing with the three armies – creating rivalry between his own commanders – but has foreseen how the chieftains will try to escape. The two men are brought before Kong Ming and to their immense relief they are released. But Kong Ming then says, 'Beware. Tomorrow Meng Huo will personally lead the attack and that is when we will capture him.' And having assigned his men to different tasks, he sets in motion the plan to capture the king.

Sure enough, Meng Huo, hearing of the disaster of the three chieftains' revolt, decides to move to the attack himself and before long he is facing Wang Ping on the battlefield. Meng Huo is splendidly dressed in fine robes studded with jewels, riding a red hare horse and bearing two bejewelled swords. Viewing his enemy, he is dismissive of the supposed skills of Kong Ming.

'You call this an army?' he says scornfully. 'This Kong Ming is no military genius! This is pathetic. Had I realized how foolish he was and how false his reputation, I'd have rebelled long ago!'

This is why, when the initial challenge match between the Man tribes' warrior Mangyachang and Wang Ping results in Wang Ping's apparent defeat and flight, Meng Huo is trapped into advancing. He is, of course, drawn into an ambush and is captured by Wei Yan, while Meng's troops are routed, with huge losses and many taken prisoner.

Wei Yan brings the captured Meng Huo to Kong Ming's camp, where he has put on a display of the Shu army's wealth and strength designed to awe the rebel chief. Kong Ming immediately orders the release of the soldiers, saying, 'I know that your families are desperate for news of you and fear the worse. So knowing you're just good people, forced into military service by Meng Huo, I release you. Go home and celebrate with those you love.'

You can imagine the joy and happiness this provokes, and the grateful troops praise Kong Ming to the Heavens.

Then Kong Ming turns his attention to Meng Huo and upbraids him for rebelling. To this Meng Huo furiously replies:

'Once, all this land of the Riverlands belonged to us. You and your lord seized it by violence and self-declared yourselves to be its rulers – even making your leader an emperor! For generations my ancestors ruled here – on the very lands you've seized without good reason. You have acted so treacherously. You are the real traitors. So what is this "rebellion" of which you speak? Answer me that.'

'Well,' says Kong Ming, 'you're my prisoner now, so will you obey?'

'You trapped me, so why should I surrender?'

To this Kong Ming replies, 'But you see I'm going to let you go. So what do you have to say to that?'

'Set me free, and I'll gather fresh men and come at you again. But if you capture me then, well, then I'll submit.'

So Kong Ming orders that the shackles be removed and Meng Huo be given food, drink and clothing, a horse to ride and be allowed to leave the camp.

Will this work?

Let's find out.

CHAPTER 88

Crossing the Lu River, Meng Huo, the king of the Man, is captured for the second time. Then for the third time.

Bewildered by Kong Ming's actions in letting the king of the Man go, his commanders ask for an explanation. 'I can catch him whenever I want,' says Kong Ming, 'but we'll only ever win the Man tribes to our side if we capture their hearts, not just their bodies.' It cannot be said this pleased the commanders.

Meanwhile Meng Huo has returned to his people, who needless to say want to know how he has managed to escape. 'I was held prisoner in a tent,' he says, 'but I killed at least ten, probably more, of their guards. So I was able to escape in the middle of the night. Challenged by one of the camp guards, I killed him as well and stole his horse and so managed to ride to freedom.'

The story delights his people, and his warrior fame increases. Soon over a hundred thousand men have ridden in to his camp to support him. Meng Huo orders all boats to be withdrawn from the north shore of the river and held on his side, the south. Here a great wall is built and fortified with watchtowers. Meng Huo's strategy is to simply wait out the attacking army of Shu. It is now mid-summer, and the heat is affecting the invading army badly.

Realizing this, Kong Ming orders his men to camp in the coolness of the hills and to build shelters. Then he sends Ma Dai to cross the river at a vantage point called Shakou, which is found to be unguarded. The reason for this soon becomes clear, for as the men wade through the waters they collapse with blood pouring from their mouths and noses. Kong Ming urgently demands of local guides why this has happened. 'During the day,' they say, 'a noxious miasma arises from the waters. If anyone tries to drink the water they are convulsed with pain and die. However, if the river is crossed at night, the miasma has disappeared, and so it is safe to cross.'

Armed with this vital information, Ma Dai crosses and takes up position in a narrow valley through which the supply line to Meng Huo passes. Once established there, he seizes the grain supply wagons as they come through to supply the rebel tribal troops. Meng Huo seriously underestimates the strength and resolve of Ma Dai, and his first attempt to shift him is a failure costing Meng Huo many men. So he sends the chieftain Dongtuna to attack, but, confronted by insults hurled by Ma Dai reminding him he has been pardoned by Kong Ming and set free, Dongtuna retreats in embarrassment. Even his own troops question the wisdom of trying to attack and outwit Kong Ming. The fact that many of them have been so thoughtfully released by Kong Ming weighs heavily upon them. In discussion with Dongtuna and the other chieftain, Ahuinan, it is agreed that they don't want to fight the empire,[24] as the empire has never done them any harm. Instead they decide to seize Meng Huo and deliver him as a captive to Kong Ming in order to seek peace.

Their plot works brilliantly. Having captured Meng Huo, they carry him off to Kong Ming's camp on the north shore.

Hearing that Meng Huo is being brought, Kong Ming orders a full display of the sheer size and military might of the army to impress the tribal leaders. Dongtuna and Ahuinan are thanked and rewarded, and then Meng Huo is once again brought before Kong Ming.

'Do you recall your promise?' asks Kong Ming. 'You said that if I caught you again you would submit.'

'But you didn't catch me by yourself. I was betrayed, so why should I now submit?'

'So,' says Kong Ming, 'if I let you go again, then what?'

'I'll return with a new army because as a leader of the Man tribes that is how it must be. But if you catch me again, well, then I will submit.'

Kong Ming releases him from his bondage and gives him food and drink.

'Ever since I left my little hut I've won every battle. So why do you think you can beat me? Why not submit?' says Kong Ming. To this Meng Huo says nothing whatsoever.

Later Kong Ming shows him the supplies and troops and asks again, 'Why on earth do you go on resisting me? Look at the troops and all the weapons. If you will but surrender, the Son of Heaven will make you a king of all the Man tribes. But Meng Huo points out: 'Even if I submit, just think of all the other rebel tribes. Let me go, and I'll bring all the men of all the tribes to swear allegiance to you.'

Delighted with this, Kong Ming releases him.

Immediately Meng Huo returns to his own camp he has the two chieftains Dongtuna and Ahuinan murdered. Then he seeks the advice of his brother Meng You as to what to do next. Together they hatch a plan. Shortly afterwards Meng You travels to Kong Ming's camp carrying tributes of gold, pearls, ivory and other treasures. He brings with him an escort of some hundred men. Kong Ming is not fooled for a moment and secretly whispers orders to his officers, who quietly move off, while Kong Ming entertains not just Meng You but also his men, plying them with drink. Knowing that as far as he is concerned Kong Ming has fallen for the plot, Men You sends two of his men back to Meng Huo's camp to say all is falling into place as planned.

The plot, of course, is that Meng You's soldiers will open the gates for an attack by the massed tribes of the Man, who will burn down the camp, scatter the enemy and, as Meng Huo hopes, capture Kong Ming.

But when that night Meng Huo and his men storm the camp they find it deserted and their men on the inside drunk and drugged, lying on the floor of Kong Ming's tent. Kong Ming secretly ordered the wine to be drugged and it has had the desired effect even on these wild mountain warriors.

Of course, an ambush is then sprung by Kong Ming, and no matter which way Meng Huo tries to go he cannot escape. For the third time he is captured. Most of his men surrender and are released at Kong Ming's explicit command – and to their great relief.

Once again Kong Ming asks Meng Huo to submit and reminds him of his previous promises.

'I failed because you tricked my brother. If I'd come instead we'd have won. Heaven – not you – has defeated me, so why should I submit?' exclaims a determined Meng Huo.

'Well, I'll have to let you go again,' says Kong Ming with a sigh, to which Meng Huo replies, 'I'll go and gather my men and let's have a proper battle. If you win that, I'll submit and never resist again.'

So Kong Ming lets him go, having suggested that he study properly the texts on war and prepare fully. On his way to the mountains he passes Ma Dai, Zhao Zilong and Wei Yan, who have taken up their positions on the south bank. They each warn him that this will be the end of him if he attacks again.

As the poet Hu Zeng[25] has written about this strategy of Kong Ming:

> For five months on campaign in this desolate land,
> Going by moonlight to the river of deadly mists,
> His outstanding audacity more than justifies the
> three visits,
> And yet despite his attacks on the Man liberty is
> given seven times!

Kong Ming again explains to his officers his desire to win the tribes by kindness not through violence. However, Meng Huo is full of anger and resentment. He sends gifts to the eight tribes of the borders, calling all the Man peoples to come to his aid. Hundreds of thousands obey but perhaps they should have noticed that when Kong Ming is informed of this, he simply smiles.

So who will win?

Let's see, shall we?

CHAPTER 89

Kong Ming tricks and captures Meng Huo a fourth time. Then a fifth time.

Kong Ming's first move is to go in his special carriage to the Western Er River. Here on the north bank his men construct fortified camps and build a bridge of bamboo. Secure in the defence of the bridge, the bulk of the army crosses over to the south side. And here they build three forts. This invasion and provocation have the desired effect, and soon Meng Huo and his vast army appear on the scene. Kong Ming rides out in his carriage to view the enemy. He is wearing his headband of silk, is dressed in white, including his crane-feather cloak, and is carrying his feather fan. Opposite him rides Meng Huo, wearing rhino-skin armour and a red headband. In his left hand he carries his shield, in his right his sword, and he is riding a red ox. He is surrounded by savage warriors. Despite the request of his commanders to give battle, Kong Ming orders a retreat back into the three forts.

'Let their rage subside, then when they have calmed down we can defeat them,' said Kong Ming.

Sure enough, a couple of days later, having observed that the tribal warriors have grown bored and have relaxed their guard, he sends out his commanders in different directions. To Ma Dai he says, 'I'm going to abandon the forts and move to the north shore. Dismantle the bamboo bridge but then rebuild it further downstream.' Leaving lights burning in the camp to make it look occupied, Kong Ming withdraws his army northwards across the river.

It isn't until the following morning that Meng Huo discovers the abandoned camps still with their stores in them. He gives orders to prepare rafts to sail across and attack the Shu army.

Little does he know that his lands have already been penetrated by the Shu troops.

Suddenly fires are ignited all around the Man army, and panic breaks out, with men fleeing in all directions. Soon Meng Huo has but a handful of soldiers still with him, and they retreat into a valley to the east. To his amazement and delight he sees Kong Ming's carriage trundling along ahead of him, and Kong Ming, seeing him, shouts, 'Hah, king of the Man! Heaven has defeated you again, but you took so long to get here.'

'Three times he has tricked me,' cries Meng Huo to his men. 'Now let's get him. Charge!'

Not many of his men follow him, but some riders do charge forward, with Meng Huo leading. Just as they close for the kill, the ground beneath them collapses, and they and their horses fall into deep pits. Wei Yan has them pulled out and binds them tight. Then he marches them off to Kong Ming's camp.

Of course, Kong Ming pardons the soldiers and sets them free. He remonstrates with Meng You and urges him to at least try to tame his brother. Then he too is released. Finally Meng Huo is brought in.

Challenged by Kong Ming to account for being captured for the fourth time, Meng Huo remains defiant, threatening to haunt Kong Ming even from the grave! The order is given: 'Execute him.' But even at this point Meng Huo is still hurling insults at Kong Ming. 'Free me, and I'll avenge all four failures.'

And once again, having ascertained that Meng Huo will indeed make another attempt, but if defeated he will – he promises – submit, Kong Ming releases him.

He joins up with his brother Meng You, and they decide to take refuge in Bald Dragon ravine until the heat of summer drives the invading army away. Bald Dragon ravine's chieftain, Duosi, assures them that this place is a perfect refuge because there are only two roads in and out. One is blocked by fortifications and is impassable to any enemy. The other road is a track across desolate landscapes and past four deadly springs – the only source of water anywhere in the region of the path. 'No one,' he confidently tells Meng Huo and You, 'will ever get through there. Only two commanders in the last three hundred years have ever made it through – the last one nearly two hundred years ago.'

As a poet[26] wrote about the heat:

> The hills and marshes are decaying, torrid places,
> A raging fire of heat overwhelms all.
> There is nowhere else so dreadful,
> Nowhere else is the wind this terrible.

And how accurate the poet is! The conditions the Shu army find themselves in are truly terrible, and the men are far from happy. But Kong Ming has come this far and knows that to turn back, even with these terrible conditions, will mean defeat. So he is, of course, eager to see if there is any way into Bald Dragon ravine. Wang Ping is sent with a detachment to try the track route but in desperation in the wilderness they drink from the first of the deadly springs and are struck dumb. Local people tell them they are doomed to die within a week or two.

On hearing this, Kong Ming goes to the spring himself. Looking around, he sees, high above, the remains of an old shrine. Perplexed by the silence of the place – no bird or animal is to be seen or heard – he climbs up to the ancient temple. He finds it is dedicated to one of the two commanders who made his way through the deserted landscape, General Ma Yuan.[27] Kong Ming prays for help, and suddenly an old man appears. From him Kong Ming learns about all four of the deadly springs and how to protect his men from their effects. 'Travel only in the afternoon, when the mists have cleared, and chew on a special herb.' To find this, Kong Ming is told to go deeper into the countryside until he comes to the valley of the stream of Everlasting Peace. 'Here you will find a hermit and before his hut flows the spring of Peace and Happiness. These waters will cure those already afflicted, and here grows the special herb of protection,' says the old man. 'Who are you, sir?' asks Kong Ming. 'I am the guardian spirit of this mountain sent to help you by General Ma Yuan.' So saying, he disappears.

The very next day Kong Ming and his affected men travel to the valley and find the spring and the hermit. He immediately recognizes Kong Ming, and Kong Ming confesses his distress at not being able to subdue the Man and thus fulfil the charge given him by the first ruler. The hermit shows the men where to bathe, and they are cured. He also shows Kong Ming the herb to be chewed as a protection.

'And who are you, sir?' enquires Kong Ming.

'I am Meng Huo's elder brother, Meng Jie.'

Kong Ming is completely taken aback at this.

'Do not be too surprised,' says Meng Jie. 'Let me explain. We are indeed three brothers. Our parents died, and my two brothers have taken to the way of evil and will not obey the king nor be part of civilized life. I've tried to stop them but to no avail, so have retreated here. I'm so sorry that their crimes have been such a curse for you and I deserve many deaths for this failure. So here I am now to beg your forgiveness.'

Kong Ming replies, 'Sir, what if I were to petition the Son of Heaven to make you king. Would you accept?'

But none of the trappings of power or wealth has any appeal to the hermit, and despite Kong Ming's best efforts he will accept nothing for the help he gives.

Having dug wells and prayed for fresh water, which miraculously arises, the army of Shu replenish their supplies. Chewing the herb, they travel only in the afternoon. And soon they arrive on the edge of the Bald Dragon ravine.

When news of the successful invasion comes to Meng Huo and King Duosi, they cannot believe their ears and go to see for themselves. 'These are deities, not humans!' says Duosi. But they all agree they have no option but to attack and fight to the end.

A grand feast is held to encourage the warriors, and in the midst of this another chieftain, Yang Feng, head of twenty-one tribes from another valley, arrives, pledging his men – some thirty thousand of them – to the struggle.

Soon everyone is very drunk, and at this point Yang Feng suggests that they need dancing women and that his women dance the sword and shield dance better than anyone else. So in they come, along with his five warrior sons. Two of Yang Feng's sons bring cups of wine to the Meng brothers but then, at a cry from Yang Feng, leap forward and seize the pair of them. King Duosi tries to flee but is grabbed by Yang Feng. The dancing women have suddenly become warriors to prevent anyone else coming into the tent.

'Why?' asks Meng Huo, who is completely taken aback.

'Because we owe Kong Ming the lives of our brothers and sons, whom he freed. We must honour his kindness, and bringing a rebel to him is how we will do this.'

With their leaders captured, the tribes scatter back to their homelands, while Yang Feng brings the three captured leaders to Kong Ming. He is richly rewarded.

So once again Kong Ming greets Meng Huo, smiling. 'Will you submit now?' he asks.

'Why?' replies the still defiant Meng Huo. 'You didn't do this. It was betrayal by my own people. Kill me if you want, but I'll not submit!'

'It was the Will of Heaven that my troops have not been affected by the poisonous springs. So given that, how much longer will you persist in this stupidity?' asks Kong Ming.

'Beyond here, in the valley of the Silver Pit hills, my ancestors lived. Three great rivers and high mountains protected them. If you can capture me there, well then I will submit, and that submission will bind all the generations to come.'

To this Kong Ming says, 'If, after releasing you, you gather your forces together to contest me and I capture you and you still refuse to submit, I'll kill all of your tribe, everyone who is even remotely related to you.'

So Meng Huo – and Meng You and King Duosi – are released.

Will this plan ever succeed?

Who knows!

CHAPTER 90

Deploying terrifying beasts, Kong Ming wins for the sixth time. Burning the rattan armour army, Kong Ming captures Meng Huo a seventh time.

So Meng Huo, Meng You and King Duosi return to their own lands – or what remains of them. In particular they go to the Silver Pit hills. Here three rivers converge at the town of Sanjiang. It is here that the main ancestral temple of the Man rulers is to be found. This temple is a place not just of animal sacrifices to the family spirits but also of human sacrifice – usually people captured from the land of Shu, or any stranger unfortunate enough to be taken prisoner. In this culture shamans, not doctors, deal with illness; law courts do not exist – instead, any crime results in immediate execution; men and women mix freely, even when bathing, and marry whosoever they wish – never seeking family approval; if it rains they plant rice – if not, then they eat snakes and elephant meat; their markets are places of barter only. This is the culture of this land of the Man tribes.

Gathering his surviving thousand or so men together, Meng Huo swears to take revenge, and his men all cry their agreement. It is also agreed that help should be sought from King Mulu of the Bana valley, who is renowned for his magical powers and at whose command tigers, leopards, wolves, scorpions and poisonous snakes come to his aid. So Meng Huo's brother-in-law is sent with gifts to entice him to join the uprising. Meanwhile King Duosi fortifies Sanjiang.

When Kong Ming and his army arrive before Sanjiang, he sends a reconnaissance party under Wei Yan and Zhao Zilong to explore what appears to be a weak point in the defences. But they encounter a storm of poisoned arrows fired with unbelievable speed. The order is given to pull back, and the Man tribesmen, thinking they have won an early victory, relax their guard – just as Kong Ming intended.

Five days later Kong Ming storms and takes the city by an extraordinary trick. He orders his vast army to all wear coats and to fill them with earth. Then they charge forward and surge up to the walls, emptying the earth as they turn to run back. By this means they build a ramp of earth that soon reaches to the top of the walls from which the Shu army then leap into the city, killing King Duosi and destroying the vast majority of the enemy troops.

Meng Huo is up-country in one of the valleys when news comes of the fall of the city, and he is lost for words, so great is his distress. Into the breach steps none other than his wife, Lady Zhurong, who is skilled in the art of knife-throwing. Taking a force of fifty thousand men, she rides out to do battle. In the battle, the Shu commanders Zhang Ni and Ma Zhong are captured and brought back by Lady Zhurong to her husband Meng Huo as hostages.

The next day Zhao Zilong takes up the challenge to fight Lady Zhurong and tries to trick her by pretending to flee. But she is not fooled. Then Wei Yan tries the same trick, but again she is not fooled. The next day this is repeated, and she ignores Zhao Zilong's feint. But after being taunted by the Shu troops, when Wei Yan attacks and then flees, she falls for the trick and is captured in an ambush.

Kong Ming, of course, treats her with due respect, and an exchange is arranged – the two Shu commanders in exchange for Lady Zhurong.

Now the Bana valley men and their king, Mulu, arrive to join the rebels. When the sun comes up the next day the Shu army get their first view of these wild people. Almost all the warriors are naked; their faces hideous to behold; they each have four daggers and they drive on their men with gongs, not horns and drums. Their king rides on a huge white elephant. With them come tigers, panthers, jackals and wolves.

At the battlefront, Zhao Zilong and Wei Yan look at each

other in astonishment at the appearance of their foe. 'Never,' says Zilong, 'in all our years at war have we ever seen anything like this!'

Suddenly King Mulu starts to chant, and instantly a terrifying storm breaks, with the wind hurling sand and stones. Riding upon the storm come tigers, panthers, jackals, wolves, snakes and scorpions, roaring and hissing in anger. The Shu troops cannot contend and retreat to the relative safety of Sanjiang. Mortified, Zhao Zilong and Wei Yan bow before Kong Ming and apologize.

'This is not your fault. I have heard of the Man magic,' says Kong Ming, 'and so I've come prepared. There are twenty wagons, ten red and ten black. Bring the red ones forward.'

When the wagons are opened, inside can be seen carved statues of fierce animals with teeth and claws of steel. They are so large ten men could sit on the back of each one. A thousand soldiers are chosen, a hundred to each wagon, and, following Kong Ming's orders, the statues are stuffed full of gunpowder. Then they are rolled forward among the soldiers towards the battlefront.

The next day Kong Ming rides to the front in his little carriage, dressed as usual as a Daoist with his feather fan. When Meng Huo spots him he points him out to King Mulu. The king immediately starts his magic chanting, and a storm billows up from nowhere as do all the wild creatures. But Kong Ming calmly shakes his fan, and the storm turns about, and the sand and stones descend upon the Man army. Then the statues are rolled forward. As soon as the gunpowder is ignited the statues roar forth flames and a terrifying noise. At this the Man army of wild animals turns tail and in fear and awe rushes back, trampling or killing many of the Man soldiers in their way. At his command, Kong Ming's men charge forward, and the defeat of the Man army is complete. King Mulu is killed, and only a fraction of the army escapes into the valley, where Meng Huo has moved his camp.

The following day a messenger comes to Kong Ming to say that Meng Huo and his whole family have been seized by one of his brothers-in-law and that he is bringing them as hostages for Kong Ming. Hearing this, Kong Ming orders Zhang Ni and Ma Zhong to take a thousand men each and to hide in the passages around his tent. When the brother-in-law and his captives arrive, they are jumped by Zhang Ni and Ma Zhong, and their men are found to all be carrying hidden weapons. Kong Ming has rightly guessed that this was a plot to assassinate him.

'You promised me,' Kong Ming says to Meng Huo, 'that if I caught you in your own lands you would submit. So will you now?'

'Hah,' cries Meng Huo, 'we came to bring death not because you have won some battle against us! I still don't believe you can beat me, so therefore, of course, I refuse to submit.'

'For goodness' sake,' says an exasperated Kong Ming, 'this is the sixth time I've caught you, but you still won't submit. What will it take?'

'If you catch me for a seventh time, well, then I'll submit and never, ever rebel again.'

'Your fortifications are now gone, so what have I to fear?' And with that Kong Ming releases them all but as they go he says, 'If I do catch you for the seventh time, that is it. If you will not submit then, I'll show no mercy.'

Regrouping once again, but with only a thousand or so men, Meng Huo is told that there is one last hope: the Wugu tribe. Their chieftain Wutugu is huge and eats only snakes and other dangerous animals alive. Their strength comes from their rattan armour. This is so strong because of the way they repeatedly soak the rattan in oil. They do this up to ten times, and it makes the armour impervious to any arrow or sword. It also floats so they can easily cross rivers.

So Meng Huo travels the hundreds of miles to their land to meet their chieftain. The people there live in caves, not houses. Wutugu agrees to help Meng Huo, and soon some thirty thousand men have answered the call. Then they march out to do battle with Kong Ming and continue until they reach Peach Blossom river. Kong Ming marches to confront them.

This battle between the armies results in the men of Shu retreating, for nothing they do can penetrate the rattan armour.

But the Wugu soldiers do not follow up on their victory, simply returning to their own camp.

It seems that they are invincible, and Kong Ming is advised that he should retreat, for there is nothing of any value in this desolate land, so why struggle to conquer it? But Kong Ming, smiling, says, 'Tomorrow I will reveal my plan. Having come this far, to retreat now would be to undo all that has been gained.'

The following day Kong Ming goes and reconnoitres for himself and finds a winding valley, like a huge serpent. He is delighted and exclaims, 'This is exactly what I hoped to find. Indeed, I believe Heaven has prepared this for us.'

Returning, he summons his officers. To Ma Dai he says, 'You take the ten black carriages and a thousand bamboo poles. Seize each end of the valley and then do as I tell you. You have two weeks to get ready.' And he tells Ma Dai his plan.

Then Zhao Zilong is given his instructions. 'Go and control the end of the valley that leads to Sanjiang and make sure you are ready.' Again Kong Ming gives his orders, and Zhao Zilong departs to carry them out.

The most complex instructions are given to Wei Yan. 'Go to the banks of Peach Blossom river. Now, when the Man soldiers attack, abandon the camp and retreat to where you will see a white flag flying. Make camp there. In two weeks I want you to "lose" fifteen battles and abandon up to seven camps. But do not come looking for me until after the fifteenth battle.'

This is not quite what Wei Yan hoped he would be called upon to do, but he accepts, even though his heart is troubled by these strange commands. Zhang Yi is told to prepare a camp with fortifications at a special place, while Zhang Ni and Ma Zhong are given a thousand of the Man soldiers who have surrendered and told of their special role in this plot.

Now everything is ready.

The plot starts well. Day after day Meng Huo and Wutugu attack Wei Yan's camps and day after day they 'defeat' him. Camp after camp is abandoned and seized by the Man tribes.

Step by step Wei Yan, guided by Kong Ming and a series of white flags marking the next camp, draws the Man army closer and closer to the winding valley and its secrets. Wutugu has been warned by Meng Huo to watch out for ambushes and not to go into any valley that is thick with trees and shrubs. Whenever such a valley is encountered, Wutugu is very cautious, but they all prove to be empty of any threat.

And so at last on the sixteenth day he is drawn into the Serpent Winding valley. Riding a white elephant and wearing a helmet of wolf fur decorated with the sun and moon, his cloak covered with gold and pearls he seems almost to breathe fire. Spotting Wei Yan, he curses him, at which Wei Yan once again retreats, and Wutugu and his men charge after him. Coming into the winding valley, Wutugu sees that its sides are bare and so has no fear of an ambush and presses on to kill Wei Yan.

To their surprise, the rebels pass a group of wagons apparently abandoned. They take this as a sign that the enemy has fled so fast they cannot save their supplies. On the tribes press until they suddenly come to the end of the valley, which is blocked by huge tree trunks. Rocks suddenly come crashing down from above, blocking the road. Wutugu orders the rocks and tree trunks removed, but while they are engaged in this, from nowhere a set of blazing wagons rumble into view, blocking the roadway.

'Back, back,' shouts Wutugu, and he and his men start running back to the entrance to the valley. But the wagons they previously passed are now ablaze, blocking their retreat.

'The carts are full of gunpowder, and we can't get out,' the cry goes up as the men start to panic. But Wutugu looks up the slopes and sees that there is no brush to catch fire so starts to lead his men up the sides of the valley to escape. Then, from nowhere, flaming brands are hurled down the sides of the valley, aimed at certain key points on the hillside and in the valley itself. The flaming brands ignite fuses, which then set off landmines buried in the soil. As if in the throes of a vast earthquake, the whole valley erupts skywards, and flames roar out across the landscape. The oil-soaked rattan armour, far from protecting the men, now becomes their funeral clothes as the rattan catches fire. Despite desperate attempts, no one is able to escape from their blazing armour. In total thirty thousand men, including

Wutugu, die that day in the burning valley, huddled together in the face of the sheer overwhelming terror of the whole event.

From the clifftop Kong Ming watches the horror unfolding, reeling from the terrible stench of burning death. He is weeping at such a dreadful sight.

'While this is in the service of the Han, it will mean my life is shortened for having to order such an attack.'

And all who stand there with him are deeply affected by both the sight and his words.

Back at Meng Huo's camp he is waiting to hear news of Wutugu's success when the thousand men who were captured earlier by Kong Ming arrive.

'Wutugu and his men have trapped Kong Ming in the Serpent Winding valley, and they need your help immediately,' the men shout. 'We've come to escort you. We were forced to surrender to Shu, but have escaped. It will be our honour to escort you to the triumph.'

When Meng Huo and his entourage enter Serpent Winding valley, they realize the scale of their mistake and that Meng Huo has once again been trapped. He tries to escape but is captured along with his wife and the rest of his group by Zhang Ni, Ma Zhong and the thousand men who fooled him into coming here. Meng Huo briefly breaks free but as he tries to escape his path is blocked by Kong Ming sitting in his little carriage. 'Ha ha, Meng Huo,' shouts Kong Ming, 'what are you going to do now, eh?'

At this moment Ma Dai leaps out and grabs Meng Huo.

When all the captives are brought before Kong Ming, he says, 'I had no option but to use these tricks but I despise myself for doing so, and the consequences of this will weigh heavily upon me in this life and that to come.'

Then he explains how he used Wei Yan to lure the enemy into this valley; how he ordered Ma Dai to prepare the black wagons and how the land mines were buried and linked with fuses – the thousand bamboo poles he had sent. He tells of how the burning wagons rolled into the far exit forced the men back and how the only way the rattan army could be killed was by fire.

'But the complete extermination of these people, of these tribes, this will always be for me a terrible burden.'

Then Kong Ming turns his attention to Meng Huo. He has him given food and drink in a separate tent and into that tent he sends one of his officers, who says, 'The prime minister is embarrassed and will not see you again. You are to be released so you can leave and gather an army to attack once again. Go, begone. Don't look back.'

Meng Huo doesn't move. Instead, with tears rolling from his eyes, he says, 'Captured seven times; released seven times! This is unheard of. I may be a barbarian but I understand the importance of morality and righteousness.'

So saying, Meng Huo and his entourage crawl on hands and knees to Kong Ming's tent and in accordance with his tradition he bares his upper body and kneels to show that he is ready to be punished.

'Your Excellency, Heaven has ensured that the southerners will never rebel again.'

'So,' says Kong Ming, 'this means you now submit?'

Sobbing, and with tears streaming down his face, Meng Huo says, 'For generation after generation we'll be for ever grateful that you spared us, so, of course, how could we not submit?'

Kong Ming and Meng Huo celebrate late into the night, and Meng Huo is appointed ruler over all the lands conquered by the Shu kingdom. And great is the rejoicing, with the Man people leaping and dancing with excitement.

A poet has written this:

Feathered fan, silk cap, jade-green canopied carriage;
The Man king captured seven times does as required.
Throughout the streams and valleys he is honoured still.
A temple on a hill stands yet raised by his former enemies.

Despite protests from some of his officials, Kong Ming settles rulership of the conquered lands upon Meng Huo and turns to head home. But they have only just reached the River Lu when storms erupt, hurling dust and stones at the men so they can go no further. Not knowing what is going on, Kong Ming asks Meng Huo for his advice.

> No sooner are the Man defeated
> Than ghosts rise in the waters.

What this all means Meng Huo will explain.

CHAPTER 91

Kong Ming offers sacrifices at the Lu River and takes his army home. Cao Pi dies.

Meng Huo looks at the storms swirling around the Shu army and divines immediately that this is caused by malicious spirits who must be pacified by offering sacrifices.

When Kong Ming asks what kind of sacrifices, Meng Huo replies, 'In the past, when these malicious spirits were driven crazy, lashing out in all directions, the only thing that worked was to offer forty-nine human heads – seven times seven – plus a black ox and a white goat.'

Kong Ming is loath to shed more blood but he knows the army is deeply troubled and anxious. When the local people are asked why they think this is happening they tell him they believe the trouble is caused by the ghosts of those soldiers – both Shu and Man – who died in the river. They have heard terrible cries and shrieks ever since the battle as well as seen strange ghostly shapes and eerie mists. They tell him yet again that only human sacrifice will work. To this Kong Ming replies 'But these ghosts are from men who've died, so why would more deaths be of any use? To be honest, I've a much better plan.'

He has forty-nine fake heads created by moulding dough stuffed with meat. These he offers in a ceremony in the middle of night, wearing his Daoist robes. A long proclamation is formally and ritually read out to appease the souls of the dead. Through this Kong Ming apologizes unreservedly for the deaths he has caused.

At the climax of the ceremony Kong Ming cries out aloud in anguish, and the whole army is moved to tears at his distress. At this soulful sound the ghostly shapes begin to disperse, and the following day the army crosses the river safely. At long last and after many months of travel they arrive back at the capital, Chengdu.

The second ruler rides out far beyond the city walls to welcome the triumphant army and its leader home. Great is the rejoicing, and as a result over two hundred foreign cities send tribute acknowledging the power and mighty reach of the new kingdom. The second ruler fulfils Kong Ming's wish that all those families who have lost someone in the war will be cared for.

Meanwhile, back in the kingdom of Wei, Cao Pi has been reigning for seven years. Cao Pi has a son, Cao Rui, whose mother, Lady Zhen, the first wife and empress of Cao Pi, was killed by his father. This was wrought through a terrible plot contrived by a concubine, Lady Guo, who wanted to be empress. When Cao Pi fell dangerously ill and looked as if he might die, she claimed this was due to witchcraft practised by Lady Zhen. After the murder of his mother, Cao Rui was brought up by the new empress, as she had no children of her own.

In the autumn of AD 226 Cao Pi falls seriously ill. Gathering the three most senior military commanders, Cao Zhen, Chen Qun and Sima Yi, to his deathbed, he instructs them to help the young Cao Rui to become emperor and to guide him as he grows into manhood. Having made sure of this, Cao Pi sheds a tear and dies. He is forty years old and has reigned for seven years.

Cao Rui is enthroned as the new Wei emperor, and all the formal responsibilities are given to the loyal supporters of the dynasty. In particular Sima Yi asks to be made governor of Xiliang and the western regions, and his wish is granted.

When the news reaches Kong Ming in Shu, he is surprised but not troubled by the accession of the young man. But he is alarmed by the rising power of Sima Yi. As a result he starts to plan to attack Wei before they have a chance to develop their armed forces, especially those under the control of Sima Yi. However, Ma Su advises against this: 'The men are still exhausted after the southern expedition, and anyway I've a plan which will destroy

Sima Yi at the hands of Cao Rui. Do you want to know what this plan is, sir?'

Kong Ming, of course, wants to know, so Ma Su points out the lack of faith Cao Rui has in Sima Yi, whom he sees as a schemer. 'Let's spread rumours in all the major cities that Sima Yi is plotting a rebellion and let's post up fake proclamations as if from Sima Yi, calling for rebellion.'

So this is what they do.

One day such a proclamation is found nailed to the main city gate of Yecheng. It is taken to Cao Rui, who reads that, according to this poster, his father apparently wanted Cao Zhi to become the next emperor. Apparently – again according to this poster – because of a charge of treason he was passed over, and instead Cao Rui was enthroned – 'a man with no discernible virtue'! The poster then goes on to say that in order to fulfil Cao Cao's original intentions, 'Sima Yi has no option but to overthrow the current ruler in accordance with the wishes of Heaven and the people.'

The fake proclamation creates great anxiety in the court, and adviser Hua Xin recalls that, 'The great august emperor told me that Sima Yi has the eyes of an eagle and the stare of a wolf and that he would bring disaster upon the dynasty if he had the power.'

Debate rages. Some say, 'Strike now.' Others say, 'Don't believe a word of this. Sima Yi is not a rebel. This all smacks of a plot by the Shu or Wu to destabilize the empire.'

In the end it is agreed that Cao Rui will go on imperial inspection to Anyi, where Sima Yi will have to officially receive him. Cao Zhen says, 'Watch how he behaves and if he shows signs of revolt, seize him then and there.' So with a hundred thousand soldiers Cao Rui goes to Anyi.

In all innocence and wanting to impress the Son of Heaven, Sima Yi brings thousands of his troops, cavalry and infantry to greet Cao Rui. Cao Rui leads the imperial vanguard and when he meets Sima Yi he demands to know why he is in rebellion. Sima Yi is appalled at this accusation and swears that this must be the work of Wu and Shu. To show goodwill he orders his army to retire. However, not even Sima Yi's bowing deep before the imperial carriage has the desired effect. On Hua Xin's advice Sima Yi is stripped of his post and ordered to return to his ancestral village – a huge disgrace. Hua Xin takes over his army.

When Kong Ming is told of what has happened he is delighted because he is fearful of invading Wei if Sima Yi has an army. So now he persuades the second ruler to go to war. He presents him with a formal petition in which he urges the second ruler to carry forward the intentions for reunification of the empire that his father espoused.

The second ruler expresses his anxiety that, having so recently undertaken the arduous war in the south, Kong Ming would be pushing himself too far in undertaking this new war in the north. Even though astrological warnings are cited, Kong Ming still insists that Heaven changes all the time, and this is indeed the time to strike. And so it is finally agreed to launch the war on Wei.

Once again Kong Ming takes the role of supreme commander. Consulting the astrological charts, he decides that the attack should start on an auspicious day in spring AD 227. As they are about to set out, Zhao Zilong steps forward and demands to be included in the invading army. Despite Kong Ming's best efforts to dissuade the old general, Zhao Zilong insists and wins the right to be in the vanguard. One of the officers, Deng Zhi, offers to help Zhao Zilong, and Kong Ming appoints five thousand of the best troops and ten officers to assist and to protect the old warrior.

News soon reaches Cao Rui of the attack by three hundred thousand men, and that the vanguard under Zhao Zilong and Deng Zhi has already crossed the border. At his own request, Xiahou Mao is given permission to lead the defence. He especially wants this role because he seeks revenge for his father, Xiahou Yuan, who died when Xuande took Hanzhong. Xiahou Mao is renowned for his ferocious temper and for being very tight-fisted. He is also married to a sister of Cao Rui. So he is put in charge despite others, including a leading minister, pointing out that the young man has no relevant experience, especially when confronting someone as skilful as Kong Ming. Xiahou Mao deflects this by asking whether the minister is himself in league with Kong Ming. 'If I don't take Kong Ming alive, then I'll never return to see the Son of Heaven,' cries Xiahou Mao. And this forces the others into silence.

> Seizing the white flags of war,
> Does this shallow youth have the ability?

We shall find out.

CHAPTER 92

Zhao Zilong kills five Wei officials.
Kong Ming takes three cities by cunning.

Kong Ming and the army stop first at Mianyang, and here various plans are mooted, not least by Wei Yan. But Kong Ming rejects them all – which especially annoys and upsets Wei Yan. Xiahou Mao has gathered his forces at Chang'an, where he is joined by troops from the Qiang tribes led by their chieftain Han De and his four sons. He is an enormous fellow wielding a huge battleaxe.

When the two armies meet the first challenge is thrown down by Han De and his four sons. Enraged, Zhao Zilong charges into battle and in the space of a few minutes kills the eldest son. This brings the three other brothers into battle with Zhao Zilong. He fights them alone, killing another of the sons, wounding one, who is rescued by his own men, and capturing the last son, Han Yao. At the sight of such slaughter, Han De flees, and his troops with him, though they sustain huge losses at the hands of Zhao Zilong and his men. It is a great victory for Shu.

As a poet has said:

> In my mind's eye I see Zhao Zilong from Changshan,
> Triumphant and vital at the age of seventy.
> Alone he fought four generals and took them down,
> Comparable to his feat at Dangyang when he saved his
>   lord's heir.

Later, when Deng Zhi congratulates Zhao Zilong on being seventy and yet still as courageous as ever, the latter answers somewhat pointedly, 'As your excellency didn't want to use me because of my age, I had to show what I am still capable of!'

Han De limps back to Xiahou Mao to report the disaster, and Xiahou Mao decides to take the field himself. When the very next day the two armies clash again, Han De rides out to avenge his fallen sons and, wielding his mighty axe, he heads straight for Zhao Zilong. After but a few bouts Han De lies dead on the ground, while Zhao Zilong, spotting Xiahou Mao, races straight towards him. Xiahou Mao turns tail and flees, and the day is once again won by the troops of Shu.

The Wei commanders meet that night to discuss what to do next and it is agreed to try to trap Zhao Zilong in an ambush the very next day.

When Deng Zhi sees the army of Wei coming so soon after their previous disasters he warns Zhao Zilong that this probably means some sort of trick is planned. But Zhao dismisses these worries, saying of Xiahou Mao, 'This child still has the smell of mother's milk on his breath! I'll finish him off today.'

So saying, Zhao Zilong charges into battle, and when he spots Xiahou Mao he goes straight for him, followed by Deng Zhi. They are, of course, swiftly drawn into an ambush. Realizing what is happening, Deng Zhi manages to pull back his own men and force his way out. But Zhao Zilong is trapped. Surrounded by the Wei men, Zilong fights against overwhelming odds and somehow manages to keep them at bay. Retreating but also determined to get to use the advantage of a small hill, he fights his way up the slope, hoping also to gain a better view of the scale of the threat. But he cannot reach the top because of a barrage of stones and logs. When night falls the Wei troops set fire to the hillside and close in for the kill. Fearlessly Zilong fights on. Down upon him rain thousands of arrows and crossbow bolts. There is no way of escape for him and his men, so he resigns himself to dying on that hill.

Then, without warning, cries go up to the northeast, and the Wei soldiers start to scatter in terror. Riding to zilong's rescue comes Zhang Bao, already bloodstained from the battle he has fought to get this far. Zilong and Zhang Bao drive through the Wei soldiers to the northwest, and then see the disorientated troops suddenly abandon their arms and flee at the sight of yet another force coming to Zilong's rescue. This time it is

Guan Xing. The two rescuers report to Zilong that they have been detailed to help Zilong and that this is why they are here. Zilong's response is not to say thank you but instead: 'Let's go for Xiahou Mao now and finish this off once and for all.'

And so they do, and that very night the Wei army is finally defeated. Xiahou Mao escapes to Nan'an but is closely followed by Zhang Bao and Guan Xing, who then besiege the city. For ten days they and Zhao Zilong and Deng Zhi try to capture the city, but to no avail. So Kong Ming comes to see what can be done.

Seeing the situation and appreciating that capturing an imperial son-in-law would be a great psychological victory for Shu over Wei, Kong Ming comes up with a plot. The two major cities in the same area as Nan'an are Tianshui and Anding. Kong Ming's plan is to fool each of the governors into sending help to the beleaguered city of Nan'an and then, when the troops have left, to seize the two cities.

Thus the governor of Anding receives a sudden visit from a messenger 'from Nan'an' by the name of Pei Xu claiming to bring a letter (very wet, soiled and not easily read) from Xiahou Mao at Nan'an asking for help. The next day another surprise visitor turns up, saying that the governor of Tianshui has already sent his men to help Nan'an and Xiahuo Mao.

Not long after, the governor of Anding, Cui Liang, sets off for Nan'an, spurred on because he sees flames in the distance. Kong Ming's men have piled up brushwood around the city and lit it to make it look like a city about to be sacked. But he still has about twenty miles to go when he is ambushed by Zhang Bao and Guan Xing. Fleeing, he heads back to the supposed safety of Anding, only to discover that Wei Yan has captured the city. In fear for his life, Cui Liang turns to retreat to Tianshui, but he is stopped by another troop of soldiers who have Kong Ming in their midst in his customary Daoist clothes and seated in his carriage. Despite trying yet again to flee, he is captured and brought before Kong Ming.

At their meeting Cui Liang is treated very well, and Kong Ming proposes a joint plot. He will send Cui Liang to Nan'an to talk with his friend the governor Yang Ling and persuade him to seize Xiahou Mao.

Cui Liang does as requested – almost. He enters the city under a truce and goes straight to see his friend the governor Yang Ling. But the governor suggests that, instead of Kong Ming's plot, they spring their own. It is agreed that Cui Liang will claim that the governor Yang Ling is willing to surrender the city and thus lure the Shu troops inside, where they can be cut down.

Cui Liang therefore returns to Kong Ming and claims that Yang Ling will surrender the city, and then the Shu troops can capture Xiahou Mao, as he has insufficient men to do this himself. To this Kong Ming replies that he will use the hundred Wei soldiers who have already surrendered and add to them Shu officers disguised as Anding men in order to get inside and seize Xiahou. He also sends Zhang Bao and Guan Xing in as well. This rather throws Cui Liang, but he realizes he has no option but to agree. 'We can kill them all anyway once they are inside,' he thinks and so agrees.

That night, Zhang Bao and Guan Xing, armed with secret missions given to them by Kong Ming, arrive at the gate of Nan'an along with the troops who have surrendered. 'Who are you?' demands Yang Ling, and Cui Liang replies, 'We come from Anding to help you.' But he also shoots an arrow over the city wall to forewarn Yang Ling about Guan Xing and Zhang Bao coming in as well.

Xiahou Mao is informed of all this, and they agree to kill the two Shu commanders as soon as they enter the city gate. The gates are flung open, and the troops enter. Yang Ling comes to greet them, but, before he can utter a word, Guan Xing draws his mighty sword and kills him instantly, while Zhang Bao strikes down the panic-stricken Cui Liang. Immediately Guan Xing sends up a fire signal for the Shu army to attack, and within moments they are swarming in through the gate. In total terror, Xiahou Mao flees to the south gate, only to be confronted by more Shu troops under the command of Wang Ping. Here he is captured.

Now Kong Ming enters the city, and his men behave so well

this reassures the people. Kong Ming goes out of his way to reinforce this message that all will be well. He had of course guessed that Cui Liang never meant to cooperate and so had plotted and set his own trap instead.

But while Nan'an and Anding have now fallen to Kong Ming, nothing has been heard from Tianshui. So Wei Yan is sent to take that city. The governor of Tianshui is Ma Zun. On hearing of the siege of Nan'an, he had held a council. Then Pei Xu had arrived with his 'letter' asking for help for Nan'an. He had been followed the next day by a messenger saying that Anding had moved to the rescue of Nan'an, so when would the Tianshui men move likewise?

Ma Zun had been ready to go to the rescue when one of his officers, Jiang Wei, told him it was a plot of Kong Ming's. Jiang Wei is a deeply respected scholar and filial son held in high regard. He pointed out, 'If Nan'an is besieged, how come two messengers have been able to escape? And who's this Pei Xu anyway? Does anyone know him? This is a trick of the Shu, and, if we leave, our city will be captured. I've an alternative plan to both capture Kong Ming and relieve Nan'an.'

Truthfully,

> No matter how skilfully you plot and scheme,
> Plans can die because of one whom no one foresaw.

So what was Jiang Wei's plan?

Let's find out.

CHAPTER 93

Jiang Wei surrenders to Kong Ming. By words alone Kong Ming causes Wang Lang to die.

Jiang Wei's plan is simple really. It is to trap Kong Ming by using exactly the same plan as Kong Ming, namely, to ambush him as he prepares to ambush them. False reports are sent out that the troops who moved out from the city led by Jiang Wei 'to assist Nan'an' were the only significant force and that only civilians remain in Tianshui. Zhao Zilong therefore approaches the city and demands entry, only to find himself attacked from behind by the force led by Jiang Wei while being mocked from the city wall.

In the clash that ensues Jiang Wei charges straight at Zhao Zilong, who to his astonishment finds himself outclassed and forced to flee, his attempt to take Tianshui foiled.

Kong Ming is seriously upset to have been thwarted and wants to know who has done this. 'Jiang Wei, a man whose filial loyalty to his mother is famous, who is clever, courageous and understands military strategy,' comes the reply.

'Well,' says Kong Ming, 'I never thought there would be one like this in Tianshui!'

Back in Tianshui, Jiang Wei is getting ready for the next attack, which he is certain will be led by Kong Ming. In preparation he takes a troop of men secretly outside the city. He orders the city walls to be bristling with flags and armed men to intimidate the enemy. In the middle of the night fires break out all around the besieging troops, lit by Jiang Wei's men, while from the walls a cacophony of noise bursts forth. Completely taken by surprise and deeply alarmed, convinced they are being attacked from all sides, the Shu army panics and melts away as Jiang Wei's men close in. Kong Ming only escapes because Zhang Bao and Guan Xing protect him and force their way through the attacking troops.

Kong Ming now opts for another strategy. He decides to use Jiang Wei's mother, given his reputation as one honoured for the filial piety he displays to her. He discovers she lives in nearby Jicheng, and so Wei Yan is instructed to go as if to besiege it but in reality to seize the mother. Meanwhile Kong Ming also attacks the supply town of Shanggui to cut off Tianshui's resources.

Jiang Wei, on hearing of the assault on Jicheng, begs permission from the city governor of Tianshui, Ma Zun, to go to protect her. With three thousand men he sets off, while a further three thousand go to protect Shanggui. Sure enough, Jiang Wei encounters Wei Yan outside Jicheng, and when Jiang Wei attacks, Wei Yan 'flees'. Jiang Wei enters the city and rushes immediately to his mother's house nearby. Likewise, Zhao Zilong allows the enemy troops to enter Shanggui.

Back at the Shu main camp, the prisoner Xiahou Mao is brought before Kong Ming, who offers him a chance to live, and Kong Ming begins to spin an astonishing set of lies. First of all he claims that Jiang Wei has offered to surrender Jicheng if Kong Ming lets Xiahou go. Kong Ming asks Xiahou if he is willing to go and tell Jiang Wei what the terms of surrender will be. He, of course, agrees. He then arranges for Xiahou Mao to meet supposed refugees fleeing Jicheng, who tell Xiahou that the city has been surrendered by Jiang Wei and that he has joined Kong Ming's side. Learning this, Xiahou turns aside and rides to Ma Zun at Tianshui instead. There he is welcomed and tells the story of the betrayal of Jiang Wei. It is at this point that the Shu army attacks Tianshui in the depth of the night. To the astonishment of the defending troops on the city wall they see Jiang Wei riding up as part of the Shu attacking force.

'Why are you fighting us Xiahou Mao?' cries Jiang Wei. 'I surrendered because of you.' Astonished, Xiahou Mao replies, 'What do you mean?' 'What do you mean, what do I mean?' replies Jiang Wei. 'You are the one who wrote to me, saying I should surrender. It was all a plot, wasn't it? Now I have joined them I've been given high command, so why would I want to go back to Wei?'

At this the battle starts in earnest, and fighting lasts all through the night.

Actually this is not Jiang Wei at all but someone dressed up from the Shu ranks to look like him in the half light of the night. Meanwhile Kong Ming has attacked Jicheng. Luring Jiang Wei out by apparently fleeing and leaving their supply wagons behind – the city is low on supplies – the Shu army takes Jicheng, so that when Jiang Wei returns from the foray, the city is in enemy hands. He and his men flee towards Tianshui but are met by Zhang Bao, and only Jiang Wei escapes alive. Seeking refuge in Tianshui, he is, of course, astonished to be greeted by a swarm of arrows fired at him from the walls. So he takes off again, this time for refuge in Shanggui. Yet again he is denied entrance, as the commander there believes he has joined the enemy. So he turns once more and heads towards Chang'an but has not gone far when he is confronted by Guan Xing and his men. As he turns to try and flee, despite his exhaustion, he finds his path blocked by Kong Ming, in his carriage, who sighs and says, 'Why are you keeping us waiting for your surrender!'

And so at last, looking at his options and realizing he has been outclassed, Jiang Wei surrenders.

After that Jiang Wei helps Kong Ming take Tianshui, while Xiahou Mao and Ma Zun flee to safety in Qianghu. Shanggui falls after its commander is convinced there is no better option. Swollen by more soldiers joining the triumphant Shu army, Kong Ming moves forward to the next stage of his invasion, setting up camp on the banks of the River Wei.

When it becomes known in Chang'an that Kong Ming has arrived on the banks of the river, Cao Rui summons his advisers. It is AD 227. The advisers recommend that Cao Zhen and the elderly minister of home affairs Wang Lang should be in command of the army to defend Wei from Kong Ming. When the two armies confront each other, heralds summon both sides for a parley and Wang Lang takes the lead from the Wei side, while Kong Ming does so from the Shu side. Each side tries to outdo the other in regalia and ceremony. After opening pleasantries, especially from the somewhat loquacious Wang Lang, Wang Lang then starts on a long speech about how the Han dynasty has been troubled by rebels and how Cao Cao, 'our august emperor', rescued the dynasty, and what a model of virtue he was. This is why the Mandate of Heaven had descended upon him, and then on Cao Pi, and why it is wrong of Kong Ming to rebel against the Will of Heaven.

To this Kong Ming retorts that he is amused by the baseness of Wang Lang's speech and gives his own version of the troubles of the Han dynasty, culminating in the Mandate of Heaven passing to his august emperor, Xuande, and now to his son. The task Xuande left unfinished – putting down rebels – is now his responsibility. 'How dare you talk to me about Heaven's Will, you white-haired idiot!' Kong Ming says. 'When you go to Hell – which will be very soon, looking at you – what will you have to say to the ancestral emperors of the Han? Ehh? Go on, get lost!'

This so shocks Wang Lang that he can barely breathe, and suddenly he cries aloud and drops dead from his horse. Then Kong Ming challenges Cao Zhen to battle for the following day.

Wang Lang's body is carried back, and the Wei commanders realize they will be at risk of attack by Kong Ming that night because they will need to perform the mourning rituals for Wang Lang. So they decide to set an ambush to forestall the anticipated midnight raid by attacking the Shu camp. Two troops of men are chosen to make a pincer movement on the camp. Meanwhile Kong Ming hatches his own, even more convoluted plot of appearing to raid but actually setting his own ambush for the ambush! In fact, what happens is that when the two battalions of the Wei soldiers break into the Shu camp it is deserted, but in the darkness each thinks the other is the enemy troop, and they fall on each other, inflicting terrible losses on their own men. When they realize what has happened, they try to retreat, only to run into an attack by Zhao Zilong on one side and Wei Yan on the other. The Wei battalions are completely routed, their commanders only just escaping. On returning to their camp, they are mistaken again for Shu soldiers and attacked, and, to finish off the battle, the actual Shu army attacks again.

It is a total victory for Kong Ming.

Over in the Wei camp, it is one of the commanders, Guo Huai, who comes up with a plan to turn the tables after such a defeat.

So what is this plan?

Well let's find out.

CHAPTER 94

Kong Ming defeats the Qiang tribes in a snowstorm. Sima Yi swiftly defeats Meng Da.

Guo Huai reminds Cao Zhen that for years the Qiang tribes have brought tribute to the court. He suggests that, if Wei offered an imperial princess to be married into the tribal chieftain's family, then they could ask for soldiers from the tribes in return. Cao Zhen sends a formal letter of proposal, and within weeks one hundred and fifty thousand Qiang tribesmen are on their way, along with their invincible iron-plated war wagons – some drawn by horses, some by camels. The army moves to the Xiping pass, where Han Zhen the Shu commander is in charge.

Responding to his call for help, Zhang Bao and Guan Xing offer to go, even though Kong Ming points out they do not know the terrain very well. Despite such a warning and his own serious personal reservations, they are off, leading fifty thousand men.

Their first engagement with the enemy is a disaster. At the crucial moment, as the Shu troops surge forward, the Qiang lines part, and out come the iron wagons. These invincible wagons are filled with archers and crossbowmen. Out fly arrows and crossbow bolts in vast numbers. The Shu troops fall apart before such an attack. Guan Xing in particular is caught by this move and has to flee, hotly pursued by a Qiang commander called Yueji.

The chase brings Guan Xing to a river, into which he and his horse leap, but a blow from Yueji's mace fells the horse and Guan Xing is thrown into the water. Thinking his time has come, Guan Xing struggles to at least rise above the water, when he sees Yueji's men riding off as fast as they can into the distance, pursued by a strange warrior. A new contender has arrived and has single-handedly scattered the enemy. Guan Xing almost manages to kill Yueji, but he fights back and escapes from the riverbank, abandoning his horse.

Guan Xing takes Yueji's horse in place of his own fallen one and rides off following the mysterious warrior whose intervention has saved his life. But no matter how hard he rides he cannot catch up with the stranger, until suddenly a swirling mist arises and surrounds the figure. Then and only then does Guan Xing realize it is none other than his father Guan Yu, riding his famous steed, Red Hare. From out of the mists Guan Yu speaks: 'Go that way my son, that way lies safety. I will watch over you until you reach the camp.' And then he disappears. Following his father's directions, Guan Xing eventually runs into Zhang Bao, who is out looking for him. Zhang Bao too has seen Guan Yu! 'I was being pursued by those iron wagons,' says Zhang Bao, 'when suddenly your father descended from the clouds and scattered them. Then he pointed in this direction and said, "Go this way and rescue my son."'

When they return to the camp, Ma Dai welcomes them and says he has no idea how to defeat the iron wagons, so he has written to Kong Ming asking for help.

When Kong Ming arrives, he surveys the enemy and their formidable wagons and draws up his plan. It is midwinter. 'Snow is coming,' he says. 'Just what I need for my plan to succeed.' So saying, he despatches various commanders and their troops with specific instructions. Jiang Wei is told to advance on the enemy lines of the Qiang soldiers and then to retreat, leaving the way open for an attack on the Shu camp. This he does, putting in place the first part of Kong Ming's plan. The attacking Qiang soldiers with their iron wagons in tow burst into the almost deserted enemy camp and see the figure of Kong Ming in his famous carriage disappearing through the back gate and so set off in pursuit. The Qiang troops led by Yueji and commander Yadan are hot on the heels of not just Jiang Wei and his men but even more significantly Kong Ming himself and so they redouble their efforts. There is some concern that they might be being lured into an ambush, but glancing around over the snow-draped landscape, they see nothing to alarm them, so the iron wagons roll on, invincible as before.

Suddenly there comes a terrible smashing sound. The iron wagons have rolled into pits, hidden under the snow, and have crashed down in ruin. From the left and from the right arrows pour down into the pits, slaying the Qiang soldiers, as Jiang Wei, Ma Dai, Zhang Yi, Guan Xing and Zhang Bao attack. Yueji himself is killed by Guan Xing, and Yadan captured.

Typically, and with his usual wisdom, Kong Ming pardons Yadan, and in return the Qiang people pledge not to rebel again and depart back to their own lands.

Confusion as to what has happened to the Qiang leads Cao Zhen to believe the Shu army has been defeated, and so he advances, only to be attacked by Wei Yan. Two of his senior commanders die in the ensuing battle. Cao Zhen and Guo Huai almost perish in the battle as well and only just escape from an attack by Guan Xing and Zhang Bao. When news is brought to Cao Rui at his court, alarm and despair overwhelm him. It is then that his adviser Zhong Yao makes a bold suggestion: bring back Sima Yi and give him responsibility for the army and the defence of Wei. Mightily relieved, the ruler agrees, and Sima Yi is ordered to proceed to Chang'an.

Back at Kong Ming's camp, now at Qishan after yet more victories, news comes which seems to offer even greater success. Meng Da, who surrendered to the Wei empire, has decided to change sides again, seize the areas of Jincheng, Xincheng and Shangyong and then march on Luoyang. With Kong Ming now planning to strike out for Chang'an, it looks possible that both ancient capital cities could fall to the Shu. But when news comes of Sima Yi's restoration and new powers, Kong Ming is deeply troubled. 'Sima Yi is formidable, and, if he takes on Meng Da, it will be Sima Yi who will win.' So saying, he sends a messenger to Meng Da, warning him to beware of Sima Yi and to build up the defences rapidly to deflect any attack.

But when Meng Da reads the message he smiles rather condescendingly, saying he has heard Kong Ming often worries too much. So he sends back a letter saying there really is no need to worry too much about Sima Yi, because he is so far away, and that gives Meng Da at least a month to repair the defences.

When he receives the letter, Kong Ming is furious and says, 'He's doomed.' When asked why, Kong Ming quotes the *Art of War*: '"Attack the enemy before he is ready; do what no one expects." He doesn't have a month, because Sima Yi will not wait for permission but will be on Meng Da within ten days, and Meng Da will not be ready.'

And sure enough, Sima Yi does not wait for orders nor go to Chang'an as instructed. He realizes that Meng Da can be taken out of the equation by swift, decisive action. So he sets out with the army towards Meng Da. En route he meets up with his old fighting companion Xu Huang, and their forces unite. Learning that Kong Ming has tried to warn Meng Da to be prepared for a surprise attack, Sima acknowledges the skills and wisdom of Kong Ming and urges on his men even faster.

Meanwhile, Meng Da has been in touch with the governors of two neighbouring cities – Jincheng and Shangyong – whom he believes are going to join his rebellion. They string him along, delaying sending their troops, on the grounds of needing more time to prepare.

Sima Yi, pretending not to know anything about Meng Da's planned rebellion, sends a message to him as if he were still a loyal commander of the Wei forces, asking him to be ready to march to Chang'an. When Meng Da asks where Sima Yi is, he is told he is already marching to Chang'an. Thinking the coast is clear for his own attacks, Meng Da is delighted by this news. He gives orders to prepare to advance on Luoyang. But no sooner has he said this than a vast cloud of dust is to be seen – clear evidence that a huge army is on its way. Rushing to the battlements, Meng Da sees the great warrior Xu Huang ride up to the gate and demand, 'Open the gates, you traitor.'

Furious at the tricks that have been played on him, Meng Da fires an arrow, which strikes Xu Huang in the head. He dies later that night, by which time Sima Yi and the whole army have enclosed the city. The next day Meng Da sees to his relief two columns of troops marching towards the city – these are the soldiers from Jincheng and Shangyong, whom Meng Da believes are on his side. He rushes out with his own troops to greet them, only to find out that they too have betrayed him.

In the debacle that follows Meng Da is not only defeated but killed, while Sima Yi enters the city as a hero.

Having dealt with the threat from Meng Da, Sima Yi now marches to Chang'an and presents himself to the Wei ruler. There, Cao Rui apologizes for having listened to bad advice and demoted him and congratulates him on taking out Meng Da's threat.

Now they turn their thoughts to the battle against Kong Ming, and Sima Yi asks that Zhang He be appointed as his vanguard commander. This is readily agreed by the Wei ruler. Together, Sima Yi and Zhang He leave to confront Kong Ming.

So who is going to win?

Shall we find out?

CHAPTER 95

By ignoring Wang Ping's advice,
Ma Su loses Jieting. Just playing a lute,
Kong Ming defeats Sima Yi.

Sima Yi and Zhang He take command of the Wei troops. They establish positions directed by Sima Yi to counter the anticipated Shu invasion heading towards Chang'an.

The death of Meng Da is reported to a shocked and angry Kong Ming. Knowing the odds have now changed, he details a defence force to Jieting to hold it against an attack by Sima Yi. Ma Su volunteers to go – even though his knowledge is mostly from books on war, not actual war itself. Kong Ming agrees but sends Wang Ping to oversee the actions of Ma Su. Meanwhile other troops are despatched to guard key passes and to prepare backup in case of disaster at Jieting. Then Kong Ming moves his main force, with Jiang Wei in charge of the vanguard.

Having reached Jieting, Ma Su arrogantly decides – against the sage advice of Wang Ping – to take up a position on a hill, which he feels gives a good advantage point to oversee the main road down which the enemy will come. Wang Ping strongly advises defending the road itself. But Ma Su, citing copiously from Sun Zi's *Art of War* – for this in truth is all he knows about war – dismisses his protests, even calling the wise older warrior a woman! In the end and with the enemy closing in, Ma Su allows Wang Ping to go with a small troop to protect the road while he stays on the hilltop. Meanwhile Wang Ping sends details of the differing positions taken up by Ma Su and himself by express messenger to Kong Ming.

Sima Yi moves forward to the attack, especially because he is encouraged when he is told that the inexperienced Ma Su is in charge. Soon Ma Su can see the vast army encamped below, completely cutting him off. Wang Ping tries to come to his rescue but is forced back. On the hill, there is no water, and soon the troops are desperate with thirst. Ma Su's army begins to disintegrate as men desert. In despair Ma Su has no option left but to lead his men off the hill and try to battle their way through to freedom. But they are pursued by Zhang He, who nearly overwhelms them, until a rescue force led by Wei Yan comes to their rescue. Wei Yan himself is drawn into an ambush and is only rescued at the last moment by Wang Ping, but at the cost of their men suffering terrible losses. And Sima Yi captures the city.

Retreating to Lieliu, they meet up with Gao Xiang, who has ridden out to assist the army after learning of the fall of Jieting. Together they decide to attack the Wei camp that night in order to retake Jieting. It turns into a disaster because the Shu men arrive to find the town apparently empty, only to then be taken by surprise when they enter. Retreating to Lieliu, they discover that Guo Huai and Cao Zhen, in their absence and in order to thwart the power of their commander, Sima Yi, are also advancing on the town. A terrible battle ensues in front of the town, and the Shu army suffer badly. So Wang Ping, Wei Yan and Ma Su flee towards the Yangping pass, fearing that this too may fall into enemy hands.

However, when Guo Huai and Cao Zhen reach the town gates, they see that Sima Yi has already taken the town. From there he directs the next stage of his plan, laying ambushes and attacks to confront Kong Ming's men.

Meanwhile, Kong Ming has received Wang Ping's map and is in despair at the stupidity of Ma Su. Then news comes of the fall of Jieting and Lieliu. He hastily advances to Xicheng, where the army's supplies are stored. With just five thousand men he is suddenly informed that the Wei army of a hundred and fifty thousand are advancing on the city, led by Sima Yi. He immediately orders that all signs of occupation, such as banners, be removed and that everyone is to be hidden out of sight and not to make a sound. Then, wearing his customary Daoist robes, and accompanied by just two boys, he sits down on the city wall and plays a lute, as if nothing were troubling him.

When Sima Yi rides up to see what on earth is going on, he

is immediately concerned that such a relaxed attitude betokens some kind of cunning ambush. Even the gates of the city are open! Convinced that this is a trick, Sima Yi orders his vast army to turn aside, and soon they are out of sight. A poet has written:

> A lute just three feet long defeats a vast army,
> For here Kong Ming forced a retreat from Xicheng.
> One hundred and fifty thousand turned aside
> And to this day people remember this with awe.

Of course, what Kong Ming has also planned is a series of ambushes on the retreating Wei army. Having roundly defeated them, Kong Ming gives orders for the Shu army to begin its own withdrawal back to Hanzhong.

When Sima Yi finds out how he has been tricked time and time again by Kong Ming, he has to admit he has met his match. So he returns to the emperor at Chang'an and asks permission for a much larger army to destroy the Shu army at Hanzhong. An official steps forward and claims that he can defeat not only Shu but also Wu.

So who is this?

Let's find out

CHAPTER 96

Torn by grief, Kong Ming has to execute Ma Su.
Cutting his hair, Zhou Fang fools Cao Xiu.

The official is Sun Zi, and his point is that sending all the army off to take Hanzhong exposes the rest of the country to invasion by Wu. Better to defend the borders, build up the wealth and security of the country, and leave Shu and Wu to argue with each other. Swayed by these arguments, Sima Yi agrees entirely, and so this is the course they take.

Meanwhile Kong Ming takes stock of the losses he has incurred and is delighted that all his commanders have survived. However, the foolishness of Ma Su has to be punished. Weeping, Kong Ming orders Ma Su's execution. His foolishness has brought about serious losses to the men and state of Shu. As Ma Su's head is struck from his body, Kong Ming suddenly recalls that Xuande told him not to trust Ma Su. Nevertheless Kong Ming leads the official mourning and the burial rites for Ma Su. He was after all like a son to him.

Kong Ming then writes a formal memorial to the second ruler saying that he should be demoted for his failures. Even though the second ruler does not agree with this, he is advised that custom and honour demand that this happen. So Kong Ming is reduced in his military titles but retained as an acting prime minister, and honour is fulfilled.

Kong Ming now sets about training and preparing his men ready for whatever engagement should now arise. This is reported to Sima Yi and Cao Rui, who start to discuss again plans for a possible attack on Shu.

It is at this point that a letter comes from Cao Xiu, commander of the Wei army in Yangzhou. He informs the emperor that the Wu governor of Poyang, by name Zhou Fang, has written secretly, offering to surrender his region to Wei and asking for troops to come to enable this to take place. Sima Yi offers to go to help Cao Xiu and Zhou Fang. But a warning note is sounded by Jia Kui. He comments that Zhou Fang is renowned for his cunning, and that this could well be a trap. Cao Rui decides to send both men to investigate at the head of a sizeable army.

Indeed it is a trap. Sun Quan has received news of the plot from Zhou Fang and mobilizes the army to take advantage of the Wei army's advance into what they thought was going to be friendly territory. However, in view of the size of the invading army, command is given to the great strategist Lu Xun. It is Lu Xun who realizes that the weakness of the Wei army is its commander, Cao Xiu, the only reason for whose appointment is that he belongs to the imperial family. So he plans an elaborate series of pretend retreats designed to lure the unsuspecting Cao Xiu into ambushes.

Meanwhile Zhou Fang has met up with Cao Xiu and, hearing that there are questions about his true intents, he dramatically tries to kill himself with his own sword to convince Cao Xiu of his integrity. Prevented – as he obviously expected – by Cao Xiu, he cuts off his hair as a sign of his loyalty to the Wei dynasty, and this act is enough to fool Cao Xiu into trusting him. He agrees to follow Zhou Fang's battle plans. This creates considerable tensions within the Wei army, for Jia Kui has received reports of the Wu army gathering and he does not believe Zhou Fang at all. Cao Xiu is furious at being challenged in this way and almost has him executed. Morale within the army is dropping fast.

And it is as Jia Kui fears. Zhou Fang leads the Wei army into the trap set by Lu Xun. The defeat of the Wei army is total, and Cao Xiu only escapes by the skin of his teeth, ironically through the skills and military wisdom of Jia Kui.

Lu Xun is rewarded for his brilliance, and the returning army bring vast quantities of arms, horses and captured men back to Wu. Elated by this success, Lu Xun now proposes that

Wu should make an alliance with Shu and Kong Ming for a joint attack on Wei. Sun Quan supports this plan, and it is agreed to send a letter immediately to Shu.

So how will things pan out now?

Let's see.

CHAPTER 97

Kong Ming urges an attack on Wei.
Zhao Zilong dies, and Jiang Wei defeats
Wei by the use of a letter.

It is in late AD 228 that Lu Xun defeats the Wei attack. Cao Xiu dies of despair shortly after at Luoyang, while Sima Yi returns to Chang'an in order, he says, to protect it against any attack by Kong Ming. For this the other commanders mock him behind his back.

In Chengdu, Kong Ming receives the letter from Sun Quan proposing a joint attack. The second ruler supports the proposal, and Kong Ming summons the commanders to a banquet to prepare for the war. Just as the banquet begins a huge pine tree blows over in front of the hall. Kong Ming consults the gods through divination and announces that this foretells the death of a great general. Almost straight away Zhao Tong and Zhao Guang, the eldest sons of Zhao Zilong, arrive exhausted, having ridden hard and fast to bring the news that their father Zhao Zilong has died. His illness took a turn for the worse and, exhausted, he succumbed. Kong Ming is thrown into deep sadness and mourning. But it is the second emperor, whose life he saved when a child, who seems most profoundly affected.

As a poet has said:

> The tiger general from Changshan
> Combined Zhang's courage and Guan's wisdom.
> Victorious at Hanshui,
> Renowned at Dangyang.
> Twice you rescued the child prince
> In service to his revered lord.
> Books record his fame,
> Ensuring this never dies.

Zhao Zilong is buried with full military and imperial honours.

Shortly afterwards Kong Ming petitions the second ruler for permission to continue the war against the north, to fulfil the mandate the first ruler gave to him before his death. In fulsome terms Kong Ming describes his war in the south and how now there is the need to strike the north. The second ruler agrees wholeheartedly with the proposal, and with Wei Yan as their leader Kong Ming launches an army of three hundred thousand on the road to Chencang.

When news reaches the Wei court, Cao Zhen asks permission to redeem himself for his earlier failure. He also brings to the fore a huge giant of a man, Wang Shuang, as leader of the vanguard. With one hundred and fifty thousand men, Cao Zhen with Wang Shuang sets out to protect the key passes.

When the Shu army arrive outside Chencang, they find it stoutly fortified and commanded by Hao Zhao. Having failed in an outright attack, Kong Ming is in despair, but Jin Xiang, one of his commanders, suggests a more subtle approach. He is a friend of Hao Zhao and offers to go and discuss surrender with him.

His first visit is a failure, as Hao Zhao refuses to discuss anything with him and drives him from the city. His second attempt doesn't even get him inside the city, and this time he has to flee as Hao Zhao takes aim from the city wall with a bow and arrow.

Through the reports of his spies, Kong Ming discovers that there are probably only three thousand men in the city. He orders a hundred siege towers built, confident that he can swiftly seize this small city. But Hao Zhao is ready, and thousands of flaming arrows not only destroy the towers but thereby burn to death most of the men inside as well. Next Kong Ming orders battering rams made and launches a mass attack, but, using huge rocks on ropes, Hao Zhao smashes them out of the way. Finally Kong Ming orders a tunnel dug under the walls, but Hao Zhao counter-digs a tunnel and slays the miners.

Soon after, news comes of the Wei vanguard, commanded by the giant Wang Shuang, approaching, and Kong Ming sends troops to counter him. Wang Shuang, on encountering the Shu army, slays the commander, causing the Shu troops to panic and flee. The demoralizing effect of this defeat on the Shu army is considerable, leading to desertions and leaving Kong Ming in serious trouble. Advised by his commanders and especially Jiang Wei that they need to create a diversion in order to trap Cao Zhen and defeat the mighty Wang Shuang, Kong Ming agrees, and the army divides.

As a result Cao Zhen suddenly receives out of the blue a 'secret' letter from Jiang Wei. He ardently states his loyalty to the Wei and points out that he was forced to join the Shu army. He now offers to desert and to help the Wei army trap and defeat the Shu so that Kong Ming can be captured.

Falling for this, Cao Zhen orders his commander Fei Yao to advance and work in cahoots with Jiang Wei, even though Fei Yao keeps saying he is sure that Jiang is going to betray them again. And so it proves to be, and it deals a shattering blow to the Wei army. Tricked by Jiang Wei and then falling into an ambush, Fei Yao flees. When he then finds himself trapped and facing combat with none other than the treacherous Jiang Wei, he refuses to surrender. Instead he cuts his own throat.

With the defending army shattered, Kong Ming and the triumphant Shu army cross through the Qishan pass and into the Wei lands. However, their victory is tinged with regret that they haven't captured Cao Zhen, nor have they taken Chencang. Panic erupts in the Wei court at the news, and Cao Rui summons Sima Yi once again, who reveals he has a plan to defeat Kong Ming without any need for force!

And what exactly is this plan?

Read on.

CHAPTER 98

Chasing after the Shu army, Wang Shuang is killed. Taking Chencang, Kong Ming wins a battle, while Sun Quan becomes emperor.

Sima Yi points out that the Shu army have over-extended their supply lines and that at the most they have a month's supply of grain. 'If we just wait, don't attack or respond to intimidation, then they will have to retreat. In the disarray of retreat, we can attack and seize Kong Ming.' Sima Yi also foresees that Sun Quan is on the verge of declaring himself an emperor and that he will then attack the north. Therefore he is holding back his army ready to attack Lu Xun when he crosses the border from the south. So Cao Zhen is told to refrain from any engagements. Wang Shuang is instructed to patrol the roads to prevent any fresh supplies reaching the Shu army. Meanwhile Minister Sun Li comes up with a plot. He has wagons prepared that look as if they are grain convoys but are actually filled with inflammable materials so that they can lure the Shu into attacking and then destroy them with fire.

Kong Ming is beginning to despair but even he is amused when he realizes that the so-called grain wagons are a trap. After all, he is the master of fire in warfare! But he sees that they could use the anticipated attack as a trap of their own by luring the enemy into attacking the Shu camp and then ambushing them.

This they do, and the Wei army is completely outfoxed and defeated. Wei Yan, operating on secret orders from Kong Ming, also traps Wang Shuang and slays him, and then Kong Ming, being a realist, orders a retreat by the Shu army, because indeed they are running out of supplies.

In the south, Sun Quan is informed of the developments in the north, and it is recommended that he attack the north while they are licking their wounds. It is then that Zhang Zhao announces that auspicious signs have been observed – a phoenix and a dragon have been seen. 'Your virtue is as great as that of Yao and Shun, while your wisdom is equal to that of Wen and Wu,'[28] says Zhang Zhao. 'It is time, therefore, to take up the Mandate of Heaven and become the emperor and then as emperor send the army to war!' Many others also suggest this, and at last Sun Quan agrees. An altar is built for the enthronement, and in the early summer of 229 Sun Quan becomes emperor.

After the enthronement Zhang Zhao says to the new emperor, 'Do not rush into war so soon after your enthronement. First of all establish law and order. Found schools, build alliances. Agree to share the empire with the Shu and take your time planning the war.'

Sun Quan follows Zhang Zhao's advice and sends an ambassador to Shu to suggest such an alliance. At first the second ruler is opposed to such an idea as he now sees Sun Quan as a rebel for having made himself emperor. But Kong Ming's view is that right now they should congratulate Sun Quan and encourage him to send Lu Xun to attack Wei. This will mean that Sima Yi will be drawn south, meaning Kong Ming can also attack Wei. So Chen Zhen is despatched with suitable gifts for the new emperor.

Sun Quan summons Lu Xun and orders the attack, but Lu Xun is only too aware that this is really for the benefit of Kong Ming. However, he sees things slightly differently as well. If Kong Ming attacks Wei, then he, Lu Xun, might well be able to actually take advantage of the chaos and also attack Wei – possibly even seizing the whole of the north.

When Kong Ming hears that that part of his plan is in hand he sends spies to see how things stand at Chencang. Hearing that the valiant Hao Zhao is seriously ill, he despatches Wei Yan and Jiang Wei to attack the city immediately. But they are only to attack when they see flames rising within the city. 'You have three days to get ready to leave!' he tells an astonished Wei Yan and Jiang Wei. Then he orders Zhang Bao and Guan Xing to carry out secret instructions, and they set out as well.

But when Wei Yan and Jiang Wei arrive at the city, it is to find that Kong Ming has already taken it. He told the others to take three days because he actually set out straight away with Zhang Bao and Guan Xing. The defenders were so demoralized by the sickness of Hao Zhao that they put up little resistance, not least because pro-Shu men inside the city fired the city gates. During the mêlée that followed, and knowing the city has fallen and all hope is lost, Hao Zhao passes away on his sickbed.

After the capture of Chencang, Kong Ming's army go on to seize the San pass and thus prevent the Wei reinforcements reaching the city. From the plains on the other side of the Qishan hills, Kong Ming sends Jiang Wei to capture Wudu and Wang Ping to seize Yinping.

Emperor Cao Rui is suddenly informed of the fall of Chencang; the death of Hao Zhao; that Kong Ming is through the Qishan hills and that Sun Quan has declared himself emperor. In deep distress he summons Sima Yi to advise him. 'Don't worry about the Wu. They are just pretending to invade because they have an alliance with Shu. They know Kong Ming wants to avenge Jieting and seize the south even more than he wants the north. Lu Xun will therefore bide his time and see which of us wins. So we only need worry about Shu.' Delighted, Cao Rui promotes Sima Yi yet again and gives him the highest level of command, even offering him the imperial seal of authority currently held by Cao Zhen – but Sima replies, saying he would get it himself.

So now the scene is set for the great confrontation.

And who will win?

CHAPTER 99

Kong Ming wins a major battle.
Sima Yi invades Shu.

It is summertime in the year 229 when Kong Ming leads his army onto the plains below the Qishan hills. In response Sima Yi moves to Chang'an to prepare for the defence of Wei. Appointing Zhang He as leader of the vanguard, he moves out with one hundred thousand men towards Qishan, until they reach the south bank of the River Wei. Sima Yi sends a relief force to aid the besieged towns of Wudu and Yinping, only for that force to discover that Kong Ming has taken the two towns and that they are trapped between different groups of Shu troops. The collapse of the Wei force is total – the only serious problem for the Shu army being that Zhang Bao fell from his horse and hurt his head. He is sent back to Chengdu to recover.

Sima Yi believes that as Kong Ming will be in the towns trying to reassure the people it will be a perfect time to attack and seize his camp. Zhang He is therefore sent to attack, but once again Kong Ming has foreseen this and Zhang He is severely trounced. However, as Kong Ming watches Zhang He trying to break through and reach him, he reflects aloud that this man of all the others is the greatest risk to their venture. 'He must be got rid of,' says Kong Ming. Meanwhile, so complete is the rout of the Wei troops that Sima Yi orders a retreat to their base camp.

Likewise, Kong Ming orders a return to his own camp, now furnished with the trophies of war. Here Kong Ming receives an imperial command which restores his lost military status. At first he refuses, but it is pointed out this will trouble the troops. So he accepts and he is back in all his formal positions of power. However, to his frustration he cannot now entice

Sima Yi to engage with him. No amount of taunting draws any of the Wei troops out to battle. So Kong Ming gives orders for his men to pack up and 'retreat' – or rather pretend to retreat in order to draw the enemy out.

Sima Yi is determined not to be tricked again by Kong Ming, but his commanders are becoming restless through inaction and long for battle. When news comes that Kong Ming has apparently retreated, they are jubilant and press for permission to wipe out the departing army. But Sima Yi is cautious. He discovers that the enemy have only retreated a short distance and fears a trap. For three days spies report on the slow movement of the Shu army, until his commanders can bear it no longer and demand action. Sima Yi gives in and orders an all-out attack.

Despite Sima Yi's best efforts and schemes, Kong Ming once again outwits him and inflicts a crushing defeat upon the Wei troops, including sacking Sima Yi's own camp. Even when Sima Yi has foreseen traps, Kong Ming has traps behind the traps! Sima Yi is incandescent with rage.

'Do you not understand anything about war?' he demands of his commanders. 'It takes more than fiery courage and a lust for blood. These just draw us into disaster after disaster. So, enough. No more of these foolish, foolhardy ventures. If any-one disobeys he'll be executed according to military law.' Overcome with shame and embarrassment, the commanders have to acknowledge that their ventures have cost the lives of huge numbers of men, the loss of untold numbers of horses and the capture by the enemy of vast stores of weapons.

Meanwhile, Kong Ming returns triumphantly home and sets about planning another invasion. This all falls apart when news comes that Zhang Bao has died of his head wounds. This breaks Kong Ming's heart, and he weeps until he makes himself ill. As a poet has said:

How brave fearless Zhang Bao was in all his deeds!
Yet Heaven gave him no support.
The tears of Kong Ming drifted upon the west wind,
For there was no one else like him.

In the light of his illness, Kong Ming has to acknowledge that his powers are failing and he quietly withdraws back to Chengdu to recuperate. When Sima Yi discovers that his enemy left five days earlier undetected, he has to admit that he was outwitted by Kong Ming – perhaps, he ponders, the gods are working with him.

It is in the autumn of the following year that the Wei seek to turn the tables and invade Shu. Cao Zhen, restored to health and eager for revenge, proposes an attack directly on Hanzhong, and the plan is given imperial permission. Sima Yi and Liu Ye are directed to join Cao Zhen and advance with four hundred thousand troops to seize the mountain pass into Shu and attack Hanzhong.

In Chengdu Kong Ming has taken the time to recover and, on hearing of these manoeuvres, calls in Zhang Ni and Wang Ping. When he tells them to take just a thousand men to defend the pass, they are deeply sceptical and troubled. How can a thousand men stop four hundred thousand?

'I have observed the night sky,' replies Kong Ming. 'The stars tell me that there is going to be a massive rainstorm for many days. This will break the spirit of the enemy troops and make any attack up the rain-soaked mountains impossible. You'll have no difficulty in holding any attempt back. I, meanwhile, will prepare our major force to be ready for the inevitable retreat of the Wei army. Then we can destroy them!'

Sima Yi arrives in Chencang to find the entire city has been razed to the ground. There is nowhere to take shelter. But he too has spotted that the stars foretell torrential rain and, despite the urging of his own commanders, he commands that they stay and build bivouacs in the ruins of Chencang rather than try to find shelter on the plains or in the mountains. And when the rains come, they wash everything away, the waters rising over three feet deep. After a month of this, the troops are cold, ill, permanently wet, the horses are dying and the morale of the whole army has collapsed. When an imperial command comes telling them to abandon the attempt and return home, everyone is delighted but also aware of the risks of a counter-attack by Shu.

Slowly the army turns around, fearing all the time that Kong Ming's men will attack.

So what does Kong Ming plan? The opposite of what they expect.

And how will this work?

CHAPTER 100

Cao Zhen is overwhelmed by a Shu attack on his camp. Kong Ming shames Sima Yi but is recalled and humbled.

Kong Ming has worked out that Sima Yi will leave troops behind to spring an ambush on any Shu forces seeking to take advantage of the Wei army's retreat. So instead he sends his forces way ahead to occupy the pass through the Qishan hills and to trap the retreating army there. He despatches Wei Yan and Chen Shi among others to guard the pass with strict orders not to advance too fast and to beware of any ambush.

Meanwhile, disagreement has broken out between Sima Yi and Cao Zhen. Sima Yi predicts that Kong Ming will set up an ambush at the Qishan pass, while Cao Zhen is sure he will not. Each competes with the other until a wager is agreed. If Sima Yi is wrong, he will dress as a woman and paint his face! If he is right, Cao Zhen will give him precious imperial gifts such as a jade belt and a warhorse.

Back at the Qishan pass, Chen Shi has become impatient with the cautious approach of Kong Ming and therefore of Wei Yan. He doubts whether the rain-sodden, depressed Wei troops have the morale to try to set up counter-ambushes. 'If we go straight into the attack now we can wipe them out,' he says. Deng Zhi, adviser to Kong Ming, argues that Kong Ming is always right, only to have Chen Shi say, 'So how come he lost at Jieting if he's so brilliant?' Refusing to be curbed, Chen Shi breaks off with five thousand men and, passing through the hills, he prepares for battle. But he hasn't gone far when suddenly he is attacked. He tries to force his way back, only to find the path blocked by Wei troops. When at last he is able to retreat into the pass, he has only four or five hundred men left alive, and all of them are wounded.

Meanwhile Cao Zhen has grown lax in attention to detail, and his men likewise, as they have seen no sign of the enemy. Nevertheless an expeditionary force of five thousand is sent out somewhat half-heartedly to see what is happening. They have not gone far when they are trapped in an ambush devised by Kong Ming; their commander is slain, and the troops surrender. Taking their armour and clothing, Kong Ming dresses his own men as though they are Wei troops and sends them off to Cao Zhen. They fool Cao Zhen and facilitate a mass attack on his camp, which destroys the Wei army there and scatters the troops. Cao Zhen himself only just escapes, rescued by, of all people, Sima Yi, who now proposes they forget their wager. 'Let's instead serve our kingdom with all our energy together,' he says. But these events cast Cao Zhen into deep depression, which results in sickness, and this too affects the morale of the troops.

Back to Kong Ming. He orders the execution of Chen Shi for disobedience but spares Wei Yan, not least because he has plans for him for the future, though he does not entirely trust him. News comes to Kong Ming of the ill health of Cao Zhen. 'He's only remaining with his troops,' declares Kong Ming, 'to boost morale, so let us destroy him.' So saying, he writes a letter to Cao Zhen and sends it with some of the men who surrendered earlier, freeing them in the process.

When Cao Zhen reads the letter he erupts with fury. The letter is a stream of subtle, pointed abuse deriding his achievements and saying that history will only remember him as a coward, a failure and a fraud. The fury this evokes is too much for Cao Zhen's weakened body, and that same night he collapses and dies. The Wei ruler orders Sima Yi the very next day to engage his full force against the Shu army in revenge. And this is what happens. Sima Yi spots Kong Ming in his Daoist robes and seated in his carriage. Sima Yi roars out his fury and defiance.

'We have historical precedents for our emperor's power and right to rule,' he says. 'He's willing to permit the kingdoms of Wu and Shu to exist because he's magnanimous and wishes to preserve the ordinary folk from harm. You – what are you but a country boy from Nanyang? You're unable to calculate

Heaven's Will. If you continue in this fashion you'll perish. But if you reconsider and withdraw, then our kingdoms can live in peace and settle issues of borders as civilized people do, thereby ensuring the ordinary folk are not harmed.'

To this Kong Ming replies, 'Our late emperor gave me the onerous charge of defeating all traitors. I'll ensure that soon the Cao family are destroyed by the House of Han. You ungrateful man! Your family benefited from the Han for generations but you've cast this aside and joined in the rebellion! You must really be ashamed.'

This exchange leads to a challenge. Kong Ming challenges Sima Yi to a battle of military strategies. Each side uses extraordinary formations based on mystical ideas and texts. Kong Ming uses one based upon the Eight Trigrams of the *Yi Jing* and draws the enemy into a supernatural maze, which ends in total defeat for Sima Yi. As a result Kong Ming captures the three leading commanders, Zhang Hu, Dai Ling and Yue Chen. Brought before Kong Ming, he dismisses them and sends them back with a message for Sima Yi. 'Tell him to do more study on military matters and then try to remember them.' So saying, he gives them and their captured officers their weapons but strips the soldiers, blackens their faces and sends them back humiliated.

This simply provokes Sima Yi into launching his entire force at the Shu army. But once again Kong Ming has foreseen this, and an attack led by Guan Xing from the rear scatters the Wei army. It is said that six or seven out of every ten men in the Wei army died that day. With no other option, Sima Yi retreats to the south side of the Wei River and does not appear again.

It is then that by accident Kong Ming sets in train a series of troubles. A minor official, Gou An, a drunkard and a lazy man by nature, has taken days to bring a vital supply of grain for the Shu army. Discovering this and knowing how vital supply chains are, Kong Ming is all for having him executed but is persuaded not to. Instead he orders him beaten eighty times with a whip. Burning with resentment, Gou An deserts and goes over to Sima Yi. Sima Yi sends him furtively back to Chengdu to spread rumours that Kong Ming, buoyed by his string of military successes, is now planning to usurp the throne.

Gou An proves to be very effective at this, and the result is that the second ruler begins to suspect Kong Ming and, to make sure he does not rebel, summons him back to the capital. When the recall arrives at Kong Ming's camp, he knows that behind it are lies and rumour. Although he is close to fulfilling his long-held desire of crushing Wei, he has no option but to return and bring the army back with him. However, he also knows that Sima Yi is the one behind this and therefore expects he will attack as the Shu army retreats. Through a cunning plan of making it look as if more troops have joined at each night's stop – by the number of fire pits left where the army has camped overnight – he fools Sima Yi yet again into thinking the Shu army is expanding, not shrinking. Sima therefore does not attack. Only much later does he realize the trick Kong Ming has played.

So what happens when Kong Ming returns to Chengdu?

Let's find out.

CHAPTER 101

Kong Ming pretends to be a god.
Zhang He falls into a trap.

When Kong Ming arrives in Chengdu he asks the second ruler why he has been summoned back. The best excuse the ruler can come up with is: 'I missed you.' Having thus established that it was rumour-mongers, Kong Ming tracks them down and has them executed, though the chief instigator, Gou An, escapes.

Going back to Hanzhong, Kong Ming starts to prepare for another invasion of Wei. It is in the early months of AD 231 when he and the army once again cross the border. Sima Yi is called to command the Wei forces, and the two armies and their leaders set forth once again for battle.

Sima Yi realizes that Kong Ming is going to need supplies, especially of grain, and that therefore he will force the Qishan pass and seize the grain fields of Longxi. Kong Ming easily takes the city of Lucheng close to the grain fields and then moves forward to the main area of Longshang close by the grain fields, only to find Sima Yi already there. But Kong Ming has expected this and now puts his own plan into action. He has had created three exact replicas of his famous carriage, and into these he puts dummies of himself, very lifelike indeed. Alongside each of the carriages walk twenty-four men dressed all in black and barefooted – like followers of some strange cult. He has the same arrangement for his own carriage but adds to this Guan Xing, dressed as an occult local deity figure. Parading in front of the enemy, he draws two thousand men away as they chase after him. But no matter how fast they go and no matter how slowly his carriage seems to move ahead, they cannot catch him. It takes Sima Yi to recognize this as a magic trick known as the Eight Doorways. Supported by local deities summoned by Kong Ming, he has managed to create what is known as Shortening the Distance. Sima Yi knows nothing can be done to counter this magic. So he orders the retreat but, turning around, suddenly encounters Kong Ming again in his famous carriage – ahead of him.

'How is this possible?' asks the astonished Sima. The effect on the Wei troops is deeply demoralizing and is increased when, taking another path, they again find Kong Ming and his carriage ahead of them. Turning again, they encounter Kong Ming once more. By now the nerve of the army has been broken and in panic they flee back to their base at Shanggui to hide!

Having used his identical carriages trick, Kong Ming now has the grain fields to himself, and soon thirty thousand men are reaping the abundant harvest. Only later does Sima Yi learn that, far from Kong Ming appearing four times, the others were in the charge of Jiang Wei, Ma Dai and Wei Yan. He has been fooled once more.

Sima Yi and Guo Huai then plan to attack Kong Ming at Lucheng while the men thresh the harvest. But once again Kong Ming has foreseen this, and through ambush and vigorous defence of the city walls the Wei army are trapped between two forces of the Shu army and heavily defeated. Sima's next strategy is to cut off the supply chain and wait until the Shu army has devoured all the grain and will be forced out to fight. But again Kong Ming outwits Sima Yi, attacking the weary Wei troops before they have time to set up a camp. The massacre is terrible, bodies piled one on top of another, and the attack drives the enemy from the passes and secures the supply route.

Then word comes to Kong Ming that Wu has sent emissaries to Wei to propose a truce. This has led Wei to try to persuade Wu to attack Shu. However, Wu is in no hurry to comply. Nevertheless the possibility of a Wu attack sufficiently alarms Kong Ming for him to order a gradual and steady retreat back towards the lands of Shu, while still holding Lucheng as a base. Wei military commanders such as Zhang He are all for charging off after the retreating army to inflict maximum damage while they can. But Sima Yi has too high a regard for Kong Ming's skills not to suspect a trick. However, he finds himself under immense pressure from his officers to attack and in the end grudgingly agrees. It is Zhang He who tears off with an advance guard of five thousand men. There is, of course, an ambush. In fact a series of feints and false trails, apparent flight and panic lures Zhang He and his select band of a hundred officers into a final, fatal trap. There, late that night, Zhang He and all his men fall to the Shu assault. This death and Sima Yi's failure to prevent this foolhardy expedition so depress Sima Yi that he retreats back to Luoyang to lick his wounds.

Kong Ming returns to Hanzhong and once again becomes the victim of vicious rumours claiming that he is hoarding supplies ready for a rebellion. When Kong Ming is challenged as to why he has abandoned the invasion, he exclaims with astonishment that Li Yan the adviser has sent a note informing him of a potential invasion by the Wu, and that is why he has returned. Suddenly he realizes he has been lied to, and this is all a plot to overthrow him.

Kong Ming can see that the plot is unfolding, so he starts his own investigation. He finds that Li Yan is supposed to have sent supplies but has failed to do so. To cover up his error, he fabricated the note and then started the rumours in order to draw attention away from his own betrayal. When the second ruler is informed, he orders the execution of the traitor. Then, reminded that his father had chosen Li Yan as one of his council of advisers, he instead takes all Li Yan's official posts from him and reduces him to the rank of a commoner.

Having dealt with this, and also having taken on Li Yan's son Li Feng as an adviser, Kong Ming rests the army for three years in order to restore supplies and build up the military strength.

It is not until AD 234 that Kong Ming comes to see the second ruler and proposes another invasion of Wei. However, the second ruler points out that the three kingdoms have arrived at a modus vivendi of mutual co-existence. Why disturb this now?

'I've been planning this every night since your father gave me the charge to destroy the traitors. I must do this in order to honour the House of Han.'

At this Qiao Zhou steps forward and says, 'Do not summon the army, my lord.'

> Kong Ming's only thought is obedience,
> Even if it costs him his life.
> But Qiao can read the past and the foretelling
> of the heavens.

So what happens next?

What has Heaven planned?

CHAPTER 102

Sima Yi captures the bridge over Beiyuan. Guan Xing dies and Kong Ming tricks Sima Yi again.

Qiao Zhou, as the official astrologer for the court, reports that inauspicious signs have been seen. For example, thousands of birds drowning themselves are clearly a warning, while at the same time astrological signs indicate good fortune for the Wei dynasty. In the city people are saying they have heard the cypress trees crying at night. He urges no action in the light of these signs, which seem to favour peace and the Wei kingdom rather than the Shu. But Kong Ming dismisses these as 'inconsequential' and certainly not enough to deflect duty. Instead he offers sacrifices at the temple of the first ruler, Xuande, declaring that he has tried five times to fulfil the command to suppress the north and restore the Han and that he will now try to do this for the sixth time. From the temple he goes straight to Hanzhong to prepare. Upon arrival, he is profoundly distressed to hear of the death of Guan Xing as a result of illness. As a poet has said:

> Life and death, inevitable;
> Our time is as brief as a gnat's.
> Only through loyal service
> Can fame last for ever.

When Kong Ming's army move out, they are three hundred and forty thousand strong.

In Wei, hearing of the Shu army's advance, Cao Rui calls for Sima Yi. He too has been observing the stars and has concluded they augur good fortune for the Wei, so he is surprised at Kong Ming's move – all the more so after three years of peace. The Wei ruler sends him off with instructions to only take up a defensive position.

Sima Yi organizes an army of almost half a million men, assembled at the River Wei, fifty thousand of whom are detailed to build wooden pontoons. He sends special troops to fortify Beiyuan with instructions to wait until starvation reduces the invading troops to foolhardy actions and then strike. His pontoon bridges span the River Wei.

Then Kong Ming comes out of the Qishan hills and, building rafts filled with combustible materials, he tries to burn down the bridges. However, his plan is revealed by spies, and the rafts are targeted by archers, wiping out all the men and defeating that plan. Wei Yan, who has led the attack, finds himself ambushed, with his rafts destroyed and on his own. Although he survives, most of his men do not. Likewise, an attack by Wang Ping and Zhang Ni is also foiled by a counter-ambush. Kong Ming suffers heavy losses that day and is humbled as a result. In desperation he sends the learned adviser Fei Yi as an envoy to Sun Quan, the Wu emperor, asking for help. Sun Quan immediately agrees to come to his assistance by attacking Wei, intending instead to use this as a cover to seize Xincheng and then Xiangyang and Huaiyang.

At the banquet to celebrate this new alliance, Sun Quan asks Fei Yi who is in charge of the vanguard, and, on being told Wei Yan, comments that this is a most untrustworthy man. When Fei Yi reports this back along with the good news of the alliance, Kong Ming comments that this shows how good a commander Sun Quan is. When pressed to take care about Wei Yan, Kong Ming replies obliquely, 'I have my plans!'

Sima Yi then tries the old deserter trick. He sends a soldier by the name of Zheng Wen to pretend to have deserted to the Shu side. He hopes that Zheng Wen will enable him to know Kong Ming's plans and thereby thwart them. But the plan backfires terribly. Kong Ming is not fooled for a moment, and on pain of death Zheng Wen is told to write a fake letter to Sima Yi claiming that, if Sima Yi himself will lead the raiding-party attack on the camp, he can capture Kong Ming. With no other option, Zheng Wen writes the letter and is then placed under armed guard. Sima Yi is convinced of its authenticity and gives orders to prepare for the attack. Back at Kong Ming's camp that night, he performs the magic dance of King Yu, portraying the stars of the Northern Dipper, and gives secret instructions to his commanders, especially Wei Yan, Wang Ping and Zhang Ni.

It is a clear, moonlit night when Sima, his commander Qin Lang and the men set out. But soon clouds arise, and a heavy mist and darkness fall over the troops. Charging into the camp, Qin Lang realizes that he has been tricked – it is empty. Suddenly he and his men are attacked from two sides, and he is trapped. Sima Yi is unable to reach him, for he too has been ambushed. That night eight or nine men out of ten of the Wei army die, Qin Lang among them, and Sima Yi only just escapes. For Kong Ming has used occult powers to bring the clouds in and then uses divine powers to clear them away afterwards.

Zheng Wen is, of course, executed, and then Kong Ming tries to draw the Wei army out to the attack, but to no avail. He realizes that what he needs is a lure, a trick to make the Wei army come out so that he can destroy them. He also needs fresh supplies of grain to feed his army and by a series of plots and plans he tricks the Wei and captures their own grain wagons. This at last provokes Sima Yi into sending out his men to the attack. And they fall into Kong Ming's long-planned ambush. Hearing the cries of his men, Sima Yi rides out himself to the rescue, but he is trapped, and his men desert, leaving him stranded.

Is this the end for Sima Yi?

Let's find out.

CHAPTER 103

Sima Yi is trapped by Kong Ming in Gourd Valley but is saved by rain. Kong Ming seeks to know from his star how long he has to live.

Sima Yi escapes, but only by throwing his golden helmet down to distract his pursuers. The captured Wei grain convoy yields vast quantities of grain. Then news comes of the invasion of Wei by the Wu. However, the initial invasion led by Zhuge Jin is a failure and costs the Wu many men. Lu Xun tries to devise strategies to defeat the Wei, but his plans all fall, through subterfuge, into the hands of the enemy. Despite his highest hopes, Lu Xun has to concede that he cannot advance, and so the entire Wu army withdraws, abandoning the Shu army to its fate. Kong Ming is on his own again.

Expecting to stay in the Qishan mountains for a long time, Kong Ming has his men join with the locals and plant crops, which are to be shared equally. Meanwhile, Sima Yi's son Sima Shi is chafing at the bit to have a go, but his father quotes the holy sage: 'Getting upset about minor issues ruins the greater plan.' But reports keep coming in of the Shu troops digging in and settling down which greatly alarm the Wei commanders. They capture various groups of Shu soldiers and from them seek to understand what Kong Ming is up to but are none the wiser – exactly as Kong Ming intends. So Sima Yi and his two sons decide to attack in order to try to disrupt whatever it is that Kong Ming is doing. His plan is to lure Sima Yi and his two sons into a narrow-necked valley and then trap them with fire – and he very nearly succeeds. Charging into the valley, enticed by the possibility of catching a fleeing Wei Yan, Sima Yi and his two sons at first suspect nothing, for the valley is empty. Then Sima Yi sees huts on the hillside and realizes the risk they are running. But it is too late. He and his men are trapped when flaming torches are hurled down onto vast stores of inflammable materials, and the whole valley erupts in flames. Arrows rain down from the Shu troops on the ridges of the valley. Mines buried in the ground explode in the valley floor. Convinced that he and his sons are about to die, Sima Yi hugs them and prepares to meet his fate. But at that exact moment a dark cloud appears, and torrential rain pours down. Within minutes all the fires have been put out. Charging out, they meet other contingents of the Wei army and together are able to drive back the attack of the Shu army on their camp.

Kong Ming sighs when he sees Sima Yi and his sons escape thanks to the rain. 'Man schemes, but Heaven decides!' he says. 'There is no way to make things go against that.' Desperate to make the Wei troops come out to fight again, Kong Ming even sends a woman's headdress and a shroud to mock and insult Sima Yi, but this doesn't draw him out. Instead the messenger is questioned by Sima Yi about the habits of Kong Ming. 'He rises early and works late into the night,' says the messenger. 'He oversees all the details, including punishments, and eats almost nothing.' This heartens Sima Yi, who tells his officers that such a lifestyle means Kong Ming cannot last much longer. His own officers try to encourage Kong Ming to lighten his workload but they cannot move him. However, such questioning disturbs Kong Ming's equilibrium, and his refusal to pay any attention makes his officers give up trying to help.

Sima Yi is also having trouble with his commanders, who want to attack, whereas Sima Yi is holding the defensive position. He even has to ask Cao Rui to confirm the order that there is to be no attack, so as to keep his officers in line.

When news reaches Kong Ming of the defeat and retreat of the Wu army, he collapses. As his officers help him up, he mutters, 'This old problem. Perhaps my end is near.' Late that night he staggers out to study the stars and then tells Jiang Wei that he has but a few days to live because the stars show that his end is near. Jiang Wei beseeches him to try magic to prolong his life, and he agrees. It is the late summer of AD 234, and a great ritual site is set up for Kong Ming to commune with his guiding star. But the next day after the ritual, he is weaker, and blood comes from his mouth.

Sima Yi sees in the stars that Kong Ming is failing and immediately orders an attack. As Kong Ming is praying with a ritual lamp burning bright – sign of his life energy – Wei Yan rushes in to announce that the Wei army is advancing to the attack. So hasty and clumsy is he that he knocks over the lamp, and it goes out. Then Kong Ming knows his time is drawing to a close. 'It's not possible to avoid one's fate,' he says.

Wei Yan falls to the ground, begging forgiveness, and Jiang Wei is so furious he draws his sword, but Kong Ming commands him to put it away.

> No amount of care can help you avoid your destiny,
> Nor is it possible to fight fate.

So what will happen now?

Read on.

CHAPTER 104

Kong Ming dies – a great star falls.
A wooden statue frightens Sima Yi.

Sending Wei Yan out to confront and hold off the Wei troops, Jiang Wei comes to sit beside the dying Kong Ming. Kong Ming hands over to him his secret formulae for the use of magic such as the Eight Main Concerns, the Seven Precautions, the Six Troubles and the Five Anxieties. 'You alone are fit to receive these,' says Kong Ming, and Jiang Wei breaks down, crying. 'I've also designed a bow which can fire ten arrows at a time. But I've never had time to develop it. Here are my plans – have it made and tested. Most of the kingdom is now safe, but watch out for Yinping. There could be trouble there soon.'

Calling Ma Dai to his bedside, Kong Ming gives him secret information, asking only that Ma Dai carry it out after he has died. Likewise, he passes to his commander Yang Yi a silk bag with secret instructions inside. 'When I've died, Wei Yan will turn rebel. When this happens, go with him and when at the front open the bag and then find the one who is to kill him.'

Exhausted by all this, Kong Ming collapses but later awakes and writes a memorial to the second ruler. As soon as the second ruler receives this, he despatches Li Fu to find out how ill Kong Ming is. In deep distress Li Fu hurries to Kong Ming and, weeping, asks how he is, to be told by Kong Ming: 'I've failed to complete my task. I've failed both the second ruler and country. When I've gone, guard and guide him. I'll send one more petition.'

Kong Ming is taken outside at his request to review the military preparations, but the wind is cold and chills him. Sighing, he regrets that never again will he lead his men into battle. And so saying, he returns to his tent, where the illness worsens. He then gives orders to Yang Yi, saying, 'When I die nothing must change. Everything must look like normal. Retreat before anyone realizes what has happened'. Then he calls for paper and pen and writes one last time to the second ruler.

'Death is what comes to us all,' he writes, 'and one's fate cannot be avoided.' He then recounts the responsibilities he was given and the battles he fought with the north, but to no avail. 'Now I am dying and I am heartbroken that I have failed to fulfil my service to Your Majesty. Please, remember to be of honest heart; self-disciplined; caring only for the wellbeing of the people. Respect your late father and follow his path. Be beneficent to all. Promote the worthy; block the unworthy – those who exploit and harm – and so ensure the righteousness and strength of your kingdom.'

He then allocates his estate in Chengdu to his children, stressing how little it is – eight hundred mulberry trees and about fifteen hundred acres – not much for all that he has done. Once the memorial is completed, he summons Yang Yi and orders that his body after death be placed in a large box, sitting up. No one is to mourn. All must keep quiet. 'Put seven grains of rice in my mouth and a lamp at my feet. These actions together will help me to stop my guiding star from falling, and this will confound Sima Yi. This will enable you to retreat calmly. If you're attacked, put the wooden statue of me in my carriage and drive it towards the enemy. That should see them off!'

Looking up into the heavens, he points to a star in the Northern Bushel constellation and says, 'There, that is my guiding star.' Then he faints. Li Fu arrives while he is unconscious, fearing he is too late, but Kong Ming rallies. He asks Kong Ming who is to take over after his death. 'Jiang Wei,' says Kong Ming. 'And to follow him?' enquires Li Fu. 'Fei Yi.' 'And who else?' he asks, but no further names come from Kong Ming, for he has died. He was fifty-four years old. The poet Du Fu has written this:

> Last night a bright star fell to earth,
> Telling everyone the Master has gone.
> No more orders emanating from his tent,
> Though his fame can only spread from now on.

Three thousand followers disorientated –
Ten thousand with no chance of victory.
The green woods, sun-dappled and beautiful,
No longer hear his chants ringing.

At his death Heaven and Earth mourn; the moon wanes, dimmed by Kong Ming's soul on its journey to Heaven. But as instructed, Jiang Wei and Yang Yi ban any mourning. They dress his body and put it in the box as they were directed. Three hundred loyal men stand guard. Giving secret orders to Wei Yan to guard the rear, they begin quietly to withdraw and return home.

Sima Yi cannot understand what the stars are doing, for one reddish one dips and then rises and then dips again three times. Hoping this foretells the death of Kong Ming, he is still so frightened of Kong Ming that he dare not try to take advantage in case this is another of his tricks.

Wei Yan, meanwhile, has had a dream. He dreams that he has two horns coming out of his head. Disturbed by this, he asks Zhao Zhi if he can explain it. Troubled, Zhao Zhi tells him it is auspicious but when later he discusses this with Fei Yi he says that actually it is an inauspicious sign but that he doesn't want to alarm Wei Yan. When Wei Yan finds out that Yang Yi has been given prime ministerial responsibilities at Kong Ming's deathbed, he becomes very difficult, questioning why Yang was chosen and not him. 'Let's attack, and this way fulfil the hoped-for victory against Sima Yi. No point in stopping now just because the prime minister is dead!'

But Fei Yi has to point out that Kong Ming's last instructions were to retreat. To pacify Wei Yan, Fei Yi promises to discuss this with Yang Yi, but when he tells Yang Yi of the conversation, he says that Kong Ming warned that Wei Yan would rebel. So instead of Wei Yan at the rear, Jiang Wei takes this position, and the army begins to move out. When Fei Yi doesn't return, Wei Yan begins to be suspicious. Discovering that Jiang Wei has on Yang Yi's command taken the rearguard position, he grows indignant and, turning to Ma Dai, asks him to help him kill Yang Yi. Pretending to agree, Ma Dai goes with Wei Yan and his troops.

Sima Yi is soon informed that the Shu army has gone. With his troops he chases after the retreating army but is completely taken by surprise when the rearguard suddenly turns, banners flying, and there, seated in his carriage, is none other than Kong Ming. Panic overcomes not just him but all his men, and Jiang Wei takes full advantage of the mêlée to slaughter untold numbers of the Wei troops.

So distraught is Sima Yi that he rides pell-mell for many miles, until two of his commanders catch up with him and slow his horse. Touching his head, Sima Yi asks almost incredulously whether he still has his head! It is a few days later that Sima Yi finds out that it was only a wooden statue of Kong Ming and that Jiang Wei had but a thousand troops with him. This is why a common saying arose: 'A dead Kong Ming puts a live Sima to flight!' As a poet has said:

> It was midnight when that star fell from heaven,
> But Sima ran anyway, shit-scared of the enemy.
> And to this day he's still mocked in the west
> For asking, 'Can you see if my head is still there?'

Sima gives up the chase, and the retreating Shu army moves on until suddenly flames are visible, rising in the road ahead. The stamp of an army shakes the very ground, and messengers speed back to Yang Yi to say soldiers are barring the road.

So who is this?

Who indeed!

國泰
民安

CHAPTER 105

Kong Ming leaves a plan in a silk bag.
Cao Rui ruthlessly seizes the Dew
Collection Bronze Bowl.

Wei Yan! He is the man who has blocked the road and drawn up his troops to oppose Yang Yi and the rest of the army. Having discovered his treachery, Yang Yi halts the army and discusses with Fei Yi what to do. 'The prime minister knew he would rebel,' says Yang Yi, 'and now he blocks our path. What do we do?' Fei Yi replies, 'He'll have written to the second ruler, making out he is the loyal one and we're the rebels. We must get our own message to the second ruler.' A back road is found, and messengers sent to Chengdu to inform the second ruler of Wei Yan's rebellion.

In Chengdu, the second ruler has had a dream of an avalanche, and when he summons his advisers to interpret this, they tell him of the star that has fallen to earth and that these portents all mean Kong Ming has died. The arrival of Li Fu confirms that this is true and the second ruler collapses with grief. All are deeply moved, and even the ordinary folk cry aloud. It is a few days later that Wei Yan's petition arrives declaring that Yang Yi has usurped power and only he, Wei Yan, stands against him. Such an unexpected announcement creates great debate within the court, with most people feeling that it is more likely that the haughty Wei Yan is the rebel. The matter is resolved when shortly afterwards Yang Yi's petition arrives. Adviser Jiang Wan says, 'Kong Ming never did fully trust Wei Yan, so you can be assured that he made plans to deal with this before his death. Wei Yan will be drawn into a trap, of that Your Majesty can be sure.'

Two further petitions arrive, one from each side, and this leads the second ruler to suggest that maybe a compromise, some form of reconciliation, could be undertaken, and he sends Dong Yun to try to achieve this.

By now Wei Yan has taken up position by Nangu, never having dreamed that Yang Yi, using back roads, could have come round behind him. Commander He Ping leads the loyal troops and, emerging behind Nangu, he challenges Wei Yan to single combat, shouting, 'Where are you, you traitor Wei Yan?' to which Wei Yan replies, 'You're the traitor, helping one like Yang Yi. Don't you try to shout me down!' 'The prime minister's body is not cold yet,' retorts He Ping, 'and you have already rebelled.' Then, turning to Wei Yan's soldiers, he says 'You men, when did the prime minister ever do you harm? Why are you helping the traitor? Go home, and we'll reward you.' A huge cheer goes up, and many of the men set off home straight away.

Infuriated by all this, Wei Yan attacks, and He Ping charges forward as well. They fight many rounds, until He Ping pretends to retreat. Wei Yan tries to follow him, but arrows drive him back. Watching his army literally fall apart, he chases some, slaying them as they run. The only troops to stand firm are the three hundred men around Ma Dai. But when Wei Yan suggests that they desert and join the Wei army, it is Ma Dai who says, 'Better that we as men of honour carve out our own lands than surrender to another. You're the best soldier in the whole land. I swear to follow you and suggest we take Hanzhong, from where we can attack the West of Shu.'

Encouraged by this, they first attack Nanzheng, where Jiang Wei is already ensconced along with Yang Yi. Profoundly worried about how to deal with this, Jiang Wei asks Yang Yi for advice. 'As he was dying,' he says, 'Kong Ming gave me this silk bag to be opened when Wei Yan rebelled.' So saying, he opens the bag and reads the cover of the envelope. It says, 'Only to be opened when you confront Wei Yan.' So, armed with this, Yang Yi follows Jiang Wei out of the city gates to confront Wei Yan and Ma Dai. Jiang Wei shouts his defiance at Wei Yan, who replies, 'This doesn't involve you, Jiang Wei. It's Yang Yi I have come to fight.'

In the shadow of the gateway Yang Yi opens the letter left by Kong Ming and then rides out to be beside Jiang Wei, confronting Wei Yan and Ma Dai.

'Your betrayal was predicted by Kong Ming,' he says. 'However, if you can shout, "Who will dare kill me?" three times, I will know you for a true warrior and will surrender Hanzhong to you.'

Roaring with laughter, Wei Yan says, 'Listen to me, you pathetic coward. I was only partially afraid of Kong Ming when he was alive. Now he is dead, who is there to fear? Eh? Answer me that! I'll shout this not just three times, but thirty thousand times – as if frankly this was of any importance!'

So saying, and holding his sword in the air, he shouts, 'Who will dare kill me?' Before the shout fades away, a voice comes from behind him: 'I dare kill you!' A sword flashes through the air, and Wei Yan falls dead from his horse. And who killed Wei Yan? Ma Dai, for Kong Ming told him before he died that when he heard Wei Yan shout, 'Who will dare kill me?' that was the signal to slay him. As a poet has written:

> Kong Ming knew his Wei Yan,
> Who would finally betray the Riverlands.
> A mere silk bag, a plan no one could imagine,
> Was what seized the day!

When news reaches the second ruler he orders that Wei Yan be buried with honours as befitted his earlier bravery and valour for the kingdom.

By now the body of Kong Ming has reached the outskirts of the capital, and everyone from ruler to peasant comes out to greet and to mourn Kong Ming. In every valley and on every hill, ordinary folk weep. Yang Yi is rewarded by being given high honours, while Ma Dai is given the high rank that was previously held by Wei Yan.

In the winter of AD 234 Kong Ming is buried with full ceremonies and ritual. The second ruler builds a temple in his honour at Mianyang. Du Fu wrote the following poems:

> Where can I find the prime minister's shrine?
> Beyond the town where the cypresses stand vertical.
> Here's sunlit, lush grass – a perpetual spring.

Orioles sing in the branches – but who to?
Three times his lord had to beg him to help the
kingdom.
He served two terms with all his heart,
But died with all his plans unrealized –
And ever since, truly heroic men weep at his death.

Kong Ming's illustrious name is known worldwide,
Highest among the high, famed for his kingly mien.
Three kingdoms split into being: he used all his skill,
One-pointed as a feather, to reunite them again.
His reputation as great as the legendary ones:
Even in his failures, he still ranks among the greatest.
The stars turned . . . the Han were fated to fall.
Working to the end, his body scarred, he never gave up.

No sooner has the second ruler returned to his palace than word comes of what seems to be military preparations by Wu for an invasion. Distressed at what appears to be a betrayal of their alliance and an opportunist exploitation of the distraught state of Shu following Kong Ming's death, he sends an ambassador to find out what is going on.

The ambassador, Zong Yu, finds that all the Wu officials are dressed in mourning clothes. The military movements are explained as being undertaken in case Wei decides to take advantage of Kong Ming's death, and so the alliance is renewed once again, and the heart of the second ruler is put at ease.

Now the second ruler raises Jiang Wei to take Kong Ming's place as prime minister; Fei Yi becomes the head of the secretariat, and others receive their rewards. But Yang Yi feels belittled, as he expected to have a higher post than his junior, Jiang Wei. He even comments that perhaps he should have deserted and joined Wei, where he would have been given real honours! When the second ruler hears this, he cashiers him and sends him into internal exile. Unable to bear the shame of this, Yang Yi commits suicide.

Meanwhile in the kingdom of Wei all is far from right. The Wei ruler has embarked upon an enormous programme of building palaces, with vastly extravagant halls and towers, and huge gardens. All are undertaken using only the most expensive and showy of materials, and over thirty thousand men are employed just on his schemes alone. Brave officials submit memorials to him complaining that this is an inappropriate use of the nation's skills and resources. Such remonstrations are dismissed angrily by Cao Rui, and one official even pays for such temerity with his life.

Finally, Cao Rui demolishes the huge bronze statue, created centuries before, which stands in Chang'an and, so legend tells, brought longevity to the greatest of the Han rulers. Its main feature is a bowl held in the hands of the statue on top of the immensely tall pillar of bronze. This bowl catches the early morning dew. Mixed with fragments of jade, it is believed that this dew is the elixir of life. And it is this that Cao Rui wants to have in his new palace.

Many inauspicious signs and events take place as the workmen try to demolish this strange monument, but nothing seems to touch Cao Rui's heart or mind. Not even when one official points out that the greatest rulers of the past – Yao, Yu the Great – only built with thatch and lived in simple homes, while the worst of ancient rulers – men such as Jie or Zhou – lived in extravagant palaces and brought ruin on their dynasties: for example, the first emperor of the Qin, whose vast palaces did not survive for even one more reign, as his son was overthrown. But all this wisdom is ignored.

Nor is the domestic life of Cao Rui any better. His first wife, the Empress Mao, is set aside for his latest love, and, when Cao Rui thinks the empress has mocked him, he slays all her staff and then 'suggests' that she should commit suicide – which she duly does. Yet, despite such abominable behaviour, no one at court makes a sound. Then news comes of a revolt. Gongsun Yuan, lord of Liaodong, has declared himself king, built a palace and set up a court. The north of the kingdom is in flames. It is the year AD 239.

How will this ruler face such a challenge?

Let's find out.

CHAPTER 106

Cao Rui dies, and Cao Shuang usurps power for ten years. Faking ill health, Sima Yi sets a trap for Cao Shuang.

Cao Rui orders Sima Yi to come to court and then despatches him to deal with the revolt of the lord of Liaodong. The enemy really stands very little chance against a commander as skilful as Sima Yi, but the weather – it is autumn – causes many problems for the Wei army, and this leads to dissent. Sima Yi deals with this with severity, showing little mercy. He has, however, the full support and trust of Cao Rui. When Gongsun Yuan is eventually captured and executed along with his son, Sima Yi rounds up the whole clan and kills them all – over seventy of them.

Back in Chang'an, Cao Rui falls ill. He has been visited by the ghosts of the empress he made commit suicide and her attendants whom he had killed, and this brings about a collapse in his health. Realizing that the end of his life is drawing near, he appoints one of his relatives, the son of Cao Zhen, Cao Shuang, to be the regent, as the heir apparent, Cao Fang, is just eight years old. Then he summons Sima Yi and appoints him to share in caring for the young king with Cao Shuang. The young boy is brought in and told to trust Sima Yi and Cao Shuang. Falling upon his father's neck, the boy weeps and will not let go. And this is how Cao Rui dies, his son weeping upon his shoulder. He is thirty-six and has reigned for thirteen years.

It is not long after the enthronement of the young king that Cao Shuang begins to usurp the imperial powers. He places his own henchmen in the senior posts; builds himself palaces; steals imperial concubines from the imperial palace and removes control of the military from Sima Yi. Seeing which way the wind is blowing, Sima Yi retires and, feigning illness, disappears from sight. His sons do likewise.

Things go on like this for ten years. During this time Sima Yi is so invisible Cao Shuang largely forgets about him, though he always fears him. Anxious suddenly to know whether the man still poses a threat to him, he sends Imperial Inspector Li Sheng to visit him. When Sima Yi knows who has come and why, he takes to his bed. He even pretends both that he is hard of hearing and that his mind is slipping by pretending not to understand anything Li Sheng says. 'Death awaits me,' he says as the visitor departs. When Li Sheng reports this to Cao Shuang, he says, 'So I've nothing to fear, because he's going to die.'

As soon as Li Sheng has gone, Sima Yi rises from his bed, calls his sons to him and says, 'When Li Sheng reports back, Cao Shuang will no longer worry about me. This means he'll go out hunting with few precautions. That is when we strike.'

The time comes for the sacrifices to be offered by the young ruler at his father's tomb. The whole court goes out with Cao Fang and Cao Shuang to attend the ritual. One official remonstrates, saying that this leaves the capital unattended and thus vulnerable to revolt. 'And who exactly would lead this? No one,' says Cao Shuang.

The 'who' is, of course, Sima Yi. Summoning his old comrades in arms and his two sons, he sets out to murder Cao Shuang.

Can Cao Shuang survive?

Well, let's see.

CHAPTER 107

Sima Yi takes over. Jiang Wei loses a battle.

Sima Yi's coup works seamlessly. Using his authority as a regent, he takes over control of the palace administration, the military and the secretariat. He goes before the queen mother and assures her that no harm will come to her or to the Son of Heaven – her son the emperor. His fight is with the corrupt official whom he plans to execute. As chaos spreads through the capital, men have to choose whether to back Sima Yi or Cao Shuang.

In the midst of all this, Sima Yi sends a message to Cao Shuang saying he only wants to scale back the power of Cao's brothers. When Cao Shuang hears of the revolt, he collapses from his horse in fear and astonishment. This terror is further increased when a petition from Sima Yi reaches the Son of Heaven Cao Fang that outlines in no uncertain terms that Cao Shuang and his cohorts have usurped the imperial power and that as a result the whole empire is unsettled, brimming with revolt and unrest. Reassuring the young emperor that his mother supports all this, Sima Yi asks that Cao Shuang and his men be stripped of their powers and authority. He finishes by pointing out none too subtly that he has already taken over military control of the city.

Cao Fang asks Cao Shuang what he wants to do. But he is paralysed by fear. Unable to make up his mind, he dithers all day and all night and when dawn comes the next day he still cannot decide whether to trust Sima Yi or flee in order to raise an army to counter-attack. Finally he decides to surrender and to accept the loss of his power and wealth if it means he can survive. So he hands over his badges and apparatus of authority and is sent to live on his estate. But the gates are locked and guarded by Sima Yi's men.

Now Sima Yi sets about eliminating all who opposed him, all who seized power and all who abused their positions. It is not long before Cao Shuang, his brothers and their entire clan are executed.

Cao Fang appoints Sima Yi as prime minister and his two sons are elevated to high positions of power. Suddenly Sima Yi recalls that one member of the extended Cao clan whom he has not killed is the great warrior Xiahou Xuan, who undoubtedly could be a threat. He summons him to court. This has the result of making Xuan's uncle Xiahou Ba revolt, and with his three thousand men he crosses over the border and offers his services to the second ruler of Shu Han.

When Jiang Wei hears he has come, he is at first very doubtful. But on hearing of all that is going on, he agrees to Xiahou Ba joining the forces of Shu. Jiang Wei is concerned that Sima might invade Shu, but Xiahou Ba points out that Sima has enough on his hands just taking over and securing Wei.

This news inspires in Jiang Wei the desire to attack Wei while the country is still in uproar. This plan he presents to the second ruler. Fei Yi strongly objects but is overruled by the second ruler. Jiang Wei, supported by Xiahou Ba, moves to Hanzhong to prepare the invasion. Despite trying to bring the Qiang tribesmen in as allies, the invasion is a disaster. The forts they build don't have enough water for them to survive the sieges they fall under when Wei retaliates. Furthermore, Chen Tai, the Wei commander, outmanoeuvres the Shu army at almost every stage. Guo Huai, the local governor, is especially ferocious in his attacks.

Sima Shi, the eldest son of Sima Yi, confronts Jiang Wei at Yangping pass. Charging at each other, they fight only three rounds before Sima Shi turns and flees. Jiang Wei travels on and takes up position in the fort at the pass. When Sima Shi approaches the fort, arrows fly out at an unprecedented rate. The ten-arrow bow machine Kong Ming designed has not only been built, it actually works!

Can Sima Shi survive?

Shall we find out!

CHAPTER 108

Sima Yi dies and Sun Quan dies. Sun Jun executes a treacherous plot at a banquet.

Sima Shi loses countless men to the arrow machines, but Jiang Wei loses tens of thousands in his failed invasion. He retreats to Hanzhong, and Sima Shi and the other Wei commanders return to Luoyang.

In late summer of AD 251 Sima Yi falls seriously ill in Wei. Dying, he passes on his authority to his two sons, Sima Shi and Sima Zhao.

In Wu, also in late summer that year, a storm blows over the tall trees around the shrine of the Sun family and the shock of this brings on a serious illness for Sun Quan. Six months later, in early AD 252, he dies. He had reigned for twenty-four years and was seventy-one years old.

A poet has said of him:

> This blue-eyed, red-bearded hero,
> Inspired all who served him.
> Twenty-four years he ruled without challenge.
> A coiled dragon; a tiger below the mighty river.

By now most of the great men of the kingdom – Lu Xun, Zhuge Jin and others – have died. It is Zhuge Jin's son, Zhuge Ke, who now holds power and enthrones the heir apparent Sun Liang as emperor. But Zhuge Ke is a foolish and ambitious man. Soon he has taken control of the whole court and country and is living a life of extravagance. Using his power, he has any who oppose him killed and brings a chill of fear over the whole land.

News of the death of Sun Quan inspires in Sima Shi a desire

to invade Wu. Despite being advised that this would be a foolish move, he insists. He marches south, and in response Zhuge Ke goes north to the border. The Wu troops, through various plots and schemes, inflict terrible losses on the Wei army, forcing them to retreat. This in turn inspires in Zhuge Ke the desire to invade Wei in revenge. Even though omens of bad fortune appear before him, so intent is he on a victory that he dismisses them. He even writes to the Shu ruler and Jiang Wei suggesting they join him in this war.

It is a disaster. The Wu army fail to capture anywhere and when they besiege Xincheng they are outwitted by its governor. Zhuge Ke himself is wounded by an arrow. The summer heat, despair and bad management by their leaders lead many of the Wu soldiers to desert, and they slip away back home. Illness makes the rest as good as useless, and so the army retreat.

Zhuge Ke is so embarrassed by his failures that he hides at home, faking illness. Resentment against Zhuge Ke and his abuse of power leads some members of the Sun family to plot against him. Sun Jun petitions the emperor for permission to execute Zhuge Ke. They plot to invite him to a banquet and at a signal from the emperor, who has long wished to rid himself of Zhuge Ke, they will kill him.

Meanwhile Zhuge Ke has experienced many strange events and phenomena. Finding a man wearing mourning clothes wandering lost in his house, he executes not just him but the guards, who swear that they never saw anyone enter. That night the main beam of the house cracks in two, and, when he gets up to see what is happening, Zhuge Ke sees the man in mourning and the guards carrying their heads under their arms. The ghosts shout at him, and he collapses in terror. The next morning, he tries to wash, but the water smells of blood no matter how often the maids change it. Other signs show that all is not well for Zhuge Ke, and although he sets out for the banquet his courage fails him, and he turns around. But he is then met by two of the officials, who persuade him to come to the banquet. At the crucial moment during the banquet Sun Jun shouts, 'The Son of Heaven has ordered the execution of a traitor!' and with one swipe of his sword he takes off Zhuge Ke's head. His brother Zhang Yue tries to defend himself but he too is slain. Their bodies are wrapped in reed mats and thrown into a paupers' burial place, unmarked, outside the city.

Zhuge Ke's wife is at home when suddenly a maid covered in blood bursts in. The woman's face shows terrible anger; grinding her teeth, she runs at a pillar and smashes her head against it, crying, 'I am Zhuge Ke, murdered by that traitor Sun Jun.' Horribly aware of the threat that this means to her and her family, she gathers them together, and their wailing fills the air. Very soon after, soldiers burst in and take them to the market square, where they kill every one of them. It is autumn AD 253.

From that day on power is given by the emperor to Sun Jun.

In Chengdu, the letter from Zhuge Ke has arrived suggesting an alliance of warfare against Wei. In response and without knowing what has befallen Zhuge Ke, Jiang Wei mobilizes the army and sets out for the north.

Will this fare any better than previous attempts?

Let's find out.

CHAPTER 109

The emperor of Wei is deposed. Cao Mao becomes emperor.

So it was that in that year, AD 253, once again Jiang Wei calls together his armed forces and sets off for the border with Wei. This time they ensure the involvement of the Qiang tribesmen through the offering of many gifts. This has the desired result, and King Midang brings his army to join the invasion. In response Sima Shi sends Xu Zhi to lead the Wei army, renowned as he is for his valour. Alongside, he sends his own brother, Sima Zhao. The first engagement goes badly for the Shu army, and Xu Zhi takes a mighty toll of the Shu soldiers.

But at the next engagement it is the Wei troops who suffer, and Xu Zhi is slain. The Shu army sweep on to overwhelm the Wei camp, and Sima Zhao is forced to find sanctuary on a hill-top, where the small spring can supply only a fraction of the water his six thousand men need. The supplies run out, and despair descends upon the troops. It is then that Sima Zhao is reminded of the story of how a former hero similarly trapped and without water prayed to the spring and it gushed forth water a hundredfold. So that is what Sima Zhao does, and after he makes the offerings and prayers the stream pours forth more than enough to slake the thirst of the men.

Meanwhile Chen Tai of the Wei army has pretended to desert along with five thousand men and joined the Qiang in their alliance with Jiang Wei and the Shu. However, his real reason is to dupe the Qiang into mounting a raid on the Wei camp, where they will then be ambushed. Believing he is genuine, the king of the Qiang, Midang, orders an attack that very night. Led on by the duplicitous Chen Tai, one of their senior commanders leads the attack on the enemy camp. Of course, no sooner have they tried to enter than the commander's horse falls into a deep pit, and, from behind, the troops who claimed to be deserting attack the Qiang and in front Chen Tai leads another detachment of Wei soldiers to the attack. Thousands of the Qiang die, and King Midang is captured. He is persuaded to leave the alliance with the Shu and rejoin his old allies the Wei, because when he arrives bound in chains Guo Huai releases him. Attacking the Shu camp, they surprise the men and overwhelm the camp. Jiang Wei has to flee but he manages to wound Guo Huai as he retreats. That night Guo Huai dies.

Once again the armies retreat. Jiang Wei has lost again, though he has managed to kill Xu Zhi and Guo Huai, so the effort so far as he is concerned is not completely wasted. As for Sima Zhao, he celebrates the defeat of the enemy attack, and this only strengthens his brother Sima Shi's control of the empire. Soon he is acting as if he were the emperor even in front of the emperor himself.

Cao Fang finds himself sidelined and retreats to his own quarters, deprived of almost all his own officers bar three. One of these is Zhang Qi, the father of the emperor's consort Empress Zhang. Together with the other two, Xiahou Xuan, whose uncle has fled to Shu, and Li Feng, he plots with the emperor to rally loyal men to come to the help of the emperor and overthrow both of the Sima brothers. To seal this, Cao Fang removes his imperial dragon-phoenix shirt and, cutting his finger, writes in blood the edict summoning men to his side. He recalls that: 'Dong Cheng was killed by my ancestor Cao Cao the august emperor because an exact same conspiracy was discovered.' But the others dismiss this, saying that Cao Cao was of a far superior intelligence than Sima Shi.

However, no sooner do they leave the palace than Sima Shi confronts them by the roadside. He asks why they have been so long at the palace, and they try to bluff their way out, claiming they were studying the Classics with the emperor. But Sima Shi is not fooled and he soon discovers the shirt with its bloody words and flies into a terrible rage. The inevitable follows. The three men and their entire clans are executed, and in his fury Sima Shi forces entry into the palace and heads straight for the emperor's quarters. Throwing the dragon-phoenix shirt on the floor, he erupts: 'Why have you turned against us? We've done nothing but serve you. Why do you see love as opposition; mistake service for failure?' Emperor Cao Fang tries to pass blame off on others, but the blood-soaked shirt cries out his offence. With no other option, the emperor confesses his role in the plot. Turning to face the empress, Sima Shi says, 'You're Zhang Qi's daughter and therefore you must face the consequences.' His soldiers drag her away, while the emperor screams for mercy – but to no avail. She is strangled.

As a poet has commented:

> Thrown outside, barefoot, is Queen Fu,[29]
> Torn from her lord, she pleads for her life.
> Today, the Sima do the same to Queen Zhang,
> Heaven repays the cost to the descendants of Cao.

Events then take a swift turn. Sima Shi calls a council of ministers and denounces the emperor, saying he is unfit to rule. Cajoling the queen mother, he arranges for Cao Fang to abdicate and with the queen mother selects another member of the Cao family, Cao Mao, to be emperor. He has no desire whatsoever to become emperor but up against Sima Shi he has no option. It is the year AD 254.

But rebellion breaks out at such a dramatic seizing of power.

What happens next?

What indeed.

CHAPTER 110

Wen Yang defeats an army on his own.
Sima Shi dies, and while Jiang Wei wins a battle he is then defeated.

It is in Huainan, under the leadership of Wen Qin, governor of Yangzhou, and Guanqiu Jian, a famous general, that the rebellion breaks out. Disgusted at the usurping of imperial power by the Sima brothers and the death of Cao Shuang, they launch their rebellion. Their first target is the city of Xiangcheng, where they set up camp. Sima Shi has just had a painful operation to have a mole removed from just below his left eye. He is still in considerable pain, and, when news comes of the revolt, is not keen to have to go himself. However, he knows that, if he does not, then the rebellion will gather strength simply because he has not come. So reluctantly he leads the army to the attack.

Paramount among the warriors of the rebellion is the mighty Wen Yang. His weapon of choice is a whip of steel. It is he who puts most fear into the hearts of the loyalist Wei troops, even though he is only eighteen years old. And it is he who leads a daring raid on the Wei camp. Inside the camp Sima Shi is in terrible pain from his eye but when he hears the shouts as Wen Yang leads the rebels into the Wei camp he rises, biting down on his quilt to stifle the cries of pain. The rebel attack initially creates panic among the Wei soldiers, and in the ensuing confusion many are killed. But slowly they regain their confidence and push back. The plan was that more troops from the rebel side would crash into the camp from the opposite direction – but none come. Instead a further contingent of the Wei troops arrive, trapping Wen Yang. Fleeing, he is pursued by a hundred of the enemy, but time and again Wen Yang turns and, driving straight into their midst, slays right and left with his steel whip until the men back off, and he is able to escape again. Single-handedly he fights all who come at him until the Wei give up and let him escape.

Despite such strength, it is in vain, and not long after, in early AD 255, the rebellion is finally quashed. Then Sima Shi's sickness takes a turn for the worse, and he knows he is dying. He summons his brother Sima Zhao. 'There is no way,' says Sima Shi, 'that I can simply pretend that the heavy duty I have does not count for anything. I must therefore pass the burden on to you. But remember this at all times: trust no one. For if you do, they will destroy our clan.' Sima Zhao, weeping, accepts the seal of authority. Wanting to ask for advice, Sima Zhao starts to speak, but his words are interrupted by a heart-rending cry from Sima Shi. And he dies. News is sent to Emperor Cao Mao (Cao Fang had died the previous year), who orders Sima Zhao to stay where he is to prevent any attack by Wu in such an unsettled time. When, however, he hears that Sima Zhao has moved his army back, he is greatly troubled. But he receives reassurances from his adviser Wang Su that he has nothing to fear. Soon after, Sima Zhao moves his army into the capital itself. Now seriously alarmed and in an attempt to win his favour, Cao Mao heaps titles and gifts upon Sima Zhao. Does he really need them? He is by now the most powerful man in the kingdom.

Once again the disorder in Wei encourages Jiang Wei to contemplate an invasion of the north. The invasion drives into the borderlands but is soon countered by the Wei army under Wang Jing. Thinking that they have the Shu army trapped – who are backed up against the River Tao – they attack, only to be roundly defeated by Jiang Wei, who, inspired by this, presses on to attack Didao. Zhang Yi protests against this, saying surely his triumph at the River Tao is enough, but Jiang Wei's blood lust is up, and he moves forward anyway. Chen Tai moves his army of Wei troops to the defence of Didao. Jiang Wei is fooled into an attack which leads him and his men into an ambush set by the experienced Wei general Deng Ai, and once again he is defeated. He withdraws to Hanzhong but he is already planning his next invasion of Wei.

Will this be any more successful?

We will find out.

CHAPTER III

Zhuge Dan raises an army.
He battles Sima Zhao.

Although the Wei commanders, Deng Ai and Chen Tai, hold a banquet to celebrate defeating the Shu, they know that Jiang Wei will not be able to resist the temptation, despite all the odds, to try to invade yet again. And sure enough Jiang Wei voices his opinion that he should invade again. This time opposition in Shu is more vocal. However, Jiang Wei dismisses this by saying there are five reasons why they will succeed.

'Firstly, the failure of the Wei army to defeat the Shu at the River Tao has dampened their enthusiasm, to put it mildly. Secondly, we will transport our troops by ship – they must march, so we will be more rested. Thirdly, we are well trained – they, frankly, are not. Fourthly, we have had a bumper harvest. And finally, they won't know where we will strike so will have to divide their forces. We can move as one unit.'

Even though Xiahou Ba points out how skilful Deng Ai is at military strategy, Jiang Wei simply brushes this aside. So once again Jiang Wei advances into Wei. And Xiahou Ba was right. Deng Ai is a better military planner. No matter where Jiang Wei advances, Deng Ai is there to confront him or has placed troops ready to intercept him. The Shu losses are great, and the gains – absolutely nothing at all. Chen Tai and Deng Ai overwhelm Jiang Wei and his Shu troops at every occasion, and once again Jiang Wei has no option but to retreat back to Hanzhong. And this time his men complain loudly, and the grieving relatives of those killed complain vociferously. Jiang Wei has to accept that he must take full responsibility for the disaster and be demoted.

The Wei commanders celebrate, and Emperor Cao Mao

changes the title of the year to that of Celebrating Victory to show how pleased he is. But everyone knows that the real ruler is without doubt Sima Zhao. It is he who takes all the key decisions without even the pretence of asking the emperor. In such circumstances it is only a matter of time before aspirations of imperial glory begin to shape Sima Zhao's thoughts. He is encouraged in this by his chief adviser, Jia Chong, who offers to go and take soundings as to how such an idea might go down in the country.

The first person he visits is Zhuge Dan, a cousin of Kong Ming, who lives in Huainan and is the controller of the forces on both sides of the River Huai. Despite being related to the former prime minister of the enemy country of Shu, Zhuge Dan through his own abilities has risen slowly through the ranks in Wei. While dining with him, as if in an aside, Jia Chong mentions that some people of worth have been saying they no longer feel the emperor is up to the task and that the Regent Sima Zhao should take over. 'They see him as more worthy, but I wonder what your opinion is?'

Zhuge Dan's reaction is immediate: 'If this were to take place, I would die fighting to protect the throne.' He also criticizes Jia Chong as the son of a long-time servant of the Wei for even raising it. All this is swiftly reported back to Sima Zhao, who is rattled by such opposition and decides to get rid of Zhuge Dan. He tries to lure him to court by offering him a new post, but Zhuge Dan immediately knows the real reason. A letter demanding the execution of Zhuge Dan is also sent to the imperial governor of the region, Yue Chen.

Learning of the letter, Zhuge Dan responds immediately. He draws together a thousand of his men, seizes the provincial capital, slays Yue Chen and his entire family and then sends a formal memorial to the emperor denouncing Sima Zhao and his crimes. Then he recruits men from the fields and within weeks has an army of around one hundred and fifty thousand. He also seeks an alliance with Wu to back up his defiance.

In Wu, Sun Jun, the prime minister, has died, and his vicious, cruel and tyrannical cousin Sun Chen has taken over. There is nothing the Emperor Sun Liang can do to control him. An appeal for support comes from Zhuge Dan, and upon reading it Sun Chen responds immediately by sending seventy thousand men.

When Zhuge Dan's memorial to the emperor arrives at the court, Sima Zhao reads it and resolves not only to send an army to crush the revolt but to lead it himself. However, Jia Chong points out that Sima Zhao might face a revolt in the court while he is away unless he takes the imperial family with him. So Cao Mao is forced to join the army along with the queen mother. The attacking army of around two hundred and sixty thousand advances like a tidal wave towards the south, while Zhu Yi of the Wu moves his army north. The first encounter goes to the advantage of the Wei troops, and the Wu have to retreat and take stock. Then Zhuge Dan moves his forces up, and the real battle begins.

Who will win?

Shall we find out?

CHAPTER 112

Sima Zhao tricks Zhuge Dan.
Jiang Wei fights to seize Changcheng.

Sima Zhao plays a clever trick. He 'leaves' supply wagons filled with grain, weapons and other materials on the edge of the battlefield. When Zhuge Dan and his Wu allies attack, the Wu soldiers, who have no real interest in the outcome of the battle, run off to loot the wagons, leaving Zhuge Dan and his men alone and exposed. They suffer a major defeat and flee to the city of Shouchun, where they prepare for a long siege. The Wu forces occupy the nearby town of Anfeng, ready to strike back if necessary. However, the presence of Sun Chen does little to help. He orders attacks which are futile and loses the Wu good men. Humiliated and furious, he then executes the commander whom he has made undertake these perilous missions, throwing all the blame upon the unfortunate man. In the end his oppressive rule leads one of the commanders, Quan Yi, to desert and join the Wei forces. Quan Yi also gets news through to his uncle in Shouchun, who also deserts and leads his men out of the city to join the Wei army. Seeing what is inevitable, Sun Chen deserts the army and its inevitable defeat and hurries back to Wu.

Inside Shouchun the fraught situation does little to improve Zhuge Dan's temper, and any suggestion of a different military strategy draws nothing but contempt from him. By this he alienates his own commanders, who begin to desert. Starvation begins to bite, and the defenders become seriously weak. Any complaints are dealt with severely. Zhuge Dan himself roams the streets, striking down any who complain. Such harshness only leads of course to more desertions.

The end is inevitable. The city is stormed, and though Zhuge Dan tries to escape he is trapped and slain. His whole family are then killed, while his faithful soldiers refuse to bend the knee to Sima Zhao, and all of them – over three hundred – are executed. The Wu soldiers caught up in the fall of the city surrender, and although Sima Zhao wants to kill them all he is persuaded to have mercy, as this will be of advantage in the long run for their relationship with Wu.

Then news comes that Jiang Wei has once again invaded Wei and is heading for Chang'an. It is in the year AD 258 when Jiang Wei attacks, seeking to take advantage of the chaos in Wei caused by Zhuge Dan's revolt. This time dissent arises within the Shu court at yet another plan by Jiang Wei to attack Wei. The adviser Qiao Zhou even writes a formal essay to the second ruler condemning such actions as a sign of a weak kingdom lacking in wisdom. 'Things are not going well generally in Shu,' he says. 'The court has become saturated with wealth and luxury, which leads to vice and corruption. They place their trust in the eunuch Huang Hao, but all he does is ignore the due processes of rule, exploiting his position for personal gain.' But it is Jiang Wei who opens the scroll and, reading this, he is furious and throws it away. He ignores all the warning signs and ploughs ahead with his schemes.

At first he is successful, overwhelming Sima Wang, a cousin of Sima Zhao, who is commander of the city of Changcheng, where Wei supplies are stored. Defeated in the field, Sima Wang retreats into the city, and Jiang Wei besieges it. Just as the Shu troops are about to overwhelm the city walls and seize the city, reinforcements arrive, led by the great Wei general Deng Ai. Stalemate ensues, but this is broken when Jiang Wei receives news of the death of Zhuge Dan and the failure of the revolt, including the surrender of the Wu troops.

'Once again,' sighs Jiang Wei, 'our hopes have become empty dreams. There is no option but to go home.'

> Four attempts – failure;
> Fifth attempt – enthusiastic but failure.

Can he get home easily?

Maybe, maybe not.

CHAPTER 113

Ding Feng plots to kill Sun Chen,
while Sun Liang is deposed. Jiang Wei defeats
Deng Ai but is betrayed at home.

Jiang Wei is able to escape, because Deng Ai knows there is little point in pursuing him, as he will try to set ambushes, and, well, frankly, what is the point in chasing him! He is going back with his tail between his legs anyway.

The failure of the Wu troops to support Zhuge Dan leads to horrific recriminations and consequences back in Wu. Sun Chen has all the families of the commanders executed. By now the ruler of Wu, Sun Liang, who is only sixteen years old, is completely in the control of Sun Chen. The weakness of his position is further exposed when he tries to overthrow Sun Chen by plotting with his brother-in-law to take over the city and kill Sun Chen. But his brother-in-law privately informs his father. He is married to the eldest sister of Sun Chen, so he is immediately informed of the plot. As a result Sun Chen deposes the ruler, claiming that he is morally corrupt and utterly incompetent to perform the required imperial rituals for the ancestors. Within moments Sun Liang has been seized and sent into internal exile, weeping as he leaves.

A poet has said:

> Quoting great leaders of the past,
> Such treacherous actions mock them.
> Mourn for Sun Liang, a wise ruler
> Who will never darken the court doors again.

Now Sun Chen simply seizes all power, appointing his relatives to all the key positions. He brings to court a bewildered relative of the deposed ruler and against his wish has this man,

Sun Xiu, made ruler. It is the year AD 258, and Sun Chen is made prime minister.

Much later that year, slighted by something the poor innocent ruler has done, Sun Chen decides to go the final step and seize imperial power for himself. Alarmed by what he sees happening, the ruler, Sun Xiu, calls for help from his adviser Zhang Bu. He summons the veteran commander Ding Feng, and together they plot the overthrow of Sun Chen. Using the occasion of a great festival, the next day they plan to invite Sun Chen to attend and then murder him.

That night inauspicious signs appear, which alarm the household of Sun Chen, but which he dismisses. In the morning, rising from his bed, he collapses but still insists on going to the festival. 'My brothers and I are in control of the palace guards. So who is going to try and challenge me?' he says. 'If there is anything to worry about, start a fire, and we will come quickly.' Sun Chen sits beside Sun Xiu, and all seems well until flames erupt around the palace. Thinking this is his signal, Sun Chen rises, only to be suddenly confronted by Zhang Bu, entering with thirty guards. Within a moment they have seized Sun Chen. He begs to be allowed to go into internal exile. Citing the names of those Sun Chen has arbitrarily killed, Sun Xiu asks, 'And when did you ever show mercy?' and he gives orders for Sun Chen's immediate execution. He is hauled to one side in the great hall and summarily executed there and then.

When the second ruler of Shu, Liu Shan, hears of these events, he sends a message of congratulations. In response, Sun Xiu sends his own envoy to Shu. When the messenger returns to Wu, Sun Xiu asks how things stand in Shu. He is informed that the country is falling apart due to the corruption of the eunuchs, the dishonesty of the court and the poverty of the people as a result. 'This is an example,' says the messenger, Xue Xu, 'of sparrows in the roof unaware that the building is about to be burned down!' Another messenger comes back to Shu to inform the second ruler that, in the opinion of the Wu, Sima Zhao is about to seize imperial power in Wei and that both Shu and Wu should be prepared for any military fallout.

Jiang Wei hears of all this and of course immediately proposes an invasion of Wei! Predictably he advances through the Qishan hills and sets up camp on the plains. Deng Ai is delighted. He is expecting this and has left the plains for Jiang Wei to occupy, but has dug a long tunnel under the area where the enemy camp is set. It is a good plan – it means there could be an attack from above and below ground. However, despite all his plans and preparations, a major night attack from above and below ground fails to overwhelm the Shu army, and Deng Ai has to admit defeat. A major battle the next day sees Deng Ai driven back by the triumphant Shu. Jiang Wei has used techniques learned from Kong Ming and his almost magical military formulae. The Wei are no match for such occult powers. However, Sima Wang tells Deng Ai that he too knows these strategies, and so the next battle is as much a battle of wits, magic and strange powers between Sima Wang and Jiang Wei as one of force. But once again it is a disaster for the Wei, and both Sima Wang and Deng Ai are roundly defeated. They have to retreat – Deng Ai even receives wounds from four arrows as he flees.

Facing military defeat, Deng Ai and Sima Wang come up with another plan. They decide to undermine Jiang Wei's credibility with the second ruler and his favourite, the eunuch Huang Hao. Bribes are taken to Huang Hao, and soon rumours circulate in Chengdu that Jiang Wei, dissatisfied with his level of power and authority, is planning to go over to the Wei. Soon the rumours are so prevalent that Huang Hao feels able to petition the second ruler to order Jiang Wei to come back.

Jiang Wei has been trying to engage the Wei army, but they hold back from open confrontation. Then the summons comes ordering Jiang Wei home. Now the Wei army surge out onto the battlefield in order to make the retreat of the Shu army as arduous as possible.

What will happen next?

What indeed.

CHAPTER 114

Emperor Cao Mao is murdered in his carriage.
Jiang Wei outwits Deng Ai.

Whatever other faults he has, Jiang Wei knows how to manage a retreat. Instead of a rout, he makes a tactical withdrawal, safeguarding his men with a strong rearguard force to protect them, so much so that Deng Ai, observing it, decides not to attack, and thus the Shu army make their way back safely to the land of Shu.

As soon as Jiang Wei arrives in Chengdu he goes and confronts the second ruler about why he has been recalled. 'We were worried that you might be worn out by such activities,' says the second ruler lamely, to which Jiang Wei retorts, 'I had victory within my grasp! I think the only reason was that someone has been spreading rumours and that Deng Ai lies behind this.' The second ruler really has nothing to say in reply, so shortly afterwards Jiang Wei returns to Hanzhong, ready for yet another attack on Wei.

Back in Wei, Deng Ai has reported to Sima Zhao the growing dissension within the Shu kingdom. Much encouraged, he begins preparations for an attack on Shu. But when he seeks the advice of Jia Chong, he says, 'This is not the right time. You're not secure at home, and any absence would provide opportunities for your enemies here.' He then tells Sima Zhao of something strange that has happened:

'Not long ago a yellow dragon appeared twice in the well at Ningling. When his imperial majesty was congratulated on such an auspicious sighting, the Son of Heaven said it was far from auspicious. For if the dragon symbolizes the ruler, this dragon is not in Heaven, nor in the fields, but is trapped underground in a well. This means imprisonment. In response the ruler wrote this poem, which is, to put not too fine a point on it, about you, sir.'

> The dragon is besieged,
> Unable to dance upon the waters,
> Unable to soar to the Milky Way,
> Unable to prance upon the fields.
> Down in the dank well is he,
> Slimy creatures his only companions.
> His mighty mouth shut, claws shielded,
> Ah, is this not me of whom I speak?

The poem profoundly disturbs and angers Sima Zhao, who says, 'So he wants the same fate at Cao Fang! He must go or he'll destroy us.' 'Just say the word,' replies Jia Chong, 'and it will be done.'

It is summertime AD 260. Sima Zhao goes immediately to the imperial palace. The Emperor Cao Mao rises to greet him, whereupon the courtiers cry, 'Give Sima Zhao the highest honours, for he is worthy of them!' When Cao Mao makes no reply, Sima Zhao rounds on him. 'For three generations my family have served the Wei. Doesn't that deserve the highest honour?' Cowed by this outburst, Cao Mao has to agree. Then Sima Zhao rounds on him: 'In your poem about the dragon in the well you describe us as slimy creatures. Not exactly respectful, now, is it?' To this Cao Mao has nothing to say. Sima Zhao, having cast a chill over the whole court, turns and leaves.

In despair Cao Mao retreats to his inner chambers and summons senior officials Wang Shen, Wang Jing and Wang Ye. 'It's obvious that Sima Zhao intends to seize the throne. Please, please help me to overthrow him.' But Wang Jing points out that Sima has secured all the key appointments, and that no one in the court will or can challenge him. 'Just live with it,' is his advice. Startled by this conversation, Wang Shen and Wang Ye decide that, to protect their families from suspicion, they must go and tell Sima Zhao of this conversation. Only Wang Jing says he will do no such thing. So it is the other two who tell Sima Zhao of the emperor's thoughts.

Shortly after this, Emperor Cao Mao summons his guard and with a crowd of servants some three hundred strong sets out to confront Sima Zhao. Taking his own sword, Cao Mao is riding in the imperial carriage, and as they leave the palace Wang Jing, weeping, prostrates himself and tries to stop the emperor from leaving. 'These few men cannot fight Sima Zhao. It's like sending sheep into the mouth of a tiger. This is pointless.' But Cao Mao will not be deterred. 'We're moving out. Get out of my way,' he says, and the procession turns out of the palace gate. In the street he is confronted by an armed Jia Chong on horseback, with Cheng Ji and Cheng Zu in attendance, followed by many thousands of armed troops. Emperor Cao Mao shouts above the noise, 'This is the Son of Heaven. Do you intend to murder your rightful ruler?' Jia Chong then turns to Cheng Ji. 'This is why you have been retained by Sima Zhao', and at this command Cheng Ji shifts his halberd and asks, 'Dead or as a prisoner?' 'Dead – by order of Sima Zhao,' replies Jia Chong. Then Cheng Ji charges. Cao Mao cries out aloud, 'You traitor, how dare you!' but these are his last words. Cheng Ji's halberd stabs him in the chest. Cao Mao struggles out of the carriage, only to be struck again in the back. Dead, he falls down beside the carriage. All his guard flee. Only Wang Jing cries out in outrage, and he is seized and bound while a report is sent to Sima Zhao.

When Sima Zhao comes to the scene of the murder, he pretends to be truly upset. Later he summons the officials of the court and asks what should be done. 'How do we punish those who have done this?' he asks. Chen Tai, dressed in mourning clothes, says, 'Kill Jia Chong. That will at least feel like some sort of apology to the country.' 'Is there not a lesser punishment?' asks Sima Zhao, to which Chen Tai replies that actually he has worse punishments in mind. 'The real traitor is Cheng Ji. I'll have him carved to death and his entire clan wiped out.' Horrified at this turn of events, Cheng Ji cries out, 'I was simply following your orders given by Jia Chong!' But Sima Zhao orders his tongue cut out to silence him and he and his brother Cheng Zu are publicly executed and his entire clan murdered.

As a poet has said:

> That year, Sima Zhao ordered Jia Chong:
> Kill the emperor.
> Cheng Ji paid for this crime, he and his clan,
> But we all know who the real criminal was.

Likewise, Wang Jing and his entire family were executed.

After the formal burial of Cao Mao, Sima Zhao chooses another distant relative of the August Emperor Cao Cao to take the throne. This is Cao Huan. Sima Zhao is back on top again.

When news of this reaches the Shu court, Jiang Wei argues that, because regicide has taken place in Wei, it gives full legitimacy for an invasion to overthrow the culprits. He writes to the Wu to seek their participation and once again follows the by now very familiar path to the Qishan hills. Here, Deng Ai is entrenched. His deputy, Wang Guan, hearing of the impending attack suggests a plot to him. He will pretend to defect and join the Wei army with his five thousand men and then from within their ranks betray them.

When Wang Guan turns up to defect to Jiang Wei, claiming he is driven to this by the murder of his uncle Wang Jing and the killing of his own family, Jiang Wei is delighted. But then Xiahou Ba arrives and when he hears the news he is not delighted: 'You can't seriously believe this, can you? I've never heard about this man before. Is he really related to Wang Jing?' But Jiang Wei laughs and confesses that he hasn't been fooled for a moment but is going to fight fire with its own fire! So plot after plot is undertaken. False information is fed to Deng Ai, purporting to come from Wang Guan. Fooled by this, Deng Ai is drawn into an ambush and defeated, almost losing his life. Wang Guan is not so lucky. Informed that the plot has been uncovered, he dies trying to escape by crossing the Black Dragon River. His troops, captured by Jiang Wei, are buried alive.

Great as the defeat of the plot is, it has been at terrible cost to the Shu army in terms of men and supplies. So Jiang Wei turns around and goes back to Hanzhong. Even though Deng Ai asks to be demoted for this defeat, Sima Zhao elevates him, loading him with titles and gifts. Deng Ai rewards his men, and Sima Zhao, realizing the vulnerability of the border, sends him extra men.

So what happens next?

Let's find out.

CHAPTER 115

The second ruler listens to rumours and recalls the army. Jiang Wei goes to take charge of the army colonies.

It is now winter AD 263, and Jiang Wei is yet again ready to attack Wei. He has rebuilt the stockades, gathered the supplies, sent ships downriver to prepare for the attack and summoned his army. But the second ruler and many of his council are opposed to yet another invasion. After lengthy discussions the second ruler says, 'Let fate determine what we do next. If he fails, then we can end this once and for all.' But even Jiang Wei's general Liao Hua is uncertain, saying that in Deng Ai there is a foe of superior talents, and the people are tired of these military adventures. To this Jiang Wei retorts, 'Kong Ming tried six times to conquer Wei. This will be my eighth, and if anyone opposes me – he will be executed.' So once again he rolls into Wei. This time he targets the city of Taoyang while also planning a side attack on the Qishan hills pass but using the attack on Taoyang as a diversion to tie down Deng Ai and his army.

Xiahou Ba is sent to take Taoyang and, arriving there, finds it deserted, and people fleeing out of the back gate. However, entering into the city, he finds himself in a trap. Soldiers suddenly appear on the walls and, closing the gates, slaughter the Shu soldiers trapped inside. Here Xiahou Ba himself perishes, along with almost all his men. Encouraged by this, Deng Ai launches a night raid on Jiang Wei's camp, which throws the Shu army into chaos. Things are not looking good for Jiang Wei, but he stoutly refuses to concede this. Deng Ai and Jiang Wei contend with each other for weeks, each trying to trick the other. Jiang Wei has just managed to get the upper hand when he is ordered back to the capital city – an order delivered three times in one day. The reason is that once again the eunuch

Huang Hao has exerted his influence over the corrupt, weak and foolish second ruler and cast doubt upon the reliability of Jiang Wei. So, with no other option open and with victory again snatched from him, Jiang Wei retreats back to Hanzhong and thence to the capital. Meeting an old friend, he learns of the schemes of the eunuch and swears there and then to kill him.

The next day the second ruler and Huang Hao are picnicking in the back garden of the palace when in charges Jiang Wei with a group of his guards. Huang Hao, hearing the commotion, flees and hides before Jiang Wei reaches the second ruler, seated in his pavilion. 'I almost had Deng Ai,' Jiang Wei says, tears coursing down his face, 'when your three orders reached me. But why?' The second ruler has nothing to say. This spurs Jiang Wei on: 'That eunuch Huang Hao has seized power – just as the Ten Eunuchs did in the reign of Emperor Ling. He must be killed. Only then will peace return and the country prosper.'

'Huang Hao is simply my servant,' says the second ruler. 'He is no threat whatsoever. I do hope you have not taken against him.' But Jiang Wei is not swayed and warns the second ruler that terrible consequences will ensue if the man is not killed.

'We live and let live – I hope you can abide by that,' says the second ruler, and he calls Huang Hao to come out of hiding. Grovelling on the ground before Jiang Wei, Huang Hao claims he only ever tries to be of service to the kingdom and has no interest in interfering in public affairs. 'I'm in your hands, general,' he says, 'and I hope you'll be merciful.'

Confronted with such unabashed fakery, Jiang Wei strides away in anger. At a loss as to what to do and fearful that if he falls the kingdom and dynasty will too, he seeks advice from his friend Xi Zheng. It is he who suggests that Jiang Wei establish military colonies where the troops can settle, grow food, train and build up supplies ready in a few years to go on the offensive again. This also has the advantage of removing Jiang Wei from the environs of the malicious and corrupt court and thus protects him as well. Inspired by this, Jiang Wei does exactly that, and soon he and eighty thousand men are en route to the region of Tazhong to set up the colonies.

When Deng Ai and Sima Zhao hear of this, they send spies

to find out what exactly is going on. They decide that a pre-emptive strike is needed, and so Sima Zhao summons Zhong Hui and gives him command. They agree that they will pretend they are preparing an attack on Wu but actually are preparing to take down Shu, especially given the disordered state of affairs due to the evil influence of Huang Hao.

As Sima Zhao sees him off, one of his senior advisers says, 'You have given him one hundred thousand men, but I don't trust him.' Sima Zhao smiles and says, 'Don't worry. I know!' He then says something to his adviser which makes him in turn smile.

What did Sima Zhao say?

Let's find out.

CHAPTER 116

A shaman fools the second ruler.
Kong Ming's spirit appears to Zhong Hui.

'Zhong Hui will confound the sceptics,' says Sima Zhao, 'who claim we cannot win in Shu, because he has a plan. However, even if he decides to revolt once he defeats the Shu, they will be broken, so he cannot use them against us, and the people of Wei will never follow him, so there is nothing to worry about.'

While Zhong Hui advances to the front, Deng Ai receives orders to advance on his front. That night he has a dream of a spring erupting below his feet. Frightened, he seeks an explanation of this from the *Yi Jing*. The explanation leaves him downhearted and troubled, for it forecasts victories in the southwest and failure in the northeast. Orders come for him to liaise with Zhong Hui for the attack on Hanzhong, while another army is sent to attack Jiang Wei at Tazhong.

As the situation escalates, Jiang Wei writes a memorial to the second ruler asking for additional help to defend the kingdom. But the letter is intercepted by Huang Hao and then interpreted to the second ruler as simply Jiang Wei trying to aggrandize himself. 'There is nothing to worry about,' says Huang Hao. 'I know a shaman in the city, and her deity can tell the future. Shall we ask her what the deity says about the future?'

So she is brought to the palace, and the second ruler performs the rituals and burns the incense. The shaman unties her hair, takes off her shoes and in a frenzy dances wildly, whirling round and round until she collapses on the altar. 'Her deity is descending,' says Huang Hao. 'Clear everyone else out.'

'I am the protector god of the Shu,' she says in a trance. 'Your Majesty's lands are at peace. Why do you ask about anything else? Soon the Wei lands will be yours as well. Have no fears, sir.' Then she collapses and takes quite some time to revive. The second ruler is completely fooled by her performance, and as a result Huang Hao is able to ensure he ignores all the letters from Jiang Wei. And so the slippery path to the destruction of the kingdom begins.

Success follows success for the Wei army, including the capture of Hanzhong. Then one night in the town of Yang'an, Zhong Hui and his men are disturbed by the sound of men-at-arms coming from the southwest. When they go to investigate, there is nobody there. The same thing happens the next night. Now thoroughly alarmed, Zhong Hui rides out to explore where this disturbance is coming from. They soon come to a hill, covered in mist. This place and its atmosphere fill everyone with a sense of deep foreboding. When asked what hill this is, Zhong Hui is told it is Dingjun mountain. Suddenly a storm blows up, and down the hill ride thousands of horsemen, who attack the troops. Terrified, Zhong Hui and his men flee, but, when they stop, those whom they think have been wounded by the horsemen have no wounds. They were phantom riders.

When he asks if there is some special shrine on the hilltop, it is the traitor Jiang Shu who tells him no, but there is the tomb of Kong Ming. Realizing the source of the disturbances, Zhong Hui prepares sacrifices and offerings and returns the next day to pay his respects to the spirit of Kong Ming. A calm falls over the region as soon as he has done this.

Then, that night, Zhong Hui awakes in his tent as a cold wind blows in. He sees standing before him a man dressed in Daoist robes, holding a feather fan. His face is like perfect jade. He stands eight feet tall and drifts through like an immortal. Rising to meet this man, Zhong Hui asks, 'Who are you, sir?'

'This morning you honoured me with your sacrifices,' says the apparition. 'So I have come to share this with you. It is clear that Heaven's Mandate has been removed from the Han. But this does not mean that the ordinary folk of Shu must suffer more. When you conquer the western lands do not kill or harm more than is necessary.' And with that he disappears.

Moved by the appearance of Kong Ming, Zhong Hui has a special banner made to be carried at the front of the army. It says, 'Protect the Kingdom; Reassure the People', and he gives orders that no harm must come to the ordinary folk on penalty of death. This results in the people trusting him, and the cities fall one after another without bloodshed.

A poet has said:

> The ghostly horsemen of Dingjun mountain
> Move Zhong Hui to pray at Kong Ming's tomb.
> He who protected alive the fortunes of Xuande,
> Protected the people of Shu even when dead.

The Wei armies led by Zhong Hui and Deng Ai advance without cessation, and place after place falls to them. Jiang Wei is driven back and back. He is almost trapped, but through subterfuge manages to escape across a ford and take up a defensive position at the Jian pass. But no sooner has he arrived than he sees before him a vast army.

What will happen now?

What indeed.

CHAPTER 117

Deng Ai scales the mountains to bypass the Shu army. Zhuge Zhan dies fighting.

To his relief it is further Shu troops, and together they hold the pass. Some commanders are worried about the possibility of an attack by the enemy directly on Chengdu, but Jiang Wei points out that the towering mountains in between will act as a serious defence.

The first attack by Zhuge Xu fails, for he is driven back by Jiang Wei. Returning in disgrace to Zhong Hui, Zhuge Xu has to apologize for being outsmarted by Jiang Wei. But this is not enough for the supreme commander. Zhong Hui orders the execution of Zhuge Xu and is only just persuaded to mitigate this to imprisonment by the earnest pleas of his other commanders. The treatment of Zhuge Xu horrifies Deng Ai, and in particular he resents the authority that Zhong Hui has taken upon himself without consultation with him. In a personal confrontation little respect is shown by either side, with both men pretending to admire the plans of the other – but in truth dismissing each other.

This leads to Deng Ai deciding that if Zhong Hui can take Hanzhong, then he can take Chengdu and gain the victor's crown. This near-impossible task he now takes on, and he sets off the very next day to cover the long and arduous distance to the capital. When Zhong Hui hears this, he simply couldn't care less, convinced that such an attack is impossible, and that Deng Ai will die trying.

It takes Deng Ai and his men twenty days of climbing and road-making to enable the supplies to follow on, but eventually they arrive at the foot of the huge mountain range known as Heaven-Scraping mountain. Despair overcomes the engineers, for there is no way they can construct a path over such rugged and sheer mountains. But Deng Ai is adamant. 'We have come four hundred or more miles, so there's no going back.' He gathers his men about him and asks if they are willing to face the greatest challenge yet. To a man they shout back their agreement. Climbing up the almost sheer mountain face, they eventually reach the top. Far below them at the bottom on the other side lies the way forward. Deng Ai orders his men to slide their weapons down the sheer cliff-face. Then he rolls himself in his felt jacket. Others do the same, then one by one they roll down the cliff-face. Those without felt use their ropes and cling on to trees and bushes as they slowly descend. This is how they overcome Heaven-Scraping mountain. To their astonishment at the bottom where they land is a stele engraved with words written by Kong Ming. It says:

Two fires commence;
A man will pass.
Two warriors compete;
Soon death will come.

Amazed at Kong Ming's foreknowledge, Deng Ai venerates the stele. Later this was written:

Heaven touching Yinping, rugged and steep,
Even the crane hesitates confronted by such heights.
Here Deng Ai wrapped in felt came rolling down,
Astonished that Kong Ming had foreseen just that.

With such an element of surprise they easily take Jiangyou. News of their advance comes to the second ruler, who is, of course, profoundly alarmed. When he questions Huang Hao, he is told that these reports are false. Yet even though the second ruler asks to see the shaman again, no one can find her. Reports pour in, and *in extremis* at last the second ruler tries to act. He calls his officials, and they suggest asking for the help of Kong Ming's son, Zhuge Zhan. Originally, at the court of Shu, he despaired of the corruption and, pleading sickness, stayed away. Summoned, he now rises to the occasion and takes command of the troops in Chengdu. It is his plans and plots that begin to turn the tide.

One attempt by the Wei to break through is thwarted by the appearance of Kong Ming riding in his famous carriage. The mere sight of him so unnerves the Wei that the men run, but are slaughtered in great numbers by the Shu. Battle after battle goes against the Wei. Deeply troubled, Deng Ai seeks to win Zhuge Zhan to his side by sending a flattering letter, but Zhuge Zhan simply tears the paper into pieces and executes the messenger.

At last Deng Ai, by using the retreat and ambush strategy, inflicts a crushing defeat upon the Shu. Surging forward, the Wei army besieges the city of Mianzhu. Desperate for assistance, Zhuge Zhan sends an appeal for help to the Wu kingdom. When the ruler Sun Xiu reads the appeal, he agrees to send reinforcements. But it takes time to get the troops ready. Before they can arrive, and not even knowing if they are on the way, Zhuge Zhan has frankly given up hope. He decides upon a last-minute attempt to break out and with his son Zhuge Shang by his side he and the army ride out to fight Deng Ai. It is a catastrophic mistake, and both men die fighting. After he has triumphed, Deng Ai, moved by the courage of the father and son, gives them honourable burial. Mianzhu falls the next day.

Now the march is on for Chengdu.

Is this the end for Shu?

CHAPTER 118

Crying at the ancestral shrine, a loyal prince dies. Moving into Shu, two generals compete.

The terrible news reaches Chengdu and the second ruler. He learns about the fall of Mianzhu and the deaths of Zhuge Zhan and his son. The second ruler calls a council of advisers. There he is informed that panic has set in, as people flee the capital, anticipating a siege or even conquest and occupation. Many advise him to flee south and to take refuge with the Man tribes prior to launching a return invasion. But adviser Qiao Zhou rejects this, pointing out that the Man tribes are not exactly trustworthy, to put it mildly. He also opposes suggestions of an alliance with the Wu. Instead he advocates that there is no other option. The second ruler must surrender.

'At no point in our history has an emperor taken refuge in another country. It's after all far more likely that Wei will swallow Wu than the other way round,' he says. 'Imagine how humiliating it would be to have surrendered to Wu only to then have to surrender again to Wei. Far better that we simply surrender to Wei. They'll surely give you a territory to dwell in and rule and so you'll be able to protect and serve the ancestral shrine as well as help protect the ordinary folk.'

The second ruler is unable to make up his mind and retires, deeply troubled. But the next morning he is still none the wiser about what course to take. Qiao Zhou then submits a memorial supporting surrender, and this helps the ruler decide. He will submit to the Wei.

Imagine his astonishment when his son Liu Chen roars out his disapproval and, rounding upon Qiao Zhou, calls him a coward for driving the second ruler into doing what no other emperor has ever done before. The second ruler has seven sons, but frankly the others are pathetic specimens. Only Liu Chen has any spirit and strength. The second ruler rounds on his son: 'Everyone else agrees. Only you want to increase the bloodshed, just because you're a shallow, warlike youth!'

Liu Chen tries to argue that they still have Jiang Wei, who can fight his way through. And denouncing Qiao Zhou as a worthless fop, he contends strongly that they should hold on.

'Take care and shut up. You have no grasp of the Will of Heaven,' declares the second ruler.

But still the young prince argues on, even declaring that he will not allow himself to live to see the day his patrimony is given away. But the second ruler will have none of this and he orders the prince be cast out of the hall. Then he gives orders for the document of surrender to be drawn up.

Soon the envoys arrive at Deng Ai's camp with the document of surrender and the seal of authority. They are treated well and return to the second ruler to inform him of what has happened. He then sends instructions to Jiang Wei to also surrender.

But Liu Chen cannot bear the shame and in his rage he returns to his palace, bearing his sword. His wife, Lady Cui, asks what the matter is. When he explains and says he will not kowtow to the Wei but will kill himself so he can face Xuande in the afterlife, she says she will do the same and asks permission to die first.

'Why?' asks a startled Liu Chen.

'My lord, you will die for your father and I'll die for my husband. We follow the same rule and values. There can be no question.' So saying, she smashes her head against a pillar and dies. The prince kills his three sons and, cutting off his wife's head, makes his way to the temple of the late emperor, Xuande. Here, kneeling and weeping, he offers up the souls of his wife and sons and then himself and slits his throat with his sword.

A poet has said:

> Ruler and courtiers happily bend the knee;
> Only one prince who could not bear the pain.
> So did the western Shu cease to exist,
> The only hero the northern lands' king, Liu Chen.

He gave his life to save his ancestor's shame,
Distraught, weeping below the blue sky.
Yet he still seems here, awesome, ever present,
Can one really say the Han have therefore perished?

The entry of the Wei troops into Chengdu is as a triumph. In relief the people cheer and strew flowers on the ground. The second ruler is allowed to keep his palace. The people are assured of good governance. Envoys are sent to Jiang Wei to ensure his surrender, while messengers are sent to Chang'an to tell of the victory. Despite Deng Ai's best efforts, Huang Hao escapes by bribing those around him.

This is the end of the Han.

A poet [Li Shangyin] later wrote:

Even the fish, birds and monkeys obeyed his commands;
Wind and rain created his defence. And yet
What his followers wrote of his strategy – gone,
The end, a prince fallen and carried river-wise away.
He emulated his models: Guan Zhong and Yue Yi,
But once they'd passed, what hope did he have really?
Perhaps next year we'll walk by his shrine,
Our songs will be sung, and completed . . . but what of
our grief?

When news of the surrender reaches Jiang Wei, his rage is awesome to behold, as is the anger of his men. They want to attack straight away, but Jiang Wei says, 'Don't worry. I have a plan by which the Han will be restored', and he shares this privately with his commanders. So Jiang Wei leads his officers to surrender to Zhong Hui, where he is treated as an honoured guest.

'Frankly, I have been so impressed by your campaigns,' says Jiang Wei, 'that I am more than prepared to surrender to you. Had it been Deng Ai – why I would have fought to the death!' This warms Zhong Hui's heart, and soon the two men are great friends once more.

When news of Jiang Wei's surrender to Zhong Hui reaches Deng Ai in the capital, he is deeply perturbed by this and immediately writes to Sima Zhao, basically saying that, in order to impress Wu and perhaps encourage their surrender, the second ruler, now simply known as Liu Shan, should be given an estate – Yizhou – and honours and kept in luxury in Shu so that Sun Xiu can see how benevolent the Wei are to those who submit. This causes considerable anxiety to Sima Zhao, who reads in this a plot by Deng Ai to take over the Shu kingdom for himself. He sends two messages back. A formal one full of praise and citing historical precedents for such a splendid general and a private letter basically saying, 'Don't go making such decisions until we have had time to consider them. Then we will tell you what is going to happen. This may well take some time, so be patient.'

Deng Ai is furious with what is clearly a rebuke. He writes back, pointing out that, historically, the commander in the field can override edicts from the court, which, because of distance cannot be as aware of the situation and the need to act as the commander. He finishes his letter by reassuring Sima Zhao that he will 'do nothing to harm the kingdom'. This only increases Sima Zhao's anxieties, and he consults Jia Chong, who recommends using Zhong Hui to control Deng Ai by promoting him. So a letter goes to Zhong Hui, giving him increased status and power, not least in Shu.

Sharing this with Jiang Wei, he interprets the promotion as a coded message that Deng Ai is not only slipping out of favour but is even being viewed as a potential rebel. Jiang Wei, flattering Zhong Hui, reinforces the impression that Deng Ai is becoming a traitor. He also shows, via a map, that this plan to establish the fallen Shu ruler in Yizhou reflects the same historical situation when Kong Ming helped Xuande set up his initial power base.

'So,' says Zhong Huo, 'how do we get rid of Deng Ai?'

'Clearly,' says Jiang Wei, 'Sima Zhao is really worried about him. Write to him outlining your reading of Deng Ai's treacherous plots and actions and then with Sima's permission you can crush Deng Ai.'

So the memorial is sent. To add to the confusion and distrust, Zhong Hui intercepts Deng Ai's own memorial explaining his actions and adds some sentences which incriminate Deng Ai even more if read by a mistrustful mind. Almost immediately Sima Zhao orders Zhong Hui to arrest Deng Ai, and he himself sets off with thirty thousand men to ensure this happens. But Sima Zhao also has another reason to go. As he reminds Shao Ti, his adviser, 'I don't trust Zhong Hui. That's why I'm going, not because of Deng Ai.'

When Sima Zhao arrives in Chang'an, Zhong Hui commences his plans to capture Deng Ai.

In Shu, an emperor overthrown, the victor he.
From Chengdu a great army descends – its victim? Him!

How does this roll out?

Swiftly.

CHAPTER 119

Jiang Wei plots revenge. A second abdication imitates the first, and Sima Yan becomes emperor.

Zhong Hui now worries how to go about overthrowing Deng Ai. He asks Jiang Wei for his advice. 'Despatch Commander Wei Guan to arrest him. If Deng Ai kills him, that's outright rebellion, and thus you'll have the excuse to march against him.'

But when Wen Guan is told to go and arrest Deng Ai with his own troop, they all realize that this is a plot to have Wen Guan killed in order to provide a valid excuse for Zhong Hui to attack. As a result, Wen Guan sends secret messages to Deng Ai's own officers warning them that he has been instructed to arrest Deng Ai, but if they join him he will make sure they are not arrested as well. 'If you do not agree, you are likely not only to die but to see your entire clan wiped out.' Only then does he set out with two prison wagons for Chengdu.

Upon arrival, all of Deng Ai's officers take up the offer and kowtow to Wen Guan at the break of the following day. Emboldened, Wen Guan breaks into Deng Ai's quarters while he is still asleep and arrests him and his son. Almost immediately Zhong Hui and Jiang Wei arrive on the scene. They mercilessly beat Deng Ai, shouting abuse at him. But Deng Ai replies with equal venom. Once Deng Ai and son are en route as prisoners to Luoyang, Zhong Hui conscripts all Deng Ai's men into his own army. Crowing at his success and the fulfilment of his dream, he is gently chided by Jiang Wei, who points out that many in the past have thought they had risen to the top, only to find it is at that point that their fall begins. He even recommends that Zhong Hui might think about retiring or possibly becoming a hermit on Emei mountain.

'I'm not even forty yet, so I've no plans to retire,' replies

Zhong Hui, and with the tacit encouragement of Jiang Wei he begins to have expansionist ideas. Jiang Wei even writes secretly to the second ruler encouraging him to have hopes for the restoration of the Han.

But all this is cut short when a letter arrives from Sima Zhao. He announces that he is en route from Chang'an, 'concerned that you need more troops to help overcome Deng Ai'. Zhong Hui is no fool and realizes that this is a covert way of saying Sima Zhao doesn't trust him, because he has more than enough men to take control by himself. Realizing that a crisis is brewing, Zhong Hui starts to plan to consolidate his hold on Shu and in effect do exactly what Xuande did in making it his base.

Then Jiang Wei comes up with a new scheme. 'The queen mother has just died, so why don't you claim that just before she died she sent you a letter authorizing you to avenge the murder of the emperor by capturing Sima Zhao? This will enable you to seize the north.'

Zhong Hui is delighted by this idea and invites Jiang Wei to join him, lead the vanguard and share in the spoils. Seeming deeply touched but worried, Jiang Wei thanks him but points out that many of the Wei officers might oppose this.

'I know,' says Zhong Hui. 'Tomorrow is the end of the New Year celebrations – the fifteenth day of the first month – and there will be a great lantern festival. I will host a banquet and invite all the officers. Then anyone who refuses to vow obedience we will kill there and then.'

Jiang Wei is secretly delighted with how well his plan is going!

And that is what happens. At the banquet the next day Zhong Hui suddenly starts crying. His officers ask what the matter is. He announces that he has a secret letter from the late queen mother. 'She commissioned me to overthrow and punish Sima Zhao for his crimes of killing the emperor and trying to take over the kingdom. You must all join me in this.' The announcement astonishes all present, and there is a moment of stunned silence. 'If anyone does not join me,' declares Zhong Hui, 'he will die.'

So everyone vows to join him. But he does not trust them

and has the entire officer group imprisoned. Jiang Wei pushes him even further. 'You can't trust them, you know,' he says, 'so kill them all now.' To which Zhong Hui, smiling, says, 'Already planned. A burial pit has been dug, and there are thousands of clubs ready to beat them all to death.'

Now this is overheard by one of the minor officers whom he trusted so has been spared imprisonment – one Qiu Jian. He has served faithfully under one of the officers now imprisoned, Hu Lie, and he sends him a warning. He in turn has a son outside the city with his own troop, and an urgent message is sent to him, asking for immediate help. The son, Hu Yuan is distraught when the letter arrives and summons all the other main officers still at liberty to join him in launching an attack a couple of days later – on the eighteenth day. This they all heartily agree to do.

On the night of the seventeenth, Zhong Hui has a dream in which he is being attacked by a vast number of snakes. The following morning he asks Jiang Wei how he would interpret this dream. To allay any fears, Jiang Wei says this is a dream about dragons, and that means it is auspicious. Zhong Hui then gives Jiang Wei the order to go and execute all the Wei officers. But no sooner has he started the executions than Jiang Wei has a heart attack and collapses, out cold. Just as he starts to come round, the din of an attack overwhelms the palace prison, and chaos breaks out, with men rushing about everywhere. 'Mutiny,' cries Jiang Wei. 'Kill all the officers.' But it is too late. Soldiers burst in, fires break out, and even though Zhong Hui fights back he is taken down with an arrow, and then his head is hacked off. Rushing out to the attack, Jiang Wei suffers another heart attack. 'I've failed. So be it, this is the Will of Heaven.' And so saying, he cuts his own throat. He is fifty-nine years of age. His whole family perishes that day. Only Wei Guan is able to restore order, but then news comes that in the mayhem Deng Ai and his son have been released by their supporters, and Wei Guan begins to fear for his life. An officer who has personal reasons for wanting them dead offers to do the deed and he sets off with five hundred men. When Deng Ai sees the men advancing, he believes they have come to support him so with no protection goes to greet them. He and his son are cut down in cold blood.

A poet has written this about Deng Ai:

Even as a youth he loved to plan and plot;
In so many ways he triumphed in his role.
He could read what the land told him,
And just as easily, the stars in the heavens.
Mountains split to allow his horsemen through,
Rocks sundered to make a path for his men.
But brutal murder destroyed all his gains,
His soul, drifts now over the River Han.

Another poet has written about Zhong Hui:

From birth he was quick-witted,
As adviser he found a role at court.
His strategies defeated the Simas,
Another Kong Ming they said of him.
His triumph was at Shouchun,
At the Jian Gate fame was his.
Not for him hiding in the hills,
His soul wanders, longing for rest.

And another has written about Jiang Wei:

Tianshui renowned as his birthplace,
His home province proud of him.
His ancestry back to the hero Jiang Ziya,[30]
All he knew, drawn from Kong Ming.
Great in courage, so what did he have to fear?
Forging forward, never considering return.
On the day he died in Chengdu,
All the generals of the Han wept.

Many fine men die that day: Liu Rui, the heir apparent; Guan Yi, grandson of Guan Yu; and so many others. It takes Jia Chong, who arrives ten days later, to restore order. The Wu army, seeing that Shu has now fallen and the Han have ended, withdraw back to Wu.

When the deposed second ruler Liu Shan arrives in Luoyang, Sima Zhao upbraids him in public for his dissolute lifestyle, for his mistreatment of good men and for destroying his own government. But then, acknowledging that Liu Shan has surrendered of his own volition, he awards him a minor title and funds of not inconsiderable generosity. But the eunuch Huang Hao is publicly tortured to death for the terrible harm he has done to the kingdom.

The very next day, Sima Zhao holds a grand banquet for Liu Shan and his men. At first the entertainment is all Wei dances and music, which deeply offends the Shu men. All, that is, bar the second ruler, who sits grinning throughout. Then come dances and music of the Shu, which cause the men of Shu to weep, so moved are they. Taken aside and chided by Sima Zhao as to why he is not moved by the Shu as his men are, Liu Shan simply says he is having a nice time and expresses thanks. Later, Xi Zheng, one of his advisers, takes him aside and tells him he really ought to look and sound distressed. 'Say something like: "My father's shrine lies so far away. I long for the lands of Shu. I remember them every day."' The second ruler goes back in and parrots Xi Zheng exactly: 'My father's shrine lies so far away. I long for the lands of Shu. I remember them every day'. This causes Sima Zhao to say, 'Why! You sound exactly like Xi Zheng!'

'Ah. Actually that is quite true. Umm . . .' says Liu Shan. And Sima Zhao, realizing the man is basically a simpleton, also appreciates he has nothing to fear from him.

In recognition of his victories and the collapse of Shu, courtiers petition Cao Huan to make Sima Zhao a king in his own right as a reward. Unable to say no, the Son of Heaven ennobles Sima Zhao as the king of Jin. But others, reporting strange omens and auguries, push for the new king of Jin to become an emperor in his own right. Encouraged, Sima Zhao enters the palace, meaning to implement this. But a sudden violent stroke renders him speechless: so much so that, as he lies dying, all he can do is to point to his heir, Sima Yan, to indicate that he is indeed to succeed to his titles. It is summer AD 264 when he dies. Sima Yan is immediately crowned as king.

Sima Yan asks Jia Chong how his father compares with Cao Cao. Jia Chong points out that Cao Cao was highly successful but feared and thought to be utterly ruthless. Under his son, Cao Pi, things went from bad to worse due to the brutality of his regime. In contrast, Sima Yi and Sima Zhao were militarily successful and also cared for the ordinary folk. 'Then your father,' says Jia Chong, 'overthrew the Shu, and his standing rose above all else. Frankly, how could Cao Cao even be spoken of in the same breath?'

This then leads to a discussion about how dynasties are sustained, and as Cao Pi appeared to continue the Han, could not he, Sima Yan, continue, on the same moral basis, the Wei? It is agreed that this precedent means he could.

That is all he needs. He goes immediately to the palace rooms of the Emperor Cao Huan with his sword unsheathed.

'Exactly who won the kingdom for the Wei?' he demands.

'Your grandfather and father,' says a cowed emperor.

'Well, Your Majesty,' says a smiling Sima Yan, 'frankly you have none of the skills or talents required to rule or command a country. Perhaps it is time to abdicate and let someone more competent take over. Now don't you think that is a good idea?'

An astonished emperor is left speechless, but an official speaks up for him, claiming that not only did Cao Cao win this, but his descendant is a worthy man. He is beaten to death for his troubles. The emperor's other advisers, seeing the writing on the wall, recommend abdication, and that way the emperor will be able to live out his years in peace.

And so it happens.

Early in AD 265 the emperor abdicates, and Sima Yan ascends the throne. Jia Chong reads out the pronouncement that the Mandate of Heaven passed from the Han when they lost it to the Wei forty-five years ago. Now they too have lost it. Heaven and Earth's choice now rests upon the Sima family. With that Cao Huan is dismissed with a minor title, and Sima Yan becomes the emperor of the new dynasty entitled the Great Jin.

And so the Wei dynasty dies.
The Han are gone,
The Wu's hills and rivers will soon no longer be theirs either.

How did this happen?

Let us find out.

CHAPTER 120

Recommending Du Yu, Yang Hu dies.
Sun Hao surrenders to Wei, and the
Three Kingdoms are united into One.

News of the overthrow of the Wei emperor by Sima Yan profoundly shocks the king of Wu, Sun Xiu, for he knows that his kingdom is now seriously under threat. This so troubles him that he becomes ill and has to take to his bed. Summoning Prime Minister Puyang Xing, and now unable to speak, he points at his heir, Sun Wan, and indicates that they should both assist each other. Having done this, he dies.

When Puyang Xing announces the late emperor's choice, disputes break out. The leading military officers complain that he is a callow youth and what is needed now is a leader – such as Sun Hao, the son of Sun He. They are adamant that he should be their ruler. So Sun Wan is given a small region to govern, and Sun Hao is proclaimed emperor. It is the year AD 265 when he takes the throne.

However, it is not long before he starts to show his true, warped nature and manifest his innate cruelty and indeed extreme violence. He elevates the eunuch Cen Hun to be his companion in crime, and when the late emperor's prime minister, Puyang Xing, and others protest, he arbitrarily has them executed. After that, no one dares complain or resist. His oppressive measures and inordinately heavy taxes bring poverty to wide swathes of the country, and he takes not just through outrageous taxes but by sequestering private funds and family fortunes as well.

Even his own appointee as deputy prime minister, Lü Kai, is moved to petition him.

'No disaster has happened, but poverty afflicts the people. Nothing is being done, but the treasury is empty. In times past the Han collapsed, and from its ruin arose the Three Kingdoms. Now the lineage of Xuande and Cao Cao has also collapsed due to abuse. Looking at this, we can see what might befall us,' says Lü Kai. He continues: 'We have less than a year of supplies, and this is already a serious problem. Your officials are loathed for the way they demand what cannot be given. The harem, which under Sun Quan was less than one hundred, now numbers over a thousand.' He finishes his petition by asking the emperor: 'Reduce the demands upon the people for military service; for labour and for other services. Limit the number of women in the palace; choose good ministers and get rid of the bad and then we can all rejoice, as will Heaven.'

In response, Sun Hao simply becomes even more extravagant, building vast palaces. He seeks advice from a fortune-teller, who assures him: 'Good news, sire. In the future a blue canopy will enter Luoyang.' Sun Hao takes this to mean that the Wu will conquer the Jin.

Sadly this also inflames his desire to campaign against Jin and to conquer lands in the north. Despite the advice of those who understand such things, he is not to be dissuaded, and plans are put in train for an invasion. The first target is to be the Jin city of Xiangyang, and the Wu forces are given to Lu Kang to command.

Sima Yan, the Jin ruler, is soon informed and asks for advice. Jia Chong points out, 'Sun Hao is deeply unpopular with his own people. Therefore it would be seen as virtuous if Jin invaded Wu because this could help launch a coup. As a result Wu would fall easily.' Sima Yan agrees wholeheartedly and orders Yang Hu in Xiangyang to prepare.

Now Yang Hu has won the hearts of the local people through good management and through having the troops plant their own crops, which means they have supplies now for up to ten years. They do not have to take the crops of the ordinary folk. He has also been benevolent to any Wu soldiers captured who wanted to return to their families. His lifestyle is modest, and he is so beloved that he moves about with no fear of attack. He has a high regard for his Wu opponent, Lu Kang, and advocates caution. Indeed, he urges that there be no invasion until civil strife actually erupts in Wu.

Over time Yang Hu and Lu Kang become real friends. They exchange gifts of meat and wine; on one occasion, hearing Lu Kang has been ill, Yang Hu sends his own special potion and physician to cure him. When such gifts are exchanged, cautious members of both entourages question whether they might be poisoned, and both men dismiss such thoughts as unworthy of the integrity of the other leader and eat and drink happily.

It is into this that the edict from the ruler of Wu arrives, ordering an outright attack on Jin. In reply Lu Kang is politely forthright about why such an invasion will not succeed and he also recommends that the Son of Heaven instead concentrate on virtue and keeping the peace at home. The ruler of Wu is furious. 'I know that he and the enemy are friends and this is what this is about.' And so saying, he demotes Lu Kang and sends instead Sun Ji to take over. No one dares breathe a word against this in the court.

Over the next ten years the ruler of Wu's abuses of power grow even worse. His execution of anyone who opposes him becomes more blatant, and the fear he generates prevents any honest discussion or plans being undertaken. Back in Xiangyang, Yang Hu has followed events closely after the dismissal of his friend Lu Kang. Now he sees that Wu is indeed ready to rise in revolt, and he petitions the Jin emperor for permission to invade. As he puts it in his memorial, 'Heaven provides the possibilities but we must do the work.' He then sets out how desperate the people of Wu are under the tyranny of Sun Hao. He has every expectation that the request for permission to invade will be agreed. But while Sima Yan agrees, his advisers do not, and so no permission is given.

Deeply disappointed, Yang Hu bemoans that a real opportunity has been lost. In the year AD 278 he travels to court and asks permission to retire to his home village, as he is unwell. Asked for his advice, he says, 'Wu is ready for revolt and consequently for conquest, but if someone virtuous were to arise after Sun Hao, then the situation would change and the opportunity would be lost.' Asked if he will lead an invasion, he declines on grounds of health and recommends the ruler find a younger man. Then he goes back to his home village.

However, the return home does not solve the problem of his health, and a few months later he is at death's door. Sima Yan makes the journey to be at his bedside. Deeply moved by this, Yang Hu expresses his gratitude and loyalty to Sima; in return, Sima apologizes for having failed to act against Wu when Yang Hu so strongly and accurately proposed it. In response to Sima's question about who else could undertake the task, Yang Hu recommends Du Yu. Having ensured continuity, Yang Hu dies.

Across the land people mourn the passing of this great and, even more importantly, good man. In Xiangyang the people remember that he loved to ride in the Xian hills. So they build a temple and carve a stele, and people go there each season to pray. Those who read the stele always cry, which is how it gained its name, 'The Stele of Tears'. A poem has described this:

Climbing at dawn to Yang's temple, I am moved.
Upon the Xian hill in spring, just fragments of a stone.
From the pines fall dew drops,
The tears perhaps of those who miss him still.

So Sima Yan appoints Du Yu as commander. A remarkable man, his greatest love is his copy of the *Spring and Autumn Annals*, which he reads every day and even has carried when he goes out riding.

In Wu, time has passed. Lu Kang and Ding Feng have died, and the behaviour of Sun Hao has got worse and worse. The tortures he has devised – such as peeling the skin from a person's face or digging their eyes out – shock and horrify the nation. Fear rules in Wu.

Yet Sima Yan, ruler of Jin, cannot make up his mind whether to attack. Sometimes he is for it, then an adviser will make some objection, and he will change his mind. Then one day a memorial comes from Du Yu. He essentially argues that unless they attack now, the south will invade them.

And so at last Sima Yan decides to go to war.

Immediately he sends commanders and troops in many directions, each with a Wu city to attack – Du Yu against Jiangling; Sima Zhou against Tuzhong; Wang Hun against Hengjiang; Wang Rong against Wuchang; Hu Fen against Xiakou, while the navy is sent down the river to attack as well under the command of Admiral Wang Jun. In overall charge is Yang Ji – to be based at Xiangyang.

When the news reaches Sun Hao, he is greatly alarmed and orders flow out of the palace to show resistance. But as he goes back to his private chambers, his favourite, the eunuch Cen Hun, can see he is troubled and asks what it is that so worries him. 'Our armies can deal with the land invasion, but I'm really worried about the naval attack.' 'Well,' says Cen Hun, 'I know how we can deal with them.' And he comes up with an astonishing plan. Iron is collected from across the land and cast into thousands of mighty chains and huge iron spikes. These are stretched across the river, and the spikes dropped into the river channel to break up the attack and sink the ships.

The first engagement of the war is a triumph for the Jin, who, playing on a fake retreat, draw the southerners into an ambush which virtually wipes out that army. At the same time, Du Yu has instructed eight hundred of his men to mingle with the fleeing remnants of the Wu troops, and thus they are able to enter the enemy city of Xiakou. As soon as they are inside they start fires, creating chaos, and very swiftly the city is taken. The knock-on effect on the morale of the Wu is immediate. The commander of the Wu navy, Lu Jing, tries to scramble ashore to save himself but is killed, while the commander of the city of Jiangling flees, leaving his city to the enemy. When he is captured, Du Yu has him executed in punishment for such cowardice. City after city, region after region surrenders to the victorious Jin. Now, led by Du Yu, the race is on to take the Wu capital of Jianye.

As part of this attack Admiral Wang Jun is heading down the river when his spies bring information about both the iron chains stretched across the river and the sunken spikes. Hearing this, he orders huge fire ships prepared and then sends them down the river. The sailors set fire to them just before they run into the chains and are grounded upon the spikes. So intense is the heat generated that the iron chains melt, the spikes fall apart, and the navy sails on.

The Wu generals Zhuge Xing and Shen Rong gather with Prime Minister Zhang Ti and recommend surrender. However, the prime minister is realistic. 'Wu is finished,' he says, 'but to let it die without dying in battle is to dishonour our country. What shame that would bring upon us.' Convinced by this and now united in this view, the commanders return to their troops and prepare for battle. And for death.

They attack, and mighty is the slaughter. The Jin troops storm through, Shen Rong and Prime Minister Zhang Ti are slain, and at that the Wu army disintegrates. A poet has written this about Zhang Ti:

> On Ba hill, Du Yu's banners flew,
> Here Zhang Ti of the south loyally died.
> No longer did regal grace animate the land,
> But he chose to act as if it did.

When realization of the scale of the disaster dawns on Sun Hao, he asks why the troops won't fight. He is then told bluntly it is because of the corruption of Cen Hun. 'Kill him, Your Majesty, and we'll go out to fight,' say the officials, But Sun Hao still cannot awake to the real problem and says, 'Are you seriously suggesting one palace eunuch can destroy a whole kingdom?' Realizing that he will never act, the officials take matters into their own hands and slay Cen Hun, feasting upon his dismembered body.

The few soldiers and sailors who remain are frightened when their banners fall in a great storm; many take this as a profoundly inauspicious sign and desert. Now there are just a few brigades between Jin and total triumph.

Wang Jun is very close to Shitou and determined to be the one to capture this last-stand city. This is greatly facilitated when Zhang Xiang surrenders his Wu army, and to test his new loyalty to Jin, Wang Jun asks him to lead the vanguard on the city. As soon as the men on the walls see that Zhang Xiang has surrendered, they open the city gates to him and the Jin army.

Sun Hao knows it is over and at first is tempted to commit suicide but is persuaded to follow the example of Liu Shan and surrender to the Jin. Wang Jun accepts his surrender and treats him as an honoured guest, as a prince.

A poet of the Tang dynasty [Liu Yuxi] has written this:

> The famous ships of Jin storm downstream,
> Jinling's kingly rule is blown away.
> The iron chains, why they sink,
> The flag of surrender flies over Shitou.
> I often reflect on the sadness of times gone by,
> Yet the mountains stand still above cold streams.
> Today the king has no place in the world to live,
> The fortifications are as bare as autumn trees.

So Wu falls to Jin, and great are the treasures and wealth and people who now are united again under one ruler. Du Yu opens up the grain stores, and at last the ordinary people have enough to eat. They welcome the new rulers.

At the victory feast in the Jin capital, and with tears flowing down his cheeks, the ruler of Jin says, 'This day belongs to Yang Hu – I wish he had lived to see it.'

When Sun Hao is brought before the ruler of Jin he makes a good impression through his use of humour. The ruler says, 'This seat here has been awaiting your arrival for quite some time!' to which Sun Hao replies, 'Funny that. I had one ready for you!' Sun Hao is given a minor role, and this generosity is extended to all the honourable officials or their descendants who have served the Wu, such as the family of the slain prime minister, Zhang Ti.

So at last the Three Kingdoms are once again made One under the Jin.

As the saying goes, 'Empires collapse into chaos and empires arises from chaos.'

Liu Shan, the emperor of the Shu, dies in AD 271. Cao Huan,

ruler of Wei, dies in AD 302. Sun Hao, ruler of Wu, dies in AD 283. All pass away naturally in their own beds.

A poet has summed this all up:

When the founder of the Han dynasty took
Xiangyang,[31]
The sun rose on the lineage of Han.
After the revolt,[32] Guang Wu restored the Han,
As a bird rises into the sky at noon.
Ahh! But then came as ruler Prince Xian,
And the Han sun sank into the darkness of night.
He Jin's foolishness empowered the eunuchs,
Dong Zhuo arose and seized the palace halls.
To strike the dictator down, Wang Yun plotted,
Only to provoke Li Jue and Guo Si to revolt.
Revolt and rebellion surged over the land,
Warlords attacked everywhere, all things.
East of the Great River arose the Sun family,
To the north arose the Yuan to power.
In the west it was Liu Yan and son.
Liu Biao took Jing and Xiang for himself.
In Hanzhong, Zhang Yan and Lu ruled,
While Ma Teng and Han Sui defended Xiliang.
Tao Qian, Zhang Xiu, Gongsun Zan – brave men,
But greatest of all, Cao Cao, the emperor's prime
minister,
Attracting to him those skilled in government
and war.
The emperor in his power, Cao was unstoppable,
His armies ruling the north.
From nowhere, though of imperial birth, came
Xuande
And his sworn brothers Guan Yu and Zhang Fei,
Partakers of the vow to defend the Han.
Without a home, he wandered the land for years,
A group of no significance, but fate decreed otherwise.
Fate brought him three times to Nanyang's
countryside,

And here Kong Ming revealed the true state of affairs.
'Three kingdoms now exist,' he said,
'Attack first Jingzhou and then Shu,
Build your home there, it will supply you well.'
How sad! Xuande had but three years,
And to Kong Ming's care he left his son.
By six invasions through the Qishan hills
Did Kong Ming try to change the fortunes of Han.
But the Mandate of Han had run dry,
Kong Ming died, a star falling to earth.
So Jiang Wei tried instead with all his strength,
Nine times he invaded the north, but to no avail.
Zhong Hui and Deng Ai came to the west,
The mountains and streams of Han became those
of Cao.
Five sons of Cao held the throne,
Then the Sima arose and usurped the throne.
In contrast, no great battle saw Wu end.
All that is left are the three kings, no longer kings.
All is change, change is all.
This is fate, it cannot be changed.
Three kingdoms, gone as if a dream,
And reflecting on this, why, we can only mourn.

雨
順
風
調

Notes

1. *From early in the second year of his reign*: i.e. AD 170
2. *In the last year of Emperor Ling's reign*: i.e. AD 189.
3. *late summer of AD 189*: All dates in the text have been converted into AD dates to help orient the reader historically.
4. *King Wen of Chu*: Chu is an anachronistic name, given that it was in *c*.1100 BC that King Wen founded the original Zhou dynasty, which later became the rump state of Chu when the seven kingdoms emerged, as stated in Chapter 1.
5. *Yi Yin or even the duke of Zhou*: Two of ancient China's most revered and famous ministers, whose wise counsel is recorded in *The Most Venerable Book* – the *Shang Shu*.
6. *the story of King Zhuang of Chu and the tassel*: The story is that at a banquet suddenly all the candles blew out, and the feast was plunged into darkness. One of the guests tried to grope the queen, who in response tore off the tassel from his hat. When the candles were lit again, she demanded that the king seize whoever was missing a tassel from their hat but instead the king ordered everyone to tear off their tassels. Later the man in question became a hero who defended the dynasty.
7. *Sima Qian*: The first of the great historians of China, *fl. c*.100 BC. He was criticized by some for not paying enough respect to some of the Han emperors. He was castrated as punishment.
8. *Kong Fu Zi*: i.e. Confucius (551–479 BC), Chinese philosopher who emphasized morality and correctness in personal, social and governmental life.
9. *the Five Elements*: In Chinese philosophy there are five elements: water, fire, wood, metal (sometimes called gold) and earth.
10. *back in the reign of Emperor Shun*: Emperor Shun died in AD 144. This is now AD 199.
11. *The confrontation goes on for month after month*: This battle took place in AD 200.

12. *qilin*: The second most powerful creature in Chinese mythology after the dragon – symbol of imperial power. The qilin has the head of a horse, the body of a dragon and the feet of a deer.
13. *Meng Zi*: (372–289 BC or 385–303/2 BC), known as Mencius, a philosopher and sage in the Confucian tradition.
14. *the time of the Warring States*: An era of warfare with various states trying to conquer the others aimed at the creation of a single Chinese empire, mostly defined by historians as lasting fronm 475 to 221 BC.
15. *the Master*: Confucius.
16. *Yi Jing*: *The Book of Changes*, an ancient Chinese divination text originally dating to the Western Zhou period (1000–750 BC).
17. *the time of Emperor He*: AD 89–106.
18. *Tai mountain*: The greatest and most important of the sacred mountains of China.
19. *we met long ago at the Zhenguo temple*: See Chapter 27.
20. *King Wen of the Zhou*: King Wen only took on the Mandate of Heaven because of the corruption of the last Shang king, *c.*1100 BC, and was presented as maintaining order and virtue, not as overthrowing a legitimate ruler.
21. *a sign of good luck*: In fact, they symbolize the forthcoming rise of Sima and his three generations, who take over from the dynasty of Cao's family and the empire of the Wei and establish the Jin dynasty.
22. *King Wu*: This is how he is known in Chinese Imperial Annals – as the first Wei emperor.
23. *Shu*: The old title of the Riverlands, revived by Xuande as the title of his kingdom; sometimes also called Shu Han to show continuity with the old dynasty.
24. *the empire*: The characters here are *Middle Kingdom*, China's own name for itself, but I have translated this as 'empire'.
25. *Hu Zeng*: A ninth-century poet. His collected poems are contained in two volumes – the *Anding Ji* and the *Yongshi shi* – the latter being a collection of poems on history from which this poem comes.
26. *a poet*: Believed to be the eleventh-century Sima Wen.
27. *General Ma Yuan*: Ma Yuan invaded in AD 42–3 to put down a rebellion by the two Trung sisters – now considered Vietnamese heroes.
28. *Yao and Shun . . . Wen and Wu*: Yao and Shun were legendary kings of the highest virtue, while Wen and Wu were the founders of the Zhou dynasty, which overthrew the corrupt Shang dynasty

in the twelfth century BC. They were all models of good governance and wisdom. See *The Most Venerable Book* (*Shang Shu*), also in Penguin Classics.

29. *Queen Fu*: This was the empress that Cao Cao had murdered – see Chapter 66.
30. *the hero Jiang Ziya*: The adviser of the first emperor of the Zhou dynasty, *c.*1100 BC.
31. *When the founder of the Han dynasty took Xiangyang*: This was in 206 BC.
32. *the revolt*: This was the revolt of Wang Mang between AD 9 and 23, after which the Han dynasty's recovery is called the Eastern Han.